"Apocalypse grabs the reader on page one & throttles them along with tunnel vision until the end. Three days later you'll awake not knowing which was is up & which is down!"

- Ronald Higgs, NewsGroup USA

"I had no idea how bad things were, until I read Apocalypse"

- Jill Linus, mother of 3, Franklin, Ohio

"Two Thumbs Up! Apocalypse is a must read, for everyone, everywhere."

- David Johnson, News USA

"So far outside the box it's almost back is again. A defiant breakthrough that shatters all perceptions of societal norms, while questioning the very foundation that humanity's built on."

- Dr. Jason Porter
New York Research & Policy Institute

"An inspirational masterpiece. A true work of art that even inspires us extreme "robotic-sheep."

- Phil Andrews, Editor & Chief of The Post

"Four thumbs up!"

- Transhumanian Society

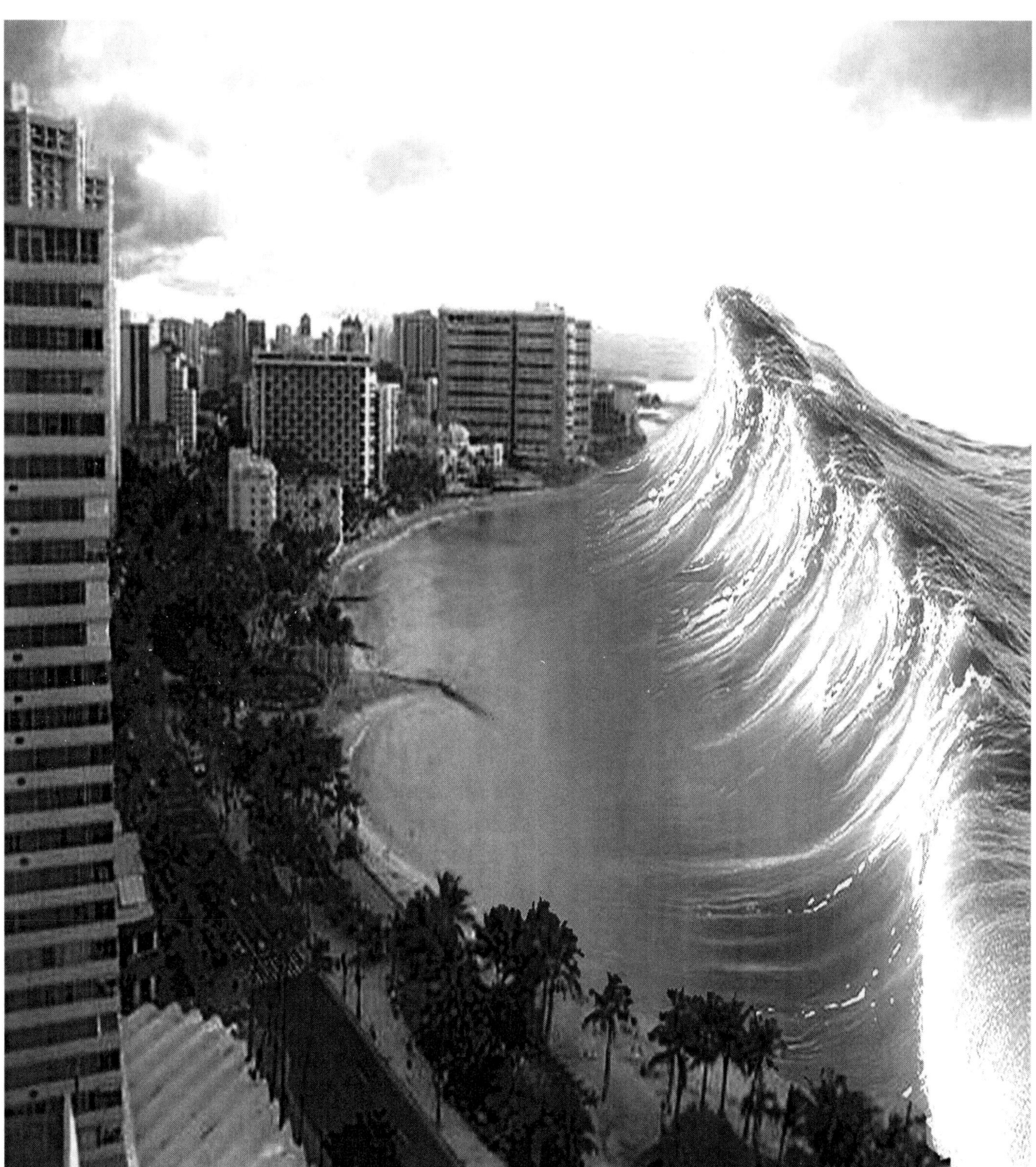

APOCALYPSE

HOW TO SURVIVE A GLOBAL CRISIS

BY

DAN MARTIN

Cover Art by René Aldrette aldrette@gmail.com
Back Cover image by Thomas Lancaster
Edited by Barbara Seiden
Text by Dan Martin, unless otherwise noted
Interior photos and illustrations by Dan Martin or public domain sources unless otherwise noted.

Printed in the United States of America.

Library of Congress Control Number: 2011928216

ISBN 978-1-4276-5185-3

Special 2012 Edition

In collaboration with Agua-Luna

www.AGUA-LUNA.com

Published by ECKO House Publishing
www.ECKOHousePublishing.com

The begging the screaming, there's no place to turn;
They're filling their pockets, and letting us burn.
The babies – the family, what's left to eat?
Our cattle are slaughtered and dumped in a heap.
The milk is polluted, the water, the air;
They're pushing in closer, but we're too doped to care.
The election's a sham, the leaders have fled;
The winners all lose, the losers all dead.
They're saving more lives, and more being born;
They're pushing in closer and there's not enough corn.
Too many mouths and not enough wheat;
They're pushing in closer, the sweat and the heat.
The concrete of buildings, the harshness, the gray;
The viaduct bridges have all spread away.
Coldly cementing me into a tomb;
Innate and inanimate, lifeless—the womb.
Moving, not breathing, begins as it ends;
Co-workers, loved ones, family and friends.

- Laura Lisa

TABLE OF CONTENTS

205778

ABOUT THIS BOOK

Will the world as we know it end in 2012? No one really knows for sure. However, it's the intention of this book and the will of the author to teach you what you'll need to know IF some type of event does actually occur on December 21, 2012, or beyond.

This book is a special 2012 edition and preface in a three part series on self-sufficiency and how to live sustainably and Independent, today. An incredible series in living cheaper, debt/mortgage-free and without bills in today's society. Where the following books show you everything you'll need to know to live self-reliantly, *"Apocalypse"* takes it one step further by utilizing and applying some of the same do-it-yourself sustainable living step-by-step methods into a post-apocalyptic world in which you may very well soon find yourself living.

When/If life as we know it ever reverts back to 'simpler' times due to any occurrence or multiple occurrences at any time, you'll need the life lessons that were once passed down from generation to generation (as well as a few additional ones I've devised) to guide you in and through the new world. In other words, this book will teach you everything you'll need to know to be able to provide for yourself and your family, without outside assistance from any group, organization, society or government, since these entities would no longer exist anyway.

The backbone of *"Apocalypse"* is filled with dozens of DIY lessons, illustrations, diagrams, charts, pictures, tables and descriptions, helping you to deal with and re-establish control over your life and your family's life. Separated into ten well- laid-out chapters is information that: deals with what will happen just before, during and after any number of different possible apocalyptic cataclysms; teaches you how to prepare for such catastrophes beforehand, during and/or directly afterwards, along with step-by-step guides that walk you through building and acquiring shelter, water, food, security, energy, medical and transportation; and finally, explains what will need to be done to create a new world order, different from the last.

You'll learn all about the following critical information: (a) practical and useful scientific, historical and religious-based supporting data, encompassing a dozen or so of the most likely possible doomsday scenarios that have the highest percentage and probability of occurring in 2012 or in the immediate future; (b) pre-preparation and post-preparation survivalist know-how based on governmental organizational studies and testimony of past catastrophe survivors; (c) skills you'll need to learn and actions you'll need to take not only to survive, but to live comfortably during the immediate aftermath as well as the months and years to come; and finally (d) how to rebuild a new, better, healthier world society all taught in an easy-to-read beginner's level format, brought to you in a series of logical, step-by-step processes.

What *Apocalypse* isn't saying, is that you need to drop everything, quit your job and head for the hills. Although the book will give you the tools you'll need through the event as well as during the 'end times'. It is also versatile enough to be applied to any number of survivable natural or man-made disasters, including: another terrorist attack like 9/11, a viral outbreak such as what occurred with the SARS or Swine Flu pandemics a couple years back, a devastating hurricane like Katrina (a category 3 storm that flattened New Orleans in 2005), a catastrophic earthquake such as the one which just struck Japan (which measured 9.0 on the Richter scale), a Tsunami or Tidal wave like the one that submerged dozens of Asian cities under a 100ft wave (caused by the 2010 Indonesian earthquake), volcanic eruptions like the 1985 Nevado del Ruiz eruption in Columbia, killing 23,000 people, an economic collapse similar to the great 1929 depression or the current ongoing global "financial crisis," a governmental collapse like what occurred with Russia in '91 and is currently transpiring in Egypt, Libya, Syria, Ireland and Bahrain, polar shift (currently the poles are moving at a rate of 34-37 miles per year), a large meteor impact like the one that hit Siberia, Russia, which was 1,000 times more powerful than the atomic bomb dropped on Hiroshima, tornadoes, fire, war, invasion, the list goes on and on.

No other nation throughout history (that we know of) has ever separated themselves (with the help of technology, society and government) so far from Earth's most basic living functions. But there's a drawback to this easy dependence. What IF it all fails one day? Will you know how to survive? How to carry on? How to sustain yourself and your family until a *"Brave New World"* is constructed?

While *Apocalypse* includes a 'How-to' manual, it's also designed to give the reader an insight into the reality of our world and the efforts our societies have taken to redirect our nations onto incorrect and immoral paths. The planet is being destroyed, regardless if it will be completely destroyed during our time or not. Wars are being fought in New York as well as the Middle East. People are starving, whether it's in D.C. or Zimbabwe. And natural disasters are reshaping the unprepared countries of today's world. ~~It's not too late; but the call for action is now.~~ It IS too late; all that we can do now is prepare ourselves for the full collapse and rebirth.

For all those who feel there's just something
not quite right with the world.

ACKNOWLEDGEMENTS

First and foremost, there's no other person in this world that has or could have ever helped in the making of this book more than my wife Lucia. She not only bought me my first Sustainable Living book, sparking the fire that led us to move off the grid (which ultimately led to this book based on that ten-year experience), but was brave enough to accept and believe in the ludicrous notion that we could live, cut off from any and all forms of society, indefinitely. She left her country, family, friends and a high-paying career as a computer engineer with AT&T and abandoned all of the many (although not known then) unnecessary extras society has to offer, in order to live literally homeless on an unknown, inhospitable "inhabitable" mountain for two years while we built our first home together, alone. We'd live and learn on the Ranch in seclusion, without leaving once in six year span, literally. At age 25, Lucia contributed to the design of our cabin and helped to physically build it, a feat not seen since the days of the old Wild West settlers. She grew, trapped, killed, cleaned and cooked our food, right alongside of me. She made ink and paper, candles and candy, built solar panels and wind turbines; all while constantly raising over a dozen rambunctious kids.

If that wasn't enough, for the last three years she'd not only follow me, but encourage me to travel all over the world teaching others how to be self-sufficient themselves, just like us. Lucia built, maintains and supports our website (Agua-Luna.com) which is specifically designed to help people find our information so that they can live a better, simpler life as well. As a last effort, she's helped out in the in-depth research and eye-witness accounts needed to complete this book as well as *Self-Sufficiency*. The sacrifices she's made are remarkable, if not super human. It takes a very special type of person to not only support, but drive, motivate and inspire someone to do such things with their life. And although those years we spent sustaining each other were physically demanding, spending 24 hours a day, 7 days a week for 6 years completely alone in an area where no one even knew we existed, with my wife being the only other soul I'd see the entire time, those years were honestly the best years of my life. We accomplished more than we ever had dreamed possible, making this book and the next possible and based on our experience, and I truly couldn't have done it without her.

I'd also like to thank my editor, Barbara Seiden, who, herself, is an award-winning journalist and great writer, with a B.A. from the University of Michigan. Some of her credits include writing for "Bewitched" and ABC-TV's "Movie of the Week." If I weren't actually born from her womb, I'm sure that she wouldn't have taken on such a large and controversial project. But, again, she stood by our decisions as well as supported our efforts, offering insight before and after, while patiently waiting years for us to resurface so she could receive word of our success/survival. Her editorial skills bring a comprehensive breath of fresh air to my incompetent, illogical writing style. She delivers a professionally-flowing, finished product to you, the reader, which I can't even comprehend, let alone construct myself.

My father, Craig Martin, who taught me about nature, hunting, fishing, shooting, along with mechanics and construction; he also encouraged me to join the military (where I learned leadership and combat).

My father's brother, Robert, and wife, Jo, who, on several occasions, "enlightened" me on how the government and world 'should be' (among other topics), up in the mountains or out in the desert, well into the night.

Thanks to Mexico and the Mexican people, (especially my brother in-law, Sergio, mother-in-law, Socorro, father-in-law, Sergio Sr., and extended family, friends and neighbors), who still live off and with the land. Thanks for explaining and showing me how to perform basic life functions long forgotten in the U.S. (as well as putting up with my 'less than perfect' Spanish on a daily basis).

Thanks to Dmitry Orlov for giving me the *Governmental Collapse* insert in *Chapter 4*. No-one could describe what's currently unfolding in the U.S. in front of our eyes, where it's going to go, and how to prepare for it, better than he has. His insight is awe-inspiring, yet, awakening; and I thank him and others who have the courage to speak up in such troubled times. There may be hope for humanity still--although, somehow, I doubt it.

I would also like to thank you, the reader, for buying my books and continuing to request the information I have amassed through our website. Your interest, need and desire to be self-sufficient and independent energize and motivates me to continue to construct and pass on these life lessons to you. I appreciate your past feedback and hope this book will not disappoint.

Thank you to my immediate family as well as my readership family for your faith, your spirit, and your loyalty which inspires me to make each new book better than the last.

And lastly, I would like to thank all rescue workers, soldiers, emergency workers and just normal bystanders who will soon fight and probably give their lives to save the lives of others during the first hours of the apocalypse, because there probably won't be another book to acknowledge their bravery in the aftermath.

EDITOR'S NOTE

Dan Martin, the author of "Apocalypse" and co-founder of Agua-Luna lived completely cut-off, independent from society, with only his wife on a homestead in the mountains of West Texas. They lived 100% Self-Sufficient, bill, mortgage, and debt-free for over six years without seeing one other person the entire time. Together they built their own cabin, grew their own food in hydroponic bays, caught and harvested their own rainwater, made their own clay dishware, generated their own wind and solar electricity, made their own ethanol and hydrogen fuel, and raised, slaughtered, milked and prepared their livestock and wild game.

To further explain the length to which Martin disconnected, Agua-Luna Ranch is 100% off the grid, i.e. no phones, no phone lines, no cell service, no electric lines, no water lines, no sewer lines, no garbage pickup, no postal service, no roads, no emergency access (911, medical or fire), no physical connection or association with society whatsoever.

Completely shut off from the world, they built and maintained their own security, fire control, waste management, entertainment, nutrition, furniture, home, climate control, etc. etc.

They were a true modern-day husband and wife Swiss Family Robinson. The extent of their compound's success and accomplishment through permaculture was incredible for being built and maintained by only two people; and the fact that they'd leave two high paying professions and go back to basics is amazing and an inspiration to us all to become self-reliant ourselves.

Before leaving it all behind, Martin was an Aerospace Technician for Boeing and Lucia, a computer engineer for AT&T with a Computer Science degree from the most prestigious school in the country. In his earlier years, Martin was stationed in Japan and Iraq and served in Desert Storm. Lucia received honors graduating first in her class. Martin is now the author of dozens of DIY style guides showing how to do exactly what they have done, based on their six-year experience--everything from harnessing renewable energy to producing alternative fuels, natural building methods, living life off the grid, permaculture designs, sustainability know-how, or just methods in greener, bill and debt-free urban living.

Since exiting their refuge, they've circled the globe promoting a self-help educational awareness campaign in an attempt to teach others how to be self-sufficient, lower their expenses, bills and debts through dozens of workshops & seminars on the topic. They've hosted some 100+ volunteers/interns in & out of the country, completed 36 client-based sustainable projects in the last four years (seven due for completion this year) & consulted on some 20 or more corporate and government-based renewable energy conversions. Martin and Lucia have conducted 14 radio, print and media interviews, been featured in seven magazine articles and over 1,000 online blogs. And countless posts & book notations in several different countries all mention Agua-Luna as well as Martin's personal efforts which he's undertaken.

"Because our lifestyle is lived completely self-sufficiently and self-sustainably for the last 6 years, we are familiar with the day-to-day aspects & how simple it actually is for regular people all over the world to make the conversion. No one else can say that."

- Lucia Martin

Apocalypse, How to Survive a Global Crisis... is a great source of Do-It-Yourself information. This guide can of course be utilized to survive dooms day scenarios, but yet won't be obsolete if the end of the world doesn't occur in 2012. It can still be applied to daily living out of or even in society to lower bills, debt, expenses, or to become completely self sufficient. In the end, Dan Martin may be literally transforming and possibly saving the lives of regular people all over the world.

Is the world, as we know it, going to end on December 21, 2012? I'm not going to sit here and lie to you in order to sell a few copies of books. I have no idea. No one knows for sure. There's a lot of evidence, as you'll read, that shows it's highly likely, but there was a lot of evidence showing mankind would fall in the year 666, 999, 1999 and 2000 as well. However, just because nothing happened at the passing of any of those dates, doesn't mean nothing will happen in 2012 or any future date in our lifetime for that matter. It's like the story of the boy who cried wolf: A boy watching a flock of sheep in the field would come running into town yelling a "wolf is coming, a wolf is coming," yet there were never any wolves to be found. Finally, the townspeople stopped believing his lies; and when a wolf finally did come, no one came to help. In the end the town lost their entire winter supply of meat and probably all starved to death. The point is, don't ignore a potential danger, just because it's never happened before, when in fact, as I'll show, it has all happened before.

The question then arises: what to do, if anything? The following is a letter I received from Jason Barr in Cincinnati, Ohio, which I think says it pretty well: *"Why worry about any of this if we can't do anything about it? I mean, everyone said that the 2000 millennium was going to wipe out all the computers and it didn't, and even if it had, so what? I couldn't have done anything before-hand to prepare for it. What am I supposed to do, quit my job, pull my kids out of school and move up into the mountains?"*

My response: "My wife, was a Computer Engineer in 1998 and 1999, tasked with the job of preparing computer systems around the world so that they wouldn't "crash" (thereby stopping business, trade and ultimately our way of life) at 12:00:01am on January 1st 2000 (the millennium). The problem at the time (which actually did turn out to be a viable one) was that since the invention of computers, the systems were built to only accept 2 characters in the year field. At the moment when the internal clocks would have gone from 11:59:59pm 99 to 12:00:01am 00, most computers around the world would think it's 1900, not 2000. So in order to keep global services operating past midnight, she went in and reprogrammed the computers to now accept 4 characters, additionally back-filling those now empty characters with data all the way back to 1900, so it would maintain continuity before switching. She, of course, was only one of many thousands of people around the world who did prepare for what could have been a catastrophic event. Can you even imagine what chaos would have ensued if services like telephone, electricity, water, sewer, garbage, internet, banking, sales, fuel, emergency services, etc. were to have shut down (which they would have)? You didn't need to prepare because it was done for you."

Looking back to the present, for the last ten years, major corporations, governmental bodies and military organizations have been on a mad construction spree again making vital preparations, building underground facilities all across the mid-western United States (and the world) in order to maintain a Continuity of Government (COG). If the government is preparing itself, I can see no viable reason why you shouldn't as well. Why would they be spending billions in sustainable, secure sites if it was known for sure that nothing was going to happen in 2012? I'm not saying that they know something IS absolutely going to happen and that there's a conspiracy to cover it up (which there very well may be). I'm only suggesting that they probably understand there's a good chance that something may occur and it's better to be safe than sorry don't you think?

However, these facilities are NOT open to the public. Only a chosen few are picked to receive admittance if the sky starts falling. The rest of us? Well, we're on our own. Does that mean you should drop everything, abandon everything you've worked to establish, and buy an abandoned missile silo site in Nebraska? No, of course not. But you can at least educate yourself on what to expect and make a few preparations that won't cost you much. And in the end, if 2012 passes without incident, at least you'll have a little knowledge of self-sustainability to guide you in the bright years to come or at least until the next apocalyptic event.

For those of you who are actually wanting to drop everything, it can't hurt to buy one of the only places on earth that <u>will</u> actually survive and sustain you and your family long after society is gone, can it? At the very least, you'll never pay for electricity, utilities, fuel or food again; and with the money saved on these expenses, you'd pay off the investment in a few years! If the world really does, in fact, end, the money you've invested and the high interest loans you've accumulated won't really matter anyway when the economy crashes & banking establishments fail. Hell, any debt anyone has now will be completely wiped clean.

Swine flu, West Nile Virus, bird flu, anthrax, destructive earthquakes, hurricanes, tornadoes, blizzards, droughts, floods, tsunamis, volcanoes, climate change, acid rain, deforestation, governmental corruption, war, pollution, overflowing landfills, chemical & toxic waste, smog, contaminated lakes & rivers, holes in the ozone, holes in the magnasphere, passing asteroids, whaling, oil shortages, epidemics, mass blackouts, economic collapse, government collapse, starvation, poverty; it's a wonder we're still around to tell you the truth.

CHAPTER 2

LIKELY SCENARIOS: COME WHAT MAY

Why would anyone abandon the comforts and provisions of society to have to provide for themselves and their own family? For most people, living, working and raising a family dependent on society is a way of life, the only way of life, the easiest way of life. But what if it weren't? What if you didn't need society in order to exist? Or what if that way of life was drastically disturbed, stripped away or terminated altogether? Now, I'm not saying your actual life, just your *way* of life. To you, however, those two things are one and the same. They seem intertwined; yet, in reality, they're really not. Let me paint a ~~possible~~ likely picture for you of several events that scientists, prophecy, religion and history all say have a higher possibility of happening than not in just the next 2-10 years...

The walls in your bright, white office rock violently as a giant explosion abruptly and without warning, shakes the entire 2nd floor. If this were the west coast, your first thought would be earthquake, but just outside of Denver? A few moments pass, followed by a second blast, a third, fourth, fifth, sixth, seventh, eighth. As the impacts continue, the power finally fails. Dust falling from the ceiling is re-illuminated a few seconds later when emergency lights and alarms kick on. The city seems to be quite literally blowing up around you, with your now seemingly-delicate sheetrock office taking the brunt of it. There are 10, 20, 30 blasts before the large blind-covered windows burst inward filling the room with popcorn-sized fragmented shards of glass.

With the windows out, you now feel warm bursts of air movement, coinciding with each explosion. These two forces combined are the result of atomic blast shock waves 20 miles away. But this isn't WW3; it's the effect of small meteorites smacking into the Earth's surface with the force of 500 megatons of TNT—a meteor shower the likes of which you've never seen before, but only a prelude of what's to come—meteorites the size of Suburbans and giant hamburger holding Big Boys statues, a debris field surrounding the forward leading region of what scientists call a "global killer." It'll hit the Earth with the force of 200 million Megatons of TNT, again causing the extinction of most planet-based life. A meteor approximately 16km (10x bigger than the one that hit the coast of Mexico about 65 million years ago) is right now hurtling through space at a trajectory that will cross through Earth's orbit at nearly 17,000 miles/hr, smashing into and collecting every rock in its path--AKA the debris field that is currently bombarding the plateaus of Southern Colorado, as we speak. This natural occurrence takes place every million years or so; unfortunately for you, a million years have passed! The date? December 21, 2012. Your lifestyle has just been disturbed, dramatically!

The office is noisy with the hustle and bustle of fellow co-workers bringing the day's business to an end. That long lunch-break though is starting to come into play as you find yourself rushing out last minute work in order to pick up the kids on time. But the little ones will have to wait today. Someone has just run in yelling, "An airplane has hit the White House!" and like clockwork, dozens of cell phones simultaneously ring as loved ones relay the same shocking news. Seemingly rehearsed, everyone heads to the break room to watch the news broadcast: *"... has hijacked an unknown number of jetliners ranging from Boeing 737s to 747s and have been continuously and systematically crashing them into civilian and government destinations in Los Angeles, San Francisco, Seattle, New York, Boston, Newark, New Jersey, Manhattan, Chicago, Washington, D.C., Dallas, and now Atlanta and Houston. Lisa, we're now getting reports that, at present, the current official count is 26 hijacked airplanes and that this may only be the first wave of what could potentially be up to 117 airplanes already airborne, not responding to FAA communications or in-flight transponders..."* The views outside the office window are even more surreal as a large, extremely slow, low-flying, ghost-like plane passes so close to the building that you can see alert, panic stricken passengers inside. At first, there's no sound; and even the office becomes quiet with anticipation. Then, the engines roar hard; the plane banks extreme left, racing behind the National Bank building, disappearing out of view, forever. Finally, you feel an impact so great it feels like the plane struck your building. Then another, almost in unison, several blocks away and finally one more several minutes later. The date? December 24, 2012. Your lifestyle has just been disturbed, dramatically!

A cool air flows through the long aisles of the local grocery store. With this headache, the rows and rows of vacuum-sealed, white plastic pill bottles make finding mere cough syrup seemingly impossible. And driving home with blurred vision, dizziness and cold sweats is problematic, to say the least. The driveway grows longer after what seems like a month-long journey across town and the scratchy throat has finally developed into a full-blown fever, making it difficult to even reach the bed. You see cases of a new virus has emerged all over the Midwestern United States, with reports of people affected now popping up in parts of California, New York and Texas as well. Designated R1N8, the virus will eventually ~~affect~~ kill 3/4 of Earth's human population. Thirty-eight thousand Americans were in intensive care with 'flu-like' symptoms even before any warnings were broadcasted on television. No one knows what has caused the outbreak--terrorists, government experiments gone awry, imported ferrets, nature. The date? December 13, 2012. Your lifestyle has just been disturbed, dramatically!

I lost my job today. But it was only a matter of time, and I knew it. Most corporations these days are making drastic cut-backs and laying-off hundreds of thousands. They say we're in a recession, but it's been almost 8 years. Corporate bailouts, incentives, tax breaks, loans, but I'm the one that needs to feed a family of four. And if that's not enough, now there's talk of discharging another 30,000 soldiers from active duty and releasing 7,000 more early parolees because of the lack of federal funding to feed and house them. That's all we need is another flood of jobless bodies looking for work where there's none to be had. The date? June 17, 2013. Your lifestyle has just been disturbed, dramatically!

You awake and again there's no change in the dire situation that's overshadowed the country since the total collapse of the economy. The shed is colder today, winter's now in full throttle. It's time to get up; and although you have nowhere to go, no job to be at, your sleep shift is over and someone else needs the cot. Memories of your 4-bedroom home now seem like a daydream and your commute to the old job at Palin and Associates Enterprises, a highway to heaven. You walk in a random direction, wondering where you'll find this morning's meal since the mission on 8th street closed down. Electricity and fuel is still being rationed, but you have no use for either on bicycle. The few UN, Australian and Japanese foreign-aid workers left have no control over the growing violence. Organized crime has taken on a new persona, adding to its ranks collage of criminals, out-of-work law enforcement personnel, evacuated prisoners and ex-military on the streets. And still not a word has come from the new United American Republic government in Lincoln since Texas seceded from the Union last month. Lucky them. The date? November 14, 2014. Your lifestyle is being disturbed, dramatically!

It was the middle of the night when they flew in disguised as scheduled overseas passenger jetliners, dropping bombs on most major cities along the way. Boston, New York, Newark, Chicago, Cincinnati, Indianapolis, Detroit, Lansing, Ann Arbor, Atlanta, Norfolk, Richmond, Charlottesville, Seattle, Tacoma, Portland, Washington, D.C., and, of course, the Los Angeles and San Francisco metropolitan areas. Later, ground forces came in through Vancouver, Windsor, Toronto, Laredo, Del Rio, Brownsville, El Paso and San Diego, subduing entire states with little resistance. At the time, most of our troops were in Afghanistan, Iraq, South Korea and Libya. When the National Guard finally did show, they had no chance. News reports show 12,000 people were killed in the first day alone. The president was rushed out on Wednesday and is probably in a secure underground bunker somewhere; but there's been no information from the White House since. It's truly surreal, to tell the truth--something seen in a movie about another country that we invade on the other side of the world. Who would have thought that it would ever happen to us? The date? January 1, 2013. Your lifestyle has just been disturbed, dramatically!

And although no one actually saw the explosion, the sound of the blast was unmistakable. The sky lit up with a blinding white flash, but the foretold mushroom cloud wasn't quite visible yet. As you turned to the clerk behind the counter to make sure she'd heard it as well, you noticed her arm still outstretched from handing you your morning coffee. The distant perplexed upward gaze on her face said she did. It was then that the second explosion was heard from the opposite side of the city. It seemed like an eternity passed, while you stood with other bystanders and watched speechless and in awe. A third explosion, a fourth, a fifth echoes in your ears. In between each, possibly several much fainter ones resounded in the distance as well. As you stare on, in disbelief, waiting for the next, there they finally are... dozens of dark brown mushroom clouds rising slowly into the sky, behind blocks of office buildings. The date? July 4, 2012. Your lifestyle has just been disturbed, dramatically!

It's only 7:30 and morning traffic is already brutal. Even though you still have a few miles before your exit, you merge into the faster outside lane anyway. Just then, the wheel begins to vibrate slightly like a flat tire, but without the distinct 'whapping' sound. As the car's vibration grows into a shaking and finally a violent swaying, it becomes clear that something's not right. Simultaneously, vehicles in all four lanes begin drifting around like plastic helmeted football players on a classic electric gyrating board game. Suddenly, the view ahead turns red as drivers slam on their brakes, pilling up and plowing into each other just dozens of feet in front of you. Some cars dip, dive and topple, end over end as the blacktop gives way below. Unable to stop, some drivers are pushed into the void by the now-ensuing train wreck. Within seconds and without sound, it's over.

People begin stepping out of vehicles to survey the grisly scene and for the first time feel the quake. As if shaking ticks from its back, giant earthquakes rock the planet as the Earth's tectonic plates are thrust thousands of feet into the air, dropping entire cities mercilessly into the depths below. Millions of bystanders are currently experiencing a dreamless state of instant free-fall, while entire continents change their shapes and locations. Cracks, which are as deep as the Grand Canyon, divide well-kept lawn from well-kept lawn. Entire countries, once above sea level, sink into the dark blue abyss while oceans violently rise, sending thousand-foot tsunamis over mountains of metropolitan concrete rubble. Every above-ground and underwater volcano known to exist on Earth (as well as a few new ones) erupt on cue, spewing scorching lava, deadly gasses, fiery rock and nuclear ash-like fallout into the atmosphere, blocking the Sun for months. Due to a lack of light, the crisis will trigger a mini ice age, killing every animal, plant and human above ground. And yet, there you stand, contemplating auto insurance deductibles. The date? March 21, 2013. Your lifestyle has just been disturbed, dramatically!

Tuesdays are the worst, worse than Mondays, worse than middle of the week Wednesdays. Tuesdays offer no hope for the weekend and promise a ton of work before it comes. But cheer up, this workday is about to get cut short when the power suddenly fails. The office fills with gasps, "Woo-Hoos," and cuss words as computer screens darken in the middle of tasks-in-progress. When the emergency power finally kicks on, computers regain life, and again, but in reverse order, "Woo-Hoos," cuss words and gasps fill the room. But before employees can complete their expressions of joy and sadness, the fluorescent lights flash, pop and rain a fireworks display of sparks upon the office floor. Computers fizzle and smoke in response, and voices start to take on an edge of concern. Smoke alarms, sprinklers and mass confusion accompany shouts of downright panic as everyone runs from the building. Once your eyes adjust to the outside light, you realize there's no major catastrophe, no 4-alarm fire or terrorist attack, no cause for alarm of any kind, until, that is, you see small groups of people congregating outside buildings as far as the eye can see. Little do you know, workers are evacuating buildings throughout the hemisphere as solar flares literally wipe out most of the world's electrical grid. Unaware, you've just been escorted out into a bright sunny lethal day, you're now receiving the same deadly doses of the radiation yourself. F*^$%-ing Tuesdays. The date? October 13, 2012. Your lifestyle has just been disturbed, dramatically!

The last bits of summer sunlight drift beyond the hills. You watch grass quickly turn an eerie off-white from a large living room window as a frost line rapidly flows across the front lawn, crystallizing the blades like a wave of water flowing over a sandy beach. The days are so short now, the air so cold. On the news they say that most of the blanket of snow now stretches all the way down to Florida, Louisiana, Georgia, Texas and California. The media continues to show "record-breaking temperatures and snowfall" followed by scenes of dead animals falling from the sky and fish washing up on shorelines. It must be a cold day in hell because birds are now flying south for the summer. This, they say, is the official start of a global ice age, and it's only supposed to get worse. The in-laws are trying to get everyone down to Mexico with the rest of the refugees, but word is that people are being shot just trying to cross the border. John's job hasn't laid anyone off yet; so there's probably nothing to worry about, at least, not yet. The date? July 17, 2013. Your lifestyle has just been disturbed, dramatically!

The mood is light and festive at the neighborhood bar, so you comment on the fairly attractive female's phone sitting next to you. Partially fueled by holiday spirit, you are proportionally driven by alcoholically-induced sexual intentions, but mostly you speak up just because the newest model iBerry 6G is cooler than shit. She replies with some meaningless regurgitation of already advertised half relevant dribble partially fueled by curiosity, proportionally driven to see where the night might go, but mostly just because stating miniscule trinkets of random information makes her feel good. She scoots closer saying something or another, while touching, swiping and tapping several screens into and out of existence. It's then that you both notice the message reading: "Sorry, Internet service in your area has been disabled." The satellite-broadcasted football game above the bar displays a similar message. Smart phones, palm devices and YouTube uploads throughout the scene are all disrupted. "Free Drinks!" the patrons proclaim and the night gets exponentially better. If excitement is what you crave look no further, the World Wide Web is no more! Think of the societal repercussions this will create. All good things must come to an end though I guess, huh? It was good while it lasted, I suppose, right? The date? November 15, 2012. Your lifestyle is about to be disturbed, dramatically!

The night sky is amazing and although I know it's not, Nibiru, now the 10th planet in our solar system, rather looks almost like a second moon tonight. So far, the catastrophic scientific predictions and so-called widespread panic it will create haven't manifested yet. Everything may be ok after all. You'll see, it may just pass by only blowing out a few light bulbs and transformers; either way, it's a stunning view. The date? September 15, 2013. Your lifestyle is about to be disturbed, dramatically!

The last thing I remember is walking into the hotel lobby restaurant for a dinner reservation. There were 4 of us on a lay-over from the all-day meeting with FINCO. That's when the shaking began. I remember looking up at a table of ready-to-go wine glasses shaking violently at the edge of the second floor balcony. It was only a matter of a few seconds, before everything crashed down upon us. I was knocked to the floor with the wind knocked from me. When I awoke, I heard the voices of my colleagues calling out to each other. Groping in the dark, I tried locating the others in what seemed to be an 8x8x5ft area. Two I recall were pinned under rubble, so I took my cell phone to light up the area. It was unbelievably dusty. Huge steel beams and concrete everywhere.

People yelled for help throughout the night, presumably in other parts of the restaurant. But it wasn't until the light came out on the second morning that I heard help. Someone pounding on the rubble from above, kind of systematically. We all started screaming and screaming. We were so excited, but there was no response. Eventually, we began thinking that they didn't hear us and weren't coming back. We were devastated. The next two days were the same, no one came; and I remember getting really cold and hungry. There had been a table of plates of scraps the busboy hadn't cleared on the floor on one side of the space, but that was gone in the first few hours. I even tried digging under the rubble around the table, hoping to find more food on the fifth day; but it was pointless. On the sixth, things started getting really bad. Tensions were high and hopes were low in those still talking. Sometime during eighth night, someone saw lights through the cracks, but again there was never a response. I have no idea what happened after that. My next memory was of exiting the debris and seeing the world in ruin. The date? February 26, 2013. Your lifestyle has just been disturbed, dramatically!

You awake, feeling wet and cold. Immediately realizing something's wrong, you instantly swing out of bed only to find you're knee-deep in water. "Mary, the house is flooding," you yell, but before you can get around the bed, the water rises six more inches. "Get the children," she screams, but you hesitate, in a semi-state of shock, unable to think, to move. "GET THE CHILDREN!" The girls are on the second floor, thank God, but by the time you get to the stairwell, you're wading waist-high through books, papers, clothes and couch cushions. Little do you know that in just a couple moments you'll watch helplessly as the eldest of your two daughters is swept away, never to be seen again. Half-way up the stairs, with the water almost matching your efforts, a Ford plows though the living room wall. Into the bedroom, you both waste no time snatching up two sleepy kids. This window opens up over the garage, but there's nowhere to go past that. Homes down the block are almost completely submerged now as the surge frantically rises. The death to which your neighbors must have awoke. Disorientation, confusion, submerged in complete darkness, you don't even realize that the rogue wave has separated you from your child. The date? April 21, 2012. Your lifestyle has just been disturbed, dramatically!

All of this must sound like science fiction; but it's actually all happened before. In fact, there's been a major rise in global catastrophic events that, in just the last few years, has truly (and strangely) skyrocketed:

- June, 1908, a 90ft meteoroid detonates 10km above the surface of Earth, near the Tunguska River in Russia. Equivalent to 30 megatons of TNT, it flattens every tree (80 million of them) in a 2000km radius. Frequency tables predict that such strikes should occur every 100 years or so. You can say that by 2012 we'll be slightly overdue.
- June 1914, more than an astonishing <u>70 million</u> military personnel are mobilized to fight in the largest war the Earth has ever known. Ultimately, World War I will take the lives of an epic 65,000,000 people.
- June 1919, an influenza epidemic known as the Spanish Flu spreads across the entire world, infecting 1/3 of the earth's population and ultimately killing more than a ridiculous 50 million people.
- Sep 1, 1939, more than <u>100 million</u> (outrageous numbers) military personnel are once again mobilized to fight in the largest war the Earth has ever known. Ultimately, World War II will take the lives of 72,000,000 people.
- Dec 7, 1941, forces attack/invade the United States in two waves, killing thousands of Americans.
- Aug 6, 1945, Hiroshima is hit with an atomic bomb, completely devastating the city and killing at least 166,000.
- Aug 9, 1945, Nagasaki is hit with an atomic bomb, completely devastating the city and killing 80,000.
- May 22, 1960, a 9.5 earthquake rips through Cañete, Chili, killing 6000 people and creating a tsunami that wreaks havoc across the entire world from the Americas to the Philippines, to Australia, from the southern tip of Argentina all the way up to Alaska. To date, it's the largest earthquake in recent history.
- March 28, 1979, unit 2 suffers a partial meltdown at Three Mile Island Nuclear Generating Station in Dauphin County, Pennsylvania releasing 481 PBq of radioactive gases and 740 GBq of iodine-131.

- Nov 9, 1979, computers at North American Aerospace Defense Command's Cheyenne Mountain, the Pentagon's National Military Command Center, and the Alternate National Military Command Center in Fort Ritchie, Maryland, all show that the Soviet Union has launched a full nuclear strike on America.
- Sep 26, 1983, the Soviet early-warning satellite system alerts officials that the United States has launched five missiles carrying nuclear warheads and are in flight and on their way to Russia.
- April 26, 1986, reactor 4 suffers a meltdown at the Chernobyl Nuclear Power Plant in the Soviet Union. The largest accident ever sends a plume of radioactive fallout into the atmosphere, forcing the evacuation of entire cities.
- Dec 26, 1991, the Soviet Union, one of the largest, strongest super power nations in history, suffers an economic collapse which leads to the fall of its government and the separation of its nation.
- Jan 25, 1995, a combined effort of American and Norwegian forces launch a rocket towards Russia causing President Boris Yeltsin to activate and direct his nuclear football at America in response.
- Sep 11, 2001, 19 men hijack 4 jetliners crashing 3 into several iconic American buildings, killing over 3,000 people, in the once thought-to-be 'invulnerable' United States, changing the lives of all Americans, (and the world) forever.
- September, 2001, (one week after the 9/11 terrorist attacks), letters containing lethal levels of anthrax are sent to television networks ABC, CBS, NBC, The New York Post and the National Enquirer magazines, as well as two democratic senators, killing the dozens of people who came into contact with the envelopes.
- March 12, 2003, a viral pandemic known as SARS (Severe Acute Respiratory Syndrome) spreads rapidly around the globe killing almost 10,000 people. This virus has not yet been eradicated.
- Aug 24, 2005, a category-5 Hurricane breaches land, wreaking havoc upon Florida, Texas, Mississippi, Louisiana, Georgia, Alabama, Kentucky, Arkansas, Tennessee, West Virginia, up to Ohio, Michigan and New York. New Orleans with its 1,333,000 inhabitants is completely and totally decimated. Evacuees are still homeless after 5 years. According to the Census Bureau in 2006, the est. population of New Orleans is 223,000—1/6th of its original count.
- March, 2007, divers cut and remove an 11km section of submarine Internet cable connecting Thailand and Vietnam to Hong Kong, disconnecting us from the region and the region with the rest of the online world.
- May, 2009, schools, buses, movie theaters, parks, shopping malls, concerts, and public and government buildings are shut down in every major city in the world and incoming flights from abroad are canceled worldwide as a pandemic known as Swine Flu sweeps the planet. The virus has still not been eradicated.
- Jan 12, 2010, a catastrophic magnitude 7.0 earthquake hits near the town of Port-au-Prince Haiti, killing over 230,000 people and displacing 1,000,000 more, making it one of the deadliest earthquakes in history.
- Feb 27, 2010, an 8.8 Chilean quake shakes Earth so hard it "moves the planet's axis and speeds up its rotation."
- March 6, 2010, a major earthquake in Taiwan severs 6 undersea Internet cables including SWM-3, disconnecting the U.S. from Asia and Asia from the world.
- April 15, 2010, undersea Internet cable SEA-ME-WE 4 which links Asia and Europe, fails. The resulting total information outage of World Wide Web services collapses Asia and most of Europe's Internet simultaneously.
- Oct 25, 2010, a 7.7 earthquake hits Indonesia killing thousands, sending a 3-meter-high tsunami across the planet.
- Oct 25, 2010, just hours after the earthquake, Mount Merapi (one of the most dangerous volcanoes on the planet) erupts, shooting poisonous gas, deadly ash and magma for miles, killing hundreds and displacing 40,000 more.
- Dec 21, 2010, reports surface of a new pandemic hitting Haiti. 18,000 people (and rising) are currently (as of publication) infected with Cholera, hampering still ongoing quake relief efforts two years later.
- Jan 5, 2011, Tampa Airport closes its main runway to realign it with the new position of the rapidly moving poles.
- Jan 9, 2011, Sri Lanka announces a state of emergency after 20 non-stop days of rain and flooding.
- Jan 10, 2011, Australia, a region known for its extreme deserts and droughts is virtually submerged underwater.
- Jan 14, 2011, Tunisia's President Ali dissolves his government and declares a state of emergency.
- Jan 24, 2011, 1000 dead and another 400+ missing after extreme flooding in Brazil.
- Jan 27, 2011, Egypt turns off all Internet and cell service for the country in response to civil unrest.
- Feb 1, 2011, Irish Prime Minister dissolves Ireland's government.

BREAKING NEWS: Just days before this edition went to print, news broke of multiple governmental collapses in Egypt, Tunisia and Yemen; a 9.0M earthquake, tsunami and nuclear power plant meltdown (bigger than Chernobyl) in Japan killing 27,000; the resulted dumping of millions of gallons of radioactive water (20,000 times the safe annual sea level limit) into the ocean; prompting the rest of world to brace and prepare for a radiation connected affects at home.

CHAPTER 3

SPIRITUAL PROPHECIES: A MAP TO AWARENESS

Much discussion has ensued over the years as to when the world will end. There have always been guesses, speculations, even prophecies describing imminent doom, the four horsemen, and fire and brimstone (among other things). Throughout history prophetic cultures like the Egyptians, Sumerians, Mayans, Jews, Hindues, Muslims, Christians and Natives have all given predictions, describing the end of the world in detail. The Dark Ages were filled with a time of day-to-day living in wait, anticipating the foretold apocalypse, rapture, Armageddon and the return of Jesus. In recent times, Merlin, Mother Shipton, Edgar Cayce, and now even a sophisticated online computer program, have all prophesied the same "Judgment Day" events the ancients did. The visions are vast and descriptive, compiling many books worth of possible translations and scenarios. I've attempted to provide many of these prophecies in full, if possible, rather than picking and choosing what fits my bill, so that you, the reader, can get a better glimpse of the full picture.

NOTE: Meanings in brackets and parentheses are this writer's additions and/or notes of explanation, in an attempt to bring some clarity to documents written hundreds, even thousands, of years ago in many different ancient languages and settings.

MOTHER SHIPTON

Mother Shipton, probably one of the clearest and most concise prophets, has been authenticated over and over as her predictions come true on a continuous basis. Reputedly born Ursula Southill in 1488 in Norfolk, England, she married Mr. Tony Shipton, and died only five years before Nostradamus. While all prophecies are open to interpretation, Mother Shipton's verses are easy to understand; and in light of recent world events, they seem to have extreme indications for our times.

She lived in the time of Henry VIII of England and accurately predicted his victory over France in 1513 in the Battle of the Spurs. She also correctly predicted the dissolution of the Catholic Church, the fall of Cardinal Wolsey, the untimely death of Henry's son, Edward VI, the horrific reign of "Bloody" Mary I, and the ascent of Queen Elizabeth to the throne of England. It is recorded in the diaries of Samuel Pepys that she also predicted the damage to London caused by the Great Fire. And even though her visions take on a poetic nature, the events themselves are unmistakably clear.

And now a word, in uncouth rhyme of what shall be in future time:

A cage without horse will go (automobile)*; disaster fill the world with woe* (sadness)*. In London, Primrose Hill shall be; in centre hold a Bishop's see* (meeting place). [The rate of accidental death has skyrocketed since 1900 with the invent of the automobile. The reformation of the Church of England by Henry VIII as its sole head occurred in the early 1500s.]

Around the world men's thoughts will fly; quick as the twinkling of an eye (telephone, radio, television, internet). *And water shall great wonders do* (work)*; how strange. And yet it shall come true.* [Steam power brings locomotion to reality; the Panama Canal cuts a ship route connecting two oceans, while hydro-electric dam power plants generate enough electricity to light several states, providing millions of people with electricity. All these things would have been of great wonder and strangeness to Mother Shipton during her time and therefore, in her visions.]

Through towering hills proud men shall ride; no horse or ass move by his side (motorcycle). *Beneath the water men shall walk, shall ride, shall sleep, shall even talk* (submarines and/or scuba divers). *And in the air men shall be seen; in white and black and even green.* [Commercial airline pilots wear white and black uniforms, while military pilots wear green uniforms.]

A great man then shall come and go; for prophecy declares it so. [Scholars link this vision to JFK, as he's always been referred to as "a great man," born 1917, assassinated 1963. He is arguably the one man who's done the most for our country and the planet through civil rights and the space program. I personally believe (since the visions at this time are specifically denoting technology-based advancements) that Mother Shipton is speaking of Albert Einstein (1879–1955) who, by far, has contributed to our technological advancement greater than anyone else throughout history. Shipton may also be referring to Martin Luther King, Jr. (1929-1968) or Mohandas Karamchand Gandhi (1869-1948), both of whom were also assassinated.

In water iron then shall float; as easy as a wooden boat. Gold shall be seen in stream and stone; in land that is yet unknown. [The first "iron ship" was built in 1843; however, now all ships are made from steel (iron). The great California (then unknown) Gold rush of 1848 is her second reference.]

And England shall admit a Jew; you think this strange, but it is true. The Jew that once was held in scorn (disrespect) *shall of a Christian then be born.* [In 1948, Israel, a new nation, was "born" of England and was given to the Jews.]

A house of glass shall come to pass, but alas, alas, a war will follow with the work; where dwells the Pagan and the Turk. [The Crystal Palace, a gigantic glass atrium, was constructed out of a million feet of glass in London for The Great Exhibition of 1851 and destroyed by fire in 1936. Following this catastrophe, England entered into a number of "Pagan/Turk" wars, including the Afghan, Indian and Boer wars in the Middle East and the Far East, when Queen Victoria began a campaign to expand the British Empire.]

These states will lock in fiercest strife (war)*; and seek to take each others life. When north shall thus divide the south; and Eagle build in Lion's mouth. Then tax and blood and cruel war; shall come to every humble door.* [American Civil War saw the north/south states at war and the American (eagle) War of Independence with England (lion).]

Three times shall lovely sunny France; be led to play a bloody dance. Before the people shall be free; three tyrant rulers (dictators) *shall she see.* [The three Republics of France: The French First Republic, founded in 1792, lasted until the declaration of the First French Empire in 1804, and, finally, the creation of the Consulate and Napoleon Bonaparte's rise to power. Napoleon was succeeded by his two sons, Napoleon II and Napoleon III; all three were, of course, dictators. This, however, could also allude to only Napoleon himself, followed by Manuel Noriega, (a Panamanian dictator who ruled in the 1970s and '80s and was later jailed for 7 years in France), and the third French dictator not seen yet.]

Three rulers in succession be; then when the fiercest strife (war) *is done; each springs from different dynasty* (ruling family)*; England and France shall be as one.* [World War II brought the three different dynasties of Japan, Italy and Germany together, with England and France fighting together as allies.]

The British olive (Queen Victoria) *then next, then twine; in marriage with a German vine. Men walk beneath and over streams; fulfilled shall be their wondrous dreams.* [Queen Victoria of England married Prince Albert of Saxe-Coburg and Gotha (now modern Germany) and was Queen of the Britain Empire until her death in 1901. Her reign is known as the Victorian era, and was a period of great industrial, cultural (including a massive bridge and tunnel-building campaign), political, scientific, and military progress within the United Kingdom, all of which, at the time, were indeed wondrous dreams come true for the people.]

Women shall adopt a craze (custom), *to dress like men, and trousers* (pants) *wear; and to cut off their locks of hair. They'll ride astride with brazen* (ugly) *brow; as witches do on broomstick now.* [At the end of the 19th century, bicycles became safer and cheaper, which gave women access to unprecedented mobility, contributing to their feeling of freedom and eventual emancipation in Western nations. This new personal freedom soon led to the "feminist movement" and "rational dress," liberating women from skirts, substituting for bloomers (pants for women), which in turn allowed women to straddle their new bicycles like men, instead of the traditional side-saddling. Finally, the feminist movement called for cutting the hair short, which is all described perfectly in the above narrative.]

And roaring monsters with man atop; does seem to eat the verdant (ripened) *crop. And men shall fly as birds do now; and give away the horse and plough.* [The mass exodus from farms into cities during the 1930s and '40s followed by crop harvesting machines, tractors and crop duster airplanes.]

There'll be a sign for all to see; be sure that it will certain be. Then love shall die and marriage cease; and nations wane (cease) *as babes* (children) *decrease. And wives shall fondle cats and dogs, and men live much the same as hogs* (pigs). [According to The National Center for Health Statistics published in the New York Times, the birth rates of the United States and Europe have fallen to its lowest level in at least a century. Combine that with the highest divorce rate of up to 73% in the world, where three out of four couples who marry today will get divorced, and a trendy abortion craze, and no wonder the above excerpt rings so true.]

In nineteen hundred and twenty six (1926), *build houses light of straw and sticks. For then shall mighty wars be planned, and fire and sword shall sweep the land.* [Japan, at this time, still predominantly built their homes from light wood, bamboo and thatch straw roofs. It has been said that Japan had planned the World War II attack on Pearl Harbor as early as 1926. Also Hitler published MEIN KAMPF in 1926, which outlines his 'political ideology.']

When pictures seem alive with movement free (television, movies)*; when boats like fishes swim beneath the sea* (submarines). *When men like birds shall scour the sky* (air warfare)*; then half the world, deep drenched in blood shall die.* [In 1928, Philo Farnsworth transmitted the first television image; and a year later, the U.S. Navy made electrical-powered submarines. A few years after that, in 1939, the American monoplane, which allowed pilots to "scour" the sky at three times the speed of the previous bi-planes, was invented. World War II began this same year, killing almost half of the world's population involved in the war.]

For those who live the century through; in fear and trembling this shall do. Flee to the mountains and the dens (caves)*; to bog* (swamps) *and forest and wild fens* (valleys). [At the end of the century, during the late 1990s, in preparation for the millennium, the government, as well as private corporations led by heads of the New World Order, began building underground bunkers and Sustainable sites in preparation for possible doomsday events, be it in the year 2000, 2012, or beyond.]

For storms will rage and oceans roar when "Gabriel" (the Arc Angel) *stands on sea and shore. And as he blows his wondrous horn; old worlds die and new be born.* [The fall of civilization and the rise of a new one, the end of the world as we know it, you can't get any clearer than that. The Hopi Indians actually believe four of these transformations have come and gone and that World War III will bring on the 5th. The end of the Mayan calendar signifies a similar transition into a new civilization.]

A fiery dragon will cross the sky; six times before this earth shall die. Mankind will tremble and frightened be; for the sixth heralds (stories) *in this prophecy.* [To date we've witnessed five of the six spectacular comets described above: Kahoutek, Halley's, Hyakutake, Hale-Bopp and Hartley 2. The sixth and final comet is predicted to pass very close by and possibly strike the planet in 2012 according to various scientists and religious texts (including the Bible). A good contender for this comet is the Caesar's comet, which passes extremely close to the earth every 200 years or so. Other possibilities include several dark comets which aren't visible until just before impact.]

For seven days and seven night; man will watch this awesome sight (the comet will be visible for 7 days). *The tides will rise beyond their ken* (normal levels)*; to bite away the shores and then; the mountains will begin to roar* (volcanoes)*; and earthquakes split the plain to shore.* [The comet would create an enormous tidal wave covering thousands of miles of mainland if it were to land in the ocean (which it most likely would). When it finally hit the ocean floor, the impact would shift the tectonic plates, creating massive and epic global earthquakes and volcanoes.]

And flooding waters rushing in; will flood the lands with such a din (loud noise). *That mankind cowers* (hides) *in muddy fen; and snarls about his fellow men.* [Of course, we'd all run for the hills. And as anyone who's been in a boat, cabin or has gone camping is aware, when you're kept in close proximity to others for long durations of time, you start getting on each other's nerves, to say the least (cabin fever).]

He bares his teeth and fights and kills; and secrets (hides) *food in secret* (hidden) *hills* (underground). *And ugly* (violent) *in his fear he lies; to kill marauders, thieves and spies.* [Food will become scarce without corporations and trucking companies providing for us. Marauders will attempt to steal what stashes of food you're able to accumulate.]

Man flees in terror from the flood; and kills and rapes and lies in blood. And spilling blood by mankind's hands; will stain and bitter (cause hatred) *many lands.* [Fighting for survival will become an everyday event for those that are left, with women, of course, having the worst of it.]

And when the dragon's tail (comet) *is gone; man forgets and smiles and carries on. To apply himself - too late; too late for mankind has earned deserved its fate.* [The days following 9/11 everyone looked on in shock and hope as the world collapsed around them. Afterwards, some tried to change the things that were destroying the world. Most people since then, though, have once again become complacent. This is human nature and will undoubtedly occur when the comet hits as well. There will be a brief time of peace while man tries to rebuild, but it'll be too late. Our fate is already sealed.]

His masked smile, his false grandeur (pride)*; will serve the Gods their anger stir. And they will send the dragon* (comet) *back; to light the sky - his tail will crack* (make a loud noise). *Upon the earth* (meteor impact) *and rent* (break open) *the earth; and man shall flee, King* (upper class), *Lord* (middle class) *and serf* (lower class). [When man becomes complacent a 7th comet will hit, and all classes of man will once again run away. Possibly the same comet described in the Bible's "three days' darkness of Judgment day."]

But slowly they are routed out; to seek diminished water spout (fresh water). *And men will die of thirst before; the oceans rise to mount* (cover) *the shore. And lands will crack and rend anew* (break open again)*; you think it strange, it will come true.* [The oceans, having been mostly vaporized by the comet's impact, won't continue the cycle of evaporation and condensation we know as reverse osmosis or rain, causing a massive dry spell or drought. When people finally run out of food and water in their underground bunkers, they'll be forced out only to find there's no water. Many will die before the water in the atmosphere starts to condense again.]

And in some far-off distant land; some men - oh such a tiny band (small group), *will have to leave their solid mount* (Mountain)*; and span* (cover) *the earth, those few to count.* [Cheyenne Mountain is an underground military base inside a mountain in Colorado (far-off/distant to England) housing NORAD, and holds enough food, water, fuel, supplies, tanks, jets and helicopters to sustain top officials, political leaders and corporate heads during the worst of possible times. Once the aftermath has subsided, they'll most likely come out and travel the globe, viewing the devastation.]

Who survives this disaster and then; begin the human race again; but not on land already there, but on ocean beds, stark (void), *dry and bare.* [Those survivors will undoubtedly attempt to rebuild or restart society; it's in our nature. These new cities will be built on the now accessible dry ocean beds which would be very fertile, vast and plentiful, full of mountains, hills, valleys and possibly even remaining rivers.]

Not every soul on Earth will die; as the dragon's tail goes sweeping by. Not every land on earth will sink (be flooded)*; but these will wallow in stench and stink; of rotting bodies of beast and man; of vegetation crisped* (burnt) *on land.* [The land (especially where major cities once stood) will be littered with dead rotting human and animal bodies. The produce piled up in delivery trucks, homes, warehouses and grocery stores will die and rot as well.]

The land that rises from the sea will be dry and clean and soft and free. Of mankind's dirt (pollution) *and therefore be; the source of man's new dynasty* (nation or civilization). *And those that live will ever fear; the dragon's tail for many a year. But time erases memory; you think it strange, but it will be.* [An island made up 100% of our plastic litter (pollution), named The Great Pacific Garbage Patch, was discovered floating in the Pacific Ocean west of California in 1997. Its size is estimated to be larger than the continental United States, making it visible from space. The second part refers to catastrophe survivors who are forever haunted by the event, forced to live in fear as they experience similar situations in life. Such is the case for New York residents as they still look out their windows with clenched teeth at the site of any low-flying aircraft.]

And before the race (human race) *is built anew; a silver serpent* (space ship) *comes to view. And spews out men of like unknown* (aliens)*; to mingle with the earth now grown. Cold from its heat* (cold fusion) *and these men can; enlighten the minds of future man.* [Possibly an alien race will come to help restart humanity, either teaching us a better way to exist or physically enlightening and elevating our spiritual plane.]

To intermingle and show them how; to live and love and thus endow (pass on). *The children with a second sight* (clairvoyance)*; a natural thing so that they might; grow graceful, humble, and when they do; The Golden Age* *will start anew.* [Many scientists and historic researchers like Erich von Däniken, Zecharia Sitchin and David Hatcher Childress believe that this has already happened many times over in the history. An alien race has come before helping the Sumerians, Incans, Mayans and possibly Atlantians and Egyptians. The resulting children of advanced DNA will be born with a brain that uses more of its capacity (currently we only use 10%), giving the offspring mental powers so that the human race can rebuild itself to be a peaceful species.]

The dragon's tail is but a sign; for mankind's fall and man's decline. And before this prophecy is done (fulfilled)*; I shall be burned at the stake at one* (1 o'clock). *My body singed and my soul set free; you think I utter blasphemy* (being accused of lying). *You're wrong, these things have come to me* (visions)*; this prophecy will come to be.* [The comet will cause mankind's fall (the end of society as we know it) and the decline in the human population. Mother Shipton predicts here she'll be burned at the stake before her prophecies are fulfilled, which she was in 1561.]

- Mother Shipton

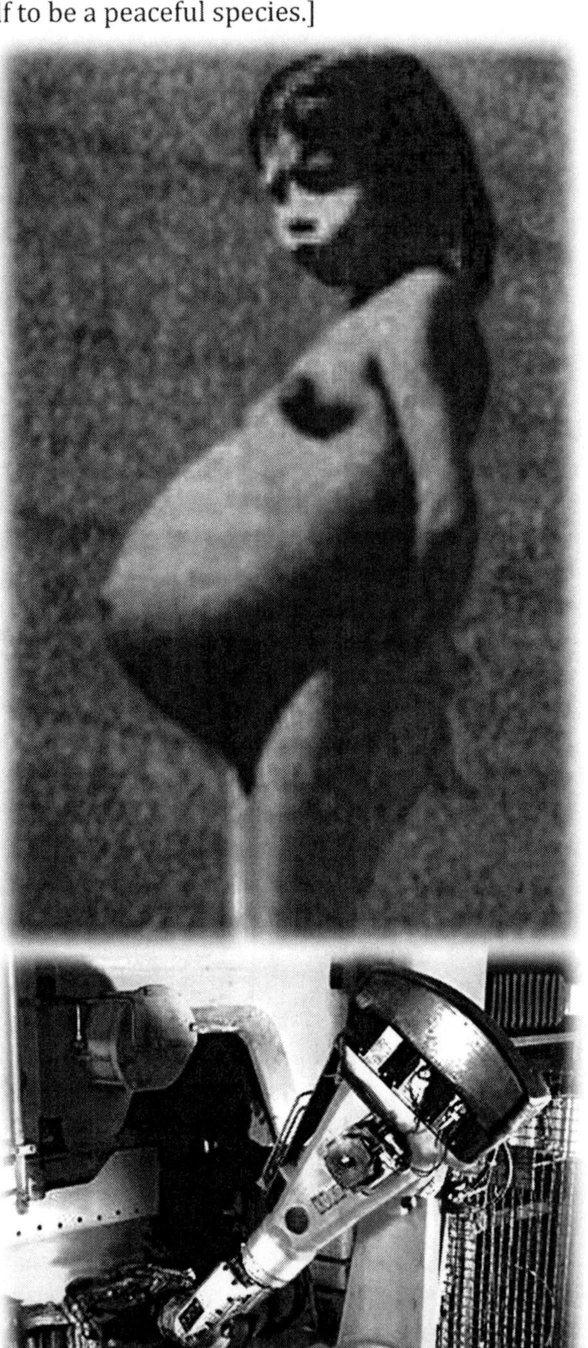

The following set of Mother Shipton prophecies were later found in a similar clay jar:

The signs will be there for all to read; when man shall do most heinous deed (savage acts). *Man will ruin kinder* (children's) *lives; by taking them as to their wives. And murder foul* (unforgiving) *and brutal deed; when man will only think of greed* (capitalism). *And man shall walk as if asleep* (robots)*; He does not look - he may not peep* (speak). [TIME reported: "A 10-year-old girl in Spain was made pregnant and gave birth last week (Oct. 2010). And earlier that same year, a 9-year-old schoolgirl in northeast China gave birth. In 2008, another 10-year-old girl in Idaho, got pregnant at age 9 and back in 1939, Lina Medina of Peru, became pregnant at the age of 5.]

And iron men (robots) *the tail* (work or labor) *shall do; and iron cart and carriage too.* [Since the 1990s industrial robots have been incorporated into manufacturing plant assembly lines, often putting mechanics out of work. Conversely, the truck replaced the cart for hauling cargo and the car the carriage for transporting people.]

The Kings (leaders) *shall false promise make; and talk just for talking's sake* (politicians are famous for talking without saying anything). *And nations plan horrific war; the like as never seen before. And taxes rise and lively down* (living standards)*; and nations wear perpetual frown* (depression). [Tony Blair and George W. Bush have been rumored to have planned the "war on terror" long before the 911 attacks; and global depression rates have since hit an all time high.]

And Christian one fights Christian two (Catholics vs. Protestants in North Ireland)*; and nations sigh* (complain), *but nothing do. And yellow men* (China) *great power gain; from mighty bear* (Russia) *with whom they've lain. These mighty tyrants* (dictators) *will fail to do; they fail to split the world in two* (nuclear war). *But from their acts a danger bred; an ague* (sickness), *leaving many dead. And physics* (doctors) *find no remedy; for this is worse than leprosy. Oh many signs for all to see; the truth of this true prophecy.* [China, the newest superpower, is said to have purchased hundreds nuclear weapons from the USSR since the collapse. Many of the world pandemics, including SARS, and Swine Flu have originated in China and/or Russia.]

Yet greater signs there be to see; as man nears latter century (2000). *Three sleeping mountains gather breath* (volcanoes)*; and spew out mud and ice and death. And earthquakes swallow town and town; in lands as yet to me unknown* (America). [Predictions from leading scientists call for a major earthquake that could essentially break off most of California, sending Los Angeles, San Diego, San Francisco, Sacramento (at the time, America was virtually unknown to Shipton) into the sea. The results are shocking when you couple that with the jump in catastrophic volcanoes, especially in China, Indonesia, Chile, Haiti and Japan today.]

- Mother Shipton

SAINT MALACHY

Possibly one of the most surreal prophets, Saint Malachy (1049-1148), was a 12-century Irish priest who had predicted (through a dream) the remaining succession of future Popes (the current Pope Benedict being the last) with stunning accuracy, ending his list with the fatal last words "... and the fearsome Judge will judge his people. The End!"

Saint Malachy's vision (which he documented and gave to the Vatican) described a continuation of just 111 more popes to reign, each with a short Latin description. In 1595 the original transcript was discovered buried in the Vatican archives and published in the book Lignum Vitae by Arnold de Wion. 500 years and more than 70 popes later, Malachy's predictions have hit the mark on every Pope. Unlike the vague and often poetic writing styles of other prophets, Malachy's predictions are short and clear, each often only containing a few Latin words like "draco depreffus" [dragon pressed down]. The clarity of this description (and the rest) comes into view only when we match this prediction with the correlating Pope of the same year. Now, one could randomly search for the best fit throughout the many Popes that have served and possibly make a connection, but to match up number for number in proceeding numerical and orderly fashion, prediction to Pope and still have the terms match perfectly is something quite different.

To use our original example: The term "draco depreffus" [dragon pressed down] is the 22nd prophecy from Malachy's list and is supposed to describe and match the 22nd Pope (after Malachy), which it does exactly. Over 200 years after Malachy, we have Clement IV (1265–1268), the 22nd Pope in sequence to reign from Malachy (the 184th starting from the beginning), whose crest literally shows an eagle with wings open smashing a dragon. And just so there's no confusion, the preceding Pope, Urban IV's coat of arms bares two red roses; and the succeeding Pope, Gregory X's crest is what looks like a castle wall, both of which are not even close to a "dragon" being "pressed down".

And as expected, the 104th term on Malachy's list "religio de populate" [religion laid waste] once again fits the 104th Pope, Benedict XV's reign exactly, which included: World War I (killing 10-20 million Christians); the Spanish flu (killing 50-100 million Christians); and the conversion of Russia and the Millions of Russian Christians into the atheist Soviet Union. In fact, we couldn't pick a Pope even out of sequence to fit the descriptions better if we tried. I've set the two lists (the list of Malachy's visions, with the list of Popes that served) for your review; the matches are uncanny, if not an exact fit. As stated before, the following lists are matched number for number in ascending sequence, the first vision correlating to the first Pope, beginning with Pope Celestine II, who was the first Pope after Malachy:

Vision	***Pope/Relation***
1. Ex caſtro Tiberis [from a castle of Tiber]	**1st Pope:** Celestine II was born in Città di Castello, Umbria, on the shores of the Tiber.
2. *Inimicus expulſus* [enemy expelled]	**2nd Pope:** Lucius II's surname Caccianemici's, means "to hunt, enemies".
3. *Ex magnitudine mõtis* [of a great mountain]	**3rd Pope:** Eugene III was from the town of Montemagno.
4. *Abbas Suburranus* [suburran abbot]	**4th Pope:** Anastasius IV was from the Suburra family.
5. *De rure albo* [from the white countryside]	**5th Pope:** Adrian IV, bishop of Albano, was born & educated in the town of St. Albans.
6. *Ex tetro carcere* [out of a loathsome prison]	**6th Pope:** Victor IV was Cardinal of St. Nicholas in the Tullian prison.
7. *Via Tranſtiberina* [road across the Tiber]	**7th Pope:** Paschal III was Cardinal of St. Mary across the Tiber.
8. *De Pannonia Thuſciæ* [Tusculan Hungary]	**8th Pope:** Callixtus III was a Hungarian born & Cardinal Bishop of Tusculum.
9. *Ex anſere cuſtode* [out of the guardian goose]	**9th Pope:** Alexander III's family coat of arms bares a goose on it.
10. *Lux in oſtio* [a light in the entrance]	**10th Pope:** Lucius III was Cardinal Bishop of Ostia. Lux meaning Lucius (light).
11. *Sus in cribro* [pig in a sieve]	**11th Pope:** Urban III was of the Cribella or Crivelli (sieve) family, whose shield is a pig.
12. *Enſis Laurentii* [the sword of St Lawrence]	**12th Pope:** Gregory VIII Cardinal of St. Lawrence; whose shield was a pair of swords.
13. *De Schola exiet* [he will come from school]	**13th Pope:** Clement III was from the house of Scolari [scholar].
14. *De rure bouenſi* [from cattle country]	**14th Pope:** Celestine III was of the Bovensis or boves (cattle) family.
15. *Comes Signatus* [designated count]	**15th Pope:** Innocent III was from the family of the Counts of Signia (Segni).
16. *Canonicus de latere* [canon from the side]	**16th Pope:** Honorius III served as a Canon in the church of Santa Maria Maggiore.
17. *Auis Oſtienſis* [bird of Ostia]	**17th Pope:** Gregory IX cardinal Bishop of Ostia's family coat had a bird.
18. *Leo Sabinus* [Sabine Lion]	**18th Pope:** Celestine IV was Cardinal Bishop of Sabina, whose arms bore a lion.
19. *Comes Laurentius* [count Lawrence]	**19th Pope:** Innocent IV Cardinal-Priest of Lawrence & his father was Count of Lavagna.
20. *Signum Oſtienſe* [sign of Ostia]	**20th Pope:** Alexander IV was of the Conti-Segni family & the Cardinal Bishop of Ostia.
21. *Hieruſalem Campanię* [Jerusalem Champagne]	**21st Pope:** Urban IV was from Troyes, Champagne & patriarch of Jerusalem.
22. *Draco depreſſus* [dragon pressed down]	**22nd Pope:** Clement IV's family coat of arms was an eagle smashing a dragon.
23. *Anguinus uir* [snaky man]	**23rd Pope:** Gregory X's family coat of arms bares a serpent swallowing a male infant.
24. *Concionator Gallus* [French preacher]	**24th Pope:** Innocent V was from France & belonged to the order of preachers.
25. *Bonus Comes* [good count]	**25th Pope:** Adrian V's surname 'Ottobono' means (good), of the Lavagna counts.
26. *Piſcator Thuſcus* [Tuscan Fisherman]	**26th Pope:** John XXI was the Cardinal Bishop of Tusculum.
27. *Roſa compoſita* [composite rose]	**27th Pope:** Nicholas III's family coat of arms (or composite) bares a rose.
28. *Ex teloneo liliacei Martini* [toll of lilied Martin]	**28th Pope:** Martin IV was the Treasurer for the St. Martin Church, France.
29. *Ex roſa leonine* [the rose from the lion]	**29th Pope:** Honorius IV's family coat of arms bares two lions holding a rose.
30. *Picus inter eſcas* [woodpecker between food]	**30th Pope:** Nicholas IV was originally from Ascoli Piceno, in the country of Picene.
31. *Ex eremo celſus* [raised out of the desert]	**31st Pope:** St. Celestine V was a hermit; his chosen name was Celestine (Cellus).
32. *Ex undarũ bñdictione* [blessing of the waves]	**32nd Pope:** Boniface VIII's family coat of arms were waves.
33. *Concionator patereus* [preacher From Patara]	**33rd Pope:** Benedict XI was from Patara & belonged to the Order of Preachers.
34. *De feſſis aquitanicis* [fesses of Aquitaine]	**34th Pope:** Clement V was Archbishop in Aquitaine. His family coat bares fesses.
35. *De ſutore oſſeo* [from a bony cobbler]	**35th Pope:** John XXII's family name 'Duese' means bones, whose father was a cobbler.
36. *Coruus ſchiſmaticus* [schismatic crow]	**36th Pope:** Nicholas V was called brother Peter of Corbarium" (Corvaro or crow).
37. *Frigidus Abbas* [cold abbot]	**37th Pope:** Benedict XII was an Abbot at Fontfroide (cold spring).
38. *De roſa Attrebatenſi* [from the rose of Arras]	**38th Pope:** Clement VI was the Bishop of Arras & his coat of arms showed six roses.
39. *De mõtibus Pãmachii* [Pamachius mountains]	**39th Pope:** Innocent VI born at Mont Limoges & was knows as St. Pammachius.
40. *Gallus Vicecomes* [French viscount]	**40th Pope:** Urban V was a French-born Nobleman.
41. *Nouus de uirgine forti* [from the strong virgin]	**41st Pope:** Gregory XI was Cardinal of New St. Mary's before becoming Pope.
42. *Decruce apoſtolica* [from the apostolic cross]	**42nd Pope:** Clement VII was CP of the 12 holy apostles (whom coat was crossed arms).
43. *Luna Coſmedina* [cosmedine moon]	**43rd Pope:** Benedict XIII was "Peter de Luna", Cardinal Deacon in Cosmedin.
44. *Schiſma Barchinoniũ* [schism of Barcelonas]	**44th Pope:** Clement VIII was an Antipope, Canon of Barcelona.
45. *De inferno prægnãti* [from a pregnant hell]	**45th Pope:** Urban VI was born Inferno, to the surname 'Prignano' (Prignani).
46. *Cubus de mixtione* [cube from a mixture]	**46th Pope:** Boniface IX's coat of arms resembles three dimensional cubes.
47. *De meliore ſydere* [from a better star]	**47th Pope:** Innocent VII coat of arms bore a star.
48. *Nauta de Ponte nigro* [sailo of a black bridge]	**48th Pope:** Gregory XII a Commendatary of the church of Negroponte (black bridge).
49. *Flagellum ſolis* [whip of the Sun]	**49th Pope:** Alexander V's coat of arms bares a large sun.
50. *Ceruus Sirenæ* [stag of the siren]	**50th Pope:** John XXIII was Cardinal of St. Eustachius, who saw a stag with a cross.
51. *Corona ueli aurei* [crown of a golden curtain]	**51st Pope:** Martin V was Cardinal Deacon of San Giogia in Velabro (golden veil).
52. *Lupa Cœleſtina* [heavenly she-wolf]	**52nd Pope:** Eugene IV was a Bishop of Siena bares a female wolf on its coat of arms.
53. *Amator Crucis* [lover of the cross]	**53rd Pope:** Felix V's surname was Amadeus (Amator) of Savoy which shows a cross.
54. *De modicitate Lunæ* [from the mean Luna]	**54th Pope:** Nicholas V was from Sarzana in the diocese of Luni (Luna).
55. *Bos paſcens* [pasturing ox]	**55th Pope:** Callixtus III's coat of arms bore a grazing ox.
56. *De Capra & Albergo* [of nanny-goat & an inn]	**56th Pope:** Pius II was secretary to Cardinal Capranica & Albergatti.
57. *De Ceruo & Leone* [from a stag & lion]	**57th Pope:** Paul II was Bishop of Cervia (stag) & as was titled "the winged lion".
58. *Piſcator minorita* [minorite fisherman]	**58th Pope:** Sixtus IV was of the Franciscans (Minorites), born to a fisherman.
59. *Præcurſor Siciliæ* [forerunner of Sicily]	**59th Pope:** Innocent VIII was the Bishop of Molfetta in Sicily before becoming Pope.
60. *Bos Albanus in portu* [bull of Alba in harbor]	**60th Pope:** Alexander VI was Cardinal Bishop with the title of Albano & Porto.
61. *De paruo homine* [from a small man]	**61st Pope:** Pius III's surname was "Piccolomini" (small man).
62. *Fructus Iouis iuuabit* [Jupiter fruit will help]	**62nd Pope:** Julius II's coat of arms bore Jupiter's sacred oak tree.

63. *De craticula Politiana* [from a Politian gridiron] **63rd Pope:** Leo X's father name "Lorenzo the Magnificent" connects back to Gridiron.
64. *Leo Florentius* [Florentian lion] **64th Pope:** Adrian VI's family coat of arms (Florenszoon/Florentius) bore two lions.
65. *Flos pilei ægri* [flower of the sick man's pill] **65th Pope:** Clement VII's coat bore six medical balls, one which held the Florentine lily.
66. *Hiacinthus medicorũ* [hyacinth physicians] **66th Pope:** Paul III's coat of arms bore six hyacinths.
67. *De corona montana* [of a mountainous crown] **67th Pope:** Julius III's coat bore mountains & palm branches in the shape of a crown.
68. *Frumentum flocidum* [trifling grain] **68th Pope:** Marcellus II's coat of arms bore a stag & ears of wheat.
69. *De fide Petri* [from Peter's faith] **69th Pope:** Paul IV used his surname Pietro.
70. *Eſculapii pharmacum* [Aesculapius' medicine] **70th Pope:** Pius IV's surname was 'Medici'.
71. *Angelus nemoroſus* [angel of the grove] **71st Pope:** St. Pius V was born in Bosco (grove) with the surname 'Michele' the angel.
72. *Medium corpus pilarũ* [half body of the balls] **72nd Pope:** Gregory XIII's coat is a half dragon & 'balls' is connected to his anointment.
73. *Axis in medietate ſigni* [axle in midst of a sign] **73rd Pope:** Sixtus V's coat of arms bares an axle.
74. *De rore cœli* [from the dew of the sky] **74th Pope:** Urban VII was Archbishop where tree sap is known as "dew of heaven".
75. *Ex antiquitate Vrbis* [of the antiquity city] **75th Pope:** Gregory XIV's father was from the ancient city of Milan.
76. *Pia ciuitas in bello* [pious city in war] **76th Pope:** Innocent IX was the Patriarch to the city of Jerusalem (the city of wars).
77. *Crux Romulea* [cross of Romulus] **77th Pope:** Clement VIII had the chosen name of Saint Pancratius (a Roman martyr).
78. *Vndoſus uir* [wavy man] **78th Pope:** Leo XI was the Bishop of Palestrina (the seafaring hero Ulysses).
79. *Gens peruerſa* [corrupted nation] **79th Pope:** Paul V appointed his own nephew to the College of Cardinals.
80. *In tribulatione pacis* [in the trouble of peace] **80th Pope:** Gregory XV's Papacy corresponded with the Thirty Years War.
81. *Lilium et roſa* [lily & rose] **81st Pope:** Urban VIII was from Florence, Italy, which bears a red lily on its coat.
82. *Lucunditas crucis* [delight of the cross] **82nd Pope:** Innocent X was made Pope on the day of the Exaltation of the Cross.
83. *Montium cuſtos* [guard of the mountains] **83rd Pope:** Alexander VII's coat of arms bore six mountains & a star.
84. *Sydus olorum* [star of the swans] **84th Pope:** Clement IX's surname Chigi (swan) was linked to Alexander VII (the "star").
85. *De flumine magno* [from a great river] **85th Pope:** Clement X was born in Rome which sits on the great Tiber river.
86. *Bellua inſatiabilis* [insatiable beast] **86th Pope:** Innocent XI's coat of arms bore a lion.
87. Pœnitentia glorioſa [glorious penitence] **87th Pope:** Alexander VIII's surname was "Pietro" who repented after denying Jesus.
88. *Raſtrum in porta* [rake in the door] **88th Pope:** Innocent XII's surname was 'Rastrello', which means "rake" in Italian.
89. *Flores circundati* [surrounded flowers] **89th Pope:** Clement XI Cardinal of San Maria Aquiro (who was adorned with flowers).
90. *De bona religione* [from good religion] **90th Pope:** Innocent XIII's family was well known for Pope production.
91. *Miles in bello* [soldier in war] **91st Pope:** Benedict XIII, all but five Cardinals rose up & led a violent war against him.
92. *Columna excelſa* [lofty column] **92nd Pope:** Clement XII saved two columns from Parthenon for his chapel at Mantua.
93. *Animal rurale* [country animal] **93rd Pope:** Benedict XIV) was from Bavaria which bore two lions on its coat of arms.
94. *Roſa Vmbriæ* [rose of Umbria] **94th Pope:** Clement XIII's Cardinal title was Santa Maria (represented as a rose).
95. *Vrſus uelox* [swift bear] **95th Pope:** Clement XIV's family crest bore a bear running.
96. *Peregrin apoſtolic* [apostolic pilgrim] **96th Pope:** Pius VI spent the last two years of his life in exile as a prisoner.
97. *Aquila rapax* [rapacious eagle] **97th Pope:** Pius VII was Pope during the rain of Napoleon (the eagle).
98. *Canis & coluber* [dog & snake] **98th Pope:** Leo XII was hated often referred to as a "Dog" and/or "snake" at the time.
99. *Vir religioſus* [religious man] **99th Pope:** Pius VIII's chosen name 'Pius' means exhibiting religious reverence; devout.
100. *De balneis Ethruriæ* [of the baths of Tuscany] **100th Pope:** Gregory XVI belonged to Camaldolese (Fonte Buono or good fountain).
101. *Crux de cruce* [cross from cross] **101st Pope:** Pius IX was stripped by Savoy (whose coat is a white cross on a red cross).
102. *Lumen in cœlo* [light in the sky] **102nd Pope:** Leo XIII's coat of arms bore a shooting star.
103. *Ignis ardens* [having an intense love for] **103rd Pope:** St. Pius X's was the first pope in 400 years to be declared a saint.
104. *Religio depopulata* [religion laid waste] **104th Pope:** Benedict XV reign included: WWI (killing 10-20 million Christians); the Spanish flu (killing 50-100 million Christians), the conversion of Russia to atheism.
105. *Fides intrepida* [intrepid faith] **105th Pope:** Pius XI condemned Nazi racism & signed with Fascist Italy, giving the Vatican sovereignty placing the Pope at head of state.
106. *Paſtor angelicus* [angelic shepherd] **106th Pope:** Pius XII supposedly received vision exercising Papal Infallibility.
107. *Paſtor & nauta* [shepherd & sailor] **107th Pope:** John XXIII was patriarch of the maritime city of Venice.
108. *Flos florum* [flower of flowers] **108th Pope:** Paul VI's arms bore three lily flowers.
109. *De medietate lunæ* [from the half moon] **109th Pope:** John Paul I was born on the day of the half moon.
110. *De labore ſolis* [of the labor of the Sun] **110th Pope:** John Paul II's life was spent in communist Poland known as the star of communism or "the sun of the workers".
111. *Gloria oliuæ* [glory of the olive] **111th Pope:** Benedict XVI chose Benedict XVI as his regal name, which traces back to the Order of Saint Benedict & the Olivetans both which use Olive branch in symbols.

In persecutione extrema Petrus Romanus qui paſcet oues in multis tribulationibus: quibus tranſactis ciuitas ſepticollis diruetur & Iudex tremẽdus iudicabit populum ſuum Finis [In extreme persecution, the seat of the Holy Roman Church will be occupied by Peter the Roman, he'll feed the sheep through tribulation, at the end the city of seven hills will fall & the Judge will judge his people. The End.] **(Wyon, 1595)**

There are several interpretations pertaining to the unnumbered 112th Pope listed on the Malachy list. Since there is no number on the original document pertaining to the last prediction of Petrus Romanus, many believe that the last-numbered Pope/prediction on the St. Malachy list (Pope Benedict XVI/Gloria Olivae) is in fact Petrus Romanus; and, therefore, the current Pope is the last Pope to reign in the Holy Roman Church. Another theory is that the next/last Pope to sit as the head of the Catholic Church after the current Pope Benedict XVI will not actually be a Pope. In order for this scenario to come true, a catastrophe would need to occur--one large enough to wipe out the entire College of Cardinals. This could be the work of a fast-moving globally-contagious virus or a solitary occurrence directed right at the Vatican during either a consistory or a conclave of the College of Cardinals. In this instance, the top surviving official of the Roman Curia would take up position as the "caretaker of the Church" and wouldn't take on a papal name since he would not actually be Pope. Peter then would be his real surname. Conversely, if Petrus Romanus was not actually a prediction of St. Malachy but added at some other time, the current Pope (Pope Benedict XVI) would, in fact, then be the last Pope anyway.

THE MAYANS

The Mayans, who we're hearing so much about today, were a Mesoamerican culture arriving on the scene as far back as the year 2,600 B.C; but they really flourished around 250 A.D.-900 A.D. One of the most advanced mathematical and astronomical societies ever; this culture could track and predict time, formulating the span of a year to the thousandth of a decimal point (unachieved by the Greeks or Romans). They were able to calculate every solar and lunar eclipse for the next thousand years based on a calendar called the 'Long Count.' The Long Count calendar lists every day starting from the "beginning of time" ending at the "end of time." In our case, December 21st 2012 (or surrounding days/months), is literally the end of days. These durations of time are separated by groups of cycles of 1872000 days known as 13 Baktuns, which is approximately equal to 5126 years or one 'World Age.' From this, the Mayans were able to predict rulers, world events, world wars, even the date that the white man would come in boats. (In 1521 A.D. Spanish invaders found empty cities abandoned by the Mayans. They had simply just packed up and left before the Spanish arrived.) Finally, they predicted the end of the world as we know it.

The difference between the Mayans and other prophetic groups/individuals is the fact that every prediction the Mayans have given has come true, every single one. This is largely not due to mythology, spirituality, dreams or insights from God, but to the fact that their visions weren't actually visions at all, but scientific calculations based solely on math and astrology. The ending of the Mayan calendar is a visual and numerical representation to the ending of a previously observed 'Earth phase' or cycle, in which the Earth was changed by some event and recorded by humans at least once already in the past. You see according to the Mayans (and most other ethnic groups) the Earth goes through various cycles every 10,000 years or so, ending in some type of great event (the last being a great flood). These cycles and world altering/re-shaping events were then recorded and passed on time after time. Everyone now knows that we're currently on the crest of a global warming flip-flop that will send the planet into another one of these "great changes." The Mayans knew this simply because it has all happened many, many times before, not because of some unexplainable, unseeable hocus-pocus; and with a 100% track record, it's a good idea to listen to what they have to say this time as well.

Our calendar (history and time) is based on a linear concept: Time continues forever in a straight line. The Mayan calendar is that of a cyclical concept, where history and time travels in an arch or circle, finally doubling back on itself, completing the cycle and starting a new. In this case, the term 'history repeats itself' really holds true. Whereas our calendar is shown (and printed) in a linear structure day after day, month after month, page after page, a new calendar replacing the last every January, continuing on forever for the last 2000 years, the Mayan calendar is shown simply as a circle, with never any need to print another. Imagine a calendar that, rather than turn the page every month, or add a new one every year, you just have a different picture representing the next month, year, age.

So how did all this 2012 hype get connected with the Mayan Calendar? Even though our two calendars are formatted very differently, they both still document the exact same Earth history (days, weeks, months, years, etc.), only with different starting points. The key is finding out where in time the two calendars overlap. Dozens of scholars on the subject have debated the point of commencement of the Mayan Long Count calendar (0.0.0.0.0) in correlation to our calendar (the Julian calendar). They've come to agree on the date of 6 September 3114 BC. When we count 1872000 days later (the total number of days in the Mayan calendar) on our calendar, it ends on... you guessed it, December 21, 2012.

Why did the Mayans, who do everything based on past, present and future occurrences, choose these dates to start and end a cycle? Is it any coincidence that the Egyptians 'Age of Picius' and 'Age of Aquarius' cycles end and start almost on the same date? The fact is that some event <u>will</u> occur at the end of the Long Count calendar, it always has. This is already proven via the Mayan's incredibly accurate astrological calculating, recording and documenting skills. Thousands of predictions concerning eclipses, solar flares, meteorological impacts and other astrological events have come true on time, every time for thousands of years with a 100% accuracy rate. To turn a blind eye now, while saying this time it won't come to pass, is completely absurd. Will every man, woman and child on earth die in a bloody apocalyptic science-fiction-based scenario? Will all humans suddenly vanish off the face of the earth as we ascend consciousness? The calendar doesn't say these things. It simply says that this cycle will end as it always has based on an event(s) that have always occurred on this same day since the dawn of time. As for the rest we'll have to wait and see.

What is the actual event? Scientifically as discussed in *Chapter 4*, it could be any number of world-changing catastrophes which the planet currently is on the verge of undergoing. Planets/galaxies alignments, solar flares, axis shifts, climate change, viral pandemics, WW3, widespread nuclear terrorist attack, global economic and/or governmental collapse (the list goes on) could all correspond with the Mayan's 'end of days.' Which one(s) will cause the most change is yet to be seen. We may, however, get a little hint by looking at how the last cycles ended: the first cycle ended with a Jaguar taking all of the people from Earth, the second ended by air (which I presume to mean tornadoes, hurricanes, etc.), the third by fire (volcanoes, meteor), the fourth in water (flood, tsunamis), which means this one will be by earth (earthquake, axis shift, crust realignment) which is what scholars have deduced from the calendar and which we're seeing an extreme spike of lately.

On December 21, 2012 the Sun will literally stand still, when it lines up with the Milky Way and the galactic equinox, something that hasn't occurred in roughly 26,000 years. The Milky Way is that cloud of bright stars in the evening sky. The galactic cosmological equinox is the axis in which the constellations move and have moved since the beginning of time, aka defined coordinates in space. It is said that we will transcend a spiritual wall into a heightened era of awareness and intelligence when the two align. What this means for us physically, is that ions, neutrons, electrons, and "whatever (other) energy that typically streams to Earth and through your body from the center of the Milky Way will indeed be disrupted on 12/21/12 at 11:11 p.m. Universal Time," Journalist Lawrence Joseph writes. According to most neurobiologists, psychologists and behavioral science experts, we don't know how the universe, particles and magnetic forces affect the brain and body. For all we know, we may transcend some fixed point in reality; descend into a puddle of mush on the floor, spontaneously combust, start barking, or worse.

Interestingly, there are numerous unsolved and unrelated riddles concerning the Mayans by which, even today, leading scientists in the field are duped by, such as:

- What caused the instant disappearance of the Mayans at the peak of their culture? From 600 A.D. to 850 A.D. the Mayan population exceeded 22,000,000. In the year 850 A.D., that number dramatically dropped to just 7,333,333, or 1/3 the population, virtually overnight. Over 14 million people basically disappeared without signs of mass graves or migration.
- While possessing the knowledge of the wheel (shown in discovered Mayan children's toys), why did they develop elaborate and sophisticated road systems, but never actually utilize the wheel?
- How and why did they paint detailed images of the dark side of the moon without ever seeing it? (The moon orbits in a fixed position; it does not rotate but is rather locked face to face with the Earth. The "dark side" or back side of the moon is never seen by anyone other than those who have traveled by spacecraft or the photos sent back by such devices.)

THE HOPI

The Hopi, a Native American people, are indigenous to Northern Arizona in North America. According to Hopi legend, their country will be laid to ruins by what to many readers, is described as an atomic bomb and nuclear fallout ash: *"Eventually a gourd full of ashes would be invented, which if dropped from the sky would boil the oceans and burn the land causing nothing to grow for many years"* as recanted by Frank Waters, an American writer known for his historical works on the southwest. The Hopi may have received their information from the same source as the Mayans, being that both crossed the Bering land bridge from Asia thousands of years earlier. Many clan leaders have seen signs that the end is near come to pass over the last 500 years or so and are seeing the remaining signs coming true during our lifetime. White Feather of Bear Clan states:

The Fourth World shall end soon, and the Fifth World will begin. This the elders everywhere know. The Signs over many years have been fulfilled, and so few are left.

This is the First Sign: We were told of the coming of the white-skinned men, like Pahana, (elder brother) *but not living like Pahana - men who took the land that was not theirs and who struck their enemies with thunder.* [As early as the mid 1600s, white men took Native American lands by force using thunderous rifles and canons.]

This is the Second Sign: Our lands will see the coming of spinning wheels filled with voices. (Covered wagons entered the scene early on, where the occupants inside could be heard but not seen.)

This is the Third Sign: A strange beast like a buffalo but with great long horns, will overrun the land in large numbers. [Cattle, with their larger horns, first introduced by Europeans have since decimated the American landscape, turning lush prairies into vast deserts.]

This is the Fourth Sign: The land will be crossed by snakes of iron. [Railway tracks quickly snaked their way across the country as the industrial revolution swung into full force.]

This is the Fifth Sign: The land shall be crisscrossed by a giant spider's web. [Millions of miles of utility and telephone lines hung from poles now literally crisscross the country, forming what looks like giant spider webs.]

This is the Sixth Sign: The land shall be crisscrossed with rivers of stone that make pictures in the sun. [Since the early 1900s almost 2 million miles

of asphalt (tar and stone) roads have been laid which produce mirages as they heat up in the Sun.]

This is the Seventh Sign: You will hear of the sea turning black, and many living things dying because of it. [Oil spills like Bp's 2010 incitement in the Gulf of Mexico dumped more than 5 million barrels of oil into the ocean, literally turning it black.]

This is the Eighth Sign: You will see many youth, who wear their hair long like our people, come and join the tribal nations, to learn our ways and wisdom. [Since the 1960s the hippies with their long hair, started a movement leading thousands of people to travel to reservations in order to learn the ways of the Native Americans.]

And this is the Ninth and Last Sign: You will hear of a dwelling-place in the heavens, above the earth, that shall fall with a great crash. It will appear as a blue star. Very soon after this, the ceremonies of the Hopi people will cease. [Many believe this last prophecy to be a comet; however because of the term "dwelling-place in the heavens", this sounds more to me like the new International Space Station which is due for completion in, you guessed it, 2012. If burning up in our atmosphere, methane inside the ISS would in fact burn blue.]

These are the Signs that great destruction is here: The world shall rock to and fro. The white man will battle people in other lands -- those who possessed the first light of wisdom. There will be many columns of smoke and fire such as the white man has made in the deserts not far from here. (The military tested the first atomic bombs in Los Alamos, New Mexico, during the 1950s, not far from the Hopi reservation). *Those who stay and live in the places of the Hopi shall be safe. Then there will be much to rebuild. And soon, very soon afterward, Pahana will return. He shall bring with him the dawn of the Fifth World. He shall plant the seeds of his wisdom in our hearts. Even now the seeds are being planted. These shall smooth the way to the Emergence into the Fifth World.* (Waters, 1993)

Is this Hopi legend likely to come true? Well, the Hopi have a great track record, 3 for 3 to be exact. According to the Hopi, the Earth has been wiped clean 3 times before, once by fire (during the Hadean Era 4.6 billion years ago, the surface of the earth was completely covered in volcanoes and lava), the next by Ice (the last ice age 20,000 years ago, covered both hemispheres with glaciers), the third by flood (according to the Bible, along with scientific evidence, the great flood occurred 12,000 years ago, due to an enormous warm-up of the planet causing glaciers from the last ice age to melt), which brings us to the present transition:

The end of the fourth world (called Tuwaqachi by the Hopi) is described by Frank Waters in his book *The Book of Hopi*: *"Eventually a gourd full of ashes would be invented, which if dropped from the sky would boil the oceans and burn the land causing nothing to grow for many years* (atomic bomb). *This would be the sign for a certain Hopi to bring out his teachings in order to warn the world that the fourth and final event would happen soon. That it could bring an end to all life unless people correct themselves and their leaders in time."*

Waters goes on to say *"The final stage, called "The great day of Purification," has been described as a "Mystery Egg" in which the forces of the swastika* (India or Germany) *and the Sun* (China) *plus a third force symbolized by the color "red"* (any communist country) *culminate either in total rebirth or total annihilation. The degree of violence will be determined by the degree of inequity caused among the peoples of the world and in the balance of nature. In this crisis rich and poor will be forced to struggle as equals in order to survive."*

The Hopi tell of three additional worlds to follow the fall of ours, that of "The Fifth World" (by the arrival of Pahana, or the lost "White Brother"), "The Sixth World" (which is The World of Prophecy and Revelation), and "The Seventh Age" (The World of Completion), which shows that the world will, in fact, not be actually "ending" but merely passing through a transition. That's not to say, however, that the human race won't incur major casualties during the transition. But the Hopi aren't the only Native American people who talk of the end times. Most American Indian cultures hold the same references:

So they knew things would happen. Things would speed up a little. There would be a cobweb built around the earth, and people would talk across this cobweb (phone, World Wide Web). *When this talking cobweb was built around the earth, a sign of life would appear in the east, but it would tilt and bring death. It would come with the sun. But the sun itself would rise one day, not in the east but in the west* (polar shift). *So the elders said, when you see the sun rising in the east, and you see the sign of life reversed and tilted in the east, you know that the Great Death is to come upon the earth, and now the Great Spirit will grab the earth again in His hand and shake it* (earthquake), *and this shaking will be worse than the first.*

- Cherokee Legend

World Wide Web

When the end is near, that when four white buffalo have been born ... then the old ways will return ... and the earth will be saved. At the end of the time White Buffalo Woman will walk again the earth. [The chances of one white buffalo being born (let alone four) are calculated to be 1 in 10 million according to some. Yet since 2005, exactly that has occurred.]

- The Lakota, Sioux Nation

NOSTRADAMUS

This brings us to the granddaddy of all prophets. Although I like Nostradamus's predictions and they make sense with a lot of current events leading up to 2012; simply put, it's the opinion of this author that he's a fake:

The year 1999 seven month (September), *From the sky will come a great King of terror: To bring back to life the great King of Angolmois,* (the Mongols), *Before after Mars to reign by good luck* (for a long time).

- Century X, Quatrain 72

1999 came and went and no "great king of terror came from the sky." Now, I could explain the misdated visions away in some type of creative secondary events which, in turn, would eventually lead up to the end of the world occurring in 2012 or beyond, except really nothing of significance occurred in September 1999, (other than Viacom and CBS merging, Aaaa). In fact, if anything, September 1999 was abnormally calm around the world. Many relate this prophecy with the events that occurred on September 11, 2001, which in all fairness would have made a LOT more sense in that (a) from the sky came not only one, but four (or three depending how you look at it) great terrors, (b) the terrorist attacks were meant to strike a vital blow to the U.S. and bring power back to Middle Eastern countries, especially Islamic nations which were once controlled by Genghis Khan (the greatest king ever known); and (c) the events which occurred on 9/11 resulted from a 'situation' that has been going on over there right now for almost ten years, a very long time indeed. But the dates just don't match up; and there's no getting around that. So I'm not going to sit here and stretch the truth and make the rest of his predictions make sense to you, the reader, in order to sell a few more books. The bottom line is that nothing happened during the date that Nostradamus predicted something would, which to me (I can't speak for everyone) disproves him as a viable prophet all together. Feel free to pick up a translated copy of his work like *The true prophecies or prognostications of Michel Nostradamus*, by Garencières and read for yourself, though, I may be wrong and he may say the world will end in 2012 also.

SUMERIANS & PLANET NIBIRU

Most have heard of planet 'Nibiru', Planet X or the tenth planet by now--an elliptical, highly-orbiting planet in our solar system on a collision course with Earth. Nibiru was first discovered by astrologers of ancient Sumer, a pre-Semitic culture of the lower Euphrates valley known as Mesopotamia and Babylon. The Sumerians had an advanced system of science, math and astronomy, far surpassing that of any culture up until just a few hundred years ago. They developed a star map which clearly shows ten planets (not the nine we currently believe to be) orbiting around the Sun (a concept that wasn't understood until just 400 years ago). What is this tenth planet? The Sumerians call it Nibiru (the planet of crossing) and say due to its highly elliptical orbit (far beyond Pluto) it travels in and out of view regularly. During the time of the Sumerians (more than 6000 years ago), Nibiru completed one of these cycles, crossing into the inner orbit of the solar system, making it visible day or night. Due to this extreme orbit (3,600 years) it crosses in front of Earth very rarely, making the chance of collision low. According to the Sumerians, a collision did occur creating our moon and the Great Band Asteroid Belt at some point in history, though. This view of the creation of our moon was derided until just recently, (along with every other major scientific revelation or discovery throughout history). NASA announced the theory of the origin of Earth's Moon as a catastrophic collision with a "Mars-sized planet" at the 30th Lunar and Planetary Science Conference in Houston on March 16, 1999.

Will Nibiru cross orbits with Earth in 2012, as all the doomsdayers preach? Who knows. If the planet is currently hidden from view behind the Sun as stated, it would have to have an extremely quick return trip, keeping it out of view until we reach the other side of the Sun in our yearly orbit. As most of you probably understand, we don't necessarily have to see something to believe in it though. Planets, no matter where they're located in the solar system, draw and pull on other planets. We can see this planetary movement and mathematically calculate and predict where and if a tenth planet really exists. According to NASA this planetary gravitational pull does, in fact, exist "on Uranus, Neptune and Pluto" indicating that there is another body of significant mass beyond them in our own solar system. In other words a tenth planet.

This 'wobble' or mathematical irregularity is so noticeable in the orbits of our outermost planets that it has prompted leading astronomers from all over the world to vigorously search for a large planet on the edge of our solar system. Astronomers, based on mathematical proof and visual planet observational effects, are so sure of the planet's existence that they've already named it 'Planet X' as the 10th planet in our solar system. In fact, on June 17, 1982, NASA officially recognized the possibility of "some kind of mystery object" beyond the outermost planets in a press release from Ames Research Center, California. Suddenly, the theory that was derided just a few years ago is now becoming fact as proof starts trickling in:

- Newsweek, June 28, 1982, an article entitled *Does the Sun Have a Dark Companion?* states: "A 'dark companion' could produce the unseen force that seems to tug at Uranus and Neptune, speeding them up at one point in their orbits and holding them back as they pass. The best bet is a dark star orbiting at least 50 billion miles beyond Pluto. It is most likely either a brown dwarf, or a neutron star. Others suggest it's a 10th planet since a companion star would tug other planets, not just Uranus and Neptune."
- The Washington Post, December 31, 1983. A reporter in an article labeled *Mystery Heavenly Body Discovered* interviewed Chief Scientist Gerry Neugebauer from Jet Propulsion Laboratories *"A heavenly*

body possibly as large as the giant planet Jupiter and possibly so close to Earth that it would be part of this solar system has been found in the direction of the constellation Orion by an orbiting telescope aboard the U.S. infrared astronomical satellite. All I can tell you is that we don't know what it is,"

- The U.S. News World reported on September 10, 1984, in an article named *Planet X - Is it Really Out There? "Shrouded from the sun's light, mysteriously tugging at the orbits of Uranus and Neptune, is an unseen force that astronomers suspect may be Planet X - a 10th resident of the Earth's celestial neighborhood. Last year, the infrared astronomical satellite (IRAS), circling in orbit around Earth, detected heat from an object about 50 billion miles away that is now the subject of intense speculation."*
- An October 1988 article in the Astronomical Journal by R. Harrington describes the mathematical modeling specifics of such a planet *"The planet would be three to four times the size of Earth, three times further from the Sun than Pluto. With an extreme elliptical orbit of 30 degrees."*
- Newsweek on July 13, 1987, published a NASA/ARC press release stating findings from NASA research scientist John Anderson which show *"an eccentric 10th planet may - or may not - be orbiting the Sun."* The article goes on to say that he *"has a hunch Planet X is out there, though nowhere near the other nine." "If he is right, two of the most intriguing puzzles of space science might be solved: what caused mysterious irregularities in the orbits of Uranus and Neptune during the 19th Century? And what killed off the dinosaurs 26 million years ago,"* bringing us back once again to the Sumerians historic documentation of Nibiru once striking Earth.

Why, then, can't we see Nibiru every year when we orbit around the far side of the Sun? Well, first assuming that scientists and governmental agencies haven't already seen the planet and aren't covering it up for fear of global and economical chaos, Pluto has a measly 248-year orbit; and our telescopes can barely see the planet when it's at its closest. The comet Kohoutek has a 7,500 year orbit (more than double Nibiru's orbit) and we don't see Kohoutek until it is almost on top of Pluto. Or there very well may be a cover-up. According to The London Daily Mail, US astronomers have been ordered that all "earth-shattering" data discovered (including solar flares, incoming comets and asteroids) must go through NASA first:

The Daily Mail report of May 15, 1998, in an article entitled, *Delayed Impact, or the Secrets of Asteroid Peril,* announced *"If a giant asteroid is hurtling in the general direction of our planet, we will be the last to know about it. For astronomers have decided that the news would be too earth- shattering for ordinary mortals to handle, and would likely cause widespread panic. In a week that sees the release of the film Deep Impact, a fictional account of just such a catastrophe, astronomers funded by the American space agency NASA have now agreed to keep asteroid and comet discoveries to themselves for 48 hours while more detailed calculations are made. The findings would then go to NASA, which would wait another 24 hours before going public."*

In fact, Astronomers Napier and Wickramasinghe have discovered unsettling evidence that there may not only be one 'black' planetary body out there hidden from sight, but thousands. They say that *"the number of known comets does not match what is predicted by theory."*

THE EGYPTIANS

The 'Kolbrin Bible' is not really any real religious text at all, rather it's a historic book that has documented every significant event known to ancient man, describing future events based on these past events, much like the Mayans, Hopi and Sumerians texts. The book was written by Egyptian and later Celtic scholars:

MAN 3.1: *Men forget the days of the Destroyer. Only the wise know where it went and that it will return in its appointed hour.* [Most people in society today are unaware that a planetary body collided with the earth.]

SCL 33.9: *It will come in a hundred generations, as is written in the Great Vault.* [1 generation = 20-22 years.]

SOF 20.2: *Ninety-two generations have to be born.*

MAN 3.7: *A hundred and ten generations shall pass into the West and nations will rise and fall.* [Add the three figures up and you'll get more than 6040 years ago, the approximate time of the writing of The Kolbrin from 2012.]

MAN 4.1: *O mortal men who wait without understanding, where will you hide yourselves in the Dread Days of Doom, when the Heavens shall be torn apart and the skies rent in twain, in the days when children will turn grey-headed?* [Children are mentally growing up more rapidly due to a sudden increase in divorce, adult-related content available to them uncensored on the internet and television, and over-anxious parents pushing modeling, beauty pageants, acting, education and other adult-like activities onto their children. There has also been premature physical development noticed as well, caused by growth and reproductive hormone additives fed to cows (to speed up production), which the children ingest.]

SCL 33.12: *When women are as men and inconsistent as women, the hour approaches when the Great Lady will wander. When man and woman meet as one in likeness, the Fiery Heralds will appear in the darkness of the sky vault.* [As described in Mother Shipton's prophecy of similar likeness, at the end of the 19th century a new movement called the "feminist movement" and "rational dress" was well underway, liberating women from skirts, substituting them for pants, while cutting the hair short. Today's women resemble men more so than any other era, not only through looks, but actions and work as well. As for the men, well, we're not as 'manly' either.]

SVB 7.21: *In those days men will be falling away from manliness and women from womanliness.* [Men of today's time are less masculine, aggressive, controlling and brave than any other time. We don't carry around swords or fight at the *drop of a hat.* Not to mention the popularity of metro-sexuality, homosexuality, bi-sexuality, transvestites, trans-gender, hermaphrodites, Pseudo-hermaphrodites, etc.]

MAN 3.8: *Men shall be divided by their races and the children will be born as strangers among them. Brother shall strive* (fight) *with brother and husband with wife. Fathers will no longer instruct their sons and the sons will be wayward* (following no path). [In the United States, families are singular nuclear families far removed from relatives, alienated and spread out geographically often living thousands of miles away. When we finally do get together for family functions and holidays, we often feud. As far as children being "born strangers" this holds true today more than ever, starting with daycare enrollment. They're raised by daycare, babysitters, in-laws and friends without much association with the parents at all. Proven when one commits some heinous crime like shooting a congresswoman or a bunch of students at school; the first thing the parents say is, "I don't know who that person is. I didn't raise him like that." That's right, you didn't. It's the same story over and over again today.]

MAN 3.8: *One worship will pass into the four quarters* (all) *of the Earth, talking peace and bringing war. They will possess great riches but be poor in spirit.* [The Roman Catholic Church (the richest religion on the planet) was the first religion to spread over the entire Earth, and have been the cause of more wars than any other religion to date.]

MAN 26.9: *It will be a time when men worship the works of men and say, "There is nothing greater than these." When the hearts of men are in turmoil and all men seek pleasure and gain.* [As we currently live in the age of consumerism and capitalism (in no other time has there been such thing as disposable products), this truth is easy to see in friends, family, and co-workers as they purchase and show off the newest I-device or purchase.]

SVB 7.18: *It will come in the Days of Decision, when men are inflicted with spiritual blindness, when one ignorance* (belief) *has been replaced with another, when men walk in darkness and call it light* (hypocrisy). *It will come when they seek only worldly things.* [Today there are more atheists and 'fake' Christians than at any other time throughout history. They sin and then sit in church pretending, for show, to save face in the community. On a similar line, people switch religions almost as often as they switch cars. The only real religious experience any of us have is when we're frantic about the newest accessory or application for that smart phone. We've cast off any form of spirituality in exchange for a new car, I-Pod, touchpad, tool, shirt, purse or kitchen appliance.]

MAN 3.10: *In those days men will have the Great Book before them, wisdom will be revealed, the few will be gathered for the stand; it is the hour of trial. The dauntless* (fearless) *ones will survive, the stouthearted* (good hearted) *will not go down to destruction* (death). [The "Great book" may be the Holy Bible, the Koran, the Bhagavad Gita, the Torah, the Sutras, The Kojiki, who knows? Who cares? Does it really matter?]

MAN 3.7: *Men will fly in the air as birds and swim in the seas as fishes.* [In our century we have witnessed the invention of airplanes and submarines. This alone should be a sure sign that these predictions apply to only our time. Conversely, it's amazing how all of the religions describe the events with exactly the same words.]

MAN 3.7: *Men will talk peace one with another,* (but) *hypocrisy and deceit shall have their day.* [The UN is a great place for any and all that wish to discuss peace, while secretly plotting for war in the background.]

MAN 3.8: *A nation of soothsayers* (prophets) *shall rise and fall and their tongue shall be the speech learned* (around the world). [Britain used soothsayers and astrologers significantly at one time, more so than any other nation. English is the most common language in schools, business, trade, in tourism, spoken in most countries.]

MAN 3.8: *A nation of lawgivers shall rule the Earth and pass away into nothingness.* [Obviously the Romans, as they developed and enforced the 'Rule of Law' on which most of the world's legal systems and legal terminology is based. The Romans have now all but disappeared from the world, let alone common knowledge.]

MAN 3.8: *A nation of* (across) *the seas will be greater than any other, but will be as an apple rotten at the core and will not endure.* [The United States is the only Super Power Nation on the other side of the ocean (the USSR, UK and China are all connected). Most wouldn't argue that America is corrupt, especially in light of recent world events. And I think it's safe to say we're about to fall just like the Soviet Union did.]

MAN 3.8: *A nation of traders* (China) *will destroy men with wonders* (America) *and it shall have its day.* [There's no arguing, China is the leading trade nation in the world; everything is now *Made in China*. Along that same line, America is definitely the land of technological wonders. I believe this verse is describing the time when China will defeat America and rise to become the one true Super Power.]

MAN 4.3: *It will be a vast sky-spanning* (as big as the Earth) *form enwrapping* (encircling) *Earth, burning with many hues within wide open mouths.* [Similar to other prophets, this verse very much resembles the foretold Nibiru planet in close proximity.]

SVB 7.18: *It will be a thing of monstrous greatness arising in the form of a crab* (from the crab constellation), *first its body will be red, then green, then blue.* [As materials or gases burn up in the atmosphere they give off different colors depending on their compound, red-iron, orange-sodium, blue-methane, etc.].

MAN 3.5: *The Heavens will burn brightly and redly, there will be a copper hue over the face of the land, followed by a day of darkness. A new moon will appear and break up and fall.* [As described above, our moon was formed very much in the same way. It sounds like we'll be getting another new moon soon out of this deal.]

MAN 3.3: *When ages pass, certain laws operate upon the stars in the Heavens. Their ways change, there is movement and restlessness, they are no longer constant and a great light appears redly in the skies.* [IF we are hit by a planetary body, it will shift the polar axis, which means the stars will spin and be located in new directions.]

MAN 4.2: *There will be the great body of fire, the glowing head with many mouths and eyes ever changing. These will descend to sweep across the face of the land, engulfing all in the yawning jaws.* [Throughout every apocalyptic description, by all sources, we see over and over again, repetitive meteor impacts. I'm not sure if it's just because it is easier to attach so many descriptions to a meteor and we're missing the bigger, unknown event, or that so many religions and prophets see the same thing. Either way, it should be interesting to say the least.]

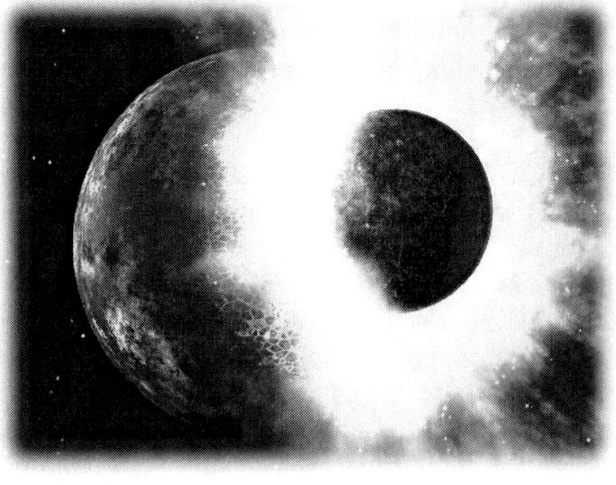

MAN 3.6: *They will be eaten up in the flames of wrath and consumed by the breath of the Destroyer.* [IF a planetary-sized comet were to hit the earth, heat in the magnitude of a nuclear bomb would be generated across the Earth, instantly burning air and boiling the seas.]

MAN 4.2: *Terrible teeth will be seen in formless mouths and a fearful dark belly will glow red from fires inside. The fangs will fall out, and lo, they are terror-inspiring things of cold hardened water.* [No idea, all I can say is let the Gods help us all.]

MAN 5.1: *The Doom Shape, called the Destroyer, in Egypt, was seen in all the lands thereabouts. In color it was bright and fiery, in appearance changing and unstable. It twisted about itself like a coil, like water bubbling into a pool from an underground supply, and all men agree it was a most fearsome sight. It was not a great comet or a loosened star, being more like a fiery body of flame.* [Since we've never actually seen this before, who knows what effects in physics would occur.]

HINDUISM

According to Hindu scriptures, the world passes through a cycle of four stages before cleansing itself and starting all over again (sound familiar?). We are currently in the 'Kali Yuga' or age of vices stage (of which there are certainly plenty). Pretty close classification for a manuscript that was written well before the 16th century, 400 years before consumerism and capitalism was even conceived of. The term "Kali Yuga" means strife, discord, quarrel, or contention and is definitely what we're currently experiencing today socially, economically, naturally, politically, and globally in wars playing out around the world. The Hindu version of the apocalypse is scheduled to come at the "end of the age of vice," according to the texts. The Hindu Book of Kalki Purana describes signs of these "far off future times" (present-day) in full detail. Keep in mind that they're written in an old language and are, therefore, sometimes hard to understand. Also, keep in mind that the ideas stated, although they sound completely normal to us today because we have lived and seen them all our lives, were absurd concepts when the book was written.

I, Verses 23-38: *Those who are known as twice-born* (Brahmins or upper class society or in the U.S., middle class) *are devoid of the Vedas* (don't associate with lower classes), *narrow-minded and always engaged in the service of the Sudras* (take on maids, chauffeurs, etc.)*; they are fond of carnal desires, sellers of religion, sellers of the Vedas, untouchable and sellers of juices; they sell meat, are cruel, engaged in sexual gratification and gratification of their appetite, attached to others' wives, drunk and producer of cross-breeds; have a low life-span, mix with lowly people and consider their brother-in-law as their only friend. They like constant confrontation and are fond of argument, discontent, fond of jewelry, hair and style* (sound like anyone you may know?). *The wealthy are respected as high-born and Brahmins are respected only if they are lenders; Men are merciful only when they are unable to harm others; express displeasure towards the poor; talk excessively to express erudition and carry out religious work to be famous; Monks* (priests) *are attached to homes in this Koli Age* (the age we're currently in) *and the homeless are devoid of any morality; Men of this age deride their teachers, display false religious affinity but trick the good people; Sudras (lower class) in Koli are always engaged in taking over others' possessions; in Koli, marriage takes place simply because the man and the woman agree to do so* (true today)*; Men engage in friendship with the crooked and show magnanimity while returning favours; Men are considered pious only if they are wealthy and treat only far-away waters* (lands) *as places of pilgrimage; Men are considered Brahmins simply because they have the sacred thread* (nicest clothes or brand-name clothes) *around their body, and as explorers, simply because they have a stick in their hand* (anyone that does any real hiking see these weekend hikers on the trails with their new "trekking poles," a clear sign that that person doesn't hike)*; the Earth becomes infertile, rivers hit the banks, wives take pleasure in speaking like prostitutes* (women used to speak as ladies, very proper) *and their minds are not attracted toward their husbands* (their marriage is not a priority, but the newest car, cell phone, pair of shoes is. Once only isolated to the U.S., recently this behavior has become an ongoing theme globally.)*; Brahmins become greedy for others' food, the low-born castes are not averse to becoming priests, wives mix freely even after they become widows* (widows used to be separated from society but are now mixed in without notice)*; the clouds release rain irregularly* (massive floods and abnormal droughts have recently swept the planet)*, the land becomes infertile, the kings kill their subjects, the people are burdened with taxes; they survive by eating honey, meat, fruits and roots; in the first quarter of the Koli Age, people deride God; in the second quarter, people do not even pronounce God's name; in the third quarter, men become cross-breeds; in the fourth quarter, men become the same* (uniform) *breed; nothing called race exists anymore; they forget God and pious works become extinct.*

The second coming of Christ or in this case the tenth (and final) coming of Kalki (the last being Buddha):

Vishnu Purana 4.24: *When the practices taught by the Vedas and the institutes of law, shall nearly have ceased, and the close of the Koli age shall be nigh* (at an end possibly correlating with the end of the year 2012)*, a portion of that Divine Being who exists of his own spiritual nature, in the character of Brahma, and who is the Beginning and the End* (22.13 of Revelations: *"I am the Alpha and the Omega, the Beginning and the End."* The similarities between Christianity prophecies and Hinduism are unmistakable, Hinduism being much older than Christianity, of course)*, and who comprehends all things shall descend upon the earth. He will be born as Kalki in the family of an eminent Brahmin, of Shambhala village* (in modern day India)*, endowed with the eight* *superhuman faculties. By his irresistible might, He will destroy all the barbarians and thieves* (corrupt governments and corporations) *and all whose minds are devoted to iniquity. He will then re-establish righteousness upon earth; and the minds of those who live at the end of the Koli age, shall be awakened, and shall be as pellucid as crystal. The men who are thus changed by virtue of that peculiar time, shall be as the seeds of human beings, and shall give birth to a race that shall follow the laws of the Kritya Age, the Age of Purity.* [Similar to the above texts]

I-2, Verses 11-15: *Afterwards, Sumati, the wife of Vishnujasha became pregnant. Kalki descended to earth* (as a human) *in the month of Baisakha on the 12th day after the full moon.*

The Hindu book of Divya Maha Kala Jnana (Divine Knowledge of Time) written by Shree Veera Brahmendra Maha Swami about 1000 years ago:

At the time of His (Sree Veera or Kalki's) *arrival, Krita Yuga Dharma* (religion of the age of peace) *will have been established with the Moon, Sun, Venus and Jupiter having entered the same sign.* [Next scheduled to occur 22nd May, 2012]

The rule of Sree Veera Dharma starts on a full moon day in the month of October during the year Chitra Bhanu. He will be born before the eighth day of full moon of the month of Margasheera (June 7-21). *His devotees will be looking forward to his glory and his arrival during the month of Karteeka* (May 10-25). *In the year of Partheeva* (2005-2006), *all the people will be able to see Sree Veera Bhoga Vasantaraya, and everyone will meditate on the Great Spirit. Sree Veera Bhoga Vasantharaya will be crowned during the year of Khara* (2011-2012). *He will be crowned three years after exotic horses drink the water of Tungabhadra River.* [In the present-day South Indian state of Andhra Pradesh]

There will be rain of blood in towns, villages, and forests. Poor quality coins will be used as currencies. In some places, there will be a rain of fire. Kings of all kinds will be destroyed, and His strength will reign supreme. Terrible wars will be fought, and no one will be able to mourn for the dead. People will be unable to rely on each other. Many incurable diseases will be present. A man will have ten women after him, which will result in extreme behavior in human beings. All the Grahas (planets) *will deviate from their paths. Non-believers will disappear. An invisible drought will occur. There will be terrible rains throughout the world.* [Polar shift]

A Star with three tails will be born in the east, due to which many villages will be reduced to ashes. (Upon entry, comets burn off most of their material in several streaks of light.) *He will rule over the Universe for a period of 108 years, and return to heaven. Preceding that, the world will be full of calamities and situations will be changing every instant. When Saturn enters Pisces* (2025), *Mlechchas* (non-believers or Muslims, specifically) *will be destroyed. When Saturn enters Aries* (2028), *a little peace will be established. When Saturn enters Taurus in June* (2030), *poisonous air will blow from the north-east, and extreme people will go to Yama Loka* (abode of death) (Nuclear, chemical or biological warfare, China is North-East of India.) *When Saturn enters Gemini* (2033), *this will usher in an era of peace.* [Keep in mind that World War III (not the war of Armageddon) needs to start, endure and end before 2025, according to these lines. The Iraq War lasted 7 years (2003-2010) and the Vietnam War 20 years (1955-1975). If World War III began on December 21, 2012, it would last at least until 2025]. *By the year of Ananda-Raksha* (2034-2036), *all Koli Dharmas* (dark actions or religions) *will be destroyed. By the year Ananda* (2034-2035), *all the countries will attain peace and happiness. The word of his glory will spread in the world. Before the year of Ananda, rice will be sold for low price. Then, all the countries will become prosperous.*

MOHAMMED: THE QUR'AN

The Qur'an is almost as old as the Bible (New Testament) and was believed to have been revealed to Mohammed (a prophet) from Allah (God) until his death on June 8, 632 A.D. The book which is considered the best piece of literature in the Arabic language, holds many similarities to the Bible, Divya Maha Kala Jnana, Kalki Purana and several other religious books. For the sake of being proficient, I've added it here as well, however; since it does repeat the same information over and over again, I've kept it short and relevant.

14:48: *The day will come when this earth will be substituted with a new earth* (new cycle), *and also the heavens, and everyone will be brought before GOD, the One, the Supreme.*

18:94: They said, 'O Zul-Qarnain, Gog and Magog are corruptors of the earth. Can we pay you to create a barrier between us and them?

20:15: *The Hour* (End of the World) *is surely coming; I will keep it almost hidden. For each soul must be paid for its works.*

27:82*: At the right time, we will produce for them a creature, made of earthly materials, declaring that the people are not certain about our revelations.* [The advent of the computer as well as the accompanying World Wide Web has been instrumental to Islam as well as breaking the Qurans numerical codes.]

43:61 *He* (Jesus) *is to serve as a marker for knowing the end of the world so that you can no longer harbour any doubt about it.* [Jesus appeared right on time as predicted and his inspired books, especially Revelations, tells everything we need to know about the apocalypse.]

54:1: *The Hour has come closer, and the moon has split.*

69:13-15: *When the horn is blown once. The earth and the mountains will be carried off and crushed; utterly crushed. That is the day when the inevitable event will come to pass.* [Again instructions of major earthquakes or polar shifts.]

JESUS: THE HOLY BIBLE

Pope Leo IX predicted the end of the world. In 1514, he said, *"I will not see the end of the world, nor will you my brethren, for its time is long in the future, 500 years hence."* If we do the math the world should end in 2014, two years after the Mayans' calculations. So the question is, who's the better mathematician? Sorry, Pope, the Mayans are world-renowned math whizzes; close, but no cigar; but thanks for taking a crack at it. All joking aside, he was pretty close. To understand what exactly to expect just before, during and after, we will need to turn to the Bible, the widely accepted, globally translated guide to the apocalypse.

The Holy Bible, regardless of the format, be it New King James (NKJ), Contemporary English Version (CEV), English Standard Version (ESV), New International Version (NIV), New King James Version (NKJV) (the list goes on), is a wealth of end time prophecies and know-how. Due to the sheer volume of data it possesses on the subject (not to mention the fact that it was written by several of the world's most trustworthy people all stating the same thing), it may be the single best source for signs that the end will occur in our lifetime. And it's exactly because of this that past cults, doomsdayers and evangelists use books like Revelations to preach fire and brimstone on any given day/month/event, which could easily be dismissed as rubbish, but today it's different. The magnitude of leaders in many different religions, backed by science, along with the enormous amount of catastrophic warnings by different and in most cases opposing factions, is clear and immense, and what's worse is that they're all agreeing with each other.

If we take a look at The Bible rationally for a moment we'll see that it's actually divided into several books written by several authors, over a span of several thousand years. However, Mathew, Isaiah, Jeremiah, Ezekiel, Daniel, and, of course, John (in the Book of Revelations) seem to have focused on the apocalypse, more so than any of the others. For example, Mathew states:

"And this gospel of the kingdom shall be preached in all the world for witness unto all nations; and then shall the end come."

- Matthew 24:14

The gospel, once only spread by missionaries and later the printing press (which allowed the Bible to be printed and distributed inexpensively to not just the churches but to the individuals), is now being "preached in all the world unto all nations," extremely quickly and easily in just the last century via television, radio, CD, DVD and internet. No other era could say that. Because of this, we can easily see that the timeframe they were speaking of is the 21st century, simply by reading the verses.

Also it's the contention of this author that John's visions (Jesus took John into the future to show him the end times) were visions of the end times and just that. Many believe John witnessed aliens destroying the world during the apocalypse, describing them as 'Gods', clouds and fire only after having no other earthly experience or objects to relate them to. Although entertaining, I don't see that the involvement of an alien race is mandatory to the extinction of humanity. We're doing a great job of that all by ourselves. I personally just believe that John simply saw the future (present day), and yes, with nothing else to relate such sights to, did the best he could in his language with his meanings. I mean, imagine if John who lived 2000 years ago, all of a sudden showed up at the Detroit Ford auto manufacturing plant, or LAX airport, I think that he'd have some very descriptive stories to tell. Instead, they attach extra-terrestrial entities to verses which describe a loud machine coming down from heaven (the sky) surrounded with a lot of smoke and fire. I just can't see that a species that has the ability to travel thousands of light years is still using combustible fuels and not some form of electromagnetism or other unknown cleaner, safer propulsion source, whereas we currently still do. That said, the future sites John tries to describe must seem indeed very alien to him, you can read it in his writings. But they're just that, alien to him and only him. Tanks, machine guns, rockets, space shuttles, computers, TVs, cell phones, cars, space stations, space suits, these things are all completely normal to us, so it's difficult for us to attach relevance of such outlandish descriptions to such normal things. So you'll have to imagine how John saw such sites, not how we see them today. And although I encourage you to review the entire Bible, for the sake of time (the world is coming to an end, you know) I'll only discuss the book of Revelations here:

1:2: *Who bare record of the word of God, and of the testimony of Jesus Christ, and of all things that he saw.* [To "bare record" means that John actually saw these prophecies with his own eyes not simply that he's conveying a message. This would imply then that John was either: (a) literally transported into the future like Scrooge and the ghost of Christmas future, or (b) viewed the events in a dream-like or trance-like state. In other words, the message given by the angel was not to have been a verbal or written message, but more like a video message. I picture John, sitting there watching the movie of the real life apocalypse, entitled, well, *Apocalypse*.]

1:7: *Behold, he cometh with clouds; and every eye shall see him, and they which pierced him: and all kindreds of the earth shall wail because of him. Even so, Amen."* [First, someone or something flying down from the clouds would definitely be newsworthy. In fact, the news via TV and internet would be the ONLY way short of the entire population of the world being in one spot, that "every eye could see him." Another hint is that the events described could only occur after the invention of national broadcasting television in 1928. The fact that he (God, an angel, an alien, or 21st century man) floats down from the sky is interesting. He doesn't actually just appear, but is coming from a specific location in the direction of, well, up. He could possibly be coming from another planet or maybe the space station. The means in which he travels isn't clear, maybe a spacecraft, aircraft or simply just a man floating down through the clouds. Either way all should prove a fascinating sight indeed.]

1:10: *I was in the Spirit on the Lord's day* (worshipping on Sunday), *and heard behind me a great voice, as of a trumpet.* [Remember, Jesus is already with John, narrating to him the sites at hand; the "voice" then, can't be God but something else. According to John, it doesn't sound like another human or a dog barking anyway, but a trumpet blaring. This 'trumpet' sound could be the voice of an alien as Erich Von Daniken and Zecharia Sitchin suggest. Even a chimpanzee, which only differs from human DNA by 1.5%, and dogs (whose bark does sound like a quick horn, if you think about it) differing by only 4%, sounds unmistakably different from us. I can't imagine what an alien would sound like, maybe trumpets, maybe not. My personal contention, however, is that he's listening to possibly simply a car horn, maybe someone yelling to John and Jesus to 'get the hell out of the road!']

1:12: *And I turned to see the voice that spake with me. And being turned, I saw seven golden candlesticks.* [Today we would say: and I turned to see who was speaking to me or, in this case, where the sound was coming from. And "I saw seven golden candlesticks," not a being, or any living thing, but more a metallic type object(s).]

1:13: *And in the midst* (middle) *of the seven candlesticks like unto the Son of man, clothed with a garment down to the foot, and girt about the paps with a golden girdle.* [John is now describing what he sees of the object or entity that's making the sound, using old terms like 'girt', 'paps' and 'golden girdle.' Before modern scientific terminology, light was measured in quantity of candles, ie. "candle watts," just like force was measured in quantity of horses, i.e., "horsepower," the 7 candlesticks then could be lights or headlights, having 7 of them would denote something large like the navigational lights of a ship or airplane. The term 'girt' (or 'girth' a measurement in width) is often used in architecture meaning "horizontal structural member," and about the paps' means "around the middle." So upon further analysis, we have a man or a man inside a ship with navigational lights wearing white and gold, possibly a space suit then.]

1:14: *His head and hair white like wool, as white as snow; and his eyes as a flame of fire.* [Sounds like a shiny white surface, possibly an astronaut's suit and some type of infra-red (which projects a red tint) or night vision goggles. Again, either way, these are not attributes I'd associate with a human, let alone a God or angel.]

1:15: *And his feet like unto fine brass, as if they burned in a furnace; and his voice as the sound of many waters.* [Now the sound is no longer like a 'trumpet'; it's changed. Maybe because the engines have turned on. And I couldn't describe the steal landing gear of an airplane or even a space shuttle better if I used my own words. So we have a man in a spacesuit in a space shuttle. Interesting.]

1:16: *And he had in his right hand seven stars* (lights)*: and out of his mouth went a sharp two-edged sword: and his countenance* (glow) *as the sun shineth in his strength.* [At this point I'm leaning strongly toward the B2 Spirit or Stealth Bomber or a yet unknown offspring, possibly able to enter space. If you look at where the mouth is, it resembles a sharp two-edged sword. I see "his right hand" symbolizing the right wing of the aircraft and its guidance lights; also the Spirit gets a strange "glow" on its back and belly when it breaks the sound barrier.]

2:10: *...behold, the devil shall cast* (some) *of you into prison, that ye may be tried; and ye shall have tribulation ten days: be thou faithful unto death, and I will give thee a crown of life."* [During World War II Japanese American citizens were rounded up and put into concentration camps, along with Jews in Germany, Poland, and Czechoslovakia. During the Iraq war, Muslims were held in Guantanamo Bay detention camp. During World War III, it is most likely the same would occur with the warring country(s). In fact, since the year 2000, many locations around the Midwest have undergone major construction efforts building what appear to be enormous holding facilities for just such an event.]

4:1: *...and, behold, a door opened in heaven* (from above)*: and the first voice which I heard as it were of a trumpet talking with me; which said, Come up hither, and I will shew thee things which must be hereafter.* [The cabin door of any large airplane or vehicle is quite higher than ground level, making the door drop down from above, with the voice coming through a intercom or loudspeaker as John is invited up.]

4:2: *And immediately I was in the spirit* (overcome, flabbergasted)*: and, behold, a throne was set in heaven, and* (one) *sat on the throne.* [Once in the cockpit John sees the captain of the aircraft in the pilot's seat. Whatever the actual flying object is, I believe the message here is during the end times if anyone comes to rescue you, go with them/it!]

4:3: *And he that sat was to look upon like a jasper and a sardine stone: and a rainbow round about the throne, in sight like unto an emerald.* [The jasper (maroon in color) and sardine (black or blood red) stones may represent the colors of the captain's uniform (which strangely happened to be the color of a Star Trek uniform, maybe John was just watching a little TV, now that would be hilarious). As far as the "rainbow," in every cockpit there are panels upon panels of different colored lights, gauges, dials, alarms, buttons, circuits, etc. around the flight seats.]

4:4: *And round about the throne* (were) *four and twenty seats: and upon the seats I saw four and twenty elders sitting, clothed in white raiment; and they had on their heads crowns of gold.* [24 additional stations with the occupants all in uniform which denotes military, which may be some other aircraft possibly in existence but yet unknown to the general public, like the X-48. (The B2 was designed in the late 1970s and wasn't rolled out and viewed by the public until the late Desert Shield in the 1990s.)

True story: After leaving the military, while still having security clearance, I was doing contractor work on large body aircraft around the U.S. One day I was sent to an international airport (I won't say the name) and asked to sit through weeks of security training classes and asked to sign confidentiality and non-disclosure forms promising not to relate what I was about to see to the public. We were then bused into a large private hanger, where I saw a very large, circular aircraft completely covered in tarps. (Since I actually didn't see anything, I have no problem saying it here, now.) A small section about one meter by one meter was opened with the paneling (cowling) removed, where I spent about 3 weeks rebuilding all the hydraulics and structural membranes. I'm not stating that it was a UFO; I really don't believe it was. I just think that we have aircrafts that aren't known to the public yet. The Air Force has actually attempted to build several types of 'flying saucers' though, including the TR-3 Black Manta, TR-3B, MX-1794, VZ-9a, Horten 2-29, RFZ's, Vril, HAUNEBU, RC360, AV-7055, PEPP Aeroshell, MOLLER International, EKIP, Avro Omega, HO-229, and Project-Y; -Y2; -1794. Who knows what they'll roll out for the apocalypse that John saw.]

4:5: *And out of the throne proceeded lightnings and thunderings and voices: and seven lamps of fire burning before the throne, which are the seven Spirits of God.* (For someone who has never seen the powering up of aircraft primary/secondary, flight, navigation and communication computer screens, it's quit an ordeal.)

4:6: *And before the throne a sea of glass like unto crystal: and in the midst of the throne, and round about the throne, four beasts full of eyes before and behind."* (Perfect description of the bridge of an aircraft which has glass windshields. At this point you can't mistake "glass windshields" for God. "Four beasts full of eyes" sound to me a lot like 4 peacocks. Peacocks being originally from Africa and India may have been a very alien sight to John.)

4:7: *And the first beast like a lion, and the second beast like a calf, and the third beast had a face as a man, and the fourth beast like a flying eagle.* [We seem to be witnessing John's description of a modern day aerial Noah's Ark (which would coincide with the end times), full of lions, cows, monkeys, eagles and who knows what else John didn't see.]

4:8: *And the four beasts had each of them six wings about* (between them)*; and* (they were) *full of eyes within: and they rest not day and night, saying, Holy, holy, holy, Lord God Almighty, which was, and is, and is to come."* (For anyone that's heard any peafowl or turkey sing, it does sound a little like "holy, holy, holy, holy".)

6:1-2: *And behold a white horse: and he that sat on him had a bow; and a crown was given unto him: and he went forth conquering, and to conquer.* [He who rides the white 'horse', the first of the four horsemen of the Apocalypse, will lead the people through tribulation. In this way he'll seem good (white) but is actually a liar; Christians call him the antichrist. He probably won't actually be wearing a crown. This just symbolizes a position of leadership or authority, possibly president Obama, possibly the leader of the UN, possibly an army general, maybe even the Pope. The bow means he's in or has control of the military and again, he probably won't actually have or be holding one.]

6:3: *And there went out another horse red: and* (power) *was given to him that sat thereon to take peace from the earth, and that they should kill one another: and there was given unto him a great sword* (powerful weapon). [The "red horse" is described above as war, (in this case World War III) possibly with the 'red' army of Russia, China, Vietnam, Cuba and/or North Korea or all of the above, symbolized with the red communist star, which makes sense being that all have or have access to nuclear missiles, the "greatest weapons" ever made.]

6:5-6: *And I beheld, and lo a black horse; and he that sat on him had a pair of balances* (measuring scales) *in his hand. And I heard a voice in the midst of the four beasts say, A measure of wheat for a penny, and three measures of barley for a penny; and* (see) *thou hurt not the oil and the wine.* [The 'Black Horse' is economic inflation, whereas the color black often denotes sickness or plague. Both of which typically occur during and directly after a war or other catastrophic event. We're currently seeing this in Haiti with the Cholera outbreak as a result of the 2010 earthquake.]

6:7-8: *And I looked, and behold a pale horse: and his name that sat on him was Death, and Hell followed with him. And power was given unto them over the fourth part of the earth, to kill with sword, and with hunger, and with death, and with the beasts of the earth.* [When someone is sick or dies they become pale. What this is saying is that 1/4 of the Earth's population (over one billion people) will die in World War III.]

6:9-10: *I saw under the altar the word of God.* [Keep in mind John is still in the aircraft or possibly an Earth built lifeboat (space ship) and what he calls an 'alter' is most likely the cockpit console. What he's seeing under the console sounds like monitors showing live video of other people in the ship talking with the captain, which he would describe as souls, since there are only the faces and voices with no actual physical bodies.]

6:12: *And, lo, there was a great earthquake; and the sun became black as sackcloth of hair, and the moon became as blood.* [This description really strikes home with us because of recent events. On October 25th 2010, a massive 7.7 magnitude earthquake rocked Indonesia creating a massive tsunami and triggering the eruption of Mount Merapi which sent deadly ash and poisonous gasses into the atmosphere. This, however, is a typical scenario. Earthquakes can often cause the built-up energy stored in volcanoes to suddenly release, darkening the Sun with ash and even dyeing the moon red from the chemical gases and smoke reflecting many wavelengths back, while allowing the red (the longest) to penetrate.]

6:13: *And the stars of heaven fell unto the earth, even as a fig tree casteth her untimely figs, when she is shaken of a mighty wind.* [Meteors crash down upon the Earth like figs falling from a tree, a pretty visual example. This actually occurs at least once every hundred years (Chernobyl). It's just luck that one hasn't hit a city yet.]

6:14: *And the heaven departed as a scroll when it is rolled together; and every mountain and island were moved out of their places.* (Giant pole-shifting earthquakes triggered by the bombardment of meteors. As I described previously, this has occurred at least twice that we know of already and often does with major earthquakes. It occurred once with the Indonesian quake in December of 2004, as reported by U.S. Geological Survey expert Ken Hudnut: *"That earthquake has changed the map, physically relocating countries as far away as the U.S."* The unusually strong shift in the plates near Sumatra Island, Indonesia, causing a 9.15 earthquake, permanently changed the region's geological landscape. It drastically relocated some countries east to west by up to 30 meters, raising submerged land masses from the sea while permanently sinking others.)

6:15: *And the kings of the earth* (political leaders), *and the great men* (engineers, businessmen), *and the rich men*

(upper class), *and the chief captains* (military leaders), *and the mighty men* (military), *and every bond man* (working class), *and every free man* (middle and lower class), *hid themselves in the dens and in the rocks of the mountains.* (So, the government/military take some people underground to find safety from such catastrophes.)

7:2-4: *And I heard the number of them which were sealed* (saved)*: sealed an hundred* (and) *forty* (and) *four thousand of all the tribes of the children of Israel.* [In the old days, if you had the seal of the king you were spared from death during war. In this case, with the next set of catastrophes being plagues, we can expect 144,000 of the 3/4 of WW3 survivors to slide through completely unaffected by the following pandemics. The only way anyone could survive a virus though, is if they had a vaccine; and what do you know, there are less than 150,000 calculated bulk vaccines stored at anytime for any given virus in the world. Funny how things work out like that.]

8:6-7: *...and there followed hail and fire mingled with blood* (poisonous rain), *and they were cast upon the earth: and the third part of trees was burnt up, and all green grass was burnt up.* [Nuclear, meteor or volcanic fallout poisons the rain, and forest fires caused by volcanoes and/or meteor impacts would kill most plant life.]

8:8-9: *And the second angel sounded, and as it were a great mountain* (rock) *burning with fire* (meteor) *was cast into the sea: and the third part of the sea became blood* (died). *And the third part of the creatures which were in the sea, and had life, died; and the third part of the ships were destroyed.* (A second meteor strikes the planet, this time in the water, wiping out most of the sea life and naval, private and commercial ships on the planet. Currently, there are an estimated 100,000 ships around the world today, which means only 25,000 would survive the tsunami created by the impact. Sounds about right.)

8:10-11: *And the third angel sounded, and there fell a great star from heaven* (nuclear bomb), *burning as it were a lamp, and it fell upon the third part of the rivers, and upon the fountains of waters* (nuclear fallout)*; And the name of the star is called Wormwood: and the third part of the waters became wormwood; and many men died of the waters, because they were made bitter.* [Today, many countries of the world possess nuclear weapons of mass destruction. Russia and the U.S. have over 100 nuclear subs each with a payload of dozens of ICBMs with thermonuclear warheads right now pointed in a particular direction. With these devices, hundreds of major cities can be laid to waste, literally in minutes. Just like the nuclear explosion that went off over the city of Chernobyl (which literally means 'wormwood') the water, meat, plants, crops and milk were and would be poisoned for years with radiation (Chernobyl is still abandoned to this day.]

8:12: *And the third part of the sun was smitten* (afflicted), *and the third part of the moon, and the third part of the stars; so as the third part of them was darkened, and the day shone not for a third part of it, and the night likewise.* [As described in the 'NASA' section, this could be easily caused by the nuclear detonations or the earthquakes themselves, essentially slowing down the rotation of the Earth and offsetting the wobble in a way that creates sixteen hours of night and eight hours of day (reverse of what is now). February 27th of 2010, a Chilean earthquake (8.8 magnitude) shortened the length of each day. Richard Gross of NASA's Jet Propulsion Laboratory in California has shown that the quake has not only sped up the rotation of the Earth, but also enlarged its wobble by offsetting Earth's mass around its axis by more than 3 inches. In 2004, a 9.1 and again last year a 7.8, both hit Indonesia, and now Japan's 9.0 all additionally shortened the day and shifted the axis. This would cause the Sun, Moon and stars to show only "1/3" of the time that they currently show.]

9:1-2: *I saw a star fall* (the 3rd meteor) *from heaven unto the earth: and to him* (it) *was given the key of the bottomless pit. And he opened the bottomless pit; and there arose a smoke out of the pit, as the smoke of a great furnace; and the sun and the air were darkened by reason of*

the smoke of the pit. [This meteor creates such an enormous crater or pit that smoke from the impact or possibly core gases block out the Sun, much like it did on 9/11 when the two 44ft jetliners crashed into the twin towers.]

9:3: ***And there came out of the smoke locusts upon the earth: and unto them was given power, as the scorpions of the earth have power.*** [The locusts will carry a virus, transmitting it to humans like swine flu and bird flu did (bug flu). The virus (like most do) will immobilize people like a scorpion. A scorpion's prey is typically fast-moving such as field mice; so the sting must paralyze quickly with neurotoxins and enzyme inhibitors.]

9:4: ***And it was commanded them that they should not hurt the grass of the earth, neither any green thing, neither any tree; but only those men which have not the seal*** (vaccine) ***of God in their foreheads.*** (Viruses usually don't affect plant life. The virus will kill many, but the people already vaccinated will be protected.)

9:7-8: ***And the shapes of the locusts*** (were) ***like unto horses prepared unto battle.*** (John's description of the virus as seen under a microscope would look like the breast plate and armoring of a horse.)

9:11: ***And they*** (the virus) ***had a king over them*** (one who set the virus loose), (which is) ***the angel of the bottomless pit, whose name in the Hebrew tongue*** (is) ***Abaddon, but in the Greek tongue hath*** (his) ***name Apollyon.*** (Both Abaddon and Apollyon mean Antichrist or, in this case, world leader. He will let loose an epidemic which will kill and sicken all but those who have had a vaccine. Many viruses today were created by and/or unleashed by government agencies on purpose or by accident, such as the current Swine Flu being released by Russia.)

9:13-16: ***Loose the four angels which are bound*** (located) ***in the great river Euphrates*** (modern day Iraq). ***And the four angels were loosed, which were prepared for an hour, and a day, and a month, and a year, for to slay the third part of men. And the number of the army of the horsemen*** (were) ***two hundred thousand thousand*** (two hundred million)***: and I heard the number of them.*** [This verse is a bit different, the four "angels" who were let loose had an exact hour, day, month and year; they were pre-programmed to fire from somewhere in the Middle East. Sounds to me like a countdown clock on a few ballistic (or sub-orbital) missiles, (in this case probably Chinese DF-4s). Some (if not all) probably even carrying nuclear payloads. This could signify that it's actually a Middle Eastern country that fires the missiles, or more likely that a communist country has leased land from one of the several countries along the Euphrates river. China then raises a 200 million man army (which they could possibly do today, but could not have before). The four nukes end up killing 2/3rds of the remaining inhabitants of the Earth which is only 1/4 of the original populations since 1/4 was already killed (2/3 of 3/4 is 1/4). In my opinion, this would be a great cleansing of the parasites that currently pollute this planet, but that's just me.]

9:17-19: ***And thus I saw the horses in the vision, and them that sat on them, having breastplates of fire, and of jacinth, and brimstone: and the heads of the horses*** (were) ***as the heads of lions; and out of their mouths issued fire and smoke and brimstone. By these three was the third part of men killed, by the fire, and by the smoke, and by the brimstone, which issued out of their mouths. For their power is in their mouth, and in their tails: for their tails*** (were) ***like unto serpents, and had heads, and with them they do hurt.*** [Sounds like a tank or tank-like machines with a canon that shoots fire and smoke (and mortars) from the front. An M2 or an M-240 typically situates a high caliber machine gun in the rear, which do tend to "hurt" a little. Now that we have a new figure, let's recalculate our math. There is only 1/4 of the original population of the Earth remaining after the nukes, which would be approximately 3,500,000,000 people left standing at the end of the nuclear attack (as of 2011 there were almost 7 billion people on Earth). Now that the nukes have done their job, the land forces invade killing another 1/3 which leaves only about 1/6th of the original population or 583,333,333 people. Keep in mind this isn't World War III; this is nothing less than World War IV. If World War IV started in 2013-2015, the human population would be at 3.5 billion by around 2019, 2020.

The question one now has to ask is, why is all of this happening? My witty translations of the book of Revelations are clever to say the least (and shockingly accurate in some cases), but they are just that. They are my interpretations of a somewhat cryptic prophecy. God, himself, (or aliens) may come down and rain fire and brimstone on the humans of Earth in punishment for the sins we've caused this planet and its inhabitants, wiping out the infection called humanity from the face of the Earth as it did at Sodom and Gomorrah and during Noah's time. We may very well even carry out the job ourselves, without the assistance of a higher deity. We've been trying so hard for so many years to do just that. Either way, we've obviously strayed off the path and need to be either erased or redirected by a being more supreme or advanced than us. We're not capable of reform or fixing the problems that we've created (disease, war, famine, illiteracy, corruption, greed, crime, drug abuse, murder, neglect). We just can't stop and don't care to. No, a complete and total reboot is the only answer.

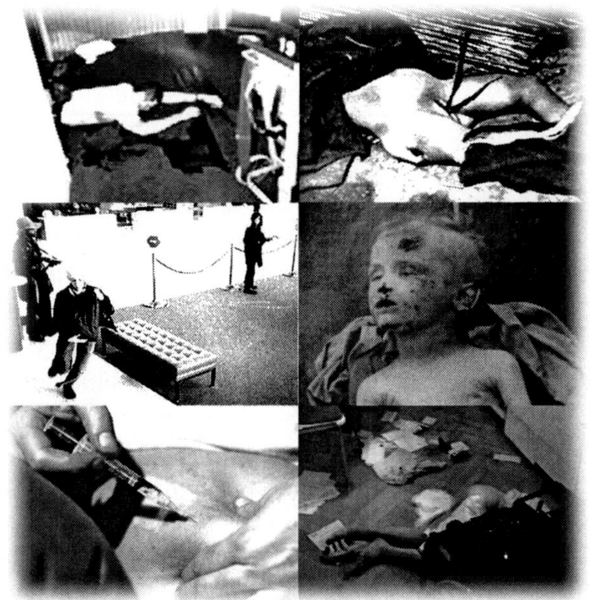

9:21: ***Neither repented they of their murders, nor of their sorceries, nor of their fornication, nor of their thefts.*** [It's all laid out right there: murder, sorcery (drug use), sexual assault and theft. For ten years global murder rates were in a state of steady decline. In 2008, that decline increased drastically and has been rising at a rate of 5.2% on average per year. Illegal drug use ("sorcery" is from the Greek word 'pharmacy' or drugs) rates have also been on a steady rise of at least 7% annually and has almost tripled since the early 60s. Fornication doesn't necessarily refer to the sexual act of actually fornicating. It comes from the Greek word "Porneia", from which 'pornography' also originates. It doesn't just mean porn either (although we've seen a huge spike in porn abuse since the internet as well), it is referring to any and all sexually-related activity outside of matrimony--adultery, sex crimes, porn, child abuse, all of which have steadily been on the rise since the late 50s and early 60s. It also includes theft, which covers all theft related crimes/acts, such as fraud, burglary, car theft, identity theft, home invasion, telephone marketing scams, financial investment schemes, credit card theft, corporate inside trading, over-inflated mortgages, high interest rates, and balloon mortgages which brings us to the current collapse in our economy along with major governmental corporate bailouts. hmm.

Sociologists can't pinpoint the cause of this backwards downward-sliding trend, be it a sense of social prowess, a lack of absolute ethics, lucrative punishments for such crimes, or just a total breakdown in human standards. Technology may also be to blame, for example; with the rise in Tweets and Facebook updates, the focus of right and wrong seems to have been repressed in favor of rises in online social statuses. In November, 2010, "The Science Guy" (known for his 1990s TV show "Bill Nye the Science Guy") fainted in front of hundreds of students at the University of Southern California. Rather than rush to his aid though, everyone instantly started uploading videos of the episode to YouTube and Twitter. Not one person went to assist the collapsed man in favor of capturing and sharing the occurrence online with friends. The internet is riddled with similar incidents including the famed 2007 YouTube video, "Don't Tase Me, Bro," where you can actually see dozens of students recording the incident with phones and video cameras; or a cop's phone video of Messy Maya's last moments, which depicts a dying man shot and moaning lying face down in a pool of his own blood. The video went viral in November, 2010. Or maybe you've seen the many videos of grotesque 'teenage girl beatings' around the U.S. currently trending on Twitter, Facebook and YouTube. One incident involved a teenage girl from Chicago captured on a cell phone video by unresponsive onlookers. Fox News reports: *"A girl was savagely beaten in a Sauk Village public park June 2, and a cell phone video captured the attack. The footage begins with two girls fighting in the dirt then quickly turns into a one-sided pummeling, with other girls rushing over to beat the victim, cut off her hair and burn her with a cigarette lighter."* Another involved a 15-year-old girl who brutally beat another young girl in a Seattle bus tunnel in February, 2010, as security guards stood by literally inches away doing nothing. Insane!

The youth of the nations are particularly susceptible to the trending downfall of society as more and more parents ignore or even encourage a lack of morals, values, ethics and standards. Ask a kid today what the

Ten Commandments are and he'll most likely say either a) changes in our constitution; b) a movie; or more likely c) I don't know. Today it's cool to not know something. If you know the answer it means that you're a nerd and, well, that's not cool. Regardless of the reason(s), we can absolutely see the trend spiraling downward at a drastic rate, possibly crashing into a dark abyss by the year 2012.]

11:7-9: ***And when they shall have finished their testimony, the beast*** (the antichrist) ***that ascendeth out of the bottomless pit*** (resurrected) ***shall make war against them, and shall overcome them, and kill them. And their dead bodies*** (shall lie) ***in the street of the great city, which spiritually is called Sodom and Egypt, where also our Lord was crucified.*** (Jerusalem) ***And they of the people and kindreds and tongues and nations*** (people from all over the world) ***shall see their dead bodies three days and an half, and shall not suffer their dead bodies to be put in graves.*** [We're seeing here the antichrist coming out from behind the scenes, into the public spotlight of the media. And again, with the invention of television and global broadcasting, 1928 allows people from all over the world to view the dead bodies in Jerusalem only in our time, which is exactly when it's happening. Since the Six Day War (also known as the Arab-Israeli war) in the 60s to the 90s, thousands of Israelis and Palestinians have littered the streets of Jerusalem (sometimes left for several days due to constant fighting) as Palestinian suicide bombers attempt to strike terror into the hearts of the Israeli nation, which we see on TV all the time.]

11:13: ***And the same hour was there a great earthquake, and the tenth part of the city fell, and in the earthquake were slain of men seven thousand: and the remnant were affrighted, and gave glory to the God of heaven.*** [Another earthquake kills seven more thousand. To give a quick number count we're currently at 583,333,333. If you subtract 7k from this amount, the remainder is 583,326,333, which is not a huge loss in comparison, considering that more than 3/4 of the Earth is now dead. Also 7 thousand deaths from an earthquake is pretty minimal; the Haiti quake caused almost 20,000 deaths from a city of 9.8 million or about 1/10th. A tenth of a city with 60,000 people would be 6,000, which is a very small city.]

12:3: ***And there appeared another wonder in heaven; and behold a great red dragon, having seven heads*** (seven heads of government) ***and ten horns*** (armies), ***and seven crowns upon his heads.*** [Again, red signifies war and possibly communism, and a crown is a position of power. This would mean that the seven current communist countries: China, Cuba, North Korea, Laos, Vietnam, Cyprus and Nepal (Moldova "was" communist until 2009 which would have been eight, see how things are coming together in preparation for the end times?), are the seven heads of government with ten armies (the horn of the rhino for example, is designed to do battle) between them. Also, here we see that a 200 million man army doesn't necessarily have to come from only China; but China will bring the 7 countries together which together could equal much more than 200 million soldiers.]

12:7-8 ***And there was war in heaven*** (in the sky)***: Michael*** (a general) ***and his angels*** (army) ***fought against the dragon; and the dragon fought and*** (with) ***his angels*** (army)." [China and company make war with Michael, whoever that is, probably us, as much as we love war, but maybe even the archangel himself, who knows.]

13:3: ***And I saw one of his heads as it were wounded to death; and his deadly wound was healed: and all the world wondered after the beast.*** [Which communist country that was once powerful but was destroyed almost to the brink of death, will rise to power again during the end times? Hmm, our options are rather slim. Could it be Russia? Many say, why would the USSR attack us, we're friends? Well, Bush was family friends with the Taliban and you see where that got us. In an article by CNN on May 17, 2001, (before the Taliban was overthrown) entitled, *U.S. Gives $43 Million to Afghanistan,* Colin Powell, (Secretary of State under former President George W. Bush) states, *"We will continue to look for ways to provide more assistance to the Afghans."* He then continues to call on other nations to donate as well. The contribution made the U.S. the leading sponsor of Taliban-fueled terrorism. So the question now is still: What would cause the USSR to attack the U.S.? We personally like to attack countries for oil (resources), to stop them from controlling others (power), and my personal favorite... to stimulate the economy (war creates lots of jobs, which fuels the economy), all of which the USSR is in great need of right now. So the question should be: Why wouldn't they attack? It's the smartest move for them right now. Actually, currently, Russia is spending almost 200 billion to upgrade and revamp its military. In preparation for?]

13:6: ***And he opened his mouth in blasphemy against God, to blaspheme his name, and his tabernacle, and them that dwell in heaven.*** [This is further proof that the country is communist, since communism bans religions of any kind. In fact, if you look up the definition of communism, it specifically says *"as the government, the vanguard party must educate the proletariat (citizens) — to dispel the societal false consciousness of religion."*]

13:11-12: *And I beheld another beast coming up out of the earth* (not literally; it just means to rise up)*; and he had two horns* (armies) *like a lamb, and he spake as a dragon* (as the communists do). *And he exerciseth all the power of the first beast before him* (the 7 nations), *and causeth the earth and them which dwell therein to worship the first beast, whose deadly wound was healed.* [According to Christians, this is the false prophet. According to the verse, he will get his power from the 7 communist nations, backed by the armies of 2 of the 7 nations, campaigning for support for the 7 countries but not actually being of them. A communist spokesperson if you will, probably from Europe, as very few Americans would support, let alone extol communism.]

13:16-18: *And he causeth all, both small and great, rich and poor, free and bond, to receive a mark in their right hand, or in their foreheads: And that no man might buy or sell, save he that had the mark, or the name of the beast, or the number of his name. Here is wisdom. Let him that hath understanding count the number of the beast: for it is the number of a man; and his number* (is) *Six hundred threescore* (and) *six* (666). [In the 1990s, the European Community (EC), which later became the EEC and finally the EU, implemented legislation for the Single Market that covers the requirements of inspected products by the EC. Once products have been screened and passed, they were eligible for sale within the Single Market. The report describing such controls specifically states: *"one cannot market or sell a product unless it has the EC mark."* This reflects almost word for word the prediction above and fits with the European profile of the false prophet. As for the mark being "666" and located on the hand or forehead, we'll need to discuss bar codes and micro chips for a moment. In the early 1970s, UPC codes (or bar codes) started showing up on all commercial and agricultural goods. Strangely enough, on every barcode ever printed you'll find the same three numbers repeated over and over again, "666." If you look closely, you'll notice that all of the vertical "marks" or bars are linked with numbers directly below. This is true for all of the numbers except the vertical lines in the beginning, center and end. Notice that the number 6 is represented by 2 equal lines "||", which are exactly the same marks as the beginning, middle and end bars.

But that's not the half of it. Cutting edge pet microchip implant technology has now been modified to safely use in humans. The device can send out a homing signal, confirm identity, monitor vital body functions, carry medical records, credit card and bank account info, as well as perform e-commerce transactions. The "VeriChip" currently is the only RFID microchip (Radio, Frequency, Identification) approved for human implanting by the FDA. In England, however, live testing with a similar chip is already underway on 45 lucky individuals. As far the numbers 666, most computer programs ASCII codes (American Standard Code for Information Interchange) begin with a starting code of 666. According to some people, a computer program (which currently runs off two separate servers) has already been set up to regulate and control all monetary transactions for the European Conglomerate Countries (ECC) through, of course, the use of UPCs (Universal Products Codes), digital chips and the World Wide Web or WWW (which in itself translates to 666 in Hebrew as vav vav vav). (Now pay attention, because this is where it all comes together) The EC backed 'one' notions like 'world commerce/trade'; the EU now backs notions like 'one world health/education', both of which are the same as communist ideas of nationally provided schools, healthcare and markets among other services.]

15:7: *And one of the four beasts gave unto the seven angels seven golden vials* (glass tubes filled with a gold- colored liquid) *full of the wrath of God, who liveth for ever and ever.* [Ok, this is where it even starts scaring me. Remember the first "four angels" in this format were ballistic or sub-orbital missiles, some carrying nuclear payloads. Here we see the "beast" (the communist allies) put seven biological payloads on seven new ballistic missiles making them "full of the wrath of God," I bet, bombing nations with virus-causing pandemics of mass destruction. Remember, the "antichrist" let loose a virus on us before, possibly just as a test or prelude to this attack, so they have the capability (as if anyone is arguing that).]

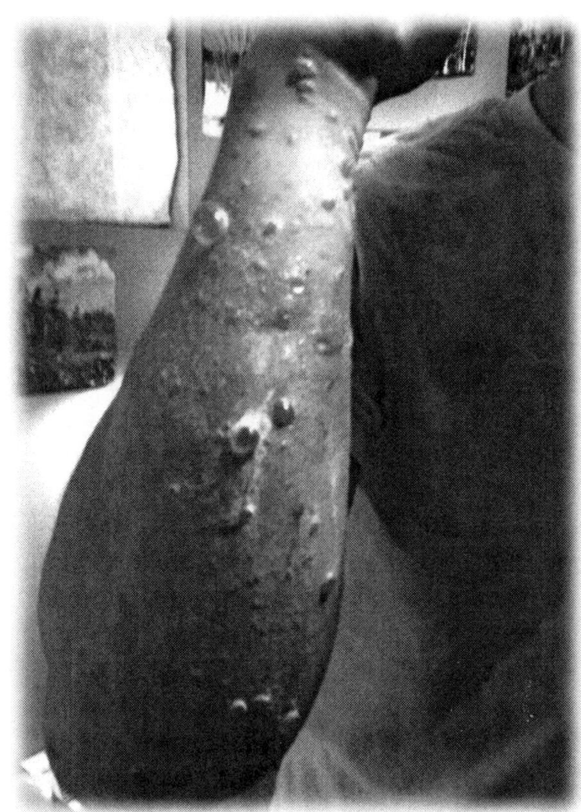

16:2: *And the first went, and poured out his vial* (exploded) *upon the earth; and there fell a noisome and grievous sore upon the men which had the mark of the beast, and* (upon) *them which worshipped his image.* [As we've already seen, "the mark of the beast" may be Europe's common commerce system. So the first ballistic missiles will hit somewhere in Europe. The Syphilis virus causes extreme sores in its victims and has been tested on Americans (1932 and 1972 Tuskegee experiments) and Guatemalans (1946-1948) for use as a weapon by at least the U.S. government.]

16:3: *And the second angel poured out his vial upon the sea; and it became as the blood of a dead* (man)*: and every living soul died in the sea.* [John could again be referring to the oceans of people or more likely just the ocean and some type of fish born viral outbreak (fish flu) that jumps the species chain killing humans like swine flu and bird flu did. Even if it didn't affect humans at all, the effect of the virus on every living thing in the sea would decimate the already crippled fishing industry, reducing humanity's already dwindling food supplies completely. In an article by TIME published on December 7, 2010, Tara Kelly reports, *"scientists predict if world leaders don't make the necessary policy changes the world will run out of food by the year 2050,"* which is right in line with the above biblical prophecy timeline.]

16:4: *And the third angel poured out his vial upon the rivers and fountains of waters; and they became blood* (poisons). [This third missile could have a warhead that contains anything from Giardia lamblia, Cryptosporidium, E coli, Leptospirosis (of the genus Leptospira), Vibrio cholera to various strains of Salmonella, which are all river and lake-living pathogens and is the reason why we always boil water before drinking it.]

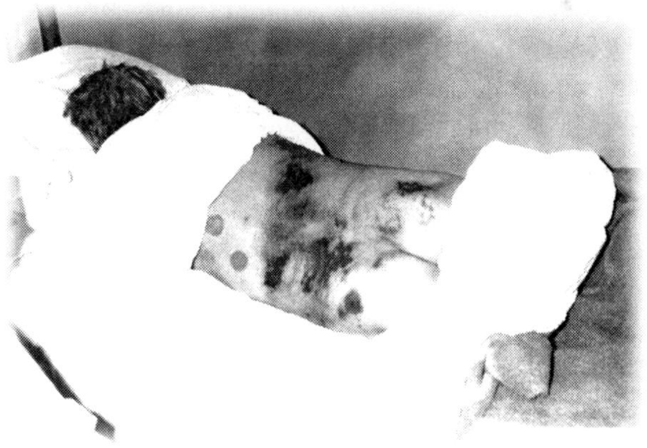

16:8: *And the fourth angel poured out his vial upon the sun; and power was given unto him to scorch* (burn) *men with fire.* [One of the deadliest viruses is Ebola, which causes extremely high fever and massive internal bleeding that will literally cook you from the inside out. Ebola virus, which causes its victims to feel as if they're "being burned by the Sun," kills 90% of people infected and is one of the only viruses that cause hemorrhagic (bloody) fever.]

16:10-11: *And the fifth angel poured out his vial upon the seat* (home) *of the beast; and his kingdom was full of darkness; and they gnawed their tongues for pain, And blasphemed the God of heaven because of their pains and their sores, and repented not of their deeds.* [The fact that a missile intended for another destination accidentally explodes over their own country is, in a way, comical, but completely relevant in the end of days. The virus sounds like Smallpox to me, which is one of only a few viruses that can cause both sores AND blindness.]

16:12: *And the sixth angel poured out his vial upon the great river Euphrates; and the water thereof was dried up, that the way of the kings of the east might be prepared.* (This verse signifies that the sixth missile hits a country somewhere in the Middle East, possibly even Israel, and that the effects of the virus will dehydrate its victims, such as a Norovirus which is aerosolized, making it airborne.)

16:16: *And he gathered them together into a place called in the Hebrew tongue Armageddon.* [Armageddon is where the future great battle will be fought. Armageddon (Har Megiddon in Hebrew or the Hill of Megiddo) is in Northern Israel and is a perfect location (many ancient battles have been fought here) because of the terrain.]

16:17: *And the seventh angel poured out his vial into the air;* [The seventh viral attack is an airborne or inhalable pandemic probably anthrax, and by the sound of it, against Israel.]

16:18-19: *And there were voices, and thunders, and lightnings; and there was a great earthquake, such as was not* (seen) *since men were upon the earth, so mighty an earthquake, so great. And the great city* (Jerusalem) *was divided into three parts, and the cities of the nations fell: and great Babylon* (Iraq) *came in remembrance before God, to give unto her the cup of the wine of the fierceness of his wrath.* [Another earthquake occurs, this one bigger than any since the creation of the Earth. We're probably talking something like a 60.0M, with the current Richter scale only going to 10.0M. Jerusalem being divided, this may be literal or that the city is divided between Palestinians, Israelites and probably Christians, which is the direction it's trending now.]

16:20: *And every island fled away, and the mountains were not found.* [This earthquake would level most mountains and create tsunamis 1000ft high, covering nearly all land masses on the planet in water.]

17:1-2 & 15: *And there came one of the seven angels which had the seven vials, and talked with me, saying unto me, Come hither; I will shew unto thee the judgment of the great whore* (the U.S.) *that sitteth upon many waters* (controls many people). *With whom the kings* (world leaders) *of the earth have committed fornication* (in league with; this is where the term "is in bed with" comes from), *and the inhabitants* (people) *of the earth have been made drunk with the wine* (goods) *of her fornication. And he saith unto me, the waters which thou sawest, where the whore sitteth, are peoples, and multitudes, and nations, and tongues.* [One of the leaders of the seven communist countries talks to John, showing him U.S. corporatism and capitalism (there is a McDonald's, Nike and Harley Davidson outlet store in almost every country except communist countries); pointing out that the U.S. sits as a world leader in goods, entertainment, military and commerce, educating and leading the world into a life of lower morals, obesity and war; drunk with naive notions of grandeur, watching *The Wedding Singer* on a 72" plasma TV, drinking beer while sitting on plastic lawn chairs under a leaky roof.]

17:16-17: *And the ten horns which thou sawest upon the beast, these shall hate the whore, and shall make her desolate and naked, and shall eat her flesh, and burn her with fire. For God hath put in their hearts to fulfill his will, and to agree, and give their kingdom unto the beast, until the words of God shall be fulfilled.* [A wake-up call for Americans (or whoever the recipients of God's will is), saying the communist armies (along with everyone else on the planet) don't like us (they like our material goods, just not us); in fact, they hate us; they will strip America of her prosperity, destroy her government, and bomb her shores, because "God has told them to do so."]

17:18: *And the woman which thou sawest is that great city* (New York or D.C.), *which reigneth over the kings of the earth.* [This verse could apply to the government of the United States, which often forces other countries to adhere to their wishes, or the financial leaders of the world, most of which are out of New York.]

18:8-9: *Therefore shall her plagues come in one day* (that's nice, thanks), *death, and mourning, and famine; and she shall be utterly burned with fire: for strong* (is) *the Lord God who judgeth her. And the kings* (world leaders) *of the earth, who have committed fornication* (been in league with) *and lived deliciously* (reaped the benefits of capitalism) *with her, shall bewail her, and lament for her* (be sad), *when they shall see the smoke of her burning.* [This verse could mean the actual bombing of D.C. and New York or more likely just the fall of our government, economy and capitalism. Either way, upon knowing the party's over, countries which have reaped the benefits and been in league with the U.S., such as the UK, Australia, Canada, Saudi Arabia and Mexico, will be saddened when she falls. Our pandemic will act quickly; in one day we'll be decimated. I do find it very amusing, however, that after several planet-altering earthquakes, volcanoes, asteroidean impacts, floods, great famines, drought, World Wars, the rise and fall of super nations and one-world orders, nightmarish viral epidemics, all responsible for killing over 3/4 of the planet, that commerce, wealth and our entire barbaric economic system (which is what got us into this mess in the first place) is the last to fall. It is truly mind numbing.]

19:11: ***And I saw heaven opened, and behold a white horse; and he that sat upon him*** (was) ***called Faithful and True, and in righteousness he doth judge and make war.*** [This is what Christians call the second coming of Christ. Who this actually is, what "white" vehicle he's on and what country (or what planet) he comes from, I couldn't say; heck, maybe it's actually Christ come again. Who knows. That said, I personally have the idea that the country is India for reasons explained in the next verse.]

19:14: ***And the armies*** (which were) ***in heaven*** (religious) ***followed him upon white horses, clothed in fine linen, white and clean.*** [White robes indicate a religious order. India strikes me as the only opposing force left on Earth after the fall of the United States that could potentially conquer a communist alliance. Currently, India has an estimated 4,768,407 troops--the largest army in the world over China's 3,455,000.]

19:19-21: ***And I saw the beast*** (the communist alliance)***, and the kings*** (communist military leaders) ***of the earth, and their armies, gathered together to make war against him that sat on the horse*** (India)***, and against his army. And the beast was taken*** (defeated)***, and with him the false prophet*** (the EU) ***that wrought miracles before him, with which he deceived them that had received the mark of the beast, and them that worshipped his image.*** [This is what's known as the Battle of Armageddon, although it's not much of a battle. The communist nations and the EU fall before the battle even begins.]

21:1: ***And I saw a new heaven and a new earth: for the first heaven and the first earth were passed away; and there was no more sea.*** [This vision coincides with many other prophets' visions including the Hindu belief, along with the Hopi's "fifth world" and the Mayan's "golden age." Each depicting not the actual end of the world (although more than 75% of the population will be dead because of the transition), but the physical and spiritual transformation into a new era, call it hyper-evolution, which will occur in a matter of a few years.]

MERLIN

Merlin, the children's storybook magician, was a real Scottish person, a druid living inside the pagan enclave towards the end of the sixth century, according to British historian, Nikolai Tolstoy, in his book *Quest for Merlin*. Merlin's predictions are in line with the rest of the prophets before mentioned; however, Merlin tends to focus more on UK and European events during the end times:

All these things shall Three Ages see, till the buried Kings shall be exposed to public view in the City of London. [The first age ran from the 6th-11th century, the second from 11th-17th century and the third from 17th-21st century. In 1908, Westminster Abbey in London, England, (the burial place of ancient kings) was opened to the public for the first time in history.]

In those days the oaks of the forest shall burn and acorns grow upon lime trees. The Severn Sea shall discharge itself through seven mouths and the river Usk shall burn for seven months. Fishes shall die in the heat and from them serpents will be born. [The Severn Estuary Sea is currently the site of a nuclear and renewable energy power plant; if a total meltdown occurred (such as what happened in Chernobyl, Three Mile Island Japan), it could easily cause the destruction and mutations described above. An enormous tidal barricade surrounds the complex which funnels tons of water in and out, cooling the plant through seven massive concrete openings, resembling "mouths."]

The baths of Bath shall grow cold and their health giving waters shall engender death. [In World War II, the once popular "health-giving hot springs of Bath," England, were declared radioactive; in 1979, it was completely closed to the public when amoebic meningitis was the cause of at least one death.]

The River Thames shall encompass London and the fame of this work shall pass beyond the Alps. [The Thames Barrier in London, England is the world's second largest movable flood barrier. In 2003, construction began on the MOSE (Mosses) Barrier in Venice, Italy, (mere hours away from the Alps), based on the same design in order *"to take into account the expected rise in sea level as a result of global warming."*]

The Hedgehog shall hoard his apples within it and shall make subterranean passages. [The hedgehog being London, which contains the largest system of underground sewers, subways and drainage tunnels in the world, is an international symbol of wealth (apples). It is a global pre-eminent financial hub, equal only to New York City as the most important location for international commerce.]

At that time shall the stones speak (cellphones) *and the area towards the Gallic coast shall be contracted into a narrow space.* [The Gallic coast (now modern-day France) has been "contracted into a narrow space" by the Channel Tunnel. The Channel Tunnel built in 1994, is a 31.4 mile tunnel connecting England and France. A trip that took days by ferry now takes 30 minutes].

On each bank shall one man hear another and the soil of the island shall be enlarged. [Since around the year 1600, Britain has greatly "enlarged its soil," annexing: Africa, Asia, Australia, the Caribbean, Scotland, the South Pacific, India, Ireland and the U.S.; the UK would eventually go on to cover 1/5th of the Earth's land mass and 1/4 of its population, that's a huge soil enlargement].

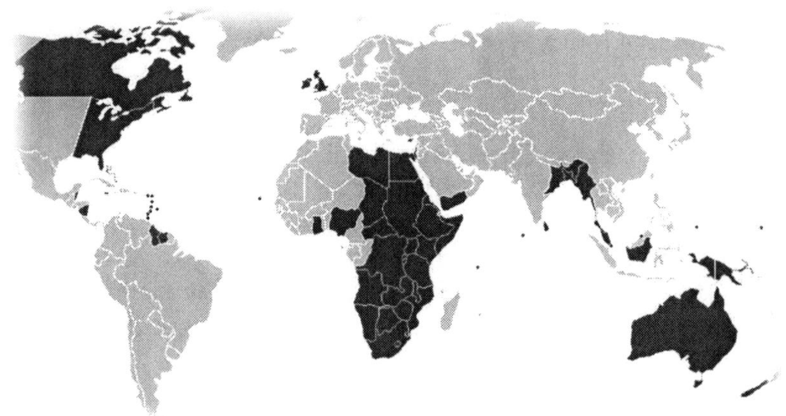

The secrets of the deep shall be revealed and Gaul (France) *shall tremble for fear.* [David Byers and Charles Bremner wrote an article in Paris published by The Sunday Times on February 6, 2009 stating: *"Two submarines carrying nuclear weapons – from the Royal and French navies – collided in the Atlantic."* Both subs had over 16 ballistic nuclear missiles and a crew of 130. A senior Navy official goes on to say, *"The potential consequences of such a collision are unthinkable."*]

ANTON JOHANSSON

Anton Johansson, Sweden, (1858-1909) successfully predicted the sinking of the Titanic, even naming one of its passengers (John Jacob Astor VI). He accurately described events of World War I in detail and foresaw San Francisco's earthquake of 1906 as well as a volcanic eruption in 1902 that destroyed St. Pierre city, Martinique. He said the Third World War would break out at "*the end of July, beginning of August,*" but was unaware of the year:

India will be occupied by China. New diseases used as weapons will cause 25 million people to die. (Might this be ballistic missiles with viral warheads?) *Persia and Turkey will be conquered apparently by Russian troops. Revolutionaries will instigate unrest and war in India and Egypt* (hmm, that's currently happening also as protestors are up heaving governments in Tunisa, Lybia, Egypt, Bahrain and Syria) *to facilitate the occupation of India and Europe. The Russians will conquer the Balkans. There will be great destruction in Italy. The red storm* (communism) *will approach France through Hungary, Austria, northern Italy and Switzerland. France will be conquered from inside and outside. American supply depots will fall into Russian hands. Germany will be attacked from the east. There will be a civil war; Germans will fight against Germans. The Eastern Bloc will cause a civil war in England. Russia will lead a mass attack against the United States, so U.S. forces will be prevented from reinforcing Europe. New weapons will cause huge hurricanes and firestorms in the U.S.A. where the largest cities will be destroyed.* [HAARP (a top secret government facility in Alaska) may very well use high-powered electromagnets, high frequency radio and microwaves, adapting Tesla's earthquake-generation technology to trigger catastrophes such as floods, droughts, hurricanes, thunderstorms, and devastating earthquakes in Pakistan, the Philippines, and may possibly be the cause of the 2010 Haiti earthquake as well].

EDGAR CAYCE

Edgar Cayce may be one of the most astonishing prophets. In deep meditation, he would answer correctly questions from (non-paying) clients about anything from farming to engine repair to heart surgery and disease diagnosis even though he knew absolutely nothing about any of these subjects. Between the years of 1901-1945, he would make 14,246 extremely accurate readings (all on file in Virginia Beach at the Edgar Cayce foundation), without ever taking any kind of payment in return. Politicians, presidents, actors and businessmen would come to Cayce from around the world, literally becoming rich and famous overnight based on his visions. He'd predict Hitler, The Apocalypse and WWII:

Question: *Please forecast the principal events for the next fifty years affecting the welfare of the human race.*

Answer: *This had best be cast after the great catastrophe that's coming to the world in '36, in the form of the breaking up of many powers that now exist as factors in world affairs* (World War II). *Then with the breaking up in '36 will be changes that will make different maps of the world.* [WWII Poland, Hungary, Czechoslovakia, Romania, Albania, and Germany became part of the Soviet Union. Conversely, communist Yugoslavia broke away from the Soviet Union and Germany was divided into East Germany and West Germany. Korea was liberated from Japan and communist China was born.]

Question: *How should we regard those changes that do come about?*

Answer: *What is needed in the Earth today? That the sons of men be warned that the day of the Lord is at hand.*

Question: What is meant by "the day of the Lord is near at hand?

Answer: *That has been promised through the prophets and sages of old, the time and half time has been and is being fulfilled in this day and generation. Soon there'll again appear in the earth that one through whom many will be called to meet those that are preparing the way for his day in the earth. The Lord, then will come, even as you have seen him go.*

Question: *How soon?*

Answer: *When those that are His have made the way clear, passable for Him to come. Don't think that there will not be trouble, but those who put their trust wholly in the Lord will not come up missing. They will find conditions, circumstances, activities, someway and somehow much to be thankful for.*

Question: *What can we do to counteract such serious happenings?*

Answer: *Tendencies in the hearts and souls of men are such that theses upheavals may be brought about. Man is not ruled by the world, the earth or the environment nor planetary influences. Rather it is true that man brings order out of chaos by his compliance with Divine Law. By his disregard of the laws of Divine influence, man brings chaos and destructive forces into his experience.* [And we have disregarded the law for the most part, have we not?]

Question: *What greater change or the beginning of what change, if any, is to take place in the year 2000-2001 A.D.?*

Answer: *When there is a shifting of the poles. Or a new cycle begins.* (The fact is that the polar shift wasn't known until almost 50 years after Cayce's death. Since 2000, there have been literally dozens of major earthquakes, several of which have shifted the poles according to NASA scientists.)

Question: *What changes will the Earth pass through?* Answer: *As to conditions in the geography of the world and of the country, changes are gradually coming about. Many portions of the east coast will be disturbed, as well as many portions of the west coast, as well as the central portion of the United States. Lands will appear in the Atlantic as well as the Pacific. What is the coast line now of many a land will be the bed of ocean. Many of the battlefields of the present* (1941) *will be ocean. Portions of the now east coast of New York, or New York City itself, will in the main disappear. This will be another generation, while the southern portions of Carolina, Georgia, these will disappear. This will be much sooner. The waters of the Great Lakes will empty into the Gulf of Mexico. It would be well if a waterway would be prepared. Virginia Beach will be among the safety lands as will be portions of what is now Ohio, Indiana and Illinois and much of the southern portion of Canada, and the eastern portion of Canada; while the western land, much of that is to be disturbed as of course much in other lands.*

Question: *Will Los Angeles be safe?*

Answer: *Los Angeles, San Francisco, most all of these will be among those that will be destroyed before New York even. If there is the greater activities in the Vesuvius, or Pelee then the southern coast of California and the areas between Salt Lake and the southern portions of Nevada may expect within the three months following same, an inundation by the earthquakes. The earth will be broken up in many places. The early part will see a change in the physical aspect of the west coast of America. There will be open waters appear in the northern portions of Greenland. There will be new lands seen off the Caribbean Sea, and dry land will appear. South America will be shaken from the uppermost portion to the end, and in the Antarctic off Tierra Del Fuego, land and a strait with rushing water.*

Question: *How soon will the changes in the earth's activity begin to be apparent?*

Answer: *When there is the first breaking up of some conditions in the South Pacific and the sinking or rising in the Mediterranean and the Etna area then we would say they have begun.* [Sea levels have risen so much in the South Pacific that about a dozen nations, including the Marshal Island are all about to be completely submerged.]

Question: *How long before this begins?*

Answer: *The indications are that some of these have already begun.*

Question: *Will there be any physical changes in the earth's surface in North America?*

Answer: *All over the country we will find many physical changes of a minor or greater degree. The greater change will be the North Atlantic Seaboard. Watch New York, Connecticut and the like. As to changes physical again: the earth will be broken up in the western portion of America. The greater part of Japan must go into the sea. The upper portion of Europe will be changed as in the twinkling of an eye. Land will appear off the east coast of America. There will be upheavals in the Arctic and in the Antarctic that will make for the eruption of volcanoes in the torrid areas, and there will then be the shifting of the poles so that where there have been those of a frigid or semi-tropical will become the more tropical, and moss and fern will grow. And these will begin in those periods 58 to 98 when these will be proclaimed as the periods when His Light will be seen again in the clouds.* [Since the late 1950s the planet has undergone a steady state of Global Warming (a term that was later changed to *climate change*) which has created the conditions above.]

DANIEL MARTIN

Now on to bigger and better prophets, me! It's no coincidence that I've saved the best (myself) for last. Actually, in all seriousness, I did have a vision of the end times (no kidding). It came in the form of a dream repeated itself the same way (more or less) almost every night for about 15 years, from as far back as I can remember (so maybe more) and may be the driving force motivating me to have written this book, possibly to warn others, possibly not. It wasn't of violence, viruses, earthquakes, volcanoes, nuclear weapons or the second comings of Christ like my predecessors. It showed no hints of a timeframe other than the décor and items lying around, but was strong enough and real enough to be added here amongst my fellow prophets. So without further adieu:

I'm leading a small group of World War III (or some type of major attack on the United States) survivors through a semi-wrecked office building. The dream is always the same with the exception of which direction and through which offices I'm traversing. There's no sign that this is WWIII, no battles going on, no destruction caused by fighting or violence, no scorch marks or blown out windows, no blood stains or decapitated bodies draped on and over desks and emergency stairwell railings. The offices are simply in disarray, as if abandoned in haste; but I know why, inside myself, inside the dream I know and understand a third world war has caused this. Filing cabinet drawers are pulled out, documents and folders discarded on the floor, half-drunk soda bottles and coffee cups strewn about, with no regard for carpet cleanliness. No, the people who were here just days ago, left in a hurry and for some reason. I'm here now with about 7-14 people dressed in casual and office-like attire (though I don't believe they worked in this building) following and looking to me for guidance through company headquarters, telemarketing call centers, insurance offices, corporate paper company regional branches, etc. We're trying to get somewhere in a hurry, yet cautiously, as if someone or something may be following us not too far behind or up ahead, ready to spring an ambush on us in a blink of an eye. We walk in single file past toppled fake black leather swivel chairs and under flickering hanging compact fluorescent lights, through 7, 8, 9, maybe even 10 rooms.

- Dan Martin 1:1

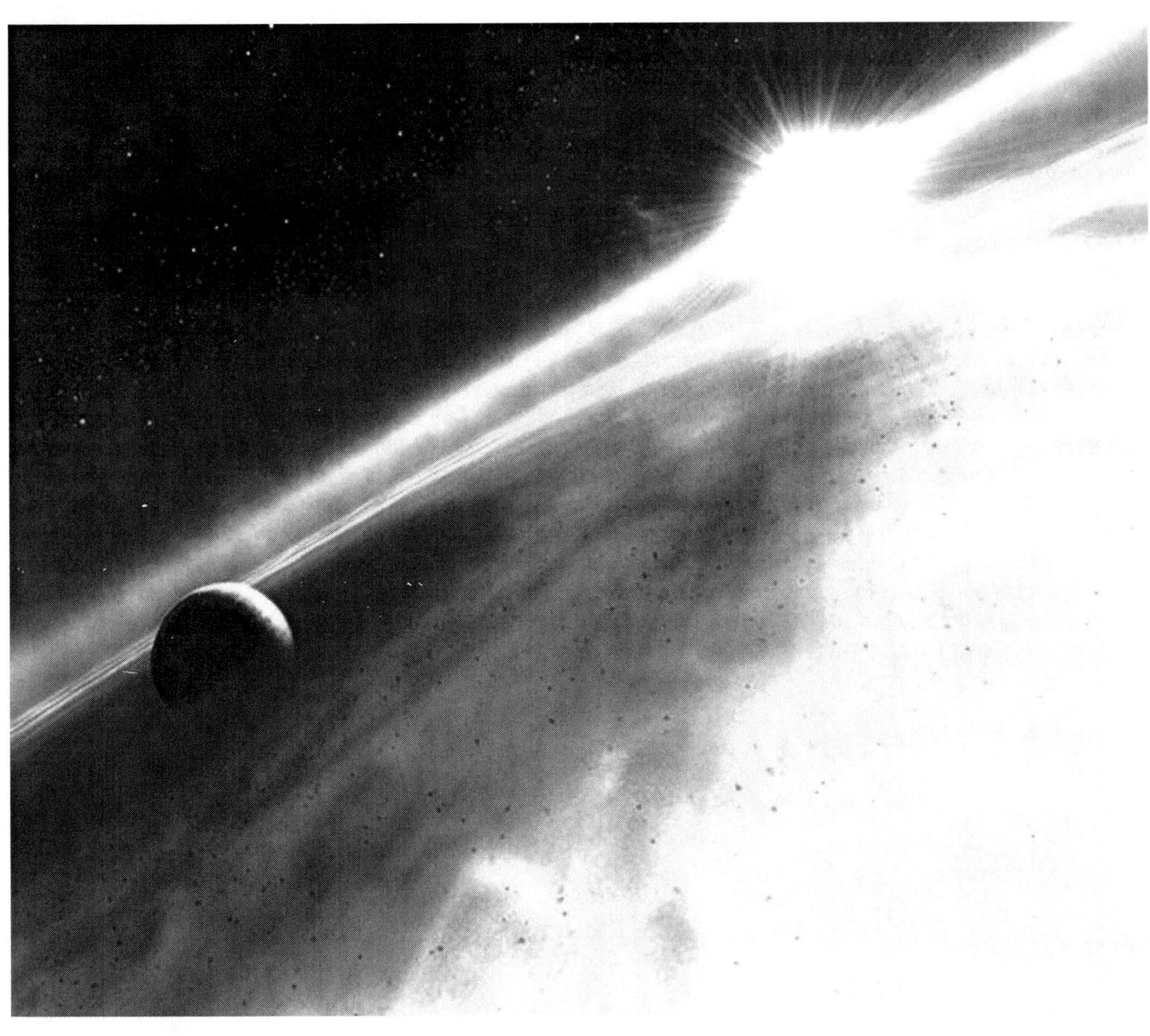

CHAPTER 4

SCIENTIFIC PREDICTIONS: SUPPORTING EVIDENCE

Now, let's put all the ancient, recent and current (me) prophets, religious texts and spiritual beliefs aside for a moment. There's real scientific evidence, as well as government acknowledgments, that support many of the prophecies coming true by 2012. Science, scientific discoveries, scientific evidence, and leading scientists of our day have no problem backing up such dark, outlandish ideas. In fact, they have a few of their own to throw into the mix.

For example, for the last few years the vibration or "hum" of the Earth has increased significantly, something that hasn't occurred since man first built the technology to record such data. Since the invention of all wave-based communication devices, we've always used a 7-cycle format as a baseline for communications, .8 different than the frequency of the Earth at 7.8. However, in the last few years that frequency has increased and exceeded 11 cycles, and therefore would, in theory, peak by the year 2012. Similarly, Dr. Paul La Violette, author of *Galactic Super Waves and their Impact on the Earth,* postulates that a "galactic Super Wave" made up of a large quantity of gamma rays, created by pulsars, will also "strike the Earth around a 2012 timeframe." You see our solar system isn't unique in any way, shape or form. It orbits around a black hole, which is only about 30,000 light years from your kitchen, located in the center of the somewhat flat, disc-like Milky Way Galaxy. Our Sun and accompanying planets pass through or in and out of this flat disc plane (called the 'galactic equator'). The "winter solstice" aligns perfectly with the galactic equator every 26,000 years or so. But don't worry, the next perfect alignment won't happen for another two years (2012) or so. This makes you wonder, out of our 260 million ancestors, why does a perfect alignment, (which promises unspeakable parallels and despicable disasters), have to occur in our generation, on a date that's already filled with enough foretold cataclysmic disasters, as well as scheduled, unscheduled and unforeseen catastrophic events to last 1,000 generations?

DISCOVER MAGAZINE: ASTEROID IMPACT

Five massive extinction events, wiping out more than half of all living things on Earth, have occurred in the last 540 million years. What would happen; and what is the likelihood of an asteroid the size of a small town (around 6 miles in diameter) crashing into our planet? If we do the math, we're looking at a mass extinction rate of every 100 million years, on average. The last of these events, known as the Cretaceous-Tertiary (or CT) extinction event, occurred 65 million years ago and almost completely obliterated the dinosaurs. So don't panic, we still have another 35 million years or so to go for another, no worries. In fact, the planet has literally been bombarded with asteroids, meteoroids and other planetary objects billions of times over the years, causing over a thousand globally destructive occurrences. Some of the most major impacts created giant craters that survive the test of time, giving us a glimpse into the devastation very large asteroids achieve:

NAME	LOCATION	WIDTH (miles)	AGE (yrs ago)
Yarrabubba	Western Australia, Australia	18.6	2,000,000,000
Sudbury	Ontario, Canada	155	1,850,000,000
Keurusselkä	Western Finland, Finland	18.6	1,800,000,000
Shoemaker	Western Australia, Australia	18.6	1,630,000,000
Amelia Creek	Northern Territory, Australia	12.4	1,000,000,000
Kamensk	Southern Federal District, Russia	15.5	646,000,000
Strangways	Northern Territory, Australia	15.5	646,000,000

Beaverhead	Idaho and Montana, United States	37.2	600,000,000
Acraman	South Australia, Australia	56	590,000,000
Glover Bluff meteoroid Crater	Wisconsin	5	500,000,000
Presqu'île	Quebec, Canada	15	500,000,000
Slate Islands	Ontario, Canada	18.6	450,000,000
Siljan	Dalarna, Sweden	32.3	377,000,000
Woodleigh	Western Australia, Australia	25	364,000,000
Charlevoix	Quebec, Canada	33.5	342,000,000
Weaubleau-Osceola Crater	Missouri, United States	12	340,000,000
Serpent Mound Crater	Ohio, United States	5	320,000,000
Middlesboro Crater	Kentucky, United States	3	300,000,000
Clearwater West	Quebec, Canada	22.3	290,000,000
Araguainha	Central Brazil	24.8	244,000,000
Saint Martin	Manitoba, Canada	25	220,000,000
Manicouagan	Quebec, Canada	62	214,000,000
Rochechouart	France	14.3	214,000,000
Decaturville Crater	Missouri, United States	3.7	200,000,000
Upheaval Dome Crater	Utah, United States	6.2	170,000,000
Obolon'	Poltava Oblast, Ukraine	12.4	169,000,000
Puchezh-Katunki	Nizhny Novgorod Oblast, Russia	50	167,000,000
Morokweng	Kalahari Desert, South Africa	43.5	145,000,000
Gosses Bluff	Northern Territory, Australia	13.6	142,000,000
Mjølnir	Barents Sea, Norway	25	142,000,000
Tookoonooka	Queensland, Australia	34	128,000,000
Carswell	Saskatchewan, Canada	24.2	115,000,000
Sierra Madera Crater	Texas, United States	8	100,000,000
Kentland Crater	Indiana, United States	4.5	97,000,000
Steen River	Alberta, Canada	15.5	91,000,000
Crooked Creek Crater	Missouri, United States	4.3	80,000,000
Manson	Iowa, United States	21.7	73.8,000,000
Lappajärvi	Finland	14.3	73.3,000,000
Kara	Nenetsia, Russia	40.3	70,000,000
Boltysh	Kirovohrad Oblast, Ukraine	15	65,000,000
Chicxulub	Yucatán, Mexico	105.6	65,000,000
Montagnais	Nova Scotia, Canada	28	50,000,000
Logancha	Siberia, Russia	18	40,000,000
Haughton	Nunavut, Canada	14.3	39,000,000
Mistastin	Newfoundland and Labrador, Canada	17.4	36,000,000
Popigai	Siberia, Russia	62	35,000,000
Chesapeake Bay	Virginia, United States	56	35,500,000
Toms Canyon Crater	New Jersey, United States	13.6	35,500,000
Flynn Creek Crater	Tennessee, United States	3.8	20,000,000
Nördlinger Ries	Bavaria, Germany	15	14,800,000
Karakul	Pamir Mountains, Tajikistan	32.3	5,000,000
Lonar	India, United States	0.75	52,000

Barringer Meteorite Crater	Arizona, United States	.75	50,000
Odessa Craters (thousands)	Texas, United States	.1	30,000
Clovis**	Great Lakes, United States		13,000
Rio Cuarto	Argentina	656	10,000
Henbury	Australia	0.11	5,000
Kamil*	Egypt	0.027	3,500
Kaali	Estonia	0.74	2,700
Haviland Crater	Kansas, United States	.01	1,000

* The Kamil Crater wasn't known to man until it was discovered on a Google Earth image review, showing us again exactly how technology is helping us to understand that we're more vulnerable than what we may have once thought.

** The Clovis Crater isn't really a crater, the Clovis meteoroid blew up over the Great Lakes setting all of North America on fire and ultimately causing the Younger Dryas cold period.

You can see by the "AGE" column, it just looks like a giant count-down clock to the end of the world. That being said, an asteroid doesn't need to be 6 miles across or form a 90-mile wide crater to end the world *as we know it.* A meteoroid or several meteoroids (since they occur in 'showers' when the Earth passes through a field) just 5-10ft in diameter (which hits several hundred times per year) striking in and around a major metropolitan area with high population masses would disintegrate most of the region's infrastructure including, buildings, economy, law enforcement, emergency services, government, as well as, of course, taking millions of human lives in the process.

An asteroid only 30ft wide (which occurs every fifty-one hundred years), would impact the ground with 1000 times the force of the atomic bomb that exploded at Hiroshima, (which killed 166,000 and flattened almost the entire city). And it doesn't actually need to land on New York, New Jersey, Detroit, Boston, London, Los Angeles, Paris, Hong Kong, Sydney, or any one of the hundreds of other major cities in the world, for the local annihilation and global ramifications to be unimaginable. For example, if the same asteroid that exploded over Siberia 100 years ago, were to hit today around, say, the desolate Pennsylvania/New Jersey state line, the same disaster area or 'blast zone' would wipe out most of the eastern seaboard, crushing our economy and ultimately devastating the world. We already see

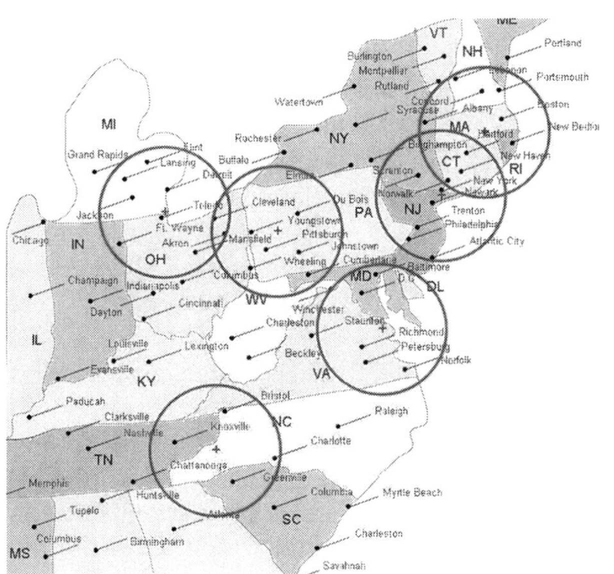

what happens when the housing market hits a little bump; we can guess what would transpire if all houses in the entire Eastern United States were wiped out by the blast radius: mass panic, millions of lives lost, Sun-blocking fallout killing most of the vegetation on Earth and ultimately starving out those not near or directly affected by the blast, triggered volcanic and earthquake activity in the region, massive flooding around the world (if it were to strike in the ocean), just to name a few.

Basically, anything larger than 5-10ft in diameter could not only destroy our already collapsing economy, but would also wreak major damage on an aging infrastructure, which would likely be irreparable. 5-15ft objects strike the planet about 500 times per year; 15-30ft meteors, approximately once a year; 30-50ft asteroids, in the range of one every 100 years; 50-100ft rocks, about once every 500 years; 150ft objects, about once every thousand years; half-mile wide asteroids strike Earth approximately once every 500,000 years; 3-mile wide asteroids, every ten million or so years; and as mentioned above, 10-mile wide objects, every 100 million years or so. And again, by looking at the time frames, regardless of what the government wants us to believe, we're due, at least, for the medium to smaller ones.

So why don't we see these 15 footers hit all the time? One reason is that most of our planet is water; and until recently, most of the land mass was uninhabited. Some people in remote areas did witness impacts, however, because of the lack of broadcasting and communication technology, these reports were never made public, or weren't believed. That's all changing now. Due to the immense growth in human reproduction and enormous evolution in technology, the entire planet is becoming populated and connected. We are, therefore, able to be a witness to these events much quicker. Secondly, many of the meteoroids explode over land. They look and sound like lightning and thunder without the clouds. Lastly, the implementation of Missile Early Warning Satellite Systems all over the planet, including America's Ballistic Missile Early Warning System (BMEWS), now allows us to detect objects before they enter Earth's atmosphere. In 1992 alone, 136 significant meteoroids were tracked. The point is that globe changing meteoroids impact the planet every few years, and I'm not talking about the little "falling star" meteorites you see flashing across the night sky (which occur hundreds of times per night). Actually, I'm not sure why more media coverage is not devoted to these occurrences now. Possibly, they want to divert attention from the likelihood that eventually one of these rocks the size of a house, is going to destroy a major city soon and we have no way to stop it. Regardless, they do hit, and their effects are obvious:

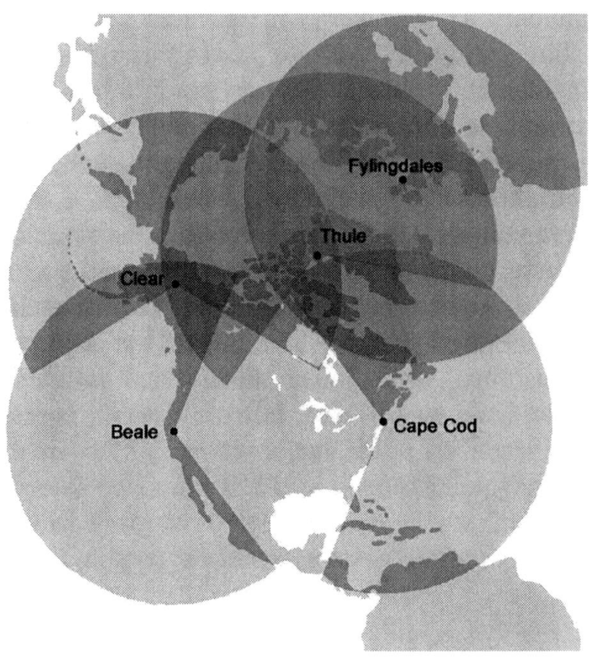

- 1443, a meteoroid strikes the ocean near New Zealand forming a 12-mile hole, called the Mahuika crater.
- 1490, a hail of "falling stones" kills 10,000 people in Shanxi Province, China.
- 1891, several rocks 5-10ft wide impact the sands in southern Saudi Arabia creating the Wabar craters.
- June 30, 1908, a 30ft asteroid explodes near the Tunguska River in Siberia, Russia. The blast destroys every tree (80 million trees) in an 830-square-mile area.
- February 12, 1947, a 28-ton meteoroid crashes near Luchegorsk Russia, known as the Sikhote-Alin event.
- March 31, 1965, a meteoroid breaks apart in the atmosphere and sprays meteorites across the countryside near British Columbia, Canada.
- January 18, 2000, a 15ft, 180-ton asteroid explodes near Whitehorse, Canada. This event was shown on The Science Channel series, Killer Asteroids.
- December 25, 2004, large amounts of gamma radiation strike the planet; moments later changes in Earth's gravity affect sensitive data-collecting equipment all over the planet. The next day, December 26, a 9.1 magnitude earthquake (one of the largest ever) rips apart Indonesia. Many scientists claim the radiation, earthquake and following tsunami (all typical of asteroid impacts) were the result of a 150-200ft asteroid striking the ocean (bedrock) that we, the general public, were never made aware of.

- May 2, 2006, a rock strikes Earth's moon with the power of 4 tons of TNT. Actually, meteoroids hit the moon all the time, which gives you an idea of the magnitude of space garbage on a direct path with Earth.
- June 7, 2006, a meteoroid impacts the ground near Troms, Norway. This event is interesting because it was a major current event, although not covered by the international news sources, again. According to British News agencies, because of the December 2004 impact, worldwide broadcasters were instructed to hold all breaking news updates related to impacts in order to prevent widespread panic, again.
- September 15, 2007, a meteoroid hurdles through space on a collision course with Earth, hits the ground near Carancas, Peru, near the Bolivian border and Lake Titicaca. The impact creates a huge crater, scorches the Earth, "boiling the water" (according to local official, Marco Limache), spews "fetid, noxious" gases, poisoning the local ground water with "arsenic compounds," and sickens local residents with an "unexplained illness." Later, Peruvian scientists postulated that the local citizens contracted arsenic poisoning after inhaling the boiling, arsenic-contaminated water vapor.
- October 7, 2008, a 15ft meteoroid named TC3 (Catalina Sky Survey temporary designation 8TA9D69) enters Earth's atmosphere and explodes 23-miles above ground raining more than 600 high-velocity fragments on Sudan. This event was the first of its kind; because it was not only seen but tracked for approximately 20-hours before impact. The ability to detect and track near-Earth objects is a new technology with TC3 being the first. However, about one hour before impact, the object entered the Earth's shadow and was lost to observational tracking.
- November 21, 2009, a meteoroid tears across the sky on a collision course with Earth, finally striking just north of Pretoria, South Africa, near the Botswana border.
- January 6, 2010, Hubble discovers a debris field surrounding Asteroid P/2010 A2m (similar to the impact story in *Chapter 2*), with a calculated orbit routing back to the Chicxulub Crater Yucatán Peninsula in Mexico (the dinosaur killer). At the same time, cutting-edge technology has shown that the Chicxulub impact was actually one of many simultaneous asteroid impacts that struck the entire planet. Craters around the world, including the Silver Pit Crater in the United Kingdom, the Boltysh Crater in Ukraine, and the Shiva Crater near India, have all been dated to the exact same time as the Chicxulub Crater. The implication here is that the asteroid that wiped out almost all life on Earth is a comet orbiting our Sun that's encircled by a large cloud of debris on a possible regular collision course with Earth.

The point I'm trying to make here again and again, is that an impact is commonly understood as an event that would cause the end of civilization, but is believed by most as something that "could never happen to us." In 2000, Discover Magazine published a list of twenty likely unexpected scenarios that would bring on a sudden doomsday-like environment. An asteroid impact placed number one as most likely to occur. Until recently, we laughed at the idea that the end of our society, race, species, world, neighborhood could possibly come to an end. The discovery and explanation of the Chicxulub Crater, eye-witness accounts of the Comet Shoemaker-Levy 9 event (where several enormous asteroids were seen impacting Jupiter), the May 2006 meteoroid impact on the Moon and double solar impacts of 1998 hopefully have changed the indestructible view of ourselves. These events should remind us, awaken us, and make us cognizant of the fact that space isn't 'void' at all as most of you may think; it's actually literally filled with cosmic rock and garbage that we crash into or that crashes into us on a regular basis, any of which could at any time, knock us back a couple steps toward the dark ages.

AVI BIOPHARMA: PANDEMIC

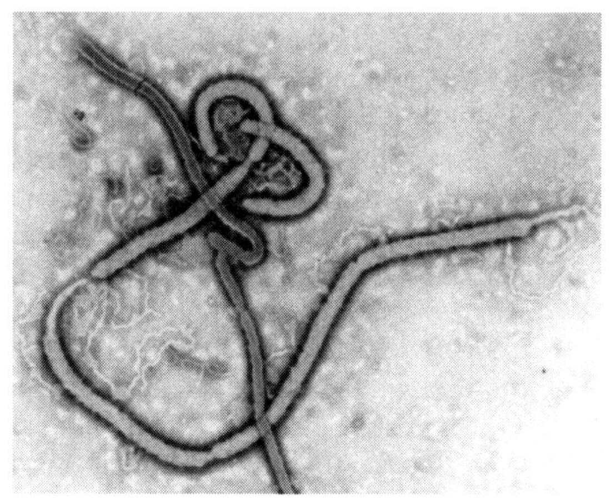

Extinction of the human race is imminent. It has happened to all of our cousin species and most other animal species that ever existed on Earth since the beginning of time. It is not a question of if, but <u>when</u> this will occur. It's just a race against time and a mystery game of what will be the cause, with a good chance of it being a global pandemic, caused by any number of natural or man-made lethal viruses administered and carried accidentally or intentionally. Patrick Iversen of AVI BioPharma said in an interview with *The New Yorker* in January, 2011, entitled *Going Viral, "I just thought, you know, flying a plane into a*

building for a sort of low cost, you create a very high-cost event. If I were a terrorist I would do a virus." "Things are a lot scarier if you could take a dog with some zoonotic virus and let him go in some neighborhood and the next thing you know people are tying up the whole medical system."

NOTE: A Pandemic is a disease outbreak affecting a vast area, sickening or killing a very high percentage of its victims. The outbreak itself usually occurs when the virus mutates faster than the human immune system or pre-inoculated vaccinations can combat.

Dan Martin's Top Ten Deadly Viruses Threatening the Human Race, Race:

The Phoenix: The Phoenix comes in 10th place in the race to wipe out humanity. In 2006, researchers in France recreated a five-million-year-old ancient human retrovirus, that can copy/paste itself onto strands of our DNA, whose current remains are now found scattered across the human genome, (similar to the HIV retrovirus). Thierry Heidmann at the Gustav Roussy Institute in Villejuif has brought one of these bad boys, (named Phoenix, after the mythical bird reborn from its own ashes), back to life. It's possible that this virus, or this virus's ancestors, was responsible for a previous mass extinction of humans (like Atlantis), or relatives of humans, (like Homo erectus or Homo neanderthalensis), at some point in history. By studying the retrovirus, we can learn what to expect if/when a new retrovirus were to attack to the human population. If the Phoenix were to 'fly' today, the results would be cataclysmic. Currently, Heidmann's team is inserting the Phoenix directly into human cells to "see what it would do." Isn't that how it always starts?

The team has discovered these ancient viruses, living dormant and uninterrupted in our genetic code for hundreds of thousands of years, may still be infectious. (Can anyone say oops?) This means that dormant, deadly viruses located in every human may soon awaken for some reason or another, and just, well, kill us all (God's fail-safe button in case this human experiment were to run amok). Heidmann acknowledges the dangers in resurrecting highly dangerous infectious viruses; much like the 2005 scare in the resurrection of one of the deadliest diseases known to man, the 1918 pandemic flu (Spanish flu), virus that killed 20-40 million people.

West Nile Virus: The 9th contestant is the famed West Nile Virus that in 2007 transformed into an extremely deadly disease in the United States and the world. West Nile virus causes a severe inflammation of the brain and spinal cord, eventually killing its host and is currently transmitted through insect, spider and tick bites. Birds, especially the American Crow, are highly susceptible to the disease. So if you happen to suddenly see an abnormal amount of birds falling from the sky, it may be a good indication to take shelter; something's "run amok" and the end is upon us.

Bird Flu (H5N1): The 8th runner-up for the next pandemic to annihilate the human race will most likely be Bird Flu or H5N1. Once thought to be only prolific in birds and mammals, (like West Nile), this virus has mutated, infecting people in Hong Kong last year. Since then there have been 50 reported cases of deaths caused by Bird Flu across Asia and many more in America. Doesn't sound like much? Well, experts say those rates are a mere taste of what H5N1 could do if it mutates again into a more transmittable form. *"The situation right now with H5N1 is very similar to what we saw in 1918,"* said Michael Osterholm, director of the Center for Infectious Disease Research and Policy at the University of Minnesota, in Minneapolis. *"Not all influenza strains are created equal, and it's more than just idle speculation that an H5N1 pandemic could mirror that of 1918."* An all-out reproduction of the 1918 Spanish Flu event is imminent. The only thing preventing billions of people from dying tomorrow is the fact that H5N1 isn't currently spread from human to human very easily (inhalable through nose and throat and thereby transferable by sneezing and coughing). However, at the time of publication of this book, that was just two mutations away. And if history serves us right, this or any other lethal virus will adapt and mutate in the not-too-distant future. They always do.

Swine Flu: Steadily rolling in at 7th place is the current Swine Flu (aka Influenza A or H1N1) outbreak. A new study shows last year's pandemic may have occurred as a result of a Russian or Asian laboratory accident in 1977. Swine Flu ran rampant during the early part of the Twentieth Century, and was all but eradicated in the 1950s. Dr. Shanta Zimmer and Donald Burke, of the University of Pittsburgh, state: *"This finding suggested that* *the 1977 outbreak strain had been preserved since 1950." "The re-emergence was probably an accidental release from a laboratory source in the setting of waning population immunity to H1 and N1 antigens."* A calculated 55 million people have, to date, been infected with Swine Flu, while 20,000 have died worldwide. 15%-30% (one out of three people) of Americans were infected according to an article in *The New Yorker* in January, 2011, entitled *Going Viral.* In fact, Britain and Cairo report a new outbreak of Swine Flu in early 2011.

SARS: 6th place goes to the infamous 2002 SARS virus. During the first phases of the SARS epidemic, (in which the disease was again predominantly carried by animals), the virus only infected an estimated 3% of people with whom it came in contact. That percentage skyrocketed up to 70% in just 2 months during the second phase, (in which it mutated to be inhalable and could now be more virulent from human to human, showing how easily a virus can mutate). During the third phase, that percentage rose higher as it mutated yet again, stabilizing and fortifying itself in its new environment, spreading even easier. Chung-I Wu, professor of ecology and evolution at the University of Chicago, says, *"What we see is the virus fine-tuning itself to enhance its access to a new host - humans. The virus improves itself under selective pressure, learning to spread from person to person, and then sticking with the version that is most effective."* The findings show that the SARS virus was, in fact, an animal-based disease that jumped the "species barrier" into humans.

Influenza B: Holding down the middle ground in 5th place is the all-too-common, human-based, Influenza-B virus. Influenza-B, or 'the common flu', is a highly RNA infectious disease that kills more than 500,000 people per year during seasonal epidemics, and millions during pandemic years. According to some reports, Influenza-B is responsible for killing over a hundred million during the 20th century. Even Hippocrates described the pandemic during his time, which then only attacked the masses a few times every hundred years, as causing millions of deaths over 2,400 years. Which raises the question, what has changed, causing the flu to have its own yearly season now and what changes can we look forward to in the future?

Rabies: From the back of the pack, making up ground in 4th place, is the mythological Rabies virus. May 4, 2009, National Geographic reported that a superior strain of the virus scoured the western United States, evolving faster than any previously known strain of the disease. This scourge caught the attention of the CDC (Center for Disease Control), virology experts say. Rabies-infected wild animals are known to attack and bite other animals and even humans for no apparent reason, transferring the disease through the wound. However, this is the first time that the virus was found to be transferred to offspring and other animals through mere socializing, much like humans would transmit a virus. Due to the close proximity of new human suburban housing developments, the chance of transferring the virus to humans is now much higher. The risk of such a disease making the jump to people *"should be a major concern,"* said Hinh Ly, a molecular virologist at the Emory University School of Medicine in Atlanta.

Zombie-ism: Surprisingly, locking down the 3rd place position, we find the star of many films like *Dawn of the Dead, Night of the Living Dead*, and the newest hit television show, *The Walking Dead*, depicted by cannibal virus-stricken zombies returning from the dead with the anger and vengeance of an out-of-work postal employee. But this is all just science-fiction, or is it? *"Though dead humans can't come back to life, certain viruses can induce such aggressive, zombie-like behavior,"* according to a new National Geographic Channel documentary, *The Truth Behind Zombies. "For instance, rabies can drive people to be violently mad,"* says Samita Andreansky, a virologist at the University of Miami's Miller School of Medicine, in Florida. If rabies were to ever mix with a flu-like airborne virus, a fictional zombie-like apocalypse may not be so far out of reality. Also, there are parasites that can take over the host's body, killing the host while manipulating the lifeless body at will. Hairworms, as scientists have named them, make the host kill themselves in obscure ways, such as *"jumping off tall structures or by drowning themselves in swimming pools"*; then they take over the body for up to several days after death.

It's very unlikely that a natural form of zombie-ism will evolve in our lifetime; there's nothing found in history 'yet' that indicates it's happened before; but what about a man-made zombie virus like that seen in *Resident Evil*? *"Sure, I could imagine a scenario where you mix rabies with a flu virus to get airborne transmission, a measles virus to get personality changes, the encephalitis virus to cook your brain with fever,* (stimulating further aggression), *and throw in the Ebola virus to cause you to bleed from your guts. Combine all these things, and you'll* (get) *something like a zombie virus,"* Andreansky said.

Ebola: Second place goes to, the Ebola virus. The extremely dangerous filo virus, Ebola (as publicized in movies like *Outbreak* and *The Hot Zone*), can kill its victims faster than most other viruses on today's market. Ebola isn't a commonly understood disease, which makes it that much scarier. It's been said that the strain "Ebola Reston" is already airborne (able to move from host to host through inhalation, sneezing, coughing, etc.),

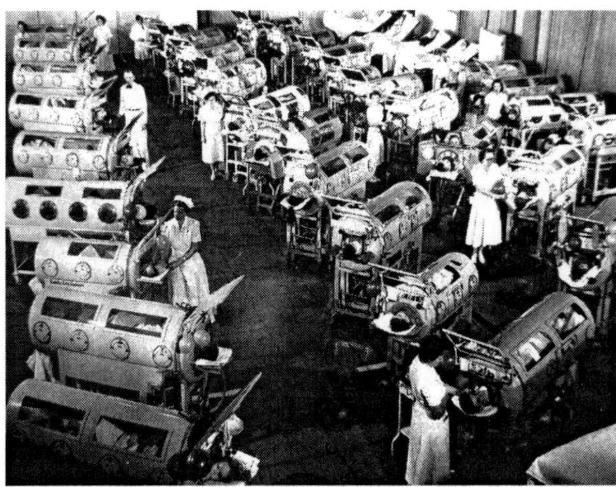

capable of transferring from primates to humans (and some say possibly plants to humans), commonly spread through simple contact or contact with the corpses, (which are highly contagious), of Ebola victims. There is currently no cure or vaccine for any of the Ebola virus strains.

Secret or Undiscovered Viruses: And The Winner Is... (Drum roll, please)... Unknown. WooHoo! Who? Typically, two new human viruses are discovered each year (since 1901) on average. Using this fact, we can estimate four new deadly species of viruses by 2012. When a known virus mutates and spreads, it's because people haven't built up any immunity to it yet, and old vaccines won't have any effect on the newest form. With new, undiscovered viruses this is doubly so, since the virus has never even been seen before. And just so you know, the chance of a never-before-seen virus killing millions, even billions of people is 100%.

Before 1901, there were several global-killing pandemics that, in comparison, dwarfed the Spanish Flu. In 1968, more than 750,000 people died as a result of the milder H3N2 Avian Flu. The death toll itself wouldn't be the most destructive element in the equation, either. The resulting drop in travel and trade as nations began locking down borders would likely have little effect in controlling the disease or any disease in today's extremely fast and mobile world; however, it will most likely completely crash the already collapsing international economy and devastate civilization as we know it, much like the effect the Swine Flu scare had in 2009.

The *Top 10 Countdown* was brought to you in part by your neighborhood restaurant bathroom door handle, the $10 bill in your wallet, and, of course, your Cousin John's wife, Susan. Keep in mind though, that the above viruses are merely the most capable contestants, possessing the best chance of wiping out the human race, and are not necessarily the most dangerous or deadly diseases, to date, known to man. An extended list of viable candidates would surely include: yellow fever, HIV/AIDS, Smallpox, Typhoid Fever, Bubonic Plague, Cholera, Anthrax, Malaria, Dengue, Hantavirus, Measles, Hepatitis B and C, Rotavirus, Leprosy, Nipah, Hendra, Marburg and many, many more, which still exist and/or are locked away in some super secret, secure vault somewhere. To date there have been more than 5,000 deadly viruses discovered (or made), killing over 5.6 million people annually; and they're discovering new potential population killers every day not in the news...... Yet!

- Dengue Fever - 25,000 caused deaths per year. W.H.O. (World Health Authority) estimates that number could rise to 2.5 billion people, (two fifths of the World's population), in the next two years (by 2012).
- Yellow Fever - 30,000 caused deaths/yr. There is no cure for yellow fever.
- Rabies - 55,000 caused deaths/yr.
- Hantavirus - 70,000 caused deaths/yr.
- Measles - 197,000 caused deaths/yr. This virus once wiped out over 1/3 of the world's population during Roman rule around 170 A.D., and has killed more than 200 million people to date.
- Hepatitis C - 500,000 caused deaths/yr. There is no vaccine or cure for Hepatitis C.
- Influenza - 500,000 caused deaths/yr.
- Hepatitis B - 521,000 caused deaths/yr. One third of the world's populations, (over 2 billion people), are currently infected with Hepatitis B. There is no treatment or cure for Hepatitis B.
- Rotavirus - 611,000 caused deaths/yr.
- Human immunodeficiency virus (HIV) – 3.1 million caused deaths/yr.
- Klebsiella pnueumoniae – 100,000 caused deaths/yr. (drug resistant and rapidly spreading in California)
- Methicillin-resistant Staphylococcus aureus – 50,000 to 200,000 caused deaths/yr. (drug resistant)

Vaccines: Vaccines have little effect on the current yearly flu outbreaks, let alone an extremely mutated form of some other lethal fast-acting virus. *"Technology has improved, but the capacity to make vaccines is not great,"* said Anthony Fauci, director of the National Institute of Allergy and Infectious Diseases at the National Institute of Health, Bethesda, Maryland. *"We have to be careful we don't assume we have everything that we need—because we don't." "You can't make a vaccine in advance, because you don't know for sure which virus will eventually be the cause of a new pandemic,"* explained Albert Osterhaus, director of the Netherlands' National Influenza Centre in Rotterdam. *"Once you have data showing that a new influenza virus is spreading rapidly, you* *need to develop a vaccine as soon as possible on the basis of the information you have on the virus."* This process would take at least 6 months, even with enormous stockpiles. Six months is like a feather thrown into the wind, compared to only a few weeks' time needed to circle the globe at the potential rate some of these viruses can travel--especially through congested super cities like Paris, London, New York, L.A., Tokyo, Sydney and Hong Kong. The likelihood of producing, or even administering, the vaccine in time, before death is highly unlikely. We could see the world death rates rise to upwards of 80% with mere thousands receiving vaccinations in time. Even then, the government decides who will receive the limited supplies of the vaccines first. Then, there's the fact that vaccine manufacturers are profit-based corporations that rely on product demand (large quantities of infected people) and are affected by lawsuits. They're not just going to start making tons of costly drugs to accommodate the world without any reason. *"At this moment if we were to face a pandemic outbreak of flu in the next year or so, the world would be basically unprepared,"* Osterhaus said. Respirators and antiviral drugs could help slow the transmittance of such deadly viruses; however, they are manufactured similar to the above vaccines and are not stockpiled in a sufficient amount to serve the masses. In other words, you're screwed!

It makes you think, then; would the drug companies ever make and unleash a virus onto the public just to sell vaccines? Run by fear, misinformation, emotions, and a lack of information by pet owners, Parvo is fundamentally one of the largest money-making diseases known to man. It is unknown exactly how or when the man-made virus was created; but based on the fact that it spread so quickly around the world, researchers now know that it was, in fact, passed on to all breeds by the vaccinations themselves, possibly as a way to make more money vaccinating, or just out of incompetence. There's no way, naturally, that the disease could have spread as fast, (a few months), and as vast, (over 5 continents), as it did naturally. In conclusion, a vaccine may not actually be the answer; rather, it may be the source itself of the disease.

What about the government? Would they ever make or intentionally unleash a deadly virus onto the public just to test its effects as well? The short answer--YES! In 1932-1972 the U.S. Public Health Service intentionally infected 399 impoverished African-Americans from Macon County, Alabama with syphilis. The victims were never told that they were being infected with, or that they had syphilis, nor were they ever treated for it (with a simple dose of Penicillin). The only thing that the Public Health Service told the men was that they were being treated for "bad blood" and that they would receive free burial insurance, according to the Centers for Disease Control.

BREAKING NEWS: Just days before this book went to print, the U.S. Government issued an official public apology for *"experiments in which* (American) *government researchers used prostitutes to deliberately infect prison inmates in Guatemala with syphilis,"* said U.S. Secretary of State Hillary Clinton, in the New York Times, CBS News, and other national broadcasting networks and news groups press release. The 1946-1948 tests *"occurred under the guise of public health,"* said Clinton. Medical historian, Susan M. Reverby, made the discovery while digging through historic papers at a Pennsylvania archive. *"In addition to the penitentiary, the studies took place in an insane asylum and an army barracks,"* Reverby said in a release. *"In total, 696 men and women were* (intentionally) *exposed to the disease"* by our government. *"The researchers induced the disease by allowing inmates in the central penitentiary to have sex with infected prostitutes,* (which was legal only in Guatemala)*, and gave the disease to the prisoners by inoculating their arms, faces or penises with a solution of the bacteria that causes syphilis. Researchers are organizing a case review to see if people involved in the study, and their contacts, are still alive. If so, they may have passed on the disease."* Reverby made the discovery "four or five years ago," she says. Why, then, is it just now being made public? Upon the find, she disclosed her data to government officials; and the government "*kept the information from us for five years.*" Makes you wonder what else they're holding from us of critical danger/importance, imminent meteoroid impacts? Known terrorist threats?

UBS INVESTMENT-BANK ECONOMISTS: ECONOMIC COLLAPSE

The 2007 "financial crisis," caused by American banking liquidity shortfalls, shows no hope of clearing, even today five years later. According to some economists, *"This financial crisis is worse than the Great Depression of the 1930s."* The combination of sub-prime lending, predatory lending and fraudulent underwriting practices, coupled with comfortable credit conditions, deregulation, inaccurate pricing risks, dramatic growth of the housing market, ("housing boom" or "housing bubble"), and a dramatic increase in the quantity and cost of commodities, all led to the current "financial crisis" (economic collapse). In other words, if you fill the bubble,

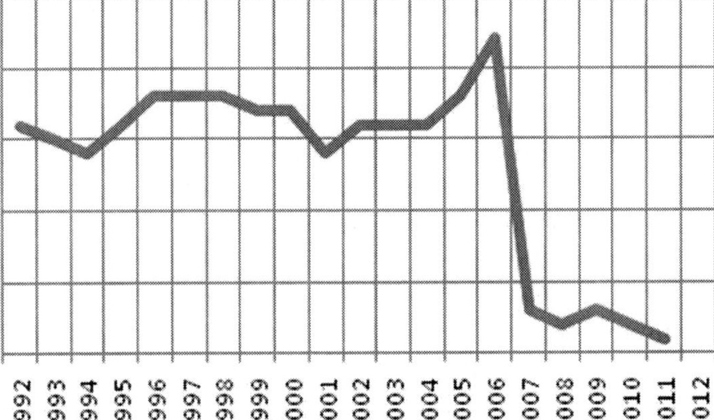

(housing bubble), with enough hot air, eventually it's going to pop. It's really just all about 'stuff'. Before people needed money to prove status, now it's stuff. The bigger the house and the more stuff the better; and it doesn't matter how ethically you acquire the stuff. You can be completely in debt; but with lots of stuff you have value and so you're looked up to and respected amongst, family, friends and co-workers in the community.

According to the International Monetary Fund, *"large U.S. and European banks lost more than $1 trillion on toxic assets and from bad loans from January 2007 to September 2009."* These losses were predicted to peak out at $2.8 trillion in 2010, where we'd then begin to see a return of the country's financial stability; however, at the time that this book went to print (2011), this "predicted" stability was nowhere in sight. In fact, the nation's deficit was actually growing faster, and the economy was collapsing further, spiraling deeper towards total global ruin by 2012. *"And the worst is still to come,"* according to UBS investment-bank economists, who stated that *"the beginning of the end has started."*

How does the fall of one country's economy affect the entire world? Well, for one thing, there is no such thing as "one country's economy" anymore, that is; it's closer to something like a one-world economy now. Changes in the American economy affect the world economy due to the percentage of foreign investors, world trade, overseas marketing, planetary aid and exported goods, services and merchandise. Until recently, they were good changes; most countries in the world reaped the benefits as America flourished. Now that our economy is almost completely devastated, the world is paying the price, big time. In fact, Northern Rock, a medium-sized British bank, was one of the first financial institutions to fall because of "America's economic financial crisis." Any other world financial institution directly involved with home construction, financing, and lending, followed closely behind. Since then, over 100 large mortgage lenders and financial institutions around the world have declared bankruptcy. Dozens of others are either failing, holding fire sales, or being taken over by government entities, such as Lehman Brothers, Merrill Lynch, Fannie Mae, Freddie Mac, Washington Mutual, Wachovia, and AIG. And dozens more, like Regions Financial, Corus Bank, Bank United, Downey Savings, MBIA and Ambac, are on the verge.

Lately, the government has stepped up unprecedented bailouts, fiscal stimulus packages and plans, monetary policy expansions and institutional bailouts, but with little improvement. Too little, too late, as the saying goes. As a result, the global stock market has been rapidly declining, for the most part, with no end in sight. In fact, in 2008, Iceland's economy completely and totally crashed with the fall of every single one of the country's major banks, as a direct consequence of the "American economic crisis," which reverberated around the world.

According to a Brookings Institute report released in June, 2009, the U.S. is responsible for more than a third of global growth and decline. "*The U.S. economy has been spending too much and borrowing too much for years, and the rest of the world depended on the U.S. consumer as a source of global demand.*" This is a formula that can only equal global disaster. Astounding annual worldwide GDP (gross domestic product) rate declines reflect as much:
-14.4% in Germany, -15.2% in Japan, -7.4% in the UK, -18% in Latvia, -9.8% in Europe and -21.5% in Mexico. Yet, according to a World Bank report published in February, 2009: the Communist and Arab worlds were *"far less severely affected by the credit crunch. With generally good balance of payment positions coming into the crisis, or with alternative sources of financing for their large current account deficits, such as remittances, Foreign Direct Investment (FDI) or foreign aid,*

Arab countries were able to avoid going to the market in the latter part of 2008. This group is in the best position to absorb the economic shocks. They entered the crisis in exceptionally strong positions. This gives them a significant cushion against the global downturn."

The failure of corporate leaders, banks, and foreign traders are minimal compared to the effect the economic recession has on those in the lower income brackets. The urban areas have suffered in far greater proportions, as evidenced by unforeseen, record-breaking evictions, foreclosures, abandonments and extended rental vacancies. A rapid rise of joblessness is leading to extreme rises in divorce, homelessness, suicide and increased migration rates. Theft, vandalism and robbery-related crimes have increased exponentially as well. More than ever, children are destitute and dying, living on the streets without shelter or food, not just in third world countries, but here at home as well. In fact, today the majority of residents in homeless shelters are children, something never seen before. As Americans are downsized and losing their jobs, less funds are available to donate to homeless shelters. And it's only going to get worse from here. Husbands will leave their wives and children because they don't have the means to support them. A 1940 poll on the Great Depression revealed that 1.5 million married women were abandoned by their husbands during the depression.

DMITRY ORLOV: GOVERNMENTAL COLLAPSE

There is a 100% certainty that the American government will collapse; it's guaranteed. Every single government throughout time has consistently and consequently fallen. Not one has survived, no exceptions. In fact, our country is more susceptible to catastrophic failure than most, because our country is based and run on commerce--something that, by its very nature, is always in a state of flux, instability and insecurity. All of the nation's money is held, distributed and traded by the dead or dying financial institutions mentioned above. Unlike the Soviet Union which experienced an economic collapse because of its governmental collapse, we could experience a governmental collapse due to our current economic collapse. How is this possible? It's actually quite simple, really. Our government can only function with money from taxpayers. If our economy collapses completely, the taxpayers are out of jobs, and, therefore, don't pay income or property tax; they stop purchasing food, supplies, goods and merchandise and, therefore, sales tax. This causes drastic government cutbacks, downsizing of departments, relocations, base and facility closures and, eventually, mass layoffs (unless, of course, government employees choose to just work for free out of the goodness of their hearts and let their children starve!) So, at the very least, you're looking at a severely weakened, barely functioning, minimally-staffed and highly vulnerable government/country, if not a completely and totally collapsed one. Basically, when the government's umbilical cord (taxes) is severed, the entity (government) quickly dies.

Dmitry Orlov, a Russian-born, American writer, has really hit the nail on the head (or in this case, the sickle), in his book, *Reinventing Collapse: The Soviet Example and American Prospects.* Orlov was able to examine precise instances, events and trends during the collapse of the superpower Soviet Union and use them to predict what he believes will occur to the United States when our government finally collapses. Although his personal insights and revelations are shocking, to say the least, the book is mostly filled with factual data on the subject, along with ways to prepare for the aftermath.

Dmitry was born in what is now Saint Petersburg Russia, moving to America at twelve years old. In his early twenties he traveled back to Russia, and personally experienced/witnessed the collapse first hand. Below he recounts exactly what happened in Russia and why it's happening all over again here in the United States, now:

- The Soviet Union (SU) collapsed almost 20 years ago.
- The United States (US) will collapse.
- The SU collapse was harder to predict because of secrecy.
- The signs that US will collapse are (all over the news) open and for everyone to see.
- The collapse of the SU has a lot to teach us about the collapse of the US.
- The differences are just as interesting as the similarities:

Both post-WWII military-industrial empires were predicated on technological advances and economic growth. Both made (peaceful) attempts to spread their ideology over the entire planet and both exercised political and economic control over many countries. Both remained evenly-matched for several decades and both eventually went bankrupt. Both have an electoral process in which the same parties rule every time and both fought together in WWII. Both fought unwinnable wars with the same countries (Korea, Vietnam, Afghanistan, and the Cold War) for the same reasons and both experienced declining oil production (SU peaked a couple years before it collapsed just like we did/will). Both had/have out of control military budgets and both had/have unsustainable deficits and foreign debts. Both had/have bulky, unresponsive, corrupt political systems, incapable of reform and both maintain/maintained delusions of grandeur.

I anticipate that some people will react rather badly to having their country compared to the USSR. I would like to assure you that the Soviet people would have reacted similarly, had the United States collapsed first. Feelings aside, here are two 20th Century super powers who wanted more or less the same things – things like technological progress, economic growth, full-time employment and healthcare – but they disagreed about the methods. And they obtained similar results – each had a good run, intimidated the whole planet and kept the other scared for almost 50 years. Many of the problems that sunk the Soviet Union are now endangering the United States, as well, such as a huge, well-equipped, very expensive military, with no clear mission, bogged down in fighting Muslim insurgents; energy shortfalls linked to peaking oil production; and a persistently unfavorable trade balance, resulting in runaway foreign debt. Add to that a delusional self-image, an inflexible ideology, and an unresponsive political system, and you have two peas in a pod. On the other hand, the USA and the USSR were evenly matched in many categories, but let me mention four: Space Race, Arms Race, Jails Race and the Most Hated Empire Race.

1. The Soviet-manned space program is alive and well under Russian management, and now offers first-ever space charters. The Americans have been hitching rides on the Soyuz while their spaceships sit in the shop.
2. The arms race has not produced a clear winner--Mutual Assured Destruction remains in effect. Russia still has more nuclear warheads than the U.S., and has supersonic cruise missile technology that can penetrate any missile shield, especially a non-existent one.
3. The Jails Race once reflected the Soviets had a decisive lead, thanks to their innovative GULAG program. But they gradually fell behind, and in the end, the Jails Race has been won by the Americans, with the highest percentage of people in jail, ever.
4. The Hated Evil Empire Race is also finally being won by the Americans. It's easy, now that they don't have an enemy country with which they can compete.

I don't see why Russia's fate should be any different from what happens to the United States, at least in general terms. The specifics will be different and we will get to them in a moment. We should certainly expect shortages of fuel, food, medicine and countless consumer items; electric, gas, and water outages; breakdowns in transportation systems and other infrastructures; hyperinflation, widespread shutdowns and mass layoffs; along with a lot of despair, confusion, violence, and lawlessness. We definitely should not expect any grand rescue plans, innovative technology programs, or miracles of social cohesion.

When faced with such developments, some people are quick to realize what it is they have to do to survive and start doing these things, generally without anyone's permission. A sort of system emerges, completely informal and often semi-criminal. It revolves around dismantling, liquidating and recycling, the remains of the old system and is based on direct access to resources and the threat of force, rather than ownership or legal authority. Whoever has a problem with this way of doing things will quickly be out of the game. These are the common generalities; now let's look at some specific differences that may prove troublesome for us:

Housing:

	TYPE	OUTCOME	REASON /RESULT		FINAL OUTCOME
SU:	owned by the state	free rent	accessed by public transportation	=	continued transportation throughout
US:	owned by banks/corporations	foreclosures/ evictions	largely inaccessible except by car	=	a flood of suburban immigrants into already over-crowded cities

One important element of collapse-preparedness is making sure that you don't need a functioning economy/government to keep a roof over your head. In the Soviet Union, all housing belonged to the government, which made it available directly to the people. Since all housing was also built by the government, it was only built in places that the government could service, using public transportation. After the collapse, almost everyone managed to keep and travel to/from their homes.

In the United States, very few people own their place of residence free and clear; and even if they did, they'd need an income to pay real estate taxes, property fees and association costs. If they didn't pay, the government would then take the home away. Simply put, in the U.S., people without an income face the reality of homelessness. When the collapse occurs, very few people will continue to have an income, so homelessness will become rampant. Add to that, the dependence of cars in most suburbs, and the lack of gas to run them and what you will get is mass migrations of homeless people toward overpopulated city centers.

Transportation:

	TYPE	OUTCOME	REASON /RESULT		FINAL OUTCOME
SU:	public	still continues to this day with fuel shortages	compact cities along railways (rails offer a maintainable transportation surface)	=	continued transportation throughout
US:	mostly private automobiles	stops running with fuel shortages	abandoned cities (roads become unusable due to lack of maintenance)	=	eventual use of bikes, walking or shopping carts

Soviet public transportation was more or less all there was, but there was plenty of it. There were also a few private cars, but so few that gasoline rationing and shortages were mostly inconsequential. This entire public infrastructure was designed to be almost infinitely maintainable, and continued to run even as the rest of the country collapsed.

The population of the United States is almost entirely car-dependent and relies on markets that control oil import, refining and distribution. They also rely on continuous government (federal at the interstate level, and state, county and city at the local road level) for investment in road construction and repair. The cars themselves require a steady stream of imported parts and are not designed to last very long. When these intricately interconnected systems stop functioning, much of the population will find itself stranded.

Employment:

	TYPE	OUTCOME	REASON /RESULT		FINAL OUTCOME
SU:	predominantly public	slowdowns, salaries delayed; massive inventory	continued access/barter	=	gradual transition
US:	predominantly private	shutdowns, massive layoffs; low inventory	liquidation	=	instant joblessness

Economic and governmental collapse affects public sector employment almost as much as private sector employment, eventually. Because government bureaucracies tend to be slow to act, they collapse more slowly. Also, because state-owned enterprises tend to be inefficient and stockpile inventory, there is plenty of it left over, for the employees to take home and to use in barter when the collapse occurs. Most Soviet employment was in the public sector and this gave people some time to think of what to do next.

Private enterprises are more efficient at many things, like laying-off their people without notice, declaring bankruptcy and liquidating assets. Since most employment in the United States is in the private sector, we should expect the transition to permanent unemployment to be quite abrupt for most people, with government employees being laid-off last.

Families:					
	TYPE	OUTCOME	REASON /RESULT		FINAL OUTCOME
SU:	3 generations under one roof	close; clustered geographically	accustomed to hardship	=	life goes on
US:	singular nuclear families far removed from relatives	alienated; often spread out geographically	feelings of entitlement, pampered & unaccustomed to 'roughing it'	=	strangers, suffering, dying alone

When confronting hardship, people usually fall back on their families for support. The Soviet Union experienced chronic housing shortages long before the collapse, which often resulted in three generations living together under one roof. This didn't make them happy, but at least they were used to each other. The usual expectation was that they would stick it out together, no matter what.

In the United States, families tend to be spread out over several states. They sometimes have trouble tolerating each other, and even fight with each other when they come together for Thanksgiving or Christmas, even during the best of times. They might find it difficult to get along in bad times. There is already too much loneliness in this country; and I doubt that even a collapse will cure it.

Money:					
	TYPE	OUTCOME	REASON /RESULT		FINAL OUTCOME
SU:	of little value	shared among family & friends	income not essential to happiness	=	broke but happy
US:	worth more than actual worth	hardly ever shared	income essential for happiness, survival & status, more important than friends & often family	=	broke & helpless

In the Soviet Union, very little could be obtained with money. It was treated as tokens rather than as actual wealth and was often shared among friends and family. Many things – housing and transportation among them – were either free or almost free.

To keep evil at bay, Americans require money. In a total collapse, there is usually hyperinflation, which wipes out any savings quickly. There is also rampant unemployment, which wipes out any income. The result is a population that is largely, helplessly penniless.

Consumer Products:					
	TYPE	OUTCOME	REASON /RESULT		FINAL OUTCOME
SU:	a cost to the government	product-based economy	shortages of products, up to you to make it work, technology heirlooms	=	fix it yourself
US:	profits for the Chinese	service-based economy	shortage of money, planned obsolescence, disposable everything	=	recycle the trash

Soviet consumer products were always an object of derision – refrigerators that kept the house warm – (and the food) and so on. You'd be lucky if you got one at all and it would be up to you to make it work once you got it home. But once you got it to work, it would become a priceless family heirloom, handed down from generation to generation, sturdy and almost infinitely maintainable.

In the United States, you often hear "it's not worth fixing." This is enough to make a Russian see red. I once heard of an elderly Russian who became irate when a hardware store in Boston wouldn't sell him replacement bedsprings: *"People are throwing away perfectly good mattresses, how am I supposed to fix them?"* (Not to mention the fact that many of our items are intentionally built with keyed screws or fused seams so that you cannot open them for repair; and you are, therefore, forced to purchase another. Some (like popular brand cordless drill recharge bases) actually has a easily replaceable common fuse inside, that cannot be accessed.)

Economic collapse tends to shut down both local production and imports; so it is vitally important that anything you own wears out slowly and that you can fix it yourself if it breaks. Soviet-made items were generally, incredibly durable. The Chinese-made products available in the U.S. are much less durable.

Food:					
	TYPE	OUTCOME	REASON /RESULT		FINAL OUTCOME
SU:	backyard gardens, local food stocks	home cooking culture	physically active	=	long food lines meant home planting, growing, harvesting
US:	supermarkets, food shipped in diesel trucks	fast food culture	obesity epidemic	=	waiting to be fed, dumpster diving, starvation

The SU agricultural sector was notoriously inefficient. Many people grew and gathered their own food even in relatively prosperous times. There were food warehouses in every city, stocked according to a government allocation scheme. There were very few restaurants, so families cooked and ate at home. Shopping was rather labor-intensive and often involved carrying heavy loads long distances. Sometimes it resembled hunting – stalking, that elusive piece of meat lurking behind some store counter. Shoppers often stood for hours in long lines to buy basic, essential groceries. So the people were well prepared for what came next.

In the United States, most people get their food from a supermarket, which is stocked by out-of-town suppliers in refrigerated diesel trucks. Many people don't even bother to shop, and just eat fast food. When people do cook, they rarely cook from scratch. This is all very unhealthy; the effect on the nation's girth is visible, clear across the parking lot. Many people who just waddle to and from their cars seem unprepared for what will come next. If they suddenly had to start living like the Russians, they would literally blow out their knees.

Medicine:

	TYPE	OUTCOME	REASON /RESULT		FINAL OUTCOME
SU:	public	free basic care	focused on basic care & prevention	=	basic care
US:	private	medicine for profit	focused on cardiology, gastroenterology, hematology/oncology, neurology, urology, obstetrics/gynecology, dermatology, endocrinology, orthopedics, nephrology, radiology, pathology, psychiatry, & of course plastic surgery	=	folk remedies, untreated epidemics, chronic disabilities, death

The Soviet government spent their resources on immunization programs, infectious disease control and basic care. As a socialist society, it directly operated a system of state-owned clinics, hospitals and sanatoriums. All doctors were trained to administer basic care. This caused people with fatal ailments and chronic or rare conditions to have reason to complain, since they had to pay for private care.

The United States medical system is built on a capitalist society. Health care is still privatized, for the most part, except for Social Security. There are very few fields of endeavor that are not motivated by profit, most Americans would agree. The problem is, once the economy is removed, so is the profit, along with the services it once helped to motivate. And if you ask a doctor you meet today what he is, he'll reply "Neurologist," or "Radiologist." No one is just a doctor here anymore. So when the collapse occurs, there'll be a bunch of jobless Neurologists and Radiologists (specialists) running around, but very few General Health Practitioners.

Education:

	TYPE	OUTCOME	REASON /RESULT		FINAL OUTCOME
SU:	public & free	8th grade SU = 12th grade US	almost all children walked to small neighborhood schools	=	the lost generation
US:	crippling lifelong student loans	12+4 years produces a semi-literate jobless young adult	children bused or driven by car to huge city-wide schools	=	illiteracy & ignorance

The Soviet education system was generally quite excellent. It produced an overwhelmingly literate population and many great specialists. The education was free at all levels; higher education sometimes even paid the students a stipend, and often provided free room and board. The educational system held together quite well after the collapse. The problem was that there were no jobs for the graduates, so many of them emigrated to the U.S., to other countries, or lost their way.

The 'higher' education system in the United States is efficient at many things – science, government, industrial research, team sports, and vocational training. But primary and secondary education fails to achieve in 12 years what Soviet schools generally achieved in 8. The massive scale and expense of maintaining these institutions is likely to prove too much for the post-collapse environment. Illiteracy is already a problem in the United States, and we should only expect it to get a lot worse.

Energy:

	TYPE	OUTCOME	REASON /RESULT		FINAL OUTCOME
SU:	minimal household needs	self-sufficient, almost 100% came from SU	surplus stock/still exporting, government-owned, price controls	=	shortages, rationing
US:	enormous household needs/demands	imports 65% of oil, dwindling domestic production	privately supplied, profiteering (price gouging)	=	blackouts, powerless homes

The Soviet Union did not need to import energy after the collapse. The production and distribution system faltered, but never fully collapsed. Price controls kept the lights on even as hyperinflation raged.

The electric companies in the U.S. are free markets. Free markets develop some pernicious characteristics when there are shortages of key commodities. During World War II, the United States government understood this and successfully rationed many things, from gasoline to bicycle parts. But that was a long time ago. Since then, the inviolability of free markets has become an article of faith. Entire electric grids will run out of fuel, leaving most of the country in the dark. The rest will have to work/live on a couple hours a day of energy. Something we're not used to, ready for or capable to handle yet. We'd lose it if we lost electricity.

Ethnic/Religious Composition:

	TYPE	OUTCOME	REASON /RESULT		FINAL OUTCOME
SU:	predominantly white/communist	no real class divisions/one religion	feelings of unity	=	for the most part, semi peaceful transition
US:	extremely diverse/ extremely diverse	predominantly white upper/middle class - predominantly Christian; predominantly minority lower class – mixed	feelings of hostility; lack of trust	=	racial bigotry, riots, destruction, religious hate crimes

Good or bad, religion for the most part, was governmentally controlled in the Soviet Union.

The United States resembles Yugoslavia more than it resembles Russia in this manner; so we shouldn't expect it to be as peaceful in this area, following the collapse. Ethnically-mixed societies are fragile and have a tendency to explode racially, which they're already doing here in the best of times.

Politics:

	TYPE	OUTCOME	REASON /RESULT		FINAL OUTCOME
SU:	ideologically hamstrung	the Communist party	able to crush protest; hid the books	=	total collapse
US:	ideologically hamstrung	the Capitalist party & the other Capitalist party	able to ignore protest; cooked the books	=	total collapse

One area in which I cannot discern any Collapse Gap is national politics. The ideologies may be different, but the blind adherence to them couldn't be more similar. It is certainly more fun to watch two capitalist parties go at each other than just having to vote for the one communist party. The things they fight over in public are generally symbolic little tokens of social policy, chosen for ease of public posturing. The communist party offered just one bitter pill; the two capitalist parties offer a choice of two placebos. The latest innovation is the photo-finish election, where each party buys 50% of the vote and the result is pulled out of statistical noise, like a rabbit out of a hat. The American way of dealing with dissent and with protest is certainly more advanced: why imprison dissidents when you can just let them shout into the wind to their heart's content? The American approach to bookkeeping is more subtle and nuanced than the Soviet. Why make a state secret of some statistic, when you can just distort it in obscure ways?

AN EYE-OPENING FUTURE

I've only discussed the Russian collapse because the country was so similar to our own in so many ways. However, in just the last year alone, there have been almost a dozen governmental collapses throughout Europe, Asia, Africa and the Middle East. The popular method being through mass protests, which may eventually spread to the U.S. In fact, we may be actually witnessing the birth of such a movement currently as tens of thousands siege the Capital in Wisconsin in a fight to maintain workers' bargaining rights. Then there's the waged governmental shut-down that was delayed literally at the last moment on April 8, 2011. Which if carried out will see the closure of many federal facilities and services. Even Donald Trump, American business mogul and self-made millionaire, has declared *"This country is going to hell; this country is not great right now. We have huge deficits, huge unemployment, we have a huge problem, and we're not respected. We're not respected in the world, the world laughs at us."* When interviewed on April 7, 2011 on the Today Show.

And I hope that I didn't make it sound as if the Soviet collapse was a walk in the park, because it was really quite awful in many ways. It was horrible for most people, many of them died; most suffered horribly. The point that I do want to stress is that when this government collapses soon, it is bound to be much worse. It took ten years for Russia to recover (and they're still not back 100%), but the U.S. doesn't have the resources and existing infrastructure (or lack of) that allowed the Soviet Union to recover so quickly. We'll have it much worse.

U.S. ACCOUNTABILITY OFFICE: INVASION

The idea of an invasion by enemy troops (or even friendly troops for that matter), may sound absurd right now, but it has already happened four times before.

- December 7, 1941, Japanese forces attack and invade the United States, killing thousands of Americans.
- April 25, 1846, 2,000 solders invade Texas with the intention of making war with the United States.
- April 19, 1775, English solders invade the east coast of America, ultimately killing over 50,000 Americans.
- May, 1962, a Russian led invasion force waits for orders 94 miles south of Florida.

And it's extremely probable in the very near future that it will happen again, especially with the economy and government in shambles. I mean that's what we do. When a country is distracted with other issues, we invade it. Just like what we did in Iraq, Afghanistan and now Libya. Are we naive enough to think that other countries, other people, other governments aren't thinking the exact same way? So then why have we not been invaded in the last 50 years? What's changed?

- August 6, 1945, The United States of America drops the deadliest weapon in the world, the atom bomb, on Hiroshima completely devastating the city and killing 166,000 Japanese within the first few months. Before this, such a weapon of mass destruction had never been seen or even imagined by most countries.
- August 9, 1945, 3 days later, America drops a second atom bomb (as if one wasn't bad enough) on the Japanese city of Nagasaki, killing 80,000 (totaling 246,000) more humans. Both bombs were dropped in retaliation of the Japanese invasion of America, which subsequently killed 2,400 (or 1/100th of Japanese people killed in comparison, not to mention the infrastructure and economy of two entire cities).

That said, when the government does fall and our military isn't able to retaliate to an attack, we'll have countries lining up for invasion, either because we, in some way, form, shape or fashion, just pissed them off, for our much-desired land and resources (which is why we invade most countries), or plainly because of religious reasons. If we were to be invaded, which direction would the infiltrating armies come from? Even without a full collapse, both our southern and northern borders are currently wide open. In fact, there are roughly a *"half million illegal entries every year"* according to the Illegal Immigration report disseminated by the United States Government Accountability Office. Half a million people entered the United States last year--that could have been an entire invading army, entering undetected. And if illegals are entering this country by the millions now, there will be no stopping a ground force from invading when our system, military and government, finally are gone.

And don't even bother entertaining the thought that Mexico would stop them. They obviously have enough problems of their own currently. They can't even stop their own people from decimating the Mexican military, police forces and government, let alone a well-trained, well-equipped, battle-hardened foreign power. And once we're gone, Mexico and Canada will be next. And as for the rest of the American countries, they have no hope. The Caribbean... forget it. Imagine, for a second, what would happen if the United States military, National Guard and police force were downsized and disbanded. Can you contemplate China's 3.5 million-man army or India's 4.7 million-man army invading Mexico, the U.S., Canada, Belize, Honduras, Guatemala, El Salvador, Nicaragua, Costa Rica, Panama, Columbia, etc. etc. etc.? It would be a complete and total massacre. Now picture the havoc that would unfold on Cuba, Jamaica, the Bahamas, Haiti, the Dominican Republic, Puerto Rico, Virgin Islands, Barbados, Grenada, or St. Lucia. It's all completely absurd. Do any of these countries even have any form of military at all? They'd have no chance of survival. This entire side of the planet will be entirely vulnerable when our government collapses. Right now these countries have unknowingly, unwillingly, and/or unintentionally been 100% protected by us for the last 70 years. Some of which maintain trade with us; some are allies; some we keep under our control; some let us keep prisons on their soil or test deadly viruses on their people; so we have always looked out for them. In the same way that the American people are so dependent on society and the government for survival, other countries are dependent on America.

PRESIDENT BARACK OBAMA: TERRORIST ATTACK

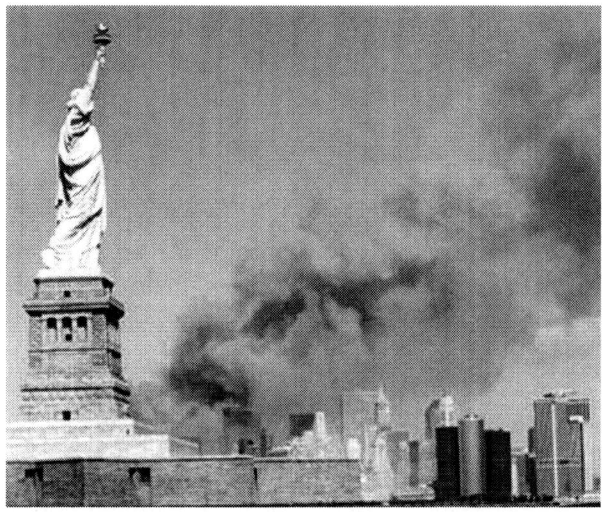

If half a million people, (and soon entire armies), can enter our country illegally, 'under the wire,' undetected every year, what makes you think 19 (probably 20) or more, terrorists can't walk down the same scratched-out desert paths, escorted by the same Mexican Coyotes and cross the same Rio Grande River? But they don't have to 'sneak in'; we let them in and even pay for their tuition to our flight schools and universities. In a speech in March 2010, President Barack Obama announced that terrorist groups "like" al Qaeda are desperately attempting to acquire nuclear weapons, and *"if they ever succeed, they would surely use it."* The most dangerous radioactive materials are found in nuclear power plants and sites where nuclear weapons are made, of which there are over 500 worldwide. Not to mention all the material Russia sold off after its collapse. In 2005, Sergey Sinchenko, a legislator from the Yulia Tymoshenko Bloc, stated: *"250 nuclear weapons were unaccounted for since the collapse of the soviet union".* Joseph Cirincione of the Ploughshares Fund told Robert Siegel: *"We have about 15 documented instances of thieves stealing weapons-usable material over the past 20 years. All of them have been in states of the former Soviet Union."*

Because of the danger and difficulty involved in getting radioactive materials from a nuclear facility, there is a greater chance that the radioactive materials used in dirty bombs would come from other sources with much lower levels of radioactivity. Low-level radioactive materials can be found in places like hospitals (used for diagnostic procedures and cancer treatments), construction sites (used to inspect welds), food irradiation plants (to kill harmful microbes), and university research laboratories. All are great sources for terrorist-based weapons of mass destruction. Also, anyone with a little DIY knowledge and some internet experience can find step-by-step plans online to build a real nuclear bomb at home simply by searching a term like "how to build a nuclear bomb" in Google, it's that simple.

But we're getting ahead of ourselves here. Terrorists don't need to fly halfway around the world and wade through muddy water or bureaucratic red tape to strike terror into an already-collapsing nation. Home-grown terrorists are plentiful; and they have been doing just as good a job at it for years:

- Januray 8, 2011, armed with a Glock 9mm, 22yr old Jared Lee Loughner shoots 19 people, including United States District Court for the District of Arizona Chief Judge John Roll and U.S. Representative Gabrielle Giffords in a Safeway grocery store parking lot near Tucson, Arizona.
- June 1, 2009, 23-year-old Abdulhakim Mujahid Muhammad, upset about the "wars in Iraq and Afghanistan," sprays a collage of bullets into the Little Rock, Arkansas, Recruiting Station killing one of the two soldiers standing outside.
- November 5, 2009, Major Psychiatrist Nidal Malik Hassan, stationed at the United States Army Base Fort Hood in Killeen, Texas, shoots and kills 13 soldiers, wounding 30, spending over half of his 400 rounds.
- September 18, 2001, (one week after 9/11), letters filled with inhalable spores of the Anthrax virus were sent to ABC News, CBS News, NBC News, the New York Post, the National Enquirer, the Sun tabloid, two Democratic Senators Tom Daschle and Patrick Leahy, ultimately infecting and killing dozens of people.
- January 29, 1998, a health clinic in Birmingham, Alabama, is bombed by the Anti-Abortion Army of God.

- February 24, 1997, Ali Abu Kamal, a Palestinian teacher shoots 7 people on top of the Empire State Building. In his pocket was note claiming the act was punishment against the "enemies of Palestine."
- July 27, 1996, the World Summer Olympics is held at Centennial Olympic Park when American Christian terrorist Eric Robert Rudolph detonates the *"largest pipe bomb in U.S. history, weighing in excess of 40 pounds"* which sprays nails and shrapnel onto 113 innocent bystanders.
- April 19, 1995, Timothy McVeigh, motivated by his desire to obliterate our *"Machiavellian government and their illegal actions concerning the incidents at Waco and Ruby Ridge,"* parks a Ryder truck holding (16) 55-gallon drums filled with ammonium nitrate fertilizer, liquid nitro methane, 18" Tovex sausages, a shock tube and electric blasting caps, in front of the Federal Building in downtown Oklahoma City. Five minutes later, a large explosion completely disintegrates the front half of the building, 324 surrounding buildings in a 16-block radius and 86 cars, killing and/or injuring 850 people and 19 children.
- January 25, 1993, as dozens of CIA employed commuters wait at a traffic light to turn into CIA headquarters in Langley, Virginia, Mir Aimal Kasi systematically walks up and down the rows of cars, spraying bullets from an AK-47 into driver-side windows.
- February 26, 1993, a Rider van pulls up and parks in the public parking area under the North Tower of the World Trade Center. 12 minutes later, a 1,310lb. bomb explodes, blowing a 100-foot hole through 4 levels of the building, killing over 1,000. The plan was to knock the North Tower into the South Tower, thereby collapsing both towers and killing all inside. It failed, of course, but was finally accomplished on 9/11. The attack was planned and carried out by Ramzi Yousef, Mahmud Abouhalima, Mohammad Salameh, Nidal A. Ayyad, Abdul Rahman Yasin and Ahmad Ajaj, all of whom entered the country legally.
- November 14, 1991, after being fired for "insubordination," Thomas McIlvane walks into the Royal Oak Post Office, in Royal Oak, Michigan, and systematically shoots almost a dozen people, including himself. (This one hits kind of close to home, as my mother worked at this Post Office and actually knew the shooter.) It was after the Royal Oak Post Office shooting that the term, 'Going Postal,' was coined.
- August 20, 1986, 14 employees at the Edmond, Oklahoma, Post Office were killed by postal worker, Patrick Sherrill.
- May 17, 1978, Dr. Theodore John "Ted" Kaczynski (the Unabomber) begins a 20-year terrorist run, sending bombs through the mail, to be delivered to universities and airlines, finally ending his siege in 1995. Kaczynski had a Ph.D. in mathematics from the University of Michigan and was assistant professor at the University of California, before giving up on humanity and becoming a recluse in Montana.

And don't forget suicide bombers, we have those too in the United States:

- May 1, 2010, believed Pakistani Taliban members park a Nissan Pathfinder full of explosives in Times Square near 45th and Seventh Ave.
- December 25, 2009, Umar Farouk Abdulmutallab, (the "Underwear Bomber"), a Nigerian citizen, attempts to detonate plastic explosives hidden in his underwear on-board Northwest Airlines Flight 253.
- February 14, 2008, Steven Kazmierczak shoots 18 people at the Northern Illinois University.
- October 17, 2008, an explosion rips through a Dalton, Georgia, law firm, killing several, including the apparent suicide bomber. Law enforcement officials describe the incident as a suicide attack.
- February 12, 2007, armed with a shotgun and a backpack full of ammunition, Sarajevo and Bosnian immigrant, Sulejman Talović, goes on a shooting spree through Trolley Square mall, Salt Lake City, Utah, shooting almost a dozen bystanders.
- April 16, 2007, Seung-Hui Cho, in an epic run through the Virginia Tech campus, unloads 19 clips (400 rounds) through two semi-automatic handguns killing 32 people and wounding almost a dozen more before killing himself, in what would later be known as the deadliest peacetime massacre by a single gunman in United States history.
- October 2, 2006, Charles Carl Roberts IV, takes dozens of young hostages at West Nickel Mines School in Bart Township, Pennsylvania, eventually shooting ten girls (aged 6–13), before committing suicide.
- March 21, 2005, commandeering a police car, Jeffery Weise drives to Red Lake Senior High School where he shoots and kills seven on campus.
- October 1, 2005, 84,501 football spectators are packed into a University of Oklahoma Stadium when a suicide bomber and OU student Joel Henry Hinrichs III ignites TATP, (the substance used in the London, 2005, bombings, and the American Airlines Flight 63 attempted bombing).

- July 4, 2002, Egyptian gunman, Hesham Mohamed Hadayet, outraged at America's support for Israel, begins shooting people in the LAX International Airport in front of an Israel ticketing counter.
- October, 2002, John Allen Muhammad goes on a three-week sniper style ~~shopping~~ shooting spree killing almost a dozen people in several grocery shopping center parking lots throughout the Washington, D.C. metropolitan area, from the trunk of a 1990 Chevrolet Caprice in the name of Jihad on America.
- December 22, 2001, self-proclaimed Al Qaeda member, Richard Colvin Reid, attempts to light a tennis shoe containing two types of explosives and blow up American Airlines Flight 63.
- April 20, 1999, 12th grade students, Eric Harris and Dylan Klebold, attack the Columbine High School in Colorado, massacring anyone and everyone in sight, shooting 33 students before committing suicide.
- March 5, 1994, suicide bomber Clifford Lynn Draper, takes dozens of hostages at the Salt Lake City Public Library (where my mother also worked), with a handmade claymore mine with a dead man's trigger.
- November 1, 1991, 28-year-old Gang Lu shoots and kills 6 faculty members at the University of Iowa before committing suicide.
- January 17, 1989, Patrick Purdy shoots over 30 schoolchildren at the Cleveland Elementary School in San Diego, California, before turning the gun on himself.

We even have the new, never before seen, first time ever, while limited supplies last, suicide SUV-ists:

- March 3, 2006, dozens of University of North Carolina students gather on campus, when Mohammed Reza Taheri-azar, an Iranian-born American citizen crashes a rented Grand Cherokee into the crowd in order to "avenge the deaths of Muslims worldwide" and "punish" the United States government.
- August 30, 2006, Omeed Aziz Popal goes on a killing "rampage" throughout the streets of the San Francisco Bay Area, maliciously and repeatedly running over dozens of people in his Honda SUV, reportedly shouting, *"I'm a terrorist, I don't care!"*

And who can forget the granddaddy of all terrorist attacks on U.S. soil:

- September 11, 2001, 19 terrorist hijackers commandeer 4 commercial airliners and meticulously crash them into several New York and Virginia targets in a series of coordinated attacks. The planned targets included the World Trade Center Twin Towers (which subsequently collapsed hours later killing all inside), the Pentagon, and a third D.C. destination, probably being the White House or Capitol Building. Several other buildings were destroyed or sustained major damage in the incident, including: 7 World Trade Center, 6 World Trade Center, 5 World Trade Center, 4 World Trade Center, the Marriott World Trade Center (3 WTC), World Financial Center complex, St. Nicholas Greek Orthodox Church, Deutsche Bank Building, Borough of Manhattan Community College's Fiterman Hall, West Broadway, 90 West Street building, Verizon Building, World Financial Center, One Liberty Plaza, Millennium Hilton and 90 Church St. Three thousand Americans were killed in the airplanes, buildings, surrounding buildings and through inhalation of toxic particles carried by the clouds of dust that swept through the city.

If this event was exactly what it seems to be, reported by the government and paraded on every channel by the media; it's devastating enough in itself. This is an eye opener, a shock to know that we are actually much more vulnerable than what our government and Hollywood has led us to believe. But if there is some type of government cover-up, as many conspiracy theorists suggest, as portrayed in the film *Loose Change*, indicating that our own country at least knew of the attack beforehand and did nothing, or even intentionally collapsed the towers themselves, ultimately killing thousands of Americans, well, that's even more disturbing. Not only do we now have to be in fear of enemy nations invading us, extremist religious groups committing Jihad on us, home-grown Right (or Left) wing activists sending bombs to us, and pharmaceutical companies infecting us with viruses, all blind-siding us from every direction; but now we have to keep an eye out directly ahead as our government systematically attacks us from the front. During 9/11 I worked as an A&P Technician (Airframes and Power plants, or engines) for Boeing and was later one of I'm sure many asked to give my opinion of damage caused specifically to the Boeing 757 (American Airlines Flight 77) jetliner after it impacted with the Pentagon. Not even the Titanium fan blades of the 2 Rolls-Royce RB211 Turbofan jet engines (which only melt at 3034°F) were found, indicating that they must have vaporized, which could only happen at about 4,532°F sustained for several days. Keep in mind that the hottest burning substance during and after the crash was the jet fuel, which only burns at 549.5°F (1800 °F if fanned), that's not even enough to melt (let alone vaporize) the steel engine itself, the steel thrust reversers, the steel core and outer steel heat shields (the big round cone thing in the back).

Sept 10, 2010, the Bipartisan Policy Center released the report *Assessing the Terrorist Threat*, which concluded that *"in (just) 2009 at least 43 American citizens or residents aligned with Sunni militant groups or their ideology were charged or convicted of terrorism crimes in the U.S."* And that's just the U.S., globally you have:

- July 2, 2007, tourists visit the Queen of Sheba temple in Mareb, Yemen, when an al-Qaeda-driven car carrying powerful bombs crashes into the tourist convoy and explodes killing 10 and injuring 12 more.
- July 11, 2006, seven bomb blasts rock a passenger train in Mumbai (formerly Bombay) India. Over 200 people lost their lives in the blast with another 700 suffering injuries.
- July 7, 2005, London's commuter train system is attacked in a series of four coordinated bombings, which detonated in different areas of the underground train system during rush hour. The fourth detonated in a double-decker bus in Tavistock Square an hour later.
- March 11, 2004, three days before Spain's elections, a series of bombs detonate in different locations of Madrid's commuter train system, killing almost 200 people and wounding almost 1,800 more.
- May 16, 2003, 45 people are killed when a series of suicide bombings go off in Casablanca, Morocco, reportedly perpetrated by the Salafia Jihadi group of al-Qaeda.
- March 21, 2002, around a dozen citizens are killed and 30 wounded when a car bomb explodes near the United States embassy in Lima, Peru.
- October 12, 2002, three bombs, including a suicide bomber, a large car bomb, and a smaller device simultaneously detonate near two popular Australian nightclubs and the United States consulate building in Bali. The attacks, killing over 200 people and causing more than 240 injuries, were reportedly carried out by a violent Islamist group.
- October 12, 2000, a small boat approaches and detonates its 1,000lbs. of explosives near the port side of the U.S. destroyer USS Cole in the Aden harbor off Yemen.
- August 7, 1998, 200 people are killed and 4,000 wounded in two detonated truck bombings of United States embassies in the East African cities of Dar Es Salaam and Nairobi.

This list goes on and on, and on, and on and on. In total there have been thousands, maybe hundreds of thousands of terrorist attacks around the world in just the last 10 years, killing and injuring tens of thousands of humans. This doesn't include foiled attacks, unknown planned attacks or cyber-terrorist attacks. Out of every section I've written, this one's the most difficult, simply because of the immense amount of data and occurrences on the subject. In other words, terrorists attack all the time, but Americans have become complacent to such events, ignoring their frequency and high rate of future probability in favor of maintaining a normal, flowing, uninterrupted life style to the point of blindness. But just for a moment, wake up, open those peepers and realize that based on everything you've just read, the chance of another terrorist attack on the United States in the next year or two is 100%. It's the contention of this author that the next attack won't be carried out in the form of a hi-jacked 757 though, but rather will be viral in nature. There are just too many possible viruses, not enough security measures in place (there are no virus-sniffing dogs or x-rays) and too many vulnerable locations to strike. For example if a terrorist can enter the U.S., attend flight school, commandeer a 30 million dollar jetliner and crash it into highly secured, pin-point target, how difficult do you think it would be for him to get a job at and release a virus into any number of lesser secured food and water supply companies, like the Aquafina/Pepsi bottling plant in Kolkata, India? Keeping that in mind, I wouldn't want to have a job or live near the following:

Hollywood	corporate headquarters	federal buildings	hospitals	hotels	landmarks
airports	religious landmarks	foreign embassies	post offices	NASA	railway bridges
oil refineries	natural gas facilities	Google server(s)	iconic buildings	casinos	churches
bus terminals	nuclear power plants	Academy Awards	education institutions	malls	stadiums/arenas
cruise ships	prominent buildings	highway bridges	amusement parks	ports	state capitols
chemical plants	energy facilities	historic buildings	medical centers	clinics	train stations

U.S. NATIONAL SCIENCE FOUNDATION: SOLAR FLARES

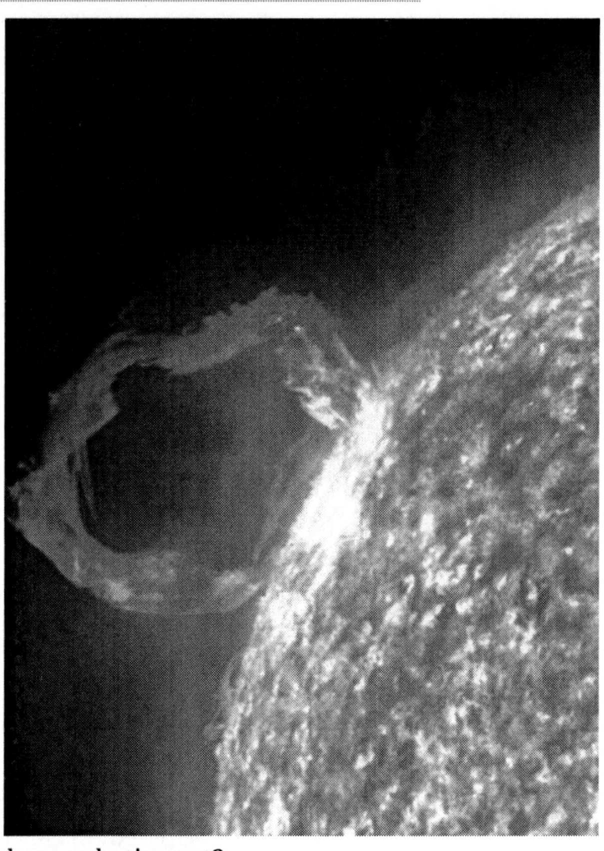

Most of you, at one point or another, have heard someone say on the radio or in the news, something about "solar activity this," "sunspots that," or "huge solar flares"; but it has never affected you right? Until now! There are three reasons to worry about the Sun's activity in 2012: (a) The Sun flips its poles every 11 years, which, in turn, brings on an increase in solar flares, sunspots, and solar activity. The next flip peak is scheduled for "2011 - 2012" according to NASA; (b) The Sun also, and separately, undergoes cycles of intense sunspot activity every 10 years or so. The *"next sunspot cycle,* (#24 scheduled to reach its maximum in 2012), *will be 30% to 50% stronger than the previous one,"* says Mausumi Dikpati of the National Center for Atmospheric Research (NCAR). Richard Behnke, director of the U.S. National Science Foundation's Upper Atmospheric Research Section, says, *"This prediction suggests we're potentially looking at more communications and navigations disruptions, more satellite failures, possible disruptions of electrical grids, blackouts, and more dangerous conditions for astronauts"*; and (c) Both of these cycles aligning at the same time is bad enough, but couple them with an enormous hole in the magnetosphere (which until now protects us from such problems) just discovered by NASA's THEMIS satellites, and we're talking about a recipe for global catastrophe of the utmost nature. Holes in the Ozone layer, holes in the magnetosphere, what's next?

And what does this mean for you, the average, non-space-walking citizen? Absolutely nothing, unless-- you happen to own or rely on any form of communicating device, (other than pen and paper or smoke signals), or may possibly have anything metallic in your home, office or vehicle. If you do, you can probably expect something similar to what occurred on September 1, 1859, during a far smaller solar eruption:

According to NASA in an article entitled *A Super Solar Flare, "telegraph systems worldwide,* (one of the only 'modern' electrical devices of the time), *went haywire. Spark discharges shocked telegraph operators and set the telegraph paper on fire. Even when telegraphers disconnected the batteries powering the lines, aurora-induced electric currents in the wires still allowed messages to be transmitted."* Doesn't sound all that bad, right? You can still use your cell phone (in a solar storm, smart) without the battery, no. Today's electronics are far more sophisticated and, in return, more delicate. Computer chips, circuits and fuses would literally fry and catch on fire in a fraction of a second, if left to such circumstances. This is exactly why Russia uses old tube technology in most of its space shuttles, rather than adapting to the new 'digital age'. Why, then, has this never occurred before? Well, I suppose we've just been lucky, is all. But to be honest, it's only been the last 10 years that our country has been 'really' dependent on such electrical devices for anything other than comfort or entertainment. I mean, really, would the world end if a pastel-colored toaster from the 70s started sparking and burnt up, or your tube style TV/VCR combo unit and 8-track player was fried? Well, I'd be devastated if my Sega Geneses melted, but I never conducted business, commerce or government with it.

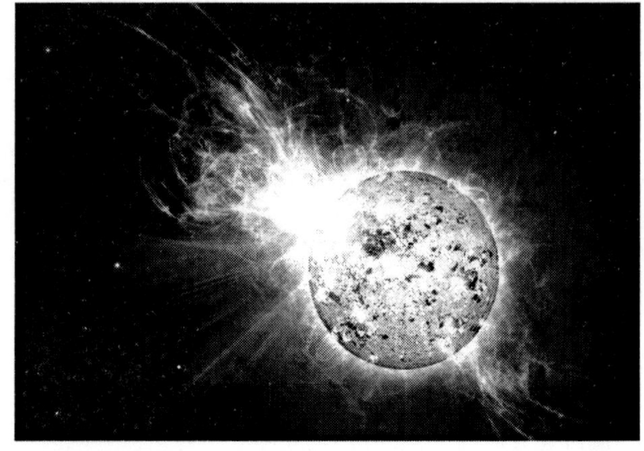

And we're not simply speaking of that new iPhone or laptop you just got. Entire electrical grids would go down as the millions of miles of electrical and telephone lines you see strung from utility pole to utility pole, all suddenly and spontaneously combusted, burning, breaking, melting to the ground, ultimately triggering widespread fires. What took more than 50 years to build would be eliminated in a flash, to be replaced in its entirety. Satellites that control global positioning systems, upon which so many of us are now dependent, national defense systems, television, communications, would all be gone. Vehicles, refrigerators, air conditioners, heaters, lighting—gone; it's back to the dark ages, literally. In fact, solar flares have crippled power grids before, as recently as the late nineteen eighties, all occurrences having been confirmed by NASA:

NASA: PREDICTS ELECTRICAL GRID COLLAPSE

You may ask, how is any of this possible? The problem starts with our complete and utter reliance, dependence and daily use of electronics; but more importantly, our reliance on power supplied by an outdated, ancient power distribution system (the electrical grid), which just happens to be *"particularly vulnerable to bad space weather,"* according to a NASA-funded study by the National Academy of Sciences, entitled *Severe Space Weather Events—Understanding Societal and Economic Impacts*. This 132-page report that predicts the collapse of an electrically dependent society states, *"Electric power is modern society's cornerstone technology on which virtually all other infrastructures and services depend."* The problem is comically simple, yet it hasn't been resolved. First, the millions and millions of miles of electrical lines wrapped up high around 30ft utility poles act like antennas, actually absorbing the grounding currents released from solar storms. This build-up melts copper lines and the copper coils inside those round metal pole top box transformers located all over the grid; which wasn't THAT big of a deal until the power companies connected all the power grids together in an effort to save money, according to the NASA report. Now, if the ground currents only strike in one area, what once would have been a localized black-out will now be distributed across entire continents.

But the problem is two-fold. Besides the fact that this wonderful electrical system which brings us such wonderful electrical comforts has basically a 100% chance of wonderfully failing, they won't be able to start it back up again even if they wanted to. Co-author of the NASA report, John Kappenmann, of the Metatech Corporation, states, *"The concept of interdependency is evident in the unavailability of water due to long-term outage of electric power--and the inability to restart an electric generator without water on site."* We're talking long term loss of *"water distribution affected within several hours; perishable foods and medications lost in 12-24 hours; loss of heating, air conditioning, sewage disposal, phone service, fuel re-supply, and so on."* says Kappenmann. And even if, eventually, they're able to replace the copper transformers (with the same susceptible copper) and restart the generators (with electrically pumped water), it's just going to happen again.

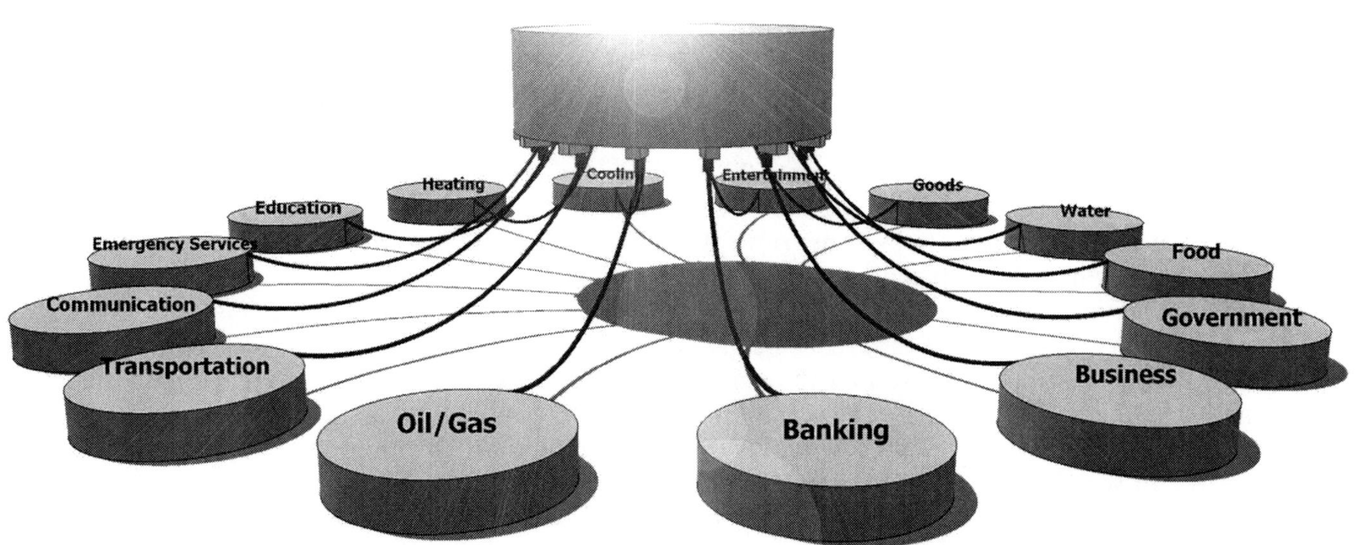

"A contemporary repetition of the Carrington Event would cause ... extensive social and economic disruptions," the NASA report warns. *"Power outages would be accompanied by radio blackouts and satellite malfunctions; telecommunications, GPS navigation, banking and finance, and transportation would all be affected. Some problems would correct themselves with the fading of the storm: radio and GPS transmissions could come*

back online fairly quickly. Other problems would be lasting: a burnt-out multi-ton transformer, for instance, can take weeks or months to repair. The total economic impact in the first year alone could reach $2 trillion, some 20 times greater than the costs of a Hurricane Katrina," NASA's Dr. Tony Phillips predicts. This is nothing other than the complete and total breakdown of the world, as we know it people, or in other words a *major global crisis.*

You remember last winter when the power in your house went out for a couple hours? That was a brown-out caused by a little wind and some ice built up on the electrical line, shorting out the transformer that powers this side of your street. Something similar happened on a much larger scale in 1989 (and again in 2003) when a Canadian power plant failed, causing a two week blackout which knocked out 100% of power for some eight eastern U.S. States, but we'll get into this more in depth in a minute. Now imagine every transformer shorting out and power failing all over the world for months, possibly years. That's the result of a NASA's 2012 solar storm prediction, which is expected to be multiple times stronger than anything ever before seen.

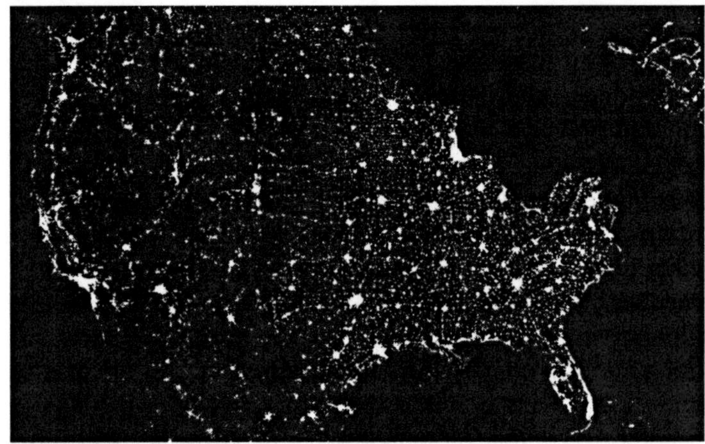

Why not just upgrade the power lines and grid? The grid is vastly outdated and extremely susceptible to power failure. (In 2009, the American Society of Civil Engineers issued an annual report card giving the U.S.'s energy infrastructure a D+). If the system was simply updated, the above catastrophe could likely be prevented. The problem, however, is the practicality of updating the entire grid before 2012. Since 2005, millions of dollars have been invested in upgrading generation, transmission and distribution; however, simultaneously, the demand for electricity has grown 25%, pushing back the completion of total grid modernization until 2030, while adding trillions to projected costs.

In short, just be ready to be on an extended camping trip in your own home (IF the copper wiring in the American style wooden walls doesn't burn it down, that is) for at least six months to a year(s). Life, as you knew it (or at least as this generation knew it) will be no more. You have to ask yourself, are you ready for that? Could you survive if the most basic forms of living, comforts which are provided for you today, things that you don't even have to lift a finger for (well, actually, a finger is about all you do have to lift) suddenly stopped working?

The light switches and wall outlets would no longer work, which means no lights, and anything and everything that you have currently plugged in is just an expensive decoration piece; i.e. phones, curling irons, hair dryers, clocks/alarm clocks, etc. But don't worry, there's no need to wake up or keep track of time now, anyway, since you don't need to bother going to work anymore, because the internet and every computer, modem, printer, and fax machine in the office will be dead (not to mention, you have no way of getting there without a working car. Got a bike?). So just relax, sleep in, hang around the house, do something you enjoy that doesn't involve electricity, since the TVs, stereo, CD player, video games, coffee maker (eww, that's a bad one, huh?) are all non-functional. Not many options of entertainment then, right? Ok, on the other hand, I'm sure there are a lot of chores that need to be done. You definitely 'have the time' now to do them, except the vacuum cleaner, washing machine, dryer, blender, microwave, dishwasher, stove (guess there's nothing to cook, though, since you can't buy anything in the grocery stores without cash registers or working ATMs), irons, yard and power tools wouldn't work because they're all electric as well. You could always go out on the town, if only that darn garage door would open. On second thought, that wouldn't help because, again, the car doesn't work without gas or (in the case of the hybrid) electricity.

Hell, man, you don't even know how to flush your own toilet now that there isn't any water pressure to your home. A non-working, electrically-driven city water pump also means no water to the sinks, tub, shower, hot water heaters or faucets for drinking, washing, showering or cleaning. On second thought, maybe you ought to stay outside. It's going to get a bit uncomfortable in your poorly designed home when the fans, refrigerators, air conditioners, furnaces (the furnace fan is electric, it won't have any way to distribute the heat) stop. You know what? I guess it doesn't really matter anyway since you don't have any way to pay your electric bill, water bill, sewer, garbage, internet, lawn care, phone, gas bill, home mortgage, house insurance, car payments, college tuition and health care without access to your bank accounts, which would be empty anyway, now that you're not working. Do you see now how a society can collapse with the loss of just one of the basics?

NOTE: This exact scenario happened in Quebec, Canada when electromagnetic radiation from solar flares in 1989 caused the loss of power for six million people.

But that's not the half of it, people. Ok, actually that is exactly the half of it. The other half was made known on December 16, 2008, when NASA admitted that the Earth's magnetosphere (which protects all life and all electronics from the Sun) has an enormous hole in it: *"The opening was huge—four times wider than Earth itself,"* says Wenhui Li, a University of New Hampshire space physicist analyzing the NASA's THEMIS data. According to the NASA report, the hole is allowing the Sun to bombard the Earth with more than 20 times the normal amount of solar particles. In February 2007, NASA sent up five THEMIS space crafts to explore and map the magnetosphere. On June 3, 2007, the five probes actually flew right through the hole, (which opens up the entire day-side of the planet to deadly solar flares, storms and radiation), amazingly during the transition of opening. *"We've seen things like this before but never on such a large scale. The entire day-side of the magnetosphere was open to the solar wind,"* said Jimmy Raeder, another University of New Hampshire scientist, after analyzing the THEMIS findings. Luckily, the Sun is the calmest it's been since 1913 (the infamous calm before the storm?), but all that's about to change. As mentioned above, not only is the Sun scheduled to flip its magnetic poles in 2012, (possibly in sequence with Earth), but solar storm activity is calculated to be *"30%-50% stronger than it's ever been."* The results will be epic.

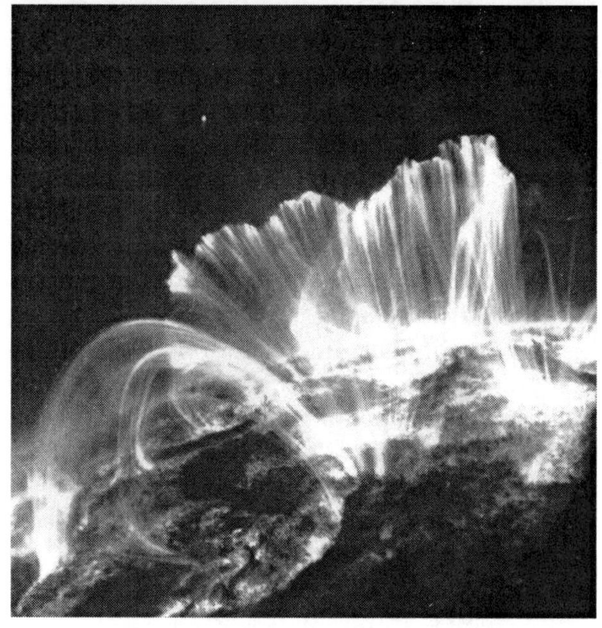

According to NASA, Solar Cycle 24 itself is actually causing this: The Sun's heightened sunspot activity will lead to coronal mass ejections (CME) filled with solar particles or plasma (deadly to humans) that will dramatically spread out through the solar wind. Increased quantities of plasma will be carried to the Earth in giant solar waves passing through the newly discovered breach in the magnetosphere. This is how one NASA scientist explained the situation: *"We're entering Solar Cycle 24. For reasons not fully understood, CMEs in even-numbered solar cycles tend to hit Earth with a leading edge that is magnetized north. Such a CME should open a breach and load the magnetosphere with plasma just before the storm gets underway. It's the perfect sequence for a really big event."* Or horrible timing, if you ask me. In other words, an enemy that can lower our shields manually, just before it attacks. Nice.

In Robert Becker's book, *The Body Electric*, Becker proves that the *"human body is a complex bio-electrical system,"* (that can't be good in an electrical solar storm, can it?); a great discovery in terms of medicine and health, but catastrophic in terms of human life and Solar Cycle 24. Basically, we're no better than that copper coil inside the pole-mounted electric transformer. Where once we only had to fear the Sun's poisonous cancer-causing radiation, we now get to visualize all of OUR bodily and cranial electrical circuitry melting in the up-and-coming 2012 solar storm as well. No problem--just stock up on non-perishable groceries, tinfoil helmets and take cover underground (or on the night side of the planet) for the duration of the storm. It may be long bombardment, says David Sibeck, a THEMIS project scientist. According to him, the breach will last for the entire span of the solar cycle: *"It should be that we're in for a tough time in the next 11 years."* **11 YEARS?** NOT GOOD,

PEOPLE! I'm glad I've got Twinkies in MY bunker! *What's in your bunker?* Again, I find it extremely consistent in keeping with humanity's trends that even NASA predicts the end of the world as we know it, and no one listens.

SVANTE ARRHENIUS: CLIMATE CHANGE

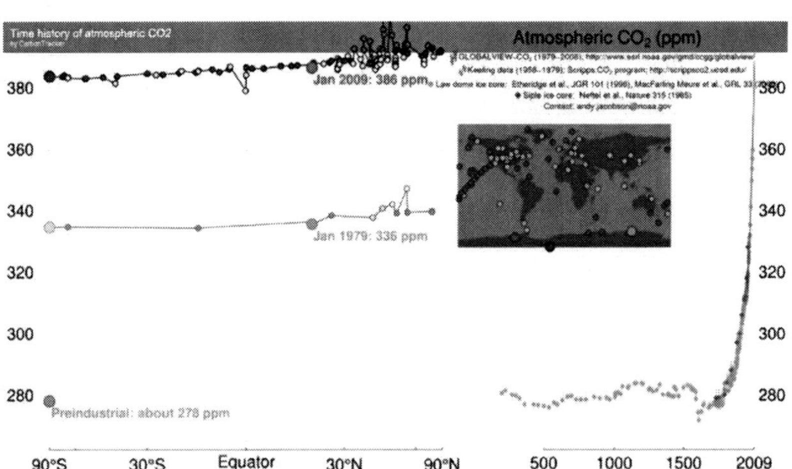

In 1896, S. Arrhenius wrote in his paper on the influence of carbonic acid (CO2) in the air and its effect on ground temperatures, that atmospheric CO2 was actually increasing. This was later confirmed in the 1930s, with the development of precise measuring equipment. In the 1970s, NASA announced we were entering into a global warming/cooling cycle. By the end of the 1990s, it was finally widely accepted (but not unanimously so) that the Earth's surface air temperature had warmed significantly over the past century. Before this, however, the idea of polar ice caps three times the mass of Everest melting in our lifetime was derided among the public and scientific communities. There's more carbon dioxide in our atmosphere today than in the last 45 million years combined, far beyond anything natural, which is why we're seeing the increased temperatures. As of the publishing of this book, millions of gallons of water were melting off glaciers around the world daily in direct response to these warmer temps.

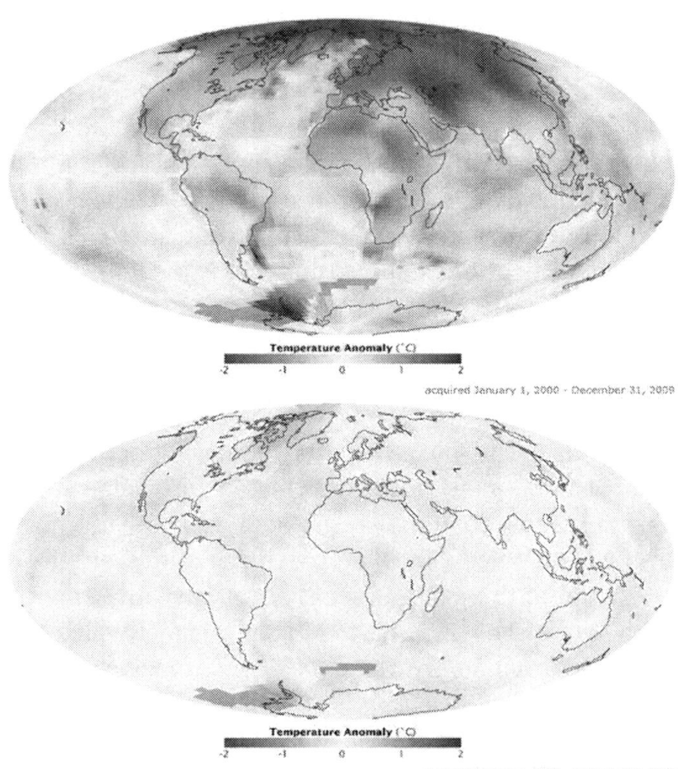

The annual United Nations Climate Change Conference has just released its findings showing that this year's climate change alone is directly responsible for over 21,000 deaths, which is double from that of last year. This includes record-breaking climate-causing disasters, record temperatures, floods, and a notable increase in sea level. This year has registered 770 meteorological phenomena: 129°F temperatures in Pakistan (which usually average 80°F), which is the highest temperature ever registered in all of Asia, and 46°F in the 'coldest' regions of Russia (which usually average -50°F,) which is causing numerous brush fires and destroying 26% of Russia's agricultural wheat fields. If this trend continues, the outcome would end in one of two possible scenarios:

1. The entire southern and northern ice caps melt. If this occurs, we'd see the ocean rise more than 200 feet, 70% of the towns, cities and major cities around the world would be completely underwater. This is known as the Great Flood and is already occurring in Bangladesh, where 20 million people are about to be homeless as sea waters rise; Papua New Guinea, where entire communities have already been displaced by the rising ocean; the Philippines, which state 80% of the saltwater is already overflowing into the community; Barbados, who reports that rises in sea levels are currently threatening settlements, living conditions and the economy; Kiribati, where many of the 94,000 people living in villages have already been relocated because of climate change; Egypt, where rising seas threaten much of the country's infrastructure and development; Tuvalu, as stated in Tree Hugger magazine, *"home to some*

10,000 people, the group of atolls and reefs is barely two meters above sea level. A 1989 U.N. report predicted that, at the current rate the ocean is rising, Tuvalu could vanish in the next 30 to 50 years;" and, of course, Maldives, which made global news last year as some parts of the nation are already entirely submerged. According to calculations, the country could be completely underwater by 2012.

2. The United States, Canada, Europe, and the rest of the northern hemisphere could abruptly fall into an ice age as soon as 2012. As millions of gallons of cold, fresh water melt off of the north polar ice cap and Greenland glaciers, pouring into the Atlantic Ocean, the Gulf Stream (which is responsible for our summers) will fairly quickly come to a complete halt, eventually triggering an all-out new ice age in as little as 2 to 3 years.

NATIONAL OCEANIC & ATMOSPHERIC ADMINISTRATION: FLOOD

Leading scientists in the field (continuing work related to Hapgood's Theory of *Global Crust Displacement*) say that the melting of the North Pole's ice cap will ultimately make the South Pole "top heavy." This, combined with the Earth's natural wobble, will eventually cause the planet to literally topple over, possibly overnight, relocating the North and South Poles entirely. Currently, the North Pole is losing mass at a rate of a couple million gallons of water per day. Its mass has already been reduced 10 times lower than the Antarctic cap, which is gaining mass (new ice is accumulating and/or freezing) at almost the same rate. The Antarctic cap now contains more than 90% of the Earth's ice. This, along with the fact that the Antarctic cap is actually growing at a rate of almost "50 billion tons per year," according to Professor Curt Davis at Columbia University, is cause enough for alarm, to say the least.

The reason for this unbalancing act could be: the abundance of high solar activity (as described above); increased axis wobble and/or polar displacement (which both bring the pole closer to the Sun) caused by the intense earthquakes mentioned above; or just global warming (now referred to as climate change or the greenhouse effect). This effect has increased since the 1950s, but is a completely natural event (the planet has been experiencing global warming long before humans ever existed). That said we certainly do help to speed up the process mostly through industrialization and vehicle emissions. In fact, we've contributed more than twice as much CO2 (and other climate changing gases) into the atmosphere in just the last 300 years (since the invention of industrialization and automobiles) as nature has in the last 800,000 years according to the National Oceanic and Atmospheric Administration (NOAA) who keeps a "Carbon Tracker" *"to keep track of carbon dioxide uptake and release at the Earth's surface over time"* on their webpage.

This difference in the Northern and Southern cap growth/reduction is most likely due to the simple lack of industrial activity and land mass in the Southern hemisphere (roughly 90% of the world's population live in the Northern hemisphere). Regardless of the reasons, Arctic ice is currently melting at a rate of its mass per year, but that's not really the problem. Because the Arctic cap floats in the water and doesn't sit on a land mass like the Antarctic cap, it already displaces any and all water it will eventually dump into the ocean in its mass. The melting, however, has produced massive changes in gravity for the last 50 years. As the Northern cap continues to lose more and more of its mass, the weight of the Southern cap is slowly causing the Earth to topple over. Eventually, the balancing act will tumble over completely, bringing the South cap into direct Sunlight, which in turn will melt the cap within days, possibly weeks, but ultimately speeding up the natural process exponentially, sending billions of gallons of water into the oceans literally overnight.

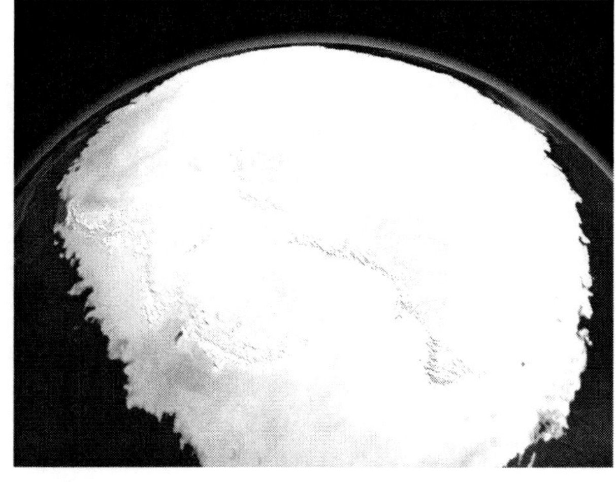

Because the Antarctic cap IS on a land mass, its run-off would raise the sea level 200 feet higher than its current height. The results would completely and epically flood most of the world's low-lying cities such as New York, Los Angeles, San Francisco, Washington, D.C. Montgomery, Juneau, Little Rock, Sacramento, Hartford, Dover, Tallahassee, Honolulu, Springfield, Baton Rouge, Augusta, Annapolis, Boston, Jackson, Jefferson City, Concord, Trenton, Albany, Raleigh, Salem, Jacksonville, Orlando, Miami, Norfolk, Philadelphia, Richmond, Panama City, Tallahassee, Mobile, Baton Rouge, New Orleans, Harrisburg, Providence, Columbia, Nashville, Austin, San Antonio, Houston, Richmond, Montpelier, Olympia, Seattle, Tacoma, Portland, Vienna, Sydney, London, Paris, Rome, Tokyo, Brussels, Zagreb, Athens, Budapest, Vilnius, Warsaw, Bucharest, Moscow, Belgrade, Bratislava, Kiev, Calcutta, Dhakacan, Shanghai, Copenhagen, Tallinn, Helsinki, Berlin, Reykjavik, Dublin, Riga, Valletta, Monaco, Amsterdam, Oslo, Lisbon, Stockholm, Saint Peter Port, Saint Hillier, Baku, Manama, Dhaka, Thimphu, Phnom Penh, Beijing, Baghdad, Jakarta, Kuwait, Beirut, Kuala Lumpur, P'yongyang, Masqat, Manila, Doha, Singapore, Seoul, Colombo, Bangkok, Abu Dhabi, Hanoi, Taipei, Saint John's, Buenos Aires, Nassau, Bridgetown, Belmopan, Ottawa, Havana, Saint George's, Port-au-Prince, Kingston, Managua, Panama, Asuncion, Lima, Basseterre, Kingstown, Port of Spain, Montevideo, Oranjestad, Hamilton, Road Town, George Town, Cayenne, Nuuk, Willemstad, San Juan, Alger, Luanda, Cairo, Tripoli, Wellington, Kingston, not to mention submerse entire nations like: Maldives, Marshal Islands, Tuvalu, The Gambia, Bahamas, Nauru, Tokelau, Cocos, Cayman Islands, Turks and Caicos Islands, Anguilla, Niue, Bermuda and The Vatican City, sending the planet into nothing short of complete and utter chaos and collapse. In fact, 70% of the world's capital cities would be under water. No levies or dikes are going to stop it. *Kevin Costner* would probably be the only person left on the planet, along with the *Smokers*, of course in this new *watery world*.

The above-mentioned cities lie under the 200-foot mark, but are only capital cities or highly populated cities with millions of inhabitants. Smaller cities and towns and surrounding capital 'suburbs' that are also located under 200ft number in the tens of thousands and would also perish. Think you're safe because your city is above 200 feet? Think again. Over 2/3 of the cities in the entire world are located under the 200-foot mark. That's almost 5 billion people dead or homeless, immigrating into the already overcrowded cities above 200 feet.

According to Dr. Henry Morris, an expert in geology and the flow of water, the "the father of modern creation science," and the founder of the Institute of Creation Research at San Diego, California--during the time of Noah when the ice caps thinned out enough, the levy broke (so to speak), flooding the entire Mississippi valley and western U.S. The Earth's crust was eroded and washed away under 300ft of water, transported, and re-deposited in an entirely new region in one fell swoop. The original form of land around the globe was completely destroyed, remolded and re-accumulated into a new shape with a new world literally emerging after the flood, or after the flood waters evaporated and began refreezing again, that is.

MOTHER NATURE: ICE AGE

Take a look at a globe or atlas. Notice that the latitude of most of Europe and Scandinavia is the same as that of ice-covered southern Alaska, northern Canada and central Siberia. Yet, Europe's weather and temperatures are similar to that of the United States, with seasonal snow, cold fronts and comfortable summers. It turns out that this phenomenon in geography is the result of air blowing over warm surface water currents that have traveled north from the equator, warming the two continents (America and Europe) along the way. This constant current is called "The Great Conveyor Belt," or specifically, in our case, the "Gulf Stream." Partially created

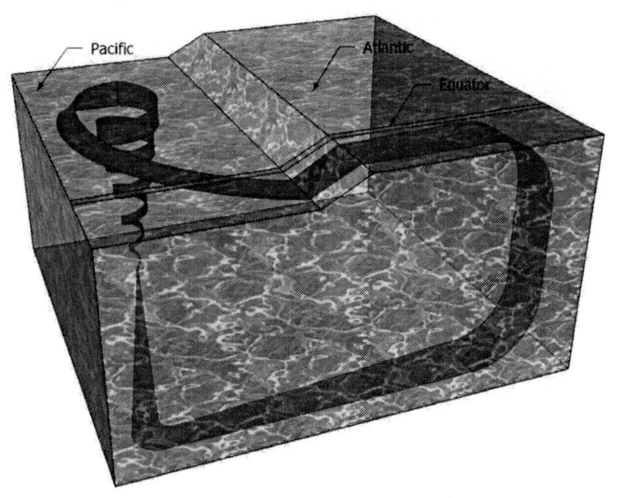

by the Earth's rotation, it is driven by the differences in the ocean's water temperatures and salinity, much like the way cold air drafts down through a house. This draft is due to the fact that the north Atlantic is so much colder and saltier than the Pacific (because it is smaller and land-locked by the Americas on one side and Europe and Africa on the other). As a result, this warm water evaporates, leaving even saltier waters. Then the predominant American winds exchange their cold air for warm, re-cooling the waters once again. Heavy, salt-ladened, cold water now sinks rapidly to the bottom of the sea just south of Greenland, actually creating a 5-10 mile visible whirlpool. When the whirlpool of cold, salt-saturated water reaches the ocean floor, it forms a gigantic underwater river 40 times bigger than all surface rivers combined. The underwater river travels south past the southern tip of Africa, dumping into the Pacific. This enormous loss of water from the Atlantic and gain for the Pacific causes the Atlantic to be slightly lower than the Pacific. In return, (because of gravity), the much warmer surface water (warm water rises to the top) flows up past North America and Europe once again to fill the void, evaporating and releasing its heat onto the continents along the way. This now cold, salty water again drops to the sea floor, feeding the gigantic deep sea river and repeating the cycle around and around, striving off any real ice age from starting.

The Great Conveyor Belt of southern flowing underwater and return northern flowing Gulf Stream water is, amazingly, the only thing stopping a full on ice age from transforming the U.S. and Europe into a year-round winter wonderland. Twenty years ago, the scientific world had very little knowledge of these facts. Finally, with new technology, scientists in Greenland recovered ice core samples from some of the most ancient glaciers on Earth for study. The results were shocking. Originally, it was believed that the transformation into an ice age comes on slowly, like a dimmer light switch. As the knob turns, darkness (an ice age) slowly takes over. But, in fact, the transformation from comfortable weather into an ice age climate comes on much quicker, more like a normal light switch. As the operator moves the switch slowly downwards, at first nothing occurs (comfortable climate with the Great Conveyor Belt working properly) until around the midway point. Here the switch finally strikes the exact position, interrupting the connection; and subsequently, shutting off the lights (the Great Conveyor Belt stops cycling and warm air stops traveling north). Still the switch continues upwards until it makes contact with the base (ice age). This 'switch', from comfortable climate to ice-age-type weather only takes 2-3 years from the time the Great Conveyor Belt stops rotating. Just enough time for any existing residual warmth in the Atlantic to dissipate entirely.

This switch from ice age to comfortable climate and back again has been occurring continuously every 15,000 years or so. Weather in Europe, for example, 30,000 years ago, was very similar to what it is today. At that time the belt stopped, a winter occurred that was colder than most and lasted longer than normal, pushing back spring by months, erasing summer almost completely. The next winter would come even earlier, as early as September, colder than any other, since the oceans leveled out and the Gulf Stream wasn't bringing warm water from the equator north anymore. Spring wouldn't come at all this year, and summer temps didn't reach much above freezing, causing snow to continue to accumulate for the next 1500 years. When summer stops, there will be nothing to push back the polar ice caps and new glaciers from creeping in and covering Europe, Canada, and the U.S. in another ice age. Humans would have to go south for the (very) long winter or die.

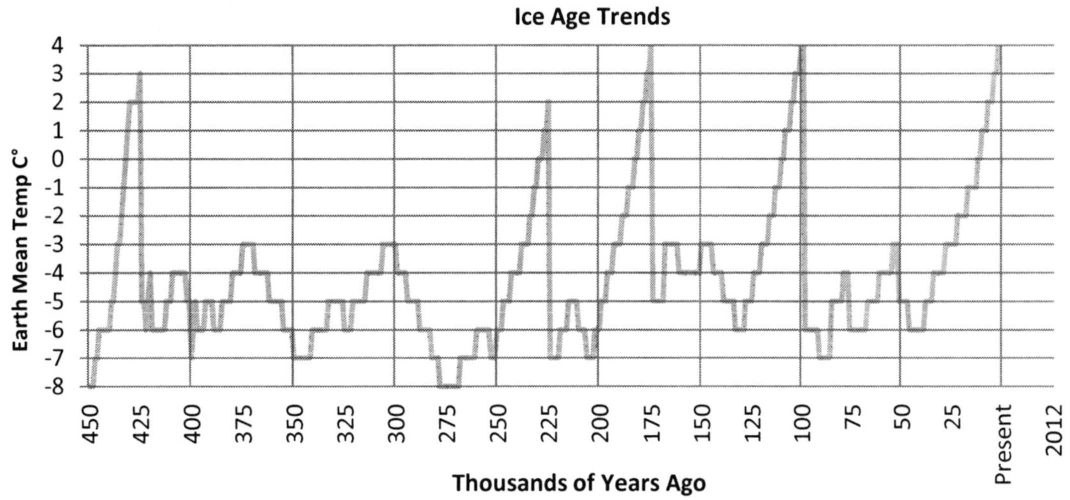

Viewing the historic graph above, we see that when the temps peak, the Great Conveyor Belt and Gulf Stream shut down (possibly within the next couple years scientists predict) and an ice age immediately and abruptly (within 2-3 years) follows. The eastern half of North America and all of Europe and Siberia will experience an immediate harsh winter, lasting a minimum of 700 years. In as early as two years, those regions would become uninhabitable and nearly two billion humans would starve, freeze to death, or have to relocate, seemingly overnight. Civilization, as we know it, probably couldn't withstand the impact of such a crushing blow.

At a certain point, the waters in the Atlantic will gain enough glacier-melted run-off (due to global warming) around the whirlpool that the "heavier cold surface water" won't be heavier or colder than the surrounding glacier water and, therefore, won't sink anymore. This will cause the Great Conveyor Belt to shut down completely. Once this critical threshold is hit, the next ice age will begin on that same day.

Exactly this occurred in the 1970s, yet recovered immediately. Since then, however, the salt-sinking water off Greenland has declined by over 80%. This leads us to the big question... When will this happen? When will the critical threshold be reached? When will the light switch flip? The same scientists who discovered that the continuous operation of the Great Conveyor Belt actually defines when the next ice age will hit, suggest that it could flip as early as 2012, and may actually be on the verge right now, tipping back and forth on the threshold, producing the extreme hot and cold weather and tornadoes and hurricanes we've been witnessing for the last few years. As stated and shown above, throughout history, always just before a glacier period, the Earth's average temperatures rise drastically before the great drop. You may have noticed the same trends in local weather recently. A few days in a row get abnormally hot and then all of a sudden out of nowhere, the next day it's suddenly cold. So get those long underwear and fleece jackets out of storage, even if it is 98°F outside.

STEPHEN HAWKING: WORLD WAR III

Astrophysicist Stephen Hawking, absolutely THE brightest man of our time, arguably ever, but at least up there with Albert Einstein, foresees the end of humanity himself. I find it totally fitting again that the human race wouldn't at least listen to what the smartest human on the planet has to say; which is, if we don't colonize other planets, and soon, there will be no hope for humankind. *"I believe that the long-term future of the human race must be in space,"* he says, in an interview with *Big Think*. *"It will be difficult enough to avoid disaster on planet Earth in the next hundred years," "The human race shouldn't have all its eggs in one basket, or on one planet. Let's hope we can avoid dropping the basket until we have spread the load."* According to Hawking, our existence has always been and currently is *"a question of touch and go,"* referring to major nuclear close calls, like the Cuban Missile Crisis of '63, as well as other current threats. Actually, *"the frequency of such occasions is likely to increase in the future,"* says Hawking. As I've stated previously, there are about 7,000 nuclear missiles ready to fire, right now pointed in a specific direction, all over the planet. What would it take to start an all-out world war? Not much. It's far simpler today with our advanced technology to just push a button and enter a code, engaging the planet in nuclear war; whereas just 50 years ago, ships, planes and troops would have to be mobilized, outfitted and transported to the region, a process that could take months of planning and preparation.

In fact, this exact scenario has transpired on numerous occasions, only halted literally at the last second, usually only because of a 'gut feeling' without evidence to the contrary. On January 25, 1995, an accumulation of American and Norwegian forces launched a rocket containing atmosphere-testing equipment which caused President Boris Yeltsin to activate and direct his nuclear football at America in response. June 3, 1979, Early Warning System displays at NORAD, SAC Command Post, the Pentagon National Military Command Center, and the Alternate National Military Command Center warn of thousands of in-flight ICBMs and SLBMs detected. Nuclear bombers were launched in retaliation but recalled later when the false alarm was found to be the work of a faulty, randomly failing computer chip. A week later the same thing happened again. Six months later, on November 9, 1979, computer radar displays at the NORAD, SAC Command Post, the Pentagon National Military

Command Center, and the Alternate National Military Command Center all picked up large numbers of Russian missiles in a full nuclear strike on America. The question to launch our nuclear arsenal in response "while we still could" was heavily weighed upon before the decision to abort was given without knowing for sure if it was again a false alarm. In the end, the alarms and supporting back-up confirmations had all been caused by a training exercise computer program used for depicting a nightmare scenario Soviet first strike. September 26, 1983, a malfunction in the Soviet early-warning satellite system alerted officials that the United States had launched five missiles carrying nuclear warheads, in flight and on a direct path for Russia. Russian officer on-duty Stanislav Yevgrafovich Petrov deviated from Russian protocol and refrained from launching an erroneous retaliatory nuclear attack. There are dozens, possibly hundreds, of such close call occurrences, where the American (and Russian) people never knew quite how close they were to a nuke impacting in their backyard.

But it's not the '80s anymore, right? The cold war is over, right? Such things couldn't happen today, right? The cold war IS over, but there's nothing to say that a new, much 'warmer' war isn't about to begin. North Korea has created and has been stockpiling chemical, biological, nuclear and radiological weapons in the last ten years. They have been conducting nuclear tests and research all while running 'war games', not to mention threatening and attacking South Korea while ignoring international entities. Iran, in the shadow of doubts set on by their nuclear program has, of course, ignored all demands from the UN and United States to cease the production of nuclear material. Negotiations with North Korea and Iran have repetitively failed, allowing for a nuclear war on the very close horizon. And then there's the collapsed Russia or, should I say, the newly-formed Soviet Union, which has still maintained most of its 10,000+ nuclear weapons. In an article published by Yahoo News in March 2011, *"Russia's military is launching its biggest rearmament effort since Soviet times, including a $650 billion program to procure 1,000 new helicopters, 600 combat planes, 100 warships, and 8 nuclear-powered ballistic missile submarines."* The report goes on to say that *"Russia will finally have a modern, top-level armed forces* (now including stealth technology as well)," which *"could create a whole new ballgame,"* according to Valentin Rudenko, director of the independent Interfax-Military News Agency.

But the real problem lies within the very likely ongoing threat of nuclear terrorism, about which we can do little to avoid, defend against or predict. Nuclear terrorism is what's known as an unknown factor in nuclear deterrence; since terrorists are a non-state entity; the threat of retaliatory attacks isn't a deciding element in their decision to attack or not to attack. In other words, the Soviet Union, Iran, South Korea or any other nuclear-harvesting country, volleying with the question to launch their nuclear weapons at another nation, has to calculate whether the risk of nuclear retaliation on their own soil, to their own citizens is worth whatever reasoning is behind their attack. Since terrorists don't have citizens, they don't have to worry. And usually their 'reasoning' or cause is "greater than the good of the people," anyway; and they just basically don't care about retaliation or future repercussions. So, in the end, whatever checks and balances, natural or manmade, have prevented so many from launching their arsenals in the past, don't exist in nuclear terrorism. We could see a much different 'cold war' in the very near future, one carried out with 'dirty bomb' attacks (waste nuclear material dispersed by normal explosives) rather than suicide attacks. No one knows how many nuclear bombs that fit into briefcases were smuggled into the U.S. by Russia before security was beefed up after 9/11.

According to a press release in September, 2008, from The National Terror Alert Institute Response Center, *"In late August, America's military and intelligence agencies intercepted a series of messages from Al Qaeda's leadership to intermediate members of the organization asking local cells to be prepared for imminent instructions."* In February, 2010, CIA Director Leon Panetta warned citizens that a terrorist attack is "likely" to be carried out in the next few months, that *"Al-Qaeda is adapting their methods in ways that often times make it difficult to detect,"* says Panetta. In a speech in March, 2010, President Barack Obama announced that 20 years after the end of the Cold War, the world faces "a cruel irony": that the risk of *"a nuclear confrontation between nations has gone down, but the risk of a nuclear attack has gone up."* And that *"nuclear materials that could be sold or stolen and fashioned into a nuclear weapon exist in dozens of nations. Just the smallest amount of plutonium — about the size of an apple — could kill and injure hundreds of thousands of innocent people."* And lastly, just a few months ago, in an official warning to Wall Street, *"Security officials are warning the leaders of major Wall*

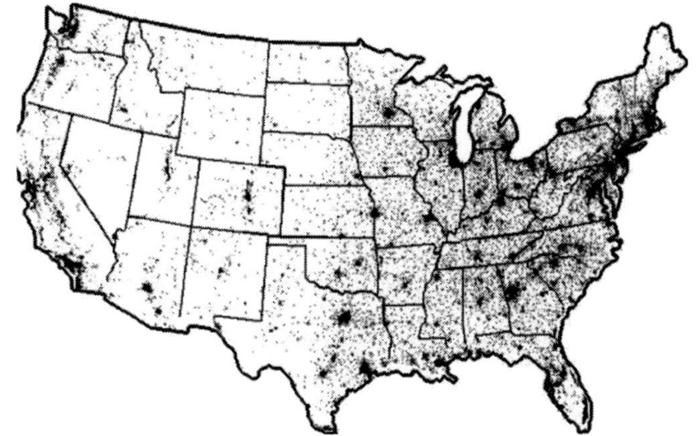

Street banks that al Qaeda terrorists in Yemen may be trying to plan attacks against those financial institutions or their leading executives," according to a press release on February 01, 2011.

In any of the above cases, probable targets would include major metropolitan areas, high population and high density locations and national and historic landmarks. For cities, this would, of course, include New York, Washington, D.C., Boston, Newark, Jersey City, and, depending on the wind direction; Elmont, Elizabeth and Yonkers. Philadelphia, Cincinnati, Chicago, Los Angeles, and, again depending on wind direction, possibly Long Beach, Riverside or Santa Clarita. Chicago, Houston, Phoenix, Arizona, Philadelphia, San Antonio, San Diego, Dallas, San Jose, Detroit, San Francisco, Jacksonville, Indianapolis, Austin, Columbus, Fort Worth, Charlotte and their respective surrounding cities/areas, all of which have a population well over 1 million people each. As far as landmarks, I wouldn't want to work at or live around:

US Embassies	Camp David	Empire State Building	Disneyland	airports	Faneuil Hall Marketplace
US Consulates	White House	military depots	Wall Street	M.I.T.	Statue of Liberty
Hoover Dam	Wheat Belt	manufacturing plants	Times Square	Princeton	Washington Monument
Fort Knox	Las Vegas	New York Stock Exchange	military bases	Yale	Lincoln Memorial
Pentagon	Smithsonian	Golden gate bridge	warehouses	Harvard	Grand Central Station
New WTC	Disney World	convention centers	power grids	dams	International Space Station

And of course, as always, the American people don't listen. Even to their own government. That said, according to the Federation of American Scientists, there are currently around 22,600 known nuclear weapons stockpiled in about a dozen or so countries, over 7000 of which are ready to fire and pointed in a specific direction as we speak:

Russia: 11,000
US: 8,500
France: 300
China: 100-400
UK: 225
Israel: 75-200
Pakistan: 110
India: 100
North Korea: 10+
Belgium: Unknown quantity
Germany: Unknown quantity
Italy: Unknown quantity
Netherlands: Unknown quantity
Turkey: Unknown quantity
Canada: Unknown quantity
Greece: Unknown quantity
Belarus: Possible possession
Kazakhstan: Possible possession
Ukraine: Possible possession
Syria: Possible possession
Pakistan: Possible possession

SCIENTISTS: POLAR SHIFT

According to a team of computer scientists, geophysicists and astrophysicists, the Earth and Sun will experience a magnetic pole reversal in 2012, a combined occurrence that hasn't happened since the disappearance of the dinosaurs approximately a million years ago. A separate and private research and analysis company in Hyderabad, India is, based on these findings and with the help of advanced computer processors and specially designed programs, predicting a major "upheaval" in 2012.

A polar shift is the manifestation of what's known as geographical and/or magnetic polar movement caused by a number of probable/predicted scenarios, including: a rogue comet, (impacting or simply passing near to Earth); a well-positioned, significantly-sized earthquake located right at the sweet spot of a reasonably unstable pressurized stack of tectonic plates; or an unbalancing act, which, as discussed prior, is triggered when enough arctic glacier ice has finally melted into the northern hemisphere, weighing down one side of the planet causing the skin (crust) of the planet to physically and violently topple or slide around on its liquid core.

Could the story described in *Chapter 2* then, in fact occur in our lifetime? Let's, for a moment, make the following assumptions: On Dec 21, 2012, the Earth's skin will indeed shift on its molten core, relocating its axis drastically, causing many continents to move hundreds of miles in a matter of minutes. Opposing subterranean forces would then cause some tectonic plates to overlap each other, slamming downward and shooting the opposite ends skyward many thousands of feet like a teeter totter. I can't even begin to visualize what the inhabitants of a city like Los Angeles (which is actually built on one of these faults) would experience. Imagine the ground under L.A. suddenly falling at 1,000ft/sec. People and buildings would suddenly find themselves in a state of free fall not seen since childhood dreams. The only difference being that there's no waking up from this nightmare.

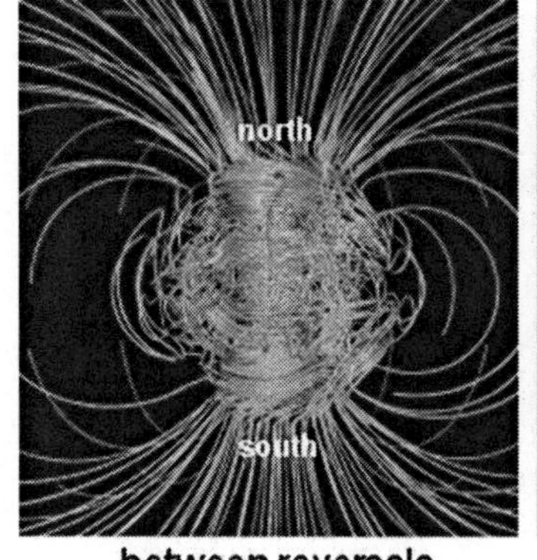

between reversals

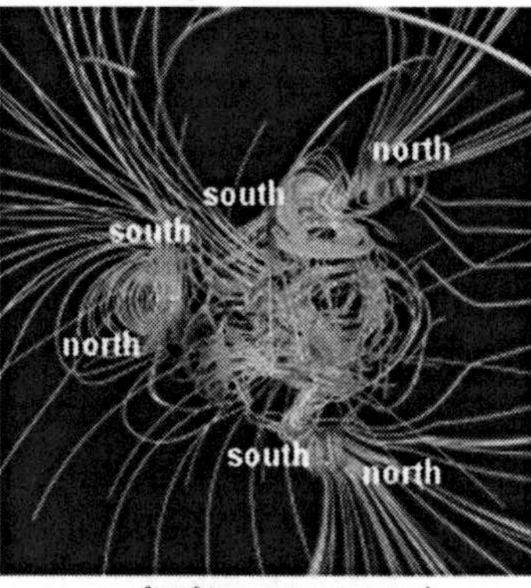

during a reversal

According to leading scientists in the field, movement of the poles has already begun! All the planets in the universe including Earth are constantly undergoing axle and magnetic changes. The north (and conversely south) magnetic pole(s), for example, have traveled thousands of kilometers in just the last 30 years, and are actually speeding up. In 1989, the North Pole jumped to the current speed of 40km/yr (25 miles/yr) from the 1831 and 1904 speeds of 9 miles (15 kilometers) a year. At this rate, it will reach Siberia in less than 40 years. *"It's moving really fast,"* says Joe Stoner, a paleomagnetist at Oregon State University, *"We're seeing something that hasn't happened for at least 500 years."* I hate when we see something that hasn't happened in 500 years, it's always, always a bad sign.

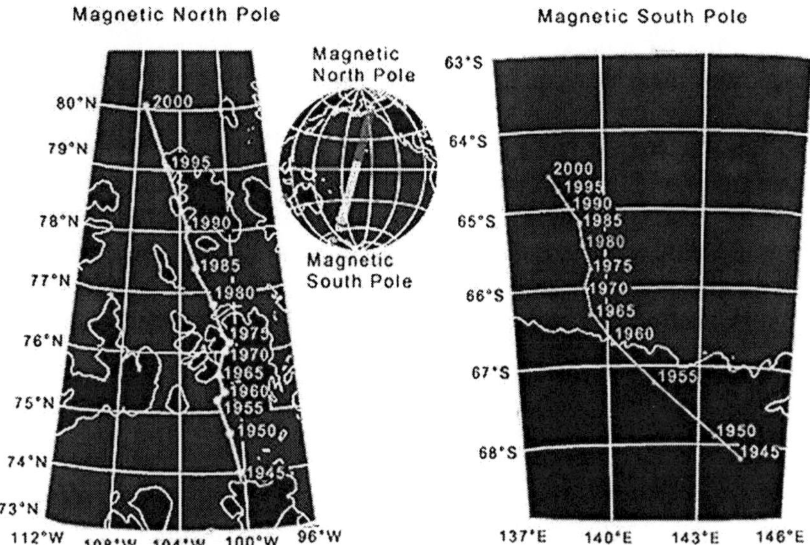

To clear things up, the "top of the world" is actually the north geographic pole (true north) which is located at the top of the Earth's "fixed" (it actually travels and wobbles a lot) axis, and is the point around which we all revolve. The north magnetic pole (magnetic north) is the top of Earth's magnetic field (where our compasses point) and is in a different location and therefore direction altogether.

UPDATE: At the time of print, news broke on this subject: A leading scientist in the field, Arnaud Chulliat, a geophysicist at the Institut de Physique du Globe de Paris in France, released never before seen data, now showing an additional jump in speed to a mind-boggling 34 to 37 miles (55 to 60 kilometers) per year.

As stated previously, NASA has also predicted a full and complete polar flip in 2012. What most of you don't know is that the Sun goes through this flip-flop (the North Pole becomes the South Pole, and vice versa) every 11 or so years. The next shift is scheduled to occur in December, 2012. It is now known that the Earth goes through the same flip-flop, randomly, on average every 400,000 years, but as little as 4 years (the last being 730,000 years ago). Because of the rate in which the North Pole is accelerating (and now with the added magnetic pull of the Sun's polar swap), we may be looking at a forced total Earth magnetic reversal within the next 2 years as well. This is how it works. Say you have two magnets close together. At first they repulse each other, but eventually one (usually the smaller one, in this case, the Earth) finally snaps over quickly and aligns with the larger's opposite pole. Because the Sun is so much bigger than Earth, it will eventually force the magnets (the poles) to simply move around (with that flip) to line up with the opposite, larger magnet. This would be extremely upsetting and unsettling to the inhabitants of Earth to say the least.

If the axis were to shift enough, or the geological poles were to flip-flop, we'd be *Mad Hatted* and may find ourselves in Alice's Rabbit Hole where up becomes down and night becomes day, literally. Those that lived in the northern hemisphere will now live in the southern hemisphere and vice versa. This would, in turn, at least from your perspective, cause the Sun to rise in the west and set in the east. You can test this point by removing a front bicycle wheel, holding it in both hands horizontally (left fist over right) while someone else spins it in either direction. Now slowly rotate the wheel 180° (right fist over left) and you'll notice that the direction of rotation of the wheel is now going in the opposite direction.

If the magnetic poles are shifted enough or flipped, we'd really have problems. The human (and all animal's) brain uses Earth's magnetic field for a whole lot of cognitive skills, such as memory, self awareness, direction and logic. The crime rate around the world the day before, the day of and the day after a full moon, for example (a time when the Sun and moon pull the Earth in opposite directions, creating a magnetic bubble) multiplies several times over from any other day during the year, especially with the quantity of major crimes such as rape and murder. If this miniscule magnetic bubble is enough to push a few people over the edge, can you imagine what a full reversal or serious shift in the magnetic poles would do? All social and economic structures would crumble within days, since humans are the only things keeping these man-made orders together.

"The sun moved from his wonted course, twice rising where it now sets and twice setting where it now rises."
- Chapter 17 of the Egyptian Book of the Dead

IDC CORP: THE END OF THE INTERNET

The End of the Internet! It would truly be the end of the world. By *"2012 about 17 billion devices will connect to the Internet,"* says IDC Corp a research firm out of Framingham, MA. What does this mean? Think 'computers' + 'the Millennium' all over again. According to, well, everyone in the field, that's the year when the world will run out of IPv4 (Internet protocol version 4) address. In other words, every smart phone, palm and iDevice you currently own, which has the capacity to tweet, check email, blog, text, take pics and/or download/download vids and songs has its own IPv4 address (not to mention every home and business laptop, desktop, fax, credit card and ATM machine in the world). What will happen in 2012? Since the IPv4 addresses only have 4 possible slots (66.248.71.113, which is your 'real' IP address, not www.lucysplace184.com, which is simply a mask and are unlimited), there are only a little over 4 billion combinations available. A third of those are already in use with another third spoken for; and the last third is expected to sell out by 2012, at the rate of current gadget purchases. But that's not the real problem, your iPhone or laptop doesn't actually own its own IP. It's only assigned an IP by your ISP (Internet Service Provider) when you get online; (so there's no need rush out and try to buy as many IPv4 addresses as you can, unless you own an ISP). But what if there are none available to issue when you connect? Well, you won't be getting online that day, no faxing and no emailing, no corporate newsletters or client updates, at least not until someone else gets off, that is. The fix is nothing less than the world-wide creation, adaptation and migration to IPv6 (6 slots) system--and you thought changing the calendar on your computer from 99 to 2000 was difficult. The problem is that no one has done anything about it yet. According to a study by the National Institute of Standards and Technology (NIST), IF everyone were to start making the necessary changes today, only 30 percent of user networks will have made the transition by 2012.

In other words, at the very least, get ready to wait hours, possibly days, to get online. How do you think the corporate, industrial, governmental, economical and business world would handle such a slowdown? Harbor no illusions; we're talking nothing less than the total collapse of the planet's social, economic, commerce, business and trade systems, ultimately leading to the collapse of world governments, again. You see, every credit transaction you make, every purchase you complete, every bank transaction, school registration, medical action, weather prediction, flight reservation, communication (even if you don't personally make them) are run through computers and the internet by the merchant or establishment. In other words, even though you think you're not currently online or aren't computer savvy, you are, or at least your records and business are; everything's handled on the World Wide Web now. And we're not talking about just waiting to download a few songs. The tasks that are carried out behind the scenes online are critical to today's capitalist functions and national infrastructure. If you walked into a doctor's office 30 years ago, the problem would have been something like: *"We're sorry sir, but we can't locate your file right now."* But in 2012, it will be more like: *"We're sorry sir, but we can't access your file right now."*

For the older generation, the internet is 'cool'; but for the new generation the internet isn't 'cool', it's just a way of life. It's like saying the refrigerator is cool. Today, though, it's exactly that, life. In fact, today it's much easier for people to actually leave society, something I've been preaching for the last 10 years. Now you don't necessarily need to physically pack up and head out, like we did, you can just disconnect, unplug, and stop paying your internet bill. By not depending on the Internet, chatting, texting, emailing, sharing, twitting, uploading, downloading, posting, messaging, Googling and whatever else, you are entirely cut off from the outside world.

And even if the world were able to make the transition to IPv6 addresses in time, we would still have the ongoing impending threat of a viral attack, orchestrated by any number of home-grown hackers or foreign technical terrorists, not to mention a generation of wired-in, bored, 13-year-old kids with nothing better to do than shut down the entire Internet. A decent hacker with a little understanding of DNS, DDOS, Bot-netting and basic coding languages like C++, could not only temporarily, but permanently (depending on the complexity of the worm) crash the current 13 (or more) key root DNS servers which make up the "Internet's spinal cord," essentially rendering the World Wide Web unusable (or in this case, inaccessible) for most of the planet's users. The coded virus would need to adapt and transverse fast enough to avoid the DNS servers' protocols though. A simpler method would be for a malicious hacker to code a virus which would spread throughout PCs and smart devices, encouraging them to download a file like this one-- http://www.internic.net/zones/root.zone--and use it as an attack list. Technically, in terms of an 'attack' on humanity, this one would be way too easy to carry out, considering how big the consequences it would have on developed countries, infrastructure and people's lives. Life, as we know it, would be no longer. It would be the apocalypse of the digital age.

And if the techy generation has too many morals to do the dirty work themselves, governments, foreign military commanders and terrorists could do the job far easier by simply destroying the structural buildings in which the 13 key root DNS servers reside (like they did with the Twin Towers). This can be accomplished with nuclear or non-nuclear explosives or simple EMP's (electro-magnetic pulses). Of course, the DNS would still be running, but for how long without a head? The 13 (actually 26) root servers are run by VeriSign Global Registry Services, the Information Sciences Institute, Cogent Communications, the University of Maryland, NASA Ames

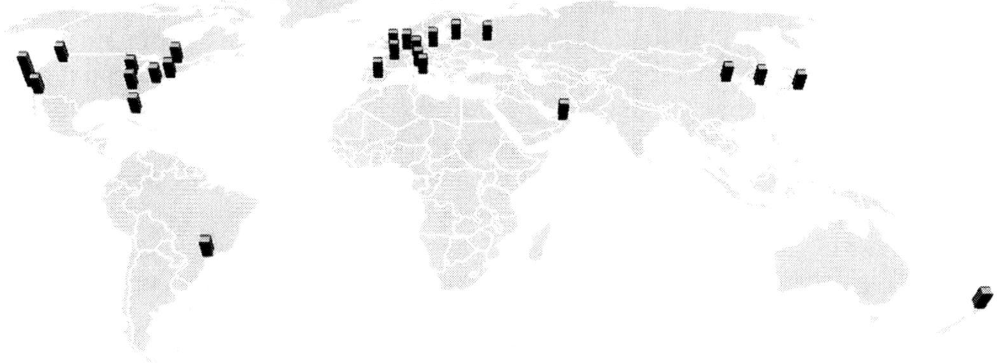

Research Center, Internet Systems Consortium, Inc., U.S. DOD Network Information Center, U.S. Army Research Lab, Autonomica/NORDU net, VeriSign Global Registry Services, RIPE NCC, ICANN and the WIDE Project and are located in their respective city/country all over the world.

HUBBLE/NASA: PLANET X, THE TENTH PLANET

On July 29, 2005, NASA announced *"A planet larger than Pluto has been discovered in the outlying regions of the solar system."* In 2005 its position was about 97 times farther from the Sun than Earth. In comparison, Pluto is half that. The tenth planet of our solar system was then photo'd by Hubble on December 9 and 10, 2005.

The comet Shoemaker-Levy, impacted Jupiter on March 23, 2003. And yet again, it wasn't until six months after the known projected heading that it was announced to the public; and the impact wasn't even on our planet. Can you imagine how long they'd wait to tell us if a rogue comet was on a crash course with Earth? I suspect not until after the fact. Do you have a big enough telescope to see one yourself? No? Then I guess we'll just have to take their word for it that none are currently coming. On March 16, 1999, at the 30th Lunar and Planetary Science Conference in Houston, NASA announced the theory that the Earth's Moon originated from a catastrophic collision with a "Mars-sized planet."

If a small meteoroid did strike Earth with enough speed, (or a large meteoroid with a slower velocity), it would hurl enough debris and dust into the atmosphere to cover and block any and all sunlight from touching the planet, sending us into an immediate ice age. The complete and total covering of the Earth with ice creates less surface friction and less heat absorption through more reflection, causing Earth's rotation to speed up, which may cause the mantle of the planet to shear loose of its liquid core, essentially free-spinning independent of its center. But we're getting *behind of ourselves.*

The simple truth here, though, is that a comet doesn't need to actually hit the planet to cause as much or more damage than just passing by. If the previous visions of Nibiru, foretold by so many, were to occur, or any other large planetary mass were to merely come close to the Earth, the cataclysmic effects would be equally as devastating as if it actually hit. If a large enough comet or planetary body were to pass from below the parallel plane upward between the Earth and Sun (causing a Solar Eclipse) the combined forces of the two masses lined up could have enough magnetic pull to offset our magnetic poles, reverse Earth's orbit, and shift the planet's skin (crust) around as described. If the moon was positioned properly, (which it will be during the Winter Equinox of 2012), the resulting effect would dye the moon "blood red," (just like it did on December 21, 2010), as foretold:

"I watched as the lamb opened the sixth seal. There was a great earthquake. The sun turned black like sackcloth made of goat hair, the whole moon turned blood red."

- Book of Revelations chapter 6, verse 6

THE DAY THE EARTH STOOD STILL

There are numerous legends from indigenous peoples around the world similar to the one above that tell of a time when exactly this happened. Either the Sun stood still, or three days of darkness occurred (depending on which part of the planet they were on at the time). A great deal of both, science and prophecy, agree that this is an essential part of ongoing Earth changes, preparing us for our great adventure. If the planet were to reverse its direction of rotation, days (and nights) would grow longer and longer as the Earth slowed its rotation to a seeming stop before reversing direction altogether. At this "seeming stop" or threshold, darkness would remain; the Sun wouldn't rise again for several days. Imagine a yo-yo that's all twisted up, you straighten the string and let it unwind. It will continue to spin far passed straight or 0, now twisting into the opposite side until the string can't take anymore and slows the spin to a stop. It's there that, for the briefest time, the yo-yo no longer rotates. But eventually, it once again begins spinning, this time in the opposite direction. We see this occurring at least once before in history, as told by the Bible in the Book of Exodus 10:22: *"And Moses stretched forth his hand toward heaven, and there was a thick darkness in all the land of Egypt three days."* Once the planet is pulled sufficiently enough in the opposite direction, the threshold would be passed and the planet would begin spinning in the opposite direction, or in our case, east to west, causing the Sun to rise in the east and set in the west, as it now does. Ancient Hindu, Jewish, Muslim, Hawaiian and Native American legends all state a time when the Sun actually rose in the west and set in the east; and one even tells of the Sun rising in the North, which would indicate the axis shifted to somewhere along the equator at one point. The position in which the Earth stops, (being day or night), is simply defined by your location on Earth and the random direction on which it finally settles in reference to that side facing the Sun.

ENDING THE MAYAN CALENDAR JUST IN TIME FOR THE APOCALYPSE

The planetary crust moves on its own without the help of comets, unknown planetary bodies, earthquakes or solar flares to such an extent as to move the position or soil of the North Pole (not the axis or magnetic pole itself) all the way to the equator and back. In other words, it would be like moving Canada (where the North Pole is currently located) to the equator. This is what is referred to as 'planetary crust displacement' and is caused by the "Precession of the Equinoxes" phenomenon. The Precession of the Equinoxes is simply a wobbling of the axis due to gravitational pulls from the Sun, Moon and other planets. The surprising element is that this cycle completes its end every 26,000 years, currently ending on December 21, 2012. The Mayans and many other ancient cultures knew this.

The end results of such a close encounter with another planet would be nothing less than widespread massive super volcanic eruptions (without cauldrons), super volcanoes (with cauldrons), super earthquakes (that dwarf the Richter scale), super hurricanes, super tornados, super tsunamis, epic flooding, fissures emitting gigatons of poisonous gas, dust choking ash causing a long term nuclear winter, and eventually the extinction of 6.5 billion people along with most other animal life on this planet; basically an apocalypse. Think it's impossible? Or was this also possibly what caused the demise of Atlantis, Mu, the pyramids, and other ancient civilizations? The pyramids show a distinct water line and water-caused deterioration 3/4 above the baseline of the structures. If this deterioration is just caused by rain, why is the water marking only 3/4 of the way up, and not all the way? Then you have sharks teeth and sea shells in deserts that sit at elevations upwards of 7000ft. We're told in school that these fossilized remains were left from when the ocean once occupied the area--at 7000ft? IF there was ever a time when the ocean sat 7000ft above its current water level it's called "epic flooding" and it's not natural. It is estimated that such a shift in planetary rotation has occurred four times (if anyone's keeping count) in Earth's human history, probably erasing any history of previously advanced cultures along the way.

"I saw a new heaven and a new earth, for the first heaven and earth had gone away, and there was no longer a sea."
- Rev 21:1

U.S. GEOLOGICAL SERVICE: EARTHQUAKE

December 26, 7:58 A.M., 2004 – The day after Christmas – An unusually strong shift in the tectonic plates near Sumatra Island, Indonesia, caused a 9.15 magnitude earthquake and made the Earth actually wobble on its axis, changing the regions' geological landscape drastically, relocating some countries east to west by up to 30 meters, raising submerged land masses from the sea while permanently sinking others. *"That earthquake has changed the map,"* U.S. Geological Survey expert, Ken Hudnut, said in Los Angeles, *"permanently relocating countries as far away as the U.S."* The quake lasted a mere 200 seconds, set tsunami waves on destructive paths throughout Asia, and killed 55,000 people (thousands are still missing today). In 1964, a 9.2M

quake hit Prince William Sound, Alaska. The strongest quake on record hit Chile in 1960 (which moved the country by 20 meters) and measured 9.5 on the Richter scale. The force with which an earthquake hits multiplies by a factor of ten for every point on the Richter scale. On February 27th of 2010, another Chilean earthquake (8.8 magnitudes) hit the country hard, actually shortening the length of Earth's day. Richard Gross of NASA's Jet Propulsion Laboratory in California has shown that the quake not only sped up the rotation of the Earth, but also enlarged its wobble by off-setting Earth's mass around its axis more than 3in. In 2004 and 2010, two more earthquakes, a 9.1M and a 7.8M, hit Indonesia, shortening the day and shifting the axis even further. Gross reports that although the Chilean earthquake was, in fact, much smaller, it caused more change to Earth's rotation simply because it hit in a perfect spot (mid-latitude, and at steeper, more unstable, angled faults).

"So they knew things would happen. Things would speed up a little. There would be a cobweb built around the earth, and people would talk across this cobweb (World Wide Web). *When this talking cobweb was built around the earth, a sign of life would appear in the east, but it would tilt and bring death. It would come with the sun. But the sun itself would rise one day, not in the east but in the west. So the elders said when you see the sun rising in the east, and you see the sign of life reversed and tilted in the east, you know that the Great Death is to come upon the earth, and now the Great Spirit will grab the earth again in His hand and shake it, and this shaking will be worse than the first."*

- Cherokee Legend

But the Earth has always experienced earthquakes; what makes these different? Earthquakes are a natural occurrence on this planet; they're well documented and well researched, which allows us to understand their properties. The shifting of the tectonic plates always occurs using the same distinct pattern: first one small quake, then another, growing in frequency, building up to the main event. Finally, a tremor occurs larger than the others (which is often confused for the actual quake) just before the main event, which dwarfs the before-shocks by at least 10 times. If we look at a historic timeline of earthquakes throughout recent history, we can see this pattern emerge very clearly. If we apply these same properties to a historical graph of all earthquakes in an attempt to predict a super quake we'll see that a super quake will hit around 2012. You see, earthquake frequency has grown rapidly in the last 500 years. It's my theory that just like the tremors of a regular earthquake, all earthquakes throughout history are the tremors of a super quake. This then would be the first sign (which have already occurred) leading us to believe that these quakes are leading up to a major, Richter scale dwarfing super quake is on the horizon. The second sign would be a final earthquake (tremor,) just before the event, larger than the others (10+M or "epic" in comparison) and finally the Super Quake of 30+M.

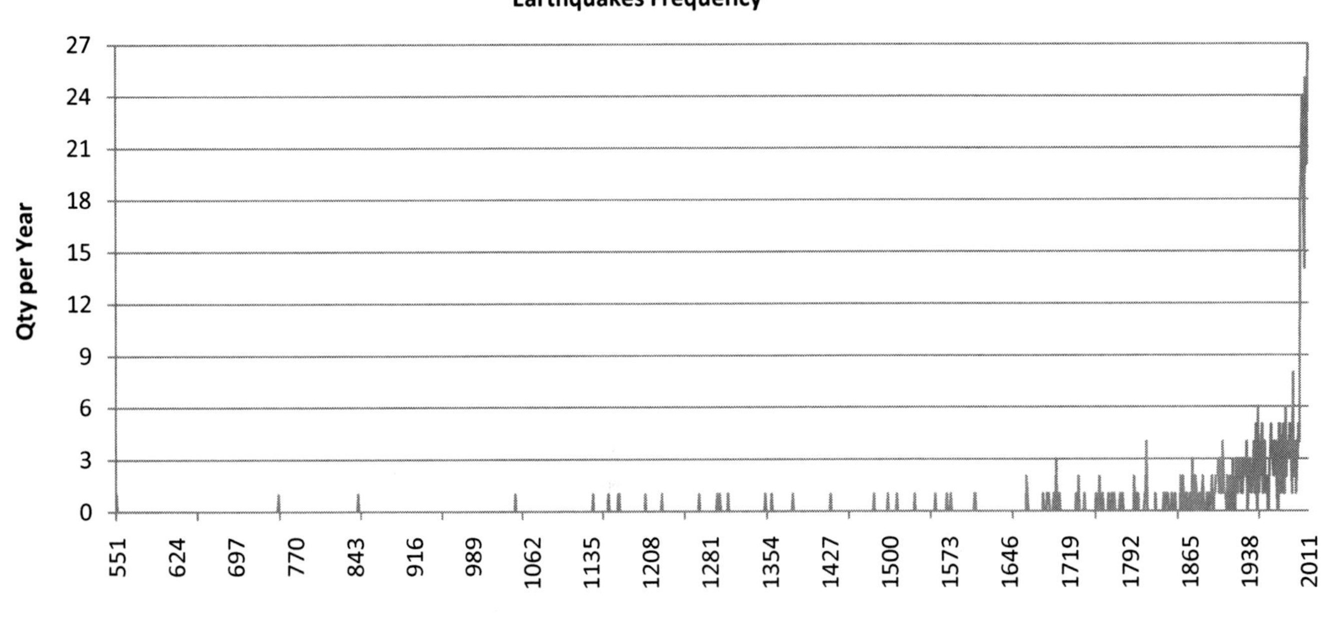

ERNST OPIK: PLANETARY ALIGNMENT

Our well-being and existence is directly affected by the Earth; while the Earth is affected mostly by the Sun (solar wind, sunspots and interplanetary magnetics). Climate, magnetics, temperatures and storm activity are therefore directly affected by peak sunspot cycles; and in return, we are directly affected by those factors. This is proven by the connection between maximum sunspot occurrences and historic revolutions, world decisions, and the start of wars. Ernst Opik, Estonian astronomer, documented these connections and their subsequent events which occurred in 1789, 1830, 1848, 1871, 1905, 1917, 1937, 1956, 1968, 1979, and 1989-90. These historic observations are only applied to the Sun. If another enormous planetary mass such as Jupiter or Planet X were to enter the picture, the magnetic influence of both planets aligned with the Sun could be devastating. However, Jupiter's perfect alignment (both longitude and latitude) with us and the Sun occurs extremely rarely.

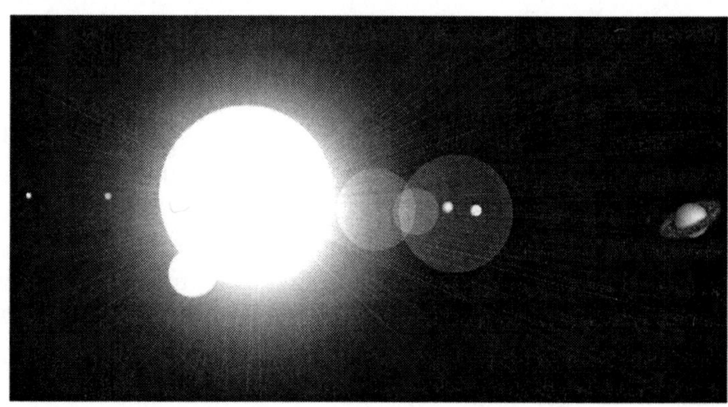

During these rare times, the Earth would be positioned directly between Jupiter and the Sun, a dangerous place to be indeed. Such a near perfect alignment could only happen when the Earth passes between the Sun and Jupiter longitudinally at the exact moment that the latitudes of each were lined up. If such an alignment were to occur, Jupiter's magnetic wind could trigger while the Sun could power a full Earth polar reversal, even without the solar polar flip mentioned above. Add to this scenario, the chances that on the same day as the Jupiter-Earth-Sun alignment a perfect Saturn-Venus-Mercury-Sun alignment, well the figure is astronomical. Now add again, the chances that on that exact same day as the Jupiter-Earth-Sun and Saturn-Venus-Mercury-Sun alignments, a Neptune-Mars-Sun alignment, and you'll come up with an image that occurs exactly once every 25,526 years, an image that will look exactly the same as the night sky on December 21, 2012, the end of the Mayan calendar. And since it's already been proven that sunspot activity is directly triggered by planetary alignments, the idea that something may occur in 2012 doesn't seem that ludicrous, now does it?

Gregor Wieser has shown through human testing that weaker changes in a magnetic field (not just its mere presence), rather than stronger magnetic fields, is the important factor in the influence of brain activity. Earth's geomagnetic field is weaker than, say, an MRI. Conversely, the human immune system seems particularly susceptible. Furthermore, Earth's outer core (specifically at the interface of the outer core and the Earth's mantle) is electrically conducting, and could be greatly influenced, by a sudden shift in polar magnetics triggering a dramatic increase of volcanic and earthquake activity. Volcanic activity occurring with solar and lunar placement/alignment results in a magnetically-triggered volcanic influence by celestial bodies. Volcanic activity is, in turn, tied directly to changes in weather and climate. [The massive flooding in the American Midwest during the spring and summer of 1993 was, according to some experts, directly caused by Mount Pinatubo's eruption in 1991.]

In addition, increased magnetic disruption or reversal would cause an increase in magma movement, (liquid iron or magma has a higher concentration of magnetic radiation and conductivity than anything else found on Earth); and, therefore, would cause shifting of the already incredibly sensitive continental plates floating in it and a dramatic increase in size and quantity of earthquakes occurring around the world. In short:

- The surface of the earth (where we live) will slide around like Jell-O.
- Major earthquakes, volcanoes, landslides, tidal waves and flooding will occur around the world. We'll be poisoned not only from above by an increase in solar radiation due to the weakening of planet's magnetosphere, but also from below by magnetic radiation from a rise in magma flow.
- Large asteroids of every shape and size will now be magnetically drawn directly into the Earth.
- And if that wasn't enough, because we know almost nothing about our own body's magnetic field, we have no idea how this transformation will affect our iron rich insides, only that it will.

TERENCE MCKENNA: TIME WAVE ZERO

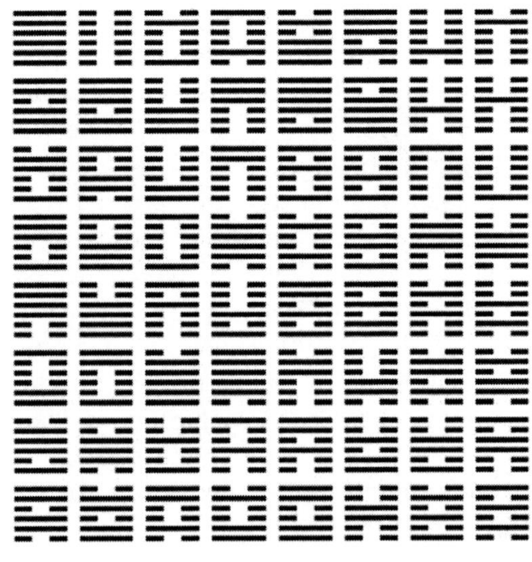

The I Ching (an ancient Chinese mathematical manuscript) has been the source for information and guidance for 5000 years. It has a simple system of 64 hexagrams, each with six levels of alternating horizontal bars and dots, which start showing movement within the shapes when placed into a square.

Terrance McKenna (an ethno-botanist and art historian) devoted most of his life to studying the I Ching. In the 1970s, McKenna had the idea to place the hexagrams not in a square formation but a linear timeline, starting from the date the I Ching was created and continuing to the present day. When fed into an advanced computer modeling program, the data instantly formed a Sparkline graph showing drastic rises and falls. When overlaid on a timeline of Earth's/human history, the results were stunning. The peak of each rise and conversely each fall, correlated perfectly with major events since the beginning of time, such as: the evolution of single-celled organisms, the extinction of the dinosaurs, the development of Homo sapiens, the invention of the wheel and tools, the last ice age, written language, the conquests of Israel, the Egyptians, Genghis Khan, the Greeks, Rome, Great Britain, the printing press, electricity, the automobile, the telephone, Internet, the list goes on. The procession of events seems to begin a sharp descent downwards around the year of Classical Greece, 700 B.C., until completely plunging off the chart into infinity around (yup) 2012.

Terrance McKenna published his findings in a 1975 book entitled, *The Invisible Landscape*. He referred to the end-of-the-world date of (November) 2012 only twice. The date of "December 21, 2012," so much discussed in the media today, wasn't correlated with the Julian calendar until 1983, with the publication of Sharer's revised table of date correlations in the 4th edition of Morley's, *The Ancient Maya*. Surprisingly, this fit so well with the end of McKenna's line graph (off by only one month) that in the second edition of his book, McKenna changed the date from "November 2012" to "December 21, 2012." Every spike and rise in the graph coincides with an event of great significance throughout our history, until around December (or November) 21, 2012, when the graph no longer fluctuates. It evens out and simply ends at zero. That is Time Wave Zero, the Omega point, the Eschaton: (Due to space limits, only 7 are shown for clarity.)

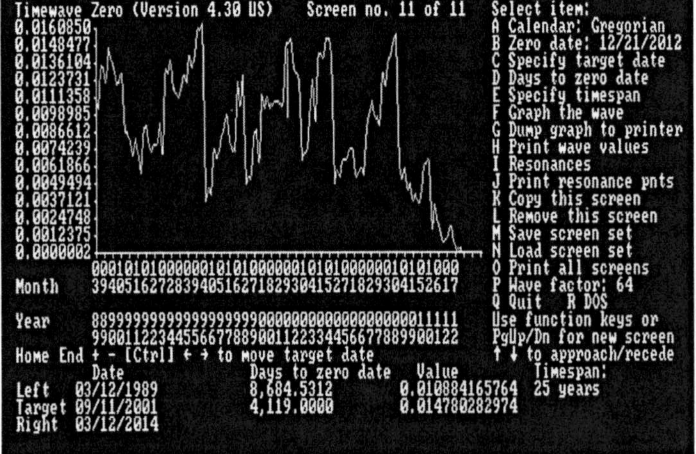

- 10,000yrs ago humans began domesticating plants and animals.
- 500yrs ago we invented the printing press.
- 100 yrs ago we began driving automobiles.
- 50 yrs ago we invented the computer.
- 30 yrs ago we landed on the moon.
- 10 yrs ago the Internet took over the world.
- 1yr ago the tallest man-made structure ever (the Burj Khalifa in Dubai) is built, reaching an epic half mile high.

The speed at which change occurs is breathtaking: Technology, space travel, population, medicine, communication, transportation, even just the mass of information out there is mind boggling, compared to a hundred years ago. And it's not slowing down, either; in fact, it's accelerating at an alarming rate. The rate at which technology is increasing is accelerating. Even the speed at which things are changing is changing. Can it be slowed or stopped? Absolutely not, at least not by us. Those born into the rapid change don't notice it at all; and those that notice it, adapt or get left behind. But if we were to invent a time machine and bring back, say, Einstein, one of the most intellectual men in recent history, his brain could possibly develop an aneurism and in reality, medically and physically pop, just due to the raw amount of foreign input. There were no mobile phones in the 1950s, no Internet; no one had landed on the moon or taken pictures of thousands of other galaxies; fossilized aliens hadn't been found yet; medical devices were much different; and people couldn't move object with their minds yet (ok, I just threw that one in there). But every child on Earth wasn't texting one another; and we didn't have cars slamming on the breaks for us or telling us which way to turn, that's for sure.

The speed at which things are changing is accelerating at such an exponential rate that every 18 months that passes, the speed in which computers process information, along with their capacity for storage and artificial intelligence, doubles. Conversely and simultaneously, the rate at which change increases and increases the duration between changes, non-change (a time of learning/absorbing change) decreases. Soon there will be a time when there is no time other then the time of change, and change will be in constant apparent motion with no time to learn or absorb the new changes. Fringe scientists who specialize in the field of Fractal Time put this point of time within the next 40 years, possibly by 2012. McKenna shows this 'arriving at an end of change' exactly on December 21, 2012, though, with lead-up base periods of 67 years. The consistency in the degree of rise and fall in the graph mimics a multitude of 64. With each specified duration of time, we evolve and progress 64 times faster than the last time over time, each of which is exceedingly shorter or faster than the previous duration. These advancements can be seen in our medical, scientific, sociological and technological fields, which are continuing to grow at a rate of 64 times faster, each time, finally coming to a boiling point around December 21, 2012. For example, from 642A.D. to 1992, a 1350 year span, society advanced at the same rate as it did and will over the next 20 years (from 1992 to July, 2012); which is equivalent to the jump in advancements society will make 4 months later (from July, 2012 to November 12, 2012); which will be equivalent to the jump it makes 39 days later (between November 12, 2012 to December 21, 2012); which will be equivalent to the jump it makes 6.5 hours later; 1.8 hours later; 12 minutes later; 13 seconds later; 14 milliseconds later and so on and so forth, never leaving December 21, 2012 and ultimately coming to an end at 8:22:13:14 PM.

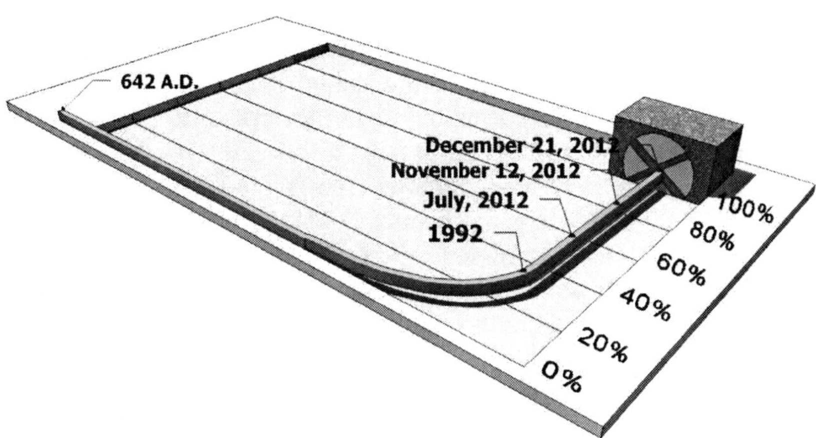

- 2012 minus 67 years = 1945 (America uses the first Nuclear bomb on Hiroshima and Nagasaki, the U.N. is founded and NASA is born.)
- 2012 minus 4,300 years (67x64) = 2300 B.C. The start of the Bronze Age.
- 2012 minus 275,000 years (4300 x 64) = The first signs of tool fabrication and use.
- 2012 minus 18 million years (275,000 x 64) = The development of Mammals in the world.
- 2012 minus 1 billion years (18 Ma x 64) = The beginning of molecular life on our planet.

McKenna's interpretation of this infinite fall and eventual disappearance of events (something which has never occurred by this magnitude since the beginning of time) is similar to that of time being "compressed," or folded over upon itself, over and over again, with the end result becoming smaller and smaller each time, ambiguously so, from the years 1945–2012. The only explanation would be that of the advent of, say, a time machine, where the linear procession of time and events as we know them would stop, reverse or jump ahead (time travel), essentially disrupting the continuation of the line graph, but not necessarily ending it, as assumed. In other words, all time is one time; i.e., all time experienced would start and stop from the time of the invention of the machine. For example, on the day of the time machine invention, one could travel 20 years into the future, live for 10 years normally as you would now, with time continuing as it currently does. (The line graph would continue, skip, but continue.) Shown on the line graph, this would look like an abrupt drop and stop of the line on the day of the invention, picking back up 20 years later, for a duration of 10 years, (because nothing was experienced during that 20

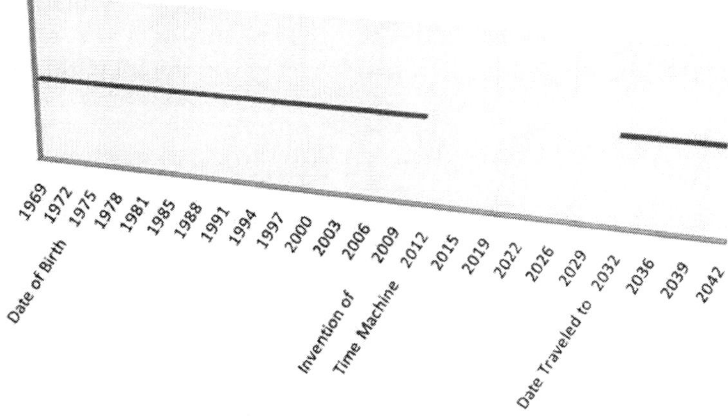

years). We wouldn't be able to see this 'skip' in McKenna's I-Ching Timeline, because it doesn't happen in our continuous state of time, explain the stop in the timeline.

The last sharp spike upwards is seen in the year 1968, arguably a time when America (and the world) experienced its most conflicted days. As the Vietnam War (one of the most meaningless wars ever fought) peaked; the hippie movement preached love, acceptance and Nirvana; Martin Luther King spoke up until he spoke no more, and U.S. presidential candidate Robert Kennedy was killed at the Ambassador Hotel in Los Angeles, California. Saddam Hussein came into power in Iraq after a coup d'état; a U.S. B-52 Stratofortress crashed in Greenland, discharging 4 nuclear bombs (Time Magazine reported the incident as *"one of the world's worst nuclear disasters"*) and Intel was founded. The Zodiac Killer made headlines; Timothy McVeigh (responsible for the Oklahoma City bombing), Zacarias Moussaoui (9/11 conspirator), and Mohamed Atta (9/11 mastermind), were all born; and Yuri Gagarin, a Soviet cosmonaut and the first human in space, died.

Medically, we're at a level where we are able to clone humans (though currently illegal), enough said. Scientifically, we're able to simulate the "Big Bang" in giant underground particle smashers; and we have walked on other planetary bodies. That is enough in itself. And don't even get me started on what sociological advancements we have made. We've covered the planet with concrete, asphalt and cable, live at a comfort level that's far surpassed any other era, and I think my brother-in-law has at least 5,000 friends on Facebook or the "maximum" currently allowed (because 5,007 friends is not healthy?). I don't think I'll have 5,000 friends in my whole life. And you don't have to look at a historic graph to see how fast things are changing technologically today compared to 10, 20, 100, 1000 years ago. The newest iPod touch pad wireless mobile phone that you purchased just a few days ago now comes in a newer version with the hottest built-in, on-the-go-smart apps for keeping current on the newest real-time-one-tap streaming Wi-Fi 5-Megapixel... wait for it... mobile phone so that you can be able to simultaneously multitask, upload, download, laterally load, text or share, from work or home, in real-time and in time for that big...

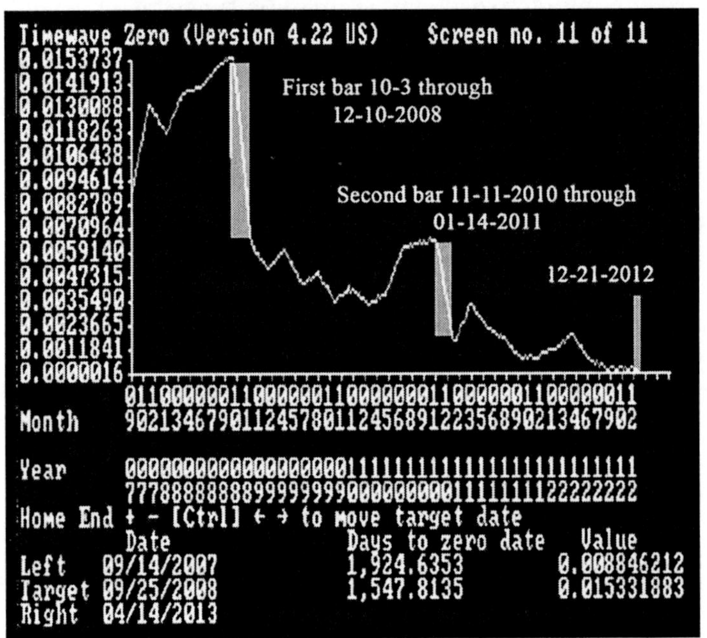

By the time this book hits the shelves, I'm sure that all of those terms (that I know nothing about) will be completely outdated not to mention subsidized, anatomized, minimalized, organized, anthropomorphized, personalized and maybe even supersized all into one or another something or other smart-ass device that everyone fantasizes about having, which I'll be criticized and ostracized, possibly institutionalized (who knows by 2012) for not. To summarize: Who still thinks that we won't implode by 2012 (or after reading this book)?

What will happen? The accelerating speed in the advancements mentioned above are truly unbelievable. According to McKenna, and other leading scientists, like Vernor Vinge and Ray Kurzweil, there are several possible options that would explain the timeline reaching 0: *"We'll either "stop advancing; invent a time machine; break through the hyper spatial barrier* (like we broke the sound barrier)*; be impacted by a planet-sized body; make contact with aliens; simply morph into a higher being; just leave our planet"*; or create Super intelligent artificial life form that will control the timeline from there on out (known as the technological singularity, discussed in the February 21, 2011 issue of Time Magazine's, *2045: The Year Man Becomes Immortal*). Regardless, something is bound to change on the infamous date, because, well, the math's all there.

THE WEB BOT PROJECT

The Web Bot Project is an internet-based bot software program established in 1997 that's able to predict future events by tracking related keywords online. Originally created to predict stock market changes, the program has literally taken over the web (watch out Sarah O'Connor, SKYNET, here we come.) By monitoring all online data (news articles, blogs, forums, website content, and other forms of Internet 'chatter') related to the

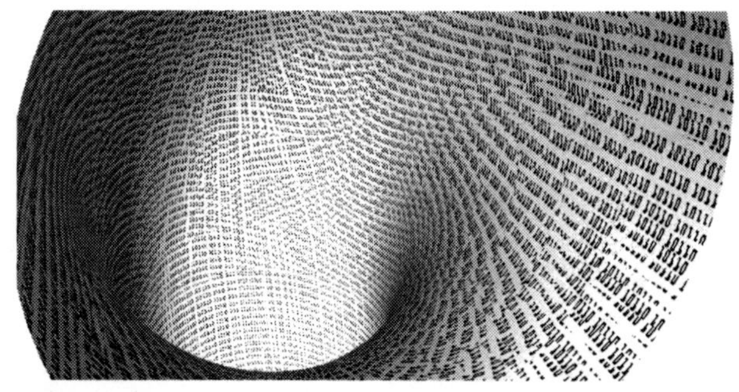

term inputted (say "2012" or "iPod") it's able to accurately make a future prediction. The theory behind it is that *"changes in language precede changes in behavior,"* say creatures Cliff High and George Ure. These changes are then communicated via the fastest form of communication available; in this case the Internet. During the Revolutionary War, messengers were used to transport pertinent messages back and forth. When caught and forced to talk, the enemy was able to predict future attacks based on the intelligence gathered. World War II radio messages were intercepted and used for the same purpose. Prison guards today monitor all incoming and outgoing mail, searching for clues of possible attacks or riots. In fact, Japan has been said to have planned the attack on Pearl Harbor as early as 1926. In May of 2002, CBS reported that, *"President Bush was told in the months before the Sept. 11 attacks that Osama bin Laden's terrorist network might hijack U.S. passenger planes - information which prompted the administration to issue an alert to federal agencies - but not the American public."* It's that simple, people talk about what's going to happen. And although communication spikes concerning man-made catastrophic events, such as terrorist attacks, governmental or economic collapse, assassinations, war, invasions and intentional viral outbreaks, would occur before the actual event, I fail to see how unknown natural disasters could be predicted in this way. Can a computer program succeed (hear) where man fails (ignores)? I suppose that is the real question.

That said, the Web Bot has heard and accurately predicted many things before they actually occurred: The September 11 attacks on the Twin Towers, the 2001 anthrax attacks, American Airlines Flight 587, the Space Shuttle Columbia disaster, the Northeast Blackout of 2003, the 2004 Indian Ocean earthquake, Hurricane Katrina, Dick Cheney's hunting accident, the BP Gulf Oil Spill, Japan's 9.0 quake and nuclear plant meltdowns, etc. etc. etc. So far, the Web Bot has a pretty good track record, and the fun doesn't stop there. The program has made several predictions concerning future catastrophic events including 2012:

- *"Six very large earthquakes during 2010;"* in 2010 there were exactly 6 earthquakes that resulted in human deaths: January 12, Haiti, 7.0M, 230,000+ dead; October 25, Indonesia, 7.7M, 435 dead; April 14, China, 6.9M, 2,698 dead; February 27, Chile, 8.8M, 521 dead; March 8, Turkey, 6.1M, 57 dead; June 16, Indonesia, 7.0M, 17 dead. It's important to note that although there were dozens, possibly hundreds of earthquakes during the year, only 6 caused human fatalities.
- *"A second depression, triggered by mass layoffs, bankruptcies, and the popping of the "derivatives bubble," will see people moving out of cities."* March 17, 2010, Jim Rogers, chairman of Rogers Holdings, told CNBC, *"We're going to have another recession, I guarantee you ... By 2012, say, it's time for another recession."* He went on to say, *"The next time it's going to be worse, because we've shot all of our bullets."*
  "After March 2011, the revolution wave will settle down into a period of reformation."
- *"A "data gap" has been found between early 2012 running through May 2013. One explanation is that "our civilization gets knocked back to a pre-electronic state," such as is brought about by devastating solar activity mentioned above."* Sound familiar? That's because you just read it in McKenna's findings as well.
- *"A new benign form of capitalism will emerge during 2017-2020."* Haven't I been saying that's what needs to happen? Ok, well that's what I'm saying.

RESPECTIVE EXPERTS: 'LESSER' EXISTENTIAL RISKS

The above events are known as existential risk, which are devastating, terminal risks on a global (affects all of humanity) level, "*where an adverse outcome would either annihilate Earth-originating intelligent life or permanently and drastically curtail its potential,*" according to Nick Bostrom, Swedish philosopher at the University of Oxford. I've left out the 'lesser' existential risks from above, for the sole reason that although they are credible and highly probable (maybe even more so than the above) in today's culture, they may sound more science fiction than science fact to most readers. It took more than 50 years for just half of the world to accept climate change; I expect those very same critics won't entertain the thought of these cases for another 50.

NON-FRIENDLY ARTIFICIAL INTELLIGENCE (NFAI)

An AI has the potential to significantly impact humanity in a negative way with global ramifications. Think *The Matrix*. As mentioned, our entire world these days revolves around the Internet, computers, computer-related technology, and electricity, the majority of which is mostly computer-controlled today. If a malicious Internet-based AI took control of the Internet, it could cause mass confusion, financial and human losses, spreading chaos around the world. It could literally transfer all world finances to one location, crash entire electric grids, stop the importation of goods, shut down hospital medical equipment, trigger (and even control) WWIII, collapse the stock exchange, change every traffic light at will, etc. etc. The possibilities are endless. And although there is major progress being made in humanoid-based AIs like Kismet, Asimo, Topio, Nao and HRP-4C, (which bring their own terrors, think *I-Robot*); the majority of advancements and global implementations are being made in online programs such as the before-mentioned Web Bot and the FBI's facial, iris, and fingerprint recognition system. eBay, Inc. (which owns Skype, PayPal, and now 28% of Craig's list) was one of the first corporations to give AIs worldwide control, accessing millions of users' information from all around the planet, in the detection of multiple and suspended accounts (which is against eBay policy) via repeat user-listing photo metadata and descriptions, computer hard disk codes, IP addresses, user e-mail addresses, cookies and credit card info.

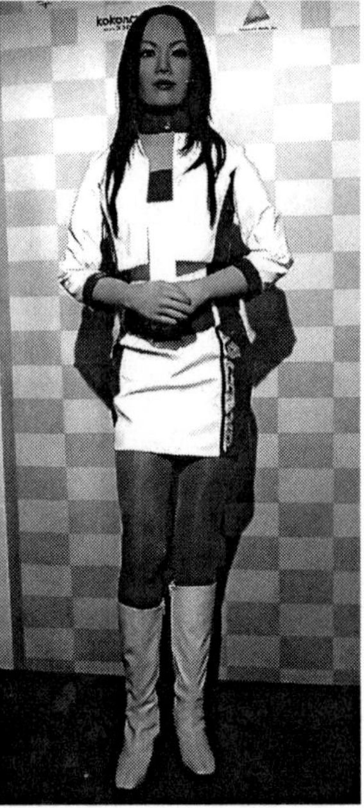

Google's Search Engine Optimization (SEO) and Search Engine Marketing (SEM) web crawlers (ants, automatic indexers, bots, web spiders, web robots, web scutters) perform a similar function in finding the most relevant search results for a specific user. In other words, anything you search, any e-mail you open, any song you listen to, any news article you read, any link you click, is all recorded and transmitted by Google's bot; so that when you type a term in the search field, Google knows the best results to show YOU, exclusively. If, for example, the same term is placed in two different computers at the same moment, the two different users will receive different and personalized search results.

Then, of course, there are the many chess AIs which are classified as 'Super Human,' or being able to perform better than humans, including: High Tech, the first program to beat a Chess Grand Master; Deep Blue, who won a 4 out of 6 game match against world champion, Garry Kasparov; Hydra, who defeated Michael Adams; and Deep Fritz, who beat the undisputed world champion, Vladimir Kramnik, 4-2. The NFAI threat is so real that scientists working in the field have formed not only one, but two organizations, to prevent or mitigate the possibility of the development of NFAIs, known as Singularity Institute for Artificial Intelligence, for the development of Friendly AIs.

GREY GOO

Grey Goo is a devastating, end-of-the-world outcome when molecule-sized, self-replicating nanobots (Nano robotics or Molecular nanotechnology) run amok, transforming the entire planet into, well, themselves, which resembles oceans of "grey goo." Here's how it works: Self-replicating nanobots would need to break down carbon (all matter on Earth, including humans, dirt, plants, water) and possibly electrons (if they weren't solar-powered) to grow and replicate. Once they reach a suitable size, they'd split or clone themselves, forming two nanobots (known as asexual, or more specifically, Binary fission reproduction). Eventually, if left to their own devices, they could rapidly convert the entire planet into more of themselves--a scenario known as ecophagy or "eating the environment." In fact, scientists at the Micro/Nanophysics Research Laboratory at Australia's Monash University have already built several quarter-of-a-millimeter nanobots, powered by microscopic piezoelectric motors, *"capable of swimming in the human bloodstream."* Again, the chance of a widespread nanobot's outbreak and infestation is so high that scientists have once again created two control groups: the Center for Responsible Nanotechnology, for safe, efficient nanotechnology; and the Foresight Institute, for safe nanotechnology, to mitigate and contain the little 'gooey' buggers.

AGGRESSIVE EXTRATERRESTRIAL (AET) INVASION

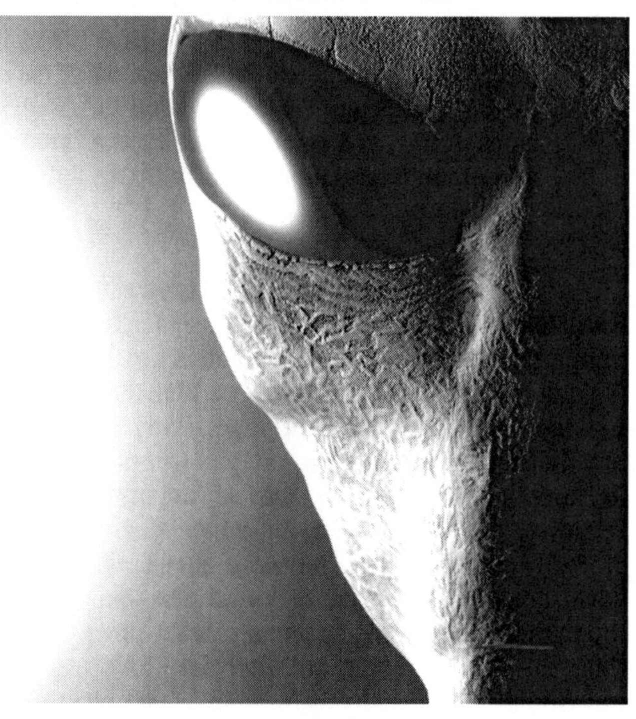

And then there's the ~~unlikely~~ very real possibility of alien invasion. I know because they told me they're coming (kidding, I wish I met an alien). Now I'm not talking the sci-fi version where monsters come down to suck out our brains or steal our organs. Your belief in the fact that there's no intelligent life out there does nothing to negate the very real danger of that life occupying Earth. Throughout history, humans have always succumbed to their very real lack and grasp on reality. First the planet was flat; then, the stars, planets and Sun revolved around the Earth; then, we couldn't travel in space, split an atom, cure certain diseases, clone humans, and on and on. Constantly, the people, religions and even parts of the scientific community, swear that something doesn't exist, or that it can't be done, only to repetitively and consequently be proven wrong. So I ask you, are you still naïve enough to believe aliens don't exist? Maybe you shouldn't be. On March 4, 2011, Dr. Richard B. Hoover, an astrobiologist at NASA's Marshall Space Flight Center published *"conclusive evidence that aliens exist,"*

along with his 10 years of supporting research and pictures of extracted fossilized aliens. And in case you're questioning Hoover's work, the findings were sent to every leading scientist in the field for corroboration.

Many Sci-Fi movies depict an alien invasion as warlike and destructive. It's pleasant to assume that any alien race capable of achieving interstellar flight would be advanced far past aggressive tendencies; however, that may not be the case. According to the Fermi paradox, the enormously high estimates of habitable planets revolving around the seemingly infinite amount of stars, calculated with the chance of intelligent life developing on such planets, says that there should be literally countless species as advanced as, or more advanced than, us. Using the same formula, one could postulate that half of these species could be aggressive for a multitude of reasons.

- The species may have one or many extraordinary, specialized reason(s) for taking such extravagant, violent first actions in acquiring a new planet that we mere mortals couldn't conceive of; such as, losing their home, starving to death, or as a result of some type of universal civil war, in which the attainment of Earth, as a stronghold, is critical.
- Violence may simply just be in their nature. We're 'more civilized than, say, a lion; and yet we kill thousands of times more often than any and every other animal on the world combined. It's "in our nature." It's like that old fable, where a scorpion asks a frog for a ride across a river. The frog of course says, "No, you'd sting me." The scorpion assures the frog he won't sting him. The frog says, "If you sting me, we'll both drown," and the scorpion agrees. So the frog lets the scorpion climb onto his back, and proceeds to swim across. Halfway across, the scorpion stings the frog; and in his last breaths, while sinking, the frog asks, "Why? Now we're both going to die!" The scorpion merely responds, "Sorry, but I'm a scorpion. It's in my nature."
- The Earth may just be in their way (think *The Hitchhiker's Guide to the Galaxy*).
- The encounter may be friendly at first, while eventually turning violent. Typically, and historically speaking, whenever a more-advanced technological civilization makes first contact with a culture that is not as advanced; immediate war is usually thwarted when the culture that is less advanced succumbs to the more advanced civilization's will. We see this throughout history with the Spanish and the Mayans, the English white settlers and the North American Natives, and the English and the Africans and Australian Aborigines. The different cultures initially accepted each other with opened arms; one culture only revolted after being abused, enslaved, raped, mass murdered, and stripped of almost everything they had, by the other culture--in other words, 'pushed to the limit'. So, never start a fight with an alien!
- Accidents happen. The likelihood that an alien race, much different genetically than us, kills us unintentionally with some foreign bacteria or virus is exceptionally high (think H. G. Wells' *War of the Worlds)* where the alien species, (in this case us), succumbs to typical viruses and bacteria not lethal to the host. If the invading alien species brought with it some type of pestilence that our bodies had no way of fighting, say silicone-based instead of carbon-based, we'd most likely perish. This was also seen when the Spaniards and Whites invaded the Americas and Hawaii, killing hundreds of thousands with measles, chicken pox, and smallpox, which the Indians had never encountered before and against which they had no immunity and no natural ability to fight off.

GAMMA-RAY BURST

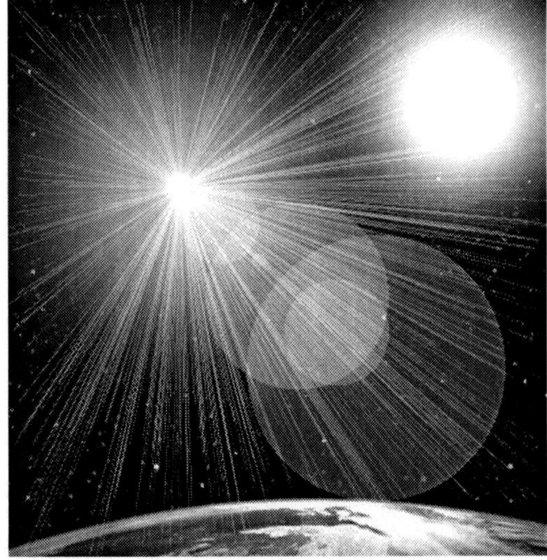

A burst of Gamma-ray typically performs a type of sterilization on planets and other galactic bodies it doesn't like, completely wiping out all life. When is the next Supernova-generating Gamma ray expected to occur? The Wolf-Rayet star (which is actually a group of stars) 8000 light years away will be the next to go. It's scheduled to go Supernova on, you guessed it, December 21, 2012. Ok, now I'm just making up and adding my own stuff for the hell of it. Scientists don't really know when the star group will explode, probably not for a few hundred thousand years, but still, if Wolf-Rayet doesn't like us, we may find our solar system being sterilized sooner than we think. In theory, we'd never see it coming though, since the light of a star, and therefore its supernova explosion, isn't and wouldn't be seen by us for many years after the actual event.

SCIENTIFIC DISASTER

Many scientists believed that splitting the atom would ignite the Earth's oxygen molecules (which are extremely combustible) in the air we breathe, setting off an unstoppable raging fire through our atmosphere, ultimately killing us all. With the creation of the Large Hadron Collider (or any high-energy particle accelerator) located underground beneath the French-Swiss border near Geneva, an entire new spectrum of fears are brought into existence, including the creation of an Earth-bound black hole by slamming protons together at almost the speed of light. That can't be good. (I tried this with my friends once, when I was a kid in my garage, and the results went badly.) And that's just the normal, everyday functions of the accelerator. If an accident occurred like the one that happened in March 2007, when a cryogenic magnet support broke, or in September 2008, when a rupture leaked six tons of liquid helium, who knows what the unforeseen ramifications of a new variable would pose. I personally hate it when six tons of liquid helium crash against protons at the speed of light (think the *Hulk* incident). The colliders are just one mishap waiting to happen. There are thousands of practical tests currently at work, involving vacuum phase transition, false vacuums, strangelet incidents, and other high-energy physics, which create their own set of apocalyptic dangers. When you mess with physics you need to be ready to suffer the consequences along with the rewards.

TRANSHUMANISM

With the use of technologies such as nanotechnology, biotechnology, cloning and cognitive science, we mechanically or chemically transform ourselves into a different or genetically-mutated race. The field is currently experiencing rapid growth due to practical applications like disease, birth defect and deformation cures, debilitating prosthetic construction and accident rehabilitation. However, the problem, and most likely cause, of transhumanism going awry (think *Resident Evil*) is that we're not very good at playing God; that is to say, we have no real practice at it.

STARVATION

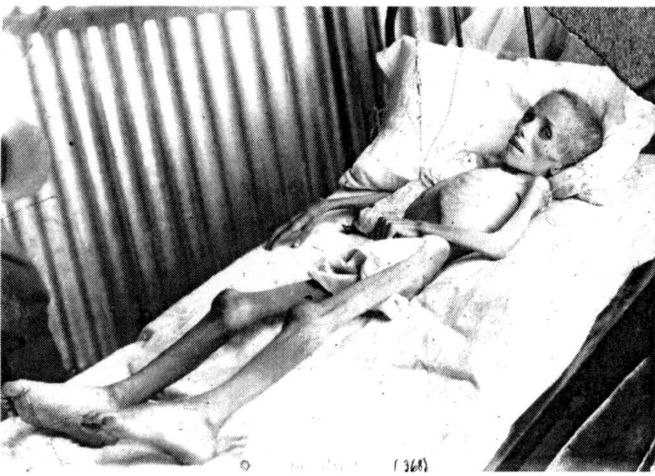

According to Professor Julian Cribb in his book, *The Coming Famine: The Global Food Crisis and What We Can Do to Avoid It*, Cribb states that a disastrous shortage of food will 'crop up' around the planet by 2050, threatening hundreds of millions of human lives. By mid-century, global populations are calculated to rise to over 9 billion, consequently doubling today's food necessities, which would far surpass that of Earth's agricultural growth ability, especially when added to current trends of extreme crop devastation, freezes and drought. The expected food shortages would ultimately lead to price gouging, riots, hoarding, and, of course, war--which is right on schedule for Armageddon. We're already seeing a dramatic increase in the cost of wheat, corn, rice, oats and soybeans, because of extreme increases in global demand from developing nations and biofuel production. The British Meteorological Office even sent out a warning in 2009 stating that *"Italy may soon be forced to import the basic ingredients to make pasta because climate change will make it impossible to grow durum wheat domestically,"* according to TIME in partnership with CNN. Even if climate change wasn't affecting crops and our population growth wasn't exceeding the possible crop growth rate, we still have a major problem with insects, or rather lack of insects, and their effect on crop growth. Many insects, and other small "meaningless" life forms, such as ants, moths, butterflies and bees, whose contribution to plant reproduction is critical, are rapidly growing extinct. Everyone remembers a couple years ago, the discovery of thousands of bee colonies disappearing virtually overnight. Well, the numbers have grown to over 90% of the country, with more than 80% in lost honey bee colonies. To give you an idea how important these animals are to humans, every third bite of food you eat is directly due to a honey bee. Possible reasons for the incredibly drastic and severe decline may be due to access to genetically modified crops, pesticides, cell phone tower radiation, climate change; we're literally killing ourselves with technology. There are no dead bodies, though, no evidence of predators; the worker bees simply don't return, leaving behind a fully-stocked colony and queen bee. Colony Collapse Disorder isn't a local problem; it's global, with states around the world reporting the same percentages of "disappearances."

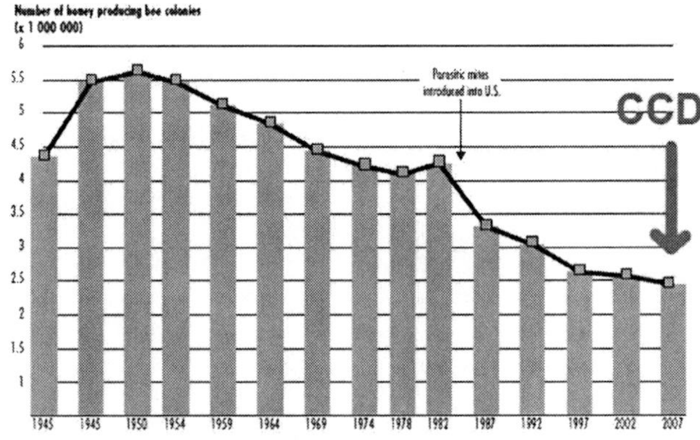

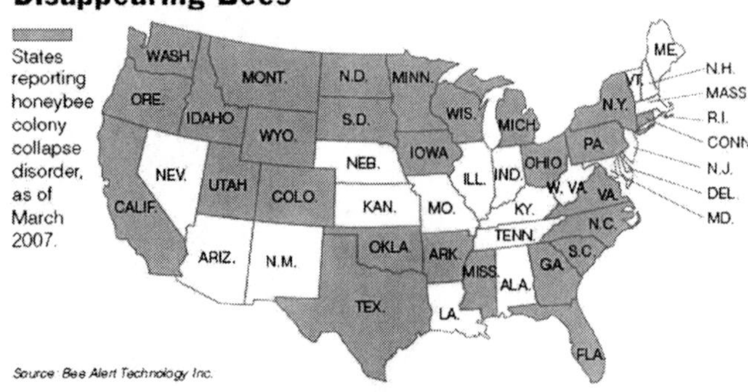

Data source: U.S. Department of Agriculture's (USDA) National Agricultural Statistics Service (NASS) NB: Data collected for producers with 5 or more colonies. Honey producing colonies are the maximum number of colonies from which honey was taken during the year. It is possible to take honey from colonies which did not survive the entire year.

This is simultaneously occurring to moth, butterfly and ant species all over the planet, as well. The fast-paced decrease is caused by the introduction of competitive predators, diminishing special requirements due to human expansion, climate change, pollution, and a number of other causes which did not previously exist. These insects pollinate, protect, aggregate, decompose, transplant, and literally plant new plants every day. For example, some species of ants are not only known to collect seeds and bury them underground in their catacombs, but feed and water the seeds as well. It's well-known in the entomologist community; if you exterminate just one of the above species (God forbid, not the bees) all life on the planet would end in a chain reaction. Here you're removing a critical block that's holding the entire structure up. But if you were to murder every single human on the Earth (except for maybe Richard Simmons, may as well leave him) in a blood-filled, extremely painful, humiliating, vengeful, super mass-murdering rampage, not one thing would happen to the planet. If anything, the Earth would start healing itself of the devastation that we have perpetrated on it. You see, we don't plant trees; we don't live with the planet; we don't fix imbalances; all we do is unbalance, cut down trees, extinct species and destroy the land, air and oceans. We plant for our own benefit only, we introduce foreign insects, animals, plants and viruses that kill or starve out the local inhabitants. You see don't live with or contribute to this planet like the other animals, we only take, we're pushing this planet to its limits and that limit has been reached.

PEAK OIL

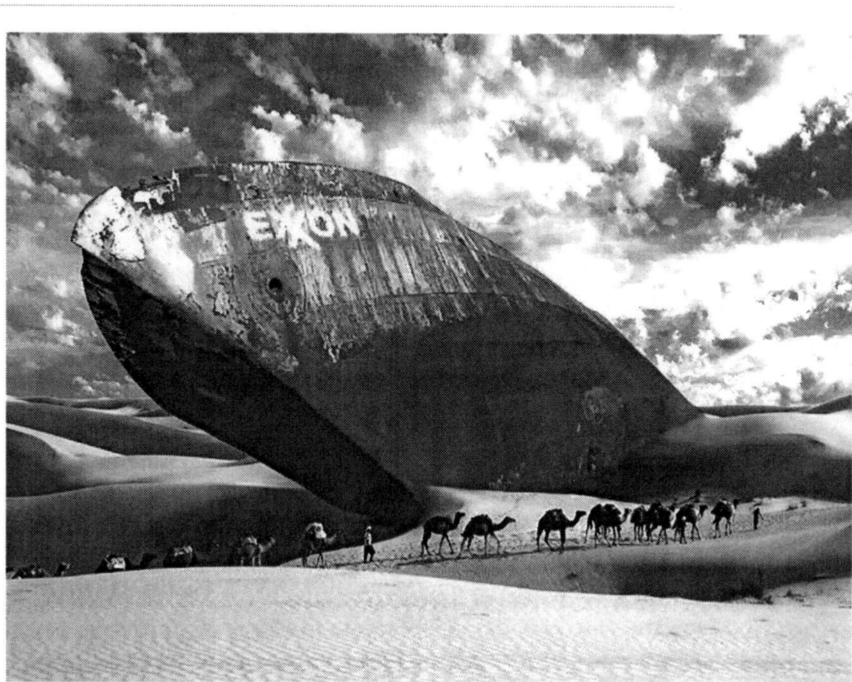

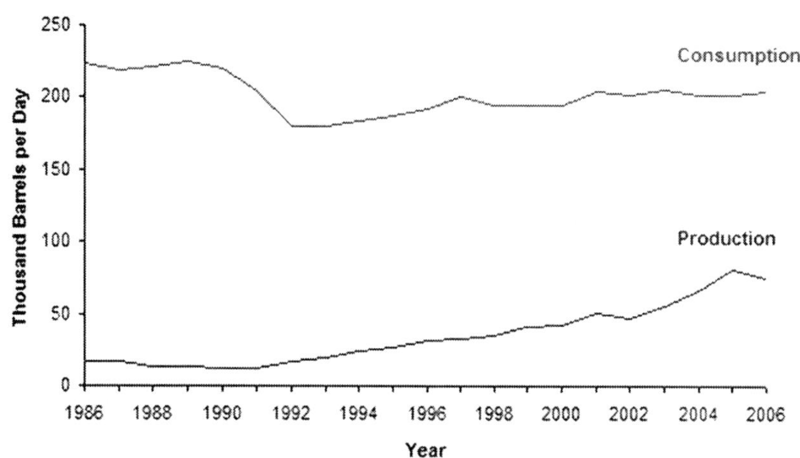

Source: EIA International Energy Annual; Short Term Energy Outlook

The attainment of the peak oil isn't a catastrophic event in itself, but is the cause of one or of many such events. For example, as we all know, the entire world is completely dependent on oil; this is Society's Calamity of the 20th Century/101. Wars are fought over it, societies collapse over it. IF a viable replacement isn't found before our oil is scheduled to run out around 2012 to 2025, the globe would experience massive ramifications: Price gouging, rationing, economic collapse, agricultural collapse, transportation collapse and finally, world-wide starvation. Pessimists and optimists argue the exact date, but it really doesn't matter, they're just arguing about 20 years. And in reality, I should be clearer; the world isn't dependent on 'oil', it's dependent on 'cheap oil'. And cheap oil will run out within the next few years either way. The price of oil will then explode as awareness kicks in; Chemicals, power, plastics, lights, agricultural, it all runs on petro. (And you thought it was bad when we just lost electricity.) I guarantee 100% of the items in your home are there via oil. In a memo leaked to WikiLeaks and published by The Guardian in February 2011, Saudi Arabia, the world's largest oil exporter has *"drastically overpromised on its capacity to supply oil to a fuel-thirsty world. That sets up a scenario, the documents show, whereby the Saudis could dramatically under deliver on output by as soon as next year, sending fuel prices soaring."*

DYSGENICS

This is the possibility of the accumulation and passing-on of defective or disadvantageous genes or traits to offspring during reproduction. Today, we're experiencing an enormous increase of birth defects in infants, again caused by hormonal disruption due to the increase in pharmaceutical drugs, hormone-soaked beef and poultry, chemical use, pesticides and fertilizers, industrial pollution and environmental changes. This can be seen in the increasing rate of children under the age of 10, giving birth, which is caused by the ingestion of livestock and poultry hormone additives that intentionally make the animal reproduce at a younger rate in order to speed up profit margins. The drug, however, has the same effect on all mammals that ingest the meat, causing reproduction to occur in children younger than normal. The same can be said of hormones that make the chicken smaller, the egg whiter, or the legs and longer (Ie. more meat). These traits are all past on the *consumer*.

In addition, there is a huge movement towards total acceptance of 'abnormal' conditions: "don't make fun of the fat kid," "don't stare at the midget," "this office building needs a wheelchair ramp," which are all well and good, but most of these conditions are passed on generation to generation. If uncontrolled or left unchecked, the human race could naturally develop into real-life X-men mutants. The Hawaiians, Egyptians and many other ancient cultures had controls over these issues. Yes, by some, they were considered barbaric. I'm not necessarily suggesting chopping off their heads, or killing them at birth if they aren't beautiful or smart enough, like the Hawaiians and Egyptians, but you can't argue with the results. According to our earliest records, Hawaiians were always famed for being the most beautiful race on Earth and the Egyptians, the most intelligent. But something in the middle may be suitable. One of the biggest supporters for such practices was none other than our own Alexander Graham Bell, who published his work on hereditary deafness and why two deaf people shouldn't be allowed to marry in his book, *Memoir upon the formation of a deaf variety of the human race.* In fact, the United States was one of the last countries to do away with sterilizing women due to poverty, race and genetic deficiencies in 1983. Until then, the practice of sterilizing women (Eugenics) was taught in all school systems in the USA, with some of the strongest supporters being Theodore Roosevelt, the National Academy of Sciences, and the National Research Council. Margaret Sanger, the founder of Planned Parenthood of America, even pressed legalization for the contraception of poor, immigrant women.

HOMICIDE

At the mention of the word many of you, I'm sure, are thinking... "We're going to murder ourselves to extinction?" Well, in essence, yes. The term "homicide" doesn't just refer to shootings, stabbings, strangulations, etc., although it covers these, as well. It means any act of murder driven by our human instinct, desire, or willingness to kill, just to kill, "it's in our nature." I'm amazed by the "hunters" or "fisherman" out there that hunt or fish just "for the fun of it," as if killing something is a pastime event. The English translation of the bible says "thou shall not kill," but the original Hebrew version of the 10 Commandments says "thou shall not murder," big difference. Killing accidentally or for food is ok, everything kills, the problem is that we kill everything. Until we evolve past the thought that we could/would harm another human, the possibility that humans will cause their own extinction (just like we've caused the extinction of countless other species) is a very scenario real indeed.

POPULATION DECLINE

In order for our society to sustain itself for more than 25 years, there has to be a fertility rate of 2.11 children/couple. No culture in history has ever come back once that number drops below 1.9. Mathematically, it couldn't come back from a drop lower than 1.3. Why? Because the society's infrastructure couldn't support itself. It requires more young people then old to keep the system going. For example, if each couple only had 1 child, there would be 1/2 as many children as there were parents, and if that 1 child had 1 child, there would be 1/4 as many children as there are grandparents. So on and so forth. Eventually, you're left with an old and dying, childless race. You see, as the fertility rate decreases, so does the population. If the population decreases, society dies. If society dies, most of you have no idea how to survive/provide for yourself and your family on your own.

The combined total of Europe's fertility rate is less than 1.3, which means that in just a few years Europe, as we know it, will be no more. This is where immigration comes in. In Europe alone, over 90% of all today's immigrants are Muslim, in America, it's Latino, which both tend to have much higher birth rates. Currently in France, there are 1.8 French children per family and 8.1 Muslim immigrant children per French family. So what's the problem? The cultural habits, lifestyles and reproduction patterns are only constant in their respective countries. When they leave those countries and immigrate to a new one, they leave behind those cultural ways and tend to take on the trends of the host nation, lowering their birth rates in unison, drastically. Germany was the first to acknowledge and accept this fact in a statement from the German Statistics Office released in November, 2006, *"the fall in the population can no longer be stopped. Its downward spiral is no longer reversible."*

Today, wealthier, higher-educated, higher-classed couples are choosing not to have children, or to have only one child. In math alone, this should equate to a decline in the human population. However, typically poorer, lower-educated, lower-classed couples have several children sometimes up to 5 or 6 and several more out of wedlock with the neighbor down the street. This would then leave one to believe that the human race would evolve towards a dumber race back towards primates (reverse evolution), think *Idiocracy*. However, this is only one theory. I personally believe that the opposite may be true: Most of the people of the world who die in wars are enlisted, uneducated soldiers, where officers are college graduates, with the soldiers dying at a rate of 1000/1. This fact, coupled with a lack of critical health care and violence-related crime, mostly concentrated in poverty-stricken, lower class, lower-educated, and higher-reproducing communities, spells certain disaster for the human race. If anything, our numbers are increasingly decreasing. In fact, if these developed-nation demographics are extrapolated, they mathematically lead to a voluntary extinction of the human race, according to John Leslie, a Scottish mathematician and physicist. World governments take this likelihood so seriously that they've devoted billions to intervening in the current reproduction trends; however, this attempt at reversal has dramatically failed to increase childbirth rates in all Western countries, and actually helped to lower it even further in China, which already employs the One Child Policy (OCP). These figures don't even account for the growing rate of infertility among international parents-to-be, or the dramatically-falling male sperm count, or the widespread effects of viruses that affects the human reproduction system. Some also say that the flood of immigrating, over-breeding Islamic nations, (of which the top 40 countries show rates of over 7.1), will fill the void in these disappearing countries, as seen with the 90% immigration rate in Europe, leading to a one-people, all-Muslim planet. Either way, it will be the end of the world as <u>we</u> know it; and there's nothing to do about it.

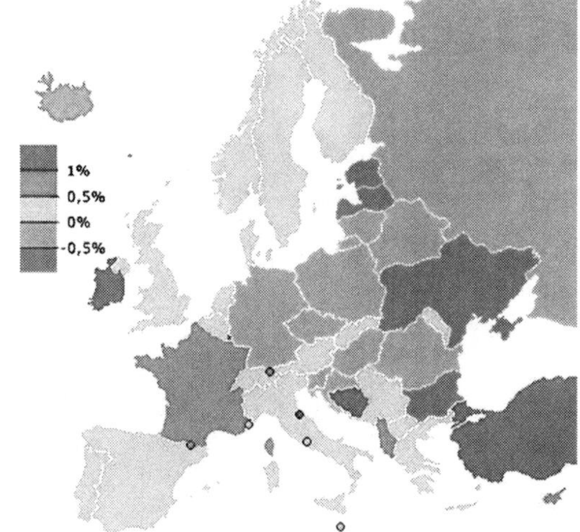

The following are the 2010 fertility rates for the countries that fall below the required "sustainable" reproduction rate and possible rebound limit. The results are shocking, and it's only getting worse:

Guadeloupe	2.1	Chile	1.9	Finland	1.8	Cyprus	1.6	Moldova	1.4	Hungary	1.2
Costa Rica	2.1	Tunisia	1.9	UK	1.8	Canada	1.5	Armenia	1.3	Slovenia	1.2
Myanmar	2.0	Brazil	1.9	Denmark	1.8	Barbados	1.5	Italy	1.3	Japan	1.2
Albania	2.0	France	1.8	Sweden	1.8	Cuba	1.4	Malta	1.3	Lithuania	1.2
USA	2.0	Sri Lanka	1.8	Serbia	1.7	Estonia	1.4	Germany	1.3	Singapore	1.2
Iceland	2.0	Mongolia	1.8	Australia	1.7	Portugal	1.4	Croatia	1.3	Slovakia	1.2
Aruba	2.0	N. Korea	1.8	China	1.7	Macedonia	1.4	Russia	1.3	Czech Rep	1.2
Iran	2.0	Thailand	1.8	Netherlands	1.7	Switzerland	1.4	Greece	1.3	Bosnia	1.2
Bahamas	2.0	Norway	1.8	Luxembourg	1.6	Austria	1.4	Bulgaria	1.3	Poland	1.2
New Zealand	1.9	Montenegro	1.8	Belgium	1.6	Spain	1.4	Romania	1.3	Ukraine	1.2
Ireland	1.9	Puerto Rico	1.8	Trinidad	1.6	Georgia	1.4	Latvia	1.2	S. Korea	1.2

ASPHYXIATION

The Earth's rain forests account for more than 20% and ocean plant life more than 50%, of the oxygen in our atmosphere, both of which are in danger of complete destruction. With the massive over-fishing, shark killings, oil spills and pollution we expend on this planet yearly, along with man's amazing ability to deforest massive areas, coupled with humanity's rapid reproduction (more air breathers means more trees and reefs needed), infestation and rapid development of this planet, we're literally strangling our own selves to death, cutting off our vital oxygen needed to breathe. Once the reefs, algae, trees and oxygen-producing plants are wiped out beyond a suitable, sustainable limit for the enlarging masses, people all over the world, but especially those living in higher elevations, will begin developing breathing problems and eventually die of asphyxiation.

Notice how the scientific predictions are the same as the spiritual prophecies. You see, such religious/mythical concepts and story's are eventually, proven. Now I don't believe in God; but I've done extensive research in both fields and am not close-minded enough to not accept the obvious similarities. For some reason, call it God, fate, Mother Nature, aliens, a form of physics we're not aware of yet (gravity wasn't discovered until 1650A.D.), something controls and guides things that was known to our ancestors. This "entity" told them about future events that we're just now proving will come true with science. Regardless, it's easy to see that most of the spiritual prophecies are the same as the scientific predictions, and those that aren't, will be.

CHAPTER 5

THE GOVERNMENT IS PREPARING: ARE YOU?

You have to ask yourself; if 2012 is a hoax perpetrated by dooms-dayers, movie-makers, money-hungry publishers, and/or religious fanatics, why has the United Stated Government (along with most major governments and private corporations around the world) made major preparations in safeguarding and sustaining political leaders and high-ranking military officials, as well as corporate heads? It makes you wonder.

2011: GAME ON

With the Cold War behind us, the U.S. military has not only maintained and stocked-piled its underground facilities since the year 2000, it has spearheaded a mass building frenzy, constructing new ones in preparation for 2012. According to many government-funded commercial construction contracting firms, the U.S. government has undergone a major underground construction campaign, scheduled to finish *"no later than late 2011."* I find the reports to be completely true, given the fact that the U.S. military (and all militaries for that matter) has always constructed underground facilities to withstand catastrophes of immense proportions. Why wouldn't they react the same way for 2012, especially after seeing all the supporting science and data? Are the governments of the world building underground bunkers to safeguard political, military and societies' leaders? Most likely, yes. It would be ignorant of them not to do so. Which brings us to project 'Global Guardian', an annual training exercise sponsored by the United States Strategic Command in conjunction with Air Force Space Command and NORAD, whose main purpose is to test the military's command and control procedures in the event of a *"dooms-day-like event."*

According to an Internet website, in an article labeled *A letter from a Norwegian politician,* the site owners claim to have received a message from a Norwegian politician, who has knowledge of, and is involved in, the mass construction of underground bunkers in preparation for a known apocalyptic event coming in 2012. The politician says that it's an international cover-up, and that the U.S. and EU have full knowledge of the impending doom, but have chosen to save only the elite. I personally don't believe that they've "chosen" to save only the elite; it's just that there's physically not enough space to hold and feed every human on Earth in an underground bunker. I highly doubt such reports to be real; not that the claims aren't real, I'm 100% sure something will occur in 2012, or in the following years, but I highly doubt that any top official from any country would send secret information, in an attempt to warn the world, to just one, fairly unheard-of website, rather than literally spamming the info to numerous (unknown) websites, media facilities, (though I'm sure they wouldn't print it) groups, organizations, anyone that would listen, all over the world. But who knows, the following letter from the "Norwegian politician" may be completely on the up-and-up. Who am I to say different?

"I am a Norwegian politician. I would like to say that difficult things will happen from the year 2008 till the year 2012. The Norwegian government is building more and more underground bases and bunkers. When asked, they simply say that it is for the protection of the people of Norway. When I enquire when they are due to be finished, they reply, "before 2011." Israel is also doing the same and many other countries too. My proof that what I am saying is true is in the photographs I have sent of myself and all the Prime Ministers and ministers I tend to meet and am acquainted with. They know all of this, but they don't want to alarm the people or create mass panic. Planet X is coming, and Norway has begun with storage of food and seeds in the Svalbard area and in the arctic north with the help of the US and EU and all around in Norway. They will only save those that are in the elite of power and

those that can build up again: doctors, scientists, and so on. As for me, I already know that I am going to leave before 2012 to go the area of Mosjøen where we have a deep underground military facility. There we are divided into sectors, red, blue and green. The signs of the Norwegian military are already given to them and the camps have already been built a long time ago. The people that are going to be left on the surface and die along with the others will get no help whatsoever. The plan is that 2,000,000 Norwegians are going to be safe, and the rest will die. That means 2,600,000 will perish into the night not knowing what to do."

Source: Svalbard Global Seed Vault/Cary Fowler

Why the secrecy? Why a big governmental cover up and why the hurry? Well do you think that the people of society would continue going to work, going to school, producing agriculture, paying their bills, paying their taxes, if we all knew that there was even a remote possibility that the world may end was true? It's also interesting to note, however, that in 2006 (in a rushed, 18-month time span) Bill Gates (along with a flurry of diverse international governments), did build the Svalbard Global Seed Vault in a frozen mountain in the Norwegian island of Spitsbergen, in the remote Arctic Svalbard archipelago, 810 miles from the North Pole. This extremely rushed construction project is very much like the Millennium Seed Bank Project, which states in its aims that it wants to *"collect the seeds from 24,000 species of plants by 2010."* In 2005, British Prime Minister Tony Blair stated that the euro will become the world's premiere currency by 2012 at the latest. The U.S. dollar has been plunging in value against the euro for years. The globalists now have America right where they want it, and are eagerly moving in for the kill. But why the big hurry? What's special about 2012 to everyone? Do they know something we don't?

"The seeds are duplicate samples, or "spare" copies, of seeds held in gene banks worldwide," according to Associated Press, *"The seed vault will provide insurance against the loss of seeds in gene banks, as well as a refuge for seeds in the case of large scale regional or global crisis."* (*"Just in case."* Good thinking. Personally, I'm going to publish a book on how to survive a "global crisis" and then head underground, also. *Just In Case*!) Yet, this is the first we're being told of such underground "seed" or "gene banks" scattered around the world. Where are the others being hidden? Maybe they're referring to the "world's first DNA bank" *Frozen Ark* launched in 2004 by the Zoological Society of London, which, to date, has collected, and is holding, more than 1,000 species of animal DNA or tissue samples in deep freeze. And what "large scale global crisis" do they know about that would wipe out every plant on Earth to a point that we'd need an immediate "Doomsday Vault" built to save genetic samples and seeds in order to repopulate the planet? That's a lot of money for a "*just in case*" scenario, don't you think? Maybe it's the *"near-Earth object that is expected to collide with Earth,"* that White House Office of Science and Technology Policy director, John Holdren, wrote about in a series of letters to Congress in which Holden outlines survival plans. Then there's Roger White the facilitator of the collection at the National Museum of American History who spoke out about the Smithsonian's "Hidden Car Cache," *"They're here for kind of doomsday thinking or Noah's Ark that someone needs to preserve these objects. We don't try to collect one of each type of cars but rather cars that represent turning points in design and usage."*

And then there's the already-established back-up government, also as a *just in case* "catastrophic scenario," now known as the "Continuity of Government," or COG. In an article dated March 1, 2002, entitled *Shadow government news to congress*, CBS reveals the existence of a 'shadow government', a duplicate U.S. government lying in waiting underground for the apocalypse: *"A shadow government consisting of 75 or more senior officials has been living and working secretly outside Washington since Sept. 11, in case the nation's capital is crippled by terrorist attack."* The article goes on to quote the then-president Bush as saying, *"I have an obligation as the president; and my administration has an obligation to the American people to put measures in place that, should somebody be successful in attacking Washington, there is an ongoing government."*

The Washington Post (who first reported on the COG plan in a March 1, 2002, article titled, *Shadow government is at work in secret*) says that they're down there all the time, even right now as you sit here reading this chapter, *"officials who are activated for what some of them call "bunker duty" live and work underground 24 hours a day, away from their families. As it settles in for the long haul, the shadow government has sent home most of the first wave of deployed personnel, replacing them most commonly at 90-day intervals."* So then the question is, why is the government actually underground right this second; and you're not even thinking about preparing yourself in two years? Hell, on the same line of thought why am I writing this book above ground for that matter?

I find it amazing that no one has a problem with the fact that the government has a *Continuity of Government* plan for its survival in an apocalyptic event; but no matter how hard I look, I can't locate the COC (Continuity of Citizens) plan. Could it be because there are no plans for the continuation of the citizens? And yet the people of our nation, the very same people that think 'your' end times preparations are a bit hokey – neighbors, co-workers, relatives – these people have no problem with the government spending billions in their own preparations, given the "extremely low chance" that such an event will actually occur. The problem is that while the government is getting ready for an event that could wipe out most of the world, building secure bunkers and stockpiling them with enough food to sustain the powerful and rich for years, they know that no bunker could possibly protect the almost 7 billion people on the planet today, even if they wanted to (which I'm not sure they do). The only recourse is to continue telling the people "not to worry." And the government wouldn't lie, right? Are you kidding? That's all they do. There were no weapons of mass destruction in Iraq; Clinton did have sexual relations with Lewinsky; Nixon did break into the Watergate building; and according to John Farmer, the Senior Counsel for the 9/11 Commission, in his book, *Truth: The Story Behind America's Defense on 9/11,* the official version of the 9/11 report was almost entirely *"based on false testimony and documents"* by government officials (which brings to mind the Warren Commission, the investigation into Kennedy's assassination and the "magic bullet"). Then there's former New Jersey state judge, Andrew R. Napolitano, who states in his book, *Exposing the Lies Government Has Told You, "the government lies to us regularly, consistently, systematically, and daily on matters great and small, but it prosecutes and jails those who lie to it."*

The point is there's no way that they could possibly stockpile enough food, medicine and supplies to sustain everyone for any duration of time (there's just not that much food in existence at this point in time on Earth) or even transport all of the people to the facilities (even if they were big enough). But do you think that they would come out and say, "We don't actually know of any global doomsday event on the horizon, but we just wanted to let you all know that at this point we do not have enough food and supplies or space in our underground bases to sustain everyone in the country/world IF any type of global catastrophe were to hit. As of now, if such an occurrence were to happen, you would have to protect yourselves. Sorry, peace be with you." Really? I honestly can't see it. It is irrelevant whether they actually know of an imminent catastrophe or not, though; they're just not going to say anything either way. In fact, since they can't protect us, it's reasonable to assume that they would say "there's nothing to worry about, nothing's going to happen," to prevent widespread panic. That's the least they can do.

Regardless, we now know that the government, along with private agencies and some of the richest and most powerful people in the world are actually preparing for a global disaster and you're not. Their plans and facilities don't and won't include you, or your family. You're on your own and can't count on anyone else but yourselves. And they'll actually tell you this in FEMA's *Food and Water in an Emergency* (PDF). They pretty much let you know that you'll probably be on your own (like the victims of Katrina) if the shit hits the fan: *"If an earthquake, hurricane, winter storm, or other disaster strikes your community, you might not have access to food, water, and electricity for days or even weeks,"* warns the report. It goes on to say, *"by taking some time now to store emergency food and water supplies, you can provide for your entire family."* Yet, I can guarantee that the head of FEMA (now the head of the Department of Defense, or Secretary of Defense) is one of the "75 senior officials" that will be, or currently already is, in an underground bunker. Also, on the FEMA website it states: *"DISASTER. It strikes anytime, anywhere. It takes many forms -- a hurricane, an earthquake, a tornado, a flood, a fire or a hazardous spill, an act of nature or an act of terrorism. It builds over days or weeks, or hits suddenly, without warning. Every year, millions of Americans face disaster and its terrifying consequences."* That means IT COULD HAPPEN TO YOU, people! They're telling you, I'm telling you, the president's telling you, people that know a LOT more than you are all telling you, but no one listens.

In the end though, something just doesn't make much sense to me. Since there is no COC (continuity of civilians) plan, the government will survive the end of the world; but when they come out from their safe bunkers, there will be no citizens left to govern. Smart. I think at this point (especially given the direction our government has taken and what it has become in recent years) I'd prefer that those facilities were left for the people. Let the government fend for themselves just as they're going to let us (based on the fact that there's no COC); and when it's all over, we'll just start a new government. A 'new world order'--doesn't THAT seem simpler than the other way around? Besides, isn't the government supposed to be "of the people, by the people and for the people"? More like "of the government, by the government and for the government," and Bill Gates.

KNOWN UNDERGROUND GOVERNMENT FACILITIES

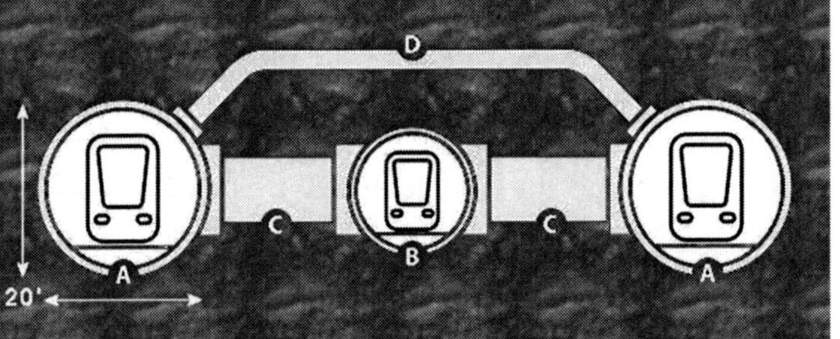

Is it even possible to build such large facilities underground? This is an extremely easy question to answer--yes. The English Channel project that I mentioned in the previous chapter was the largest engineering project in Europe at the time. Eleven boring machines used in the project drilled (3) parallel, 20ft high (and wide), tunnels 31.5 miles long, ultimately connecting France to England. Can you imagine how many people could fit into such an underground facility? If the tunnels consisted of 2 levels, and 2 people could live for an extended time in a 10ftx10ft living space, the tunnel would accommodate approximately 200,000 people. If train-style cabins are created, the number would then double to 400,000 people.

The Mount Weather Emergency Operations Center, on the other hand, is FEMA's underground command and emergency habitation in Virginia. According to the Continuity of Operations Plan, the 600,000sq.ft. underground facility ("Area B") is a major relocation site for the highest level of civilian and military officials in the event of national disaster.

Another secret bunker code-named "Greek Island," was built under the 340,000sq.ft. award-winning (five diamonds) luxury Greenbrier resort, just outside of White Sulphur Springs, West Virginia. The hotel, a facade, was also a front for the massive underground structure, which was kept *"stocked with supplies for 30 years in case of catastrophic disaster,"* until 1992. Seems like a lot of catastrophic disaster, "just in case" buildings were constructed. Are we still entirely sure nothing is going to happen?

The Raven Rock Mountain Complex (RRMC)

is a back-up Pentagon (shadow Pentagon) and entire military base located inside Raven Rock Mountain, east of Waynesboro, Pennsylvania. The deep underground base sits just 6 miles from Camp David, Maryland.

The Presidential Emergency Operations Center (PEOC) under the White House and, of course, the famed Cheyenne Mountain, home of NORAD, is another completely underground base, built 2,000 feet deep inside a mountain southwest of Colorado Springs, Colorado. The base is home to the Cheyenne Mountain Air Force. Coincidentally, the Cheyenne Mountain Zoo is also part of Cheyenne Mountain, again "just in case" I suppose. It can't hurt to have a secure underground facility to save the animals I guess. Which raises the question, why is everyone building underground bunkers for seeds, animals, DNA samples, and government heads, but not civilians? There should be at least one FEMA bunker in every city! Is it not obvious, by now (400yrs later) that we'd need them?

Next, the Denver International Airport, according to some, not an underground bunker or base, but an entire underground city—a city the elite can easily access, a short flight right to the airport on short notice, centrally located from any city in the U.S. The airport does raise unbelievable suspicion by itself. Built in 1995 on 34,000 acres, the airport is 10 times larger than any other airport in the world, making it as big as a "small city."

- The airport shut down its predecessor, the Stapleton International Airport with more gates/runways.
- The allotted construction costs were set at $1.7 billion and quickly escalated to $4.8 billion (double the cost of most airports) with 110 million cubic yards of earth moved (comparatively speaking, an extreme amount), although it was built on fairly flat ground.
- Enough fiber optics for communications, electrical and water pipes were installed to run an entire city.
- Enormous tunnels for "luggage conveyor belt" systems were included, that could accommodate three lanes of trucks simultaneously.

- In all, there's over 6 million square feet of space, an incredible amount for any "airport," anywhere in the world.
- And, of course, the murals. The murals are, beyond any doubt, at least haunting depictions of end-of-the-world scenarios, if not some type of cryptic message in themselves. [Notice the shooting star (asteroid impact), the military general with viral face mask killing peace in the form of two white doves (WW3), the destroyed buildings (earthquake, terrorist attack), all nations of children (black, white, brown) hiding underground amongst destroyed brick (bunkers), and everyone else weeping and carrying out some type of major exodus. If that's not apocalypse related, I'm an alien!]
- Freemason plaques and plaques referring to a non-existent "New World Airport Commission" abound nearby. All very suspicious indeed.

PRIVATE CORPORATION BUNKERS

Rest assured that Microsoft, Exxon Mobil, BP, Toyota, Samsung, GE, Volkswagen, AT&T, Ford, Nestlé, IBM, Sony, Hewlett-Packard, Trump, Google, Virgin, Boeing (I know, because I used to work for Boeing), and any other major corporation (or at least the intelligent ones) all have their own underground facility as backup, *just in case* something happens. At the first sign of trouble, they'll whisk their executives and the families of the executives away in helicopter to the site and lock them in with enough food, water, supplies and entertainment to last the long run. Sorry the general public isn't welcome. These aren't basic military bunkers mind you; we're talking nothing less than high end, luxurious (for an underground habitat) settings, with the finest comforts. Chef service, private medical teams, movie theatres, bowling alleys, absolutely only the best for the rich and famous. No, there's no need to make any kind of lifestyle change for these few, at least not until the supplies diminish and they're forced to come out that is. If nothing else though, it's good to know, though, that when everything else is gone, and the shit really hits the fan, Google will still be around. Thank the Gods!

PRIVATE CITIZEN BUNKERS

There are dozens of private underground bunker builders (including myself) that are the only other entities offering a safe haven during the end times for citizens. However, many are 'membership only' or sold as investment opportunities. Some even claim to pick and choose their occupants, which actually makes sense since you'll probably be the only ones left to repopulate the planet. A few provide the option to rent rather than buy (which may be a better financial alternative for many) where some are complete and total scams. In most cases, the structures are built underground, of course, pre-stocked with food, supplies, furniture and even entertainment (plan on being down there for quite a while). On notice of pending disaster, simply pack a few bags, throw the kids in the car and head for the shelter. If nothing else, it's nice for us mere citizens to know we have our own COC plan, a place to go that's safe, where our family and children can be protected IF a catastrophe ever were to occur, you know, "just in case." Think of it as just another insurance policy, if you will. You have life insurance, home insurance, car insurance, boat insurance, motorcycle insurance, RV insurance, flood insurance, fire insurance, earthquake insurance, hurricane insurance, title insurance, art insurance, probably insurance on your new smart phone, travel insurance, fraud protection against identity theft. Hell, you may even have insurance on your Shih Tzu. All of which will be null and void when the insurance companies and banks get destroyed or collapse along with the rest of society. Why not get a life insurance that will last?

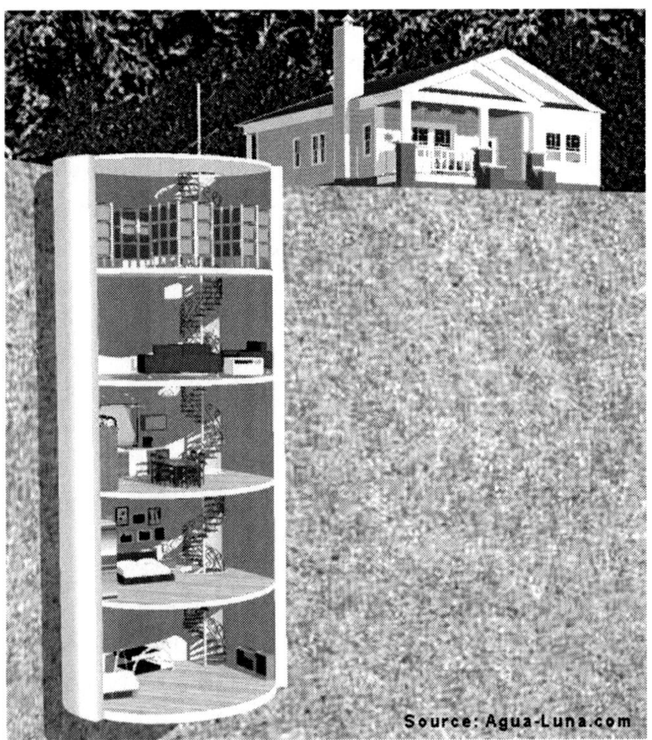
Source: Agua-Luna.com

ABANDONED UNDERGROUND MILITARY SITES FOR SALE

Or you could always just buy your own underground bunker, missile silo or mine; and stockpile it yourself with the supply list provided in the last chapter of this book. There are many current abandoned military silos and underground ammunition bunkers scattered around the United States, especially throughout Nebraska, Oklahoma and Kansas, which have already been converted to living quarters or are ready to be converted, available on the market today. A quick search may result in a new Armageddon-proof, summer home for you, your family, friends, co-workers, or just you and your girlfriend (let the wife fend for herself, right?). And of course you can build your own. Again, in the last chapter, I describe how to build a simple steel reinforced underground bunker, as well as a temporary emergency shelter that will withstand nuclear fallout.

BEFORE

AFTER

GOVERNMENT-RUN CITIZEN UNDERGROUND EMERGENCY SHELTERS

Sorry for the lead-up; like I said, there are none, because the government doesn't have a Continuity of Citizens plan. You'd think that FEMA or the National Guard would already have ready-made underground sites for us, around the U.S., just like they have for the government. But they don't. Hurricane Katrina victims were just bussed to the New Orleans Convention Center (which proceeded to flood) then to the Superdome (which proceeded to flood) and then to the Houston Astrodome (which was hit by hurricane Rita and... proceeded to flood). Does this system not sound ridiculous to anyone else? Yet, if ANYTHING like Katrina happened to a government facility, or to government leaders, members would be driven by limousine or flown by helicopter to the closest underground facility, which would, of course, be stocked and ready for them. The victims of New Orleans were mistreated, abandoned, ignored, starved, and forced into inhuman and dangerous conditions. FEMA's 'efforts' in New Orleans are negligent, if not criminal, to say the least. There were many horror stories: people actually died from heat exhaustion in facilities that were not climate-controlled; there were five-hour food lines, gang activity and drug deals. According to many survivors, women were found raped with their throats slit; children were found in bathrooms raped with their necks broken; and bodies piled up in corners and freezers. *"At times the screams became so loud, it was barbaric,"* said one survivor. Even if these are all untrue rumors, there were two official criminal rape charges filed, one involving a small child, along with ten deaths, all of which should have never been allowed to happen. In an article by CBS on August 31, 2005, entitled *Katrina Disaster Blog*, it states: *"The police chief in New Orleans is describing a horrific situation at the city's convention center."* Hoards of survivors broke in and started occupying it, because FEMA stopped picking up people at the location, destined for the Superdome. The blog continued, *"at least 15,000 hurricane refugees are trapped there, and beatings and rapes are taking place,"* said the police chief. The chief said he sent teams into the convention center, but that they were *"beaten back soon after they got inside."* Police Chief, Eddie Compass, further states, *"We have individuals who are getting raped, we have individuals who are getting beaten."* Again, "officially" there were "only" 10 deaths. These were ten people who had planned on government rescue, not dying. If you've ever been convicted of a felony charge, forget about government aid. FEMA and emergency aid workers have strict orders not to accept anyone with a felony into shelters. That is one way to prevent homicides (not that it worked). In fact, why not just bar felons from cities altogether, with that logic, then we'd have no crime?

But in my opinion, the way FEMA, the state and federal government handled the emergency shelter situation wasn't the worst of it. Several private businesses and organizations stepped up when they saw FEMA doing squat, only to be pushed aside, threatened, and sometimes even arrested by FEMA (the same thing occurred during the BP oil spill). The day after Katrina made landfall, over 50 different civilian aircrafts responded to dozens of hospital (and other agency) requests for help during the week that FEMA did nothing. They blanketed New Orleans from all directions only to have each and every effort blocked by FEMA. When asked why FEMA waved off pilots' evacuation attempts, the government's response was simply that the aircraft operators where not "authorized rescuers". I actually had no idea that one needed to have a "rescuing license" to help people. I wonder if that specialty requires a 4-year degree as well; (and you wonder why the world, as we know it, is coming to an end?). *"So they did absolutely nothing for fear of imprisonment"* said Thomas Judge, executive director of *Life Flight* of Maine, and the immediate past president of the *Association of Air Medical Services* (which sounds like enough "authorization" to me). *"Many planes and helicopters simply sat idle,"* Judge said. FEMA then proceeded to turn away even the Coast Guard as it was trying to deliver much-needed diesel fuel (the coast Guard isn't qualified either?) In September, 2005, Bob Herbert, reporter for The New York Times, confesses: *"Incredibly, when the out-of-state corporate owners of the hospital,* [Methodist Hospital in New

Orleans], *responded to the flooding by sending emergency relief supplies, they were confiscated at the airport by FEMA."* In another case, FEMA officials refused to allow Wal-Mart 18-wheeler trailers loaded with bottled water inside the evacuation zone. And *"doctors* [from the Chalmette Medical Center (now they must be qualified!)] *eager to help sick and injured evacuees were handed mops by federal officials who expressed concern about legal liability; And so they mopped, while people died around them,"* according to a September 16, 2005, article by CNN. Then there's FEMA's cry for "community service and outreach," (this one's my favorite). Two thousand trained (and, oh yes, "licensed") firefighters show up, "answering the call," only to sit for days in a hotel *"undergoing training on community relations, watching videos, and attending seminars on sexual harassment."* but they were well paid by FEMA for their time; and they now know all about sexual harassment in the workplace, a critical tool in any catastrophic situation? Eventually, the rescue workers were sent into the field to perform "secretarial or public relations" type tasks. Huh?

Another incident involved 91,000 tons of ice ($100 million of frozen water) that FEMA ordered for food storage, hospitals and relief efforts. But the ice never made it to New Orleans. According to The New York Times, the trucks were once again turned away by, you guessed it, FEMA. This isn't even funny anymore. Astor Hotel hires 10 buses to evacuate 500 people with their own money. When FEMA found out about the procession, they commandeered the buses, and told the people to *"join the thousands of other evacuees walking."* In fact, at one point, FEMA actually cut the Jefferson Parish district's emergency communications line. The sheriff discovered the incident and who was responsible for the terrorist act, restored the communications line and posted armed guards to protect it from FEMA. I mean, are we serious here? This sounds like a freaking, demented teen murder movie where the plot involves some psychotic, malicious villain and the deaths of innocent civilians. On the other hand, maybe this is exactly what it seems. But I really have no idea what they were trying to do; neither did the Select Bipartisan Committee that felt the need to investigate FEMA's actions.

Then on September 8th, finally FEMA did the unthinkable. After preventing American media coverage of the catastrophe, (on which CNN filed and won a lawsuit), FEMA began illegally (without warrant or cause) rounding up all civilians carrying legally-owned firearms, stating, *"No one will be able to be armed."* New Orleans Police Chief, Eddie Compass, said, *"Guns will be taken. Only law enforcement will be allowed to have guns."* (It's all fun and games until you mess with our freedom to bare arms). In other words, don't even think about barricading yourself in your own home in an attempt to protect yourself, your family, and your belongings during a crisis. Controversy regarding the September 8th order quickly sparked national attention when a 58-year-old New Orleans woman, barricaded in her well-provisioned house with a firearm for protection, was asked to relinquish it by several police officers who had illegally entered her home. When Patricia Konie refused, they jumped her, took the revolver and removed her from her home by force, for "failure to surrender her firearm." The entire event was captured on film. Instead of saving lives, the police were tasked (by FEMA) to round up all dreaded guns. The Second Amendment was written for these exact situations, where law and order and the 'protectors' of society are non-effective or non-existent. This was the case after Katrina and is what occurs after any catastrophe. Wayne La Pierre, the CEO of the National Rifle Association, said it best by stating, *"What we've seen in Louisiana - the breakdown of law and order in the aftermath of disaster - is exactly the kind of situation where the Second Amendment was intended to allow citizens to protect themselves."*

But when they try to do it again (and they will) know this: On October 9, 2006, a federal law prohibiting the seizure of lawfully-owned firearms during an emergency (the Disaster Recovery Personal Protection Act of 2006) was enacted into law (because of the Katrina instance). If you're going to try and tough it out on your own, don't trust anyone, especially not FEMA or the government. If you believe nothing else in this book, I say believe this... You don't want FEMA or any other government agency's help in a time of global catastrophe or any catastrophe for that matter! If you see FEMA, the police (or any *law enforcement* agency), or especially anyone with a patch on their arm, designating any of the following insignias, RUN FOR YOUR LIFE!

Africor LLC	Custer Battles	Pathfinder Security Services	MPRI, Inc.	Titan Corporation
Air Scan	MTCSC, Inc.	Global Enforce, Inc.	Raytheon	Vinnell Corporation
AONN	IANO Group, Inc.	Sharp End International	Red Star Aviation	Versar, Inc.
DynCorp	ITT Corporation	Northbridge Services Group	Triple Canopy, Inc.	Xe Services LLC
KBR	Northrop Grumman	Defion Internacional	MVM, Inc.	Xeros Services

These are Private Military Companies (PMC) or mercenaries, several of which are currently cleaning up the mess in Iraq and Afghanistan, and if they're cleaning up for the government here, it's not a good situation.

PUBLIC UNDERGROUND SHELTERS

But don't panic, there are public underground areas like subways, basements and malls, possibly near you, where you may be able to go in an emergency, IF they don't lock the doors on you that is:

- Albany, New York – Empire State Plaza is an underground city with banks, a YMCA, restaurants, food courts, retailers, a police station, a bus station and a visitor's Center.
- Atlanta, Georgia – Six city blocks of underground shopping centers/restaurants.
- Chicago, Illinois – Chicago Pedway is a layout of four disjointed tunnel systems, the largest covering about 10 blocks, connecting several buildings and stations.
- Crystal City, Virginia – A residential and commercial underground city of 173 shops, restaurants, banks, medical and other services centers. The site also connects to above-ground hotels, office buildings, and apartments, and is located near the Ronald Reagan Washington National Airport.

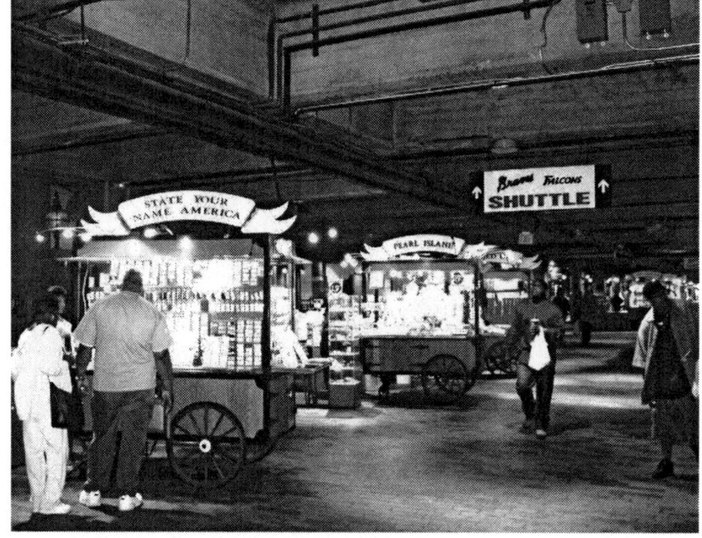

- Dallas, Texas – Dallas Pedestrian Network, tunnels connecting downtown buildings.
- Duluth, Minnesota – Convention Center Network is a system of tunnels under the Federal Courthouse and Convention Center.
- Houston, Texas – A seven-mile tunnel system under downtown Houston linking offices, hotels, banks, restaurants and stores.
- Irvine, California – A system of underground tunnels under the University of California connect campus buildings to the central utility plant.
- New York, New York – Subway stations traverse an enormous labyrinth of underground tunnels, eventually reaching an underground city located beneath the Rockefeller Center.
- Oklahoma City, Oklahoma – The Oklahoma City Underground is one of the country's most extensive underground systems, connecting 30 downtown buildings in 20 square blocks.
- Orland, Florida – Walt Disney World has tunnels for staff transportation, rest, preparation, and first aid.
- Philadelphia, Pennsylvania – There's a maze of underground concourses including the Suburban Station, Market East Station, the Market-Frankford Line, and Broad Street Line.
- Richmond, Virginia – Many of the underground tunnels are locked; but some still remain open connecting public and government buildings. Strangely, the purpose of the tunnels is not known; some say that they were built as part of an emergency evacuation plan though.
- Rochester, Minnesota – The Mayo Clinic's 'subway' connects downtown buildings via underground tunnels with the clinic.
- Rochester, New York – Nazareth College and the Rochester Institute of Technology, both have a system of underground tunnels going from dorms to campus buildings.
- Seattle, Washington – The new city of downtown Seattle was literally built right on top of the old one which can be accessed through several street and hotel locations from Westlake to the bus tunnel and from Two Union Square to Rainier Square.
- Washington, D.C. – Every building in the Capitol Complex connects through underground tunnels, which provides passage from legislative office to legislative office. The tunnels connecting office buildings are open to the public, but those to the Capitol require security clearance.

Source: tequilamike

CHAPTER 6

DOWN THE RABBIT HOLE: DAY 1

The scenarios following a doomsday-type event are easy to predict and document, even easier than calculating the actual event itself. How is that possible? It is because they've all occurred before. To some degree, every catastrophic event has taken place on this planet at some point in time. By combining historical data results of the different disasters with today's statistical reports, we're able to predict and foresee future aftermath scenarios. Although many of these scenarios have global consequences, most only affect a localized area, but by multiplying the smaller outcomes by several times, we're able to contemplate possible planetary cataclysms. For example, in the summer of 2005 we witnessed the surreal aftermath of mass confusion, chaos and death from Hurricane Katrina days and weeks after the hurricane made landfall. It was an eerie scene to our otherwise normal existence. We observed, first-hand, what only a class-3 hurricane and relatively small 20-foot tidal surge would do to a major metropolitan city of over one million occupants. The same situation transpired on the other side of the planet earlier this year when several earthquakes thoroughly wrecked Japan, the largest of which measured 9.0 on the Richter scale. As casualty reports, already in the thousands, just started to trickle in, an enormous tsunami (which would ultimately hit the U.S.) would further massacre the region, washing society out to sea. And yet the tragedy didn't stop there. The region then experienced multiple nuclear power plant explosions and evacuation due to radiation of Tokyo and other major cities, widespread fires, radioactive food found around the world, including United States and radioactive water dumped into the ocean.

The 2005 and 2011 accounts and results are much smaller than anything that would cause the world, as we know it, to end; however, by multiplying the size of the hurricane/earthquake and tsunami several times, a viable working model of the demise of the human race could be created. In our model, dozens of class-5 or 6 hurricanes and hundreds of 30+ magnitude earthquakes (or larger) hit continental coastlines worldwide with enough force to unearth sidewalks and disintegrate every manmade structure in sight. Following immediately in their wake, multiple 200ft+ tsunamis would submerge thousands more cities. Hundreds of millions of people would instantly wash out to sea or inland into neighboring countries; many more would die in place while gasping their final breaths, flapping aimlessly amongst floating, soggy sheetrock and shingling. Later, thousands of bodies will wash back up on the surrounding shorelines (which is what occurred in Japan).

We're talking massive, devastating effects on social order and structure, ridiculously delayed response times due to larger damage areas, the unavoidable collapse of trade, economics and most governmental bodies; all of which equal one example of an 'apocalypse' of human civilization as we know it. In the following sections, I have compiled the results of historical and statistical data and applied reconstructive computing tools to document current sociological, psychological, individual, and group traits. I have investigated and documented 20 years worth of recounted testimonies, and used reactions and behaviors during past emergency situations to calculate and describe actions, reactions and circumstances that would unfold immediately before, during, and after an event of epoch proportions. These illustrations will show you accurately step-by-step what will transpire, and conversely, what you'll need to know in the few hours leading up to several likely events, the day of the event(s), the days, weeks and months after the event(s), and future years to come.

Short term survival in the form of food, water, shelter, security and warmth, (all things that until now have been provided for you and therefore have been taken for granted), will need to be obtained by <u>ANY</u> means possible just before or during the immediate aftermath. This is a critical time for survival--not just the event, but the following weeks to come, as well. It will be an enormous shock to your psyche, considering that just last week the most important elements in your life were your Facebook page, American Idol (or Sunday Night Football), that new Smart Phone, graduating from high school or college, breast implants (yours or hers), brand-name clothes, hair styles, that promotion at work, or just making sure your $200,000 house and $35,000 car were cleaned and polished. These 'all new' necessities will cause you to take stock of your priorities. It may cause you to make some ethical decisions or take unethical actions, just to keep you and your family and children alive and safe--decisions you may not have deemed justifiable a few days ago. You may sit here, even now, reading this and say that you wouldn't sacrifice your values for any reason, that you would show your children that even in the face of all evil and destruction, being a "good" person is what's most important in life. But during these times it's not about right and wrong, good and evil; it really only comes down to whether you want your family to live or not, but that's completely up to you. Or maybe you're the type of person to whom such a dilemma is not an issue; maybe you have no moral compass to speak of, so making the following essential 'questionable' choices won't be a problem. You then, my friend, are one of the lucky ones. Point is, only you can save your own family.

In all fairness to 'humanity' and our great devotion to ingenuity, and although I discuss all likely possible end-time instances, it's the personal opinion of this author that we'll probably meet our maker at the hands of ourselves. We were literally on the verge of nuclear war for around 50 years straight; and now it looks like we're heading in that direction again with North Korea, Iran, Russia and who knows what dirty bomb-carrying Islamic or home-grown terrorist(s). Contrarily, we've never been on the cusp of a super earthquake (except for California, that is), or an imminent viral pandemic, or a long-term impending asteroid strike. This is why I've chosen to discuss in depth, more so than the others, what will happen, and how to prepare for and survive an all-out nuclear attack. On the same note, the occurrence of some types of events will most likely directly, or unilaterally, cause or trigger the onslaught of several others. For example, the impact of a major asteroid would trigger massive global earthquakes, which would produce super volcanoes and giant tsunamis. A disaster of this magnitude could possibly create a polar shift, ultimately triggering a full, planet-wide economic collapse, which would, in-turn, create horrible living conditions and pandemics (just as we see unfolding in Haiti). The resulting climate change would also generate massive flooding and probably even the next ice age. A major nuclear endeavor on the other hand, would most likely create an economic strain and failure, prompting a full collapse of multiple government structures, which would finally elicit the invasion of the fallen countries themselves. To illustrate these conjoining and often overlapping life-altering timelines, I've tried to list them in an understandable, yet, relatively chronological order, again starting with the most likely:

WORLD WAR III: DAY 1

"I know not with what weapons WW3 will be fought, but WW4 will be fought with sticks and stones."

- Albert Einstein

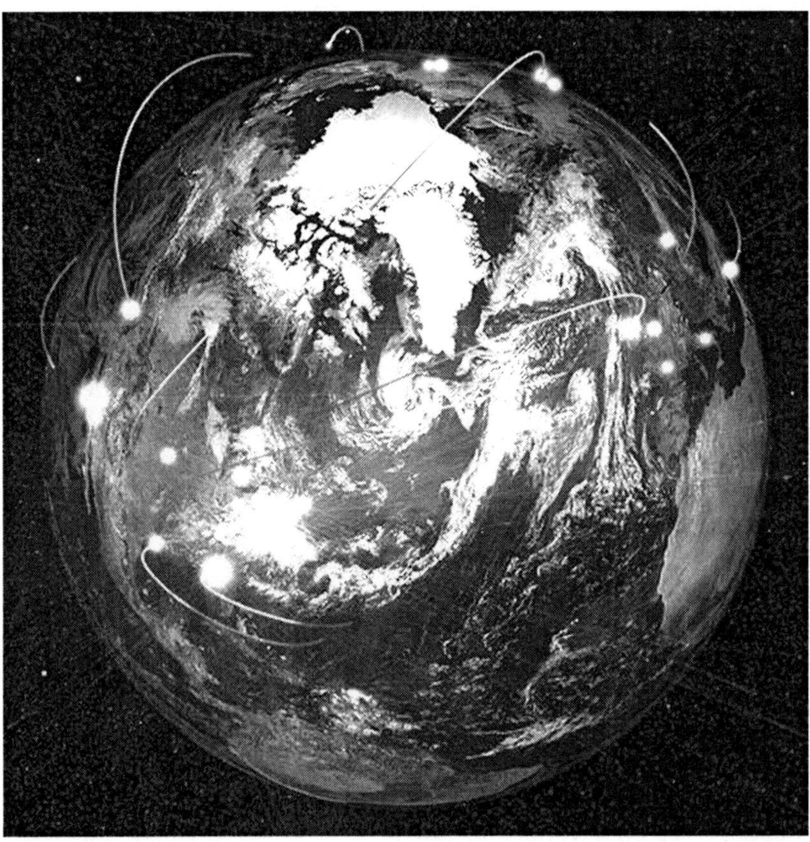

Although World War III could be fought with conventional weapons (tanks, soldiers, fighter planes, etc.), strategists know that it probably won't be. That's why whenever someone talks about WW3 today; he's probably referring to an all-out, full-scale nuclear war. Several, possibly dozens, of countries would be volleying land, air, sea, and sub-aquatic-based ballistic missiles at each other. Eventually, probably within days to weeks, this would end with the total annihilation of the highest populated regions on the planet. The good news about this type of cataclysmic event is that it's very survivable, IF you can make a few preparations well before, or even just before, during or immediately after any actual bombings or explosions take place.

More than likely, the days leading up to a nuclear attack will be filled with total news coverage talking about some country or another, probably communist in structure, breaking some Nuclear Non-Proliferation Agreement Treaty or what not, which is now testing or gathering nuclear material for use in a "nuclear power plant." The reports will announce how the U.S. and the U.N. are trying to "get them back to the table" to "have talks"--in other words, channel 7 news every day of the week lately. Almost as likely, though, an out of nowhere surprise attack will come with no warning of any kind whatsoever (like what happened on September 11), in which case we (or another nation, if we're the ones doing the surprising) will retaliate with our/their nuclear warhead arsenal. Either way, the Ballistic Missile Early Warning System (BMEWS) would notice an incoming missile about an hour or two out; and IF conveyed to the public in a timely manner, there would be plenty of time for most of us to take shelter. However, the unfortunate truth is that, more than likely, the people wouldn't be notified of such a danger until it was actually too late to do anything about it. In the end, the *interruption of your originally scheduled program for a national emergency broadcast* may be the only notice you get, if not the sound of the actual nuclear bomb, itself, exploding on the other side of town. If you suspect imminent disaster but believe you're being kept in the dark, tune multiple A.M.-F.M. radios or televisions to surrounding nearby cities or radio stations. When one suddenly goes off the air, you can calculate the approximate arrival time and the fallout's direction and speed by wind speed and direction in reference to the location of that station.

The first sign of a nuclear detonation is the characteristic white, blinding flash and resulting EMP (electro-magnetic pulse). Then comes intense pressure from the blast often described as tornado strength winds, coupled with concentrated thermal energy that will melt clothing and flesh right off your body. Both are easily avoidable by merely taking immediate cover behind a large vehicle, building, or just lying on the ground, flat (which minimizes exposure by 800%). But whatever you do, don't hesitate. The blast from a 500kt (kiloton) explosion over 2 miles away, will arrive at your location in less than 10 seconds. If you're close enough to hear the blast and see the mushroom cloud, but not feel the thermal winds, you are one of the lucky ones and will only have to deal with fallout.

Fallout is a baby powder-like substance of visible or non-visible radioactive particles that "falls out" of the sky. It will contaminate anything that is not sealed or covered up. Although it is extremely dangerous initially, it dissipates rather quickly. For example: Fallout emitting gamma ray radiation at a rate over 500R/hr (fatal, if exposed to for one hour), weakens to $1/10^{th}$ the danger in 7 hours and $1/100^{th}$ two days later. The trick will simply be to have adequate shelter until it dissipates, which again I'll discuss in the last chapter. The mushroom cloud carries the matter up into the sky rapidly, but the heavier, more dangerous debris falls back down within a matter of minutes. Lighter, less-contaminated particles will take several hours, possibly days or weeks, to

drift back to the ground, carried for hundreds of miles by trade winds. Rain concentrates fallout into localized areas, forming hotspots of intense radiation, yet, also preventing it from blowing and traveling great distances.

At the first warning of an imminent nuclear or terrorist 'dirty bomb' attack, getting to, or quickly building and stocking a suitable shelter will prove crucial. You'll only have a matter of minutes if you are close to ground zero (within a 10 mile radius). You may have 30 minutes to an hour preparation time if you're further away (30-mile radius) with the wind blowing towards you. If you're even further away (50-mile radius) with the wind blowing towards you, you may have a couple hours to get situated before the fallout hits. First, depending on how much time you have, you'll have to decide whether to make a run for your home/shelter, or stay put. Those located outside the 30-mile radius and against the wind from ground zero, should try to get as far away from the area as possible; but you'll have to take into account that (a) the roads will most likely be blocked/barricaded by debris, officials, or fallout, or completely congested and impassable with the now ensuing mass exodus of vehicles; and (b) the winds may shift, in which case you'd be stuck in the open with no protection of any kind. Either way it's important to prevent inhalation or absorption of dust by covering your mouth and nose with a dust mask (preferable N95 rated) or folded t-shirt (folded a few times) and your eyes with sunglasses and a hat.

If you decide to evacuate, make sure that you understand the direction of the blast in relation to the direction and speed of the wind. But make your decision quickly; it's better to be somewhere two hours too early, than two minutes too late, exposing yourself and your family to a horrific fate. If you flee traveling with the wind with ground zero behind you, the dust will quickly overtake you, since the wind is always traveling faster than the speed at which you are able to walk (2 mph) or are even able to drive in a disastrous and chaos-filled region (about 5 mph). On the other hand, if you travel at a right angle to the wind, you'll eventually hit a crosswind going in the opposite direction, neither with nor against the fallout wind. The best case scenario, of course, would be that the wind is blowing away from you, away from the direction you need to go and towards the explosion, which would carry the fallout away from you. With multiple detonations, judging wind speeds and calculating fallout direction can get a bit tricky, making navigating safely through radiation free areas and escape all but impossible. With fallout, it's all about the winds.

If you chose to flee, but now find you'll soon caught in the fallout, don an N95 particle respirator or dust mask, hooded rain poncho, rain boots, rubber gloves, shop dust glasses and take Potassium Iodide (KI) or Potassium Iodate (KI03) tablets (for thyroid protection against cancer-causing radioactive iodine). If you don't have tablets, topically apply tincture of iodine or Betadine. Adults apply 8ml (one measuring teaspoon is roughly 5ml) of a 2% tincture of iodine on the abdomen or forearm daily, at least 2 hours prior to possible exposure. Children 3 to 18 yrs old or weighing less than 150 lbs., apply 4ml daily. Children 1 month to 3 years apply 2ml daily. Newborn infants to 1 month, apply 1ml daily. Do NOT ingest iodine skin applicants. If you don't have any of these supplies and there's no shelter in the immediate vicinity, your only hope is to find a washout going under the road or some other subterraneous void or cavity and barricade the entrances. Or as a last option take shelter under an overpass or bridge.

Eventually, the fallout will most likely come, though, so time is critical. First and foremost, you'll need to go to your shelter (if you have taken the time to build one) or any previously discussed adequate community underground area. If you don't have access to a bomb shelter, subway or underground ammunition storage bunker (which most of us don't) fortifying a basement, cellar or just the lowest floor of the nearest building may be your best option. Contrary to popular belief, you can last up to 10 weeks without food (25 if you're obese) and 10 days without water (in cooler weather), but only a few hours in radioactive fallout without protection. If you have more than 2 adults in your party and at least several hours warning, it's a good idea to divide up work with women and children building the barricade (refer to the last chapter in this book), while men go for supplies (in accordance with the shopping list in the *Preparations* section), as it's extremely likely that water, food, fuel, batteries, ammunition and any other necessities will go fast. It's also important to realize that the food and supplies aren't critical to sustain you through and survive the fallout. That's not the reason you're gathering them now; it's to help you survive after the fallout in a post-apocalyptic world where such supplies will be completely non-existent. If you don't take the time to round them up now, there will be nothing left when you come out of your shelter. And what a shame it would ultimately be if you were to survive the end of the world, only to die of starvation in the new world. Those tasked with the fallout shelter should also divide up the work; mother and a child building the shelter, while another child/children or friends go for household supplies and water.

Source: lazzarello

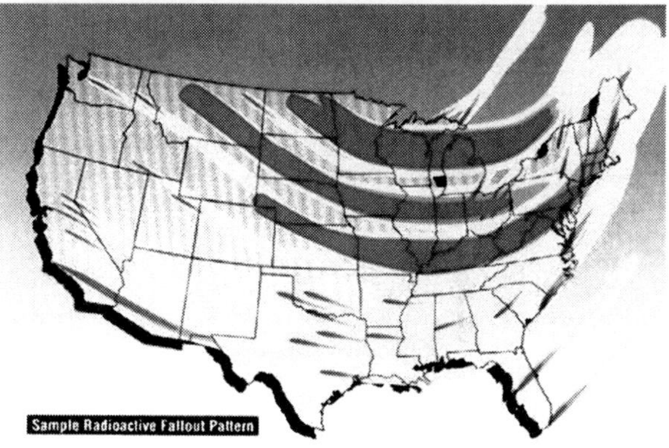

Sample Radioactive Fallout Pattern

Source FEMA

WATER

It's important to start storing water as soon as possible, before city water is disrupted from the blasts and/or the pressure fails as everyone in the city begins filling up bathtubs.

1. Turn on the faucets and let all bathtubs, sinks, washing machines, etc. fill up. Simultaneously, make use of the hose by filling buckets, kiddie pools, swimming pools, garbage cans (cleaned with bleach), ice chests, water beds, blow-up beds, cardboard boxes (lined with garbage bags), or anything else that will hold water. The containers of water without lids will need to be covered and taped off with plastic; in the same manner the sinks should be covered with garbage bags and the bathtub with the shower curtain. Also, it's a good idea to place the larger containers, like garbage cans or cardboard boxes, near the shelter before filling, since once containers are weighed down with water they become immovable.
2. While filling large containers, take a minute to pull the refrigerator out from the wall, cut the 1/4in icemaker hose in back, flip it over onto, open the doors and drape the flowing icemaker hose inside.
3. Once the sinks are full, fill up pots/pans, plastic jugs (water is more important and doesn't go bad without refrigeration like juices or milk, so dump out the contents), plastic food storage containers (Tupperware), by submerging them into the full sink. These items will all go directly inside the barricade.

NOTE: Upon exiting your bunker, the water heater, toilet tank (the upper tank, not the bowl), will all be suitable to drink or use for cleaning and showering. But if there was ever the time, conserve! If any of the water containers will be used for long-term storage (longer than a few weeks) or in order to purify questionable water, add 1 teaspoon bleach per 10 gallons water, or bring to a boil.

4. While the rest of the containers are filling, begin transporting food from cabinets, the pantry, and refrigerator to the shelter. These goods should be plentiful since the typical person keeps months' worth of supplies in their cupboards at any given time and don't even know it. If you don't believe me, check. Take all your food out, put it on the floor and calculate how much you have. Food from the refrigerator and freezer should be the last to be transferred, and the first to be consumed. The cardboard box water storage containers and garbage bag liners can be used to transport large quantities of food, along with plastic grocery bags and back packs, all of which will prove useful upon exiting in a collapsed society. Give yourself plenty of time here; it takes awhile for 1 or 2 people to move 2 months worth of food and

water. Any food and water that won't fit in the shelter, place directly outside in easy arms-reach distance and covered in plastic drop clothes or tarps. Don't bring anything that needs to be cooked, and don't cook anything you bring. The potential for fire in what looks like a garbage heap is high and could be disastrous, not because of injury, but you'll burn down your only defense/protection from the radiation.

5. Lastly, don't forget to gather hand (not electric) can openers, (at least 2), batteries, flashlights, (candles and matches as a last option), battery-powered and wind-up radios, bowls, silverware, scissors, knives, first aid materials, prescribed medicines, smart devices, pillows, blankets, bedrolls (small mattress or cushions from couches), books, playing cards, toilet paper, toothbrushes, toothpaste, soap, clothes, plastic grocery bags, etc. Tools (possibly needed for digging out) such as small shovels, crow bars, car jacks, fire extinguishers, and the building supplies used in sealing off the house (plastic tarps, staple guns, staples, duct tape), should be placed just outside the shelter as well.

The remaining people should be well into building the shelter by now. If you manage to get caught outside in the fallout DON'T GO IN YOUR SHELTER! Not only will it defeat the point since you're already contaminated, by bringing the contamination inside you'll also be poisoning the only clean place around and everyone else in the process. As mentioned before, a cheap plastic emergency rain poncho and rubber boots (which can be easily hosed off), dust mask and dust goggles make traveling outside your shelter easy and safe.

SHELTER OCCUPANCY

Front of shelter removed for clarity.

When the shelter is complete and the supplies gathered or the fallout is well, falling, seal around, lock and barricade the last door (used to bring in supplies) with plastic and duct tape (especially if it's an exterior door), enter your shelter and pull in the remaining objects (mass), closing the crawl space behind you. If the crawl space is deep, leave some objects like books, bricks or sand bags inside which can be easily pushed into position from inside.

Patience and security at this point are all that's required to survive, at least for now. A few days, a few weeks, living in an area as big as a tent (1/20th the size of a prison cell) with several other people can be *Mad Hattening* to say the least; but trust me, it's better than the alternative. Games, books, sleep and storytelling, all of which I'm sure will be very foreign to your family, should help pass the time. Vulnerability from outside attack while being locked in a basement, blind, is very real. Keep guns and ammo close and make sure everyone can reload and use them, even in the dark. Information of any source is vital for the duration of shelter occupation; that's not to say, however, that you should run outside at the first mention of an 'all clear'. All incoming facts can be misleading, misstated, incomplete, or simply just lies.

Bathroom facilities will be carried out via a plastic grocery bag or bucket with a plastic grocery bag liner. (A small plastic office garbage can holds a regular plastic grocery bag perfectly.) Once the deed is done, a bit of sawdust, peat moss, sand, kitty litter or dirt gets thrown on top and the potty is ready for someone else. Once the bag is approximately 2/3 full, it can be tied off and placed outside the shelter. A sheet can be tacked up in a corner for privacy and the bag/bucket can be hung under the upper (exhaust) vent. For cleanliness (there's no shower) and toilet bag space reasons, toilet paper isn't a good idea. Stock up and clean with baby wipes instead.

Letting pets run free inside or outside the house is a bad option, both for their potential to die a miserable death and their ability to get into your supplies. Preparing for them inside the bunker is ideal, but if limited space and resources is an issue, at least keep them inside the house/building while safeguarding your supplies from them, keeping the option of 'putting them down' in mind. Aside from the family's love for a pet, a dog will prove a critical warning and security system after the event in a lawless land. Small pets can be caged in small (just larger than the animal) cages and placed or hung (for space) inside the shelter. Keep in mind however, that these animals won't serve much use, (other than food) in a post-apocalyptic world. Larger animals or livestock also should at least be brought into the home/building and kept in additional rooms with ample food and water supplies. It's not the best case scenario, but it's better than being trapped outside in the fallout. Once the emergency has passed, the livestock can still be eaten or used (discussed in *Chapter 9*) safely.

If you happen to have any radiological instruments such as Geiger counters, survey meters and/or dosimeters, their use will be a deciding factor in determining when it's safe to leave the shelter. If not, monitor radio updates or online information on area-specific radiation levels for as long as possible/practical. All electronics should be powered down, unplugged, with the antenna removed and placed in a Faraday EMP cage or wrapped in a non-conductive insulation material (paper, bubble wrap, plastic, etc.) and buried or stored in a grounded metal container or aluminum foil in order to reduce the chance of damage from the EMP.

WHEN IT'S SAFE TO COME OUT

After a few days, it may be safe to come out. Don your rain poncho and other gear and check the scene. If you're waiting for broadcasted conditions, or have your own Geiger counter, listen/watch for ratings lower than 30R, which is still 1000 times higher than normal levels and would be dangerous to pregnant women and infants, but should be safe enough for you; 50R—some sickness felt; 200R—radiation sickness, vomiting, loss of hair; 400R—extreme radiation sickness, 50% will die within 3 weeks; 600R—100% casualty rate within the first week or 2.

Source: lazzarello

No matter the time of day, it will be dark outside and there will still be large quantities of semi-radioactive dust all over. Rooms where windows weren't protected will also be filled with radioactive fallout dust. If you have a stack of firewood or a garden, for example, that you wanted to keep safe, it should have been covered with tarps beforehand. Questionable or stagnant water not touched by fallout needs to be boiled or bleached with 1/4 teaspoon of bleach per gallon before drinking to kill any bacteria. Boiling or bleaching water DOES NOT KILL RADIOACTIVE DUST! How long should you boil water to make it safe to drink? The correct amount of time is 0 minutes. That's right, zero minutes. According to the Wilderness Medical Society, *"water temperatures above 160°F kill all pathogens within 30 minutes and above 185°F within a few minutes. In the time it takes for the water to reach the boiling point (212° F), all pathogens will be killed, even at high altitude."* Upon returning, rinse everything off before re-entry. Contrary to popular belief, you don't become radioactive by coming into contact with radioactive fallout. If you believe any outer garments, skin or hair has been contaminated, just rinse outside with shampoo thoroughly. Leave the shampoo and water outside before you leave, otherwise, you'd have to come into the shelter, contaminated, in order to retrieve it.

Any food or water stored in sealed containers left outside the building or just outside the shelter can be easily made safe to consume by simply brushing or hosing off. Any radiation that entered the contents will be safe as long as no dust has entered the container. If, for any reason, anyone does happen to come down with what's called "radiation sickness" (nausea) it's 100% recoverable and cannot be passed on to others.

Keep in mind before departing, though, that you alone are responsible for the safety and well-being of yourself and your family or group, no one else, and especially not the government. Don't wait for government calls for evacuation or steps of home protection. In order to ensure you have enough food and supplies to last the duration, you must take ANY and ALL actions necessary, regardless of what anyone else says or directs you to do.

ASTEROID IMPACT: DAY 1

On January 7, 2002, a 300-meter-wide Near-Earth Asteroid dubbed "2001 YB5" just missed colliding into the Earth by a mere 830,000km., (only twice the distance to our moon). The miss, however, isn't the scary part; there are literally almost 20,000 of these asteroids in the inner solar system racing around us all the time. The disturbing part is that there was almost no warning from December 25th on, when the 3-football-field- by 6-football-field-wide rock was discovered.

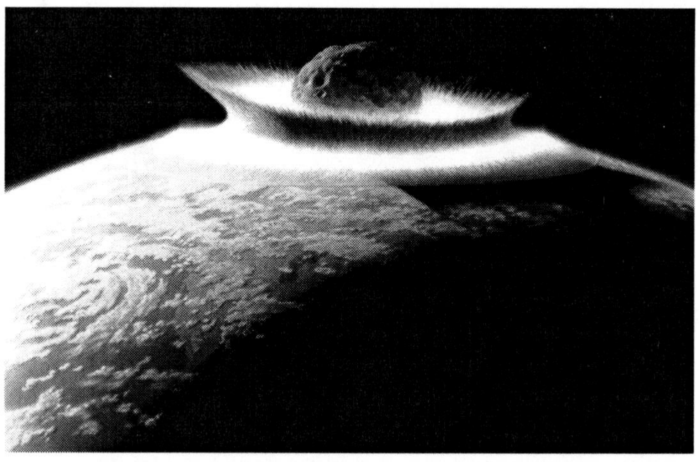

With less than two weeks notice, you'll have barely enough time to stockpile and travel to an underground location before impact. In many cases, the comet won't be noticed at all by optical observations. However, NORAD'S early missile detection system and NASA's network of space-directed satellites should get a radar lock on any incoming, leading debris fields several hours before a main, large-body impact. Although not globally devastating, these smaller Earth collisions will destroy major cities worldwide, creating panic and chaos among the masses. When the smaller impacts finally subside, there will be a brief time of "peace" leading up to the major event, which will subsequently be followed by a similar duration of calmness, before the tail end of debris again rains down upon us, wiping out whatever's left. It's important to utilize these times of temporary peace to gather supplies and make a dash for an underground secure bunker, such as a bomb shelter, building's basement or local sub-terrain subway system. You may only have hours, maybe minutes before the shockwave and thermal blast from the main collision completely obliterates any above-ground structures, so time is critical.

Even though the total duration of the entire meteor episode shouldn't last more than a day, it would essentially bombard the entire planet with a spray of high velocity rocks, since Earth completes a revolution in 24hrs. Imagine holding a globe at chest level and giving it a spin while a mate slowly pours out a bag of pebbles (with one nice-sized stone mixed in) upon it. The resulting destruction and effect would cover the entire planet, making for uncomfortable above-ground living conditions, to say the least.

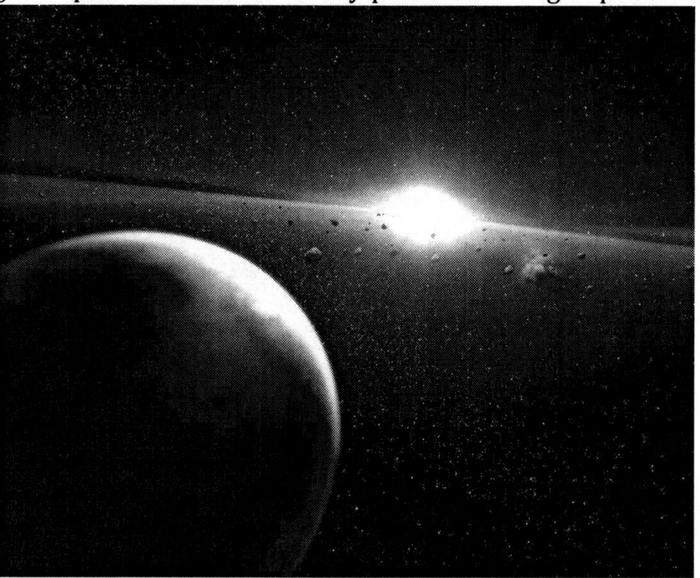

Because of the size of the asteroid and the velocity at which it hits, it won't matter if it makes contact in the ocean or on land; both are land impacts, burning off almost unnoticeable amounts of the rock's material mass upon entry. The Earth's crust will be the only thing stopping it at this point, exploding and incinerating most of the object and soil in the region, sending massive amounts of debris into the atmosphere and super-heating the air like an oven. At 500°F+, almost all living things and buildings will reach their flash point, spontaneously combusting, setting off planet-wide forest and field fires, sending a few million more tons of ash and smoke into the air, completely blocking out what sunshine remains, while sending the planet into a nuclear winter for several days, possibly even weeks, maybe months. The impact will most likely shift the already unstable tectonic plates and probably the axis itself causing massive earthquakes, super tsunamis, and global super volcanic eruptions, just like what occurred in Japan this year.

Although due to a different cause, the results are extremely similar to the nuclear Armageddon described in detail above. Using the same preparation list, round up as much food, water and supplies as possible before heading underground. A short stop at the local store should yield several weeks worth of necessities; but act quickly; everyone and their brother will be thinking and doing the same thing. Once underground, although not mandatory, it's not a bad idea to barricade the entrances with insulated, non-flammable materials, like rocks, sand bags, refrigerators, freezers, metal garbage cans filled with dirt, etc. This will keep the shelter cool until the heat dissipates outside; and since hot air rises, you shouldn't be affected in the tunnels (or basement) below. However, a small plastic kiddie pool filled with water isn't a bad backup plan to keep cool, *just in case.*

This extreme heat will dissipate fairly quickly (days, weeks) especially once the Sun is blocked out, in fact you may even see snow in the summer time. Still, wait as long as possible to step outside. Once a suitable time has lapsed, test the outside air by sticking a long broom, board or pole with a sheet of paper or plastic taped to the end, (not your hand). It may still be uncomfortably warm, but if it's not enough to melt the plastic tape, burn the sheet of paper or straw bristles, it will be safe to traverse. You won't have to worry about nuclear ash as much as during an all-out nuclear attack, but wearing an N95 dust mask and raincoat can't hurt. Full safety glasses are also a good idea since the tissue of the eye is the most sensitive surface on the human body. Limited supply expeditions are recommended for the first few days; even if it's may be dead winter, the nights outside will be scorchers, making heat exhaustion, heat stroke, and dehydration dangerously real scenarios.

Upon your return to the world, you will notice that most structures and trees will be entirely destroyed or still burning, power and utilities a thing of the past. Dark, dust-filled clouds dominating the sky for up to a year will constantly rain fine particles of soot and ash upon the planet, covering everything and anything that may have survived with a thick, snow-like coat. If you didn't stockpile enough food to outlast the ordeal beforehand, rounding up food and water will be critical and almost impossible now. Besides existing underground stashes of food or surviving houses/buildings with full pantries, there will be pocketed areas of life that were protected from the blast, located on the far sides (from ground zero) of mountains and hills, and the near sides of valleys and river banks. The mountains, hills, valleys and walls of river banks will protect plant and animal life in the area from the blast, since the wave emanates out and away from ground-zero. Gather as many of these resources as possible as soon as possible, as they will eventually die out from the heat, lack of food, sunlight, drinkable water and nutrition if they haven't already. If you can sustain yourself in such a fashion until the Sun shines again, new growth will appear as life begins anew.

SUPER STORMS: DAY 1

With climate change we're seeing an increase in unpredictable, abnormal storm activity across the globe. Multiple and more frequent massive earthquakes and hurricanes bring on repetitive tsunamis, numerous tornados, uncharacteristically dry, seasonally-induced forest fires, torrential rain causing mudslides and epic cold front-producing blizzards, all of which have steadily grown in size and frequency over just the last 10 years. In the next 10, we can expect the same increase to the point that they will occur together around the globe or in the same location, continuously. And although you may be safe from hurricanes where you live, the problem with this scenario is that your region is most likely affected by or vulnerable to at least one of the above catastrophes annually.

EARTHQUAKES

Earthquakes are famous for hitting without warning. Most earthquakes are actually foreshocks to the main event, which, in itself, should be warning enough for any who know this. Given the magnitude of earthquakes it will take to bring on the end of the world, taking the appropriate measures at this point really won't matter. So if you haven't already made the necessary preparations, the only thing you can do is take cover (which isn't really much of an option).

The best place to be in a massive world-destroying earthquake is on a different planet. The second best place to be is in your car driving down a deserted, interstate highway (which can actually be fun, trust me, I know.) However, not too many people spend the majority of their life driving down obscure back roads. If you're in a house or office (where most of us spend our time) try to make it outside and away from the building(s). I know most "experts" in this field say to remain where you are; but if you've ever been inside and outside a building during a good-sized earthquake, you'll pick the latter. Outside, in the open (where you don't want to be in a lightning storm) is the single best place you can be in an earthquake. If you can't get outside to safety before sh&# literally starts falling on your head, push a strong desk or coffee table into the corner of a room towards the center of the building, away from any glass or windows; open as many doors as possible so that at the very least if the building shifts, you won't be trapped inside, and dive for cover. You'll often hear people tell you to head for a doorway; however, most doorway frames, (especially in modern home construction), aren't load-bearing; and because of the lack of girth protection, they are just a little better than anywhere else. Conversely, close proximity to the façade of the building, that is to say, any outside wall, would be the most dangerous place to be, as façades usually fall away first.

If, in the end, you find yourself trapped (but not pinned) under rubble, try to determine the shortest route out (of the rubble, not necessarily the building), and start moving away the loose debris in that direction. In this case, you Do Not want to wait for help, since (a) help is probably trapped as well, and (b) you'll soon start running out of energy (and maybe air) and won't even be able to dig yourself out soon. Studies have shown that many earthquake survivors died just feet from safety, but were told to do nothing and wait for help. Keep a cool head, pace yourself, and remain calm. You don't want adrenaline racing though your body. It will only eat up your calories that much faster. Most likely the sprinklers will be triggered in the chaos, replenishing whatever water you'll be losing as you attempt to escape (if the water lines are still intact). Catch the water with whatever means possible, building

a small dam, or even soaking it up with clothes, you may be here for awhile. Yelling for help is really inefficient; try tapping on metal (with metal) or even clapping, both of which will be carried a much further distance. In a concrete or brick structure (which is what most office buildings are made of) always keeping a simple rock pick hammer and small jack under your desk can help facilitate escape by several magnitudes and can mean the difference between life and death. Although many earthquake-prone areas have strict building codes minimizing potential damage, non-earthquake-prone areas have no such construction regulations and will fail drastically in a super earthquake scenario. All power to even the unaffected parts of the city will be lost as power plants and nuclear reactors fail from sustained damage. In the long run, expect gas and fuel explosions, widespread fire, nuclear leaks, radiation contamination and hundreds of thousands missing.

HURRICANES

If Katrina is any sign, your mayor will wait until the last moment to give the call to evacuate. And for most, that will again be too late. I'm not sure why time after time we pass through the same disasters only to react in the same way. But I suppose that's how sheep act. First come the winds, in access of 150mph, flipping cars, toppling homes and sending anything above ground into the next county. You'll most likely be at work in some high-rise office, unable to make it to safety. In this case you don't want to head to the basement as it'll soon be flooded; and since the winds increase in a hurricane with height, don't head past the 10th floor either. On this note, keep in mind that the strongest winds will hit when the right inner side of the eyewall passes directly over.

TORNADOS

April 19, 2011, a Supercell covering 19 states releases an epic 1,500 cases of tornadoes, high winds and belts of hail with 51 tornadoes touching down in Illinois alone in a 6 hour period. April 27, 2011, a Supercell stretching from Texas to New York unleashes over 30 tornadoes, completely wiping out the town of Pleasant Grove, Alabama, killing over 200 people. Similar accounts unfolded every single day throughout the month of April, breaking all subsequent records ever held. Tornadoes, especially when they're numerous and focalized, can be more destructive than both a major hurricane and earthquake combined, demonstrating increased levels of both's devastating traits. For example, while hurricane winds can register as high as 150mph, tornado winds can surpass 300mph. This is due to the fact that a tornado is much smaller in diameter, and the rate at which the force of rotation is factored is by circumference of the circle. We see this in a spinning wheel with the outside spinning much slower than the inside. The difference in wind speeds can be the determining element in major destruction, especially in areas not prone to such occurrences. If you're not underground, expect your wood or even brick home to implode like the World Trade Center, trapping you and your family inside. Keeping food and water, a chainsaw, pry bar and car jack around will come in handy working your way out of the rubble.

Once free, for the briefest of time, you'll witness a moment of serene silence as the world literally crumbles around you, quickly broken by the faintest of panicked moan-like screams as survivors open their eyes to the devastation unfolding. Horrific, widespread panic will ensue within seconds. Instantly, caused by shear fear, adrenaline (technically epinephrine) dumps into the body. It expands air passages, stimulates glucose in the muscles and excites firing electrons in the brain, awakening you from a robotic sheep-like trance for the first time in years. Self-preservation will kick in automatically, driving you to safety; but, once there, you'll feel the desire to double back and save others. Everyone will be a bloody mess; dirty, dying, dead.

TSUNAMIS

In the super hurricanes, super earthquakes, super volcanoes and asteroid impact scenarios you'll have super tsunamis, which are numerous walls of massive water that raise the level of the sea by 5-30 meters, engulfing and flooding the already devastated seaboard cities far and wide. The water will fill up your home or office (on lower floors) before you have a chance to even wake up. Entire subdivisions will be physically disconnected from the grid, severing all phone, gas and electric lines, catch on fire and literally be swept out to sea like a Viking funeral. Days later, thousands of bodies will wash up on shorelines among the rest of the debris. Eventually, the economy will take hit after hit from the incident, with total collapse imminent. Sound familiar? It's exactly what transpired in Japan.

In the end, you'll most likely save several lives today, which later may prove to help and/or harm you, as these very same people begin to prove dangerous competition for what little food, shelter and supplies are left in a world without structure, order and control. But we're getting ahead of ourselves. As the adrenaline subsides and shock and cold set in, your panic dissipates. You begin to feel fear which, in this case, is actually a good thing. This part of the brain has remained pretty much dormant, unneeded, unwanted, asleep, ever since you were a teenager, living life to the fullest. This part of your brain had no place in yesterday's society; but this new-felt fear will awaken you and be the driving force, pushing you to survive in a society that's collapsed, literally. This emergency mode/survival instinct will transform into an actual cognitive thought process that will, at least for several weeks, guide your every decision, action and reaction.

VIRAL OUTBREAK: DAY 1

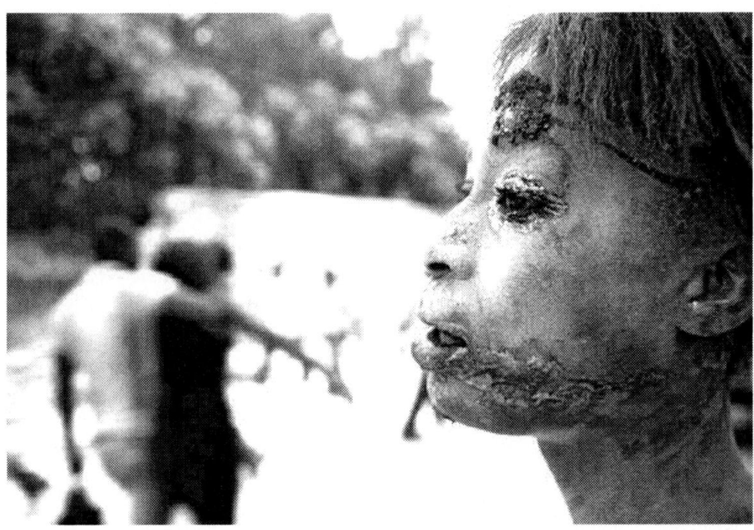

Don't expect any forewarning with a global viral outbreak or pandemic; there hasn't ever been any before. When the Swine Flu hit, the only notice anyone received was from local news networks weeks after the pandemic was already well underway. News reports announced, *"There's been a viral outbreak of dozens of reported cases in California, Mexico City, London, Madrid and Paris."* And definitely don't wait for any vaccine handouts from the government. They'll make sure to inject themselves, the military, federal employees and family and friends way before the supplies are distributed and reach the public; but by then they'll most likely run out anyway, so it won't much matter. This time, the best thing for you to do, in this instance, is to not go to the grocery store to stock up as advised in other developments; and barricade and seal off your windows and doors as described in the nuclear fallout shelter. The only thing that will save you and your family is my '0-contact' list:

Don't touch anyone!
Don't touch anything!
Don't talk to anyone!
Don't sit next to anyone!
Don't stand next to anyone!
Don't have sex with anyone!
Don't hold hands with anyone!
Don't kiss anyone!
Don't go anywhere!
Don't be in the same room as anyone!
Don't even be in the same vicinity as anyone!
Don't even look at anyone!
No one! No matter! No reason!

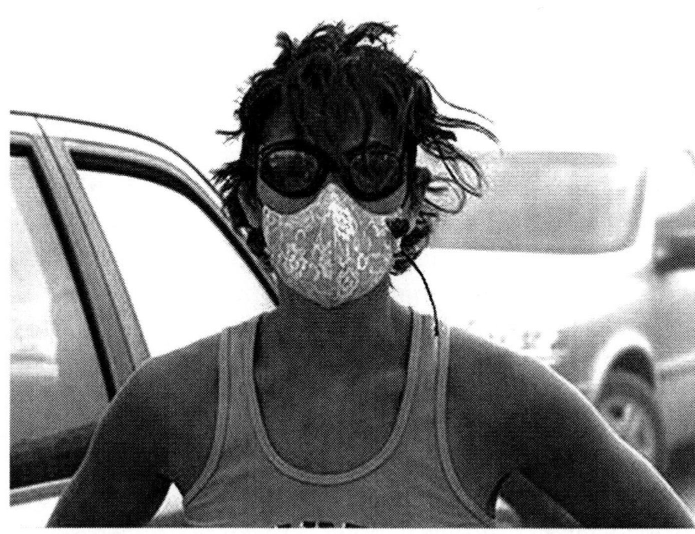

It doesn't make any difference if they're sick or not, if they need help or not, or if they're a family member or friend or not. If possible, wear an N95 medical mask, surgical gloves, and sealed goggles/glasses (they'll have a rubber seal that makes contact all the way around your eyes) or, even better, a forced air mask face shield or filtered air respirator; but I understand not everyone carries one of these around with them. Don't touch your face and definitely don't touch your eyes, nose or mouth. These areas are the quickest receptors to foreign matter.

Just seal yourself in and hunker down for a few weeks or so. As mentioned previously, you should have more than enough food, water and supplies currently in your home already, until everyone infected dies. This is what we did in Mexico during the Swine flu; and it will work for any airborne or non-airborne virus. The good thing about a deadly viral pandemic that wipes out most of humanity in a painful, disgusting and humiliating way is that power, water and utilities should, for the most part, stay on; so you'll have plenty of cold beer and movies to watch while humanity gets the big K.O. This is simply because most power plants have continued automation protocols allowing back-up fuel supplies to operate the generators for several weeks without human intervention. Hydro-electric dams, like the Hoover Dam, would be the last to go, continuing to power suburbs of the southwest and Las Vegas for several months, maybe years, according to the Hoover Engineering Team:

"the dam can continue to operate on its own for months, maybe years, keeping the Vegas Strip alight. Only the eventual accumulation of quagga mussels, an invasive species, in the cooling pipes of the power plant–currently being cleaned by humans–will shut down the dam."

Since the electric grid is bound to stay in operation, you'll also have toilet pressure and water. When you reemerge, you'll find that the gas stations probably still have fuel, since they store several 10,000 gallon tanks of each type underground (the little manhole covers you see near the pumps), which are also pumped electrically. However, you may have to familiarize yourself with their master functions (usually inside near the cash register), since many dying operators will turn the pumps off to avoid possible explosions, vandalism or theft. If you see any dead bodies, avoid them, as they'll still be extremely contagious at this point. Viruses, like any living organism, need food, warmth and water to survive. Once the host dies, it's only a matter of time before the virus dies as well. So, give the virus time to kill everyone off, and die itself, before exiting your home and re-populating the planet with other survivors.

TERRORIST ATTACK: DAY 1

It's no secret that it has been a long-standing goal for terrorists to topple governments; that's what they do, they're government topplers. The concept is simple, chop off the head and the body will fall. It's a long process composed of many attacks of terror. But with the advent of 'dirty bombs,' suicide bombers, anthrax (and other biological warfare agents), along with suicide jumbo jet pilots, the outcome could be rapidly expedited. If, for example, a jumbo jet crashes into the White House and kills the president, of course the country nor the even the government would fall. The fact is he's extremely replaceable. And the terrorists know this, but they're sending a message telling us we're vulnerable. And the message would be well received. It would devastate our already crippled economy and plunge us into a bloody, long-term campaign of retaliation and foreign occupation.

I'm always surprised when I leave the Agua-Luna compound to do a lecture, workshop or seminar in Seattle, Las Vegas, Houston, New York, London, Madrid or some other major city or tourist attraction, to see so many happy-go-lucky people, carrying on with their normal daily activities without a care in the world. I mean, don't get me wrong, being happy and content is great; I wish I could feel the same way… in a war zone. But ignorance is bliss, I suppose. I'm not sure if the people don't know--(it's announced in every airport and news channel on a daily basis)--or just don't care; but the National Threat Advisory is currently at Yellow or "Elevated,"--two away from Red, which, according to the Department of Homeland Security, means, there is a "significant risk of terrorist attacks" to the United States. In other words, THIS IS YOUR WARNING! They're warning you right now and you probably won't receive another. Run for your lives, scream and beat the walls, anything other than sitting in your office waiting to die in another terrorist attack. These 'authorities' that supposedly know what is happening are telling you all is not good, happy and go lucky; the 'all clear' has not been announced; shit is expected to hit the fan any day; we're about to get screwed again. I'm just not sure how else to say it to wake you people up.

As we've seen from past occurrences, there is little to no warning with terrorist attacks, at least not for us the general public, that is. But the government receives a lot of chatter from known/suspected terrorists, along with Israeli and British intelligence, but not once have you seen: "This is not a test, This is not a test. We interrupt this regularly scheduled program for a Terrorist Warning! A terrorist attack is likely to occur today between 3:00P.M.-5:00P.M. in the D.C. metropolitan area as several hundred thousand of you exit your place of work. Thank you, we now continue with your regularly scheduled program." No sorry, one day, everything's hunky dory; then, the next minute, skyscrapers as far as the eye can see are on fire and falling.

In the beginning, many people standing around will video phone the bellowing smoke rising out from the shattered windows to friends and family. Others will be running from the scene screaming for their lives (oh, <u>now</u> you're screaming for your lives!) Still others will be standing around, talking nonchalantly with each other. But after an instant of paralyzing commuter shock, the buildings containing 100+ stories (and thousands of employees) will once again begin to crumble and topple under the great force of gravity. An ensuing giant cloud of poisonous dust will hurl itself through the cramped streets at speeds of up to 20mph. Again, an N95 dust mask and full eyewear will definitely come in handy here; otherwise, the folded T-shirt method will suffice. In times like this, a t-shirt is usually all that's on hand. If you're in the general area of these buildings and you hear any secondary explosions, it could be due to additional, coordinated terrorist attacks, possibly nuclear in nature. Taking shelter, as described in the nuclear attack scenario above, would be a great idea right about now. If you're not in the immediate vicinity, don't stand around gawking at the tragedy like everyone else--just run away!

As entire cities (and London bridges) fall down, remaining rescue workers will be dispatched to search for survivors. A few firemen will spend the next several days combing the rubble for bodies with absolutely no luck; and Homeland Security will change the National

Threat Advisory to Red, (better late than never, I suppose). People will post pictures and notices of missing loved ones that read: "Have you seen me?" or "MISSING;" but not one person will be reunited. And finally, several days later, when all rescue attempts seems futile, additional attacks will take place, utilizing a different form of transport and delivery, such as the U.S. Mail, or city water systems, or packaged food, etc.

The real, overall destruction won't be physical in nature (although such damage is nothing to minimize), but will be (like killing the president) seen in the economic repercussions these attacks will have caused on the global market. Although many have died during these days, the majority of casualties are yet to come.

ECONOMIC COLLAPSE: DAY 1

Typically, a total, global economic collapse is gradual; the effects are felt slowly over several months, even years. However, the end result is still the same. We're currently already experiencing this stage of the collapse, felt all around the world. In fact, at a certain point, the outcome is irreversible, with almost everyone out of work, homeless, suffering and literally starving to death or dying of disease in the streets. This is day 1 of a full economic collapse.

Differing from most events I've described, an economic collapse offers plenty of forewarning. All you have to do is turn on your television or pick up a paper, any day of the week. There's so much warning it can be overwhelming. After hearing and seeing the same thing every day, we eventually come to consider such times as normal and thus ignore these warnings, which again is the current case. So you don't have the excuse this time that there wasn't any notice and that you couldn't make the appropriate preparations beforehand. But humans, in general, are blind and ignorant, especially when it comes to our daily routine activities; so we can assume that yes, it should come as no surprise we did not, in fact, heed the warnings and take the appropriate measures. But there are still some things you can do, however:

The extra monthly food in your home (unless you stockpiled beforehand) won't be enough this time to last you through this crisis. So, goods such as electronics, jewelry, knick-knacks, family heirlooms, money, etc., should all be traded off for needed supplies like ammunition, non-perishable food, shoes and 'tools of a trade' as soon as possible, before the bank repossesses the house and such things lose their value as the market becomes flooded. Don't hesitate because of personal attachment, sentimentality or desire to have 'nice things.' Act now while these items still hold any value at all. If you wait, you and your family will be on the streets, starving to death and locked out of a house full of junk you tried to keep. Keep clothing, blankets, tools, food, a couple of plastic Tupperware containers, hardware, or anything you can use to perform a job, ie., sewing machine, woodworking tools, cooking pots, fishing or hunting equipment, materials, lumber, etc. These items will soon come in handy now that private sector businesses have closed up shop, service counters aren't answering calls, and 'lifetime warranties' are null and void. Your services (anything you know how to do), will now be worth something, which you can exchange for other services and/or supplies. Unfortunately, most Americans don't really know how to do anything (other than watch TV, we do that well) anymore. If you have a rental property, keep it. Jobless tenants will not be able to pay their rent with cash and money will have little value anyway, by now. Tenants will need to trade their services for rent (no, not sexual favors, although some probably would and will), or supplies, in exchange for a roof over their and their children's head; in which case you can then employ their sewing, cooking, or building skills, in return.

With most people unclothed, starving and living out in the elements when that first winter hits (with little help from a failing government), you'll finally start to see a rapid decline in the surviving population. Women (and girls) will quickly turn to prostitution just to earn a meal. Without health care, many will perish from simple ailments, curable diseases and minor injuries. Even small accidents in a world without hospitals can prove deadly. Water, electricity and fuel will be rationed, for the most part, while food, basic supplies/items and blankets will 'supposedly' be rationed; but, in reality, they will be non-existent. Whereas money and status used to be vital, now relationships with family, friends and neighbors will be critical for safety, security and survival. Depending on others (a trait that has never been strong in Americans) will prove a necessity and way of life, as gangs of thugs, unemployed police, and newly-released prisoners rule and run the streets. This new-age, jobless, rent-a-cop/prisoner/law enforcement/organized-crime collage of bandits will most likely demand a percentage of your monthly supplies in exchange for "protection". That's just how it's always been.

The city will quickly turn into a literal cesspool right before your eyes and the government's only recommendation will be for you to "shop your way out of the recession," (they're really saying that now.) Your best chance for survival, is to leave the many and take your chances among the few. Even before a total economic collapse, the country will see a major migration, as farmers and ranchers move into the cities in hopes of government aid. This migration now provides endless beautiful locations of opportunity for someone who can get to them and knows how to benefit from them. A spot near the beach would be optimal. You can continue your business (even bringing your already-established workforce), exporting products up the coast via sailboat. In fact, now that there is a land factor added to the equation, you can expand your venture into the agricultural market, sending not only goods up and down the coastline, but food as well, to collapsed cities in need. Since all economies are now linked together, expect similar situations unfolding in all nations, around the world.

GOVERNMENTAL COLLAPSE: DAY 1

There may be several reasons that would take down a government: a hostile takeover or coup (which happened in the Soviet Union in 1991; invasion and foreign military overthrow (which we just witnessed with Saddam Hussein), economic collapse (which we're currently seeing in the U.S.), revolution and upheaval (which has just happened this year in Egypt, Yemen and Tunisia); or the government is lethally removed through the all-too-familiar tactic of assassination and intimidation (which is what happens more often than not). In any case, when 7 million people (the current quantity of U.S. military, federal employees and federal contractors), all of a sudden find themselves out of work, a bad situation (economic collapse, poverty, starvation) is about to get a whole lot worse. Soldiers, with no other training other than fighting, will turn to any source of income possible that will utilize their unique skills. Since no one is looking for 2 million security guards, they'll join the growing gangs who are already strong-arming vulnerable citizens to survive. This is exactly what's happening today in Mexico with the Zetas, who are a powerful drug cartel made up entirely from out-of-work Mexican Special Forces and federal, state and local out-of-work police officers, who initially worked for the Gulf Cartel, nothing less than an army of mercenaries. In February, 2010, Los Zetas went independent and became enemies of their former employer, which is when all hell broke loose. In February 2009, Texas Governor Rick Perry announced an "Operation Border Star Contingency Plan" to safeguard the border if the Zetas decide to attack the U.S.

The cause determines how much warning you will receive. For example, the current economic crash would signal a governmental collapse within the next 5-10 years; the growing impatience and vocal dissatisfaction with the governmental leaders is another sign; but a planned governmental coup or assassination attempt is likely only known by those conspirators constructing and participating in it. Either way, if the government were to suddenly fall and the military disbanded, the floodgates would be open to confusion, mayhem, anarchy, lawlessness, pandemonium and, finally, outside invasion. The best bet for surviving now is just to leave, pick a country (preferably a third world country, since there would be little that could collapse) and bail out before the collapse even begins, while the getting's still good. That's what any smart investor would do; and that is what you are--an investor in the American government. Your investments are automatically deducted from your paycheck in the form of bi-weekly tax withholdings. If you decide not to leave, my only other advice would be to buy guns; buy a lot of ammunition; fortify your home as best you can; and stock up on food and water (all described in the *Preparations List,)* because things are about to get a little hairy. Again, keep in mind this won't just be happening to us. As you can currently see, such things are transpiring today on a global level.

INVASION: DAY 1

Once our military is out of work, it won't be long until other powers start invading. We're talking about days, maybe weeks, since by now, many countries must feel they have a very large debt to settle with us. The U.S. is, most likely, at the top of everyone's invasion list. With our military out of work, there will be no one monitoring the billions of dollars worth of coast-to-coast radar systems. And with the rest of the world experiencing their own sets of problems, don't count on any Israeli or British intelligence to help us out this time. No, there won't be any signs--no chatter, no warning in this case. One day, suddenly, you'll just start seeing thousands of parachutes in the sky, or a mile-long procession of trucks and tanks on the highway leading into town. Asian troops would land in California, Indian troops in Mexico, with Europeans and/or Russians making landfall on the east coast, in separate occurrences or possibly all at the same time, taking up as much land as quickly as possible before agreeing on a boundary line somewhere in the Rockies. I can see it now: The Soviet Union in the north, China in the southwest, India occupying eastern South America, the new United States (*United American Republic*) forced back into the center of the country, with Islam controlling territories in the east (which they mostly already occupy today anyway). Although hostile to you, this really isn't the same type of occupation we're currently seeing in Iraq and Afghanistan. This incursion is as much to help a failing, starving, collapsed nation as it is to convert 'heathens' and fill the pockets of those invading to stimulate, maintain and save their own country's governments.

Regardless of the reason you really just have three options, (a) live and work under the control of a new foreign regime (which may actually be better than the current one) (b) leave, or (c) fall back and rebel. At first it will be automatic to put up a fight (we Americans do enjoy a good melee). In order to achieve this, the gathering of information will be crucial. What's happening? Where are they coming from? Who are they? How many are there? Anyone who survived the initial onslaught will congregate just outside of occupied areas/towns, in woods, mountains, swamps, and fields as chatter passes through the growing crowds and retreating newcomers bring with them the first bits of information. Leaders will be chosen based on past military experience, tactics will be planned, hit and run attacks carried out, supplies gathered/stolen. The whole thing sounds so fitting for America. Trenched in battle to win back what's 'rightfully yours' (which we took from the natives,) you'll most likely live (and eventually die) the next several years engulfed in war.

SOLAR FLARES: DAY 1

Solar flares are all the talk of the town these days--"the Sun is going to be very active during this month"; "a solar storm is scheduled for this week"; "a Coronal Mass Ejection (CME) disrupted two NASA satellites last week"; "a devastating solar flare is coming to a city near you" (no kidding that's a real one). Whereas we seem to have little warning with most tragedies, solar flares again flood the news with warnings, which are overshadowing the real dangers. No matter, though, you'll know when the Sun sends its will our way; if we don't get an indoor 4th of July show on December 21st, the least that could happen is a total and global electrical grid shut-down. If it's a CME you may receive up to a day's official notice. Take this time to stock up on supplies, fill up anything that will hold water (again, as described in *Preparations List*); and ground all four corners of your home. If there's

any sensitive or important electrical equipment you want to keep, like a dynamo flashlight, solar panel, laptop or shortwave radio, insulate/shield it with non-conductive material and tinfoil (Faraday cage) and ground or bury it at least a foot underground. Also, make sure to flip your main circuit breaker, disconnecting your home from the grid; because once this thing goes off, every electronic unprotected will be fried.

All in all, a little loss of electricity (up to a year) isn't bad compared to some of the catastrophes I've been describing. Almost no loss of life seen on day 1, with the exceptions of those associated with traffic light accidents, failed medical equipment, falling elevators, industrial machines gone haywire, heating/AC (or rather lack of), nuclear power plants, and other large machines or electronics that become dangerous with a loss of power. However, those numbers are still very minimal compared to the big picture. Just stay away from any rollercoasters or giant Ferris wheels; don't stand under any low-flying airplanes or helicopters; and for the love of God, keep your kids away from those escalators. If the magnetosphere still has a gaping hole in it, those that don't take shelter underground however, will start dropping flies from radiation exposure on days 2-10.

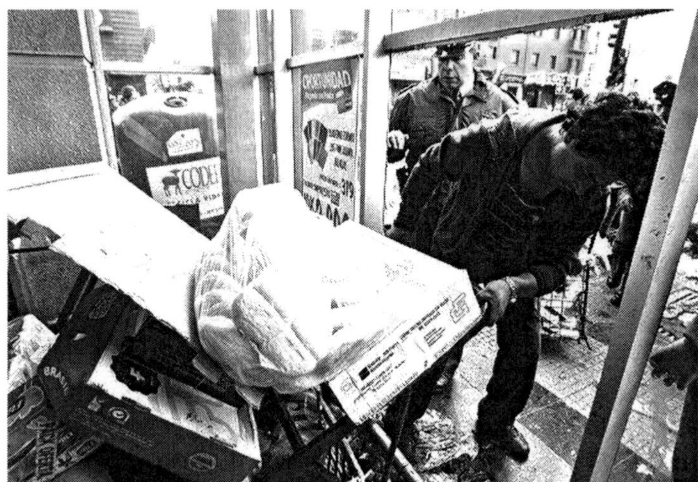

During the first days you'll have plenty to eat, since perishable foods will be the first to spoil without a working fridge. If you didn't store water, it's critical to get some now; as a last resort you have a full water heater and toilet water tank. You can bleach or 'boil' any water collected from rivers and lakes on a gas barbeque grill, or even better catch as much rain water as you can store. Once the water situation is taken care of, it's important to hit the local grocery store buying up more food for two reasons: (1) as in your fridge, their perishable foods will also go bad within a few days and (2) everyone in the neighborhood is eventually going to get the same idea and hoard groceries.

Bring along a crowbar, since the sliding doors probably won't be sliding today, and cash, since the registers probably won't be registering today (if there's anyone there to check you out, that is). Getting around on a bicycle will probably be your only option of transportation in a world without cars; but today, in this situation, you'll probably be better off walking so that you can push carts full of goods back to your dwelling. Once again, use the *Preparations List* as a shopping list with an emphasis on non-electrical items. I don't suggest a gas-powered generator or solar panels in this situation, for the simple fact that the odds are good that both (along with any other electrical item not originally sheltered), were permanently damaged in the storm. The storm, or even a series of solar storms, shouldn't last more than a day or two; and it won't really matter that your electronics are fried, since there won't be any electrical grid to plug them into now anyway.

NIBIRU - PLANET X: DAY 1

If you happen to look up one day and you see a second moon in the sky the size of, say, a quarter of our moon, that's warning enough that something BIG is about to happen and to take adequate shelter. (Actually I shouldn't say that, the Earth really has several 'moons.' The first, of course, is the large one in the sky we see every night; but there are many more. 2002AA29, for example, actually doesn't orbit us at all, but rather follows us around the Sun locked in place with us, as well as 3753Cruithne, which is scheduled to be closer than it's ever been, every November between 1994 and 2015.)

Since the entire planet is going to move, shift and generally discombobulate in reaction to the event, I really have no idea where "adequate shelter" may be--up in an airplane would be my best guess; although, you'd have to be up there for several hours, maybe days, even weeks, possibly months. For long-term preparation, just know that every catastrophic event discussed so far and hereafter will most likely present itself during this event in a very unpleasant manner. Polar shifts, super earthquakes, super tsunamis, super hurricanes, super volcanoes, widespread supercell tornadoes and, well, just a regular ice age. But it'll be a super winter wonderland with the North Pole and Santa literally transported to your door. Too bad there won't be a single cookie left on the planet for your new neighbor; unless, that is, you count the several thousands of gallons of cookies tossed when the planetary merry-go-round starts. I truly make light of the event, but if such a scenario did actually unfold, there wouldn't be a *day 2*.

POLAR SHIFT: DAY 1

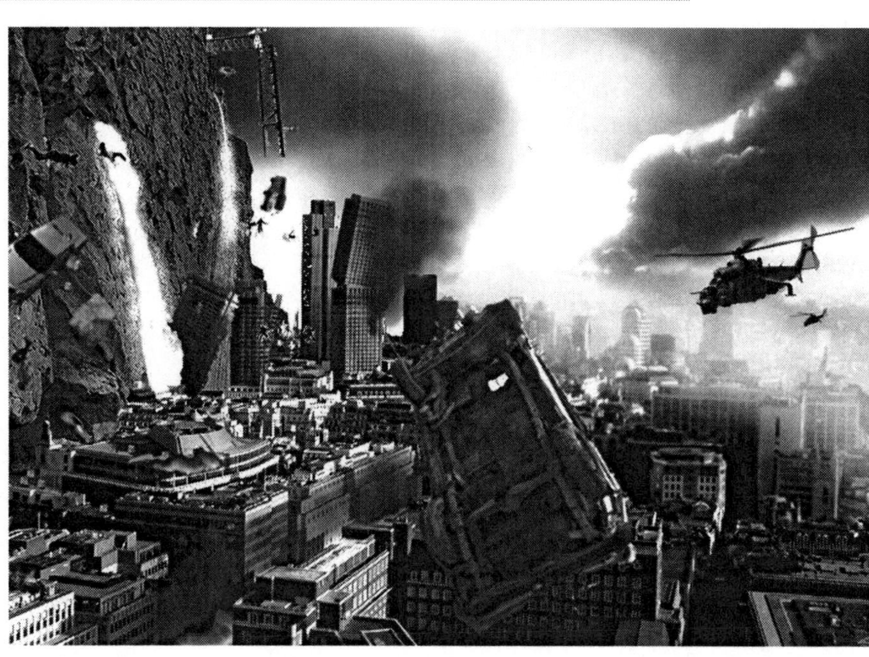

I couldn't even begin to describe the early moments of a magnetic or physical polar shift, not only because the expected devastation and destruction from such an incident is so massive it's almost unavoidable, but for the simple fact that because it's never happened before (during our time), we honestly don't really know for sure what to expect. I mean, obviously, the surface of the Earth would conduct some extraordinary feats of nature; and you should seek safety underground or in space; but we may also experience several new characteristics of physics never before known that may redefine today's laws of science. For example, we all learned in 5th grade that the reason we don't float off the planet is because of gravity; and yet gravity would undergo major alterations during this time, increasing or decreasing exponentially. We may then, in fact, float off the planet or be squashed like watermelons under our own weight. The end results also may be permanent, or, at least, long-lasting, maybe not causing us to float off the planet, just up to the living room ceiling with the same weightless movement or thrust that's on the moon, or buckle to our knees with the weight of the world literally on our shoulders. The Earth may continue for quite some time to undergo a lower or higher magnitude of gravitational pull. Physical conditions on our planet, and the impact it would have on our daily lives, our living, our growth and the development of all other living things on this planet, would be drastically altered and therefore so would we, both physically and mentally.

There's one thing I can guarantee in the aftermath of such havoc--there will be no help--you're on your own. Any and all rescue workers who could help, either took shelter, were killed themselves along with everyone else or are currently on the ceiling contemplating their options. In this case, survivors will simply sit and cry or pray/plead to God; what else is there to do when you're brought to your knees, literally? The good news is: it's now an all new world—no, it really is. There will be new continents, new islands, new oceans, and new places to explore and settle. Life will go on, probably. At least we're pretty sure it will. And there should be plenty to eat; it will all have just been relocated. You will need to relearn the old ways, how to hunt, trap, fish, gather; and you'll survive. We always have. In fact, many historians and archaeologists believe that this collapse and rebirth/rebuilding of evolved man/society has happened many, many times before. So relax, brew some cold beer, and take over a newly-formed island. Hell, you can even name your own ocean.

THE GREAT FLOOD: DAY 1

The warnings associated with a massive flood will be cryptic and misleading. Officials and reporters will talk more about secondary developing disasters then the deluge itself. They will say things like, "the Boston area is being pounded with torrential rains," or "hurricane Lucia is now on a direct path with East Texas"; but you'll never hear something like "your area is about to be submerged under 200 feet of water, head for Denver!" Yet, that's exactly what would materialize, with New York, Houston, L.A. Atlanta, Miami, Boston, San Francisco, Seattle and any other city below 220ft elevation. Any city above 220ft is the place to be, however, with hundreds of millions (2/3 of the planet's population) heading for higher ground, you may decide to look for other non-highly populated regions. Instead, officials and reporters use terms like 'flood watch', 'flood warning', and my personal favorite 'urban and small stream advisory'. What does that even mean?

A flood can materialize in several ways, (1) heavy, non-stop, torrential rains simply fill the city with water, like a glass under an open faucet; (2) hurricanes, earthquakes, underwater volcanoes or other feats of nature cause significant shifts or depressions in the ocean, literally pushing salt water up into the cities, like a kid splashing water out of a bathtub; or (3) the southern icecap (and/or Greenland) melts causing the current sea level to rise 220ft, similar to what occurred when the last ice caps melted, sending Noah around the world on a *three hour tour*. For whatever the reason, this flooding process should be enough notice alone to evacuate to higher grounds (or buy a boat); however, as I've stated over and over and over again, most people are too complacent to view this as any type of warning sign that the end of days is upon us.

Calamity from flooding is easy to avoid with a little common sense. Again, the problem is, as I've already established, most people, today don't have even a little to spare. They'll rely on city officials to tell them when to evacuate. Unfortunately, though, by then it will most likely again be too late, just like it was with Katrina when the mayor called for an evacuation of New Orleans less than a day before the hurricane made landfall. And the government knows that it won't react quickly enough. FEMA's website actually says, *"Do not wait for instructions to move!"* In other words, this means DO NOT WAIT FOR THEIR INSTRUCTIONS TO MOVE! It's actually pretty clear cut. Not only will there be massive deaths due to a lack of emergency planning and management, a lack of warning, a lack of common sense, and an overabundance of stupidity, but many more lives will be lost during the mass exodus itself as well.

Source: Phillip Perry

Of course, the first wave of upper class residents (about 16% of the U.S.) won't have a problem getting to Denver, Dallas, Las Vegas or wherever; it's just a quick flight away. For the working class and middle class (accounting for about 24% of the U.S. each) it's just a tank of gas away. The problems will start when the ~~herds~~ sorry, hordes of vehicles begin migrating along the same interstate highways towards the same cities. Gas stations will run out of food and gas, roads will become congested (soaking up even more gas) and buses will be bogged down and oversold, turning a 2-day trip into a month (or more) long voyage. Add to this probable foul weather, road rage, traffic accidents and lack of emergency services and the situation quickly turns into its own catastrophe. You're talking about over ten million people consecutively heading down I-15 (or wherever), from Los Angeles to Las Vegas, which doesn't handle more than a few thousand cars on any given day. Then you have the multitudes of lower class and homeless (which are by far the largest group, at around 35%), who have no means of getting out of the city anyway (most of the victims in New Orleans fell into this category), let alone to a city several hundred miles away. How do they get there? What money do they have for bus tickets? They don't own cars; and, if they did, they couldn't afford the gas. Some will attempt (and die in the process) to walk the great distance, a feat that took the original settlers weeks with supplies (which they won't have); while others will hold out on rooftops, waiting for rescue that will never arrive, ultimately getting swept out to sea with the rest of the garbage.

Lastly, you have the cities themselves, toward which everyone will be converging on like a swarm of locusts, sitting high and dry and pretty above the flood plain, already affected by a failing economy and lack of jobs, suddenly flooded by--not water--but millions of uprooted refugees seeking safety, food, shelter and eventually jobs. This will be the proverbial 'straw that broke the camel's back,' collapsing what little societal structure is left standing in these regions, eventually resulting in the deaths of millions more.

So to recap--How to Survive a Doomsday Flood-Type Apocalypse? Leave, and fast! Head for the mountains (not a city), maybe a small town, some place at least 250 feet above sea level at the first sign of apocalyptic precipitation; otherwise, you'll get stuck in the exodus and Die! If you plan it right now and find a destination at about a 235-240ft elevation, in a few years you could end up with a really cool resort-style beachfront property. Even better, you can possibly even lock down that newly-formed, private tropical island previously mentioned.

That said, if you find yourself trapped with rising waters all around, your best bet is to find something big that floats while you can still walk on dry land. Of course, a boat would be your best bet; but not everyone has access to a 30ft Cutter. So you'll need to make your way as far inland as possible to the water's edge, stroll leisurely into any of the already-abandoned homes in the area, unplug the kitchen fridge or freezer nonchalantly, flip it mercilessly on its back and wait for the flood waters to rise. And like I've always said, while you're waiting, it never hurts to gather a few garbage pail lids. Once the waters are high enough, you'll be able to walk the floating fridge right out the door, rather than dragging it tirelessly through the house and across the city. If balanced correctly, a fridge makes a half decent boat. A normally-sized fridge will displace about 1,000 pounds of water; which means your cargo, you and any other occupants can't exceed 1,000lbs. Since most men weigh less than 250lbs and women less than 150lbs, and since there's not much additional space for supplies anyway, I don't think that you could exceed the weight limits. The problem is balance. Fridges weren't designed to float securely and will be top heavy, naturally wanting to flip sideways. To resolve this, you'll have to tie heavy items onto the back steel netting (bottom of the boat) for ballast. Just make sure not to exceed the 1,000lb limit. Now, don't get me wrong. You're not going to be navigating the seven seas in search of booty in this rig. Just shoot for the nearest outcropping of mainland, which at this point shouldn't be more than a few miles inland. Grab your garbage pail oars and go at it. Good luck, and happy paddling!

ICE AGE: DAY 1

Since freezing to death is one of the most passive means to achieve death, the unconscious, dead, or dying are the lucky ones in this scenario, because they won't have to experience what you will in the months to come. But again, we get ahead of ourselves. We still have a massive migration south to attempt. The onslaught of an ice age will show advanced signs with a plethora of time and years' worth of signals--epic winter storms, extreme summers, massive flash flooding--in other words, what's currently become apparent all over the planet as we speak, or I speak/write, you read. The problem, yet once again, is that very few people are currently seeing, listening, understanding and/or accepting these clues; not to mention, when announcements are made to the general public, people ridicule and laugh at the news. When you decide that the long winter is actually upon you, you'll really only have one option: head for the lowest elevations, or even better, towards the equator. The problem again is everyone will be doing the same thing, congesting the roads, running the pumps dry and wiping out all food supplies between you and the Mayan pyramids (or Egyptian pyramids, depending on which side of the world you're on). It will be like a giant human infestation on Central American (or African) countries. But like I said, it's your only option. So fly, drive, walk or swim; but go south (or north, depending on which side of the hemisphere you're in) for the winter.

Withdraw as much cash from your accounts as possible. The ATM machines and even the bank branches themselves, only keep limited cash on hand; and once the panic starts, it will go fast. Use credit cards to purchase all supplies. Cash currency will have some (although much less) value, whereas a piece of plastic will soon have absolutely none. Follow your *Preparations List,* as the supplies needed will be essential to you and your family's survival. And fill up everything and anything that will hold gas, storing the extra containers in the trunk, back seat, or bed of the vehicle.

Didn't make it, huh? Thought as much, but no worries, now we get to prepare you for living in extreme cold with no hope of summer in sight, at least not for a several years, that is. First and foremost, you'll need to build something underground; it's the only way to stave off the cold. Earth or dirt not only offers incredible insulating properties (R-1 per every cubic foot of dirt), but great U values as well (U-.5 per every cubic foot). Earth-sheltered designs aren't as dependent on insulation as regular homes, since the "basal" temperature of the Earth as a medium is always an average temperature of the entire year; Underground temperature's will always be consistent, so you aren't working against the swings of temperature found on the surface. In other words, it will always be warmer below the surface in the winter and cooler in the summer, making it always more efficient to build something below ground rather than above it. I'm actually surprised that we don't currently all live underground, always, in hot OR cold regions. I describe a couple of ways to build quick, efficient subterranean dwellings in *Chapter 1*.

The rule of engaging Father Frost is to keep warm and hoard. Just watch how Mother Nature handles him. Squirrels, bears, chipmunks and other cold-region animals spend most their time stockpiling before winter. Don't worry about spoilage; you'll soon have a giant freezer just outside your door. As far as violence, marauders and theft goes, these elements become rare in colder climates. If you don't believe me, take a look at the crime rates for Canada, Greenland, Iceland, Norway, Denmark, Sweden and Finland. They're the lowest in the world. It's just too damn cold. If you do go out in -50°F air, rub Chap Stick or Vaseline on your face, hands, ears and any other exposed skin. Cover the eyes with goggles, ears with earplugs and nose with cotton. If your clothing isn't designed to take such elements, stuff newspaper or couch/mattress stuffing between each layer But there will be ~~warmer~~ less than freezing days, so if you have rounded up enough fuel (you'll need to bring what you need, don't expect to find any in route,) it may be a good idea to make a dash for the border.

THE END OF THE INTERNET: DAY 1

Similar to an all-out, electrical grid collapse described in the *Solar Flare* section above, the collapse of the internet has devastatingly long-term effects. Gone are the days of tweeting information to friends, family, loved ones and business associates, or texting to let someone know that the business meeting has been postponed, or that you'll be late for dinner. You're going to have to return to the old archaic means of letter writing. No more watching the sports game on your favorite iDevice or Plasma TV since both run off of a digital signal; I suppose you'll have to watch that antic analog boob tube, except, unfortunately, the government phased out analog signals a few years ago in a move to go digital.

Now that I've gotten your attention by removing your addictions, you may not view the collapse of the World Wide Web as a real global 'doomsday'-like catastrophe, or maybe for you, this is the worse one yet. The thing is that: (a) the internet is worldwide, hence the term WWW (World Wide Web) and not AWW (American Wide Web); therefore, the collapse of it will be "worldwide," and (b) major services, critical resources, and vital daily actions today can only be carried out online. There are no more paper records; and it will take quite some time before the web is rebooted or we devise alternate methods of carrying out such functions. Either way, expect an economic collapse of epic proportion from just this miniscule hiccup in the movement of information. This is a real cataclysmic event in today's society, and people don't even know it.

One day you're online updating your Facebook page, and BAM!, some homophobic AI (fear of homo-sapiens, before I get the gay community on my *~~ass~~*) just wiped out the web. My only suggestion is to separate yourself now, as much as possible, from the Internet. But don't get me wrong. I don't mean go cold turkey, or that you even have to alter your daily lifestyle that much. Just don't allow yourself to depend on it 100%, or on anything 100%, for that matter. If you're completely reliant on something, when it's gone, you're lost, devastated, destroyed; literally, in the blink of an eye your entire world is gone. Diversify! Learn how to live as humans did just 20 years ago. Then you won't be in the dark when the system crashes and the lights go out.

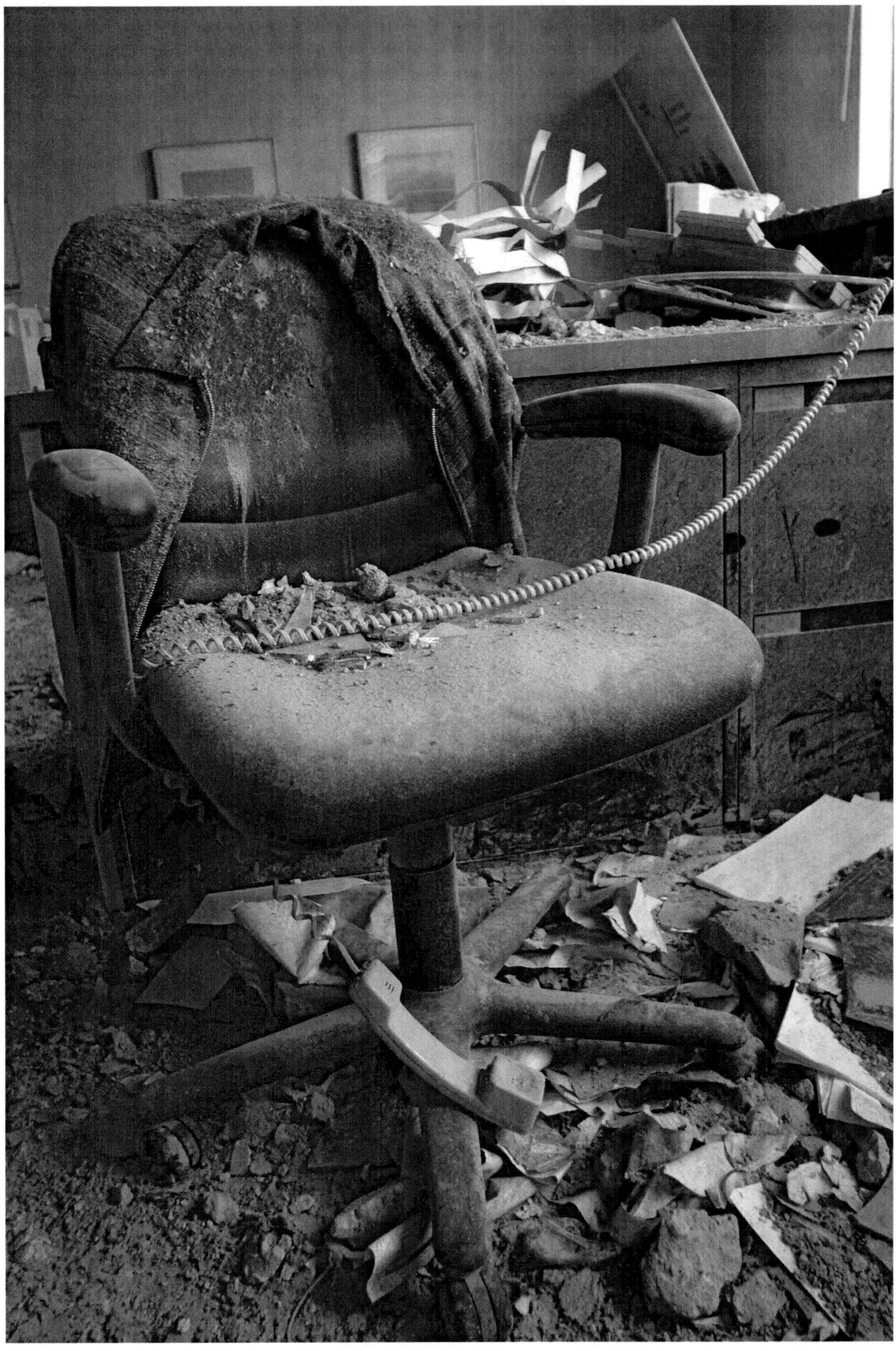

CHAPTER 7

AWAKING TO A NEW REALITY: DAY 2

As you may have glimpsed, the short and long-term aftermath of most events are generally the same, i.e., the same destruction, non-existent civil structure, confusion, lawlessness, and individuality--in other words, a complete and total collapse of everything you once knew to be the 'society' or *the end of the world as you know it.* Therefore, the proceeding measures that will need to be taken will be, for the most part, the same. For the first day or so, between fleeing for your life screaming, rescuing others (if the mood prompts), smaller post-catastrophes, and the overall stress of the situation, you'll receive little sleep. However, it will be important to eventually find safe shelter. Again, because most end-of-the-world-type events usually don't include flattening every structure on the planet, there should be many buildings left standing in which to take refuge. Taking shelter in an office, in office stairwells, or barricaded behind locked office doors (what can I say, there are a lot of offices in America) should prove adequate enough for a few nights. Wedge a chair up against the door with a few bottles on top. If nothing else, you'll be awakened/alerted by the entry of some unwanted post-apocalyptic guest.

LOOTING: OOH, OH, I WANT THAT, AND THAT, AND THAT!

It's early morning and a lot of the car and business alarms are blaring from broken windows. Looters have already started wreaking havoc throughout the city in search of supplies. Although slightly scary, this is actually great. Once a catastrophe hits, supplies like bottled water, canned food, blankets, fuel, batteries and ammunition will all but disappear from store shelves within just a few hours (even days or weeks before). The concept of capitalism trends like 'legal ownership' and 'mine', a thing of the past. It's critical to collect enough of these commodities initially to: (a) last you and your family as long as possible, or (b) to trade with, just like paper currency, which will, in fact, soon have little to no value. Before yesterday, collecting supplies in such a matter was illegal; but today is a brand new day and a whole new world; and the police and the institutions that once made and enforced such 'laws' are non-existent. Most people (including the owners of these buildings), are very much dead; and no one will respond to any alarms or cries for help now. It's every man for himself (and every woman for man's self) at this point; and if you don't act and get in while the getting's good, your family will be in a tough way in the following days to come.

Contrary to what the media and law enforcement agencies portray, looting isn't a violent activity. Anyone who has participated in such an event (like myself), knows looters are often helpful, even brotherly, in their rebellious grand theft pilgrimage. My personal experience as a kid in Detroit in the late '80s, during what was then called Devil's night, seemed to be almost euphoric, exciting and joyful in nature, as dozens of people gathered together on an annual basis to stick it to the system that oppressed them for so long. The only real problem tends to be in logically carrying out such activities. You'll notice women's arms filled with baby diapers (like poo control is now the most important necessity in the world,) followed by several teams of two-man groups carrying 60in flat screen, plasma TVs, although the electrical grid will almost certainly be long gone. Since this isn't an everyday event, and most people really don't have a clue of what they need or don't need in the aftermath of cataclysmic occurrences, and since people tend to think that they need to rush in order to get away with something or from someone, a well-laid looter's plan is non-existent. So let's lay one out...

DELIVERY METHODS

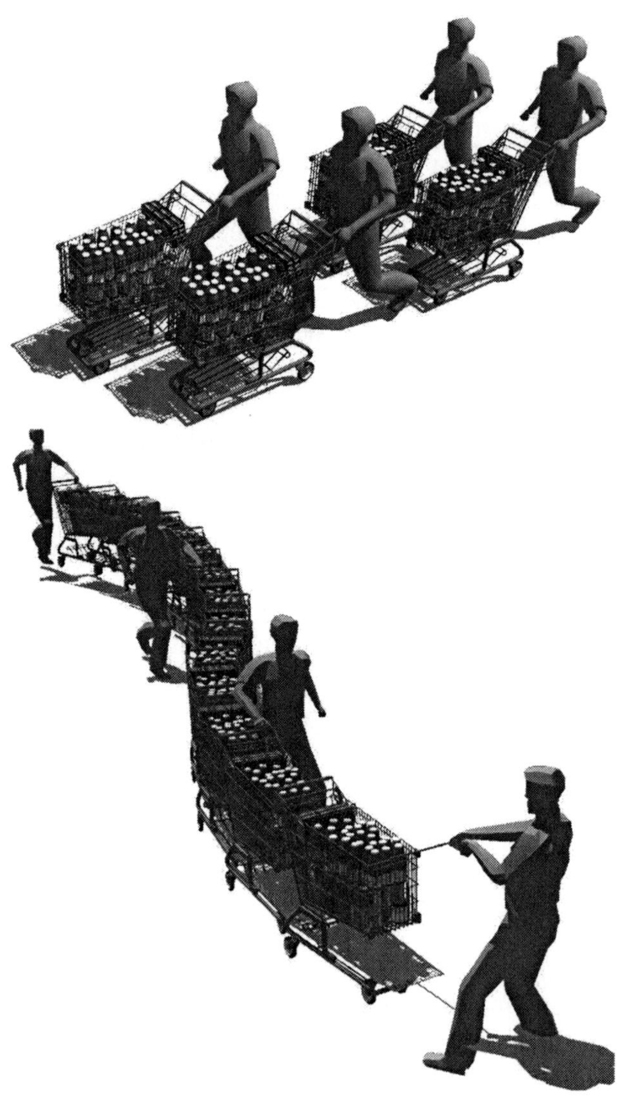

Since, most likely, vehicles of a petroleum-based nature will either be incapacitated, or the streets will be too congested or dangerous to pass safely, you'll need to secure another means of supply transport for your groceries. Shopping carts make great, well, shopping carts. Try to acquire as many as possible/practical, depending on your ability to protect them. Your first thought would be to take and fill as many as one person can push; so, for example, if you have 4 able bodies, you may hope to walk away with 4-6 carts (some men are able to push/pull an extra cart) worth of supplies. But, by tying (not clipping) the child seatbelts of the cart in front to the front of the cart behind, forming a train-like procession, you can walk away with a much higher quantity of carts and, thereby, supplies, only limited by the number of carts that can be pushed and pulled at once by the total numbers in your group. With this method, however, the 4 people can walk away with almost as much supplies as 10-14 with 10-14 walking away with 10 times as much as they could have otherwise. By additionally having one or two extra people push and pull, you can either add more carts or gain greater mobility. You're only restricted by how many people can get a hand on a cart. This makes protecting them easier as well, forcing the bandit(s) to physically untie each cart from the entire procession, or untie two carts (front and back straps) in order to steal anything other than end carts (where the most important items should be located) and which, for this very reason, should be guarded more thoroughly. This arrangement is far more practical and efficient, and is why the old chuck wagon caravans of the Wild West would travel in the same manner. In fact, by arranging the wagons (or in this case the carts) in a circle around the group (essentially forming a mobile barricade) you can better defend against a marauder attack.

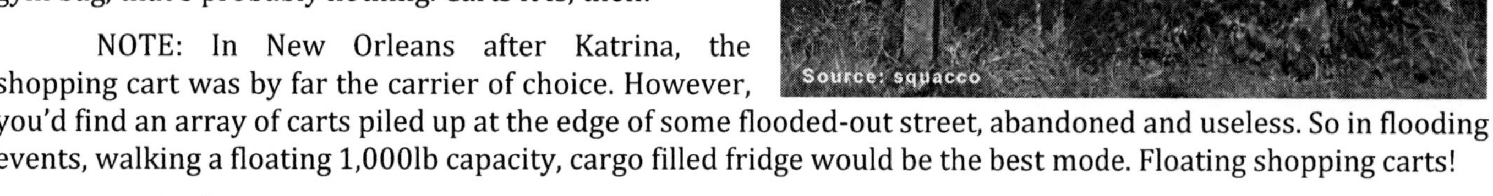
Source: squacco

The question must be raised at this point, however, is it better to make one trip for supplies, walking away with, say, twenty cartloads, or a lot of smaller trips with, say, only filling backpacks? Both create risks: Utilizing backpacks you'll remain quick and mobile, fleeing at the first sign of danger, able to jump over fences, walls and other obstacles. However, it's not likely you'll find 4 backpacks in any one store, especially once the looting begins or while you hesitate to contemplate moral looting decisions. *To loot or not to loot, that is indeed the question.* Carts, however, are usually plentiful and already on site for the taking; but they're slow and awkward and only manageable on flat surfaces (you won't find anyone climbing over walls or fences with one). You can always abandon the carts, if need be, and flee, getting away with only slightly less than what you would have fitted into a backpack. Your choice of transportation, in the end, will probably be based on how far away your temporary shelter is, how fast the shelves are empting (multiple trips = potential lost inventory) and what you currently have on hand; and since you're not a student with a book-filled backpack, or a sports enthusiast with a dirty socks-filled gym bag, that's probably nothing. Carts it is, then!

NOTE: In New Orleans after Katrina, the shopping cart was by far the carrier of choice. However, you'd find an array of carts piled up at the edge of some flooded-out street, abandoned and useless. So in flooding events, walking a floating 1,000lb capacity, cargo filled fridge would be the best mode. Floating shopping carts!

Grocery bags are also abundant on site, but are small and weak, and, therefore, should only be used as a last resort. That said, if plastic grocery bags are all that's left, be a good consumer and always double or triple bag your groceries. As far as supplies, as I stated earlier, bottled water, canned food, batteries, ammunition and fuels will be the first to disappear from the shelves. Although heavier to carry, canned foods like beans, chili, peanut butter, meat, tuna fish, spam, fruit, vegetables, etc., typically provide more calories than say a bag of noodles or chips. Although bags of chips and noodles are lighter in weight, they're much bulkier and more fragile, not to mention, nothing can take a beating when the shit goes down like a good-ol' can of beans. Perishable foods like unpreserved meat, ice cream, and milk should be obtained as a last resort. Don't waste cart space on food that will probably go bad before you have a chance to consume it. Again, if perishable food is all that's left, take it and trade it off quickly, or feast the next couple days before the food spoils, eating several (6, 7, 8) meals per day. It will convert mostly to post-stress energy and reserve fat, but that's better than nothing at this point. Eggs, surprisingly, aren't perishable foods. Eggs can be left out for over 30 days at room temperature without refrigeration. However, given their fragility, they should be treated like a perishable food and traded or eaten (raw if necessary) as soon as possible. Oil for cooking isn't a priority either. There are several types of cooking methods (baking, roasting, broiling, grilling, frying, simmering and steaming); only one requires oil (frying); and of course any item can be eaten raw. The fat of any animal can be cooked down into oil if needed. For a full apocalyptic looters shopping list, refer to *Chapter 1* in the back of the book.

Now you're starting to see why it's important to get in on the looting early. You'll be hurting bad if you can't get enough sustenance to last you a few days, or enough energy to think clearly, to formulate a plan and to practice hunting/trapping or acquiring; or if the occasion presents itself, flee, fight for and/or defend your food/family in order to get to the next food supply before you run out of energy. Until now you've never had to deal with, or think about, running out of energy before the next source of food presented itself, or about what obstacles will unfold between you and your next meal, for which you would need energy reserves. Before today, if you got hungry, you went and got a Big Mac. Too bad you don't have that luxury anymore. Now you'll have to plan your actions and needs based on the availability and accessibility of food and the ease of acquiring it.

GROUPING: THE MORE THE MERRIER

It's important to make alliances not only for protection but assistance and companionship as well. Anyone who's ever seen any reality TV show knows that a good alliance beginning on 'day one' is critical to survival and not getting voted out or, in this case, dying. Best case scenario is that you were able to arrange such a deal with friends, neighbors and/or family before the collapse, and won't currently find yourself now making pacts with strange people. But if such is the case, you get what's left; and you can always abandon, trade up, or get rid of them later, if need be. Keep in mind that these strangers will, in all probability, be around you and your wife/kids when you're sleeping and could just rob, rape and/or kill you and yours at anytime. In one sense, it's better to find strong men who are an asset in security and labor; however, these people can easily rise up and overpower you at any given point. On the other hand, women are much less likely to murder and eat you in your sleep, and are typically much more willing to take a subservient role; however, they're much more of a liability when the shit hits the fan, as well. I find an equal combination of men to women is ideal for security, labor (on all levels) and balance; as well as keeping sexual hostilities to a minimum also. At first, keep the group fairly small, around 12 or so, although there is definitely safety in numbers; more numbers also mean more food/supply requirements. Once you've established a close-knit, reliable group you can trust, expansion can be considered.

FIRES: MMM, PRETTY

Often, I'm not sure why, looting eventually turns into setting fires. Ok, so we tend to get carried away a bit with our 'sticking it to the system' mentality. Trash is the first to be set ablaze, followed closely by vehicles and buildings. In a post-catastrophic situation, I see no immediate benefit to this trend other than totally cleansing the Earth, as fires do. This is one of many "post-catastrophe scenarios" I mentioned earlier. In 1967 and again in 1992, major race riots unfolded across the country: Los Angeles, Chicago, Detroit, New York. In just three days, more than 200 buildings were destroyed by fire during the Los Angeles riots. The same events transpired in Tampa and West Las Vegas with hundreds more fires. Similar proceedings arose during the 2000 Democratic National Convention protest, the 2001 Cincinnati riots, the 1999 World Trade Organization ministerial conference protest and the 2005 Toledo riots.

PROTECTION: THE BIGGER THE BETTER

At first I thought I didn't need to add this section; it must be pretty obvious that you'll need to carry knives, guns, bats, swords or any type of weapon, it's IS the end of the world, for Christ's sake! But then I thought, probably not everyone is as paranoid as me; or rather, most people are more trusting than me. I'll get into it more in later chapters, but for now know, at least assume, that everyone's out to get you. Of course, there will be people who honestly want to help, and people who honestly need help, but walk into every situation thinking the worst. This rings especially true for the females. Women, don't let a strange man walk up to you or come into close proximity to you, for any reason, even if they seem to need help. It's literally the only way you can defend yourself from attack from us, I don't care how many kickboxing classes you've taken, you won't win against a man in a street fight. If you don't have a firearm, a crowbar makes a formidable thrashing device; and it will help open doors and windows while looting. In either case, carry something; and don't hesitate for an instant to use it in a threatening situation. Even if you're wrong, it's better to be pleasantly, than horrifically, surprised out there.

RACE VIOLENCE: CAN'T WE ALL JUST GET ALONG?

Now this is where things start getting interesting and a little violent, and in most cases is what's confused for actual looting. But in actuality, comes much later and is not connected with looting at all. When law enforcement has been removed from the picture, races tend to group up again for protection, dominance and security--Black against White, White against Hispanic, Asian against--well, they tend to get the short end of the stick in situations like this. We can see this clearly in today's prison system, where you'll find, most notably, the Aryan Brotherhood, Black Guerilla Family, and the Mexican Mafia. These people have grouped together when their society collapsed and all was taken from them. This is the most basic nature of humans. In the 1992 Rodney King riots, bands of Korean citizens fortified and pushed back gangs of Black rioters by firing AR15s, AK47s, shotguns and UZIs into the masses after seeing the abandonment of Korea town by police. Most people are aware of the beating of Reginald Denny, a White truck driver, who was pulled from his vehicle and beaten almost entirely to death by four Black men in response to the acquittal of all four police officers involved in the Rodney King beating; but not many are aware that just minutes later, on the same intersection, Fidel Lopez, a Guatemalan construction worker, was beaten in the same manner by the same men. The point here, is that, no, we obviously can't "all just get along," especially in a post-apocalyptic world, where there's no societal structure or law enforcement. Expect looting, city-wide fires, and racial violence to start; but it's about to get a lot worse!

MARTIAL LAW: FIGHT THE POWER!

Marshal Law (or a quarantine) isn't a bad thing for the government and the country as a whole; it truly benefits them and keeps law and order intact through the duration of the instability. But for the individual, it removes what little rights you currently have and restricts your movement and ability to protect yourself. You're forced to rely 100% on the government, which is something I'm understandably completely against in any situation. We're already a policed state with the CBP, FPS, ICE, USSS, TSA, FAMS, ATF, DEA, FBI, USMS, CIA, BOP, USPIS, DSS, DOC, IRS-CID, TIGTA, USMP, DCIS, FDA-OCI, Bureau Of Indian Affairs Police, Bureau Of Land Management, Park Rangers, Department Of Fish & Wildlife Services, Federal Reserve Police, Library Of Congress Police, NSA Police, Smithsonian National Zoological Park Police, United States Capitol Police, United States Supreme Court Police, Veterans Affairs Police, Attorney General's Office, Department Of Conservation & Natural Resources, Wildlife & Freshwater Fisheries Division, State Lands Security, Department Of Corrections, Revenue Enforcement, Department Of Mental Health Police, Department Of Public Safety, State Bureau Of Investigation, Highway Patrol, Capitol Police, Protective Services, State Port Authority Police, Securities Commission, Sherriff's Department, Constable Agency, Police Department, Fire Marshall, University Police, Rangers, Gang Task Force, Bureau Of Tobacco & Firearms, Bureau Of Gambling Control, State Hospital Police, Game Wardens, State Police, Division Of Parole, Bridge & Tunnel Authority Police, Harbor Police, Probation Officers, Railway Police, Airport Police, The list goes on, it's insane. As of 2008, there were 14,169 agencies that employed 883,600 law enforcement officers on local, city, county, state and federals levels, And this doesn't even include all of the private security guards and agencies, all and any of which can set up a road block or implement a form of martial law in their jurisdiction, if need be, not to mention the hoards of gangs and locals setting up their own blockades.

EVACUATION: RUN AWAY! RUN AWAY!

In most situations, the instinctive response is to evacuate the area as soon as possible. In hindsight? Obviously a mistake. Not only will it most likely be physically impossible with the masses of traffic, but even dangerous depending on the aftermath of the actual event. In most cases, it's safer and easier to just stay in place, hunker down and ride out the storm. If, however, you're able to get out before the masses or before martial law is implemented, you'll be much better off to evacuate than to wait. Either way, make sure you have enough supplies to make the trip or ride it out.

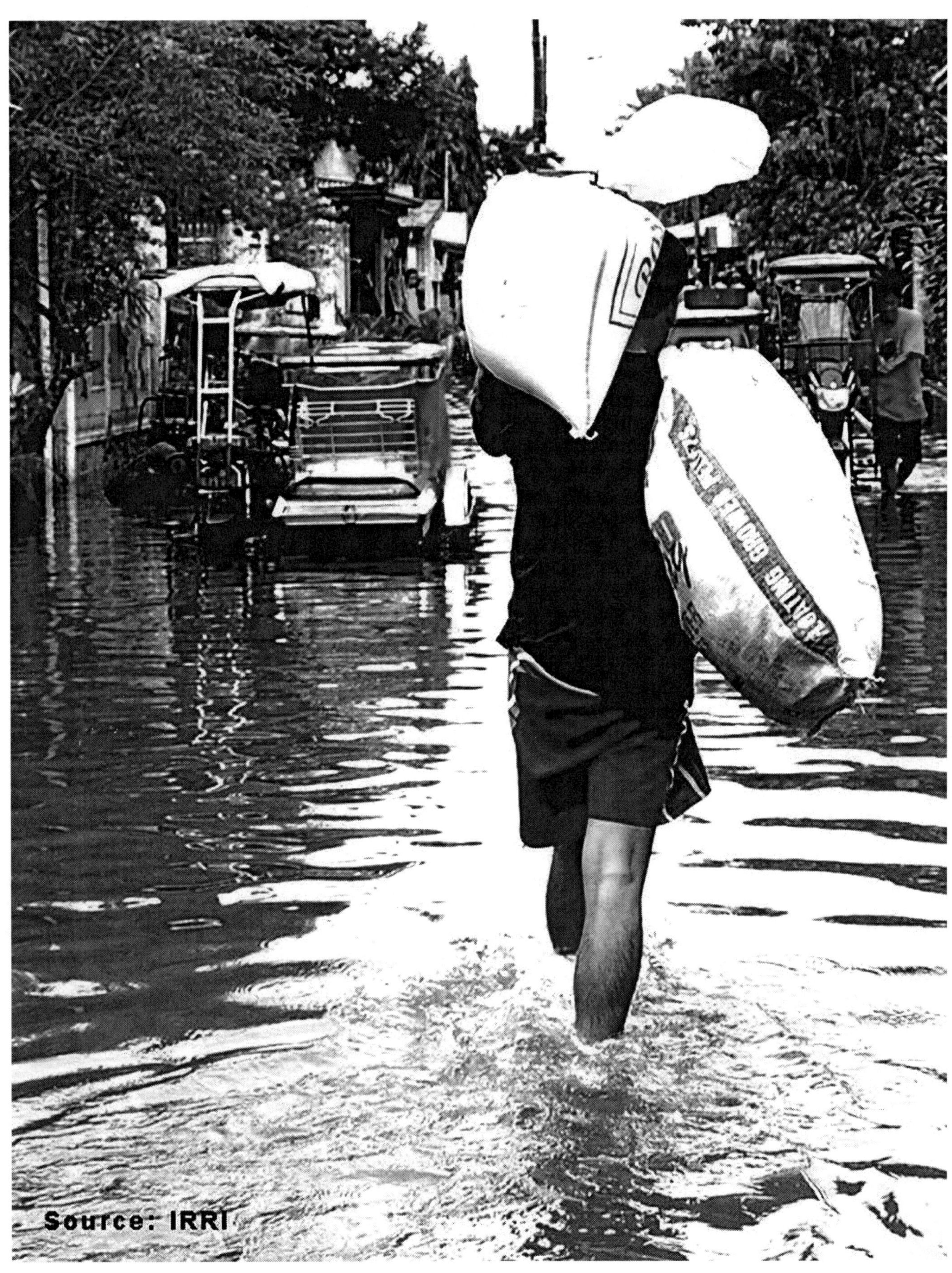

Source: IRRI

CHAPTER 8

ACCEPTING A NEW EXISTENCE: WEEK 2

Since the beginning of time, humans have always done what was needed to survive. All you have to do is look at the aftermath of past catastrophes like Noah's Flood, the Spanish Flu, WWI and II, the World Trade Center, Haiti and Katrina in order to get an idea of our potential resilience in the face of annihilation. But as you can see, we've had plenty of practice. It seems like attempts to smite us out of existence were set into motion since day one; yet, we persist, but not without major losses in numbers, that is. Pesky little infestation, aren't we?

For example, many countries lost over half their population during the Spanish flu; the Great Depression affected an alarming 92% of inhabitants of developed nations; and over three-fourths of the U.S. Navy stationed in Hawaii were completely wiped out in the attack on Pearl Harbor. There will most likely be 'some' survivors scattered around the world. Some countries will be almost entirely devastated; other less-developed regions, like the Amazon, will recover fairly well. Strangely enough, these backwoods, out-of-contact communities and villages would, in fact, be where most of the survivors will be found. It is not surprising, then, that we have no recollection of former, more advanced cultures, since only the less advanced cultures survived. An Amazonian villager has probably seen an airplane before; and when it's all over and he's carrying on humanity, he'll tell stories of a flying machine from heaven or space, possibly attributing it to God or even aliens. Either way, the technology and knowledge of how to build such a thing will be lost; and it will require reinventing the wheel again, literally. In fact, at the beginning of our involvement in WWII, American troops created airbases on remote pacific islands. To the natives that never witnessed a White man or any form of technology before, these giant metal birds looked to them like Gods, coming down from heaven. When the war ended, the airstrips were abandoned and the islanders sat around for awhile wondering what just happened. In the 80s' the islands were again revisited by White men (American anthropologists) studying island societal structures, only to realize that the tribes now had entire religions around the planes and for the last 40 years been building life-sized, wood mock-ups of the planes on the abandoned runways. When questioned about the displays, they informed the scientists that Gods had once come down from heaven and blessed the nation, but had left many moons ago.

If you've taken the necessary long and/or short term precautions, and have secured an underground bunker in time, you may be one of the lucky ones who live to tell their grandkids the truth about airplanes, nuclear bombs and the Internet. But for now, the real challenge begins with your and your family's immediate safety. The following weeks will test your resolve like you've never been tested before.

GRADUATION DAY: ON TO BIGGER AND BETTER VENTURES

Once major caches of free food, supplies and materials are completely exhausted from storefronts and warehouses, the attention will then turn to domestic storage sites (home invasion). The graduation from looting to breaking and entering will transpire in a matter of days, possible a week or two, depending on the size of the city, its available/unprotected resources, and the magnitude of the lingering population. Don't be naïve, though; this next level of food acquisition is no joke; it will occur as soon as people run out of food and start getting hungry. At this stage of looting, stealing, foraging, acquisitioning, or whatever you prefer to call it, the game becomes much more dangerous. Not only will you be attempting to enter homes that are possibly occupied/protected, but you need to worry about someone entering into your shelter/home as well. No need for crowbars today, as most homes have some form of concrete-like landscaping, bricks, walkway stones, or even just regular old rocks that will do the job just as efficiently. They make perfect tools for literally breaking and entering in a post-Judgment-Day world. Bringing your own B&E tools is a futile waste of energy at this point when there are so many enormous, fragile windows

around. The larger the window the easier it will break—double-paned, security alarm protected, argon-filled, it won't make one bit of difference. If you plan on occupying the home, a smaller upstairs window would best suit your needs, something that can easily be boarded up later.

And don't get bent out of shape over the thought of breaking into someone's house and robbing them, because you're not. These people were killed in the event or haven't made it home yet. Either way, they'll be doing the same thing to someone else's place IF they're going to survive themselves. But you're right, there's no harm in knocking first. No need to be impolite. We're not barbarians, well, not yet. If someone is actually home, simply move on to the next house. At this point, there will be more vacant homes then not; and there isn't any need to steal from other survivors—again, at least not yet. It's not yet worth risking injury to yourself, either, "yet." Again, if you don't jump on the bandwagon though, quickly, expect these urban sources of food, water, supplies, useful clothes, jewelry and other necessities to be stripped clean as well. Again, reference your *Preparations List* for suitable supplies, materials, clothing and goods you'll need to keep an eye out for.

If the day of reckoning does, in fact, occur on or around December 21st, it wouldn't be a bad idea to pick up a Bible; and, luckily, there's one in almost every home. Now, I'm not saying the book is filled with the gospel word of God passed down, though it very well may be; but, at this point, it should become obvious that it does actually contain instructions on what to do from here, wherever it may have come from; I don't think it much matters right now. As most of you must know by now, I don't believe in God, or any religious, spiritual, moral or structured "right and wrong" path or obligation for that matter. I think that humans can be free to live without chaos OR leadership OR God telling them what to do. But that's just me; and I may be wrong. The rest of the world may need guidance; and the Bible is as good a book as any to accomplish finding it. Now, I'm not saying Christianity is the right way, in general, or even the way to go in a world of upheaval and ruin. Any religion accomplishes the same thing in my mind; but it will be the most available book, at least in the U.S., that is.

ATTIRE: WHAT'S 'IN' THIS SEASON

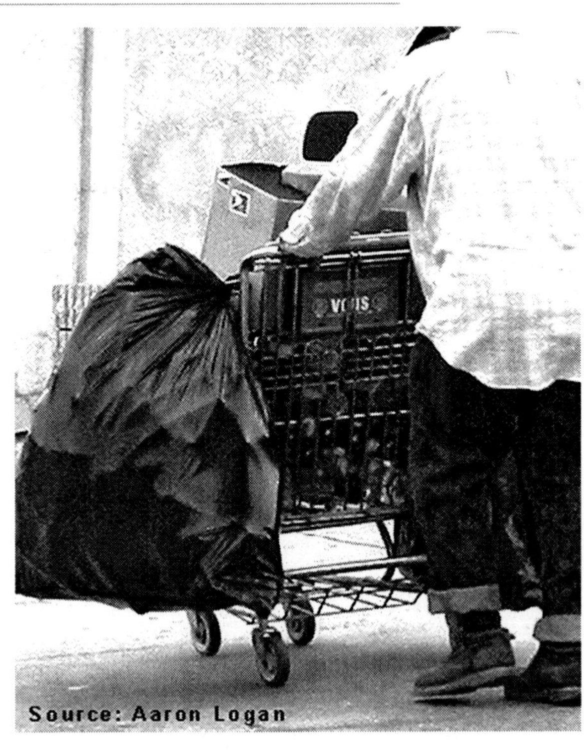
Source: Aaron Logan

By now, many of you are feeling a little overwhelmed, especially knowing that in an end-of-the-world scenario you'll have nothing that goes with your shoes. Once again, I'm here to advise you on proper catastrophe attire...

It's important to remain warm (or cool in the heat) and dry; this is *Common Sense 101*. However, since it's not easy to find people who have taken this course, I'll lay it out: If you get wet, you'll get cold. If you get cold, you're more susceptible to catching a cold because your body is too busy making heat. (I've seen people die of hypothermia in the desert, no kidding. One year, near Agua-Luna Ranch, we began seeing several helicopters flying real low. Next, park rangers and the border patrol asked us if we'd like to join the search. It seems that they had found a backpack and wallet of a hiker. The next thing you know, the body of a 25-year-old male was recovered.) If you catch a cold in a world without a structured society, medicine and medical care, you're probably going to die because you don't know what to do and no one in society has ever taken time to learn what to do to help you; they've always just assumed that doctors will always be around. So staying protected from the elements is CRITICAL! So, while rummaging through the deceased's personal belongings, show a little class and stay away from high heels, purses, funny-looking hats, dress slacks, dress shoes, dress shirts. All these items aren't durable, won't stand up to the elements and conditions and generally just serve no purpose other than for looks. As far as shoe-ware, there's been a lot of debate on what type of shoe is better, especially now that you'll be doing much more walking. Tennis shoes are extremely lightweight and comfortable requiring less energy to lift, but break down rather quickly; military boots are extremely heavy, but virtually won't ever deteriorate. I find the typical waterproof hiking shoe/boot to be the perfect blend of comfort and durability in urban survival environments. And because this new world isn't sexist or biased at all, women get to shop in the men's department for the next few months. Trust me for now, (I'll explain later) women, you will want to dress like men; it's for your own good. Look for durable pants and long-sleeve tops, wool is always a plus since it keeps you warm even when it's wet.

WATER: DISCOVERING HIDDEN SOURCES

The human body is made up of about 33% water which it uses to help circulate blood, process food, cool and assist with other critical internal functions. Dehydration is the process in which your cells shrink and stop circulating, causing your muscles to receive too little oxygen to function. But you don't have to lose 66% of your stored water to experience dehydration because the body is using almost all of the 66% all the time. Studies have shown that if you lose just 2.5%, you'll lose 25% of your efficiency and motor skills. For an average-sized man, that's just two quarts of water. The resulting mental and physical impairment could mean the end of your life and the lives of your wife, your children and those now depending upon you in the survival situation which you are currently experiencing. But you're in luck. There should still be plenty of drinkable water around in the aftermath of most catastrophic situations:

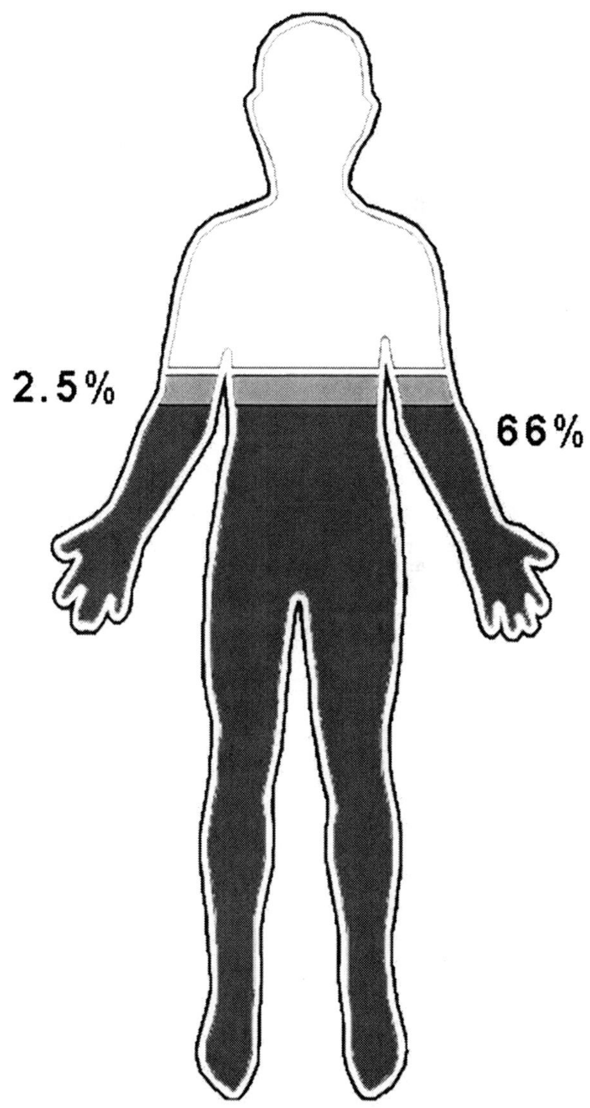

- City water: If there is no pressure to faucets there's still water inside.

a. Open a faucet on a top floor to relieve pressure; then the lowest faucet (basement or outside hose). This will allow gravity to drain any water remaining in the home's pipes. Move on to the next house and repeat.
b. This same method can work on a much larger scale by traveling to the lowest side of a neighborhood, town or city. There are enough leaks in the system's pressure so that you can skip the first step.

- Toilet: The top rectangular tank of the toilet holds about 5 gallons of safe drinkable water. The actual toilet bowl water isn't safe to drink for humans, but it is for animals since they have far more germ-fighting bacteria in their mouths.
- Freezer: Ice trays would have melted by now. All freezers, including deep freezers, also usually have a water catchment tray to hold the water runoff that melts from ice built up on interior walls.
- Fridge: Often people store water in the fridge to keep it cool, so check there also.
- Vending machines: Most vending machines now keep bottled water; it's just a matter of prying them open with your trusty crowbar. Also, soda contains 12% water (99% if it's diet) which is better than nothing at this point. Not to mention the sugars and stored calories in soda will provide energy as well.

- Water heaters: As I've mentioned repetitively, water heaters are a great source of 40 or so gallons of good drinking water; and with thousands of homes now abandoned, that's enough to last you and your group a very long time.

1. Connect a 2ft hose to the lower spigot on the water tank.
2. Open the top pressure relief valve so that the handle is sticking straight up.
3. Open the lower spigot and fill your containers.
4. Close off when finished and save the remaining water for next time.
5. Repeat on neighboring homes.

- Office building: Companies keep several 5gl water bottles on-hand for the coolers; and with hundreds of offices per building and thousands of buildings per city, that's a lot of portable, potable water.
- Garden hose: After every use, there is still 5-10 gallons of water left sitting in the hose, depending on size.
- Rain: Set out any empty containers, kiddie pools, even sheets of plastic to catch rain. Unless the event was nuclear in nature, rain water is safe to drink. It's already undergone reverse osmosis filtration; and without any industrial activity now, it may be cleaner than the bottled water you're currently holding.

Water is lost through eating, sweating, respiration and urine. Climate also plays a role, with, of course, hotter temperatures demanding more intake; as well as strong dry winds blowing across the skin that can literally suck the water from you. Conversely, high humidity content can replenish water through the skin rather than orally. So if you don't have access to water, there are a few tips you should know, to at least slow down loss:

1. Don't eat. You can last ten times longer without food than without water.
2. Stay relaxed and cool. Don't move; don't become active; don't perspire.
3. Shut up. I tell my wife this one all the time. She has no idea I'm just trying to help her conserve water. Since your mouth is filled with water all the time, every time you open your mouth to talk or breath, that moisture evaporates.
4. Store pee. Although pee is always safe to drink, I'll show you how to turn it into tasty drinkable water.

Any questionable water should be purified as previously described.

WASTE: IN A WASTED WORLD

Trash quickly builds up in a disposable, product-based nation. Although you'll be more refined, 'wasting not' and recycling everything in these murky times, the items are still cheaply built; there's no getting around that, and they'll need to be thrown away eventually. Without twice-a-week garbage pick-up, it won't matter how many survivors still exist, this trash will pile up rapidly in the streets, especially if the devastating event is just economic, or caused by government collapse, which will leave plenty of survivors and plenty of garbage but no pick-up. To resolve this issue, once the garbage cans (metal) or dumpsters fill up, burn, baby, burn. Without water pressure, toilets won't work either. This, however, can be easily remedied by pouring a 5-gallon bucket of water directly into the bowl itself, or by filling the top bowl each time after use.

TRANSPORTATION: PIMP MY NEW RIDE

Because most types of events will wipe out most types of people, there will be plenty of vehicles lying around to acquire and utilize for transportation or parts. Currently, there are 230 million functioning automobiles in the U.S. alone, an average of three per family. That's a lot of dope rides. I often have people contact me, asking, *"What is the best means of transportation to have in the end times?"* They want some big, jacked-up, V-8 truck that will roll over all the abandoned cars in the street, crash through road blocks or head off-road, if need be. But a truck wouldn't be what I'd suggest. The best option in times when there is no fuel, no parts, and no service is simplicity and fuel efficiency. A small, Japanese combination street-dirt bike is perfect when civilization is non-existent. It can weave in and out of the abandoned cars, go off-road, gets the best gas mileage at around 60 mpg, is easy to repair, is easy to hotwire and if nothing else (unlike a car or truck), you can push it to the next gas source. The only reason I would suggest a truck would be for the armoring and hauling of people or supplies through dangerous zones, where crashing your way through may become a regular pastime.

If you're going to go with a truck, though, your best bet is diesel with a steel cattle guard (not a brush guard). It has enough torque to push through obstacles while getting good gas mileage, which will be critical now. Also, diesel fuel takes a lot longer to expire (up to 25 years, in some environments), while it only takes a couple years for gas to go bad. In addition, there will be major sources of diesel with the semis and their double 200-gallon fuel tanks out of commission. When the fuel finally does run out, you can always run the vehicle on kerosene, bio-diesel or even straight oil. Conversely, though, the gasoline guzzlers can run on homemade ethanol or methanol. In the meantime, if you need to get through congested streets, might I suggest a more passive route: by siphoning out the fuel of abandoned cars (for later use); you'll lower the vehicle's weight, making it easier to push off the road to pass. The rear of any vehicle (especially trucks), will always be the lighter half, even with a full tank of gas; because the engine and transmission (weighing an average of 1000 pounds) is located in the front of the car; whereas, the gas tank is the heaviest component in the rear (weighing 150-200 pounds); and if that's empty, you can almost swing the car around (from the back) by hand with a few men.

That said, you should always pull vehicles out of the road rather than push, by hooking a tow chain (or strap or cable) to both back ball hitches or rear axles. 3/4in tow cables can be cut from highway dividers or telephone poles, and tow straps can be made from built-in building fire hoses. If you can't acquire an adequate tow chain, strap or cable, you'll need to push the vehicles out of your way. Drive up slowly, touching the rear corner panel with the cattle guard (you don't want to go crashing through the wreckage at high speeds like in the movies,) and gently push and swing the car around until you're able to pass. If you don't have a cattle guard or something protecting the front of the vehicle, wire a couple 4x4's to the front or back into the rear corner panel, pushing it around in reverse. Otherwise, you'll puncture your radiator and be completely out of commission. As mentioned, there are no vital components in the rear of your car or truck, just an empty trunk or truck bed. So if you'll be crashing through roadblocks, do it in reverse with a trunk or bed full of firewood or rocks.

After my advice, people usually thank me for my input and inform me that they'll be going right out to buy a motorcycle or truck; but here's the thing. There will be plenty of vehicles lying around just after the collapse, ripe for the picking. You <u>will</u> have to learn a couple of basic principles about the mechanics of ignition systems to get it started, though:

HOTWIRING

In most cases the keys aren't left in the ignition or visor as depicted on TV, not because people don't want you to steal their car when the world ends (I don't really think they care at this point), but because, for the most part, people don't really think about what will happen to their stuff after they're dead. So you'll need to (a) rifle through the contents of pockets or purses of the dead, decaying corpses (as long as they're not infected), or (b) learn how to hot-wire an ignition:

1. Gaining access to the interior of the vehicle is the hardest part of hotwiring a car. Slim Jims, lock picks, hangers are all well and good; but they don't work very well in newer vehicles. Your best bet is to jimmy open the sliding back window, front triangle windows, or door handles on older trucks (on most vehicles

when the interior door handle is pulled, the locks release); but nothing beats a good, old-fashioned rock to a back window; in most scenarios (you don't want glass all over the front seats).

2. Now you can't just go in with a flathead screwdriver and start sticking it in the key slot. This WON'T WORK because a screwdriver is not a key; and it doesn't have enough torque to break the ignition pins. And since we don't have the key, you'll have to by-pass the key ignition system all together. In order to work on the other side of the key switch, you'll need to rip out the key switch barrel itself along with any console and steering column panel around it. A good crowbar will knock this out in less than a minute (if you don't have a Phillips screwdriver that is).
3. Once the paneling has been removed, you'll see a bundle of 4-6 wires going into the back of the barrel. Pull all of these out. One is the main hot (usually solid red); one is the primary power supply to the car's instruments, (including the fuel pump), the coil and cylinder (usually red and white striped); another wire goes to the starter (it can be any color but is usually thicker than the others). The rest make little difference. They're usually the radio, turn signals and other accessories.

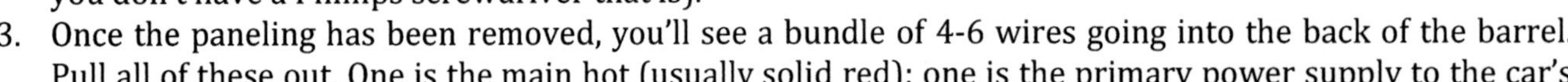

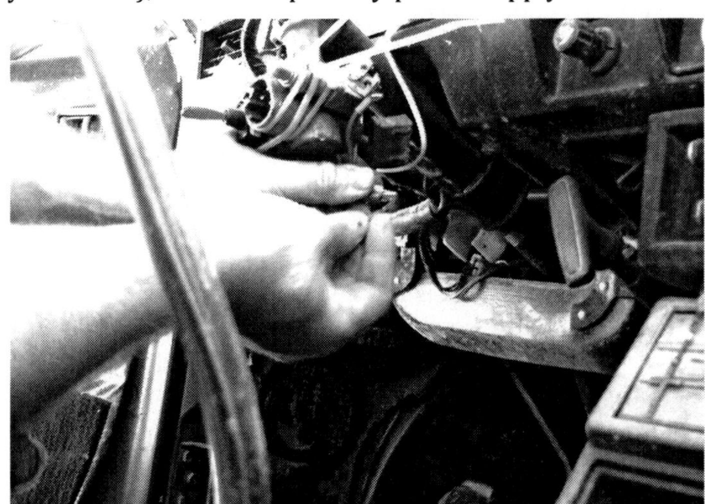

4. Take the two reds, pull the quick connects out of the assembly or cut/strip the plastic off the ends about an inch, and hold or twist them together. You should hear a click and see the dash instrument lights come on.
5. Take the thicker starter wire, pull it out of the assembly or cut and strip it down about a half an inch, and touch it against the other two reds. You'll hear the engine turn over. You may have to pump the gas, but once it catches and the engine begins to run, you can release the larger starter wire from the other two, and away you go.

NOTE: On new cars you have two anti-theft devices that may prove difficult getting around, (1) the wheel lock and, (2) the gear selector (on automatics). Both, however, can be forced to work in the following manner:

a. Unlock the steering wheel by taking a flat blade screwdriver and placing it at the top center of the steering column. Push the screwdriver between the wheel and the column, and then find and push the locking pin away from the wheel.
b. Unlock the gear selector by getting into the back seat; and while someone depresses the shifter button, kick the shifter forward--in automatic transmissions.

Another, sometimes easier, method is to simply break off the key lock cylinder (the front half of the ignition barrel), with a hammer or brick. If you look inside towards the back of the barrel, you'll see a small flat slot. That's the female end of the key lock cylinder. NOW you can stick a flathead screwdriver in and turn, bypassing all of the security features just as if you had the key.

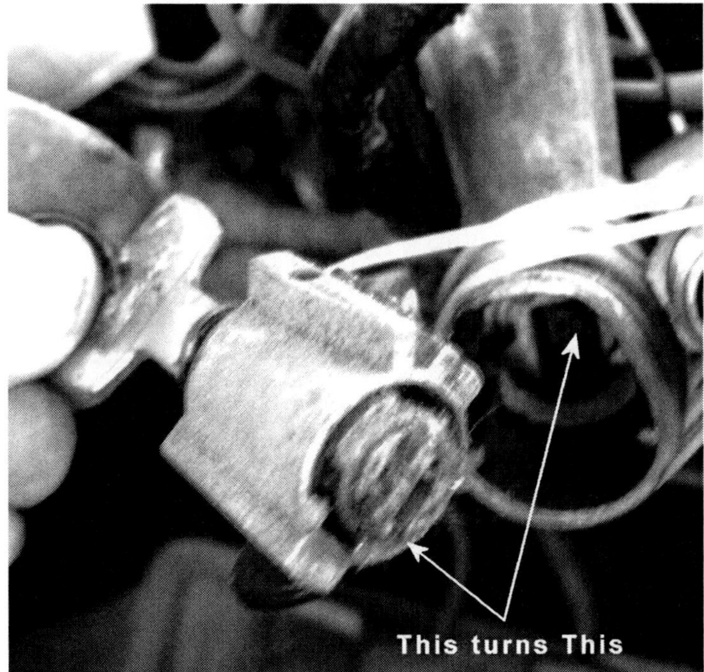

MOTORCYCLE IGNITION

Hotwiring a motorcycle is almost child's play:

1. Locate the key ignition switch barrel and find the 3 or 4 wires that connect into it.
2. Follow the 3 or 4 wires down until they connect into a plastic square quick connect.
3. Disconnect the quick connect.
4. Place a wire about 6in long with both ends stripped into 2 of the 3 holes until you hear a click.
5. If you don't hear the click, see the dash lights come on, or have power to the bike, keep trying other combinations.

6. That's it. Now press the ignition button; and away you go.

NOTE: If the bike is equipped with a steering lock, simply have one or two people sit and stabilize the bike, while another one or two forcibly turn the handle bars until the lock breaks.

SIPHONING

Siphoning gasoline from another car is extremely simple. If you haven't done it at some point in your life, here's what you'll need to do:

1. Cut a section of garden hose about 6-10ft long from someone's dead, brown front lawn.
2. Remove the vehicle's gas cap and stuff the hose as far as possible down the gas tank.
3. Mark the stopping point of the hose in relation to the gas cap opening, and remove the hose completely.
4. If the hose is wet, stick it back into the tank to the same mark. If it's not, try again, or move onto another car.
5. Now place the other end lower than the car's gas tank (about 6in above the ground), and start sucking, making sure to cap off the end of the hose between each breath with your thumb.
6. When the fuel gets to the end of the hose, stick it in a gas can or other adequate storage container. The key is to swallow the least amount of gas, but to get a good enough suction going to maintain the siphon.

You can also remove the plug from beneath the gas tank and drain the contents directly into an oil pan container or other flat container like a plastic gas can, or a 1-gallon antifreeze or oil container with the side cut open. This is also a beneficial method for draining what's left in the tank (a few gallons) after others have already siphoned off everything possible through the siphoning method. Another option is to just cut the fuel line leading out of the front of the tank and letting it drain its contents into a container in the same manner.

EXTREME ACQUISITION: A MEANS OF SURVIVAL

Once supplies from stores and abandoned homes are exhausted, it will eventually become necessary to move on to occupied homes. However, vacant home supplies should last several weeks longer than store supplies since there are literally hundreds, if not thousands of homes to any one store. But again, it all depends on how many survivors remain, the type of event, if you were able to secure any sustenance for your own group before all was taken, and the size of your group. With a larger group and fewer supplies gathered initially, this situation could unfold in as little as the second or third weeks. Keep in mind, though, that if you're starting to consider such acts, it's likely that everyone else is as well. This is where 'just living' starts getting really real, and the term "Survival of the Fittest" takes on a whole new (or rather very old) meaning.

Everyone knows their neighbors, whether it is a subdivision or an apartment building. If not physically, at least you know who lives where and which ones are more, let's say, vulnerable to invasion. Of course, widows or single elderly folks would be the most vulnerable, elderly couples after that, followed by single women with children, single women, young couples, entire families and finally single men last. Single men should be the last on your list to hit as they'll put up the greatest fight for two reasons: (1) because at this point they've just lost everything and, therefore, have really nothing to lose and/or live for; and (2) they simply have no distractions. The man with the family obviously has more to live for; he'll be more willing to give you everything you demand, while murmuring something like: "take whatever you want just, don't hurt my family." If he actually decided to fight for the food, however, from battle logistics, he would have to always keep his back to his family/wife, significantly restricting his movements and stances. Not to mention, he'd have to maintain a defensive posture

technique and never offensive, keeping himself close to his family, which significantly shifts the fight. As everyone knows, you always need both a good offense and defense. You may think (especially if you're a female reading this), that the wife or teenage sons could help in this scenario; but it's my experience that it's typically just not quite enough to shift the scale to their advantage; and in the end, they just turn out to be a liability rather than an asset. The only advantage to entering the home of a single man rather than a family man is the fact that the single man has nothing to remain for, either. He can opt to just run away leaving you everything, where a man with a family cannot just flee from them. (This may have been where the phrase "the old ball and chain" came from. If not, it's definitely appropriate.) Additionally, there is a good possibility that if he actually chooses to make a stand and loses, raping, pillaging, beatings and murderings will most likely ensue. (Sorry, ladies, but it's in our most basic instincts.) This isn't to say you should give anyone everything and don't protect what's yours. But if you haven't made the necessary shelter reinforcements yet, and don't have the upper hand, you'll now know what to expect.

And yes, if you can't muster the stomach for such things (at least the breaking, entering and theft part, not necessarily the rape, pillaging, beating and murder parts) realistically, how can you expect to survive this, let alone provide for your group and family? If another societal structure isn't built soon (which it probably won't be), most single men or men who lost loved ones in or after the disaster will, in fact, eventually turn to rape, pillaging and murder. Deep down inside it's who we are; and we have tens of thousands of years practicing it. It's programmed not only in our DNA, but most animals' DNA. Actually, it's just in the last 100 years or so that we've migrated away from such living patterns, adapting a more 'civilized' style of living. And don't kid yourself, the only thing stopping us today from rape, theft or murder is law and order. The idea of imprisonment, not morals, values or ethics, trumps or subdues the wants and desires of man's animal instincts--well, I should say, most of us. There are some who even today, actually do give in to these primitive desires. But, needless to say, during the end-times, the enforcement of society's laws will deteriorate; and we haven't evolved 'that' much in the last 100 years not to revert back to more primordial, primitive behaviors. Hell, all this talk has gotten me in the mood to throw down a little raping and pillaging, myself. I joke, (before I get the police hounding me,) well, kind of...

SHELTER REINFORCEMENT: PIMP MY APARTMENT

The abandoned office stairwell is fine for a week or so; but as more survivors begin looting habitable homes/shelters, a more long-term, secure dwelling will need to be acquired and fortified to withstand these types of attacks. There are some military defensive guidelines that will help you in choosing the perfect dream home:

Source: © BrokenSphere / Wikimedia Commons

- Height – A height advantage is critical to any battle. If you have the 'upper hand,' literally, you'll have gravity and a visual range point of advantage.
- Surveillance – Similarly, post a watch 24 hours a day. Keep on hand a set of binoculars, or better yet, a telescope (which has a much greater visual range).

- Material – Of course, steel-reinforced concrete at least 8in thick is the best. Fortunately, the great civilization of the past was thoughtful enough to make enough buildings (especially multi-level parking structures) out of the stuff. Just push a couple cars onto the ramp for a barricade and block off the stairwell(s) and you're good to go.
- Supply – All forts throughout history that didn't have long-term access to water, food and supplies to outlast the enemy, has always fallen. A source of water inside the compound is critical, with reserves of food backups capable of lasting weeks.

I don't put much emphasis on building your own shelter here because (a) I think it's a waste of time and energy with so many semi-suitable, easily-modifiable structures that will most likely remain in existence and available to take over; and (b) water, food, supplies and security are going to more than occupy most of your time and energy in the days to come. That said, if nothing else, take refuge in a brick or rock home with small windows and/or steel window bars, preferably with a clay, tile, or metal corrugated roof, as wood or tar shingles will quickly ignite and burn you out of your stronghold before the battle even begins. The only 'sure thing' advantage when it comes to a shelter is impenetrable walls and doors in a windowless, non-flammable structure. Brick up the lower level doors and windows permanently by laying brick and mortar on the outside window eave, as well as the inside on the window ledge. This will prevent admittance if anyone's able to break through the outside layer of brick. If you don't want to or can't seal off the lower level doors and windows, at least install bars made of 1/2in – 3/4in rebar on them. I'll cover how to make a simple arc welder and personal power plant in a later chapter to assist in this process.

Since the shielding of your shelter is useless if you leave... don't leave. If you must leave for food and supplies, here's a simple bullet-proof vest (Flak jacket style) you can make with common items:

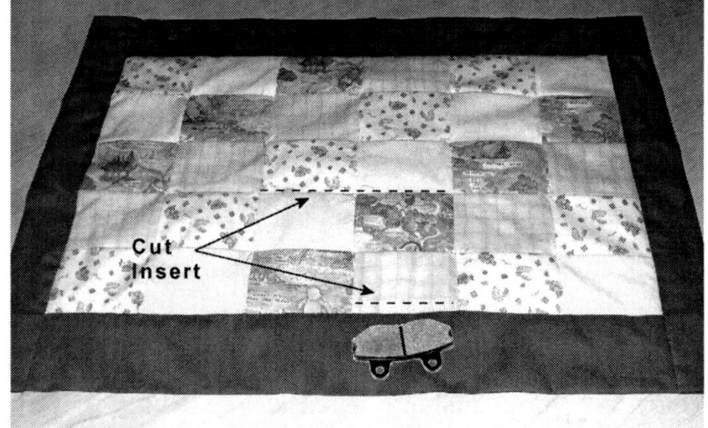

1. Collect about 20 brake shoes pads (armor, fiber bullet-stopping plates).
2. Cut the tops of each square out of a baby/child quilt (the type with smaller square patterns) and fill with plates.
3. Cut a 1ft slit in the middle of the quilt for your head and you have a bullet-proof vest. Don the vest like a Mexican poncho, tying a rope or strap around the middle. The vest is much heavier than Kevlar, but will work sufficiently for your needs.

As for town or community fortification you can consider. Of course this wouldn't apply to large cities; but a small town, that's not connected to any other on any of its sides, can be blockaded, locking off all major incoming roads and access points with spike strips, abandoned cars or manned roadblocks.

LAW OF THE JUNGLE: SURVIVAL OF THE STRONGEST

"We have a lot of backwards to go before we can even think about going forwards again."

- Me

We've strayed so far down the wrong road that we have a lot of backtracking to accomplish before we can even find or see the right road again, let alone start traveling up it. But don't get me wrong, I'm not talking about utter chaos here. There will be law, the law of the jungle, that is, which is, in fact, natural order. You see, an animal (if the term didn't apply before, it definitely applies to humans, in this case) has several food and territory-related guidelines that it very seldom breaks. For example, an animal won't attack something if it feels it may get hurt in the process itself (Law 1). The animal has learned this lesson after millions of years without hospitals or medical care; whereas, we take hospitals for granted and, therefore, take risks we otherwise shouldn't/wouldn't normally. Now there are no hospitals, no 911, no first aid, no medicine, no antibiotics or antiseptics; so a virus, bacteria, cut or broken bone will most likely spell certain death. The only time an animal would break this rule is if it were diseased, cornered, protecting its offspring, or extremely hungry.

Applied to humans, if two men of relatively the same size approached each other in a shattered world wanting each other's goods/women/children, they would most likely both cause injury to the other, because neither has a 'sure-thing' advantage over the other. In this case, the smart thing for the two men to do would be just to walk away. But they won't, not during the first few weeks at least; no, they'll have to learn this lesson the hard way. At first they'd attack everything and anything in their paths, trying to prove their masculinity to earn a position in the group or maybe to impress a female, acting as they do now in a hospital-rich, pre-apocalyptic society. Yet, eventually, after receiving some type of injury, possibly characteristically 'minor' in nature, the man would be out of commission for several days, maybe even weeks, if infection sets in. And without help/treatment, it's very likely he'll either starve to death, being unable to collect food and water, or die of infection. At the very least, he'll put a tremendous strain on his group or wife and kids, all because of a historically and societal-created small fatal error in judgment.

If he does somehow manage to beat the odds and survive, he will most likely have learned his lesson and will evaluate the situation much closer next time, making sure not to enter into a fight without the 'sure-thing' advantage. I suppose this is where the saying "what doesn't kill you makes you stronger" comes from. Now, if there were, say, ten men confronting one man (with or without a wife and child), or one of the previously-mentioned two men had a gun and the other didn't, the chance of an injury to any of the ten men (or the man with the gun), would be slim to none. In other words, a gun or numbers is a 'sure-thing' advantage and, therefore, the reward is well worth the danger.

Another rule of nature is not to attack and kill anything that doesn't at least replenish the energy exhausted in its meat (Law 2). A lobster is a prime example of this law. We only eat lobster today because they taste good, well, very good. But if you were to have to catch, kill, clean, prepare, cook, de-shell and eat lobster in the wild to live, you'd have spent considerably more energy and will have lost more calories than what the meal could replenish. The higher the calorie count of the animal or hoard of protected supplies, subtracted by the lower the loss of calories acquired by the food, equals a smart meal in the wild. In other words, if you were, say, stuck on an island and the only food supply was an endless supply of wild yet delicious lobster, you'd literally starve to death with a full stomach.

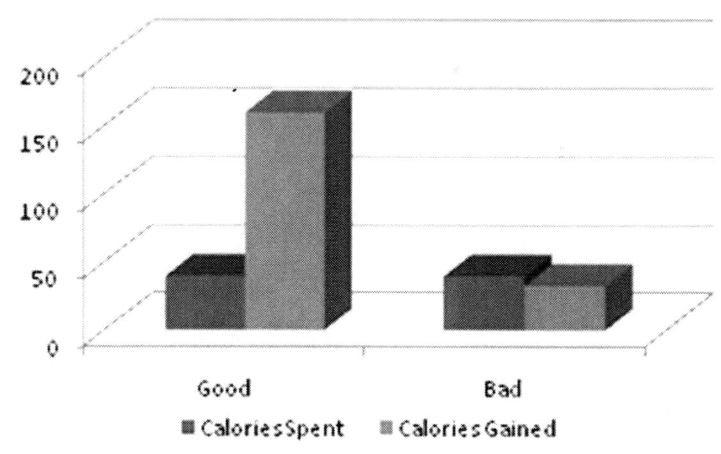

Such is the way of the animal kingdom; and such will be the way after the day of reckoning. Using these two prime rules of the jungle, we see that robbing the weaker, slower, and older people, along with women and children first is the best case scenario to prolong you, your group and your family's life, amounting to the least amount of energy loss, as well as the least chance of injury. Don't think you have it in you? Or possibly you think I'm crazy. Either way, people will be carrying out the acts I'm describing; it's what they've always done. You can accept what I'm saying and prepare defenses for it; do the deed yourself and give your family a better chance of survival; or ignore what I preach and die along with your wife and children. It's up to you; but I'm not going to sit here and be quiet, beating around the bush, delicately describing events which WILL transpire after the world, as we know it, has met its maker, in order to keep from offending today's unprepared sensitive pansy-ass masses. The truth is, it's all just in our mind. I mean you don't see animals feel bad about such actions. And yet they run-down, attack, kill and eat the weaker, older (or younger) and slower as a general rule of thumb. It's natural.

As far as defending your own hoard, wife and/or children, you can use the same two laws. Is your stash worth possible injury? How much of a stash do your 'would be' attackers possess? Is their stash worth your injury? How much energy, ammunition and supplies will be spent in this ordeal? Do you (or they) possess a 'sure thing' advantage? Now, when referring to a wife and children, the same questions may not seem relevant (or maybe they do to you, ha!) Regardless, there are preparations that you can make to help safeguard your family, group, food/supplies and shelter:

DEFENSE & OFFENSE: BRING YOUR 'A' GAME

The first rule of defending your possessions is, *look the part.* Don't have, wear or make anything that looks nice; and if you have anything nice, make it look, well, not nice. It's fairly obvious that pretty things are more prone to attracting attention. You're basically manufacturing a situation that triggers lust. I mean, these people don't have anything nice now, either; but they still want to have nice things also. Why should you have something nice and they don't? On that note, if you do have females in your group, like a girlfriend, daughter, friend, wife/wives (hell why not now?); shave their heads; make sure they don't wash their faces or armpits; and definitely (I have to say it) don't let them put any make-up on, wear anything seductive, tight-fitting, or even of female origin (men's clothes, remember) for that matter. You want them to stink and look rough, like a male.

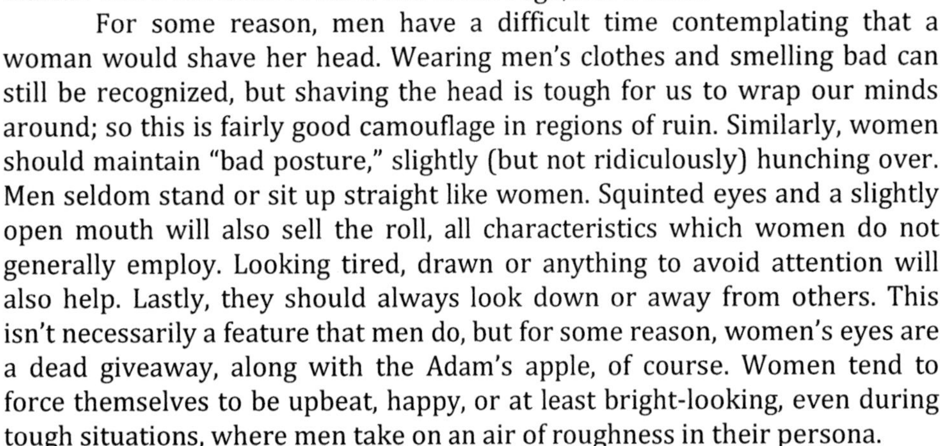

For some reason, men have a difficult time contemplating that a woman would shave her head. Wearing men's clothes and smelling bad can still be recognized, but shaving the head is tough for us to wrap our minds around; so this is fairly good camouflage in regions of ruin. Similarly, women should maintain "bad posture," slightly (but not ridiculously) hunching over. Men seldom stand or sit up straight like women. Squinted eyes and a slightly open mouth will also sell the roll, all characteristics which women do not generally employ. Looking tired, drawn or anything to avoid attention will also help. Lastly, they should always look down or away from others. This isn't necessarily a feature that men do, but for some reason, women's eyes are a dead giveaway, along with the Adam's apple, of course. Women tend to force themselves to be upbeat, happy, or at least bright-looking, even during tough situations, where men take on an air of roughness in their persona.

These precautions don't guarantee that even if you're ugly things won't be stolen, though, or that your wife, girlfriend, daughter or other group members won't be kidnapped, raped, tortured and killed, even if they look like boys, hell, even if they are boys. Life is hard on men in a post-apocalyptic world, but for women and children it can be unbearably brutal and downright archaic. But you don't need to believe me right now. I know it's a lot to take in. Such a big change to "civilized" society seems impossible, improbable; but you'll believe it as soon as you start seeing happening to others right in front of your own eyes on a daily basis, or you see someone else watching as it's happening to you.

WEAPONS

Weapons are a no-brainer, especially, long distance hunting rifles. I personally prefer a 30-06 with a 300+ yard day/night scope and traps, (which I'll discuss in depth in *Chapter 9*). These types of weaponry let you attack or defend from an attack from a distance, without the danger of injury. This is a 'sure thing' advantage; whereas, if you go face-to-face with knives or shotguns or such, everyone walks away injured, if anyone walks away at all. Handguns aren't mandatory like shotguns and rifles, but can definitely come in handy IF the other person is, say, wielding a knife or bat. If it weren't for this, I'd almost prefer a sharp knife over a handgun, simply because of weight ratios, along with the fact that knife ammunition never runs out. As far as size, a 9mm is large enough for both men and women to shoot comfortably; and because it's the most used firearm in the world, finding ammunition for it will be much easier. If you don't have a knife or don't know how to sharpen a knife, a box cutter will do. And when there aren't any sharpening stones available, a car window will work.

A high draw-weight compound bow with several dozen arrows will come in handy once all the ammunition runs out. A compound bow can be shot at almost the same distance as a rifle with great accuracy (if learned well); yet, the ammunition can be replenished and reused over and over again; or if broken, new arrows can be made. Actually, typically, more specifically, the tips of the arrows are usually what always breaks. So by stocking up on tips you'll have a long supply of ammunition. Once your tips though, finally do run out, you can still find readily available bolts and screws with the same thread pattern (typically 10/32) and cut off and sharpen the heads to make new tips.

Traps are also a great weapon for attacking or, again, defending from a distance. Traps can be mechanical or mental in nature. Mechanical traps can level the playing field for the 10 on 1 battle described in the example, providing the one person with a 'sure thing' advantage and now a large acquisition of supplies as well. Mental traps are also effective, such as a half-naked woman tied up on the side of the road (the bait). No kidding, men lose all intellectual cognitive skills when they see a half-naked woman (just go into any strip club), and more so in a lawless land. Also, a plea to a passing stranger for help to feed small children starving and dying of thirst is also a good mental trap, especially for women (women lose all intellectual cognitive skills when they see children suffering). I mention these here not only for use in acquiring supplies, but for precaution and defense as well. If you see a half-naked, beautiful woman on the side of the road, or a couple kids, or an abandoned baby crying, it's probably a trap; use extreme caution, turn around and go the other way; or survey the situation from a distance for several days before continuing. If the situation is real, they won't die in a day or two.

Like I said, shotguns are a must as well, preferably 12-guage assault or tactical style (sometimes called combat, sawed-off, short-barreled, SBS or assault shotguns) with large rounds like buck or 0, or 00 load. On this note, it may be pertinent to explain how to build, or rather convert, a regular shotgun into a tactical shotgun, along with how to make several other types of useful weapons. If you are ~~ignorant enough~~ misfortunate enough to have no weapons during the aftermath of an apocalypse that is:

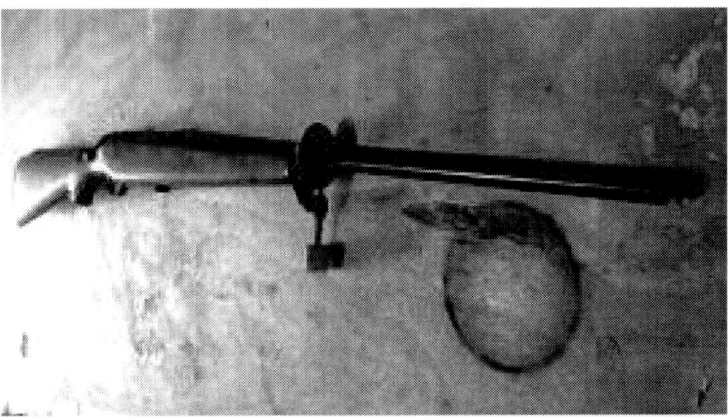

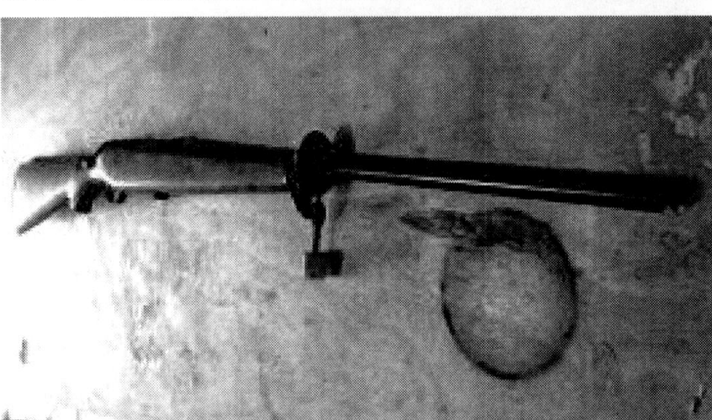

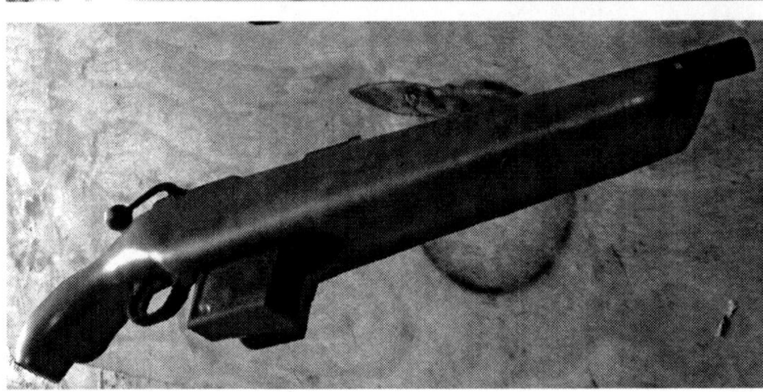

- Sawed-off shotgun:

A sawed-off shotgun is lighter, more maneuverable, and more concealable while retaining its power. The recoil will increase while the stability decreases with the modifications. And, of course, the load or pellet spray will naturally spread out wider and faster through the shorter barrel, making it perfect for mid to close rang encounters.

1. Using a tube cutter or hacksaw, cut the barrel to the desired length (the barrel itself is not hardened steel and will cut easily). Legally it must be 18in, while maintaining an overall length of 26in; but who's left to enforce such laws? Cutting flush with the hand guard is usually good enough in non-pumps (pump style would determine the barrel length for you); but cutting into it won't affect performance either, and will make the gun lighter. I'd leave 6-8in to grip onto, though.
2. File any nicks, burs, or rough spots left from the cutting with a round file or chainsaw chain tooth file inside and out.
3. Wrap a piece of tape, or draw a comfortably curved line just behind the protruding hand grip front of the shoulder stock.
4. Again, using a band saw, circular saw (with wood blade this time) or miter saw, cut along the tape edge or drawn line.
5. Again, round off the sharp corners with a wood file; and sand smooth if needed.
6. Rub a little fat or automotive oil on the cuts to prevent rust and wood splitting.

- Pipe shotgun:

1. Using a tube cutter, hacksaw, band saw, circular saw with a carbide blade, or chop saw, cut a 1ft long section out of any standard 3/4in steel electrical conduit piping and place a 12-gauge shotgun shell inside one end making sure that the head rests securely on the lip of the pipe. This will be the barrel.

2. Cut a standard 1in steel water or gas pipe to 9in long.
3. Drill a 1/8in hole in the top of a 1in pipe cap and insert a 1/8in metal screw into the hole.
4. Screw the 1in cap onto the end of the steel water pipe nipple. This will be the firing pin.

5. When you're ready to fire, place the shotgun shell inside the first pipe and the first pipe inside the second; and slide them quickly together, making sure to keep a grip on both pipes.

If you kept the barrel from the sawed-off shotgun, it would come in handy now for the first pipe. The weapon isn't very accurate; however, make no mistake, it's deadly up close with any size load.

- Gun powder:

To make black powder or, even better, gunpowder to reload shells or as improvised explosives, you'll need some potassium nitrate (also known as KNO3 or saltpeter), which you can find in its granular form in *Grant's Stump Remover* (or any stump remover), found at Home Depot, Lowe's or similar garden stores, which is 99% potassium nitrate; wood charcoal; granular (not powder) sugar; rubbing alcohol (optional); 3 bowls and a round-handled screwdriver (mortar and pestle), and a small scale found in any kitchen.

1. Add 50% (by weight, not volume) KNO3 to the bowl, along with a few drops of rubbing alcohol (which helps to bind the powder); and crush into a fine powder with the screwdriver.
2. Add 25% charcoal into a separate bowl and do the same.
3. Add 25% sugar into a third bowl and do the same.
4. Mix the three together until the color is a constant, soft grey.

At this point, you have black powder or BP, a weaker, slower-burning form of gun powder or GP. For a more powerful GP, re-granulate the mix by:

1. Adding more alcohol to the BP and stirring into a clay-like consistency.
2. Add more BP or alcohol as needed to get the consistency to the point that, when you squeeze it, it should hold its form and no alcohol should drip out.
3. Rub the clay ball through a tea bag or spaghetti strainer onto tinfoil or a paper towel until it's completely granulated.
4. Let the granules dry for a day or so indoors (so they don't blow away) and then collect.

Don't worry about the powder exploding from friction or static electricity while mixing; it requires at least 572°F to ignite. By adding a little sulfur (found in insecticides, pesticides, matches or fireworks) to the mix you'll again get a much stronger GP.

- Smoke bomb:

1. Cut up 50-100 ping balls into tiny pieces.
2. Wrap them in several layers of tinfoil.
3. Punch a hole in one side of the tinfoil.
4. Light several of the pieces in the hole, flip, drop, run.

Similarly, burning tires also creates a LOT of smoke, perfect for a smoke screen.

- Molotov cocktail:

1. Fill a bottle (wine or other thin-walled bottles work best) with gasoline 1/4 – 1/3 from the top.
2. Add 1/4 - 1/3 motor oil (used or new) to the mix to get a longer burn ratio.
3. Stuff 2ft of paper towels or a thin rag into the bottle, leaving about a foot or more hanging out as a wick.

4. Wrap electrical or duct tape around the neck and wick where the wick enters the bottle. This is so the gasoline (a) doesn't dump out accidentally when you throw it, and (b) doesn't evaporate during storage.
5. Shake the oil/gas mix up.
6. Tie the remaining wick up in a very loose knot and store for later use.
7. When ready, untie wick, light, and immediately throw (underhanded if possible, over handed throws often result in flammable liquid pouring all over the throwers arm).

If you'll be using methanol or ethanol as a fuel, you won't need oil, since it's a much slower burning combustible liquid. As far as wicks go, if you don't have rags, the light brown paper towels found in public bathroom roll-out dispensers work really well since they're stronger, less absorbent, and don't have perforated tear marks. You can also use the blue shop rags, which are actually paper towels, also. One problem with Molotov cocktails is that you're out in the elements when you're trying to light them; and if you have ever tried to strike a lighter or match in the wind, you know it's virtually impossible. A constant flame source, such as a pit fire or torch, should be in the vicinity during lighting. Lastly, don't get any gasoline on your hands while you're lighting it; the flame will instantly jump over.

- Shank:

1. File down the handle end (flat end) of a cheap toothbrush or other household plastic tool on the concrete to a sharp point on all sides.
2. Grind off the bristles on the concrete as well.

A shank can be made out of literally anything. I like the toothbrush method because (a) it's extremely easy and quick to make, (b) it's lightweight and fits in your pocket, (c) a toothbrush can be found virtually anywhere, anytime, and (d) it can pass through military checkpoint metal detectors. (Why/where would military check points be in an apocalyptic world? If there's any form of government left or a foreign military takes control after the event, they <u>will</u> declare martial law, restricting movement through even the smallest of occupied/controlled regions.) The fact that it's plastic doesn't make it any less deadly. Keep in mind a shank works a little differently than a knife in that you don't want to slice/slash with it, but rather stab or jab repetitively around the throat, front or sides of the chest area, armpits or groin areas--10, 20 even 30 stabs anywhere, though, will drain the human body of blood faster than the person can seek assistance or that assistance can seal them up. Another good way to make a plastic shank, if you have time and don't have a toothbrush, is to dig a small trench (form) in the dirt about 1-1/2in wide by 6-8in long. Melt down anything plastic (toothbrushes, combs, Styrofoam cups, spoons, forks, knives, Zip-Lock bags, grocery bags, etc.) and pour the plastic into the trench. When the plastic cools, remove and sharpen on the concrete, road or side of a building. Again, tape the end with electrical or duct tape, or tie a rag around the handle.

- Acid gun:

1. Remove the 2 plastic caps from a car battery.
2. Place the head of an empty lemon squeeze bottle inside a hole or cell and suck up some sulfuric acid into the plastic container and replace the cap until ready to use.
3. When the time is right, remove the cap and spray at the face and eyes area or any exposed skin.

The small plastic container filled with acid weighs very little and can fit in a coat pocket very easily. The stream of spray can reach up to 10ft or more making this a short range, projectile weapon. Any household spray bottle will also work with less range coverage. Conversely, if you want to maximize the coverage exposure or use it for crowd dispersal, you'll want to utilize a Super Soaker Water Canon, which can shoot 35-50ft.

WARNING: This is an extremely painful, yet, not necessarily deadly form of attack/defense. If you happen to be hit by one, quickly rinse the area with water as soon as possible. If no water is available, pee on the area, throw up on it, or pour any liquid available on the area to dilute the acid and stop further burning. If you receive treatment, the skin will eventually heal, but you will be left with deep, horrific scars, both mentally and physically.

- Pepper spray:

1. Similar to making BP, mill some red pepper seeds in a container.
2. Once the seeds are powder, add black pepper (regular household pepper from the shaker) and grind down further.

3. Add rubbing alcohol, approximately 1/4in – 1/2in above the powder and another 1/4in of baby oil and stir for about 3 minutes.
4. Pour the mixture through a paper cloth filter to remove any remaining solids.

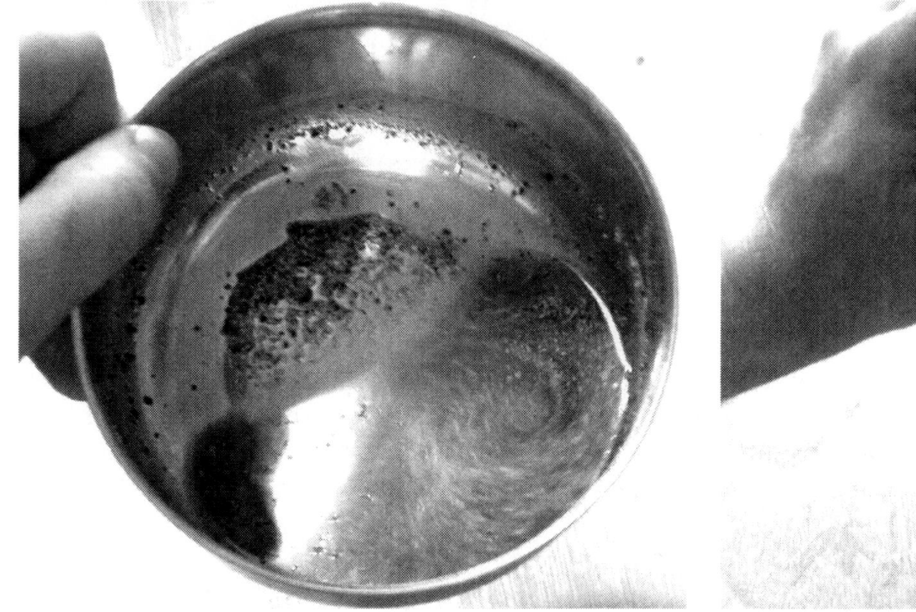

5. Pour the filtered contents into a 1-2 ounce travel-size spray bottle.

6. Replace the cap and you're ready to go.

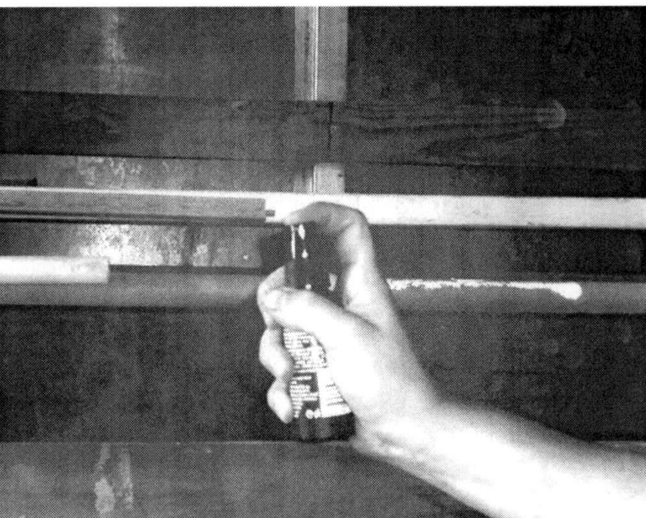

The baby oil acts as an adhesive, causing the spray to stick to the skin, while the black pepper acts as an inhalant attacking the victim on two fronts, the eyes and the nose. It's a good idea to use the spray on yourself (no kidding) before you use it on anyone else. I know this may sound weird; but you'll want to test the potency before finding yourself in a real life situation where, if the mix isn't strong enough, all you're going to do is just really piss someone off. Spraying yourself (or your wife) will be extremely uncomfortable for several minutes, but will not cause any long-term or permanent damage.

- Modified clubs:

Construction equipment, farm tools, and sporting goods have made great weapons since the beginning of time--hammers, bats, crowbars, pitch forks, pipes, and anything else that will do bodily damage will work, while keeping an amount of distance (the more the better) between you and your attacker/victim. Feel free to spice up your weapon as necessary to fit the new chaotic world. For example, it can't hurt to wrap barbed wire or nail several nails around the business end of a wooden bat, leaving 1/4in or so protruding, while clipping off the heads with a pair of wire cutters, or taping pieces of protruding glass around the end of a steel pipe, adding a lacerational aspect to the blunt force trauma.

- Spear:

The spear is one of the oldest weapons in history, even older than the club, in fact. The Indians originally flaked off shards of rock (usually flint) forming a replaceable spearhead which would attach to the spear. For now, we'll just sharpen our spear to a point. A broom or mop handle works great for this. Whittle off slices of wood at one end with a knife, cutting away enough to form an 8-10in long point. This will allow and facilitate an easier penetrating surface. In the middle and about a foot from the other end, cut 1/8in deep vertical chunks from the spear making gripping points. You won't be able to throw this spear in an attack, since there is no counter balance weight in the tip. What you don't want to do is to tie your knife to the end of your spear pole like you see in the movies; this will only lead to a broken, lost or captured knife. A spear doesn't need to be thrown to cause mortal damage, anyway. In fact, by maintaining a hold on it, you're able to inflict multiple deadly punctures as opposed to just one. If you are going to use the spear as a projectile, however, you'll need to weigh down the front by taping something like an appropriately-sized wrench about a foot from the tip and practice throwing until you master the weapon before using it in any real battle. Otherwise, you're just going to miss, break the tip, or hand the would-be victim a nice, new weapon.

- Weapons to stay away from, or use as a last resort: axes, bats, steel pipes.

Even though I've listed some of these weapons above, they should only be used as a last resort if nothing else is available, simply because they are incredibly heavy, bulky, and hard to conceal if you're walking around. If you're driving and don't have to be burdened with the load, however, that's a different story.

- Weapons that aren't really weapons at all: chains, shovels, hockey sticks, chain saws, golf clubs.

Contrary to what many think, most weapons portrayed in movies aren't weapons at all and in real life would cause little to no damage whatsoever. For example, if I were to hit someone with, say, a 6ft long chain, it would simply just wrap around him, accomplishing virtually nothing. The same physics go for a golf club. I wouldn't count on a hockey stick to do anything other than break on impact; the teeth of a chainsaw aren't designed for meat (there are meat saws however) and would bog down in the fleshy mess, creating only superficial tears; and the only thing a shovel's good for (other than shoveling shit) is grinding the head down to a point to make a spear. The metal's mass just isn't enough to knock anyone unconscious, as seen in the monster films. All that these things will do is just piss someone off more than what they already are.

HAND-TO-HAND COMBAT (STREET FIGHTING)

You should not, for any reason, ever fight anyone hand-to-hand in a street fight, especially with no help, no cops and no society. You have no idea what this person will do, or whether he has a weapon that he'll use in an instant to incapacitate you if he can get close enough. Always, no matter what, use your projectile weapons from a distance, or at least your close proximity weapons. A couple feet advantage versus a couple inches can make all the difference in the world for you to win a fight. That was the entire point of the invention of the sword (and, later, longer swords). It was to inflict mortal damage to the opponent's body while remaining a suitable distance away from the opponent's short thrusts. This is the entire key to fighting. As time went on, we would separate ourselves further and further from our enemy's attacks while still achieving ours--making longer swords, guns, artillery, bombers, and finally, ballistic missiles that can be activated, and an attack accomplished, by a press of a button from a secure underground bunker, anywhere in the world. That said, if you find yourself surprised and suddenly in a hand-to-hand fistfight, there are a couple of tricks that can help:

1. Wake up! When you become aware of a potentially unstable situation, become alert as possible. Look around for anything that could become a weapon. Search for an escape route.
2. Try first to talk the guy down. Apologize if necessary; just avoid a fight, without coming off weak that is.
3. Maintain alertness and walk away backwards, while facing your opponent.
4. If the idiot pursues, try running, if you think you can outrun him.
5. If you have nowhere to go, try to get in the first hit to the face (sucker punch) and/or a kick to the groin.
6. Keep your fists in front of your face and your mouth closed and teeth clenched.
7. Don't fight fair! Go straight for the groin, eyes, nose, throat, knees.
8. Take off any upper body clothes such as a coat and shirt; it will not only keep you cooler, insuring better performance; it'll prevent your opponent from easily grabbing you. On this note, a shaved head is also important.
9. If your opponent has a knife, wrap your clothing around one arm and use it as a shield.
10. If your opponent is bigger than you, keep your distance, throw long kicks and punches.
11. Conversely, if you are bigger, get close and take him to the ground; use your weight to your advantage.
12. If you get knocked down backwards, keep your chin close to your chest; otherwise, you'll hit the back of your head on the concrete and knock yourself out.
13. If he's advancing fast, don't immediately try to get up. Stay on your back; and start kicking up at the balls, and knees.
14. When your attacker backs off to nurse a blow or comes in for another attack, don't get up on all fours; this will provide a perfect opportunity for a face, stomach or ribs kick, get up sideways.
15. Slam his head on the concrete floor, walls or furniture as many times as possible.
16. Head-butt the face. The top of your head is one of the hardest surfaces on your body, use it when in close.
17. If you can't dodge a punch, lower your head and walk into it. This way your attacker may miss the mark or strike the top of your head, hopefully damaging his hand in the process.

18. Give your best war cry and scariest, craziest face. If you can create doubt, fear, intimidation, distraction or just second guesses, you'll keep your opponent off step, giving you the advantage.
19. When the fight is finished, don't hang around; get the hell out of there before his buddies show up.
20. Lastly, make sure that your wife, daughter, girlfriend or any other female friend has directions to leave at the first sign of a brawl. That way, once you've gotten your ass kicked, are unconscious (if not dead) on the ground, out of the picture and unable to defend her, she's not next.

Let it be known I'm a big guy, bigger than most with military training, but I would flee (if possible) before I had to enter into a fair fight with someone. Just the name alone, "fair fight," goes against every element of a 'sure thing' advantage. Blow for blow, YOU are almost guaranteed to lose against the average person; and if you've never been in a fight before (which I'm sure you haven't) you have no idea how painful and disorientating it can be. In fact, as a little taste, stand in the road as a 'friend' punches you in the face (avoid the nose) or kicks your feet out from under you to see how it feels. One such real life experience is worth every page in this book.

SECURITY SYSTEMS

There are several methods of building homemade security systems--anything from simple alarm trip wires, to motion-activated sirens, to security cameras. Since the Agua-Luna 2012 bunker is completely underground (like most) and located in a typically flat field, it is not only invisible to the naked eye (a security feature in itself), but a perfect location for a Garmin 18 Radar system (or a similar model). Boat radar systems complement underground homes very well, since: (a) they run off the homes' existing 12v solar system (boats run on 12v also), (b) the flat, treeless terrain bounces, or echoes, back the radar undisturbed just like water, and (c) the dome antenna is almost unnoticeable when painted tan. Similarly, I've also installed vehicle back-up cameras around the perimeter and dash monitors in the bunker, which also run off 12v power, of course.

That said, animals can be the best, foolproof method of maintaining security on all levels, though: alarm, defense, protection. On the ranch, we use guinea, turkey and pea hens (female peacocks) as warning systems, which all let out a loud alarming sound upon smelling, hearing or seeing an unwanted visitor (man or animal). After just weeks of hearing the alarm and seeing the intruder, the dogs and donkeys have learned to connect the two meanings together. They understand that when the alarm sounds, there's danger upon the facility. Now, whenever the fowls screech, the dogs and donkeys (which are highly territorial and protective in nature, anyway), literally charge and attack the trespasser. This scene actually takes place on a nightly basis at the Agua-Luna compound with mostly coyotes (although neighbors have fallen prey occasionally as well), so they get plenty of practice. All animals, of course, free range in a complete radius around the dwelling, preventing intruder entry from any direction.

Rock-filled cans at the end of a trip line are always a safe bet; although animals, and the wind, tend to give false warnings. Also, a can doesn't sound very loud to begin with. If you have a perimeter wall, you can't miss by filling the top with broken bottle glass. As far as fences and barbed wire, they'll slow a would-be marauder down; but that's about it.

REALITY CHECK: 1 2 CHECK, CHECK

I want to end this chapter with a little insight. I've realized over the years through observation, dedicated evaluation, real-life experiences, and from people wiser than me, something that will help you to survive--and you can quote me on this: In general, naturally, all people are bad, corrupt and even evil, if you will!

I once heard, (or probably actually heard many times) that for the most part, all people were naturally good at heart. And so I always believed this to be true like probably so many of you; no matter what bad things someone did to me or to folks around me that I witnessed, I always told myself that this was an exception, that people in general were actually good, and that there were just a few bad apples. I'm not sure where this saying came from and it doesn't much matter, or even that it was wrong at the time it was originally stated, but times have changed greatly. And those "few bad apples" have since ruined the entire bunch. The problem was, I had no proof, just a theory and the following observations: It's all over the TV and the news; we see it every day; and yet we continue to think that it's not so. So I decided to get proof.

On June 7, 2001, I purchased 100 pairs of new sunglasses in bulk on eBay and left them on a sink in the same gas station bathroom in an average-sized city with a below average annual crime rate, about one per day over a four-month period. I then taped a sign that read "please return any lost items to the cashier" on the door and sat back and waited for the results, which were even surprising to me. First off though, before I get too far, in order for this misnomer to be proved correct, at least 51 (51%-- "most") of the 100 culprits--would need to turn in the sunglasses to the cashier's "lost and found" as a good member of society should. In the end, eight citizens out of the 100 actually returned the sunglasses, while six just left them on the sink, busting this myth wide open. In reality, only 14% of people are "good" people, or 86% of people are "bad" people. This saying may have been true 60 years ago, but definitely is not true today, no way. I completed this statistical study as part of a Sociology class assignment, and with the help of the gas station attendant (who was a good friend of mine at the time) discovered the truth about people, at least in America. You may say there's a lot of difference between stealing and stabbing; but it's not the level of bad in someone's heart; it's the lack of good in someone's soul. The feeling of doing what's right or helping someone who's in need is missing in 86% of humanity; and this is why we must restart the race. As I mentioned earlier, this is especially true in today's youth who watch iPhone videos of destructive, humiliating, violent and often lethal attacks on peers while laughing and cheering out loud.

Back then, this fun factoid had no relation to this book, and I only include it here to show how naturally evil people are and will be even more so after the fall. Don't trust anyone. Don't turn your back on anyone. Always prepare and assume the worst in someone. (Remember, it's better to be pleasantly, than fatally surprised.) If I'm wrong, then no harm done; but if I'm right, and you didn't listen, heed my words and take my advice, well all I can say is that you're family counts on and looks to you and you alone for protection, not me!

In the end, it's the personal opinion of this writer that in order to keep on surviving, one must maintain a survivalist mentality. Learn an area and stay there. You see in the movies they're always traveling down the highway where they're most susceptible and vulnerable to attack. There should be no reason to travel down an abandoned highway (let alone leave your home) where bandits and marauders are plentiful. Keep secure and hunker down, only leaving your shelter for more supplies, so that you can stay hunkered down that much longer.

You may also realize that the majority of things discussed in this chapter are about food or directly relate to the acquisition of food, with shelter and water secondary. That's because food will prove to be the single most difficult undertaking for which you'll find yourself diverting the majority of your resources, time, and energy in the afterworld. Not to mention, over 70% of this planet is covered in water; and unless it all gets blown out into space during the apocalypse, you'll have plenty. Like I said, finding decent shelter "shouldn't" prove to be a problem either; but I'll discuss how to build your own later in *Chapter 1*, just in case. Security is another major concern, discussed in detail; and it becomes an even a bigger factor with a larger percentage of human survivors.

GRASPING AT STRAWS: MONTH 2

If you thought the last chapter was a bit 'over the top,' I promise you *Chapter 9* (and living in a vestige) doesn't get any better. In fact, with starvation really starting to set in, those that haven't prepared well enough up until now, combined with the total disintegration of any society instilled notions of morals, ethics or values, people will begin to literally do anything for food (just like I said they eventually would). Cannibalism is a very natural occurrence in the wild; in fact, humans are the only animals that don't partake in this tradition—well, most humans, I should say. Hell, we can't even wrap our mind around eating dog meat for that matter; the thought of eating Fido actually physically sickens most. Yet, Fido wouldn't think twice about eating you, if need be. How, then, would you feel about not only eating another person, but hunting and killing someone for food?

Depending on many common denominators, this level of starvation could occur anytime within the first 2 or 3 months. But again, we are getting much ahead of ourselves. We still have plenty of dog meat to feast on; the problem is catching the pesky varmint. So let's get to it. Time's a wasting, and we need to get serious about this whole survival thing if we want to, well, survive. No more scrounging and foraging for food or lying awake at night fearful of intruders stealing yours. The stores and homes are all empty, the people all robbed and pillaged out, you're going to have to now learn how to hunt and trap all types of game in order to feed your family, children, group and yourself. You say you're already an avid hunter, hmm? Not for this prey, and not in this environment, you're not. Get ready for some good old-fashioned Urban Hunting!

FAMILY PET: MORE MORAL DILEMMAS

62% of U.S. households have at least one pet, that's 71.4 million homes with family pets--dogs, cats, turtles, gold fish, ferrets and parakeets--after the collapse. 39% own at least one dog. More than half of these homes then will (approximately 77.5%) contain starving, trapped dogs with full bladders, waiting for their dead owners to come home and let them out to pee (I joke, of course they'd piss all over the house). Most hungry, orphaned and desperate dogs left locked up in backyards, homes and kennels, will chew through doors, sheetrock, siding, and slat and chain-link fences, break out glass windows and scratch off or pull though chained collars. Those that don't or can't, will die of starvation or, hindered and disadvantaged by man's devices, be preyed upon by us or some other predator. The escapees will then enter through neighboring broken out windows, fences and doors searching cupboards, pantries and low cabinets for snack food as well as parrots, hamsters, fish, cats or other trapped dogs to munch on. When the miniscule amount of neighborhood grub accessible to our four-legged, non-opposable thumb/can opener wielding friends becomes scarce, the larger of the once docile K-9's will form packs of 8-12 or more. They'll immediately scour the surrounding woodlands in hopes of finding prey or stray runaway small breed dogs like Pinschers, Cocker Spaniels, Terriers, Poodles, Chihuahuas, Beagles, Dachshunds, Pekingese, Pomeranians, Pugs and Shih Tzu's. But the previously claimed territories will prove too competitive a food source, forcing the packs to retreat down the deserted interstate highways towards the now abandoned major metropolitan cities where most life these days will to be congregating.

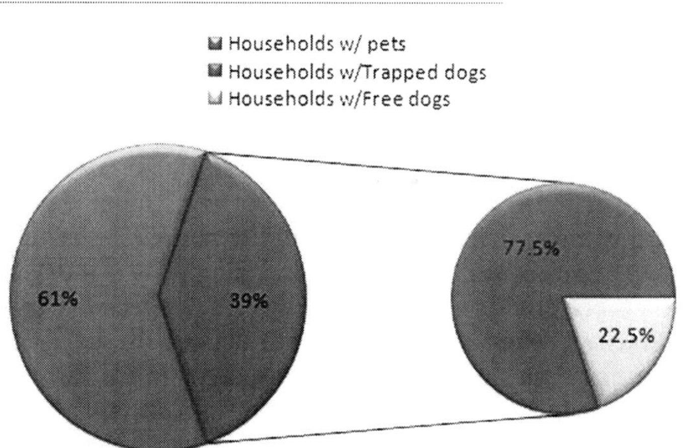

This exodus opens suburbia to all wall-burrowing, crack-squeezing rodents, insects and reptiles, which in reverse will flood into urbania from the once popular, thriving city life. These animals are able to devour the packaged food storages located in the higher cabinets or locked away in closed pantries, previously inaccessible to dogs, as well as fruits and vegetables which the carnivores usually avoid. The cats will then come out of hiding as well, now that the dogs have left, to feast on this new infestation of crunchy critters, which in turn draws the larger existing predators out from the surrounding woods. Within a matter of a couple of months, the once safe suburbs are as wild as the deepest jungle. How quickly nature takes back what's rightfully hers.

Back in the city, life isn't getting much grander at this point, but the rural life isn't what it used to be that's for sure. Things are about to turn around, though, as hundreds of packs of dogs complete their trek and begin flooding in from surrounding suburbs and townships, providing us with an ample supply of much needed nutrients, IF one is skilled enough to kill a dog and has no remorse in eating what was once man's best friend. As you can see in the photo of the coyote, I for one have no problem killing and eating any source of protein, be it dog, worms, crickets, cat, donkey; I'm what you would call a meatatarian and try as much as possible to stay away from the greens.

At one point while living in Asia, we ate dog meat (Nureongi or Hwangu) on a daily basis. In fact, over 60% of the world's population currently dine on dog; yet, the practice of eating canine or feline really disgusts the western world. That's not to say it was always this way; most of these very same 'cultured' countries currently do (to some extent), or have in the past, consumed canine, including: Canada, Mainland China, Hong Kong, Taiwan, East Timor, France, Germany, Ghana, Hawaii, India, Indonesia, Japan, North Korea, South Korea, Mexico, Nigeria, Philippines, Poland, Polynesia, Switzerland, Tonga, United States and Vietnam. It's notable to 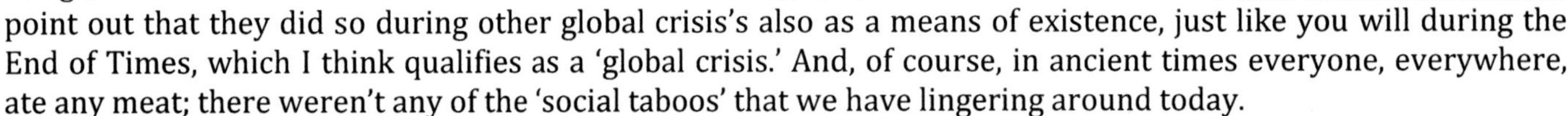 point out that they did so during other global crisis's also as a means of existence, just like you will during the End of Times, which I think qualifies as a 'global crisis.' And, of course, in ancient times everyone, everywhere, ate any meat; there weren't any of the 'social taboos' that we have lingering around today.

Dog meat Nutritional value per 100 g	
Energy 1,096kJ	Vitamin A equiv. (0%)
Ash 0.8g	Vitamin C3mg (5%)
Dietary fiber 0g	Calcium 8mg (1%)
Carbohydrates 0.1g	Iron 2.8 mg (22%)
Protein 19g	Phosphorus 168mg (24%)
Fat 20.2g	Potassium 270mg (6%)
Water 60.1g	Sodium 72mg (3%)

US % recommendations for adults.

Eating rat, however, (surprisingly) is a much more accepted practice around the world, especially in dire situations, even though rats are known to carry more diseases than dogs (and obviously carry much less meat). Maybe it is because we saw an actor in a survival situation eating rat in a movie one time; maybe it's just because we're so close to dogs and we consider rats the enemy. Either way, if you're going to stay alive, you'll need to eat; and like I always say, meat is meat.

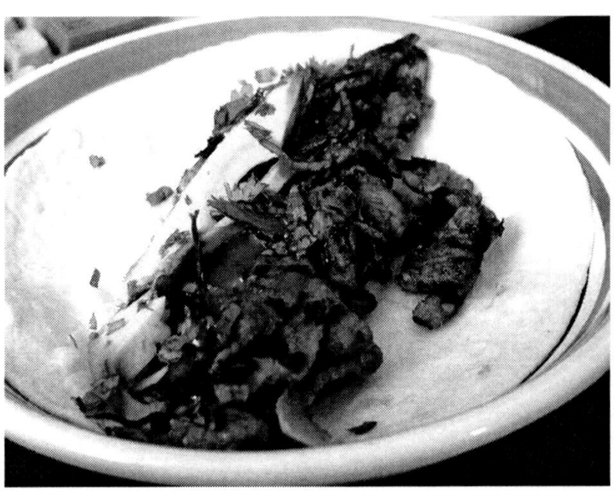

Dog meat is actually really nutritious and surprisingly tasty. My wife makes some mean puppy chow tacos made from real puppy (no kidding). Because wild game (any wild game) can be a little tough, she lets it soak in hot water for a few hours, then chops it up into really tiny cubes and puts it in the tortilla, mmm-mm (all joking aside, her dog tacos really are very flavorful).

Protein is the best source of energy (which you'll require a lot of), not to mention, without human care the fields and gardens will dry up, die and blow away. Wild plants will be your only source of greens; and without knowing which are safe to eat, they can be deadly by themselves. So without me re-writing an encyclopedia, filled with the world's most edible natural plants, we'll just stick with meat right now since it's safer to consume.

TYPES OF MEAT

The following is a list of animals and their culinary names that humans eat; (we can eat all meat safely).

Beef:
buffalo
Carabao
Cattle
Veal (calves)
Yak
Canids:
Dog
Fox
Felidae:
Domestic Cat
Tiger
Lion
Equines:
Horse
Donkey
Zebra
Lagomorphs:
Hare
Pika
Rabbit
Marsupials:
Kangaroo
Koala
Opossum
Wallaby
Ovis (sheep):
Lamb
Domestic Sheep
Bighorn sheep
Caprae (goats)
Domestic Goat
Ibex
Wild goat
Barbary Sheep
Dall Sheep
Mountain Goat
Suidae (swine):
Pig
Javelina
Wild boar
Red River Hog
Bush pig
Venison:
Reindeer
Deer
Moose
Antelope
Giraffe
Red deer
Primates:
Gorilla
Orangutan
Chimpanzee
Bonobo
Human
Monkey
Rodents:
Beaver
Guinea pig
Capybara
Muskrat
Rat
Squirrel
Cane Rat
Paca
Nutria
Groundhog
Cetaceans:
Whale
Dolphin
Pinnipeds:
Walrus
Seal
Other mammals:
Bear
Elephant
Raccoon
Rhinoceros
Weasel
Camel
Llama
Pronghorn
Poultry (birds):
Chicken
Duck
Goose
Turkey
Game birds:
Dove
Quail
Ostrich
Emu
Guinea fowl
Pheasant
Grouse
Partridge
Crow
Quail
Pigeon
Woodcock
Ptarmigan
Reptiles:
Turtle
Lizard
Snake
Iguana
Crocodile
Alligator
Amphibians:
Frog
Salamander
Toad
Fish:
Anchovy
Basa
Bass
Catfish
Carp
Cod
Crappie
Eel
Flounder
Puffer fish
Grouper
Haddock
Halibut
Herring
Kingfish
Mackerel
Mahi Mahi
Marlin
Orange Roughy
Perch
Pike
Pollock
Salmon
Sardine
Shark
Snapper
Sole
Swordfish
Tilapia
Trout
Tuna
Walleye
Echinoderms:
Sea urchin
Insects:
Grasshoppers
Chapulines
Ants
Escamoles
Honeypot ant
Bees
Cockroaches
Beetles
True bugs
Jumiles
Larvae:
Grubs
Caterpillars
Maguey worm
Crustaceans:
Crab
Crayfish
Lobster
Prawn
Shrimp
Arachnids:
Spiders
Scorpions
Mollusks:
Abalone
Clam
Conch
Loco
Mussel
Oyster
Scallop
Snail (escargots)
Cephalopods:
Cuttlefish
Octopus
Squid

ROCK BOTTOM: AGGRESSIVE ACQUISITION

Throughout history, when man's body starts to literally starve, it's proven time and time again that we will eat dog, man, rat, bugs or anything else for that matter that provides a source of sustenance. For example, the Uruguay Soccer Team plane crash in the Andes in 1972 resulted in the survivors eating their dead within days. In the end, the back straps and thighs of almost a dozen humans would be snacked upon during the 2-month period they remained *alive* in the mountains (October 13 - December 23). Before the Andes crash, colonists resorted to cannibalism during a time of starvation in colonial Jamestown from 1609-1610. The sinking of the Luxborough Galley in 1727, the Donner Party during the winter of 1846–1847, Sir John Franklin's expedition of 1848, the famine of Ukraine in the 1930s, the Siege of Leningrad in World War II, the Chinese Civil War of 1930-1949, the Great Leap Forward in the People's Republic of China 1958-1961, World War II Nazi concentration camps and Japanese Pacific-based soldiers 1933-1942, North Korea 1995-1997, and the wreck of Dumaru in 1930 all turned to cannibalism to fight off devastating, debilitating hunger pains.

I may seem nonchalant about eating the

meat of a fellow man; but the simple truth is, and there's no getting around it, at a certain point it will become the highest quantity of protein available, not to mention the most easily accessible/attainable food source out there. If the idea of eating dog physically turns your stomach, then this is likely to cause some permanent mental damage. Again, I'd have no problem hunting and eating human meat for sustenance, as time will tell, especially (but not only) if I were hungry and the guy or woman (don't want to be sexist) were already dead. Also, I have no religious, cultural or spiritual belief etiquette slowing me down as many of you may. It's all protein, carbs, vitamins, minerals, water and carbon. The question, however, right now shouldn't be which meat you prefer, but which is easier to obtain and more readily available (remember *Law 2*).

Applied to this situation, what this means is how much of and how easy it is for you to take down a certain type of prey. For example, in the entire eastern seaboard today there isn't much wildlife left. We've taken over, flattened, concreted and built on most of their habitat, killing or pushing them completely out of the area; this applies to farming areas as well. But in New York City alone at this very moment there are almost 20 million humans--people who, for the most part, have no idea how to defend themselves or use a weapon and probably wouldn't conceive that someone would want to hunt them for a meal. This fact alone should be enough to convince you to throw away your moral obligations and obtain the only food source around for hundreds of miles. But if you're still not convinced, ponder this. How much easier do you think it would be to take down a female human with your bare hands than say a female wild dog or bear or deer or even a speedy little female rat or rabbit for that matter? You could run down and overtake (just like in the wild) a woman far easier than any other female animal in the world, besides maybe a turtle. I honestly can't think of an easier or slower prey, can you? Women will and always have made easy targets; and this is exactly the reason men have preyed on (abused, raped, mugged, molested) women since the beginning of time.

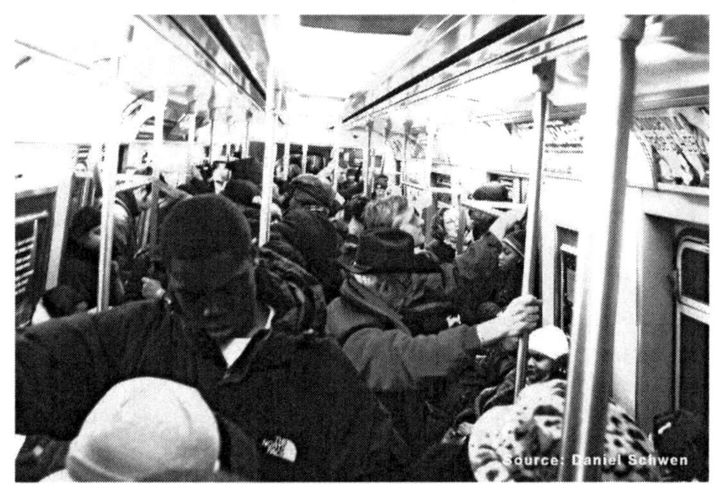
Source: Daniel Schwen

Actually, I would consider eating worms and crickets as hitting rock bottom, not human. People meat is surprisingly nutritious and tasty compared to slugs, maggots, worms and crickets. But society has brainwashed us to believe it's wrong or evil; and I can absolutely understand this. To a system built on law, order and growth, cannibalism is a trend that works against itself. However, that all goes out the window in a world where law, order and growth is a thing of the past. I say happy eating, my friends; you are all welcome to be my *dinner guests* anytime after 2012!

TRAPS: ALL THAT GLISTERS IS NOT GOLD

The main problem in this over-abundance of protein (dog, cat, human, rat or whatever), is simply catching it. Anything and every living thing will attempt to put up a fight when faced with its own mortality, potentially hurting you in the process, which is exactly what we don't want (remember *Law 1*). Traps offer automation and distance, providing not only ease of food collection, but a greater range of protection from other crazy, blood thirsty, barbaric cannibals as well.

There is an assortment of different types of traps to choose from. Some of the easier traps to build utilizing everyday parts that will be available in the aftermath include: Snare, Bear, Bait, Trip-line, Pit, Door, Bucket and Dumb Dolly, all of which work equally well on almost all forms of prey. The following describes how to build and use these types of traps to secure 'meat' and protect your establishment from meat seekers as well.

- Quail trap – A quail trap is a very effective, effortless method of collecting dozens of meat sources daily. It can be used on any type of fowl, simply by adapting the door size. The trap doesn't need to be checked daily since the critters caught are not killed and are protected inside the cage:

1. Strip the upholstery off a single bed box spring. There aren't any springs in box springs anymore but we can still use the frame.

2. Secure two 2x4 boards on each side to the four corners with nails, screws, hanger or wire.
3. Angle the boards in towards the middle leaving about a 5in gap.
4. Staple screen over the top and left and right sides, leaving the smaller front and back sides open.
5. That's it. Now place the trap in a field or sidewalk somewhere where there's been a lot of bird traffic.

The size of the tapered 2x4 openings need to be relevant to the size of the intended catch. For example, to catch quail or pigeons, the openings will be adjusted to around 5in wide. For dove and other small "Tweety" birds, no more than 3-4in.

- Rate/Mouse Trap – A rat or mouse trap is built similar to the quail trap, without the frame and the inlet door. It is actually a funnel with the hole a couple inches off the ground and slightly smaller than the rodent itself. This way it can squeeze in through the hole and drop down, but has a hard time finding and squeezing back out the opening.
- Snare Trap – A snare trap is one of the simplest traps; however, it's because of this simplicity that it won't work on a human's logic and cognitive skills.

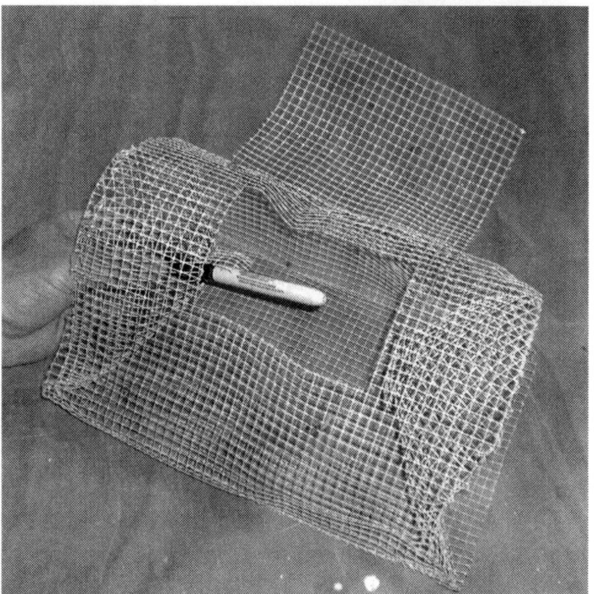

1. Tie or cinch off a loop on one end of a 3ft-steel cable or wire.
2. Loop the steel cable or wire around on itself, sliding one side through the loop.
3. Locate a well-traversed path typically in a fence line and secure the end to a post or part of the fence.
4. Open the loop to about 8in to 1ft, and tape one side up vertically to traversed fence path with scotch tape.

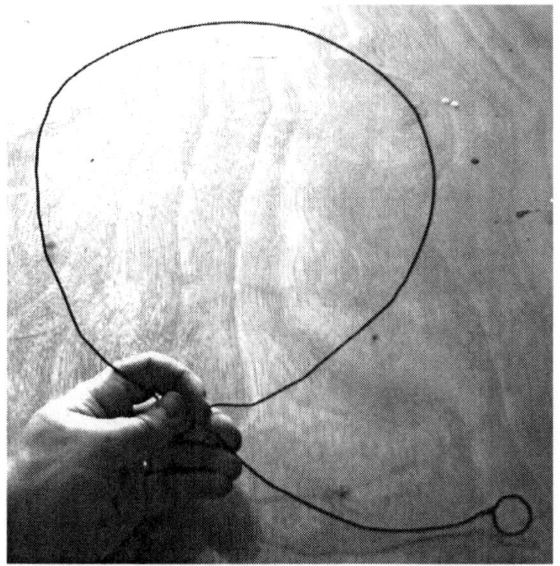

Operation: When the critter travels through the path as he always has, he'll become snared in the trap. The animal's own pulling pressure will either choke him or trap him long enough for your arrival.

NOTE: It's important to check these traps daily so that: (a) the animal doesn't escape, and (b) no other animal takes your prey. Also, try not to leave any human odors in the area, possibly even wear rubber gloves when handling the snares.

- Bear Trap – Bear traps are great because you don't have to make them. This adds to the efficiency of the trap, since I guarantee that you're not a skilled trap maker, by far. However, you would not only have to find the traps in a world of waste, which will be difficult to say the least, but carry the heavy contraptions to the location needed, as well. Bear traps are pretty straightforward:

1. While depressing the two side springs, swing the pressure plate into position and lock in place.
2. Stake or secure the chain as needed.
3. Cover with light debris, such as leaves, paper, plastic bags, or other garbage.

Operation: When the prey steps on the plate, the claws are thrown shut, locking the leg in place.

NOTE: It's a good idea to set several traps in the same high traffic area. This means though, carrying around and finding even more traps. Once they're triggered, they'll require pressure to unlock them.

- Pig trap – A pig trap or cage trap can be baited to catch any medium-sized animal, not just pigs. For example, if I wanted to catch a coyote or mountain lion, I'd place some type of raw, or even living, meat inside. A cage trap should have a strong steel frame and metal fencing welded on four of the six sides. You'll need (8) steel bed frames or equivalent steel pieces, 8ft of wire, dental floss or fishing line, a street sign bent in half or piece of plywood, about 25ft of fence, and plenty of coat hangers or welding rods.

1. Place 2 of the 8 bed frame bars on a level surface.
2. Swing out the connecting arms and weld or tie together with hangers to form a rectangle.
3. Cut 1 frame in half and weld inside the rectangle, equally spaced. This will be the bottom piece.
4. Cut another frame in half and 2 more about 2/3 and weld each vertically in the 4 corners.
5. Repeat step 2 and 3 building the top piece and weld in place.
6. Cut 8 appropriately-sized pieces of 1/2in rebar and weld in place on the sides, back and top front as trusses or supports.
7. Run a piece of fence around the entire structure and weld or tie in place with hangers.
8. Do the same for the top, leaving the front open (the bottom doesn't need to be fenced in).
9. You may have noticed that the front bars extend

up and over the top of the cage. This will be the track that the door sits on and from which it drops down.

10. Bend a piece of appropriately-sized 1/2in rebar into a square and weld to a slider that will slide on the front vertical track.
11. Weld 2 more 1/2in pieces of rebar as supports and some more fencing inside the square. This will be the door.

12. Drill a 1/8in hole in the slider track and place a nail inside the hole, from the back so that just a fraction of the nail tip is protruding through the front side.
13. Drill a hole in the middle on each of the two sides of the street sign or plywood, locate it and inch or 2 off the floor in the middle of the cage, loop a small piece of hanger through each hole and a link in the fence so that it's floating and balanced. This will be the trigger, activating and pulling the pin once the animal steps on it.
14. Drill another hole in each of the 4 corners of the sign or plywood and run two 4ft pieces of wire, fishing line or floss through each pair of holes forming two upside down triangles.
15. Tie (2) 5ft pieces of wire, fishing line, or floss onto the large upside down triangles (you may have to melt the knots of the fishing line or floss so that they don't slip), run them through the links on top of the cage to the front and tie to the head of the nail.
16. Place the door on the top track so that it rests gently on the nail tip.
17. Place the bait inside the trap, put the trap in a shady, high-traffic area and wait. For live bait traps, if you want the bait to survive, place it in a small cage and the small cage inside the bigger cage in the back.

Operation: When the animal enters the cage, it'll inadvertently step on the balanced bottom plate, pulling the pin and dropping the door in place.

- Trip Line traps (shotgun version) – A trip line can be adapted to trigger any type of lethal device: mines, spears, or a highly-pressurized spraying barrage of glass shards. I, however, prefer a simple shotgun. I saw one of these set-ups (close up and personal) in action in a marijuana farmer's field, which he was using to prevent unwanted intruders (me) in the jungles of Hawaii. Luckily, the morning rain had washed away most of the ground cover, exposing the steel wire trip line. The traps in Hawaii aren't usually mortal in design since the shotguns are loaded with skeet shot or rock salt rather than double 00 buck. But they will leave a rather large nasty scar. Our shotgun traps will however, be loaded with buck or, at least, turkey or goose shot; no need to take any chances.

1. Tie off one side of several feet of fishing line (we'll use fishing line because it's transparent and harder to see) to an immovable object approximately 1ft off the ground in a room.
2. Now run the line across a well-established path or hallway, through an open doorway into the next room.
3. If the walls are Sheetrock or thin wood paneling, punch out several holes all over the walls and run the line through one that is approximately halfway down the hall into the next room. You can also run the line simply through the door, but this is a much better scenario as: (a) the victim is more likely to be focused on the open door down the hall, not the hole in the wall; and (b) by running the line through the open door, it's more likely to be discovered since, again, they'll most likely be focusing on it.

NOTE: The BBs from the blast will penetrate through sheetrock or thin paneling of the wall unhindered, providing the best possible camouflage.

4. Place the shotgun on the floor inside the next room, angled up into the hallway towards where the victim's torso would be, and secure with concrete blocks, sandbags, books, etc. We want a clean kill, no suffering. If a mortal shot isn't desired or if the prey is a dog or some other shorter target, position the shotgun at a shallower angle aiming at the legs instead of the upper body, and load with skeet or dove shot.
5. Now pull the line taught and tie a slip knot around the trigger and the back of the trigger guard.
6. Load the gun, cock the trigger (or pump the barrel), take off the safety and you're ready.

Operation: Similar to the *snare trap*, once the victim triggers the trip line, BAM!!! The trap is deadly and just as effective with a high percentage of success; there's no denying that. Also, the blast of the shotgun will signal when the trap has been triggered, so you won't have to check the trap often. However, there are a couple of rather significant downfalls to this trap:

a. You're without your shotgun on a daily basis; once the trap's been set, there's no point in removing the shotgun for any reason. This type of trap isn't designed for that and could actually be dangerous. And, for God's sake, don't walk down the hallway thinking you can step over the line.

b. If the victim is actually able to spot the line/trap before it's triggered, you could potentially lose your weapon, and now the prey could essentially become the predator.

NOTE: Hand grenades can be substituted for the shotgun, if you just happen to have boxes lying around.

- Bait – One of my personal favorites. The only problem with this kind of trap is that you often lose the bait. The bait trap is one of the oldest tricks in the book, I'm actually extremely surprised why anything or anyone would continue falling for it after all these years, but they do. Real simple, here we go:

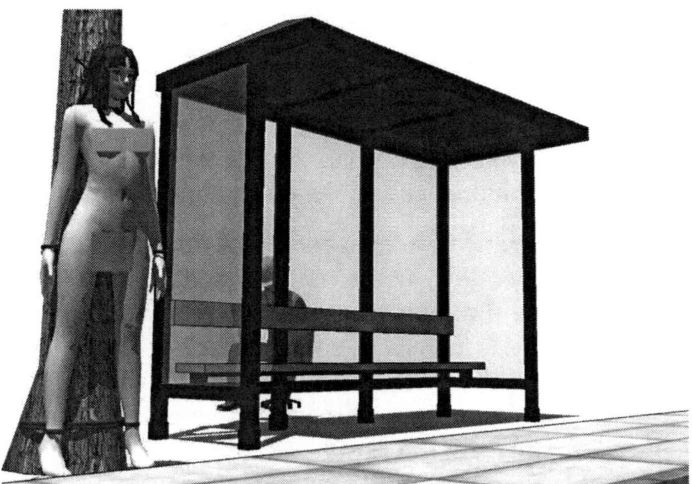

1. Take something someone wants, needs or draws attraction/attention, say water, food, ammunition, a naked woman tied to a tree, a crying baby, a goat, a chicken, 27 crates of gold bullion--(your lack of imagination is the only limiting factor)--and place it in a well-traversed path with plenty of obstacles to hide behind.
2. Hide and wait.

Operation: When an innocent passerby takes the bait (quite literally), you jump out and scream "BOO!" No really, you kill the sorry bastard, or at least take his stuff at gunpoint, up to you. A couple things to remember:

a. You're probably going to lose the bait; that's pretty much a given. I don't know why, but the bait is always the first to go in such situations, go figure.
b. If your bait is alive, consider it will be sitting out in the hot Sun all day; maybe leave it in some shade with food and water.
c. Because of your close proximity to this trap and the many unknown factors associated with it, like the number of likely victims (could be an entire mob), the trap could backfire on you.

The whole physiology behind using naked women for bait isn't based on me being sexists (though that's probably true also). The fact is that men become literally retarded when they see naked women, again, check out a strip club sometime. They just can't think properly, and would run to rescue the damsel in distress without hesitation or concern for their, or anyone else's, safety. On the other hand, a woman wouldn't necessarily fall for this trick, or at least they'd evaluate the situation a bit more thoroughly first. What I'm saying is they don't lose their senses over naked women (well most don't). For a female it would have to be something like a crying, suffering baby, in which case they too do lose all common, rational sense.

- Pit trap – The pit trap is the oldest trick in the book, cavemen were digging holes to capture cave women during my great, great-grand-daddy's day. But it is practically guaranteed to work because it's foolproof, in that only fools fall in ~~love~~ giant holes. That said, I don't really like this trap because there's a bit of labor involved; and, well, for the most part, I'm just generally lazy. Now, if you can get one of those women you stole during the house pillaging crusades to dig the hole; well, then you're in business.

1. First locate an area with soft soil (you don't want to be digging through rock) as always in a well establish path, trail or hallway.
2. Dig a hole slightly smaller than 4ft by 8ft wide, by at least 8ft deep.
3. Place a 4ft by 8ft sheet of thin, fake wood, wall paneling over the hole. Where do you get thin, fake wall paneling? From the numerous abandoned homes, of course.
4. Cover the sheet with a thin layer of dirt, leaves, grass, carpet, debris, or whatever the surrounding groundcover may be.

Operation: When someone walks over the trap, the victim causes the paneling to buckle under their own weight, dropping him/her (again, not sexist) into the pit. There are a couple downfalls to this trap however:

a. If there is more than one assailant, the trap most likely will only catch one, leaving the other(s) to attack, retreat or rescue their needed associate.

b. Also, although the walls of the hole are too high to climb, the victim can reach the outer edge of the hole. He won't be able to do much more than grasp handfuls of dirt; still, eventually he may pull enough dirt into the hole to climb out on his own, so you'll need to check the trap frequently.
c. The paneling needs to be replaced after each activation, creating a demand for 4x8 sheets of paneling.
d. The trap IS, however, fairly effective at capturing without causing injury, if that's your thing.

NOTE: This trap can be especially effective located directly in front of your home's front or back door, catching any marauders before they can attack. A framed-out fake, grey spray-painted, paneling porch can be used for the cover itself, which would easily collapse under a man's weight. You can test it this winter holiday season on unwanted relatives and co-workers as they bombard your home for the Thanksgiving and Xmas.

- Door traps (not 'trap door') – A door trap is one of the easiest, safest, most practical and easiest, easy-no-brainer traps out there. No labor or digging is involved, either (which I fancy); but the trap can only work in an existing building such as a warehouse, factory, or restaurant freezer. In a secure room (one without windows, wood paneling or sheet rock walls), simply switch the door handle around so that it now locks from the outside. That's it, there you go; didn't I say it was easy? I used to do this to my sister all the time when we were kids. As an added bonus, I would spray hairspray under the door. Yeah, not sure what the point was there, but it probably had something to do with murderfication of a sibling with pressurized VOCs in aerosol form.

Operation: Once the victim(s) are in the room (for who knows what reason) simply shut the door. A spring-closed system or more elaborate automatic door-shutting device can be rigged, but the simple human power scenario is the least likely to fail. This trap can also be carried out on the roof access door of high buildings as long as they don't have fire escapes or other escape routes. The victims may be lured into the room on some false pretense, like the world is going to end (oh, that already happened), or the never failing tied-up naked lady (that one always works, trust me.) The best case scenario is that the door already automatically closes, and then you don't have to have any involvement, whatsoever. Again, in this case just check the trap often, by simply walking up, knocking on the door and asking "hello, is anyone in there?" People are so ~~dumb~~ trusting; they'll answer back "yes, we're trapped in here (duh), please help!" And so you walk in with a shotgun and blow everyone's heads off, game over, GG, thanks for playing, see ya next time, the end.

- Bucket mines – Bucket grenades were a trap made famous for decommissioning many small American U-boats on Vietnam Rivers, and are efficient homemade underwater mines for protecting that newly-acquired island beachfront property discussed in *Chapter 5* from water-based sieges.

1. Punch two holes on opposite sides and in the middle of a large empty soup can.
2. Pull the pin of a hand grenade, and place it on its lever inside a smaller can, one that will fit the grenade snuggly.
3. Insert the smaller can inside the larger, and place the can in the desired location in the water.

Operation: The trapped air in the two cans causes the device to float like a bobber while the weight of the grenade lying in the lower can causes the can to sink just below the surface of the water, out of sight from vicious hell demon boat captains. The vacuum in the cans will also prevent the cans from separating prematurely. However, as the vessel passes over the can, it tips the can over, releasing the handle of the grenade causing it to explode directly under or to the rear of the boat (where the engine is). This is a fairly effective hindrance from water-based assaults, especially once one or two have been discovered or set off. The fear of additional underwater mines is enough to repel future attacks. Again, a couple issues to consider though:

a. Setting the traps without dropping the grenade can be difficult to say the least, especially while working in the water.
b. I'm pretty set as far as stocking up on supplies for Judgment Day goes, but even I don't happen to have a couple crates full of grenades stored up. And I don't think if you do that you'd want to let them sit out in the salt water corroding. But who knows, the world is ending for a reason, might as well be because of stupidity. You can utilize the gunpowder described earlier instead of grenades, though.
c. Lastly, the device can't be set in any location that has significant waves and if there is a current, the cans will need to be anchored in place.

- Dumb Dolly – Dumb Dolly is another hand grenade (or homemade explosive)-based trap that surprisingly works very well for the simplicity of the attack. Merely pull the pin, place the grenade on the ground in a well established path, walkway or hallway, and place a relatively heavy, wide object of importance, (the bait), directly on top, such as meat (for animals), a backpack filled with, say, small rocks, plastic bag filled with fruit or a baby in a bassinet. Of course, I personally wouldn't use a baby (probably). I'm just putting it here because: (a) some people might, you never know, and (b) I got tired of using the tied-up naked lady scenario. But if you prefer, you can have a naked woman sitting cross-legged on the device as well. You can also use the hollowed out *bucket mine* method above. Mmm chili, POW!!!

Operation: The victim will see the object and, not knowing a grenade is underneath, pick it up and KABOOM! CAZOWEE! KABLOOEY! You get the idea. There aren't too many downfalls to this trap due to its simplicity; except, again, you'll probably lose your bait, and placing the grenade can be difficult.

Good luck and happy trapping from all of us here at Agua-Luna.com!

HUNTING & TRACKING: ALL THINGS COME TO THOSE WHO WAIT

Hunting is a very difficult subject to teach someone through a couple of paragraphs in a book. It takes most people several years of guided hands-on training to become an adequate hunter to the point where they can provide 100% of their family's needs with the activity. By spending weeks on end in the mountains living, listening, learning the animal's habits, sounds and movements, you're able to evaluate and compose what techniques and tactics would bring the greatest gain in respect to a specific animal and environment. The same can be applied to humans and urban areas.

In the wild, the creature, especially if it's a predator itself, always has the upper hand, even if you have a rifle. This doesn't mean that it'll win in a one-on-one fistfight (though it would), simply that it knows everything about you, your location, speed, size, etc. and you virtually have no information on it. It can smell, hear and see you a hundred times sooner/farther than you can perceive it. It can outrun you, outfight you, and has no moral obligations about killing and eating you, your wife and your babies. However, I have a few tricks that could level the playing field greatly:

- Spotlighting – By using spotlights, car headlights, or very powerful flashlights, humans are able to see a further distance at night than many animals. As the light reflects and shines off the animal's eyes back to the hunter, this effect creates a miniature beacon of illumination, if you will. For some reason the effect even stuns the animal (deer-in-the-headlights look), so much so that in many cases you get off a much closer, better, non-moving shot.

- Feeders – By setting out food in a specific location at specific times daily, you're able to lure the animal into a behavior of habit that you can now predict.
- Flushing – The critters of the forest already outnumber us thousands to one, but by lining up several dozen people in a straight line ~~and killing them all~~, sorry, I get excited, and walking through an area together, you'll push anything in the brush into hunters on the other side. Indians and ancient man would use a similar form of this technique by simply driving the beasts off a nearby cliff or into a river.

- Circling – Circling or circle flushing is another form of man forcibly pushing the animals around, manipulating their movements at will. In this manner, however, a group of people will surround an area, slowly working their way in towards the middle and the animals in towards each other.
- Dogs – Dogs have been bred into all different types, sizes, shapes and temperaments for thousands of years, specifically for our needs, hunting being the most predominant reason, and, therefore, are very effective tools at your disposal. The smaller breeds, such as Terriers, are meant for chasing rabbits and other small tunneling rodents, while scent hounds were manufactured for tracking foxes, cats and those that don't typically fall for the 'silly' human tricks listed above. Site hounds on the other hand, are built lean and fast, able to chase down their prey, whereas Labradors and other retrievers were made for bringing back dove, quail, ducks, pheasants, geese and any other land-based birds after a kill.

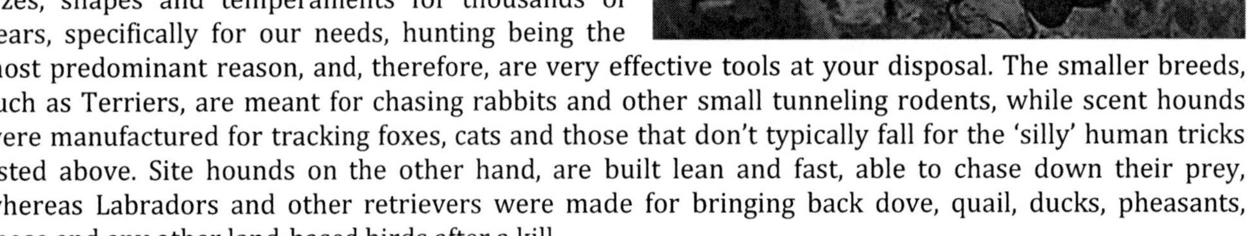

- Decoys – Fowl are fairly stupid animals and can be tricked very easily with decoys. Decoys are fake, usually plastic or wood structures made to look like real birds, which lure the duck or goose down to the location to frolic joyfully and eventually hump its wooden kin. (Brings a new light to the term woody.)

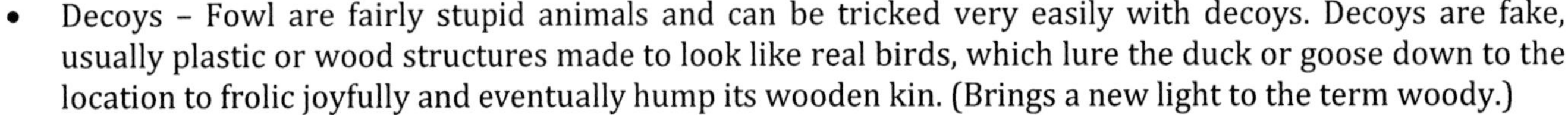

- Night hunting – Birds won't usually fly once it's dark. So if you can sneak up on a duck floating in a pond after hours, you can literally stone it to death without it fleeing (I know from personal experience). In fact, waiting until after dark or just before dawn to hunt grazing animals is a critical tactic as well for the same reason.
- Day hunting – Conversely, carnivores sleep when the Sun's out, making daytime a better time for hunting them.
- Vehicles – Adding a truck to the mix can raise your land speed equally to that of most prey.
- Tree stands – Comparably, tree stands, or other high spots, can provide you with a visual advantage while camouflaging you and your odor as well.
- Trapping – Trapping I've discussed in detail above; now it's time to put what you've learned to the test.
- Tracking – There are many methods of tracking, but all incorporate several of the same elements:

1. Keep quiet – By walking 'lightly' and avoiding and walking around noisy land cover like dry leaves and sticks, you're able to minimize the ruckus you create.
2. Travel slow – You're not going to catch any animal in the woods with speed, don't even try. Walk slowly; if you hear something, stop and wait, often for 20-30 minutes at a time.

Source: HAM guy

3. Free the funk – An animal relies on its sense of smell more than any other sense, especially in thick brush. That's why it's important to mask your musk either by rubbing animal shit or piss (not a predatory animal) over your body and clothes (especially the armpits, groan area, feet, face and head) or as a last resort, standing in front of a fire while letting the smoke saturate your clothing. Never use deodorants, soaps, shampoos, or any other man-made chemicals.
4. Tracks – By learning to identify the age of a track, you can decide if it's a waste of energy (*Law 2*) or not to pursue it. I mean, if a track is a month old, what's the point? The problem with track identification is that 80%-90% of the Earth's many different surfaces aren't the right materials to create or hold tracks. Add the fact that rain or other sources of moisture is a critical condition needed for track formation (not to mention the animal then needs to walk through the area), and the likelihood of finding an animal based on footprints is extremely low. My point is that one can't just go out into the wilderness and track something like a scene in the movies. There are a couple things to look for though, but they mostly depend on day-to-day weather conditions in the region and your knowledge of them. Did it rain this morning? If the track isn't filled with water, it means the beast has passed through the region since the morning's rain. If there is any water puddling in the footprint however, it's most likely that the animal passed by before a previous rain (since most mammals won't travel in the rain), in which case the rain just filled up an old hardened print that was possibly 2 months old. If you hunt the same area over and over, everyday, you'll become accustomed to the daily soil conditions and, be able to spot changes. Specific animal identification (hoof print vs. paw print vs. cat vs. dog) isn't as important to us, since we'll want to eat any animal at this point. Everything's in season! No tags required! No limits!
5. Broken branches – Typically, animals in the wild don't break branches as they pass by, as depicted on TV. This is simply because trees aren't rigid, dry or brittle, and flex as the animal brushes past them. Even if they did break, you wouldn't be able to accurately tell when the break occurred and especially not what broke the branch (could have been the wind), making such information useless.
6. Urban tracking – Tracking game in a city-like environment is even harder. As humans, we like things flat and solid. Although this isn't seen once in nature, we flatten our hills, roads, streets, floors, beds, tables, etc., making tracking by footprint impossible. As always, there are some things that you can do beforehand, to prepare an area to be tracked unnaturally easier later:

a. In an enclosed area, protected from the elements, place several articles of garbage in a narrow passage-way like a door or hallway. Place enough so that when something walks through it will be disturbed. Check the area daily so that you have a time frame if something is later disrupted. Memorize the configuration, or even draw a small map somewhere in the building to help determine if something actually has passed through or not.
b. Ball up a piece of paper; and while exiting a building, reach your hand inside and place the ball just on the other side of the door. Upon re-entering the facility, open the door just slightly, enough to reach your hand back in and feel for the ball. If someone did enter, the paper would not be in its location having been pushed away by the unsuspecting opening of the door.
c. Baby powder, ground up sheetrock or some other powdery substance sprinkled in an area can create an unnatural footprint-setting condition. The problem with this type of method is that if it's a human you're tracking, it's probably now aware something is awry.

7. My best advice in both a non-urban and urban environments is to stumble around an area until you find some resource worth coveting like water, shelter, food or even just a well-traveled path. Locate a high position downwind and wait. Maybe for days, but wait. Keep quiet; don't pee or shit in the area, just wait. Eventually, whatever has come here before will come again.

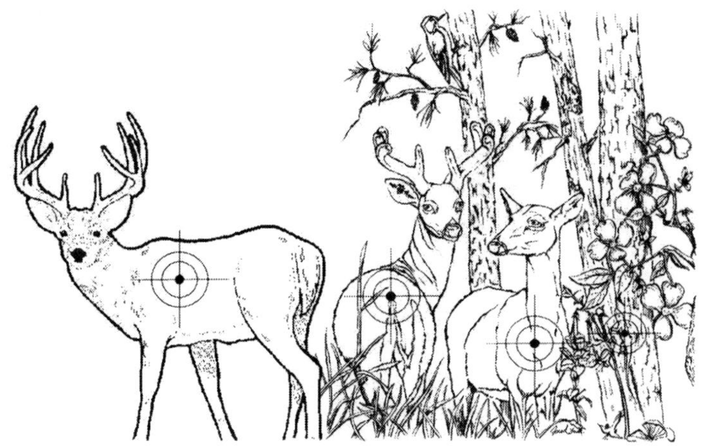

- Shooting – When you finally find something living on four legs, you'll need to know where to aim. If it's a side shot, aim for the area just behind the front armpits. This way, if he moves forwards or backwards, you still have a kill shot on the vitals. If the animal is facing you straight on, you'll want to target the upper chest region just below the neck so that if you miscalculate your distance too close or too far, you'll still have a kill shot on the vitals. From the back, aim at the butt just below the tail, and from the top, aim between the shoulder blades. You never want to aim at the head unless it's the only appendage in view; always aim at the chest cavity, since there are more numerous vital organs in this region (lungs, heart, kidneys, liver, etc).

Hunting humans is a similar ordeal to hunting animals except it's much, much easier. Like I said, they can't see, hear or smell you and tend to be much less cautious to traps or strange situations; whereas animals seem to have a sixth sense with such things, knowing when something's just not right. One time while hunting up in northern Utah for elk, I'd come across a female elk. I instantly froze in my tracks for several minutes, hoping a bull would follow. Eventually, she decided to come and investigate, assumedly because of my smell. Once I was out of view for a moment, I slowly backed up into a large bush and stayed perfectly still as she began examining me no more than a couple feet away. She looked straight at me, up and down; she knew something just wasn't right with that bush, but couldn't tell what. Eventually, she walked off unsatisfied with her findings; but she knew there was foul play in the air. A human, on the other hand, would fall for such a ruse instantly. This is seen time and time again, as we hide just behind a door or inside a cupboard, waiting to jump out and scare the ever loving sh!* out of our loved ones. A bear, dog, cat or any other wild animal, in a sense, sees right through the door or cupboard and knows something's there, hiding.

Ultimately, I would prefer to hunt and eat only human meat anyway. Not simply because they're an easier prey, but because I value animal life above human. Honestly, though, and you may not believe me, I hate killing anything. After every life I've ever taken, I swear that I'll never do it again, until that savory meat hits the grill. Then I'm again ready for action. That said, I'd definitely rather kill something that's had a chance to live life instead of an animal which has been raised, locked up in a pen, and is meant solely for eating; that's no life at all. On this note, many vegetarians and vegans come to me and ask, *"If I'm so into being self-sufficient and an animal lover, why do I eat meat? How can I take another life, or eat a baby animal or egg?"* I tell them, every apple that they eat is a baby tree, every berry a baby bush, every leaf of lettuce a living thing. If there was some magic source of nutrition with protein, minerals and vitamins that was never alive, I would eat only that, regardless of the taste, instead of killing or eating anything that could continue living, again except for maybe humans, that is.

FISHING: LIKE SHOOTING FISH IN A BARREL

I consider fishing a form of hunting, without the backbreaking labor involved. Again, though, without taking you out and holding your hand through the process, there's very little I can do to fully prepare you to catch fish, other than relay several tricks I've learned over the years that should get you started:

- Trotlines – Not sure why they're called *trout* lines; they should be named fish lines, in general. Either way, using a trotline can be the easiest way to obtain an unlimited source of protein. They're simple to make and use. It's like having dozens of full-time, non-eating, non-sleeping fisherman on the banks for several days, providing you with a 100% chance of catching food without burning much-needed calories in the process (*Law 2*).

1. Run a fishing line, cable or rope from one side of the shore (river, pond, lake, lagoon, etc.) to the other side or from the shore out to an anchored milk jug. On larger bodies of water, this is easily accomplished in a boat.
2. Tie a variety of different lengths of baited and weighted fishing lines several feet apart, spanning the entire distance of the first line. This will provide bait for numerous different types of fish who live at different depths in the water.
3. Daily, traverse the line, checking each individual hook for a catch.

- Traditional fishing – Trying to fish with a pole is an inadequate form of fishing, generally only performed for sport or relaxation. Commercial fishing or fishing for food would never incorporate such devices.
- Gator lines – Similar to a traditional pole and line, you can rig up and anchor a steel wire/cable with a large 3in baited hook on the end to catch snakes, gators or any other predatory animal. Land fishing! Who'd have thought?

- Crawfish traps– Also known as funnel traps, are perfect for our needs, again allowing us to set it out and leave. There are several benefits crawfish traps over a trotline worth mentioning:

a. A crawfish trap can be left out for days without checking it, with no fear of other fish taking your catch.
b. Since the traps are submerged and therefore hidden from view, you won't have any pirates finding/taking your booty either.
c. Crawfish traps aren't just for crawfish, they work on any type of crustacean or fish and can be built with the following common household items:

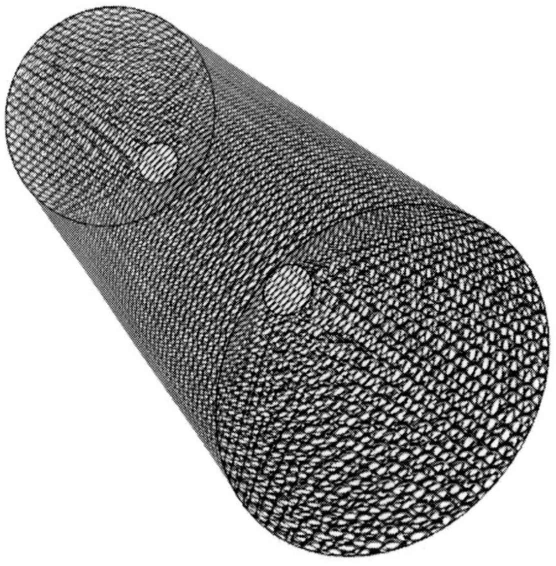

1. Loop a piece of window screen making a tube 24-36in long by about a foot in diameter.
2. Wrap two more pieces of screen into a funnel shape about 1ft in diameter, leaving about an inch open in the middle smallest point.
3. Sew the cone screens together and onto each end of the tube so that the contoured cone is inverted using strands of speaker wire.
4. Cut a three-sided square opening on top about 6in by 6in and latch shut with a strand of speaker wire, safety pin or a paper clip.
5. Tie some bait (usually the carcasses of your last catch) to the bottom of the cage.
6. Tie a 20ft piece of nylon rope on the cage and launch it into the nearest body of water.
7. Crawfish walk along the bottom of various fresh waterways so, if necessary, place a couple rocks inside the cage to keep it anchored. The same trap will work for shrimp in salt water as well.

The size of the cone opening needs to be relevant to the size of the intended catch. For example, to catch catfish the cone openings will be at least three times larger (3-4in) than the crawfish trap. Catfish, especially mud cat, are also bottom feeders; so, again, placing the cage on the floor will greatly enhance the possibility of trapping fish. When you'd like to check the cage simply pull it up with the rope. If you have a catch, use the access door to remove it, place new bait inside, shut the door and re-launch.

- Bait – There are obviously hundreds of types of baits one can use to catch fish. Conversely, different baits work on different fish. The following are some typical baits, that typically work on an assortment of typical fish found in typical regions around our typical planet:

a. Insects – Crickets, worms, grasshoppers, slugs, maggots, beetles, caterpillars, you name it, they'll eat it! I discuss how to make traps for such bastages in the *Edible Insect* section below.
b. Animal parts – Save those guts and extras for bait, especially the liver of any animal even human. Catching fish with human bait, who would have thought it?
c. Bubble gum – If nothing else, bubblegum usually works well, not because it's tasty, but because it's colorful, which, for some reason, draws a lot of fish in.
d. Fly fishing – If you're crafty enough and have some spare thread, feathers, cotton and a whole lot of spare time, you can make your own hand-made bait. Simply place a few small feathers, cotton and blades of grass against a hook, and wind with thread. The design should remain small enough to pass as a fly or other insect.

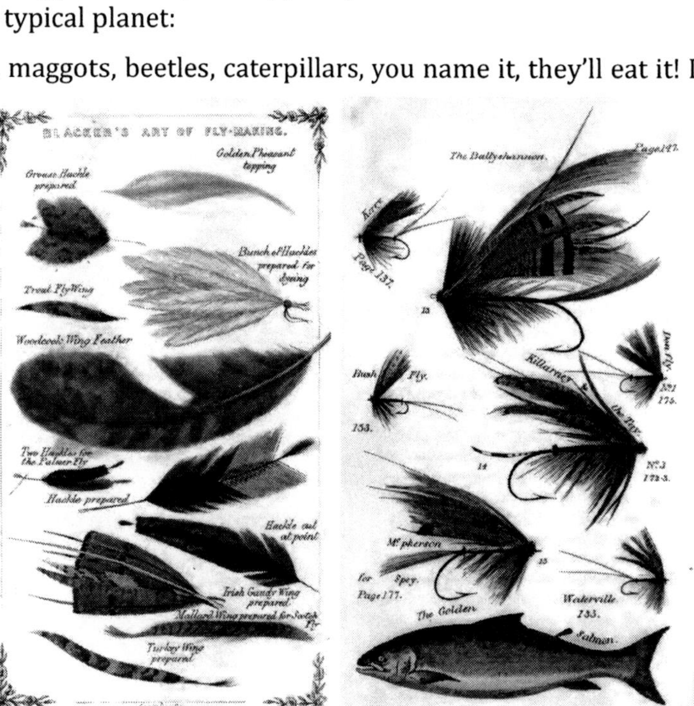

e. Ticks – If your K9 fishing companion has ticks (which most due) he's constantly carrying around a tackle box of bait for you. Surprisingly, ticks live a long time when submerged underwater, dastardly bastards!
f. Fish – Smaller fish always attract larger fish. Hook placement is critical here, since you want the fish to remain living as long as possible. I usually pass the hook twice through the tail region for live bait. For dead bait, I'll pass it through the forehead (skull) and back out through the mouth or bridge of the nose.

- Baiting – Baiting or chumming fish is different from bait for fish. It's similar to the deer feeder method mentioned, in that a plastic water bottle punched full of holes and filled with dog or cat food pellets, scraps or guts and rocks, is submerged in an area you intend on fishing regularly. The food leaches out of the holes slowly, which attracts the fish into the region on a daily basis to wait for more food. When you're ready to fish, rather than submerging a bottle, drop a hook, instead, with the same bait, and—voila! They fall for it every time. You can also use a regular can of dog or cat food, with holes punched directly in it. Using this method is the only way I'd suggest for pole fishing as a daily source of food.
- Spotlighting – Not sure what Mother Nature's obsession is with bright lights, but by keeping a light shining on the water all night, fish will begin congregating in the area daily. Partly I assume, because it attracts bugs which die and fall into the water, becoming a food source for the aquatic varmints themselves. But I also believe that, just like everyone else, fish have an underlying desire to be in the limelight--got to get those five minutes of fame.

GUTTING & SKINNING: BEAUTY IS ONLY SKIN DEEP

Gutting a kill is the most important factor in hunting. Left inside the body, the guts putrefy rapidly; and, if not removed, will spoil the meat. Gutting, skinning and sectioning a dog, deer, horse, cow, donkey, cat, human or any other large mammal is a simple but tedious matter. That being said, the only reason I would actually remove the skin would be to use it to make leather and/or fur blankets, coats or other article of clothing. Otherwise, leave the skin on as a source of vital nutrition and just burn the fur, hair or feathers away over an open fire. Equivalently, the stomach and intestines make great water containers, and leg and arm bones make good knife blades and/or knife handles that would pass any metal detector. On this note, sectioning out the meat isn't necessary either, especially after an apocalypse. No one's going to care if they receive tenderloin, sirloin, rib eye, rump roast or just leg, pelvis, ribs and hip, unless you need to carry out the animal, that is. So for the sake of keeping this manual from becoming 4 inches thick, just cut loose whatever meat you can.

1. Tie two ropes around the back ankles and hoist the animal up into a tree or other suitable structure.
2. Slit the throat with a box cutter or sharp blade and let the blood drain out into a clean container, making

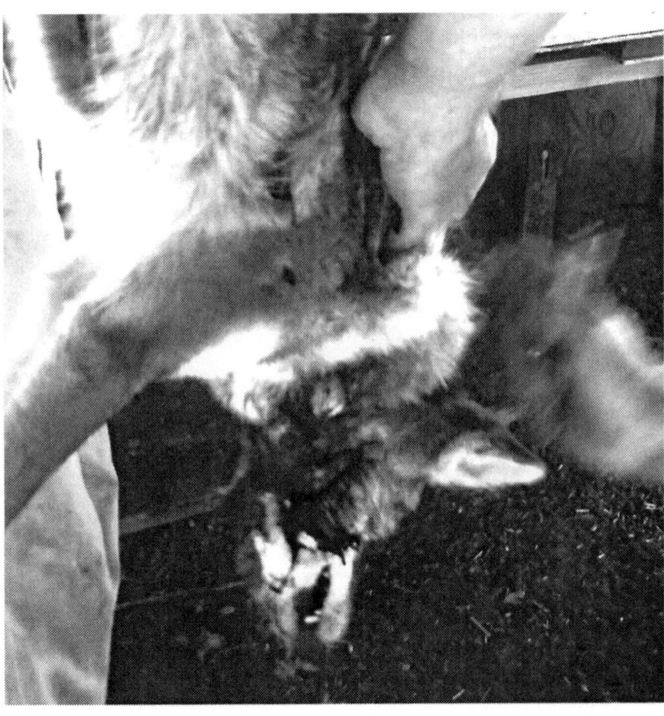

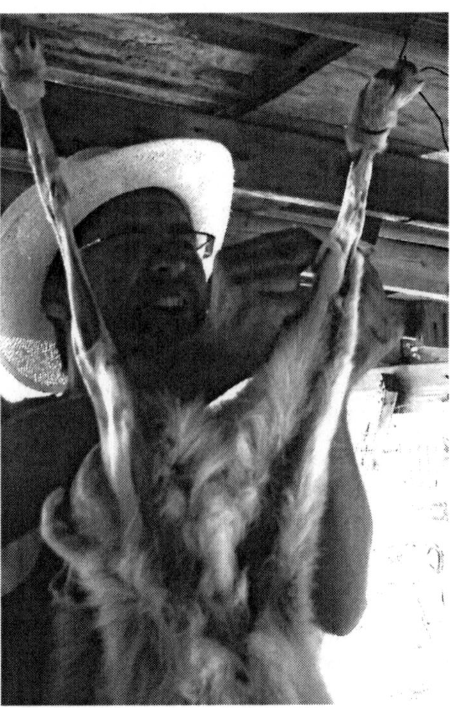

sure not to lose any. Blood constitutes 55% of the body's liquid and is composed of 92% water, minerals, sugar and proteins, making it not only a valuable source of nutrition and water, but it can be made into ethanol as well (which I'll describe in detail later in this chapter.)

3. When the blood stops flowing, make a cut around each ankle, and from the ankles up the inside of the legs towards each armpit, essentially forming two large V's at the chest and abdominal regions.
4. Make a third cut down the chest connecting the two V's and slightly cut away the fur on each ankle. Once you have at least a few inches flapping, grab with both hands and pull the skin entirely off the body. On larger animals like cows, moose, elks, donkeys, horses, etc. a vehicle and chains (or highway cables) can be utilized to help facilitate the process by hooking them into the flaps of skin and driving away.

5. Stringing the animal up by its hind legs rather than its front allows the innards to become trapped in the chest cavity and not fall out onto the floor, which we can then scoop out and place in another clean container (you'll want to keep these to consume or to use as bait as well). If you prefer to just drop the internal organs rather than digging them out, hang the animal by its front legs instead.
6. Next remove the lungs, this may entitle breaking the ribs with bolt cutters. Everything on any animal is edible EXCEPT the gallbladder (which is poisonous,) brain, eyeballs, internal organs, anus, neck, stomach, blood. The gallbladder is a green sack connected to the liver (the big bright red flat meaty substance).

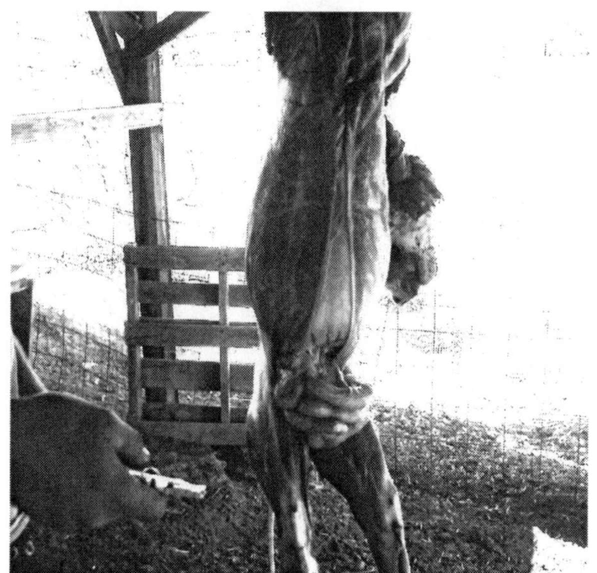

Gutting and skinning a furless animal such as a human, snake, lizard, alligator (funny how we're closer to reptiles in that way,) even the vulture shown below (Yes you can eat vulture. They sterilize themselves with an antiseptic in their urine. Actually, you can operate with it.) is identical to animals with hair, except you don't have to remove the skin (again, unless you want to make leather) or burn off the fur. Fowl is a bit different. The feathers and quills will burn off over a fire also, leaving the fat inside the first part of the quill to help further cook the food. Pulling or plucking the feathers is another option, but it typically takes a little more work:

1. As soon as the bird is killed, start pulling feathers. Pull great big handfuls as close to the root as possible and as quickly as possible. As the bird's core body temperature drops, its pores close and making the task perpetually harder to the point that you'll need to soak it in hot water and begin again.

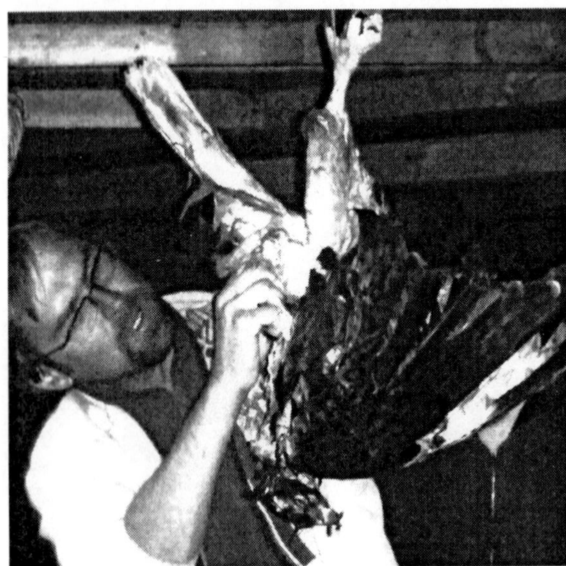

2. Cut open the lower abdomen just like before, letting the blood drain out (into a container) and remove the innards (keeping everything except the gallbladder).
3. Clean out the inside with water, and cook the entire bird without sectioning. All birds can be eaten.

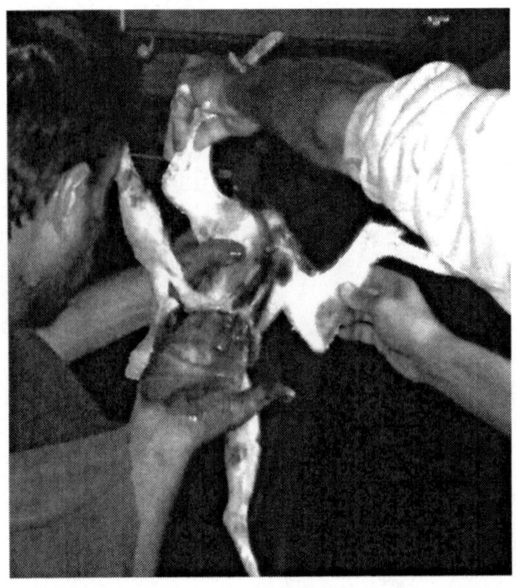

EDIBLE WILD PLANTS: BITE THE HAND THAT FEEDS YOU!

This may be the only survival guide that doesn't devote an entire chapter to edible wild plants. It's not for a lack of knowledge on my part. The problem is that there is an overabundance of knowledge. There's just too much area-specific information that would need to be relayed and described in detail to do you any good. This coupled with the facts that: (a) many wild, edible plants share many similarities with poisonous plants of the same region (there are more than 700 poisonous plants in North America alone), (b) some parts of a plant may be edible while other parts of the same plant are toxic, and (c) some plants or plant parts are only edible for certain periods of the year; you can see why there is no universal method for identifying all plants everywhere for everyone. I would highly suggest you purchase an in-depth, region-specific edible plant guide with detailed photographs (not drawings) of each plant and how to prepare them, if you're interested in eating wild produce.

In the meantime however, there is a basic test to determine if a plant or part of a plant "may" (or may not) be edible. Keep in mind this system only determines if a plant isn't extremely poisonous; it doesn't determine its nutrients or if your body will agree or disagree and purge it. The following could take up to several days testing a single plant type; so it's important not to waste your time checking what's not readily available in the area. Also, remember eating large portions of even common plants like beans, lettuce, berries, etc. can cause diarrhea, nausea and cramps. If you locate an edible plant, eat in moderation. Lastly, in most cases, the test will leave you hungry and weak. Make sure not to attempt the test when you run out of food, but rather while you still have plenty in reserve to replenish your losses once complete.

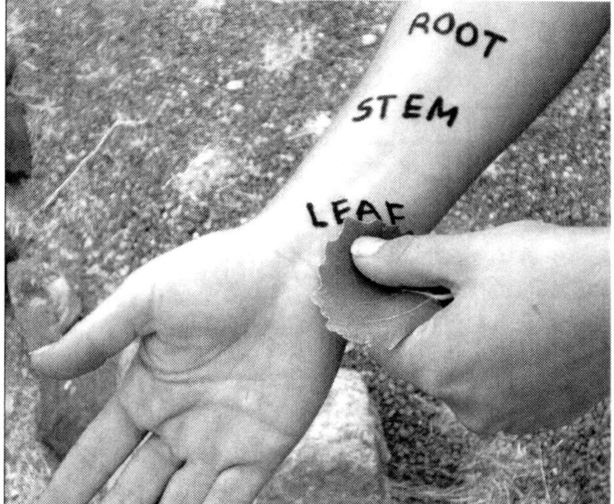

1. Don't eat anything for 8 hours to insure any effects felt come from the subject.
2. Don't pick or touch the plant before the 8 hours.
3. Pick the questionable plant and separate the flowers from the leaves from the stem from the root.
4. Rub a portion of each part of the plant against different spots on the inside of your wrists.
5. Remember, or mark with a pen, which areas on your wrist signify which piece of the plant.
6. Wait 10-30 minutes for a reaction. If no stinging or burning occurs, apply one part to the lips.
7. Wait 10-30 minutes for a reaction. If no stinging or burning occurs, apply the same part to the tongue. Do not chew or swallow, just rub.
8. Wait 10-30 minutes for a reaction. If no stinging or burning occurs, perform the same tests with the other sections of the plant.
9. This concludes the first half of the test. If you experienced any reaction during any stage of the test, that plant failed and is not safe for ingestion.
10. Boil any passed sections in water for 5-10 minutes then chew one section for 3 minutes. Do no swallow!
11. Wait 10-30 minutes for a reaction. If no nausea, stinging or burning occurs, chew the remaining sections in the same manner. Do not swallow!
12. Wait 10-30 minutes for a reaction. If no nausea, stinging or burning occurs, chew/swallow a section.
13. Wait 8 hours for a reaction. If you experience any discomfort, induce vomiting. If no reaction is felt, you may eat the remaining boiled sections.
14. Wait 8 hours for a reaction. If you experience any discomfort, induce vomiting. If no reaction is felt, eat a larger portion of a boiled section.
15. Wait 8 hours for a reaction. If you experience any

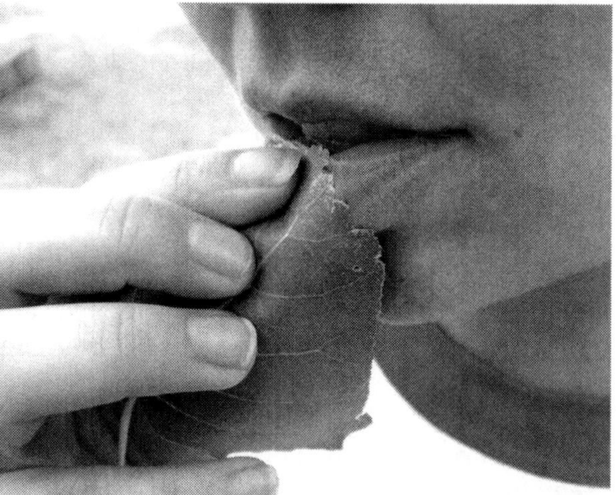

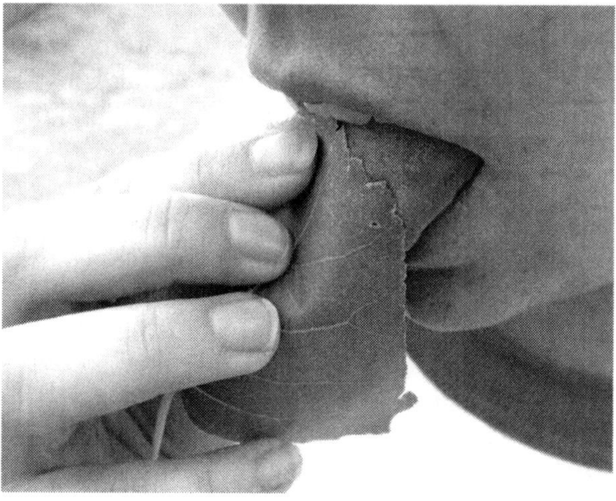

discomfort, induce vomiting. If no reaction is felt, eat larger portions of the remaining boiled sections.

16. Wait 8 hours for a reaction. If you experience any discomfort, induce vomiting immediately. If no reaction is felt, the plant, or at least the 'passed' sections of the plant, are safe to eat. If in doubt, don't eat. It's better to be hungry than to poison yourself.

On a final note, without human care, watering, maintenance and upkeep, normal home potted plants will dry up and die; and unkept home gardens and crops will either die or run overgrown and rampant, making farm lands and backyards a good place to start looking for now wild, edible plants.

BREAD & TORTILLAS: THE BREAD OF LIFE

The world has always revolved around three main staple foods: corn in the Americas, wheat in Europe, and rice in Asia, all of which are milled down into flour and used to make bread, cakes and tortillas. Wheat will be the most difficult to obtain; you'll have to actually collect the seeds from the grasses by shaking the stock tips into a burlap bag, a labor intensive job with short results. On the other hand, pulling corn from the stock is much simpler and needs no preparation to eat. Rice falls in the middle. You'll have to paddle through the rice fields, bend over the stems and knock out the spikelets into the boat. All of which will still need to be milled down into a powder with a grain mill, or by grinding a round rock over a flat one to make flour.

WHOLE GRAIN FLOUR

The term whole grain only applies to the state of the grain in its original or natural form. There are many, many different types of 'whole grains'. Some of the most common that humans grow and sell industrially are: Amaranth, Einkorn, Faro, Oat, Spelt, Quinoa, Barley, Emmer, Millet, Rye, Tiff and Wheat. But what about the other thousand plus wild grasses growing in ditches, fields and through cracks in the streets which, to a lesser or greater degree, resemble wheat? Some really look like wheat, while others only resemble wheat because they have a cluster of seeds at the end of a long slender stalk. Can these grass seeds with a similar nutritional content to wheat be harvested, ground into flour and eaten and digested safely by humans as well?

Source: Stuart Wilding

In short, ALL seeds from ALL wild grasses are safe to eat and can be used as flour or cereal. Some, however, are better than others for nutrition. Most of the grasses have tiny seeds, so grinding them loosely and then letting the wind or a fan blow/separate the chaff from the seeds is the easiest way to process them. The chaff will not hurt you if ground finely and consumed; it is simply not always digestible and will pass out unchanged. In some grain species, the "chaff" is also a source of nutrition and is often actually better for you when left in. At the very least, it's a bulk substance, which will provide a feeling of fullness even when it doesn't provide nourishment, staving off the feeling of starvation. Starving or hungry people do this often. And although we, humans, don't have the enzymes to process the actual grass stock itself, it can be cut finely and added to breads, soups or tea. Again, it is not usually digestible, but there is vitamin C and other nutrients in grass which will leach out into soups or tea. The same applies to pine needles. There are NO poisonous grasses; just be sure it is actually a grass and that there's no fungus present. From a survival standpoint, however, the amount of energy gained from eating bread, would barely exceed the amount of energy lost harvesting, milling, making and baking it (*Law 2*).

First, you'll need to know when to harvest your wild grain. Wheat usually drops its seed (which is actually a fruit) twice per year, once in June or July and again in November or December, depending on location. The seed head has to be brownish/tan in color. Remove one head from the stalk (one head per stalk) and grind between the palms of your hands. If you get hard little seeds, then the grain is ready to harvest. This stage of maturity is called the hard dough stage, because when you try to chew the seeds they are hard and will crunch when you bite into them.

1. The simplest method of harvesting grain by hand without a grain harvester is to walk down the rows of grass with a burlap sack or tarp, shaking out the tops where the seeds are kept, onto the bag.
2. As the bag fills up with seed pods, carefully empty them into a suitable container.
3. When enough containers are filled, grind seed into flour with a grain mill or by placing some seed onto a large flat rock or concrete sidewalk and rubbing with a long round rock. This is called a stone mill.
4. This method naturally allows the chaff to blow away from the seed with the wind.

CORN FLOUR

When ground down, corn yields more flour, with much less bran, than wheat does. Corn bread and corn tortillas are much simpler to make than wheat bread; and, of course, you can just eat the corn on the cob itself, making the energy loss to gain ratio within very acceptable limits:

1. After picking the corn cob, boil for about 5 minutes.
2. Shave and separate the kernels from the cob with a knife.
3. Place the kernels in the solar dehydrator described below until the corn is completely dry.
4. Mill the corn kernels as described above to produce corn flour.

ALTERNATIVE FLOURS

Thought I'd say a quick word about mesquite and some other not so common ingredients from which you can make flour. Mesquite is a leguminous tree or bush (if you can call it that) which grows profusely throughout the Americas, but especially all over the western United States. Its pea-like pods can also be dried and milled just like corn to make mesquite flour. Ancient Indians, and even today's Mexicans, rely heavily on the mesquite plant as a source of food in dry regions that can't sustain corn, wheat or rice. I've also made flour from milled crickets. The process is simple. Just dehydrate the crickets in the solar dehydrator (again, mentioned below) and grind into flour. The flour mix can be made directly into bread or tortillas or mixed with a grain or corn flour for added nutrients. Potatoes make exceptional flour. Just boil them and mash the potatoes as you normally would (no need to remove the skins) and spread them out on the dehydrator tray. Once dried, you can mill them into flour. Of course, rice is another option, prepared exactly the same way as the rest... boil - dry - mill. Acorns, oats, beans, pumpkin (or any other type of gourd), banana, hell, even banana peels, the sky is the limit. If it can be dried, milled and ingested, we can make flour out of it!

YEAST

Yeast isn't an ingredient in making tortillas, which means that much less energy lost. In fact, the most difficult part of making bread will be producing your own yeast, if you don't have any on hand already. The good thing is that it's everywhere in the air, always. The trick is getting some to grow on a usable substance for you:

1. Simply fill about 1/4 of a jar full of raisins or other dried fruit (dried in the solar dehydrator, lots of work for the dehydrator).
2. Fill the jar to a little more than half full with rain or purified water and place and screw the cap securely on top.
3. Once a day shake the contents and unscrew the top to let some air in, then replace and screw the lid back on tightly again.
4. When all the fruit rises, it will begin fizzing and the lid will pop when you try to open it. The yeast is then ready to propagate.
5. The process should take about seven days. On the eighth day, or when the fruit has all floated to the top and is fizzing, dump the contents through a strainer, pour the liquid back into the jar and close up tightly again.
6. After another week, mix in a cup of flour to a paste-like consistency; and place the lid back on loose so that air can enter and escape.
7. After a few hours you should see the dough rise considerably. It may help to initially mark the jar with a ling so that you can actually tell when the dough has risen and is ready.

8. Spread the dough out onto a tray to once again dry in the Sun.

9. Once dry, break up and place in your mill to grind into a powder.
10. At this point the yeast is ready and you can make bread or alcohol (as described below).

BREAD & PASTRIES

There are hundreds of recipes for making breads, cakes and other pastries and, of course, you can experiment to create a better, simpler method than mine. And although mine may not be exceptionally tasty (it is actually pretty good), it uses the least amount of energy while providing the greatest calorie gain:

1. Place 3 cups of flour (corn, wheat, mesquite or whatever else you'd like) in a mixing bowl.
2. A pinch of yeast (very little yeast is needed).
3. A teaspoon of salt.
4. 1-1/2 cups of water and mix. No kneading required.
5. Cover for about 12 hours in a cold place so that it has time to come together (natural kneading).
6. Pour out the contents onto a lightly floured surface, add a little more flour to the top and you're set.
7. As far as cooking the bread, you can just leave it in the Sun to rise naturally or cook on simple campfire or in any of the stoves described below. Preheat a medium pot as hot as you can, and set the dough inside.
8. Place the cover on the pot and cook until the dough rises, colors to a caramel color and starts smelling.

TORTILLAS

Making tortillas is a 3-step process. But I'll also explain how to make the smasher as well:

1. Fill a mixing bowl with as much corn flour as desired and mix enough water into the flour to attain a dough-like consistency.
2. Roll dough into a hand-sized ball and flatten between 2 plastic-covered boards (grocery bags work well).
3. Cook on a flat skillet or frying pan until lightly colored.
4. To make a tortilla smasher, simply take (2) 1in by 8, 10 or 12in by 8, 10 or 12in boards (depending on the size of tortillas you wish to make) and hinge them together on one side leaving a 1/8in gap. That's it!

EDIBLE INSECTS: YOU ARE WHAT YOU EAT!

There are 200 million bugs per person on this planet. I always look at eating them as the lowest form of food acquisition, not because they're "dirty" or "disgusting," but because they're small. The amount of energy that would need to go into finding and gathering up large quantities of any type of insect barely offsets the amount of energy spent in the act--making it. For example, catching, killing, cleaning, preparing, cooking and eating, say, an ant is an extremely simple ordeal compared to, say, a deer or even a human for that matter. (Yes, a lot of energy is burned just eating and digesting food.) But we're not just interested in catching one ant; we'd literally need hundreds to satisfy our daily nutritional needs. According to recent studies, insects "could" account for over 60% of your daily protein requirements, which is comparable to poultry and beef, as well as being high in lysine and threonine, which would be equivalent to a diet of wheat, rice, cassava or maize.

Malnutrition, which is what we're primarily concerned with, isn't a matter of protein as much as potential calories, though. Without calculating the energy spent in labor, stress, fleeing, fighting or food acquisition, a typical human requires <u>at least</u> 2,000 calories per day to maintain body mass, in other words, to hold off starvation and keep the body from eating itself. You can double that for overweight people or those of us involved in daily strenuous activity. That said, a recent analysis of common insects done by Ramos-Elorduy and Pino (1990) shows insects on average have a higher caloric value than soybeans, corn, beef, fish, lentils and beans and wheat and rye grains. The highest were: caterpillars at 6.6cal/g, beetles at 6cal/g, leafhoppers (or potato bugs) at 5.6cal/g, ants at 5.3cal/g and grasshoppers at 4.1cal/g. To be more specific, 100 grams of grasshoppers (at 75% protein) or crickets (at 67% protein) have more nutritional value than 100 grams of red meat (at 57% protein).

Then there are also other factors like fatty acid count (with insects essential fatty acids being similar to that of poultry and fish), vitamins (all typically high in B1, B2, B3 and B6), minerals (very high in iron, copper, phosphorus and zinc), carbohydrates and calcium all equating to 100% (respectively) of essential daily dietary requirements per one to two pounds of substance. These crucial nutrients are highly concentrated in the eggs and larvae forms of said insects, which lack the indigestible chitin or exoskeleton (outer shell-like coverings). From personal experience, not only are bugs a healthy food substitute in a world without hot dog stands, deli counters and produce aisles, they're actually quite delectable eaten raw or, as some prefer, cooked in some outlandish, absurd and ridiculous fashion, if you can get past the fact you're eating creepy-crawlies, that is. Most all bugs are edible; just stay away from any that sting, are brightly colored, smell bad or have fur. Once again, though, the only real problem lies in catching enough while exerting little energy:

- Ants – There are ants literally everywhere, accounting for 25% of the mass of all land animals. That's to say, if you add up the mass of every animal on land, ants would amount to 25%. That's a lot of ant. Every bit of land, with the exception of a few small islands, contain ant colonies, which is good for us since we dwell on virtually every land mass as well, making Formicidae (ant) a good starting point for lunch:

1. Locate an ant mound. A simple enough endeavor since you're probably standing near one now.
2. Dig a 3-6in trench all the way around the base of the mound, approximately 3in deep.
3. Line the trench with tin foil, shiny side up and

with your mouth an inch or two above the mound, blow a few light bursts of air into the hole. This will create the effect of a wasp's wings or other predatory flying animal's arrival and attempted invasion, causing all of the mound inhabitants to flood out of the entrance in defense of their abode. Once they reach and fall into the tin-covered trench in search of dastardly wasps, the slippery metal walls will prevent their egress.

Typically one ant contains two calories, so you would have to catch and eat 35 ants to equal the calorie count of one egg, mmm-mm ant--that's delicious!

- Caterpillars – A healthy person in a caterpillar-rich area could pick up to 20 liters or about 100-200 (depending on size of species) of the larval butterfly (or moth) per day. Caterpillars aren't as intelligent or mobile as ants and won't attempt to protect their domain or fellow kin from would-be marauders, so the same trick won't work on these critters. Similarly, caterpillars maintain the same family structures as Americans and are spread out all over the place, which make them a bit more laborious to round up. Start by looking for half-eaten leaves of nearby plants, since there's no point in searching a plant that isn't a typical food source for the bug or is a hike to get to. Once you find munched-on vegetation, focus your attention on that specific type of plant throughout the area. Then, it's just a matter of picking and moving on. Once you find one, inspect each leaf of the plant thoroughly as there's likely to be more. Typically one caterpillar contains 11 calories, so you would have to catch and eat almost 7 caterpillars to equal the calorie count of one egg.
- Termite – Termites are abundant in wooded lands; but with the literal collapse of society, pesticides and insect control companies, along with our ridiculously timber-framed home building methods, I expect they'll soon be running rampant in suburbia as well. Look for the above-ground dirt tunnels on walls or sidewalks termites make to protect their translucent bodies from the Sun, or the eaten grooves and trenches in the wood itself. Trapping termites is another rather simple process:

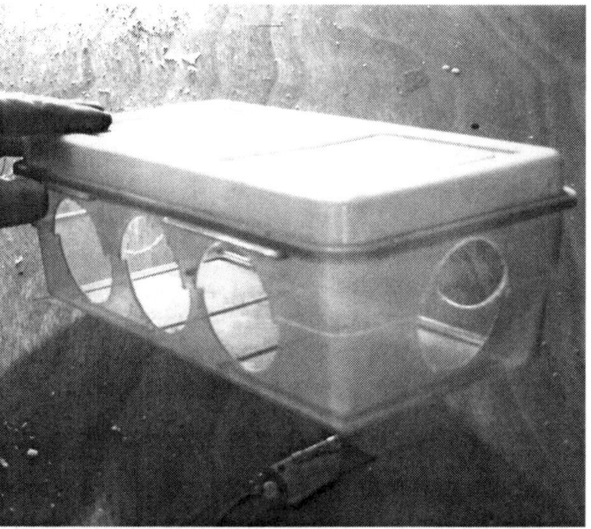

1. Take a shoebox-size plastic container, similar to the kind that kids use to hold their crayons, scissors, pencils, markers and frogs in.
2. With a box cutter, cut out several openings on all 4 sides, a few inches in diameter.
3. Locate a termite nest; and dig a hole the size of the plastic container about a foot away from the entrance.
4. Place the container in the hole so that the lid is flush with the surrounding surface.
5. Fill the box with moist (not soaked) cardboard, shut the lid and cover the top with a thin layer of dirt.

Wet cardboard is a tasty treat to these wood eaters. Eventually, they'll build a network of tunnels going to and from the box. Once this super highway system is constructed, there could be over a hundred termites in your trap at any given moment. After a few days, simply lift the lid, shake the insects out into a separate plastic container, replace the cardboard or add more as needed and close and cover the lid with dirt. Several of these traps can be located all around the one nest or multiple nests, bringing in thousands of termites per day. Typically, one termite contains 1 calorie, so you would have to catch and eat a whopping 70 to equal the calorie count of one egg!

- Cricket – When I worked nightshift at Boeing, by morning almost the entire hanger floor would be covered in thousands of dead crickets. If they weren't swept up every night, dayshift would arrive to piles, sometimes a two feet high by several feet wide, blown and piled up against the aircraft's landing gear. At first I thought that the chemicals we used on a daily basis poisoned the bugs. It wasn't until years later I learned that the bright hanger lights would lure the varmints into the building where they'd search frantically all night for food, only to die of starvation by morning. Abandoned cities would simulate that Boeing hanger perfectly, but only if power to the surrounding street lights were still on. It would then only be a matter of making your morning rounds, gathering up as many bodies as possible. If power, however, has indeed failed, we can build our own smaller trap version using the same trick:

1. Place a stove, fridge, washing machine (drum removed) or other similar appliance or container with lid, on its back. This is the trap body.
2. Place a well-charged, solar-powered (actually, solar-battery charged) lantern inside the center of the trap. There will be plenty of these in the front yards of the now decaying homes.
3. Place any green veggie scraps (leaves, lettuce, grass, whatever) inside and around the lantern, enough to sustain the beasts for the duration of the night.
4. Open the door of the fridge, stove, etc., turn on the light and you're good to go.
5. Check the trap before daybreak, then quickly close the door.
6. Extracting the insects can get a little tricky, especially with smaller numbers. Typically I just let them die of starvation, which usually occurs within a day or so. The problem with this is that they'll either: (a) eat each other for food, or (b) burn off critical calories that I want, sustaining themselves.
7. Once the bugs have been removed, let the lantern sit in the Sun to recharge, and then set the trap again for the next night.

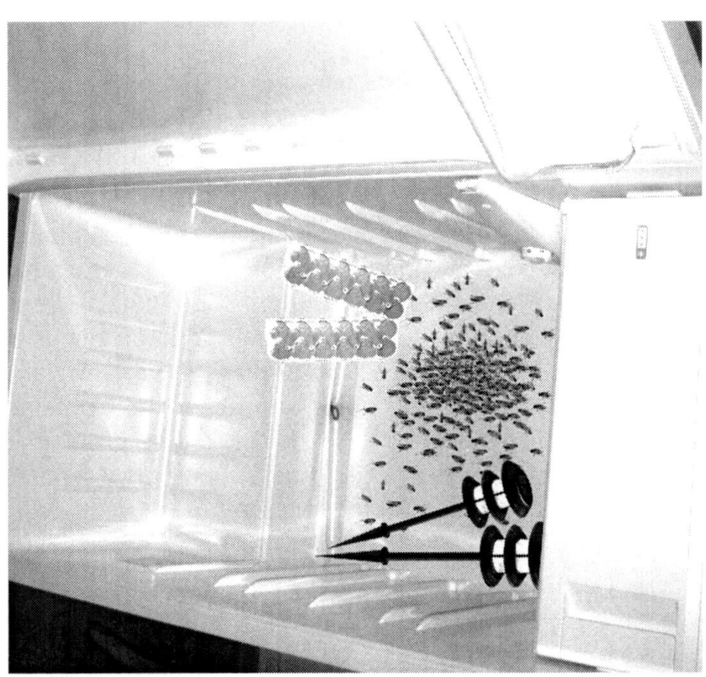

A couple things to remember about your highly sophisticated, Boeing Cricket Appliance Trap or BCAT:

a. By maintaining several of these traps around the city, one could literally feed an entire army on crickets.
b. It's better if the appliance is located outside so that the light of the lantern can be seen from far and wide.
c. The door needs to be propped wide open and supported in case of high winds.
d. If the fridge walls are high, a sheet of plywood or screen will need to be propped up against the outside surfaces as a ramp. The slippery inside walls will prevent any trapped bugs from just walking out.
e. In the morning you'll also notice that not only crickets are caught in this trap, but all types of night dwelling, light-loving creatures. These are a bonus, just extra nutrition.
f. Crickets hate human beings; they consider us mortal enemies in real life, so place the trap away from the movement of people.

Lastly, typically, one cricket contains 4.8 calories, so you would have to catch and eat 14 (and a half) crickets to equal the calorie count of one egg.

- Grasshopper – Grasshoppers are the cannibals of the insect world, they love chowing down on their fellow segmented brothers (and sisters...), making catching grasshoppers a simple enough matter:

1. Fill a kiddie pool (or other suitably large container) with soapy water.
2. Place a couple handfuls of hand-caught, smashed-up grasshoppers or other bugs in the water and let sit.

After a couple days, the decaying stench of dead in-laws will attract the attention of other hungry grasshoppers (and who knows what else). As they jump into the pool to take a long needed refreshing bath, the broken surface tension caused by the soap will submerge them to the bottom. And lastly, since insects have the swimming abilities of a holeless brick, they'll meet their maker within minutes down in Davey Crocket's locker. Boil the food source to kill off any harmful bacteria festering in your high-tech water trap before eating. Typically, one grasshopper contains 5 calories, so you would have to catch and eat 14 to equal the calorie count of one egg. That's a hopping good time right there good buddy!

- Worms – Worms are found in every landscape on the planet from the desert to the jungle, from mountains to valleys. The problem is that they enjoy the subterranean world, only venturing above-ground for our glamorous and rich entertaining nightlife. So it just comes down to a matter of creating the glamour and appeal that the inspiring wannabe worms seek, locally. Red worms can be harvested by uncovering and breaking up horse and cow shit in the early, moist hours; while earthworms and night crawlers can be raised by thoroughly soaking an area of dirt the night before and covering with a piece of carpet or cardboard, causing them to rise to the surface magically overnight. Typically, one worm contains 16 calories, so you would have to catch and eat just over 4 worms to equal the calorie count of one egg. Mm-mmm, worms. Don't they make you feel all *worm* and tingly inside?

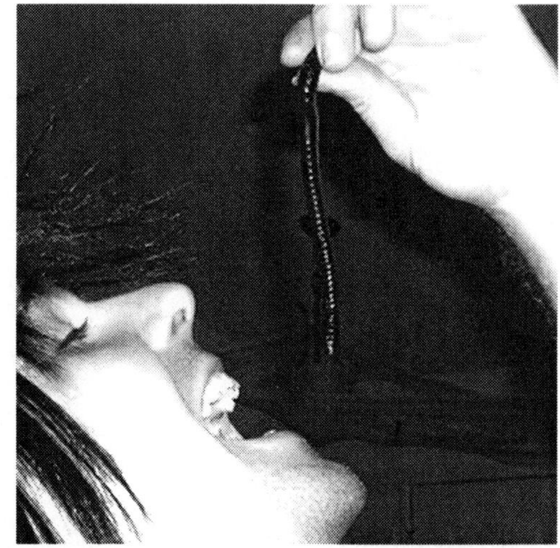

- Beetles – Beetles are plentiful on this planet. In fact, about 25% of all known life forms and 40% of all insects fall into the beetle family. The only problem with catching beetles, is that because they are so prevalent, their food supply is vast and various. Basically, they can eat anything--meat or plant it doesn't matter--making baiting the trap nearly impossible. On the other hand, some types of beetles only dine on a singular type of plant their entire life, regardless of what goodies you present them with. But I've learned with a little ingenuity one can build a better beetle trap:

1. Cut the tops out of several plastic milk jugs, leaving the handle intact.
2. Place the containers on the ground on their sides; handle up in the grass (cut the grass to the bottom of the opening if need be). If the trap will be located in the concrete jungle, place some debris in front, leading up to the hole, again forming a ramp.
3. Place a stone or other object inside the container towards the back, to not only weigh down the trap, but to cock it upwards a bit, as well, as making the exit ramp harder to traverse.
4. Place a couple of collected banana peels, skins, grinds, cores or other fruit and vegetable scraps inside the container along with about a cup or two of water and wait.
5. As anaerobic and aerobic bacteria begin to rot the produce, the trap will omit a nice smell, causing the critters to casually stroll in for a *happy* meal. They'll climb up the nice grassy or debris-ee ramp and slide in for a tasty treat. Unable to negotiate the slippery slope on the way out, they'll be done.

Beetles are opportunity eaters and won't normally be drawn into your rotting produce by smell alone unless they're extremely hungry, which they may be when most plant life on Earth has been wiped out. They will, however, make a detour into your trap for a little drive-through action if they're actually passing by.

That's why it's important to literally litter one area with traps, rather than spreading them out around town so that you have a better chance. Typically, one beetle contains 7 calories, so you would have to catch and eat 10 beetles to equal the calorie count of one egg. You've definitely got a *hard day's night* ahead of you!

- Maggots – If grasshoppers are the cannibals of the bug world; the maggot is the pig. It'll eat anything that was once living, the rottener and smellier the better.

1. Drill several 1/2in holes around the top side and bottom of a 5 gallon bucket, placing meat scraps inside.
2. Place the bucket inside another bucket, a lid on top and set in the Sun.

When the meat begins to rot, it will attract flies that will fly through the side holes and eat and lay eggs on the meat. When the eggs hatch a couple days later the pupae will borrow down to the lowest area possible, ultimately falling through the bottom holes into the bucket's second chamber below. Several hours later the pupae will hatch into maggots in a clean environment and be ready for consumption. Typically, one maggot contains 1-2 calories, so you would have to catch and eat 35-70 to equal the calorie count of one egg!

- Snail – Pro Tip: Snails love beer, but if you're like me you have already drunk your 20-year Cerveza stockpile and haven't gotten around to brewing more yet. Luckily, they enjoy a good fermented wine just as much; or, in this case, we'll skip the wine and go simply with the fermenting/rotting fruit:

1. Start collecting your fruit scraps in a 5-gallon bucket of water with lid.
2. After month of storing the bucket in the Sun, the contents will start fermenting. Dip a foot or two of 3/4in to 1in hose (depending on the diameter of snail in the area) into the 5-gallon bucket of rotting scraps.
3. In the evening, place the hose on the ground under a fallen log or just cover with a soaked cardboard.

By morning you should have a hose filled with a few dozen drunken snails and probably several slightly tipsy slugs, as well. As the beasts cram inside and around the tube for a nightcap, they're unable to escape when the ale is tapped out because of the crowded and blocked doors, just like at a New York night club. Sure, some of the outside snails break out of the bar; but in the end, the remaining slow-moving Mollusks aren't fast enough to notice or react in time and make a mad dash for the door. Make your rounds at first light, picking up any stragglers in the area along the way. Typically one snail contains 10 calories, so you would have to catch 7 to equal the calorie count of one egg! That's a sn-*hell* of a bar!

- Bees – If bees weren't so damn protective of their honey, a bee hive would be a treasure in a collapsed world void of sugar. It just so happens I know a few tricks (big surprise) to extract the honey without injury (or with the least amount of injury). On that note, if you're allergic to bee stings (which you're probably not), you should get some other poor sap to do this:

1. Dress up like a bee (not a bear, bees don't like bears); and sneak up on the hive casually. Don't run, it will panic the bees because they'll think that a fellow bee is being chased by something--kidding! Once you've located the hive, build a small fire (you don't want to burn them out) under or near it.
2. When you have a good set of hot coals, move them to directly under the hive (compensate for any winds) and pile plenty of grass, leaves or other green material onto the hot coals. This will produce a lot of

smoke, which doesn't harm the bees, but does set them into a mode of work (not war). They'll be too preoccupied to bother with any would-be honey thieves (if only bears were so smart).

3. Give the smoke as long as possible to work deep into and around the hive.
4. Carefully reach into the hive through the entrance hole (which will be remodeled and enlarged by your obese hand) and very slowly and gently break loose a portion of honeycomb and remove it.
5. Trust me, if you do this slowly and carefully enough, you won't get stung... well "probably" not.
6. Don't knock down and destroy the entire nest in a hunger-driven frenzy. One broken honeycomb can be rebuilt within days by the bees; and you can repeat the process on a weekly basis. Whereas, if you destroy the entire hive, they'll abandon it and relocate altogether, leaving you with a few days' worth of honey at the most.

Source: Florian

Again, throughout the world, everywhere other than the Unites States, people eat insects as part of their typical diet, especially snails (Escargot), crickets (Grillo) and worms (Noke). And again, we're left out of the fine dining culinary loop, continuing with our close-minded lifestyles, still considering eating bugs gross, vile and disgusting, which we may pay the price for in the end. And lastly, if you're worried about viruses, germs and the like, carried by insects, birds or any animal for that matter, don't. Most animals and insects carry and transmit viruses they pick up from the filth and waste of humans; and without society polluting the world, the insects, animals and water will be much safer to consume, just like it's been for millions of years before us. IF an insect or any other living thing has some type of virus, it will already be dead from it. Hence, don't eat anything already dead. This means, if it's alive, it's healthy.

WATER: WATER WATER EVERYWHERE & NOT A DROP TO DRINK

Eventually, city and urban water supplies will become exhausted, making long-term water procurement critical to maintain real survival. Societies have fallen or moved on due to failed water supplies more than all other reasons combined (famine, war, religion, disease, natural disasters, American Idol, etc.). Locating a good, clean source of water which will sustain not only your entire group but its expansion as well, is crucial. Although many cities are built on or near major water reserves or reservoirs, these may prove contaminated during the end times (if they're not already) or completely useless without the power grid as far as filtration and distribution. This may mean acquiring other sources or even venturing outside city limits in search of water:

- Rain – Rain catchment and harvesting systems have been around since ancient times; but not until just recently, with alternative building methods in the southwest, have they really gained popularity among home builders. We can incorporate this system into the current reclaimed urban life by taking advantage of the already existing catchment surfaces (roofs) and distribution systems (gutters) available. All we'll need is the storage aspect, which we may already have as well:

1. Locate the one home (there's always one in every neighborhood) with the swimming pool.
2. Remove several downspouts and elbows from neighboring homes and connect them in series from gutter into the pool.
3. Drain the pool of chlorine/water (don't worry about residual water left over; a little chorine will help to keep out algae growth). If there is no water in the pool, you'll have to add the chorine (bleach) at a mix of 1 teaspoon of bleach per 10 gallons of water.
4. Stand back and watch as the next rain storm fills up your newly-acquired water supply.

- Existing bodies – Rivers, streams, creeks, ponds, lakes, even snow are all, of course, obvious water sources; however, locating them could prove altogether a different matter. Once again, we'll need to turn to Mother Nature and watch how wildlife reacts, finds and lives with water:

1. Most animals can smell and, therefore, find water up to 20 miles away and will tend to congregate and live within the vicinity of a year-round watering hole. So keep an eye out for animal tracks or paths worn into the landscape. It doesn't really matter which way you follow the path; since, in most cases, they'll eventually circle back to the same water source from which the track originated.
2. A patch or line of lush green vegetation is also a sign of potential surface water in the area.
3. Most flying insects such as mosquitoes and gnats can only fly 1-2 miles/hr and need to drink water up to 10 times/day; therefore, more often than not, you'll never see a mosquito more than a few miles away from water.
4. Many fowl, such as ducks and geese, must bed down in or around water. Keep this in mind during the early or late hours of the day and take notice from/to which direction they're flying.
5. When searching for water, hike at a downward horizontal angle to the landscape. Since water always travels downhill, you're more than likely to come across a stream or creek this way. If not, you'll almost definitely find water congregated at the bottom, in the form of a pond or lake.
6. Whenever searching, make sure to keep quiet and stop frequently to just listen and look around. Rivers, creeks and waterfalls can be seen up to 6 miles away and heard up to about half that (3.5 miles away).
7. Muddy areas sometimes signify groundwater just below the surface. Dig down a couple feet and wait a few minutes; water should start to percolate up from below.

Once again, unless you find the source itself, or a spring, you'll need to kill possible bacteria living within the water with 1 teaspoon of bleach per 10 gallons of water, or by boiling it for at least 0 minutes before drinking. For just washing clothes, bathing or cleaning, you don't need to purify the water.

- Unconventional Bodies – Oceans, swamps, dirt, tree branches, urine, or any other source of water or moisture is a potential source of hydration. Through the construction of a solar still and reverse osmosis, we can not only purify even the harshest sources, but make water from dirt, animals and even branches:

a. Salt water is an exceptional source of drinkable water, anytime. In fact, since the planet is covered mostly by it, I'm always dumbfounded to hear that there's a shortage of water somewhere in the world. All that needs to be done is separate the salt from the H20, a fairly simple task even without electricity.
b. Although there's an exceptional amount of life growing and thriving in swamp water, this, too, can easily be separated and made into potable water.
c. Dirt, tree branches, cactus, animals, insects--basically anything that sucks in, drinks or holds water--has water held for us to remove, even urine.

By constructing a simple, below-ground still, we can purify all of these forms of water, separate salt or contaminants from nutrients and even retrieve water where there seems to be none at all.

1. First, choose the perfect location. The ground should be damp but able to receive sunlight for the duration of the day. This could be an area on the east side of an eastern facing cliff or house/building, which would become shady in the evening, acquiring more dew during the night, or an area previously covered by a tree or structure, which can be tied back, moved or cut down.
2. Dig a cone-shaped hole a few feet across and a couple feet deep.
3. Place a can, pot or flat plastic Tupperware container on the bottom of the pit.
4. Place about 3ft of car vacuum hose (removed from anywhere under the hood of any vehicle) inside the container and drape it up and out the side of the pit.

5. Place a clear, plastic, painter's tarp or rain poncho over the pit extending at least 6in out on all sides.
6. Cover the entire edge of the plastic with rocks, sand or dirt, making an air- tight seal all the way around.
7. Place a small stone that could fit in a closed hand in the middle of the plastic sheet, creating a nice gentle inverted slope sagging down, directly above and almost touching the inside container. If the plastic starts pulling, add more stones/dirt.

The greenhouse effect inside the still created by the clear plastic sheet causes the moisture in the surrounding dirt to evaporate, travel upwards, make contact with the inside bottom of the plastic sheet itself, condense and drip back down towards the small stone into the container. The process is identical to what occurs on the Earth everyday; moisture in the ground or ocean evaporates because of the Sun and condensates in the sky, dripping back down to Earth via gravity in the form of rain.

Placing vegetation, leaves, grass, green leafy twigs, insects, rodents or any other object that retains water into the still will increase the amount of evaporation/condensation that's produced. Placing a second container, or bottom plastic lining, inside the still and pouring saltwater, swamp water or urine in it will separate and evaporate the H20 from the other components while transferring it into the neighboring container. You can then use the vacuum hose like a giant straw and drink directly out of the clean fresh water container without danger of bacteria or contamination or destroying your still. If the drinking water is still too salty, simply repeat the process a second or third time. If you let the water sit for a half a day and settle, it will taste even better. If you don't have a vacuum tube, you'll have to disassemble the still to get the container out, a real hassle in the long-term scheme of things. This solar still should produce at least a quart of water per day. Build several in the area, each separated by at least 6ft for greater quantity collection.

NOTE: A healthy person's urine is made of about 95% water and completely sterile, with the other 5% being mostly nitrogen, potassium and calcium, making pee safe to drink even without the still. Don't let it sit, though. Fermented pee can build/collect pathogens and bacteria within a matter of days.

- Bag still – A simpler, quicker, but less efficient method is to just tie several large Zip-lock bags over a bundle of small, leafy tree branches. Again, place a small stone that would fit in a closed hand inside the bag to weigh the branch down or tie the branch all the way down to the ground. Either way, the bag should be lower than the opening so that the accumulated water won't drip out. Again, place several of these around the trees in the area, especially on the south sides as they will receive more sunlight (in the northern hemisphere). Throughout the day the plant will transpire, releasing moisture which will condense in the bag.
- Bucket filters – Don't happen to have any bleach or pots and pans to boil water in? Here's a simple filter better than any Aquafina model:

1. Place a 5-gallon bucket upside down and punch a small hole in bottom center.

2. Place a layer of 1 1/2 in charcoal (made by dousing hot coals with water) in the bottom with a bowl-like contour.
3. Fill the remaining space with alternating layers of sand, dirt, cotton and charcoal, each in the shape of a bowl, leaving a few inches on top free for water.
4. Pour water into the bucket and allow a few moments to percolate through the layers.
5. Once dripage begins, place a second, clean container underneath to catch and store the now-filtered water.

Each layer separates and filters out a different element of the water's contaminants. The bowl shape of each layer prevents the water from simply traveling around the sides of the bucket and out through the bottom hole, bypassing the entire filtration process altogether. If the water isn't clean enough for your standards, simply pass it through the filter again. If a 5-gallon bucket isn't acquirable, a 5-gallon Igloo water cooler, a clean plastic 30-gallon garbage can, or several plastic bags would all work just as well. Eventually, the layers will become saturated with the filtered toxins and will need to be dumped out and refilled with clean materials.

- Ground water filters – If you don't have any plastic sheets, bags, containers, pots, bleach, etc. dig a 5ft hole about 20-50ft from the edge of a lake, swamp, pond, river, ocean, etc. Place several rocks inside the bottom of the pit and around the sides to keep the dirt from coming loose and caving in your hole. Wait a few hours and voila--a gallon or more of filtered water. What's happening is that the surface water you see in, say, a pond is only a small percentage of the water that's saturated into the surrounding dirt. By digging a hole into this soaked earth we're essentially building a small well.

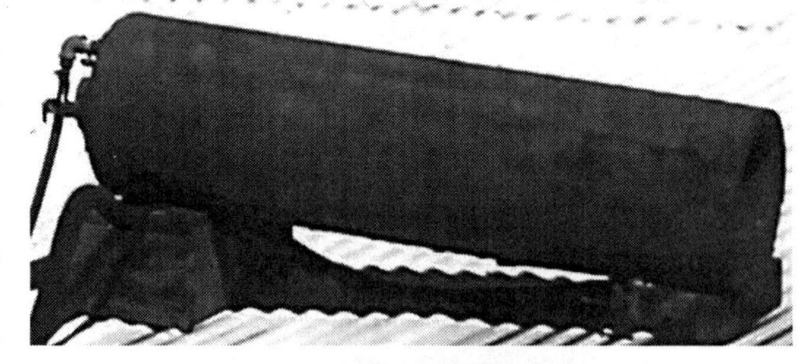

- Shower – The loss of water heaters, in some cases, can be one of the most disrupting elements of a societal collapse (which shows how spoiled we are). That said, it's actually fairly easy to heat water. All we'll need is an old water heater.

1. First, remove the outer jacket insulation and paint the actual tank flat black.
2. Place the heater on something so that it sits at least 6ft upright; and connect a 1ft piece of hose to the bottom spigot.
3. Remove one of the top 3/4in plugs, fill with water and let sit all day in direct sunlight. At the end of the day, just before the Sun goes down, everyone can take showers. A typical 40-gallon tank holds enough water for 8 showers, conserving water.

- Toilet – Squatting in the woods can get tiresome, trust me. Eventually you'll want to return, at least partially, to the civilized world and sit while you shit. Since there's no longer any functioning flushing toilets, and you don't want to waste all your water dumping it down the drain, we can build a simple waterless commode:

1. First remove a toilet seat from any abandoned home and trace the seat out on the lid of a 5-gallon bucket.
2. Now cut out the impression on the lid and screw the seat down (stainless screws/nuts won't rust).
3. Add some sawdust or dirt to the bottom and after each use. Once that bucket fills you can replace it with an empty one, placing it in a dry area with a second lid punched full of holes to fully decompose.

It takes about a month or two (depending on temperatures and humidity) for aerobic bacteria (which has no smell) to convert feces into fertilizer, which you can then mix in with the crops described in the next chapter. What you don't want to do is pee in a bucket toilet. It will quickly fill with liquids, creating a cesspool septic-tank-like environment of anaerobic bacteria, which is the stuff that stinks. If you must urinate in the toilet, punch a few small holes in the bottom of the bucket and bury it halfway down in a sandy location.

FIRE: & BRIMSTONE

Making fire shouldn't be difficult in a post-apocalyptic world. Heck, most of the world should still be burning. Either way, we're not talking about rubbing sticks together here; there will be plenty of modern tools to facilitate combustion. Lighters and matches are obvious choices; and with almost 50% of Americans being addicted smokers, you'll have a 1 in 2 chance of finding a lighter on a corpse or in an abandoned home, if not still neatly stacked on display racks in gas stations and grocery stores. Don't like the idea of rummaging through the pockets of nicotine-soaked dead folks? Here are a few ways to make fire using everyday items that 'should' still be available even during the worst of times:

- Fresnel lens – A Fresnel lens is today's magnifying glass. It's a foolproof method of starting a fire in sunlight with a lens in hand. You may have noticed the screen of many big screen TV's are very coarse or textured. This is a Fresnel lens and helps to magnify the image out to the viewer. It's just a big plastic sticker really, so peel it off and you're good to go. Theatre lighting also has a Fresnel lens covering to magnify the light onto the stage during productions as well as headlight lenses. Use the lens much like you would a magnifying glass, by lining up the Sun's focal point through the lens with the item you'd like to set on fire. Paper, cotton, newspaper, trash, dryer lint, bark, wood, even metal will all spontaneously combust when in contact with the light of a Fresnel lens.

- Spark plugs – With millions of discarded cars now littering the streets and parking lots of the world, and with at least four plugs per motor, we're talking a cache of igniting tools:

1. Remove the spark plug cable, the spark plug from the engine block, and reconnect the spark plug cable.
2. Place a piece of gasoline-soaked paper between the plug prong and the igniter pin.
3. Touch the plug prong anywhere on the engine, crank over the engine and voila--fossil fuel combustion at its finest.
4. If you don't happen to have the keys to the engine, no problem. Just lay a hanger across the positive and negative terminals of the battery and stand back as the sparks fly.

- Batteries – A 9v battery alone is a portable lighter in waiting. Without any need to modify, it has enough current to not only start kindling but burn steel, and with at least one required by law in every single home (smoke detectors), there will be plenty for the taking:

1. Get some steel wool (under most home sinks).
2. Pull the steel wool apart making it thin and fluffy.
3. Place the bundle of steel wool under a pile of kindling like dryer lint or scraps of paper.
4. Touch the 9v battery to the steel wool.

- Beer can – I suspect there will be much celebration once folks know the world is coming to an end. This provides us with plenty of empty beer cans (or soda cans) littering the streets. And since everyone's dead and won't have any further need to fight plaque disease and gingivitis, there'll be a lot of half-used tubes of toothpaste lying around as well:

1. Squeeze out some toothpaste onto the bottom of the can.
2. Polish with a piece of t-shirt for 30 minutes – 1 hour. This will create a mirror-like surface on the bottom of the can that will reflect back sunlight into a focal point approximately an inch or two away from the can, just like a parabolic mirror.
3. Pull out a 6in piece of automotive wire and strip the end off; or you can use a thin stick split on one end.
4. Place the top of the can against a solid surface, like your leg.
5. Place a piece of thin black cotton cloth in the stranded wires and hold steady at the can's focal point.

Any beveled surface such as a cooking pot lid or a satellite dish (with tinfoil glued onto the face) can be similarly used. The larger the surface, the less polishing is needed.

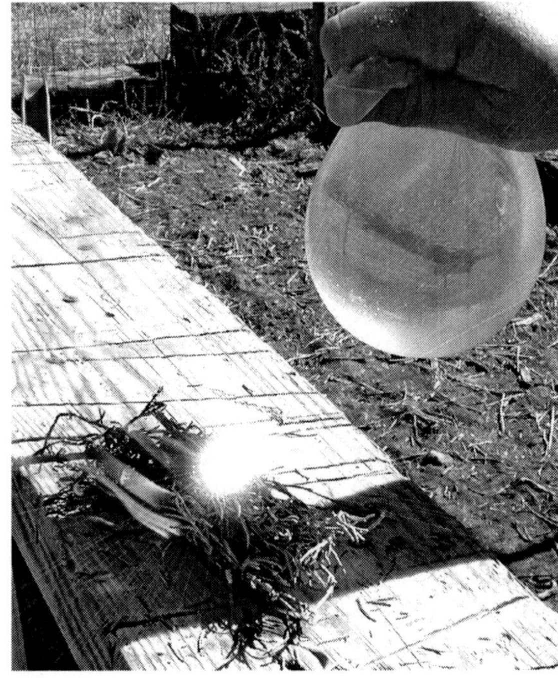

- Water – Many people aren't aware that water is actually a great fire starter. If poured into a small balloon or condom, it will refract and focus enough light to start most kindling, just like a magnifying glass. You can now finally put that old condom in your wallet to use!
- Ice – The ice method is similar to using water; but the ice needs to be formed into the shape of a lens to work. Ice is a great fire starter during an all-out ice age:

1. Chip off a small piece of clear ice (no bubbles, cracks or dirt) about 6in by 6in by 3in deep.
2. Form the top side of the ice into a slight dome by rubbing and melting it with your warm hand.
3. Form the bottom side of the ice into the same dome curve, this time inverted.
4. Focus the light as described above. Don't worry about the ice melting with the Sun. As long as it's below 32°F outside, your ice-made lens will remain intact, no matter how much Sun hits it.

- Magnifying glass – Yes, some people, especially older citizens, still keep them lying around in dens or home offices. If not, check schools, libraries, stores and office buildings. No instructions needed since most of you grew-up burning ants with these medieval torture devices as kids.

- Glasses – More than 2/3 of Americans wear glasses, so there should be no shortage of them floating around (possibly literally). Glasses make great fire starters when used just like magnifying glasses.
- Binoculars – If you've packed, or come across, any binoculars, a spotting scope or telescope, they'll work the same as the magnifying glass although the lens may need to be removed.
- Ice pack – Ice packs, like the ones you find in coolers or freezers, are made from ammonia nitrate in granulated form and can be used not only to make fire but explosives as well:

1. Open the ice packs and ammonia nitrate package.
2. Place a teaspoon of ammonia nitrate in a bowl along with a half teaspoon of table salt.
3. Grind the ammonia nitrate and salt down to a powder and add a teaspoon of zinc powder. You can get the zinc powder by sanding down a brass water pipe fitting found under any sink.
4. Grind the mixture down into a powder (careful, sweat can set off the chemical reaction).
5. Add water and stand back.

Kindling can be made out of any dry, oxygen-rich material; but in a collapsed society dryer lint, cotton balls, cotton stuffing from a sofa, bed mattress or car seat, tree bark scrapped into thin fibers, toilet paper (new or used), paper towels, cardboard and newspaper/junk mail will most likely be prevalent. Any of these items soaked in hairspray, gasoline, rubbing alcohol, paint thinner, starting fluid, Vaseline, petroleum jelly or any other accelerant will greatly help with combustion. Blowing on the kindling after the spark starts to ignite is also a critical step in the above forms of fire starting. Look at all these great fire options available all around us all the time. It's amazing we don't burn ourselves down more often.

COOKING: WHAT'S GOOD FOR THE GOOSE…

First off, there is absolutely no reason to cook food after a global catastrophe. It's a waste of time, energy, and is a sure *fire* way to draw unwanted attention from other less-fortunate, hungry survivors eager to sample your culinary skills. And before I get every FDA agent and grandmother pointing their germ-ridden finger at me, bacteria <u>aren't</u> everywhere, and <u>isn't</u> an issue in fresh kill. It has to be transported from an infected animal or area to other animals through food, water, soil, waste, humans or insects. That said, most meat and poultry that you receive from the store today <u>is</u> completely covered in bacteria like E. coli, Salmonella and Clostridium perfringens and <u>does</u> require cooking. But normal meat doesn't and, therefore, doesn't need to be cooked before consuming. On that note, you shouldn't rinse the meat either. Rinsing meat with water does nothing to kill or remove bacteria (bacteria isn't allergic to water) and will only spread the bacteria around further.

If any animal (except ruminant animals) had dangerous levels of any virus or bacteria in their body, that animal would have died before you had a chance to kill it, or else there would be billions of sick zombie deer walking around. But they don't and there aren't. This is simply because, just like us, there are gazillions of antibodies racing around the animal's body, constantly fighting and keeping at bay such bacteria. It's only when the animal is killed and these antibodies cease that the bacteria has a chance to multiply and infect the animal's meat. This, however, takes several days under the best of growing conditions: ie., pH levels of 6.7–7.5, temperatures between 41°F and 135°F and a constant supply of proteins, carbohydrates, water and oxygen. The problem really arises when these animals are forced to live penned and stacked up on top of each other and each other's feces (which is where bacteria festers), in which case their antibodies don't have time to fight off so much constant bombardment. The animals are under ongoing attach by bacteria to the point that their always sick and the meat is always infected, just like humans living in society. In nature, animals (and humans) rarely ever get sick because there not living in or coming in contact with any bacteria.

Animals in the wild shouldn't carry even a fraction of such critters since any ingested are killed upon initial consumption by the animal or in the intense stomach acids themselves. In fact, there are no recorded cases of animal-borne outbreaks of gastroenteritis before humans began mass herding and transporting beasts. Actually, only with the increase of mass-produced meat, trucked to market inventory and prolonged storage conditions do we really see an incredible spike in food-borne bacteria and viruses. The only way that fresh meat can go bad is by humans handling it. In fact, cooking food at this point can only bring negative results, such as:

- Nutrient Loss – Once the interior temperature of meat reaches 100°F, all fat tissues (regardless from which animal) become liquid. Eventually, the fat will leave the meat entirely. With extensive cooking methods like frying, the fat will evaporate completely, equating to major potential calorie loss. Water content of the meat, on the other hand, accounts for up to 20% of the meat's protein value which start to cook away at 120°F causing the meat to shrink, since many proteins are water soluble. This is one of the reasons that you don't see commercial producers shipping out cooked meats to market, even though cooked meats are 'safer' and easier to transport over raw meats. The fact is that they get paid (and you buy) meat by the pound. Why would they sell cooked, shrunken meat at a smaller profit per pound, when they could sell uncooked, inflated meat for a larger profit per pound and let you take the loss after you cook it? Fruits and veggies containing vitamin C also both elute the vitamin into the cooking water, degrading the vitamin's value through oxidation. If there's "absolutely no reason to cook meat," there's even more reason not to cook freshly picked fruits and vegetables. In fact, even just peeling fruits and vegetables can substantially reduce the vitamin content, since most of the vitamin is usually located in the skin itself. On this note, there's no reason to store produce in containers or plastic either, all produce already comes in a vacuum sealed bag (skin, peel, shell, etc.), which preserves the insides.

- Making Poisons – Cooking any type of food, but especially starchy foods, until toasted, produces acrylamide, which is a carcinogen. Many studies since the early '90s have shown that cooking meat also generates heterocyclic amines (HCAs), which, when consumed, increase the risk of cancer in humans. Actually, researchers at the National Cancer Institute discovered that *"human subjects who ate beef rare or medium-rare had less than one third the risk of stomach cancer than those who ate beef medium-well or well-done."* On the same line, researchers at the University of Toronto suggest that *"ingesting uncooked or unpasteurized dairy products* (raw milk) *may reduce the risk of colorectal cancer"*.

Since, by now, I'm sure most of you understand that I can't change what society has instilled in you over 30 years in 3 pages, you'll still prefer to fruitlessly cook your food, going against the second law; and since there will no longer be any gas or electricity to fuel your old stoves, let's do some post-apocalyptic cooking! I'll discuss a few simple methods to build different types of stoves in the new world, so that if you must leave food out unpreserved for several days, you won't die from bacteria (or paranoia). All food needs to be heated up to at least 131°F for one hour, 140°F for 30 minutes or 167°F for 10 minutes to kill any living organisms that "may" be present. And if you also must rinse produce and meat (against my advice), do not soak it in water. I suggest boiling them in soups or stews to retain most of the vitamins that would otherwise be lost.

ALCOHOL STOVE

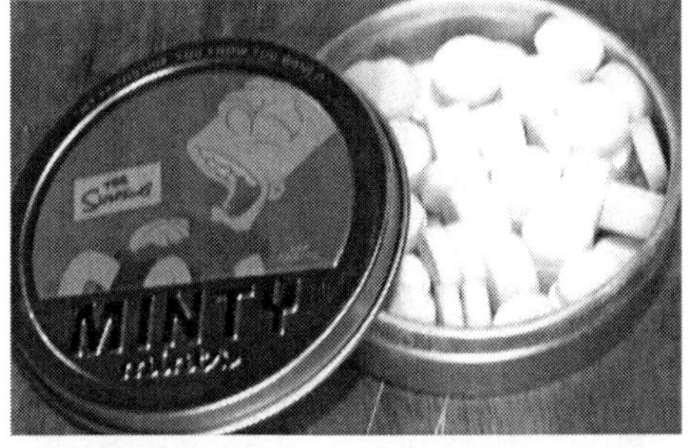

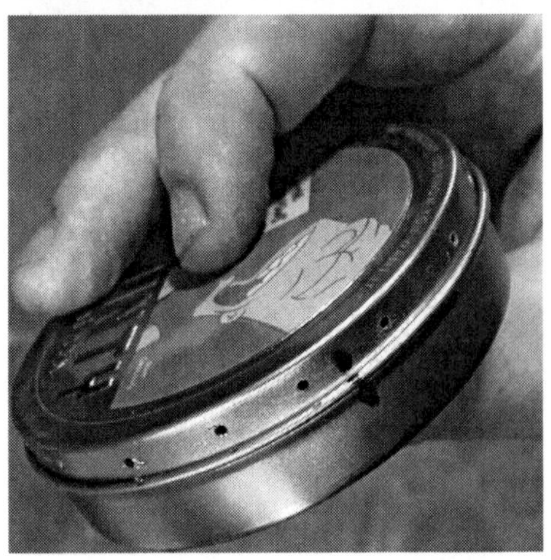

An alcohol stove will be the easiest stove to build out of the five I describe, taking no more than a couple of minutes to fashion. This simplicity doesn't come without a price, though. It's also the only one for which you have to have or make your own fuel for. Though, I often prefer this stove since you can use any flammable liquid available at the time as fuel just by twisting the lid and making the jet holes smaller or larger. The fuel will need to be the consistency of a thin oil-like diesel fuel or kerosene. If these two aren't available in the aftermath, you can make your own by mixing alcohol or gasoline with 25% oil from a car's oil pan, cooked-down fat, used cooking oil from restaurant waste vats, or ethanol or methanol, which I'll describe later. An alcohol stove, on the other hand, is just a simple, temporary or portable type of cooking apparatus to hold and burn the fuel in a controlled environment. For now, you'll need (1) small can of some sort with a lid (I used one to store candy), a thumb tack and a handful of fiberglass (just punch a hole in any Sheetrock wall).

1. Place the lid on the can and with the thumb tack, punch several 1/16in holes spaced 1/4in to 1/2in apart, about halfway up the side of the thinner top lid all the way around. This way, when the lid is rotated, the holes won't line up and you won't lose and waste the un-burnt fuel when stored.
2. Now, open the lid, place the insulation inside, fill the stove with

about 5-6 tablespoons of fuel or about 1/4 of a stove worth and close the lid.

3. Heat from the bottom to create sustainable jet vapor pressure, or pour a little fuel over the top to prime, light and place the pot with lid on top to trap as much heat as possible.

Since the stove burns clean, without fumes or smoke, it can be used as an inside heat source as well

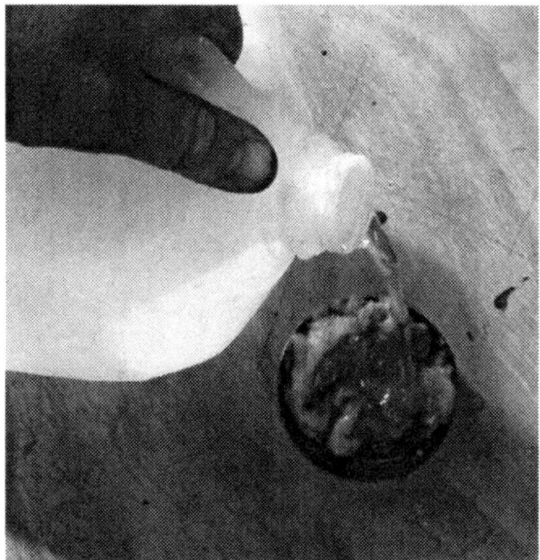

ROCKET STOVE

A rocket stove is similar to an alcohol stove except it uses just a few sticks, twigs, leaves, or brush as fuel, or anything that burns, wet or dry, to a near 100% efficiency, or about 1/8 of the fuel typically required to cook a full meal. You'll need a large metal can like a 1 gallon paint or coffee can, (1) medium soup, stew or juice can, (1) regular-sized soup or chili can, insulation or ash, (3) 1in screws and metal tin snips or sharp scissors.

1. Place the medium can over the bottom of the paint can and trace.
2. Cut the hole 3/8in smaller and cut 1/4in tabs to compensate.

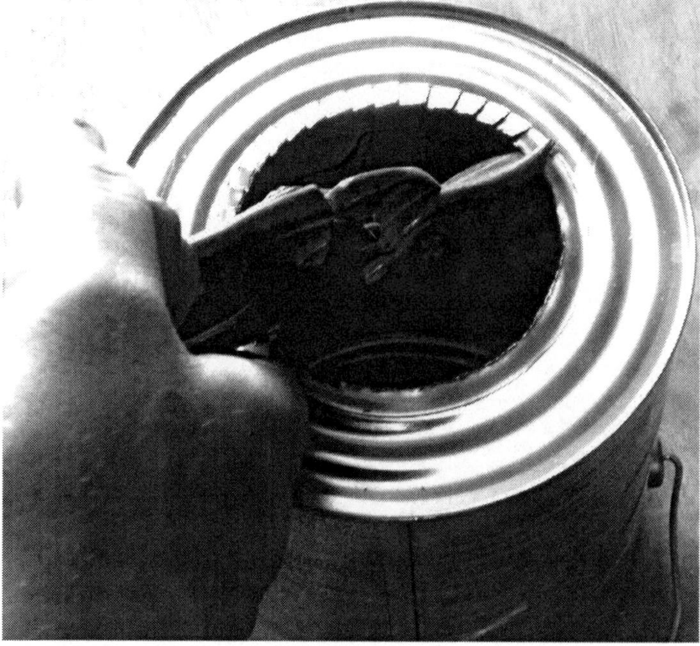

3. Place the regular can on the side of the paint can about 1in up from the bottom, trace and cut tabs.
4. Do the same for the medium can except trace and cut the small can directly onto the bottom.

5. Push the medium can inside the paint can forming a pressure fit with the tabs leaving 2in sticking out.
6. Do the same for the regular can, pushing it through the large can into the medium can inside.

7. Install the screws around the top of the large can, leaving 3/4in out to act as a pot stand.
8. Fill the inside of the outer chamber with as much insulation or ash as possible. This will keep the heat focused inside the inner chamber where the temperature will increase dramatically, forcing the hot burning air to rise like a 'rocket,' while at the same time, protecting the can itself from melting.
9. Place the lid over the large can and tap around the edges firmly until snug.
10. Cut the second soup can into a 'T'-like pattern as shown, and place inside the first, forming an upper platform (fuel feed) and a lower platform (air inlet).
11. Now, light and drop your paper or other kindling through the top chamber and feed a few twigs in.
12. For now, keep the pot off the cooking surface so that the chimney is free to full draft.

13. Place the wood inlet directed towards the prevailing wind, light the paper and stand back.
14. Blow through the air inlet onto the paper to fully ignite the sticks if needed.
15. As the twigs burn down, just push them in more, adding additional twigs as required.

SOLAR STOVE

It may come to a point where there is no fuel of any kind available, like out in the desert or floating in a *water world*. It's then that we can harness and cook with what energy is plentiful, the Sun. My solar cooker has an internal cooking temperature reaching almost 300°F and consists of (2) cardboard boxes (medium and large), (2) hangers, a mirror or tin foil, glue, a can of flat black spray paint, insulation, grass or ash, a thin-walled black pot with glass lid, duct tape and a piece of glass or Plexiglas about 20in by 20in or so.

1. Mark a line on both boxes, starting about 2in up from the bottom of the medium box and about 4in up on the larger box at about a 45° angle. You can make a 45° template by simply folding a piece of paper.

   NOTE: The angle may be steeper or shallower depending on your location. In most U.S. states, 45° works well enough; whereas, if you were at the equator, it would be 0°, and higher the further north you go. This angle won't change daily, only seasonally, as the Sun drops for winter and rises back up for summer.

2. Cut this line all the way around both boxes and paint the inside of the medium box flat black.
3. Place the medium box inside the larger box and fill all around with insulation, grass or ash.

4. Measure, mark and cut the medium box so that it's level inside the large box.
5. Measure, mark and cut the large box leaving the top flap in place for a reflector.
6. Spray-paint the inside black, coat the flap with glue and install a section of the mirror or a sheet of tinfoil, shiny side up. It may be necessary to place duct tape or aluminum tape along the edges to prevent peel back, as well as weighing the mirror or tinfoil down with books to achieve maximum bonding.

7. Place the glass or Plexiglas on top of the large box and trace the outside edge onto two sides of the glass.
8. Cut off the excess glass or Plexiglas by scouring the glass with a sharp instrument several times, and then breaking off (do this for the mirror as well in substitution for the tinfoil).
9. Place the modified glass onto the structure and tape around the edges as needed to prevent air leakage.
10. Cut the (2) hangers about a two feet long. Place the pot inside and the lid on top, open the reflector fold, stick the (2) hangers into the cardboard stove and reflector lid on each side at the desired angle, (you should feel heat build up at the center of the stove window); and you're finished.
11. In addition, by adding a reflective solar shield to the front like the kind found in every car windshield, you can double the inside cooking temperatures while lowering the overall cooking time.

At this point, you're ready to start cooking. You can add a regular kitchen thermometer found in any house to the cooking chamber if you desire, to help facilitate cooking times. You can also substitute the glass or Plexiglas for regular clear plastic wrap if necessary. Constant adjustment of the stove will be required to facilitate cooking. This is achieved by rotating the stove about once or twice an hour, maintaining equal amounts of shade on both sides of the stove. This stove can also be made in a regular shoebox or pizza box without the extra layer of insulation with reduced results. To give you an idea of cooking times, the stove will cook a whole defrosted chicken in about 5 hours (noon-5pm, when the Sun is at its highest), a loaf of bread in 8, pancakes in 1, tortillas in 30 minutes (by preheating the pan for 30 minutes first) and boil water in 1.

BARBECUE GRILL

Also, it's very likely that there will be lots of barbecue grills left on every back deck with propane tanks still attached. Americans love their barbecue! This would be my first option to use as a stove, charcoal or gas--it won't matter. A regular stove can also be removed from the house and used as a barbecue grill or smoker by placing the wood or charcoal directly on top of the heating element or burners. Just open the lower drawer (where the pots and pans are stored) for an air inlet and the oven door a crack for an exhaust.

WOOD GAS STOVE

Also known as a hobo stove, Chinese stove, camp stove and a biogas stove, a wood gas stove is, once again, similar in design to other stoves, especially the rocket stove, with one important difference. The wood gas stove recycles its own exhaust and burns it a second, third, fourth time--well, repetitively. This is carried out so that air enters through not only the bottom of the stove but the top as well. The bottom inlet air is sucked up into the stove but blocked from entering into the combustion chamber by the upper inlet air and is forced up through the sidewalls instead, entering into the combustion chamber through the upper jets. Simultaneously, inlet air is sucked down into the combustion chamber from the top, through the fire into the bottom of the stove where it's blocked from exiting because of the bottom inlet air which is entering and therefore is forced also into the sidewalls and out through the jets. By now, the sidewall air is super hot, pre-heating the wood in the combustion chamber causing gasification (or the release of stored gases like hydrogen and sometimes methane in the wood) which are otherwise released and wasted into the atmosphere in a normal fire. Now the incoming upper inlet air pulls these fuels back down through the combustion chamber before they have a chance to ignite, back into the sidewalls and back out through the jets above the fire where they finally ignite under pressure, creating a second source of combustion. In other words, two forms of combustion occur from one source of fuel--very efficient.

In order to build a wood gas stove, we'll need a quart paint can, a medium fruit cocktail can, a 4in tuna or chicken can, a can opener, a can punch or large and medium drill bits, a pair or large scissors or tin snips, kindling and your fuel (which can be sticks, sawdust, leaves, twigs or anything else that's combustible.)

1. Using the large bit, drill air inlet holes in the bottom side of both cans, equally spaced 1in apart.
2. With the medium bit, drill the jets around the top side (1/2in down) of the medium can 1in apart.

3. Place the medium can inside the paint can, and press firmly until the outside lip of the medium can is snug with the inside lip of the paint can. Because of the size differences, the medium should sit perfectly inside the paint can, leaving about 3/8in gap on all sides and bottom for the gas chamber.

4. With the large bit, drill several equally-spaced holes around the 4in tuna can about 1in apart.
5. Cut the top and bottom off with the can opener and a door out of the front with the snips. This can will serve as a wind shield, fuel feed and pot holder.
6. Light and place tinder into the combustion chamber followed by wood, adding until full.
7. You'll see only the jets on fire; this is gasification.
8. Place an appropriately-sized pot on top with lid.
9. When you're finished, dump the water onto the coals, this will make what's called 'biochar,' which is a highly concentrated form of charcoal.

The same principle of the wood gas stove can and has been implemented on a much larger scale to fuel spark plug or fuel injection combustion automobiles with zero modification needed to the engine. The alcohol stove, rocket stove, solar stove and wood gas stove are all smokeless, and since you don't want to draw unwanted attention to your nice home-cooked meals, they make great options to cook without sending up huge smoke signals. In the end, though, it really all comes down to what fuel sources and construction materials are available and are prevalent to you in the area that you're in. There are circumstances, however, where even cooking won't be enough--for instance, when you'll need to store the meat or produce for long term in a time without electricity/refrigeration. Short-term storage fine, just try to keep the food covered, clean and cool. For anything longer than a couple of days in warm climates though, you'll need to preserve the food in some way so that it's safe to eat later, which I discuss in detail in *Chapter 10*.

AUTOMOTIVE: ANOTHER ONE BITES THE DUST

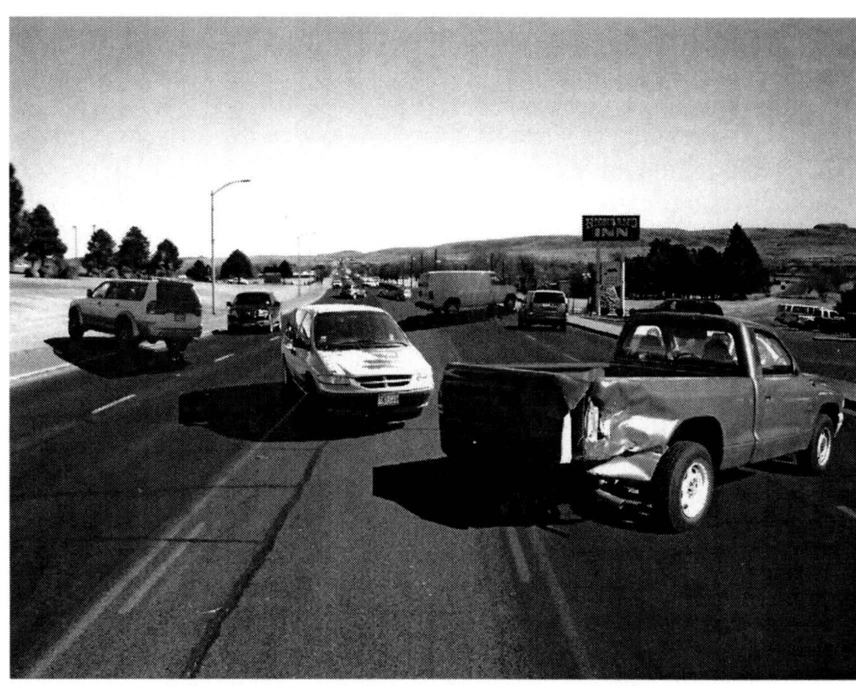

Your dope ride will eventually die out, especially with no attention to scheduled maintenance, unmaintained roads, rough environments, and the many unintended or engineered uses. The good news is that most people aren't allowed to take their cars with them into the afterlife. So there should be plenty of abandoned vehicles available for the picking on roads and in parking lots. You can simply swap yours out for another newer model or rob parts at will. Because there aren't any tow trucks and no one to call to come get you, it's important, after Armageddon, to always travel, at least, in pairs of vehicles, 'just in case' something were to occur (among other reasons). In the meantime, there are several basics that you should at least know how to resolve yourself in order to better and extend your chances of longer-term transportation:

- Flat tire – You'd be amazed at how many people, especially living in a city, have no idea how to change a tire. There are really 2 types of fixes depending on what type of flat you have:

1. Blow out. Keep at least 2 spares, since you don't know where or when you'll find another tire.
2. Slow leak. You may come out to find the tire sitting on the rim. This doesn't necessarily mean the tire needs replacing, it could just have a very small hole and slow leak. It's important to keep at least one12v air pump onboard. You can probably get away with this temporary fix for quite some time. If the leak gets faster, try sticking a screw or nail coated in tar, rubber cement, soap or Vaseline in the hole, if you don't have a tire repair kit. Find the hole by dumping soapy water around the wheel when it's pressurized.

- Overheated radiator – Always carry at least a couple gallons of spare water in the vehicle. Or you can always pee in it, no kidding. Any water-based liquid will do, temporarily. It's been my personal experience, though, that it takes several people's worth of piss to fill a radiator. On this note, in February of this year (2011), an 84-year-old man stranded in the desert outside of Phoenix drank windshield washer fluid for 5 days to stay alive. Now that is one thing I've never done.
- Broken drive shaft – This will be especially common in trucks and SUVs after the disaster with everyone crashing through barricades, over obstacles and driving off-road. The U-joint bearing is the Achilles heel in the off-road world; it's the first thing to go out when driving rough. They're just not designed with the same structural strengths as the rest of the vehicle and, therefore, aren't meant to take much of a beating. That's why it's important to keep several spares onboard. If you don't have any spares, you can usually engage the 4-wheel drive and limp back to your shelter in front wheel drive or visa-versa, removing one from another similar vehicle when time permits.
- Loose linkage or pulley – Heavy, rough driving on uneven terrain always shakes loose some bolts or nuts, stopping the vehicle dead in its tracks. Keep several extras in misc. lengths, widths and threads.
- Punctured gas tank or radiator – This is a trip stopper. If you're leaking fluids onto the ground through a relatively small puncture or crack in the gas tank or radiator, it can be temporarily fixed by rubbing soap over the hole. Soap doesn't break down with radiator fluid or gasoline very well and will last quite awhile. If it's a big, gaping hole, stick a screw in the hole along with the soap. An oil leak isn't as urgent, as long as the oil level is within limits. Without a new supply of clean oil, however, you'll be forced to drain/use other vehicle's used oil.

- No Brakes – If the brakes fail, there are a couple of things you can do to slow down and stop:

a. Pull the emergency brake. The emergency brake or 'parking brake' controls the pads via cables and mechanical levers not hydraulics and, therefore, shouldn't be affected by brake failure.
b. Drop the clutch. In a manual transmission vehicle, by downshifting into a lower gear and releasing the clutch, the engine will slow down/stop the vehicle for you.

- Dimming lights – Not that you'll be pulled over by any cops, but dimming headlights signal a low battery and failing alternator. This, again, wouldn't be that big of a deal except that the sparkplugs run off both; meaning you could potentially find yourself soon with a sputtering engine and without power. Turn the headlights (and all electrical devices) completely off, and drive by the light of the moon or flashlight. There shouldn't be much traffic on the road, that's for sure, and you 'may' even make it home in time.
- Car won't start – This should be an easy one, except most people have no idea why an engine wouldn't start or how an engine works in the first place. Could be several reasons; but the most common are:

a. Dead battery. If you hear a click but the engine doesn't turn over, it's most likely either a dead battery or loose battery clamp. Swap out the battery from any of the surrounding vehicles and try again.
b. Loose battery terminals. Open the hood, find the battery and manually try to move back and forth the red and black cable clamps. If there's a lot of white powdery build-up on the terminals, this is likely the problem. You'll need to remove the cable clamps and clean with a wire brush, although sometimes twisting them will force a connection temporarily.
c. Bad coil or solenoid. Make sure the key is turned on, locate the solenoid (on older vehicles it's separate from the starter), bridge the connections between the two terminals with a screwdriver or piece of wire and, voila! You should see some sparks and hear the starter kick on.
d. Loose connection somewhere other than the battery. This can be a little more difficult to troubleshoot, but starting from the battery, disconnect and clean with a wire brush all terminals from the battery, to the solenoid to the starter, including all grounds. On newer vehicles you may also want to check the brake pedal and park/neutral (on automatics) safety switches. When they go bad it will activate the security feature and prevent the engine from starting. You'll need to bypass them as described in the *Hot Wiring* section or find a replacement if you want to ever start the car again.

- No power – A loss in horsepower is typically due to a clogged fuel or air filter. Some filters can be cleaned by hand, others need to be washed out or replaced. Either way, just to get home, simply remove it.
- Engine doesn't start – If the starter is too weak to turn over the engine and you don't have another battery, you have real problems. Gone are the days of hand-crank motors; so if your starter goes, what can you do? Always try to park on a hill, for one thing. By parking on a slope, you can release the parking brake; and when you begin rolling fast enough in first gear, pop the clutch. Of course, this only works with a manual transmission; and you'll need to have the key on with power to the instruments.
- Whap, Whap, Whap – That's the sound of a broken belt (or a retarded Chinese duck) and although neither is critical to driving, it will stop the alternator, power steering, a/c and, most importantly, the water pump, which will ultimately overheat and crack the engine block, stopping you permanently.
- Engine dies – If the engine dies while driving and you haven't checked the fuel gauge lately... All I can say is keep extra fuel on-board. If it's not because of a lack of fuel that the engine halted, there's no telling. I wouldn't even mess with trouble shooting it at this point, just get another ride.
- Locking your keys in the vehicle – You'd think that it would take the end of the world to teach us not to leave our kids or keys locked up in the vehicle when we leave. In fact, locking the door in a chaos-run world is pretty pointless, as this will only lead to someone either: (a) just breaking your window for the hell of it, or (b) breaking your window because they want what you 'may' (or may not) have inside. If you leave the windows rolled down and the doors unlocked, any would-be thief will inspect the inside contents (don't leave anything inside, of course) and move on. This way you will never lock yourself out in a time of few locksmiths. If you must lock up your vehicle, keep a spare tied somewhere underneath. In the event you pay no attention to what I say, which is the most likely scenario, just break out one of the back side windows again, so that you're not sitting on glass.
- Pulling the ECM fuse – The ECM (Engine Control Module or your 'computer') powers the fuel pump among other critical starting and driving components. Once removed, the vehicle isn't going anywhere

with our without the keys. This is a great theft deterrent in a world where car alarms are a thing of the past. The module is small enough to fit in your pocket, making it easy to remove, walk around with and reinstall. If the vehicle is older and doesn't have an ECM fuse, pull the starter or fuel pump fuse, or even the main distributor wire coming from the center of the distributor cap, which are all small enough to fit in your pocket.

- Lastly, keep an assortment of tools on board, along with a 20ft siphon hose and a 4-star lug wrench or deep socket set, ratchet, 8in extension and breaker bar. The tools will help remedy most of the above problems; and the extra-sized sockets will come in handy when you need to remove a wheel from another vehicle.

WELDER

Having a welder, or better, a cutting torch on hand could literally be the difference between a life and death situation in a world without rescue workers. Although I can't tell you how to build a cutting torch, I can teach you how to build a quick and easy arc welder with just a simple set of car jumper cables. You'll need: jumper cables, welding goggles or dark sunglasses, 1/8in electrodes (which can be found in any welding shop) or metal hangers and brown paper bags and (2) car batteries.

1. Connect the two batteries in series so that instead of 12v, you end up with 24v. I prefer to use the batteries from a diesel truck because: (a) they already have two of them and when they drain down can be easily recharged onsite, and (b) they're deep cycle and are designed for and can take rapid full discharges without damage.
2. Switch the cross cable that's already connecting the two batteries together from pos-pos to pos-neg to that you end up with 24v instead of 12v. (To start the engine or recharge the batteries, you'll need to switch this cable back to its original position)
3. Place one end of the jumper cables on the one battery's free positive terminal and the other's on the other battery's free negative terminal. This way we have all 24v flowing through the cables.
4. Connect the ground clamp from the other side of the cable to the object that you'll be welding (make sure there's no rust, paint or anything else blocking direct contact).
5. Place a flux-covered electrode in the jaws of the positive clamp. (If you don't have access to welding electrodes you can use metal hangers wrapped in a wet paper bag, but they're far less efficient and take a lot of time to get used to working with.)
6. Strike the electrode gently against the work surface until you see a bright flash, then hold it steady retaining that particular gap, slowly feeding as necessary.
7. When the flash turns into a molten pool of liquid metal, slowly slide and feed the electrode into the weld, while moving down the joint.
8. If the electrode gets stuck, break loose and start again. If you run out of spark, recharge the batteries.

That's it, let cool and the weld should be as strong as any professionally built rig. With this setup, I've been able to weld up to 1/4in steel, that can withstand two tons of pressure or four tons of tensile pull. For larger/thicker projects, connect more batteries in series which will raise the working amperage/voltage considerably. For longer working times between charges, connect sets of batteries in parallel and series so that you're left with a 24v system. This will keep the duel battery, 24v amperage while extending the working time.

FUEL: BREAKING THE BARRIERS

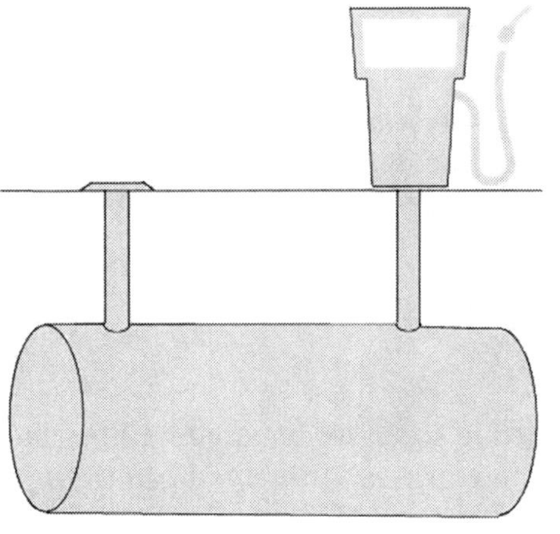

Eventually, with all this automotive use, your existing stock-piled fuel supply will come to an end. Replacement gasoline will need to be siphoned from the surrounding abandoned vehicles, possibly the fuel station USTs (underground storage tanks) themselves, which should still be full of gas to use in the new world. You see, when the power fails, there's no way to bring the gas from the underground tanks up to the pumps and not too many people know this or that they even exist. They'll think the pumps have just run out; meaning, there may actually be an enormous, untapped supply of fuel under every city block. Even though most gas stations have several (one per each fuel type) of these 6,000 to 10,000 gallon USTs, accessing and removing them can be trickier:

1. First, using a crowbar or pick, pull up the blue, yellow or red manhole cover near the pumps.
2. Cut off the padlock securing the fill port with a pair of bolt cutters or break off the entire quick connect with a pipe or pole.
3. Push down the pressure plate and insert a garden hose (this one will need to be at least 15-20ft long).
4. Since we can't use the gravity siphoning method this time, a hand crank or a siphon pump will need to be incorporated. These can be found still attached to a 55-gallon oil drum in the adjoining automotive shop.
5. Place the garden hose directly into the vehicle's tank and crank away. Pay at the pump? I think not people.

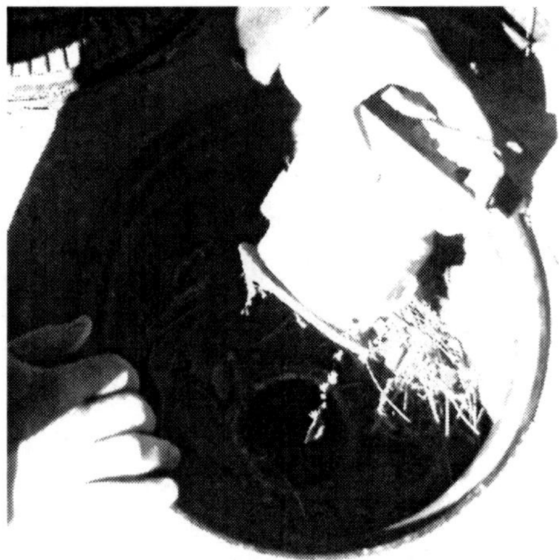

MAKING YOUR OWN FUEL

What about when there's no more fuel to be siphoned? What do you do then? Make your own, of course, (or abandon those pieces of sh#! combustion engines altogether and opt for animal transportation). In the aftermath, there will still be several types of ingredients with which to make bio-diesel, ethanol, methanol and even hydrogen fuel.

ETHANOL

This will be in the form of high grade alcohol (yes, the same kind you drink), aka ethanol. First off, before we get started, a couple of interesting realizations:

- You're already running on ethanol right now and don't even know it. In 2005 the *Energy Policy Act* was made a law ensuring that all gasoline sold in the United States contained a minimum volume of renewable fuel (ethanol), called the *Renewable Fuels Standard*. You may have even seen the stickers on the pumps saying E85, E10 or E15, which are percentages of ethanol (Ethanol 85%) you're putting into your tank on a daily basis.

- 100% of all vehicles in Brazil (the fifth largest country in the world) now run on ethanol.
- Since the 1980s most major car manufacturers were forced to make all vehicles FFV (Flex Fuel Vehicles). Basically, this just means that the O2 sensors were modified and rubber O-rings, gaskets and seals were switched for non-degradable synthetic materials. But they don't highly advertise that all vehicles can now run on ethanol rather than petroleum. This fact has been written in small print in the owner's manual for over 20 years, though.
- 180 proof ethanol is considered to be rated at about 105 octane.
- The Indianapolis 500 race cars have used straight ethanol as their primary fuel for over 80 years now.
- Most American and German military vehicles and airplanes switched to ethanol during World War II.

The first step in fermenting ethanol is building something to process it in. This is called an alcohol still, although ours looks more like a methhead's teapot. You'll need to "acquire" the following: teapot, turkey thermometer, 5-10ft of 1/4in copper tubing (cut from any kitchen sinks or from behind a fridge), (2) plastic or glass 3-5 gallon containers (with lids), 9in or so of 1/4in plastic clear tubing, (3) garbage bag ties or zip ties, (5) tablespoons of yeast, (5) pounds of fruit, honey or candy, a small funnel, a cork, and (1) gallon of water.

1. Drill a hole slightly smaller than 1/4in in the lid of one of the plastic or glass containers.
2. Loop the 1/4in clear plastic tubing around on itself as tight as possible and tie off with the garbage bag ties or zip ties leaving about 2in straight on each end.
3. Place the looped plastic tube inside the hole of the plastic or glass container lid.
4. Add the gallon of water and the 5 pounds of fruit, honey or candy (or anything else that contains sugar) into one of the containers.
5. Smash and mix the fruit, honey or candy and water until you have a pasty mash.
6. Sprinkle about 5 tablespoons of yeast onto the top of the mash and secure the lid firmly.
7. Fill the looped plastic tube with enough water to create an air block.
8. Within a few hours the yeast will begin breaking down the sugar inside the mash, transforming it into alcohol, releasing carbon dioxide which will then bubble out of the tube on top. Once the percolating CO2 has finished, you can move onto the cooking phase; but in the meantime, while you're waiting, continue building the still:
9. Bend the copper tubing several times around a 6in log or mailbox pole or something of similar thickness, making sure to leave about a foot straight on each end.
10. Now drill another hole slightly smaller than 1/4in into the teapot lid or cork.
11. Drill a final hole slightly smaller than 1/8in (the OD of the turkey thermometer) next to the first in the teapot or cork.

12. Insert one end of the copper tube inside the 1/4in hole and the turkey thermometer inside the other.
13. When the tube has stopped bubbling, give the mash mix a little shake. If bubbling doesn't continue, place the funnel inside the teapot's spout and fill to about 2/3 full.
14. Place the other end of the copper tube inside the second container touching the bottom and add a small amount of gasoline (or alcohol from a previous batch) to the container so that the end of the tube is under the liquid.
15. Place the teapot on the stove (or fire) and set the temperature to 180°F.

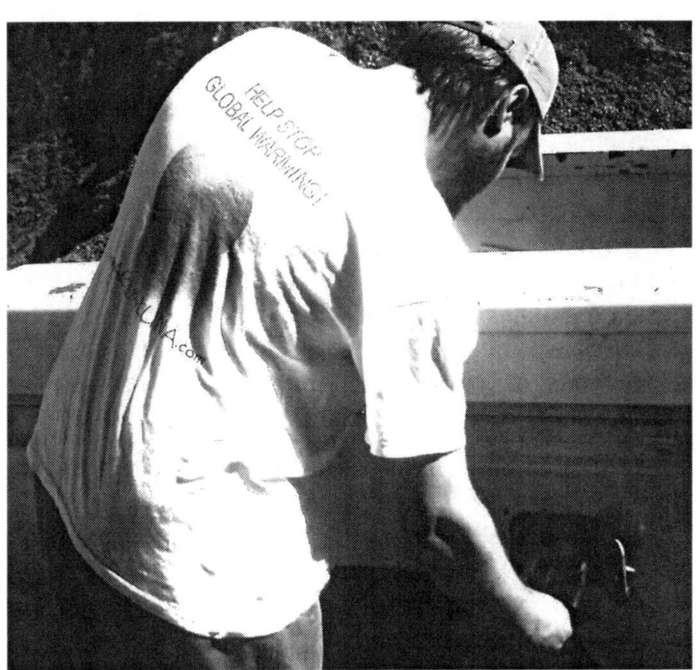

NOTE: Do not add gasoline if you intend to drink the ethanol. Also, this isn't moonshine, and it won't make you "go blind." This is simple distillation; however, if you add gasoline and drink it, it will.

Within a few moments you should see bubbling coming out of the end of the copper tube. This is alcohol that has separated from the water in vapor form and is now re-condensing in the second container. You should witness the liquid level rising as more and more alcohol (bubbles) are separated. Make sure to monitor the thermostat on the teapot. It should stay around 176°F, (which is 2°F higher than the condensation point of alcohol). This way, the copper pipe and container don't have to work too hard turning the alcohol back into a liquefied form. No matter what though, the temperature should never get below 173°F, (which is the boiling point of the ethanol), or above 212°F (which is the boiling point of water); otherwise, you'll just be transferring the liquid in the mash from the teapot into the second container. Of course, these temperatures would differ above sea level. When the conversion is done, attempt to light a teaspoon of the fuel with a lighter. If combustion takes place you have a high enough grade alcohol to use as fuel.

Don't bother with any starch-based products such as corn or potatoes; the yeast has to work too hard to convert the starch to sugar and the sugar to alcohol. Sugar beets, sugar cane, pineapple, grapes, berries, melon, carrot, cans of soda, honey and candy are all high in sugar content.

METHANOL

By placing any type of wood pieces or sawdust into the teapot instead of the ethanol mash, you can extract what is known as methanol or wood alcohol. This IS moonshine and can be poisonous to drink and will make you go blind IF you drink too much. Methanol has equal combustion properties to ethanol and, again, makes a great source of fuel to our alcohol stove or car. The good thing about making methanol over ethanol is that you don't need yeast or high sugar content plants to do it, just lots of wood. Make sure you keep the thermostat temperature a little above 147°F this time though (the boiling point of methanol); with, again, anything over 212°F resulting in the addition of water. Lastly, with both methanol and ethanol, it's a good idea to throw out the first and last half cup or so IF you'll be drinking it; it's full of toxins and just tastes crappy.

HYDROGEN

We can very easily convert regular tap water or, even better, sea water into fuel for cooking, heating or driving by separating the hydrogen and oxygen (H20). Let me start off by saying hydrogen is a great option for free energy. I built my first hydrogen cell about 10 years ago. I have converted over 50 vehicles in the last 10 years & now currently run a truck, my home gas hot water heater, stove, & a back-up generator on hydrogen for free with captured rain water & the help of a cheap solar panel. Hydrogen generators are a bit different from the Hollywood versions, such as the type seen on *Chain Reaction* with Keanu Reeves that tend to explode violently every time cameras are rolling and a film is being shot. In this case, we'll be extracting and storing both the hydrogen and oxygen (known as Brown's gas, Oxy-hydrogen or HHO). It is actually safer than storing gasoline since the mixture isn't as volatile as gas fumes and isn't combustible at all in its liquid form (water), like gasoline. Basically, there are three ways to split water: chemically, electrically and molecularly. The first two are easily accomplished without a lab environment and with the common materials that will be available to you.

- Chemically

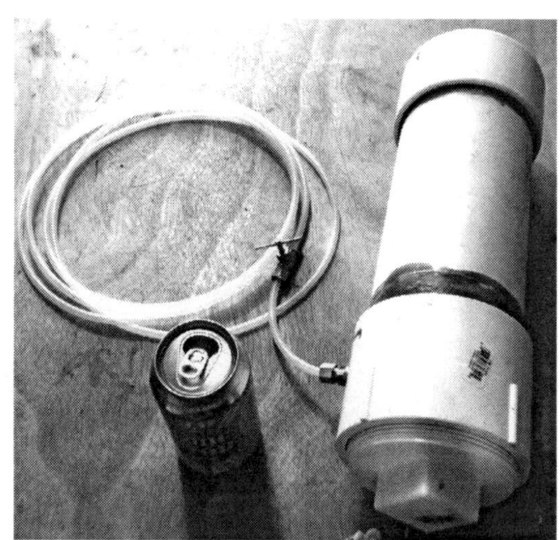

1. Cut a section of schedule 40 PVC sewer pipe 1ft long.
2. Superglue or PVC (cement) a 6in cap on the bottom & a 6in threaded male adapter on top.
3. Drill a 3/8in hole in the side of the generator near the top; and screw in a 1/4in copper shutoff valve.
4. Install the generator vertically in the engine compartment; insert 2ft of hose into the shutoff valve with the other side going into the hose of the oil blow-back hole of the air filter (or into the filter box itself.)
5. Now crunch up a couple aluminum cans (beer cans, soda cans, etc.) & drop them into the PVC pipe, along with a couple cups of lye. You can make your own lye by soaking wood ash as described below or just add crystallized Red Devil or Drano drain/pipe cleaner.
6. All that's left is to add your fuel (water) & wait a minute.

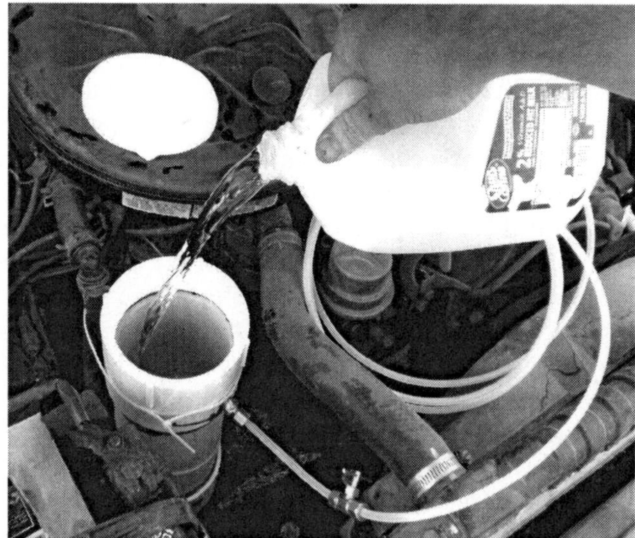

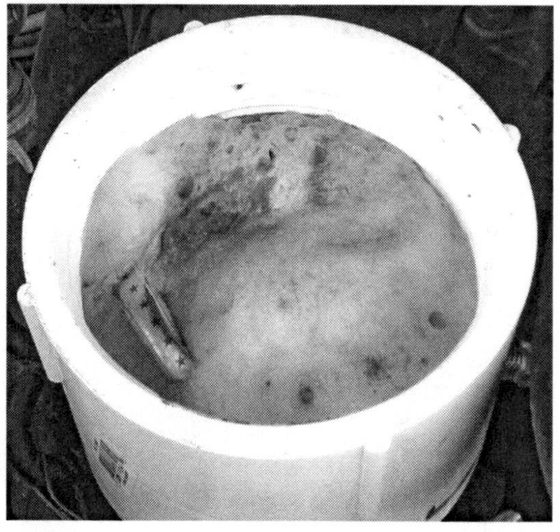

A car that runs off beer (cans) just like me, who would have thought! What happens next is that aluminum & lye don't really get along very well, so they battle; and as always, it's the innocent (in this case water), that suffers the most casualties. In the violent chemical reaction, water splits and releases its hydrogen & oxygen (2 hydrogen bubbles for every oxygen) which then builds up in the pipe's chamber and is ready to be vented into your engine by opening the valve. You may need to install a fuel shutoff valve in the car's fuel line if you want to run 100% on water. Start the engine with the fuel on, open the HHO generator valve, and once the vehicle begins running on hydrogen and oxygen, shut off the gasoline. Otherwise just let the computer or O2 sensor, automatically adjust the gasoline intake to match the extra fuel coming in, thereby extending your fuel efficiency of MPG.

- Electrically

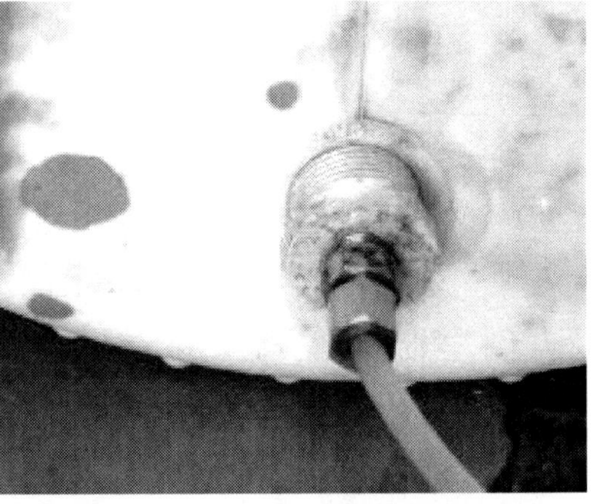

1. Drill a 3/8in hole in one of the plugs of a 30-55 gallon drum and screw in a copper shutoff valve. Again, installing the hose to the valve to the air filter as described above.
2. Drill another 1/2in hole in the other plug and place a 1/2in by 1/4in threaded to barbed hose fitting inside supergluing or siliconing the threads to prevent airleaks.
3. Run the two wires of a solar panel (the size determines the speed at which the process works) through the fitting, filling the fitting with silicone. I prefer to use a threaded hose fitting rather than just drilling a 1/8in hole in the plug because; (a) it has more inside surface space to hold the silicone in place (otherwise the silicone will just blow out with the pressure) and (b) the threads help hold the elements.
4. Tie (2) conductors to the end of the wires. Platinum works best and breaks down the slowest followed by gold, silver, stainless steel, lead, aluminum and finally, copper. Since I expect you'll have plenty of lead wheel weights or battery plates, I would suggest using them. For the sake of this book however, I'll be using two scraps of aluminum held together by rubber bands and separated by plastic bottle caps.

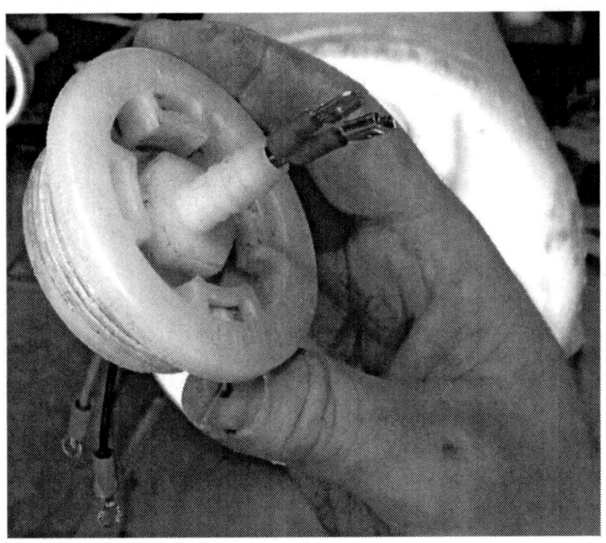

5. Fill the tank with water or better sea water, insert the elements, screw the plug back on tight and point the solar panel south (if in the northern hemisphere).

After awhile, tiny oxygen bubbles will form & rise off one conductor (anode), and even smaller hydrogen bubbles that just look like foam will rise off the other (cathode). In both setups, instead of connecting the hose to the air filter, you can also run it directly to a propane stove, barbecue grill, gas heater or generator. The by-product or exhaust of HHO gas is, of course, water, which conversely tends to rust out the cylinders, pistons, intake and exhaust systems of an engine after a few years. But at this point, when you have no other source of fuel and with plenty of replacement cars just laying around, I don't think a little thing like corrosion will bother you too much.

BIODIESEL

Biodiesel requires a big setup and separation process to convert used cooking oils (found in any fast food, truck stop or restaurant waste oil bins) into fuel, a lengthy process that isn't suitable for this book or the aftermath. That said, most diesel cars and trucks built after 1990 are able to run on what's called SVO (Straight Vegetable Oil) or WVO (Waste Vegetable Oil) by simply filtering it. There is, however, one issue that needs to be mentioned: Vegetable oil, when cool, is much thicker than diesel and, therefore, creates a film when it passes through the vehicle's fuel filter, eventually completely clogging up the system entirely. However, this can be resolved by: (a) thinning the oil with ethanol, diesel, gasoline, alcohol or some other flammable solvent, (b) placing a second tank and fuel line in the bed of the vehicle, always making sure to start and end on diesel; (in this way the fuel filter will be flushed out after every use); and/or, finally, (c) manually cleaning or replacing the filter after each use. I choose option a or c. Lastly, before dumping the raw waste oil from the vats into my fuel tank, I often filter it through a couple layers of T-shirts which is equivalent to around a 70-100 micron filter. That's it, it's that simple; collect used oil from cars, fry vats, or restaurant waste oil/grease bins, filter and pour into your tank. Another option would be to use a hot water heater to store the oil, connecting wires from the battery to the heating element, so that the oil always remains warm (around 100°F) and therefore thin.

PERSONAL POWER PLANT: SOMETHING FROM 'NOTHING'

It will become useful to build a source of electricity generation, especially, one that's mobile. With an on-the-go source of 110v energy, you can use almost any type of electrical tool. This is a great help in building better and stronger shelters, tools and devices, not to mention mechanically gaining access to places previously unavailable. If you don't have access to a generator, this can be accomplished with a 12vdc to 110vac by 1000w-2000w inverter connected to a car battery or a renewable energy battery bank. Whatever your preference, the inverter will clip directly onto the battery's (the power plant) positive and negative terminals, converting the 12vdc energy into usable 110vac, which is what most household appliances and power tools utilize. Always try to keep two inverters on-hand, just in case the first burns out; and be careful not to draw too much load while working. Inverters are great. With a flip of a switch, it's like the power grid is back up and running; but they're useless without a source to power them:

CAR

The easiest form of recharging batteries is with a vehicle. The problem is that the engine requires fuel to run. Regardless, if you're going to be driving anyway, an onboard power plant (inverter) is great if you suddenly find yourself in a pinch and need the 110v electricity; but if you plan on using the vehicle just as a generator, you'll find yourself out of fuel in a hurry. Just connect the pos-pos and neg-neg or plug it directly into the cigarette lighter.

SOLAR POWER

Solar panels, on the other hand, can charge your battery bank free of fuel and will actually be everywhere in the new world. You see, presently most traffic, communication, railroad, electrical and cable relay boxes require solar panels to charge back-up batteries in different locations in case of power outages. You may have seen these panels on the side of the road or up on a pole in obscure locations. You'll need (1+) deep cycle batteries (the type found in diesel trucks, boats, golf carts, RVs or these relay stations), (1+) solar panel, (1) 1000-2000 watt 110v inverter, several dozen feet of automotive wiring, and a couple sets of jumper cables.

1. Put the panel (or multiple panels) on a flat surface at about a 45° angle facing south, near where your batteries will be and run the wires from the panels to a battery (black-neg and red-pos).
2. Strap the corners down with pipe strap or wire so that the panel can't blow away. Be careful not to damage the panel or cover too much of the glass. Now you're powered by the Sun! If you want longer-lasting power though, add a 2nd, 3rd, 4th battery in parallel:
3. Connect one set of jumper cables between the (2) batteries (black to neg and red to pos). Repeat with additional jumper cables for all batteries. This is what's known as a battery bank linked in parallel, which means that the combined voltage of the batteries will remain at 12v, but the amperage (and, therefore, reserve

amp hours) multiply exponentially. If you, conversely, prefer a higher voltage, simply connect the cables in series (neg-pos).

4. Connect the inverter to one of the batteries (it doesn't matter which).

You now have power to the inverter and can operate any 110v appliances, electronics or power tools. A couple things to keep in mind:

- Laying the panel flat is fine for trickle-charging your bank or near the equator; but anywhere else, if you want to optimize the panel's potential, you want as much direct sunlight as possible striking the face at a direct 90° angle. This is easily achieved, however, by simply: (a) placing the panels in direct unobstructed sunlight, (b) tilting the panels towards the Sun so that there is little to no angled shadow behind the panel (just like your solar stove) and (c) facing the panels south (in the northern hemisphere).
- The panels "should" have a blocking diode installed to stop reverse current at night or when shady from sucking the electricity out of your batteries. If, however, you see that your batteries have power at the end of the day, but are dead by morning, just disconnect the panels at night.
- You can link as many batteries as you wish to extend reserve times. And by linking the batteries in series (pos to negative, positive to negative) you'll increase your voltage just like with the welder.

WIND

Wind turbines top my list of most beneficial forms of electricity generation, especially in coastal, plain regions, or anywhere that receives a constant breeze, essentially producing electricity 24 hours a day. Wind generators are similar to solar panels in that it takes a force of Mother Nature (wind) and converts it mechanically into usable 12v power, which again charges our battery bank. Building a wind turbine system is a little more complicated than installing solar panels, in that you need to actually build the turbine itself, a tower, and wire everything up since turbines are highly available like panels; but ultimately, the wind turbine system will gain much more electricity as it can also function during the night, which equates to being able to use power and tools longer. A wind turbine is composed of several different sections:

- Blades – Blades can be made out of anything, wood, metal, plastic, PVC pipes, cardboard, computer fans, or desk fans. Since you won't be powering a $200,000 house full of appliances, correct blade degree, orientation and efficiency won't matter much; so we'll be using plastic bottles.
- Generator – The generator is the most important part of the wind turbine. Electricity is generated when the mechanical rotating motion of the windmill turns an electrical generating motor externally. Not just any motor will work, though. For example, car alternators won't do, since they require a high RPM and electricity just to activate them. What we need is called a PMM (Permanent Magnet Motor) which generates electricity at a rate equivalent to the speed of rotation. So, even if you rotate the motor by hand (low winds), you'll receive some energy generation. The old cars had PMMs which were simply called generators before alternators where invented. However, some regular electric motors today, that are designed to create mechanical motion internally can be used instead, such as motors from toy cars, VCRs, cordless drills, air compressors, treadmills, exercise bikes, stair steppers, etc. The key to finding the right

generator is voltage, not amperage, in relevance to the size of batteries you have. For example, if you have several 12v car batteries linked in parallel, the PMM would need to be able to generate a minimum of 10v to a maximum of 16v at full revolution, which is the charging parameters of a 12v battery. Conversely, if the motor only put out .2 amps at 13v, this would still be enough to trickle-charge the system. Also, you need to make sure that the motor is putting out dc current not ac. Many motors put out ac current and renewable energy enthusiasts convert it to dc by soldering rectifiers and diodes in place, then convert it back to ac with an inverter. This is a complete waste of time, energy, and electricity. A cordless 18v drill motor will suit our purposes well and can be found in most garages these days.

Since a vertical-axis wind turbine or VAWT will suit our small electrical needs, the assembly won't need a tail section, swivel mount or tower, which greatly enhances the simplicity factor, making it perfect for easy/quick construction and use in and aftermath environment. To begin, you'll need (3) plastic bottles, (1) large plastic screw-on lid, (1) 1/4in step or carriage bolt, (6) small screws or rivets, super glue, box cutter, (1) cordless drill (preferably 18v), pipe strap or (2) clamps, 10ft of 12awg wire, volt meter (optional), all of which can be found in most any home garage.

1. Remove half of each plastic bottle by cutting from in front of the cap to around the bottom as shown.
2. Super glue and screw or rivet on the 3 caps equally spaced on the sides of the larger lid *hubcap*.

NOTE: Make sure that the caps are located where they'll need to be with the blades angled in the correct direction before screwing. If not when you go to screw on the bottles, they'll be pointed in every which direction.

3. Cut out or drill a 1/4in hole in the center of the hub cap with the box cutter or a drill bit.
4. Drip a couple of drops on the inside ledges of the carriage bolt and push the bolt through the 1/4in hole, pressing firmly so that the corners of the step press through the plastic circle hole locking it in place.
5. Add a lock washers and a nut, place the bolt in the drill motor's chuck and tighten.

6. Level and clamp the motor securely to the roof or other stationary object that receives high winds.
7. Connect the 12awg wires to the 2 metal tabs in the drill where the battery would normally connect with the other side connected to the battery bank.

NOTE: With most cordless drills, you won't have to remove the casing. However if your drill has a lock clutch or reverse current blocking diodes, you will have to remove the casing and these devices before installing. At which point you can then reinstall the motor and chuck back into the drill housing or leave free, it's up to you. If you decide to leave it free, you'll need to silicone around the gaps and cracks to prevent water infiltrating and shorting out the electric motor. Also, it's a good idea, in either case, to fill the chuck and air vents with silicone also. This will not only prevent rain from gaining access from above, but also lock the chuck in place around the bolt permanently. On Agua-Luna Ranch we have 8 of these wind turbines around the cabin, 2 that were siliconed, 6 that were not and haven't seen a difference in the performance of any of the units, but that's the desert.

WATER

Watermills are almost identical to windmills in that they generate electricity 24 hours/day, the difference being that they utilize the flowing water in a creek or river to spin the PMM. So, by simply laying the VAWT on its side and clamping it to a cinderblock or log, you have an instantly-made water turbine.

WAVE

Wave generators are again in line with wind and water turbines or rather river turbines, producing constant power throughout the day, all day, every day. In order to extract energy from waves, we'll need to convert either their up and down motion, or the in and out motion first into circular motion which will turn the PMM, once again giving us usable electricity. In order to convert the up and down motion you'll need some type of weight, bobber and clutch pulley, along with a lot of cable and wiring. Conversely, it's much simpler and requires a lot fewer materials to convert the in and out motion. In fact, we can once again use our wind turbine setup to accomplish this by bolting the wind turbine horizontally, just like we used on the river to a dock anchored out far enough. You'll notice that the surface of a wave a dozen feet out acts just like a river, always flowing in, while the bottom flows back out, which will satisfactorily turn our motor and trickle-charge our battery bank.

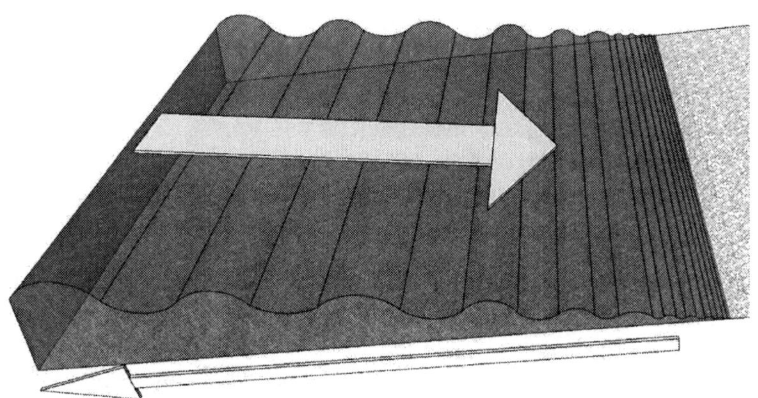

1. Utilizing a pre-existing dock simply lay the wind/water turbine on its side perpendicular to the flow of the waves, and strap down with pipe strapping or 2in clamps. (Block added for spacing)
2. Connect the wires to the battery bank as before.
3. Make sure to set the rig in relation to high tide so that your generator won't be submerged underwater.

MANUAL

If all else fails, you can force the lower class citizens in your group into slave labor just like we have always done throughout history. I joke, since, at this point, there should no longer be classes; but this setup still requires physical motion to turn the PMM, converting calories into electricity. This system is a very simple setup. All you'll need is a 1/4in by 3in bolt, large flat washer and lock washer, strapping or 2in clamps, (4) 1in sheetrock screws, (2) 8x8x18in cinder blocks, drill motor and a handmade sprocket gear.

1. Make the sprocket gear by utilizing the same lid *hubcap*, bolted in the chuck but without the bottle blades.
2. Lay the drill on its side, and strap or clamp it to the floor.
3. Place the rear left or right bike fork on top of a milk crate or two cinder blocks so that the rear tire rests gently on the gear. Add spacers as needed, or remove a little air from the rear tire to help facilitate a better lock with the gear.
4. Tie the front brake handle down so you don't roll and lean the bike on a wall or secure to maintain balance.

That's it; just run your wires once again to your battery bank and you're good to go. As you pedal the bike, the tire in contact with the sprocket will spin at a high RPM, generating electricity. I actually designed a similar system for a university-run underwater habitat in 2009.

HOARDING: GONE WITH THE WIND

When your group's survival is taken care of and electricity is again flowing, it will prove important to stock up and hoarding certain types of 'non-critical' items before the cities are picked clean. The following items will soon cease to exist, and making them ourselves would be extremely difficult without industrialization and manufacturing equipment/machinery. Things that you may not have paid much attention to or put much value on will now become important materials/replacements for building, backup parts and valuable trading items.

- Wire – Both household and automotive wiring will prove an important resource in not only electrical use, but building, tying and securing stuff together, as well.

1. Remove the cover of a plug and the plug itself with a screwdriver.
2. Punch out the Sheetrock directly on either side of the plug.
3. Follow the wiring to the next plug, fixture or switch, knocking out Sheetrock as you go.
4. Remove the next fixture, plug or switch cover and plug, switch or fixture.
5. Remove that run of wiring and repeat the process for the next, until all wiring in that home is extracted.
6. Repeat on the next house/car.

If the wire will be used for construction or electrical applications, the plastic jacket can remain on. However, copper is also an important and valuable chemical element, which was once melted down in a kiln and used to make weapons, tools, coin and jewelry. In order to melt copper, returning it to its nugget form, you'll need to build a large fire and throw the wire rolls inside. This will melt off the coating, leaving the copper wire behind. Now roll the wire up small and place in a thick cast-iron pot with a lid back in the fire. Copper's melting point is just under 2000°F and a typical wood camp fire is only around 1000°F, so you'll have to build the fire in a pit and stoke up the temperature by burning cow patties, covering the top with a metal street sign and dirt.

If you have a form, make the negative from clay or carve it in a board and pour the liquid copper into the template. On a side note, the same process can be used to melt down gold, silver or even aluminum cans which have many of the same properties as copper. Who knows, our immediate future may be known as the 'Aluminum Age,' which has never occurred in history before. Larger quantities of copper and aluminum can be cut down from the many hundreds of thousands of miles of electrical wire, strung from pole to pole across the country.

- Garbage bags – Say good-by to all plastic products; and stock up on them while you can.
- Stuffing – There isn't much in the way of soft materials besides down and feathers anywhere other than in society; so stock up on cotton balls, dryer lint, couch, pillow and mattress stuffing. It's great for not only making bedding, but as tinder or making candles as well. To make a candle, simply coat some stuffing with petroleum jelly or a string repetitively in hot wax and cold water and light.

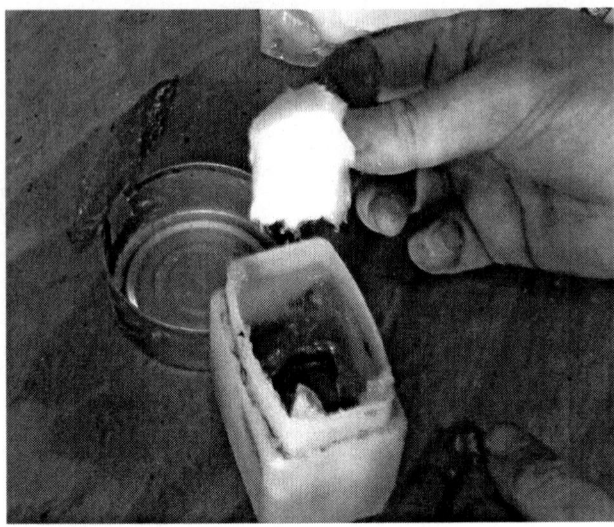

- Candles – On that note, unless you'll be harvesting wax from beehives, or live near the desert and have several dozen Candelilla plants laying around, candles will to be a thing of the past. So grab any you find.
- Fire – Sure, we can make fire with any number of materials and means, but isn't it easier to collect as many lighters and matches as possible?
- Fuel – At this point, there shouldn't be much in the way of fuels left over, which makes having some stored up still a VERY valuable commodity.
- Food – Imagine a world without canned weenies, Twinkies, Snickers, candy bars, or Coca-Cola, and how much these items would be worth to someone who hasn't had one in a year. Don't worry about spoilage; these items are rated to last between 10 and 100 years.
- Soap and shampoo – Even though we can make our own soap, with the process I've listed below, fairly easily, I always prefer not to make something that already exists. So make sure to pick up any bars of soap, bottles of shampoo, even dish soap (which can be used for bathing and washing hair) and, of course, tubes of toothpaste and toothbrushes (which can be sterilized through boiling). You'll need ash from a fire, mixing bowl and spoon, thin tray and the fat from an animal (2 shovels of ash and 2 gallons of water, makes 30 ounces liquid lye that when mixed with 1/2lb fat or lard makes 16 bars of soap.)

1. Place some ashes and coals in a container and fill the container up with water.
2. Let the container sit for a few hours/days until the water turns rust-colored.
3. Drain the water out, leaving the ash and coals in the container. This is liquid lye or potassium hydroxide.
4. Repeat the process until the water runs clear, then add enough fat or lard so that the mix is thick like mashed potatoes, and stir for 20 minutes.
5. Spread the mix out on a tray or piece of plastic and let dry in the Sun for several days until firm.

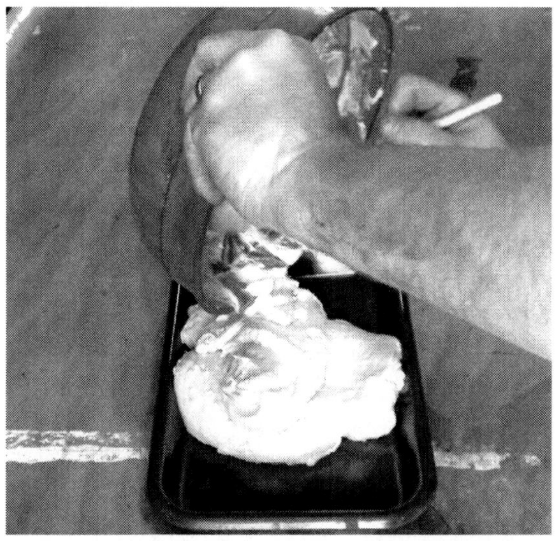

- Medicine – Of course medicines will always have a place in every American's heart, we love our medicine. It doesn't really matter what kind, pick up any you find. I'll explain their uses later in *Chapter 10*.
- Precious metals – VCRs, TVs, computers, cell phones or any other electronic item--all contain precious metals used in microprocessors found in the internal gold wires, gold plated contacts, chips, pins, silver-plated contacts, copper traces, etc. Most sparkplugs now also contain platinum along with the catalytic converters; and the air bag switches (located in the front and back bumpers) have gold in them.

- Silverware – I'm not talking about pewter or stainless steel cutlery here, but the real stuff handed down from mother to daughter made from real sterling, Britannia or Sheffield silver. This can be in the form of forks, spoons and knives or tea sets and candlesticks, all of which can be melted down via the kiln method described above. Real silver will blacken a white rag when rubbed hard, or look for any stamps.
- Screen and windows –Each are very useful in a range of alternative applications.
- Box spring – Box springs can be used as traps, shelving, tables, corrals, walls, etc.
- Corrugated metal – On the same line, metal roofing will be non-existent after the collapse. The sheets are only screwed on by screws. You will need the right-sized socket to remove the screws, however.
- Fencing – Chain-link fencing is another valuable resource that will no longer be manufactured.
- Blankets and coats – Even though Americans have enough clothing to last several lifetimes, most families only keep a few blankets due to man-made heating and climate control throughout homes, vehicles, offices and restaurants. We literally leave our climate controlled home for our climate controlled office for a climate controlled store for a climate controlled restaurant, finally returning to our climate controlled home, all via a climate controlled car. Couple this with the fact that, for some strange reason, most people in the world live in colder climates; when the gas stops pumping and the electricity goes out, there's going to be a lot of uncomfortable people and a real shortage of blankets and coats.
- Adhesives – Glues or tapes, both of which you'll find will come in very handy, to say the least.
- Paperclips and safety pins – Who would have thought that such miniature, minuscule objects would ever be worth their weight in gold? Without the machinery to tightly wind them though, they will be.
- Clothing – I'll discuss clothing more in *Chapter 10* and how there's no need to wear clothing and that there will be an abundance of it left over, the question, then, is why the need to hoard it? Because even though style and trends are a thing of the past, humans once brainwashed don't change easily and will always feel the need to wear clothes, and therefore, will be forever looking to upgrade. It's like that old saying 'out with the old and in with the new,' regardless of whether it's necessary. People just can't stand the thought of wearing the same thing over and over again.
- Rope, twine and string – Rope and string are another item we use in our everyday lives; and even though it's actually fairly easy to make, many people won't know how. In fact, since I haven't described how to make them in this book, you probably won't either. They can be a valuable item to trade if you happen to have extra, that is. Fishing line and floss belong in this category, as well, since they both do the same job.
- Salt and sugar – Salt is a must, since there's really none that's easily accessible in the wild. There is plenty of sugars, though, but it never hurts to have more of anything and everything, that's for sure.
- Coffee and cigarettes – These items are like the snack foods, except that people were/are addicted to them, which makes them that much more desirable in a world void of such vices.
- Toilet paper – If you come across a roll of toilet paper in decent condition a year into the collapse, you're one lucky SOB. I foresee toilet paper becoming a national treasure in the future. You can make your own soft, triple-ply TP by crumpling up, soaking/drying paper products like junk mail, newspaper, magazines.
- Jewelry – Jewelry is another object that carries the same meaning to people as clothing. It's completely useless even today (more so in the new world), but we (especially women) feel the need to acquire and keep it. Same will be the ways in the next; and with so many keeping such things in their homes, there will be plenty available. The value of jewelry or coins will drastically decline, initially, being pushed out by food, water, fuel and ammunition, but eventually the dust will settle.
- Plastic bottles – Any type of plastic bottle or container that can hold water as mentioned previously. New, used, in the garbage or on the streets, these can be cleaned out with bleach and refilled for storage.
- Belts and shoelaces – Yes, even the items we take for granted will disappear after a year or two; and at the rate at which we go through them, they'll not only be valuable to trade but to use for yourself, as well. On this note, belts can also be cut from tires (especially bike tires) as well as the buckles themselves; whereas shoelaces can be made from wire or twine if, that is, I ever decide to teach you how to make it.
- Batteries – Most batteries will be destroyed from not being kept charged all this time; but if you find any, any size in working order, prize them. You can, however, make your own battery and even a flashlight as described in *Chapter 10.*
- Tarps – I've always said that the one thing I'd take with me if ever stranded on a desert island would be a good quality, heavy duty, clear plastic tarp (beautiful naked women are over-rated and now over-used).

You can make your own fire, construct your own knife, but a tarp has so many applications it's mind blowing.

- Jeans – Not for clothing, as we've discussed repetitively; but they do make excellent floatation devices, sandbags, bags, are useful just for the raw material, and will definitely come in handy sometime.
- Chemicals – Not that you'll need them much for their original purpose, but most chemicals are flammable and can be used as a weapon or fuel. On this note, any bleach is a positive, as well, for stated reasons.
- Garden hoses – This is yet another item that we'll no longer be able to make adequately; and there's no better method to transport water than a modern nylon, polyurethane, polyethylene or PVC hose.
- Dog food – With or without a dog, pet food is a definite keeper for food (it's rich in nutrients) or bait.
- Steel wool – In combination with 9v batteries for fire-starting as described previously.
- Flashlights and solar landscaping lights – Without electricity flow and with all batteries dead, alternative lighting will eventually be your only source; and if you've ever gone several days/weeks/months without it, you'd know why even landscaping lights top my necessity list.
- Tools – Especially box cutters and blades, but any and all tools will eventually come in handy.
- Camping gear – A no-brainer, the rest of your life will be spent practically camping.
- Bags and backpacks – Always useful.
- Weapons and ammunition – Critical!
- Driveway bell line – This is the long hose-looking line you see at full service gas stations. You may have noticed a bell ring inside when you drive up. The hose is pressurized with air and connected to a bell on one end and capped at the other. When the car drives over the line, the weight of the vehicle depresses the hose causing a plunger in the bell to move, striking the bell. The system uses no electricity which is perfect as a security device in a powerless world. Place several of these at key entrance points around your shelter. On this note, many of the motion sensors and all vehicle 'back-up' cameras are 12vdc and can run off a car battery as previously stated.
- Books – You may or may not realize that people looove collecting books. Every household has several books sitting on shelves collecting dust, not to mention the thousands of libraries, bookstores and schools. What to do with all these books? There has to be some great use for them! In my personal opinion, we don't want to keep any record of the past civilization, and their 'ways' of doing things. One may say that "we need to keep the books to learn from our mistakes." But it's my experience that books are not used to learn but to copy, since copying is much simpler than learning. I would say, have a good old SS book-burning party, if it wasn't for the fact that books make horrible fuel. Even though they originally come from wood, the oxygen has been removed from the pages, making combustion virtually impossible (trust me I've tried). Even fanning the pages open offers little success. Books, however, do make great insulation, and they're fire resistant, a great replacement for that pink fiberglass sh!#.

It's not likely that you'll run into a house, building or room that you can't gain access to by breaking out the window with a rock/brick. But if you do, that's actually a good thing, since it means that no one else has yet to gain access to it either, which means who knows what kind of great supplies are inside, untouched. That said, if you do run into a locked door, here are several methods for gaining entry ranging from simple to difficult:

- Crow bar – Place a 36in crowbar between the handle (or deadbolt) and trim and pry back. This will rip off the trim molding and give you access and visibility to the locking bolts, which you can then work away from the frame with the bar.
- Chain and truck – Access to the door or window

is sometimes blocked by security bars or roll-down security walls, both of which are no match for a tow chain and a four-wheel drive truck.

- Bolt cutters – The simplest method to remove any padlock, any size, is with a set of 48in bolt cutters.

- Sheetrock – Most interior walls are hollow with Sheetrock on both sides. I've seen extremely strong doors, equipped with radically expensive, high-security locks that were surrounded by Sheetrock walls, which could be busted through with a closed fist or someone's head (again, personal experience). Then simply reach through and unlock the lock from the inside, or make a big enough hole to climb through.
- Axe – If the door is solid or the walls are anything but Sheetrock, an axe will make short work of it. If the door is hollow core, just hack out enough again to reach through and unlock the lever from the inside.
- Gasoline – If all else fails, burn it down, is what I always say. Typically you'd never want or need to burn down a door when you have tools, since it could burn down the entire building and all the supplies in the process. But if the building is cinderblock or metal and the door is wood, this may be an option.
- Hinge pins – If the hinge is located on this side of the door just tap it out with a hammer and screwdriver.

- Credit card – Yes, the credit card method is actually very efficient. Remove the molding as described above, then work the door bolt out by pushing against the tapered side with the card.
- Sledge hammer – A well-positioned blow just above or below the door handle or deadbolt with an 10lb sledge will rip through any wood or metal door frame. If not, it will knock a large enough hole through the door so that you can again reach through.
- Lock pick – Picking a lock isn't too difficult, but you need to know how the lock works first, so that you know what to feel and what's going on when you attempt it. After picking a few locks, it will become second nature. Inside every lock, regardless if it's a padlock, door lock, deadbolt or cabinet, is a barrel filled with several tumblers or pins. These pins need to be raised to their individual heights while keeping rotational pressure on the barrel so that they'll stay in place. If just one isn't in its proper position, the barrel will not turn. But once all are up, the barrel will turn freely, just like if you had the key.

This is a good option if you want to relock the door to protect it from others for later entry, since you can just re-pick the lock over and over again. You can fashion a lock pick set from a windshield wiper blade or a hack or coping saw blade by bending the blade end to 90° (torsion wrench) and filing down the rake pick as shown.

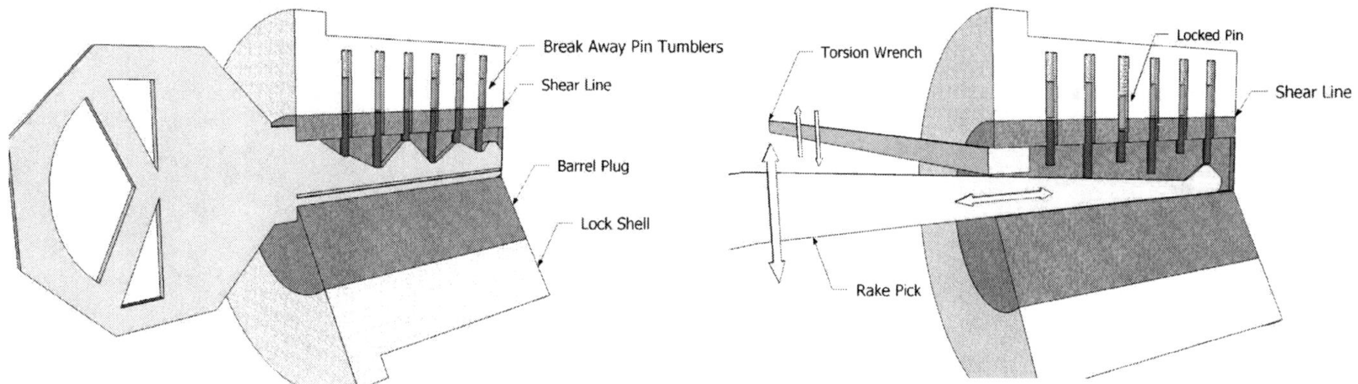

1. First, insert the torsion wrench inside the wider portion of the lock and place a little pressure on it.
2. Now, insert the rake, pointy side up all the way to the back of the key slot. Press firmly up and pull out hard, "raking" the pins. This will cause most to be seated in their "unlock" position. All that's left is to find the one or two that aren't, and work them up with the tip of the rake tool.

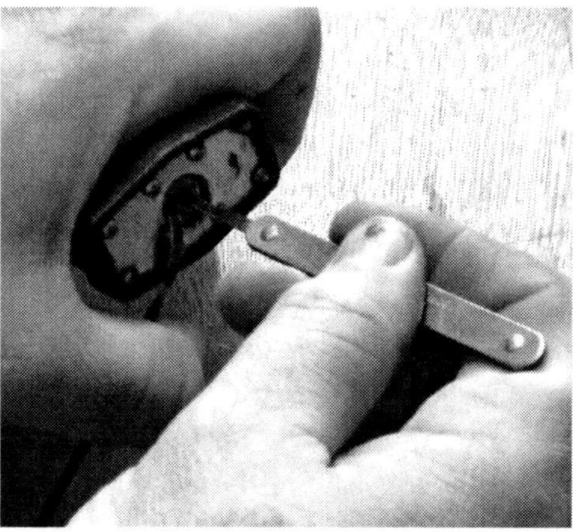

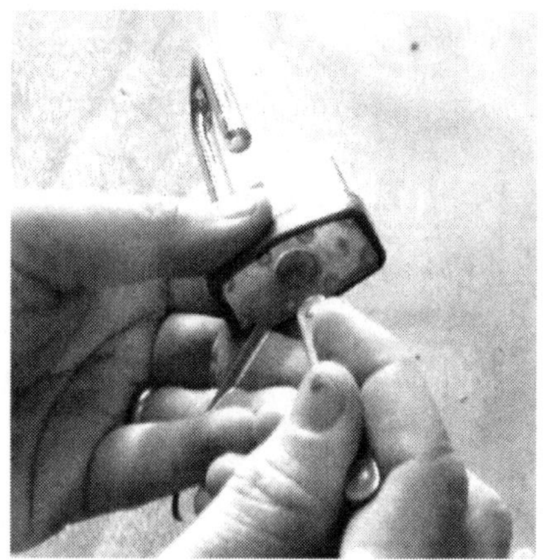

Now that you have worked so hard to build up supplies and food sources, it would prove pertinent to spread out the goods throughout the area, rather than stockpiling them in just one location, for several reasons:

a. If someone conquers your home and you're forced to flee, at least you still have your stuff.
b. If you were to keep all your supplies in one place, someone looking to steal your stuff doesn't have far to go; it's all in one spot. On the other hand, if you keep it spread out, and an intruder manages to take what's on hand while you're gone, you still have 90% in safekeeping. The following are several ingenious (if I do say so myself) locations to safeguard your goods in a collapsed society:

- Stove top – The typical kitchen stove top pops up for cleaning. Most people (especially Americans) don't care about cleaning under there and don't know that it actually is removable.
- U-Trap – For those who don't know what a U-trap is, it's the bend in the pipe that looks like a 'U' under the sinks in your home. For those who do know what a U-trap is, you'll know why no one would ever want to look in it. The U-trap has a quick disconnect that can be unscrewed if something valuable like a wedding ring, gets accidently dropped in the drain, trapping the item before it flows into the sewer. It doesn't matter if there's water to the sink or not, the item won't go anywhere. You may want to place the goods in a Ziploc bag however; otherwise, you'll be in for a treat(s) when it's time for removal. Just make sure all the air is removed from the bag or else it <u>will</u> float away.

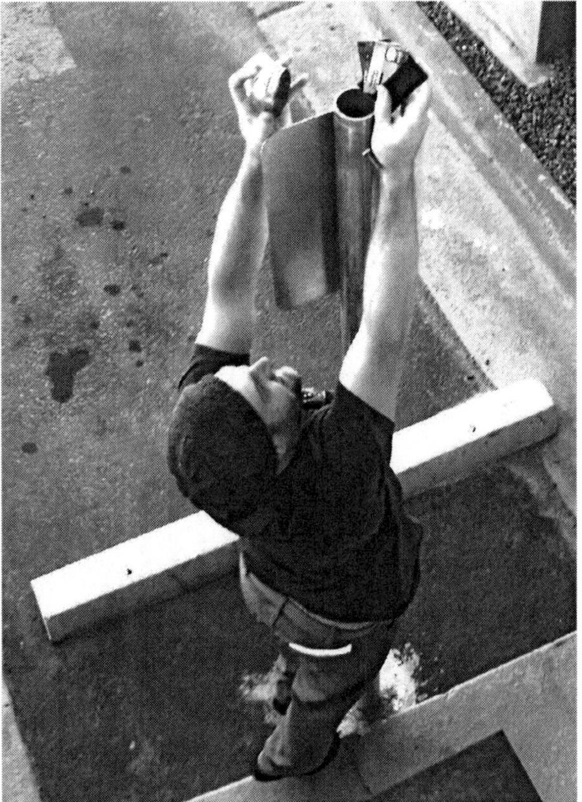

- Fence pole – The inside of all metal chain-link fence or sign posts are hollow. Many of the industrial ones or the larger residential corner posts are wide enough to hold a can perfectly. Just make sure to incorporate some sort of removal system beforehand.
- Spare Tire – With so many forsaken cars, there's tons of possible hiding places. The spare tire is a perfect example of such a place. Today, it is used to smuggle narcotics from Mexico; we can do the same with supplies. Unless you have access to a tire removal tool (tire press), you'll need to cut an incision big enough to insert your items in the back. If the spare is located under the vehicle, as seen in most trucks, this is an even better spot, as most people have never owned a truck. Regular tires on a vehicle can be just as useful. Anyone seeing a car with all four tires flat would simply assume someone slashed the tires during the initial rioting/looting.

- Underground – Burying booty is a no-brainer. The odds of anyone knowing exactly where the supplies are located are ridiculous. And the hole can accommodate any quantity of items at any size.
- Utility box – The big green metal boxes you see at the end of every street are either transformer relay or central connection boxes used by the telephone and electric companies. They have a regular padlock that can be cut and replaced with your own or picked as described above. There are several cubic feet of space behind those steel doors, making for a great vault.
- Post Office mailbox – In a pinch, the blue metal boxes on every corner make great safes. If the item is

valuable, you can get into the box later, whereas, anyone else wouldn't waste the energy.

- Door – Most interior doors have a hollow core. Accessing it without cutting into it can be a tricky, however. The best way to accomplish this is to remove the door as described above; and with a chisel or other sharp instrument, punch through the top 1in wood frame piece. Install the door back on the hinges when you're finished, filling it with goodies; and no one will be the wiser. It's not likely that anyone would try to look at the top of a door for items, would YOU?
- Business door – This one's a little different from the interior house door. Any glass door you see at the entrance of a business, restaurant, office, etc., has a couple inches of hollow tract into which the extension arm retracts. Plenty of good hiding spots in a capitalist nation.
- Ice box – Saving the best for last, the inside of an empty gas station ice box is as big as a storage room.

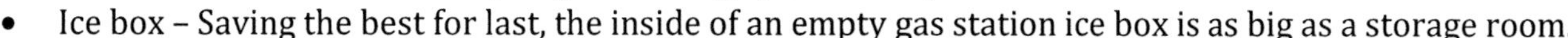

COMMERCE & TRADE: TO THE VICTOR GO THE SPOILS

This is a tricky subject. On one hand, I'd say it's better/safer to have nothing to do with other people. There should be no reason (IF you follow the advice and direction of this book, that is) that you should need anything from, or would need to have anything to do with, anyone else. It's just a bad situation that can too easily be avoided, especially during the first few months. Eventually, however, you may find that you're producing more than you need and wish to trade some supplies/materials for different- or to replace broken-items. This should be done with people you know and trust first and foremost; then with people against whom you know you could win a fight; never trading in situations where the people outnumber you and your group. And lastly, if trading with people you don't know, or with whom you have a 'bad feeling' about, try to pick an environment where they can't access you or your merchandise easily, like from your car window with the doors locked and the engine on; (and don't hesitate to run over someone if the SHTF), a drive-thru, fast-food window (if the building is fortified), or a bank teller window (perfect, since it's already built to take an assault).

As far as a source of commerce, paper money will have little value. Coins will have a bit more; but since our coins aren't made from real silver or copper anymore, anyway, not much. You can forget about check or credit cards; without the financial institutions to back them up, they're a thing of the past. Things like toilet paper, coffee, cigarettes, alcohol, sex, women, girls, (hell, boys,) drugs (all the main vices), weapons, ammunition, salt, fuel and some types of jewelry will have real monetary value. When dealing in a trade-like situation, it's important to remember two important, all holy, rules:

1. Everyone is trying to rob or rip you off! If you speak to any pawnshop owner or clerk he'll tell you *"no matter the customer, I always walk into the deal thinking I'm being scammed, it's only then I may walk out, not."* Or a cop or highway patrolman pulling someone over *"assume everyone's a criminal with a gun."*
2. Only trade merchandise that you don't need or can replenish, rebuild or reproduce!

You have to believe that there are no exceptions to rule one; otherwise you'll just get yourself or those in your party robbed, raped and/or killed, possibly in that order, possibly in reverse. There's an old saying: "You can't judge a book by its cover;" but that's exactly what the cover is for. It tells you what the book's about, at first glance, I mean that's what this book's cover did right? That's why we put images there, otherwise they'd just be blank. Then there are the morons who have no concept of living in the real world. The good thing about dealing with these survivors is that they will have no street smarts and minimal experience face-to-face with people, so they won't know if you're lying or manipulating them. This is because all communications in their life up until this point have been followed with an LOL, LMAO or :) emoticon signs. They don't know what real body language or expressions look like. I say this because 60% of people in the United States occupy an office (white collar) job and have no 'significant' daily contact with the type of people who will dominate this world—i.e., the 40% who know what it takes to survive and have actual, real-world hands-on, daily experience working as laborers and service workers, and, therefore, are able to, and will have a definite advantage over, the weaker 60%.

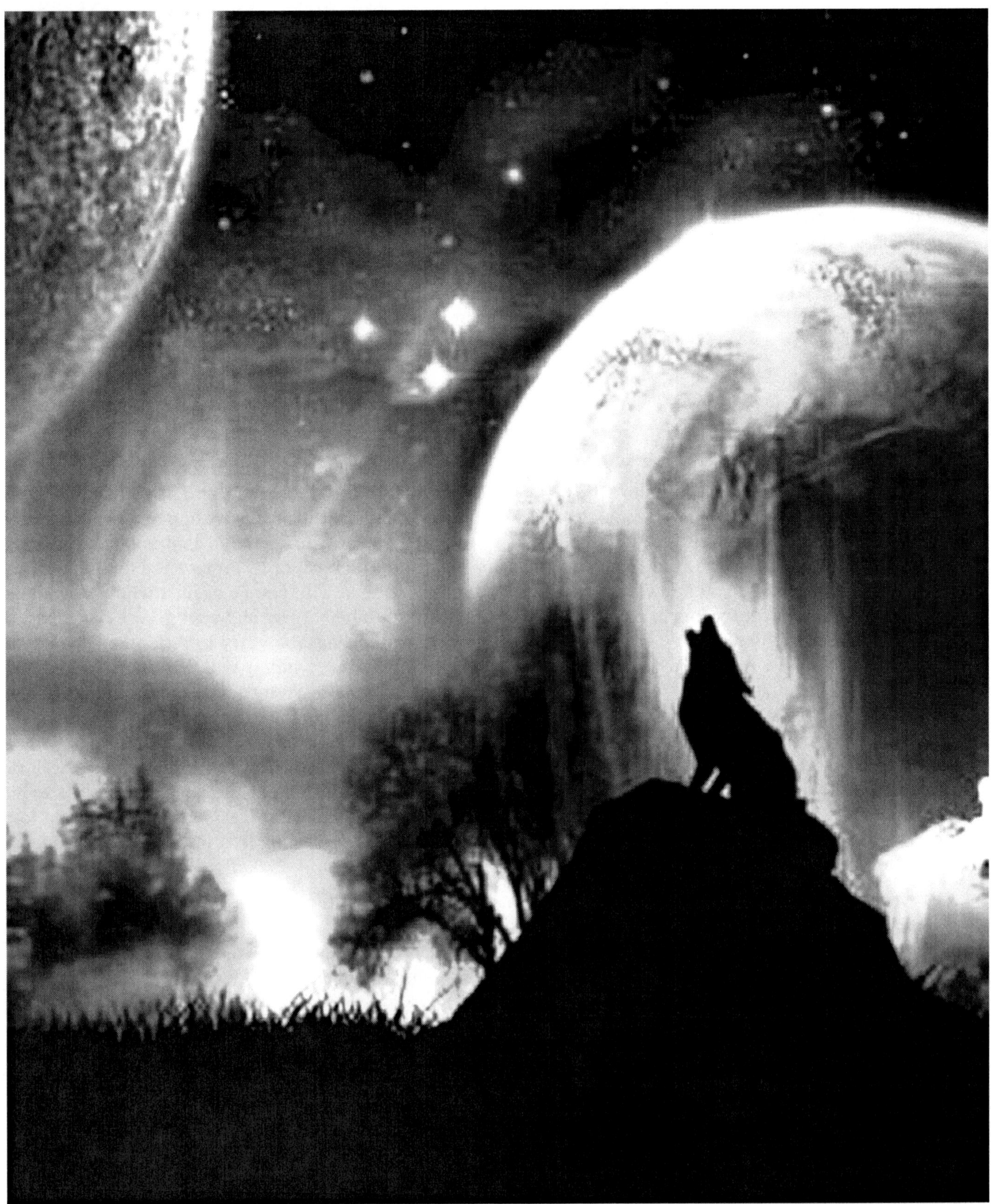

CHAPTER 10

A NEW BEGINNING: YEAR 2

At a certain point things will calm down, at least a little. New societal and political structures will most likely attempt to develop anew, or at least rebuild themselves. It's important to thwart these efforts before they even begin, unless you enjoy a good apocalypse every now and then. DON'T make the same mistakes over and over and over and over again. The founding fathers left Europe's tyranny to start a "free," "better" nation; but it was a dream, there was never such a place. In fact, this country is now more tyrannical, more corrupt and has higher taxes than England ever did/was. 'IF' we really are so "cultured," why do we still need governing or societal structures? 'IF' we're so "evolved," why can't we live alone without these entities, in peace, without fighting? 'IF' we're so smart, why can't we think for ourselves, without others making decisions for us? Conversely, if the answer is that we're not, in fact, evolved, cultured, or smart enough to live independently without a governing body and societal structure, then we're obviously not evolved, cultured or smart enough to live with one, either. I mean, it hasn't worked for the last 5,000 years, why would it work for the next?

On that note, Belgium has gone without a government for almost one year now. Before that, in 1977, the Netherlands went 208 days; and in 2009 Iraq went 289 days. Somalia has no government at all and hasn't had one since 1991; and now, with Egypt's president firing his entire cabinet before stepping down himself at the demands of the people, who knows how long it will be until they have a governing body as well. This proves that for whatever reason, people all over the world can and do govern themselves efficiently. Belgium is a founding member of the EU, houses the EU's and NATO's headquarters, and boasts one of the highest global economies, GNP and export per capita, not to mention one of the lowest crime and homicide rates. Belgium is leading the way, proving a convincing model of how the rest of the world can function in a new governless world.

MAKING IT RIGHT: ONE STEP AT A TIME

During the first couple of years, another 3rd of the remaining surviving population will die from starvation, homicide, infection, ignorance, natural elements and natural causes. The smaller groups will disband into newly-created, larger, semi-functioning communities that will start popping up all over the world--some good, some run by different tyrants. (These, unfortunately, will most likely then develop into societies because of sheer population growth.) Either way, you'll need to start preparing for long-term survival. I'm not talking about voting for a new leader or remarrying and settling down, but rather controlled procreation, controlled planting and controlled trade. It's time to discard any still lingering, pre-dawn, societal concepts, notions, views, perceptions, beliefs, rules and rituals. No more sucking the Earth dry, polluting the sky/seas, over-populating the planet, over-hunting, meaningless killing or abusing the other animal species, over-planting the crops, mass-producing hormone-soaked meat, government controlling corporations or people controlling governments.

Over the next few months, new life will most likely emerge; crops that were decimated will show signs of life; the Sun may even start shining again in the case of a nuclear winter, impact or super volcanic activity, and who knows, we may even have a new moon or 2. With the now-flourishing eco-system, cannibalism once again isn't a necessity and will even become frowned upon once again; rape, theft and murder are no longer needed for survival, and will, again, most likely be punished as a result. The Earth has destroyed the infestation that was infecting it; it's a new beginning on so many levels. With lawlessness now generally a thing of the past, there's no need to harbor the convictions, practices and outlooks that carried you through the first months of immediate aftermath either. As much as you were able to adapt to that time of transition and achieved what then needed to be done to endure, you'll once again need to adjust to and thrive in this new world, if you want to survive as well.

NEW GROWTH: AS YOU SOW SO SHALL YOU REAP

When the pH levels return to normal, Mother Nature will begin to recover and new growth will emerge. With plants it's all about the right pH. Different types of plants will only grow or will grow better in certain types of soils or rather certain pH (acidic to alkaline) levels. The way the pH scale works is that the number 7 represents 0 or middle ground. I know it's silly but, hey, we're human. Anything lower than 7 needs, or has more,

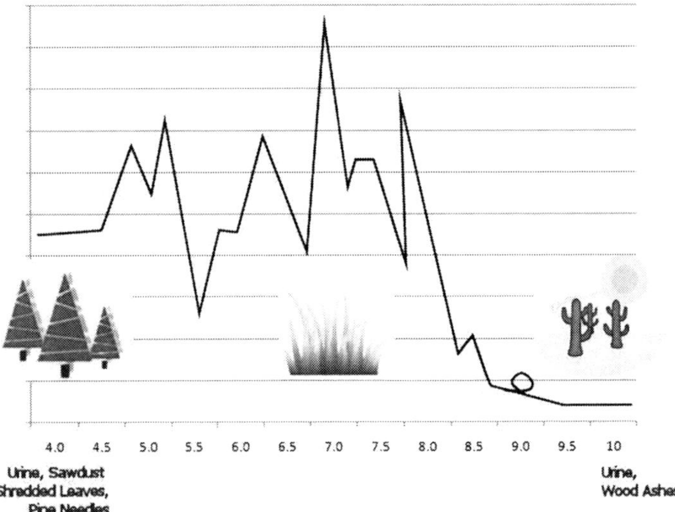

acidity; whereas, anything more than 7 requires or has more alkalinity. For optimal plant performance you'll need to (a) know what pH level soil a specific plant needs (listed below) and (b) what pH level is the soil itself. If you don't happen to have a home soil test kit or pH meter tool at your disposal, you'll need to actually taste the soil. If it has a sweeter taste or smell, it's more alkaline rich; if it has a more sour taste or smell, it's more acid rich. Also, a fairly accurate rule of thumb is that if the soil receives heavy annual rainfall or it is near thick forest cover, it probably has higher acid content. In regions of highly concentrated sunlight, moderate rainfall or near prairie cover, the soil tends to be near neutral pH levels. And finally, drought-plagued or desert-like regions are usually higher in alkaline content. If all else fails, keep the soil more acidic then alkaline as most plants prefer acidic conditions to grow.

In the best case scenario, I'd add more sulfur for more acidity and more limestone for alkaline; but I'm not even going to get into how to locate and mine for limestone reserves or make sulfur in this book. So, as always, we'll need to make do with what we've got--piss, and plenty of it! In all humans (who aren't vegetarians) the body uses urine as a way of releasing excess acids from the body, more so during the first waking hours of the day; therefore, human urine, in general, will usually have a higher acid count (around 4.5 pH) then alkaline. On the other hand, animals that only eat grains and grasses (or vegetarian humans) will have a higher alkaline count, (around 8 pH). Ok, so you can also use pine needles, shredded leaves, sawdust and peat moss (all of which are high in acidity) to lower the pH levels, as well. I just like the idea of pissing on my food. As far as raising the pH levels, wood ash is a great source of alkaline. It contains up to 70% calcium carbonate, potassium, phosphorus, and many other trace elements and as a dust-like substance, it works quickly as a liming agent.

Plant whatever crop is most hardy and natural for the region. This is no time to take risks; go with what has the best chance of survival for the climate. There are many types of produce and many facets of growing them. As important as it is to pick the right plant, it's just as important to choose the right method of planting:

FARMING

- Beans – Beans are a sure thing in most regions; they grow extremely fast, are resistant to extreme conditions, and are one of the highest sources of protein, complex carbohydrates, folate, fiber, and iron on the planet. Beans thrive in cooler shady climates when planted a couple inches down in soils with pH levels between 6.0 and 7.0.

1. First, find a barren field that receives frequent rain, at least 1in/week during sprouting.
2. In a straight line, poke your finger into the rich soil down to the knuckle or about 1.5in-2in, 6in or more apart, about a month before spring or the last frost.
3. Place one bean seed in each hole and pat down the soil lightly. (A quarter of these probably won't germinate, so plant that much extra.)

In less than a week or two, you should start seeing sprouts pop up. Once the flowers die off, bean pods will begin to grow in their place. The beans within will start to bulge out from the sides when the bean pods get large. This is a sign that they're ready to be picked. If the taste is odd, it's because they're old and you waited too long to pick them. It's better to pick too early than too late when it comes to beans.

- Potatoes – Potatoes are one of the best sources of carbohydrates as well as vitamin C, potassium, vitamin B6, magnesium, phosphorus, iron and zinc. They are equivalent to whole grain breads, pastas and cereals as far as fiber content. Growing potatoes is extremely simple. In fact, as anyone who has left a bag of potatoes on the shelf too long knows, they'll start sprouting all by themselves, even without dirt or water. Potatoes are very adaptable. They thrive in high Sun, mild, cool, or cold climates, and in soils with a pH count of 5.3–6.0.

1. Find a barren field that receives full sunlight.
2. Dig a 1ft-diameter hole about 10in deep every foot or so, about a month before spring or the last frost.
3. Fill with a shovel full of manure (donkey, horse, cow, it doesn't matter).
4. Cut a potato in half or quarters (as long as each piece has 3 eyes) and place in the hole, cut side down.
5. Cover with a shovel of dirt and pack lightly. Potatoes need about 1.5in–2in of rain per week.

In less than a week or two, you should start seeing sprouts pop up. Some potatoes may grow much faster than the others. You can harvest these early sprouters as soon as seven to eight weeks after planting. Harvest the rest about two weeks after the tops have died back, but before the first hard freeze.

- Corn – Corn is a summer growing crop, planted best well after the last freeze in at least 70°F temperatures and in full sunlight in soils with a pH content of 6.0–7.0. Corn roots love nitrogen. This can be in the form of blood poured directly on the stock base, manure planted with the seeds, or by rotating beans with a legume crop after every harvest.

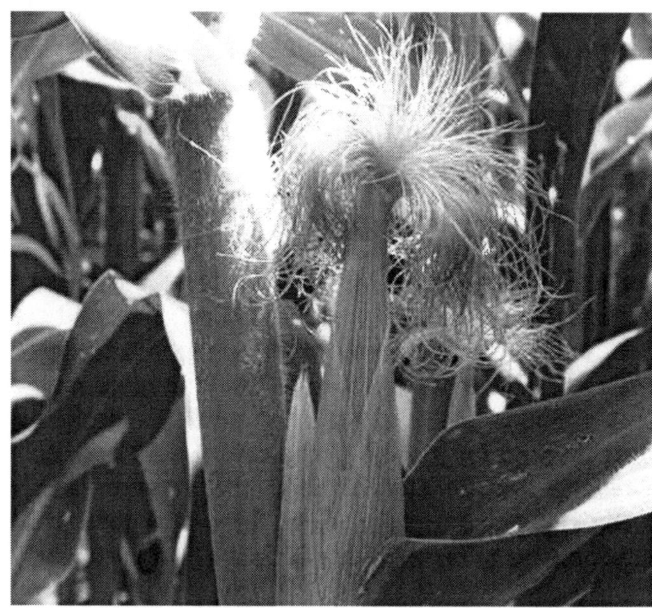

1. Pull 2 nice deep trenches side by side about 2ft apart with a hoe as long as desired.
2. Mash or crush up enough manure to line both trenches and side walls with a thin layer.
3. Put just a little of the pulled dirt back into the trench, just enough to cover the manure very lightly.
4. Place your corn kernels (seeds) about a foot apart inside each trench, cover with 1in-2in of soil and pack.
5. Corn plants need an environment that receives at least 1in of rain per week.

The 2 rows should be ready to harvest in about 70 days. You can tell it is ready when the silk starts to turn brown, about 3 weeks after it first appears (green). Corn silk is a long stigmas fiber that looks like a girl's ponytail. At this point if you pull back the husk a little, you should notice the kernels appearing full and juicy. You want to plant corn in pairs since the plant pollinates (hence the dual rows). If you'll be planting more than 2 rows, space every set of rows 3ft-4ft from one another to facilitate a path for easy picking. Plant 2 rows every 2 weeks or so (depending on how much corn you consume in a two-week period), so you get a row of corn ready to harvest every two weeks in 70-day increments. An ear of corn contains around 300 seeds, plenty for the next planting. That said, it's a good idea to collect and plant seeds from several different stalks just in case one plant isn't fertile. Lastly, just so you know, corn typically isn't yellow or golden yellow; that's corn that has been genetically modified specially for us Americans. Natural corn (like we grow in Mexico) is usually blackish, bluish-gray, purple, green, red and/or white in color and is much healthier with higher nutrient counts than store-bought corn. Hopefully, we'll never see the yellow stuff again!

- Tomatoes – Tomato plants are easy to grow, don't need much water and provide a good source of niacin, potassium, phosphorous, antioxidants and vitamins A, C and E when planted in soils with a pH level between 6.0–6.8. After the last frost, dig a trench in a sunny area, add manure or compost, and cover with dirt (just like you did with the potatoes). Place seeds approximately a foot apart, cover with earth and firmly pat down the soil. Water lightly a couple of times per week.
- Beets – If you'll be making ethanol, you'll want some type of sugary plant such as beets or strawberries. Beets are extremely fast-growing plants when planted in soil with a pH of 6.0–7.0, and can even be sowed in

winter months. Soak the seeds in water for about a day to strengthen them, plant each seed 2in apart, and water about once per day. Start planting in late winter to early spring; and they'll be ready to harvest within just a few weeks.

- Strawberries – Strawberries are unbelievably hardy when planted in early spring in a sunny area with pH levels of 5.5–6.5. Strawberries are another plant that requires plenty of water to grow. Plant the seeds a little deeper than usual and about 2ft apart. It's also important to pick any berries the day they ripen to avoid spoilage and other critters from stealing them.
- Lettuce – Lettuce is a good source of folic acid and vitamin A, but requires watering every morning and soil pH levels between 6.0–6.7. Sprinkle manure or compost throughout the planting area followed by the lettuce seeds separated about 8in-16in apart and cover with a couple inches of earth.

SPROUTING

There are literally hundreds of easy-to-grow, edible plants, too many to describe in detail or per specific region. Beans, corn and potatoes, which will grow in most areas, are a proven, simple source of much needed nutrients. Beets and strawberries are also grown easily and have high sugar/carbohydrate counts. However, you may not have the time or patience to grow any of these plants in their entirety; in this case, sprouting may prove an efficient form of sustenance instead. Sprouting is the act of planting seeds and caring for them just long enough to get sprouts in return. The seed and, therefore, sprout contains the most nutrients and vitamins per unit volume, since it's designed to provide food for growth to the actual plant, like an egg. The only downfall of sprouting is that you don't get back a replenishing supply of seeds for next year; but it's a quick means of making food for just a few days' work.

CLONING

Sprouting plants from seeds is one way to go; but without seeds, then what? Cloning is the physical act of cutting a clipping from an existing plant or tree and re-growing that same plant in a different location. This is not the offspring of the plant but the same exact plant, which means that you can expect a similar result, shape, size, and efficiency of fruit production.

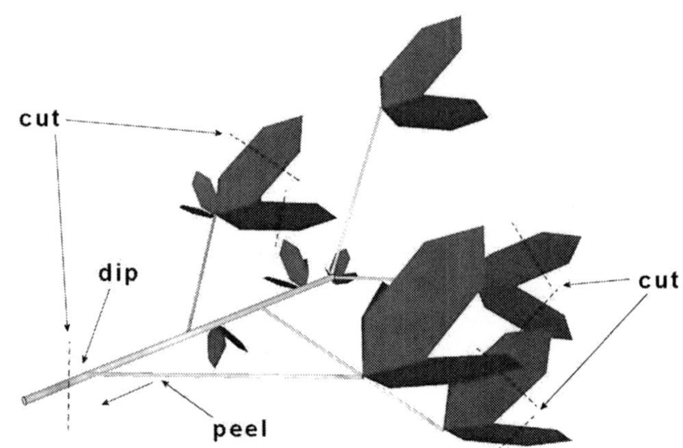

1. Pick a branch form a healthy plant that is strong, has new growth and is fruitful. The branch should be at least 6in long and have 5 big offshoots of leaves to one stock, with each offshoot containing at least 3 nodes from the top clusters of the plant.
2. Fill a plastic bottle cut in half with dirt and let soak in water for 30 minutes (never add a seed or clone to dry dirt and then add water.)
3. Cut a 45° angle horizontally 1/4in below the first knob and peel one side about 1/2in off above the cut.
4. Break the branch off the first knob and peel the skin loose from the stock.
5. Cut the middle leaves in half to prevent drying out (leaves are large solar panels for the plant.)
6. Dip the entire lower 1in-2in in root clone gel, insert into the plastic pot of moist soil and place the top section of the plastic bottle back on top to maintain humidity.
7. Keep the roots above 75°F and the soil at a pH level between 5.5 - 6.5 for 10-20 days before planting.
8. If any leaves become brown or dry, remove them immediately.

HYDROPONICS

Then there's hydroponics, which introduces nutrients directly to the leaves and/or roots, thereby eliminating the need for soil altogether. This is a great option for underground bunkers or if the soil hasn't yet recovered from the cataclysm itself. There are many, many different types of setups; I designed and built the following systems keeping in mind what basic supplies and materials will be on hand after the fall. I came up with a few different systems depending on your level of automation:

- Storage container setup – The most important factors in a hydroponics setup are a waterproof membrane and root access, both of which are achieved by utilizing a plastic storage container found in any home or garage. For this setup you'll need at least (1) (preferably 2) large Rubbermaid (or equivalent) plastic containers, a tack or needle, a 5-gallon bucket, a box cutter or hole saw, manure (preferably goat, deer or rabbit) and a lime squeeze tool.

1. Drill or cut out (12) 1-1/2in holes equally spaced throughout the lid of one of the containers.
2. Soak a quart of manure in a plastic container for about an hour until it becomes soft and moldable like clay but not runny or soupy.
3. Now scoop out a handful (don't worry, there is no harmful bacteria; this is only fertilizer) and place it in the lime squeeze tool. Squeeze firmly to form the mix into a cup and let dry overnight. Do this 11 more times.
4. Place several large rocks or 1-gallon milk jugs filled with dirt or water into the container. This will not only prevent the container from blowing away when it's empty, but will also displace the amount of necessary water so that our 5-gallon bucket fills up the entire container.
5. Place the lid on the container and the fertilizer cups in the holes. They should fit about 1/2-3/4 of the way into the holes without falling completely through.
6. Place a seed of your choosing inside 11 of the 12 fiber pots (one of the corner pots will only be a water fill port plug) and add some soil on top.
7. Heat a pin and poke a small hole in the middle of the container about 1 to 1-1/2in from the bottom.
8. Place the container in the proper amount of Sun depending on the plant type and add 5-gallons of water.
9. Adjusting the pH levels as described above, adding manure or blood (which are pH neutral) for nitrogen. I prefer goat, deer, rabbit or any pellet-type-droppings over patties for nutrition, because they release nutrients into the water in a self-contained, timed capsule.

For the first several weeks, you'll need to lightly pour or spray the water from the bucket onto the fiber pots until the plants' root systems grow and dangle down long enough (about 3in) into the container to reach the water level itself. Once this happens, you can lift out the fiber pot plug and pour the entire 5 gallons into the container, replacing the bucket underneath the pin hole to recover the liquid again. This should be performed a few times daily, the slow draining water will keep the roots damp and full of nutrition throughout the day, still allowing the roots to breathe, while replenishing oxygen at the same time. Because the drain hole is located 1–1 1/2in up from the bottom, there will still be plenty of water in the container to provide the roots with sustained moisture from evaporation when empty. By placing the second container upside down over the plants, you'll be capturing further evaporation from the plant while still allowing sunlight in--a miniature greenhouse, if you will. Once the fruits or vegetables are at a pickable size, remove, without pulling out the entire root systems and starting over. This way, time isn't wasted re-growing a new mature root system over and over again.

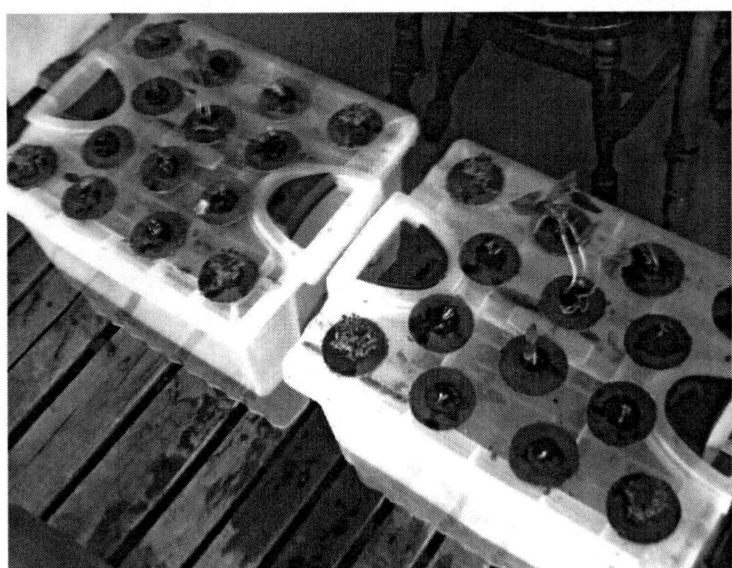

If you don't have your own seeds, and Bill Gates's worst case scenario plays itself out where all plant life on Earth is completely obliterated, it would prove critical to store seeds in several 'doomsday' seed vaults around the world. Luckily, there are over 1,400 such seed banks located in almost every country on the planet. The only problem is that the exact locations aren't common knowledge or even highly publicized. They are, in most cases, kept secret, so the typical survivor (you) won't have any clue where to find them, which completely defeats the purpose of constructing them, at least the purpose for constructing them that we've been told, which is to *"replenish the worlds plant life if it's every completely obliterated."* That said, I'm pretty sure someone somewhere out there may know where some are located and have the key to access them; but the likelihood of that specific person surviving is extremely low. If anyone comes across a list of the 1,400 or so establishments currently storing seeds to replenish the Earth's plant life, and how to access them, please let me know; and I'll add it to the next edition of this book.

GREENHOUSES

With the enormous amount of currently abandoned homes, there should be no shortage of building materials and glass for greenhouse construction. The hundreds of thousands of discarded cars or buses will also provide us with quite a few pre-made greenhouses with their numerous windows. Children and dogs left inside can attest to that. A greenhouse remains warm throughout the summer and winter months, presenting a nice, hospitably-growing environment for crops. This is accomplished by the Sun's radiation passing through the clear surface unhindered. The long light beams are then absorbed by the plants and/or soil. What's not absorbed bounces back in a refracted state and, for the most part, isn't able to pass back through the glass. This ping-pong, ricocheting action continues until all light is absorbed or transferred into convective energy and heat.

LIVESTOCK

Eventually, keeping and raising livestock without the fear of poaching will become a practical endeavor. Not just for food production (meat, milk, eggs,) but for materials (wool, leather, bone) as well. Once the chaos has calmed, that is, and it will... eventually. By raising goats, chickens, turkeys, ducks, geese, donkeys and/or pigs, you get the same nutritional value without the extra work and danger of hunting and trapping wild animals. All these animals are capable of surviving on their own; therefore, you'll be able to locate them now either roaming in the wild or on/around abandoned farms, with the exception of chickens. There will be a great decline in chickens in the new world for several reasons: (a) there is no such thing as a chicken--in the wild. Humans made chickens just like we made German Shepherds, Cocker Spaniels, Labradors, Terriers and every other domesticated dog breed; and (b) chickens are just downright stupid. They have little hope of surviving on their own in an environment unprotected by humans from predators. So without going overboard, piling animals on top of each other and their own waste, farming and exporting to the entire world, overworking 'beasts of burden' or destroying all the landscape, you can make enough food and materials to sustain yourself, your family, or a small group, and even have enough left over to preserve and store, trade or contribute to a community.

CLOTHING: A STITCH IN TIME SAVES NINE

I mention clothing in the last part of the last chapter in this book because there will be an enormous over abundance of it after the collapse; and therefore, there will be no need to fight over, stress out about, or stockpile, beforehand. The United States is unhealthily excessive in our need for clothing (among other things). On average, we spend over $2,000 per family per year on clothing. In fact, Americans keep enough clothing in their closets to clothe the entire world twice over. This doesn't even account for the $600 (per family) worth of still perfectly good but 'out of style' items that are thrown away or donated to Goodwill or the Salvation Army each year. The average American woman owns 20 pairs of jeans and another 15-20 pairs of other pants, 20-30 T-shirts and another 15-20 long-sleeved shirts, including sweatshirts, dress shirts and sweaters, 60-70 pairs of undergarments, including underwear, socks and bras, and 27 pairs of shoes (of which only 4 would be suitable to wear after the collapse)—in-all only 50% of which they will ever wear again. Men and children, on the other hand, keep about half that, which is what we really care about. (Women can wear men's clothing; but it's difficult for us to pull off a strapless dress). That's over 20 different outfits available in the aftermath per person per average household. And with a current population of over 300 million Americans, 225 million (or 3/4) of which are estimated to perish during or as a result of the event(s), that's almost 5 billion garments available in the aftermath. Between the 75 million survivors, that's over 175 outfits per person. From personal experience, I know that one article of clothing can be worn every day for more than a year without breaking down, even in abnormally high wear/working/washing conditions, more so with jeans and nylon fabrics. That's 175 years worth of clothes per person, which is well over the current typical life span of any human. And this is just what we have in our closets and dressers; you'll still have almost twice that in warehouses, Goodwill stores, malls, factory outlets, Wal-Marts and other clothing stores around the world.

In actuality, it doesn't matter how much clothing is left over; because all you'll really need is 50-70 outfits, and maybe a few extra pairs of undergarments to last you your entire life. And with the fall of society, you won't have to worry about styles/trends anymore. It won't matter if you wear the same 7 articles of clothing over and over again for the next 5 years. The point is, although many survival books talk about how to make your own clothes, in reality, with the bulk of leftovers available, in a situation like this, you most likely won't ever need to make anything for as long as you live. I should also mention that the need for clothing has been greatly inflated over the years by capitalist bandwagon jumper-on-ers. Clothes were never meant to protect you from the physically environment. In fact, they do a very poor job of this, snagging, ripping and rubbing through on every little thing. They're meant to protect you from and keep you warm in cold elements and, therefore, should never be worn in warm regions. Actually, they're debilitating in the heat, because they prevent the body's ability to cool through evaporation. A good rule of thumb is, if you begin sweating, remove clothing, if you're cold, put it back on! I know it sounds dumb, but I hear Agua-Luna interns saying all the time "I'm cold," put on more clothes?

Shoes, on the other hand, are a different story. Today, shoes are designed and built so cheaply that they often don't last 6 months. And besides women, men don't have 30 pairs lying around; so you'll find that running out of well-fitting shoes may actually become a problem. That said, we were never meant to wear shoes. We used to have thick pads on the bottoms of our feet, before the invention and use of shoewear. Actually, up until just a hundred years ago, most Americans didn't *wear shoes* at all. No Indians ever wore shoes unless they lived in snow-covered regions; and most aborigines, Africans, and Amazonians still don't. But I don't expect everyone to just disrobe, kick off their shoes and walk around like cavemen. So, just like anything else, we can make our own:

- Tire sandals – I've made shoes with leather, fiber and yarn; the strongest, longest-lasting shoes I've ever fabricated were made from a car tire. I suppose this is because tires are made (and warranted) for 50k-100k miles. Actually, shoes are a relatively new invention; throughout history, though, many advanced civilizations like the Jews, Egyptians, Mayans, Greeks and Romans always wore sandals. To make your own indestructible footwear, you'll need (2) backpack straps, a box cutter, a Sawzall and a tire.

1. Cut a section of tire about 16in long, cutting off half the sidewalls with a Sawzall and the inner steel cords with a large set of cable cutters or toenail clippers.

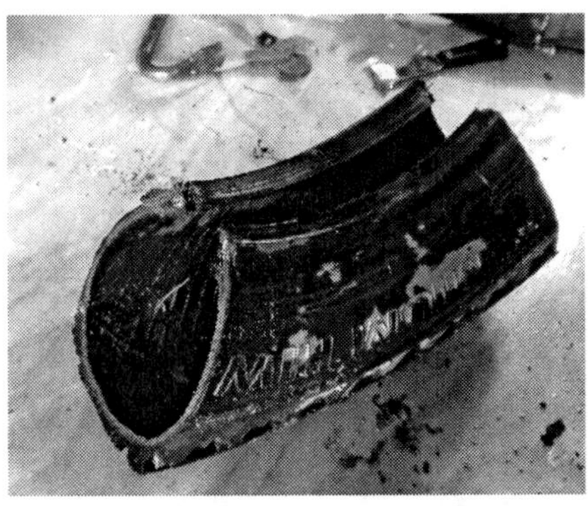

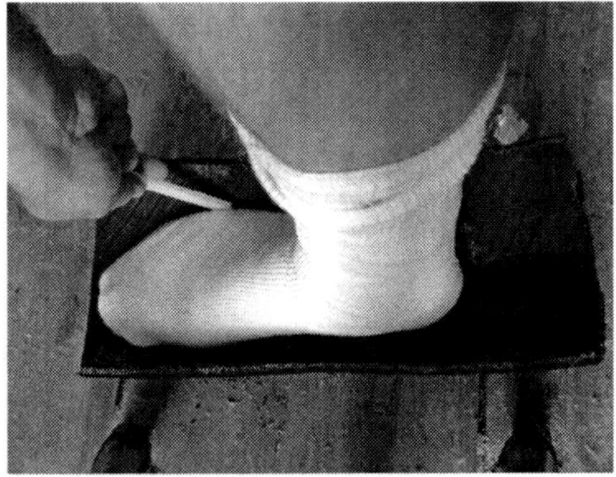

2. Place two socks on your left foot and your foot on the inside lower portion of a tire above the tread.
3. Trace your foot out on the tire and repeat the step for the right foot adding two 1-1/2in flaps at the widest and narrowest parts of your foot and one centered at the heel, as shown. The extra layer of sock will give plenty of room for growth and comfort.
4. Cut out the two patterns with the Sawzall, box cutter or sharp wood chisel (flushing the area with water as you work will break friction, helping to facilitate cutting) passing the blade a couple times over areas that are reinforced with nylon or rayon threads.

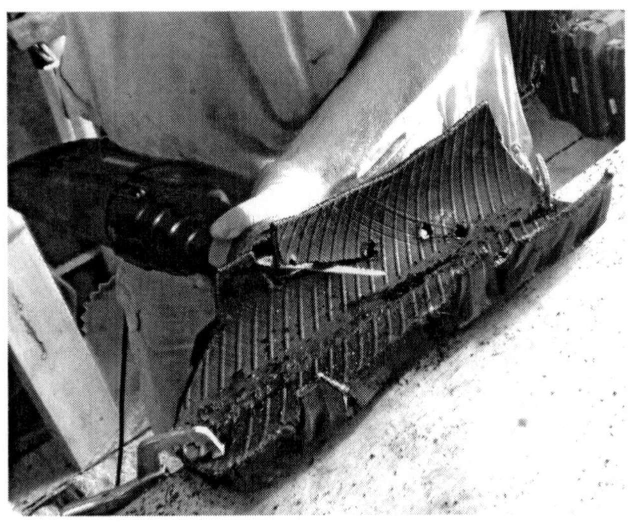

5. Make two vertical slits 1in long in each of the three heel flaps and one horizontal slit in the two toe flaps.
6. Bend up the flaps, making a slice in back half way and run the straps through the slits as shown.
7. Do the same for the opposite shoe.

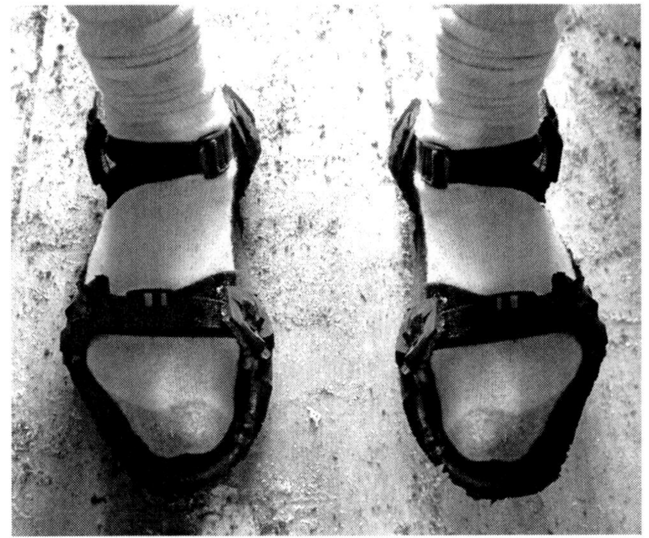

The custom sandals can be worn in any climate with or without the use of socks. By wrapping a plastic bag over the sock before putting on the sandal you can make your new footwear waterproof as well. In Germany after WWII, there weren't any shoes or shoe manufacturers for years. The same situation will soon present itself in the United States. Germans were forced to make and wear these exact same tire sandals until the economy and government revived. Three pairs of sandals can be made from one tire while the extra material can be used to make tires for a bicycle. Without air the ride is much rougher, but it's far better than riding on the rim.

BASIC HEALTH CARE & SURGERIES: IGNORANCE IS BLISS

Health is one of the most important lessons in self sustainability. Without health, there's no need for anything else. Stitches, casts, surgeries and especially childbirth have been accomplished for hundreds of thousands of years before health insurance, health care, doctors or hospitals were ever invented. This is how I know we can do so once again with a little education in the end times; and yet people don't seem to care enough about themselves or their children to seek that education. People rely on the services of society too much; this is well-documented throughout this book. The question, though, is what happens when those services are gone? It doesn't really matter to most people that they have no idea how their own body functions or what they'll need to know and do to save the lives of their loved ones. They've never even looked at a medical book before. I mean, would you buy a car and not read the owner's manual? (Ok, bad example, you probably would.) It is the same with "religious people." People claim to "follow God's words" but they have no idea what those words are because they've never read the word of God in its entirety. If you want to be able to live, at least learn about basic health care, simple emergency treatments and how to perform some minor surgeries before it's too late. For now though, I can of course, give you a few basics I've picked up over the years that you'll need to know to cure the most common injuries and ailments:

HYGIENE

Really, there are just three basic rules when it comes to hygiene: Don't touch your mouth, Don't touch your eyes, Don't touch your nose. You'd think that this would be a common sense thing, but it's not. Daily, I see people rubbing their eyes in the morning, putting food into their mouths with their fingers at lunch, and biting their nails, or even picking their nose at night. Doesn't matter if you washed your hands or not; there's still bacteria (and who knows what else) lurking under those nails. On this note, the nose hairs have a sticky-like substance (snot) that causes foreign matter to cling to it, stopping it from entering the body. If you put your finger into your nose to scratch an itch (or for whatever other reason) you only push the bacteria past those safety blockades into your body. The eyes, nose and mouth are soft tissue membrane receptacles, sponging up anything and everything that comes into contact with them. No one really seems to care today, because if they get a little stomach ache or a slight fever, they simply go to the doctor's office and get treated; well, not any longer. I wanted to start out this section with these seemingly minute tips to point out that even the smallest health problem can become a major debilitating condition and even cause death in a post-apocalyptic world.

The good news is that without society, most of these bacteria's won't exist, so you won't get sick. For example, growing up I got the flu, like everyone else, at least 2-3 times per year. However, when we spent 6 years on the ranch, not leaving even once, we got sick exactly 0 times. Conversely, the week we finally did leave, we both were instantly sick and virtually remained sick on and off that entire year. But it's a catch 22, when living in society; you're bombarded with bacterial attacks every day, so your immune system builds up a resistance. Not being in society for 6 years we had no such immunity, and therefore couldn't fight off anything until our bodies built the necessary defenses. Never coming in contact with society, we would have never gotten sick.

Every day I'm amazed at the "stylish" hardships people endure in the name of fashion and trends. While waiting outside a New York ticket counter last year, I overheard a bald, clean-shaven man say, *"I'm cold as hell."* Besides the fact that the adage makes no logical sense, over 50% of total body heat is lost out the head. He not only removed all insulation from his head, but didn't even have a hat. It's like you pull out all the insulation from the attic, and even remove the roof (hat) itself. Again, all in the name of style. Well, you won't have to worry about style in the aftermath; so you can stay warm and healthy by following these extremely non-chic tips:

1. Don't cut your hair (in cold climates). There are no more hair styles, no beauty secrets, and no shampoo tips to make your hair look richer and fuller. Body hair, armpit hair, facial hair, cranial hair, even ear hair--all exist for one purpose and one purpose only, to keep the human body warm. If you're now in a cold environment, there will be no more shaving your legs, armpits (besides the head, the next biggest source of heat loss), beard, and no more haircuts of any kind. If you can't stand the idea of not shaving your armpits, ladies, you may want to travel somewhere where it's much warmer. On that note, for men or women, a shaved head and armpits in hot regions will greatly help to cool the body.
2. Don't cut your nails short. As dull as our nails are, they're still designed to be used as tools/protection.

3. Don't wash frequently; it's not important. That's right, I said bathing isn't important; and before I get the health department pounding on my door, I'm not saying it's not necessary, just that it's not as critical as we've been led to believe. Contrary to popular belief, you don't need to bathe or wash yourself, or your hair, regularly. In fact, it can even be unhealthy, especially if you're not doing much labor and are in a cold region. Humans (especially Americans) have gotten into the habit of taking 1, 2, even 3 showers a day, which is not only a waste of water, but actually a health risk. The skin and hair creates natural oils--"oily hair," "oily skin," to protect the body, a protective shield, if you will--a condition most people deplore. When you strip this shield away on a daily basis, you make yourself susceptible to attack.
4. As far as washing with hot water, the thought is absurd. In order to kill any bacteria on your skin, you would have to wash yourself in boiling 212°F water (hence, boil drinking water to kill bacteria). And if that's something you're interested in doing, I say, go for it! Why not? I've advised worse in this book. Otherwise, a good weekly wash down in cold weather is more than enough. In hot weather, you sweat a lot; as moisture drains out of your pores, it takes dead cells with it. As soon as the moisture comes into contact with the air, it evaporates and cools the body. Once the water has evaporated, however, the dead cells remain stuck on the skin's surface and decompose, creating a perfect breeding ground for bacteria. Because of this, you will want to 'rinse off' (only), without soap on a daily basis in warm climates.
5. Don't wash clothing frequently. Similarly, clothing hardly ever needs to be washed, especially outer garments in cold regions where you don't sweat. This will only wear down the fabrics that much sooner, a luxury you no longer have. Again, wash undergarments once a week, and I'd even say, once a month for outer, especially if you're outside and away from anything man-made. Society and everything it creates produces its own breeding grounds for bacteria and viruses; and every other creature on the face of the planet transports and transmits them. Conversely, Mother Nature has a system of checks and balances, such as crustaceans, shellfish, worms, slugs, termites, maggots and other insects, larvae, algae, and slime molds, to control such filth. That's why there's no need to wash clothes that come in contact with nature. But we've tried desperately to eradicate these necessary balances in the city with pesticides, detergents and cleansers; which again, creates a wonderful atmosphere for bacteria.

If you've managed to scrounge up some toothpaste and a toothbrush, it IS important to clean your mouth, maybe not three times a day or after each meal as your local dentist advises, but at least once. You see, the mouth is warm, dark and moist, and doesn't have the strong acids as dogs or other carnivores, which makes a perfect breeding ground for bacteria and germs feeding on leftover food scraps caught between the teeth. If you aren't able to brush your teeth, then you should at least wash it out with some type of sterilizer, like alcohol, hydrogen peroxide, vinegar or citrus juice, daily. Also, the way Americans 'wipe' themselves, even today, is absurd. We take a dry piece of paper and smear the contents around blindly. How utterly filthy and barbaric. I mean, you wouldn't just wipe your hands on a dry paper after going to the bathroom, would you? And yet it's not for a lack of understanding how bacteria works that's led to this ridiculous habit. We know that bacteria can only be washed away with soap and water or an antibacterial agent; we clean our hands and face (normally much cleaner areas of the body than the butt anyway) this way. The Europeans are better at this form of hygiene than us with their bidets (a sink with soap and water for your anus). So let us take on a more hygienic form of sanitation, especially in the aftermath, when you won't be taking too many showers: use soap and water or, at least, baby wipes, when wiping. Women, it's especially important for you to wash your feminine parts daily also, as you'll be more prone to infection without showers. It's amazing the basics I've resorted to teachings humans.

NUTRITION

I once knew a Polish man named Kalute who died of starvation with a full stomach while stranded in the wilderness. Turns out, the area was heavily infested with rabbit, but little else. As he feasted on rabbit meat, his bones became weak, his teeth and hair fell out, his eyesight failed, and his circulation deteriorated. The problem is that a rabbit doesn't contain much fat and almost no carbohydrates; and he didn't know to eat the rest of the critter's innards to compensate. Parts like the kidneys, liver and heart are all great sources of vitamins A, B2, B3, B7, B9, B12 and C. The blood contains sugars and iron. The tongue and brain are the only real sources of fat, iron and vitamin B12 on a rabbit. The juicy skin and eyes retain essential sodium. The stomach and its contents contain vitamins A, B1, B3, B9, E, K and protein. The stomach lining and intestines contain vitamin B12 and protein; and, of course, the actual meat or muscle itself is full of protein, B2, B5, B6, and D (which again was all he actually was eating.)

- Vitamins – Known as commercial fortification, in today's society, vitamins are artificially added to your store-purchased foods, like vitamin D to milk (milk is actually a poor source of vitamin D), allowing you to receive all of your essentials without eating the essential foods. However, after the collapse, you'll be on your own; so in order to stay physically healthy and stave off vitamin-deficiency diseases such as: vitamin B3 deficiency (pellagra), vitamin C deficiency (scurvy), thiamin deficiency (beriberi), vitamin D deficiency (rickets) and vitamin A deficiency, you'll need to consume a full range of animals, fruits, vegetables, nuts, seeds and dairy products. Below is a complete list of different sources of these vitamins:

Type	Function	Sources	Importance	RDA
A	Helps with vision, organ & muscle growth. Is critical in immune system operation.	Liver, beef, fat, milk, eggs & leafy green plants.	Medium	.001g
B1	Helps mucous membranes, cardiovascular, nervous & muscular systems.	Pork, whole grains, beans, bacteria, fungi & plants.	Low	.0015g
B2	Helps red cell production, bodily growth, healthy skin & good vision.	Muscle, liver, kidneys, eggs, milk & green leafy plants.	Medium	.0017g
B3	Builds calories from protein, fat & carbohydrates, assists in digestion, nerves, appetite & skin regeneration.	Liver, milk, eggs, chicken, beef, fish, poultry, grains & legumes.	Medium	.017g
B5	Also helps to form calories from protein, fat & carbohydrates.	Lean meats (human meat contains twice as much B5), poultry, fish, grains, beans.	Medium	.006g
B6	Assists in brain functions & helps to form calories from protein.	Muscle, poultry, pork, fish, eggs, oats, whole grains, nuts & seeds.	High	.002g
B7	Helps to produce fatty acids & glucose.	Liver, salmon, whole grains & egg yolks.	Critical	.00008g
B9	Is critical during pregnancy & in child development, helping to produce & maintain new cells.	Leafy vegetables, mushrooms, legumes, fry beans & peas, egg yolks, breakfast cereals, seeds, liver & kidneys.	Critical	.0004g
B12	Helps maintain a healthy nervous system & assists in creating new red blood cells.	Muscle, stomach lining, fish & shellfish, meat, liver, poultry, eggs & milk.	Medium	.00002g
C	Assists the body in regeneration, inhibits cell damage, promotes healthy gums & teeth & prevents sickness by increasing the immune system.	Kidneys, liver, citrus, berries, potato skins, pine needles, peppers. We're genetically mutated & are the only mammals that can't produce vitamin C.	Critical	.06g
D	Aids in bone & tooth development & sustains muscle & nerve performance.	Sun, cold water fish, mushrooms, eggs & meat.	High	.00005g
E	Assists with good circulation, blood clotting & healing.	Stomach, liver, seeds, nuts, whole grains, leafy vegetables, crab & rockfish.	High	.01g
K	Helps blood clotting, without it you'd bleed to death from a minor laceration.	Stomach contents (from foliage eaters), liver, milk & edible dark leafy plants.	Critical	.00008g

- Carbohydrates – Strictly speaking, carbohydrates in today's society, are our main source of energy. They are mostly found in non-meat products like honey, sugars, fruits, cereal grains, and root and stem tubers; although some meat products like beef, insects, dog and horse contain carbs as well.
- Fats – The human body is incredible. If you eat too much or certain foods, the body literally has sacks or bags to store it in. These are located near the neck, around the arms, the breasts, around the waste, in the back and throughout the legs. When in need, the body burns these bags of fat first as a source fuel. On a side note, I always tell folks if the end does come, I'm hooking up with a fat chick, the fatter the better since she'll (a) have plenty of reserves and, therefore, require a lesser amount of substance I have to provide for her, and (b) if I ever start starving... well, let's just say I'll also have plenty of reserves also.

Fat molecules are the opposite of carbohydrates and mostly found in animal tissue, with the exception of a few plants like mushrooms and nuts. Wild game, of course, would have a much less fat content than domesticated livestock; whereas, cow and humans (especially Americans) would have a much higher fat percentage than, say, an antelope or deer. The best time to kill any animal, wild or domesticated, is at the end of summer, just before winter, after the animal has had all year to build and store up its mass (fat) for the colder months ahead. Conversely, in spring, the animal has most likely burnt off any fat reserves to keep warm during winter.

- Protein – Proteins serve a couple of purposes in the human body, (a) they're broken down into essential amino acids, (b) help to build muscle content, which in return helps us to perform work or labor using the lesser amounts of energy, and (c) to provide us with a food supply during starvation. Once the fat content is all burned up, the body literally eats its own muscle. Proteins can be found in any animal meat, eggs, fish, milk, nuts and grains.

These 3 organic compounds are critical in producing energy during the aftermath, again something that you've never had to consider or prioritize for with society providing for you. In fact, many of you have grown up believing that these 3 things are actually bad for you. The side table contains animals that 'should' be prevalent after the collapse and their calorie, protein, fat and carb counts.

Meat Nutritional Values (per 110 grams)				
Type	Calories	Protein	Fat	Carbs
Rabbit	125.4	24.5 g	2.6 g	0 g
Beef	400	36 g	30 g	25 g
Deer	132	25.1 g	2.6 g	0 g
Antelope	128.7	24.6 g	2.7 g	9 g
Bear	179.3	22.1 g	9.1 g	3 g
Donkey	130.9	24.8 g	2.9 g	7 g
Horse	143	29 g	4 g	14 g
Raccoon	232.1	27.1 g	12.9 g	1 g
Possum	243	33.6 g	11.6 g	0 g
Chicken	160	28 g	7 g	0 g
Pheasant	146.3	25.9 g	3.3 g	0 g
Quail	134.2	24.5 g	3.8 g	0 g
Turkey	173.8	22.3 g	7.8 g	0 g
Lamb	250	30 g	14 g	0 g
Pork	171.6	24.2 g	8.36 g	0 g
Fish	130	23 g	4 g	0 g
Frog	80.3	18.5 g	.33 g	0 g
Turtle	97.9	22 g	.66 g	0 g
Dog	43.23	20.9 g	22.2 g	.11 g
Cat	166	69 g	15.7 g	.3 g
Squirrel	130	23.1 g	3.8 g	0 g
Rat	102	66 g	7 g	8.8 g
Human	190	17 g	25 g	0 g
Insect	475	70 g	10 g	10 g

- Minerals – Besides elements like hydrogen, carbon, nitrogen and of course oxygen, we also need mineral chemical elements like calcium, sodium, iron, potassium, magnesium, sulfur, phosphorus, zinc, iodine, chlorine and chromium. Remember when mom used to say drink all your milk (calcium), eat the rest of your potatoes (potassium) or finish off that bowl of pig blood (iron)? Ok, so my mother was a bit different than most. In addition, salt water may be boiled or evaporated away to produce sodium, and eyeballs also contain a lot of salt ("now eat all your eyeballs before leaving the table son!").

Type	Function	Sources	Importance	RDA
Potassium	Form clots merging adenosine triphosphate-sodium.	Legumes, root & stem tubers, tomatoes & bananas.	Critical	4.7g
Chlorine	Required to produce hydrochloric stomach acid.	Salt.	Medium	2.3g
Sodium	Another electrolyte like potassium.	Salt, sea vegetables, salt water fish, milk & spinach.	Critical	2g
Calcium	Helps the muscle, heart & digestive systems.	Milk, fish with bones, green leafy vegetables, nuts & seeds.	Critical	1.0g
Magnesium	Break down adenosine triphosphate for bones.	Nuts, beans & cocoa.	Medium	.4g
Iron	Helps prevent anemia by processing proteins, enzymes & hemoglobin.	Muscle, leafy green vegetables, fish, eggs, dried fruits, beans & whole grains.	High	.008g

In my personal opinion, sodium or salt is going to be the most problematic to acquire, especially for those living inland and without access to sea-derived goods. So much so that it will be similar in value to precious metals like gold, silver and even platinum is today. People who derive the bulk of their diets from commercially prepared foods purchased at grocery stores or restaurants have virtually no idea how much salt they currently consume or need and, therefore, must find when the shit hits the fan. In fact, again, they're led to believe that salt is bad for them, which is mind blowing. An ordinary round box of Morton's Salt is almost 2lbs worth, 50lbs of salt represents a little more than 30 boxes of salt, which equates to 'maybe' a year's supply for one person.

Salt intake is almost as important as water intake for the human body, not to mention its importance in preserving foods as well. Sodium is a primary electrolyte in the body and helps retain water and stave off dehydration. Today we don't have to worry about getting the proper amount of our daily needed sodium because almost everything we purchase is packaged or canned with added salt. If anything, you now need to worry about too much salt and the resulting high blood pressure, which has created the current misconception and false notion that humans don't need salt in their diet. But what happens when all the cans are used up and the restaurants are gone? You'll have to find your own sources. Desalination of saltwater for potable water (discussed in the last chapter) and the byproduct, sea salt, is a good source, but it requires living by, trading with, or even traveling to the sea. In the meantime, try to eat plenty of any and all of the following foods which contain higher than normal sodium levels: eyeballs, shellfish, prunes, bananas, pineapples, celery, parsley, eggs, apples, figs, berries, peaches, chili peppers, milk, apricots, pears, melons, tomatoes, cinnamon, carrots, fish, dates, avocados, citrus, basil, ginger and beets.

MEDICAL

- Cuts and scrapes – Again, the smallest cut can and will get infected and possibly cause zombism or permanent death without being properly cleaned. Just like the nose, mouth and eyes, an open wound becomes an open door to bacteria, viruses and any other living dead like microscopic entity. If the wound is open enough so that it won't stop bleeding on its own, you'll need to stitch or cauterize to close.
- Punctures – In Medieval times a puncture would most likely result in death. Punctures push bacteria and germs into the meat/bloodstream of the body and can't be cleaned with topical antiseptics. Cauterizing the wound is one option if carried out immediately. Ingestion of Penicillin is another; although, unless you have your own, you'd probably die faster than it would take to make a batch (typically 2-3 weeks). That leaves amputation, which is how my great, great... stopped the spread of the infection in his day.
- Stitches – Stitches or suturing a wound will most likely become a daily occurrence in a group of idiots, for the one person who knows how to do it. You'll need a couple items including a suture needle which is a bent needle about the size of a thumbnail tip; (if you don't have a suturing needle you can use a regular needle; but you'll need to pinch the skin together when working;) suturing thread or regular thread; (separated floss works well if you don't have suturing thread;) hemostats, tweezers, latex gloves (if possible), antiseptic (iodine, rubbing alcohol, hydrogen peroxide), and a container of boiling water. If you don't have any of these items, you can use superglue to close the wound. Actually, this is what superglue was originally invented and used for during the Vietnam War. If you're going to take this route, though, don't apply it into the wound; clean the wound with antiseptic, pinch the skin closed, and topically apply a thin layer to 'bridge' the gap. No kidding.

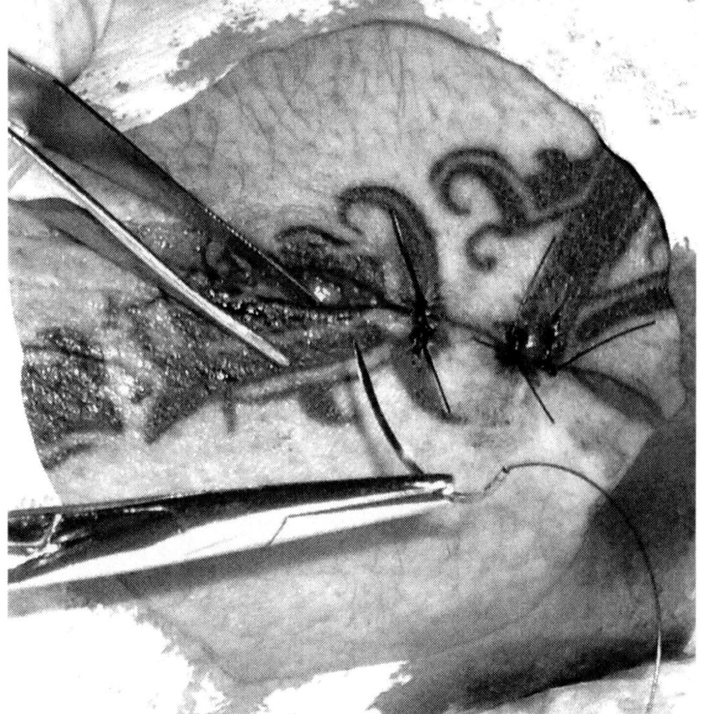

1. Sterilize all tools and materials in boiling water (even the thread).
2. Thread the needle with and sterilize the area around the cut with an antiseptic.
3. Place the suture needle facing down in the tip of the hemostats as far back as possible on the needle so that you can get as much needle through the hole before resetting in the hemostats.
4. Puncture the skin about 1/4in from the opening edge, half way down the opening, bisecting the wound (closing the middle first) with each suture.
5. Push the needle through completely, making sure not to puncture the muscular tissue.
6. Grab the other side of the needle being careful not to touch the tip (it will break off) and pull all the way through the opening, leaving about 1in of thread left outside.
7. Repeat steps 3 and 4, puncturing the skin straight across the opening, this time from below, and again about 1/4in out from the opening edge.
8. Again, push the needle through as much as possible and grab from the other side, being careful not to touch the tip, pulling all the way through the opening.

9. Now place the hemostat in the middle of and directly above the wound, loop the thread around the tip with your other hand, open the hemostat, grab onto the leftover 1in of thread and pull through the loop just tight enough so that the skin on both sides meet but doesn't buckle. Repeat the knot 4 or 5 more times (or as many times as necessary) in opposite directions.
10. Cut any extra thread from the knots down to about 1/4in so they don't interfere with the next sutures.
11. It's important to move the knot entirely over to one side, so that it's touching the skin on that side. This way when you remove the suture, you can cut the thread on this side between the knot and skin and pull out the least amount of thread possible. The larger portion of thread on top along with the knot is most likely covered with bacteria, so you don't want to go pulling bacteria into and through the tissue.
12. Repeat the procedure again starting from the middle (or quarter in this case) and so on and so forth until the entire wound is closed up or the sutures are 1/4in or so apart.
13. Remove the suture as described in step 11 after about a week.

- Cauterizing – Placing a fire-heated piece of metal over an injury is a painful way to go, but cauterizing will help stop the bleeding, kill any lingering bacteria in the wound and close the laceration entirely, especially in the case of extreme blood loss or amputation:

1. Prepare the patient by giving him/her some type of pain reliever, even the consumption of alcohol will ease the situation they're about to undergo. At the very least, place a stick or piece of wood between the teeth to bite down on, avoiding additional injury to the tongue, mouth or teeth.
2. The flatter the metal object the better, making it able to cover a larger area at once. Boil the instrument to kill any bacteria; then heat it in a fire or other heat source until hot, but not red hot.
3. Place the metal instrument firmly onto the wound but not forcibly, for durations of 2 seconds at a time. You want to melt the skin together, while coagulating (clotting) the blood in order to close the wound but not kill the healthy tissue. If held on too long it will act like plastic, cool and stick to the tool, which is bad.

- Tourniquet – By wrapping and tying off a belt, rope, T-shirt or other device a few inches above (towards the heart) the damaged area, you restrict and minimize blood loss in excessive or severe wounds.
- Snake bite – The chance that you'll survive a global cataclysm only to be killed by a poisonous or venomous snake is preposterous. Even today, with a population of over 300 million, (4 times larger than what it will be after the collapse), there are less than a dozen fatalities due to snake venom poisoning per year, according to the Department of Public Health. Actually, there are only a few types of snakes that even call for any special action, other than ignoring:

a. The Copperhead: Highly visible by its off-color copper or rust head. Sometimes, however, the entire body is a similar copper color in some species making classification difficult. Copperheads inhabit a region that runs from Northern Mexico throughout the Southern and Eastern United States.
b. Cottonmouth or Water Moccasin: Distinguished by its rich dark black color. Cottonmouths are often found in or near bodies of water or swamps in the southeast.
c. The Rattlesnake: Known for the distinct rattling sound it makes to warn off anyone from coming too close. Typically, the rattlesnake will vibrate its tail at the first sight of a would-be attacker; unfortunately, the snake's eyesight isn't great, and humans tend to move through the brush quickly and clumsily, so the alarm isn't often sounded or heard until we're right on top of the snake. Rattlesnakes have a large range, roaming throughout the Americas from Argentina up into Canada.

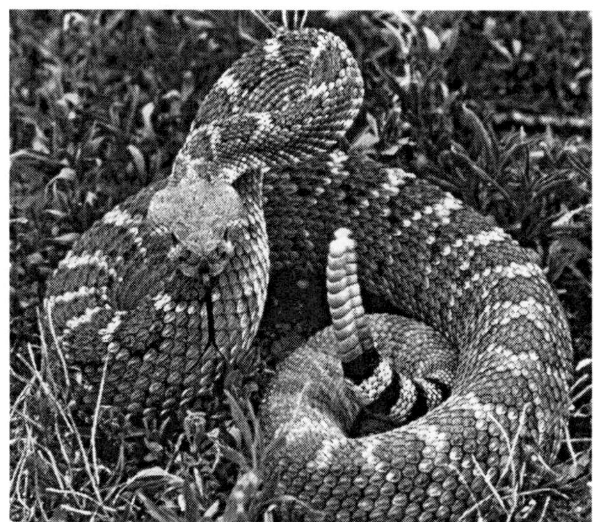

All snakebites, or any type of bite for that matter, is survivable and therefore ~~can~~ will be treated by you since there won't be any anti-venom accessible/available. The last thing you'll want to do is go sucking the venom out with your mouth, since the fasted way for any chemical to enter your bloodstream, besides injection, is orally. You see, there are many pores and glands in your mouth that will soak up the poison for you, even without swallowing.

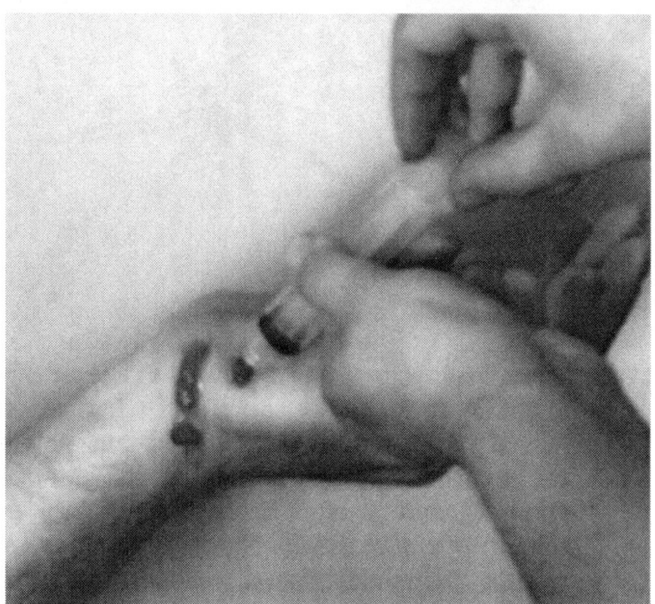

1. The first thing you will want to do is remove yourself from the situation. The snake bit you for no other reason than you got too close to it; so don't worry about it chasing you, it doesn't want to have anything to do with you. On this note, when hiking around, try not to walk past anything that's closer than 3ft, as most snakes have a less than 3ft attack or lunging radius.
2. One red blood cell will travel from the heart to the foot for example, and back in 2-3 minutes. If done immediately, you can, however, suck the poison or venom-soaked blood out of the bitten area with a syringe (without the needle of course) by placing the nipple of the syringe in each puncture and steadily withdrawing the plunger, repeating the process 2-3 times.
3. Quickly restrict return flow to the heart by tying a series of loose-fitting tourniquets above the bite, starting from the area closest to the heart, working your way away towards the bite. This will allow for much smaller amounts of the poison to make it to your heart at a time, so that the heart doesn't receive such a shock at once.
4. Lastly, don't panic and run, this will only increase your blood rate and dump more of the chemical into your heart. Stay calm, keep the bitten limb lower than the heart, remove any tight-fitting clothes or jewelry in preparation

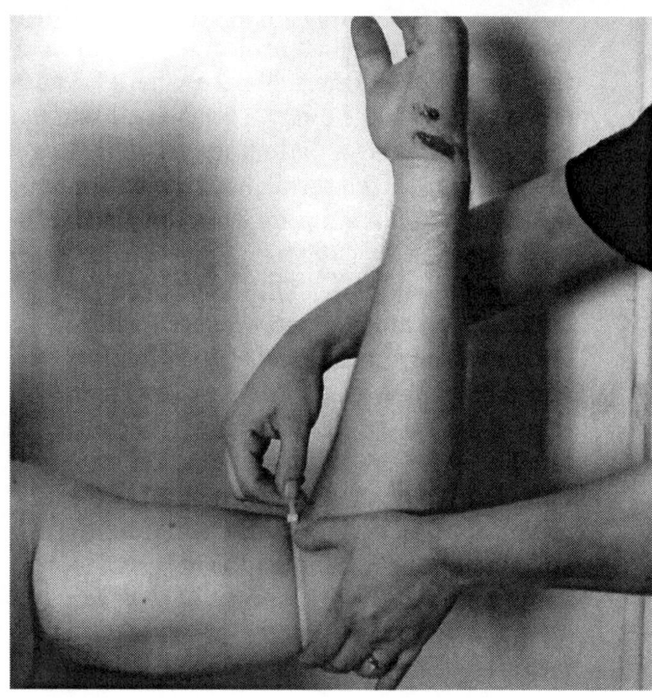

for extreme swelling and ride out the pain (which will start in as little as 5-10 minutes) as comfortable as possible which shouldn't last more than 24 hours.

5. Lastly, take a lot of pain reliever and swelling-reducing medications (which I'll go over below). Although the incident most likely won't be fatal, I know again from personal experience (what can I say, I've been through a lot) that without drugs it is extremely painful to the point you'll wish you were dead.

- Spider bites – There are many poisonous spiders in the United States, but none that are truly 'deadly.' Some of the ones that will cause the most damage or pain are:

a. Brown Recluse: A semi-small (about the size of a quarter overall) light brown, small bodied, long-legged spider with a dark violin shape design on its back. Its bite often leads to eventual nausea, vomiting, fever, rashes and sometimes skin decay around the bitten area. Often the victim doesn't even know they've been bitten until the symptoms set in.

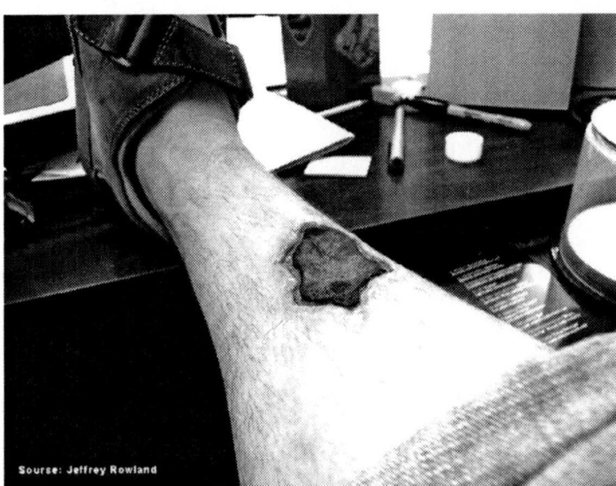

b. Black Widow: A small (about the size of a nickel overall) dark black, shiny, large-bodied, short-legged spider with two bright red dots or a bright red hourglass shape design on its stomach (in females). Its bite often leads to acute pain around the bitten region usually within 20 minutes, muscle cramps, abdominal cramps, weakness and tremors.

- Scorpion sting – No North American scorpion is fatal. In fact, I was on a project once for 3 months in the deserts of Northern Mexico where I was getting stung almost twice a day, every day. I compare the feeling to sticking a 9v battery on your tongue, but the sensation is felt throughout the entire body for a few hours. In a way, aside from the actual sting, the poison is actually euphoric.
- Centipede sting – The centipede is another misunderstood insect whose sting can only cause swelling, discomfort and pain, which usually doesn't last more than 8 hours or so. This one I became familiar with in Saudi Arabia. On that note, I've been stung or bitten by all of the above species several times while doing sustainability projects (rattlesnake twice, a few centipede stings, dozens of scorpion stings, a few black widow bites, even a tarantula bite) as well as who knows

what else, and I'm still here to talk about it. My best description of each is pain and confusion, but nothing plenty of Ibuprofen, alcohol and aspirin won't help.

- Burn – Unfortunately, there isn't much that can be done for a severe burn. I mention it here more for a source of what not to do: Don't apply any oils or butter, as it will only trap in the heat. Don't cover or bandage. Don't remove any embedded clothing or other materials melted to the skin, as this will facilitate bleeding. Never pop blisters. Rinse or submerge the area with cold water and take plenty of pain relievers. There are basically 3 types of burns:

1. First degree: The first layer of skin is reddish with some small blistering. Most sunburns fall in this category.
2. Second degree: The burn has burnt through the first layer and has affected the second layer of skin, accompanied by swelling, blisters and some first layer skin loss.
3. Third degree: A third degree burn is, of course, the most severe, having burnt through all 3 layers of skin. However, since the burn has usually destroyed the underlying tissue and nerves as well, third degree burns are often the least painful, sometimes even painless.

- Acid or chemical burn – Acids and most chemicals are water-based and should be washed off with water, pee or any water-based liquid available immediately, in order to halt the burning process. Otherwise, the acid will continue burning through and down into the skin as long as it's left in contact with the flesh.
- Injections – I'm amazed at the amount of people that don't even know how to give a shot. There are several types of injection methods, but basically we'll only ever need to use the IM or intramuscular method for vaccines, insulin, medications or drugs. Giving yourself or someone else an IM shot is very simple. It can be in any muscle on the body, but I prefer the butt because of its girth and you don't have to hunt around for it.

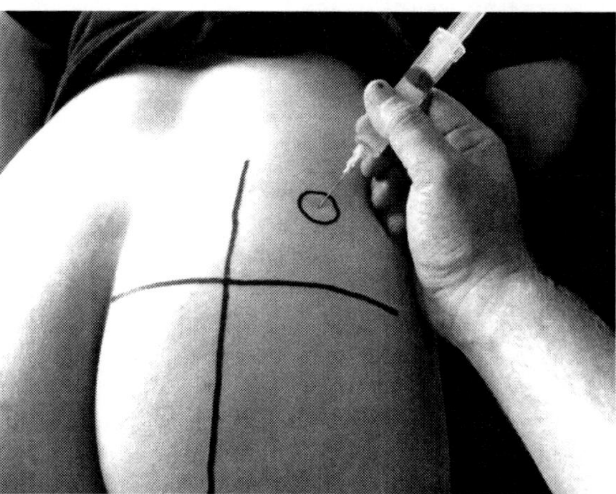

1. First, divide one cheek up into four quadrants by drawing an imaginary cross from the bottom center of the cheek up to the hip bone and from the side of the leg to the intergluteal cleft (butt crack people).
2. Now do the same for the upper outer quadrant. The center of this second bulls-eye, if you will, is your injection target/point, which is far enough from the sciatic nerve to be administered safely.
3. Sterilize the area with an antiseptic and load the syringe by sticking the needle into the medicine vile (it typically has a small rubber lid on top) and withdraw the plunger until the proper cc count is met. Keeping the needle pointing up, tap on the syringe until any bubbles have floated to the top and expel them by pressing slightly on the plunger.
4. Place your wrist on the buttocks of the patient and while holding the syringe at the lowest part of the fluid tube, quickly firmly punch the needle through the flesh into the muscle.
5. Once the needle is in the muscle, remove the plunger slightly so that you know you haven't hit a blood vessel. If you did, it will look like red dye has entered the tube;

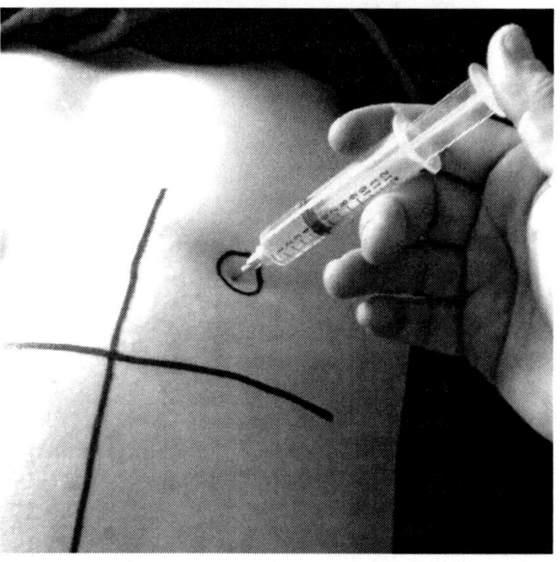

in which case, simply remove the needle just slightly and attempt to remove the plunger again. Repeat this until you don't get any more blood return.

6. Administer the medication by depressing the plunger slowly and smoothly.
7. Once the liquid is fully dispersed, swiftly pull the needle out of the muscle and gently rub, slap or smack the butt on females only (personal tip, ok so you should know me by now).

- Shock – Shock occurs when an insufficient amount of blood reaches the brain. In treating many of the above conditions, you'll need to watch out for signs that the patient is going into shock. Shock can be caused by an allergic reaction, a lack of food or water, a loss of a substantial amount of blood or severe burns. Symptoms may include confusion, bluish lips, rapid breathing and clammy skin. Without blood to the brain the person will die, so it's critical to stop the bleeding and then arrange the person's body so that it's higher than the head, allowing the blood to fall/flow towards the brain via gravity.
- CPR – Cardiopulmonary Resuscitation is a first aid maneuver performed on unconscious victims who aren't breathing in order to stimulate breath and continuous heartbeat. First check for breath and heartbeat by placing your ear to the mouth or nose, and finger (not thumb) to the neck artery or wrist.

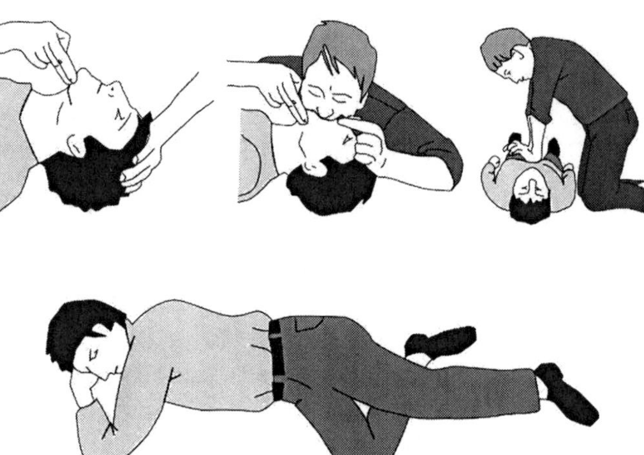

1. Locate and place the palm of your hand on the compression area. This spot will be located in the middle of the victim's chest about 2in up from the bottom of the ribcage, usually in the middle of both nipples. The same rule, however, won't apply to large-breasted women (or men), since the nipples are, of course, much lower.
2. Put your other hand on top of the first with your fingers interlaced.
3. Lock your elbows and press down firmly, compressing the chest at least 2in 30 times in an 18-20 second period, or at a rate of at least 100 compressions per minute. Make sure to allow the chest to completely recoil before administering the next compression.

NOTE: You may experience popping and snapping sounds or sensations, you're not breaking the patient's ribs; this is natural, so continue. The patient is dying; no need worry about making them worse at this point.

4. After 30 compressions, lift the neck, tilting the head back and the chin up, opening the victim's airway, pinch off the nose and blow into the mouth making sure to keep an air seal between your mouth and his.
5. The breath should be large enough for the chest to rise; if so, repeat a second time, if not, reposition the head to open the airway and try again. Regardless, however, if the second breath raises the chest or not, repeat the next set of compressions, continuing the process of 30 compressions to 2 breaths until the patient regains consciousness.
6. After a few minutes of this, check the victim for breathing and heartbeat. If after 3-4 minutes no heartbeat or breath is felt/sensed, the patient has flat-lined and you can try electrocution (defibrillation) to stimulate the heart to bring the poor sucker back to his pitiful life.
7. Keep in mind, at this point the person is dead for all intents and purposes; nothing you can do short of shooting the guy in the head is going to make the situation worse. So I would personally try anything, this includes pounding on or punching the chest and electrocution:

Defibrillation – The process of electrocution to restart a heart is actually a viable one in that our body and brain start, run and stop due to the presence or lack of electrical current.

1. Since I highly doubt you'll have access to a medical defib unit, we'll have to use a vehicle (an arc welder would also work). Start the truck (a truck alternator puts out more amperage than a car); disconnect the battery and place a set of jumper cables directly on the positive and negative terminals of the alternator.
2. Rub some Vaseline or petroleum jelly (water, if you have neither) in a 3in area on the left side of the body, towards the front bottom left side of the ribs.
3. Do the same on the right about 3in above the right nipple.

4. Pull out a flap of skin on the lubricated left side and clip the positive cable clamp directly onto it.
5. Redline the engine's RPMs and with one hand, and no other body part touching the victim, briefly touch the teeth of the negative jumper cable clamp to the lubricated area above the right nipple. This will send a current of 50-80amps straight through the heart from directly under and to the left up through the upper right quadrant just like a defibrillator does at 60amps, hopefully restarting the heart.
6. Repeat step 5 as necessary (or until crispy).

- Heimlich Maneuver – The Heimlich Maneuver is a procedure one can perform on another to dislodge an object or morsel of food from the throat or esophagus when a person is choking.

1. Encourage the victim to continue coughing; this alone may dislodge the item by itself.
2. Position yourself on the backside of the individual, placing your fist on their belly button.
3. Place your other hand over and around your fist and quickly push in and up, twisting your fist wrist thumb upwards. This is known as the 'J' thrust as the movement mimics the shape of a letter "J."
4. Continue this motion several times with enough force to slightly lift the person up onto their toes.
5. If the person looses consciousness in the process, lie them down on their side and, using a flashlight to see and a long pair of hemostats, attempt to gain physical access to the object orally.
6. If the item still can't be removed, perform an emergency tracheotomy as described below.
7. Once the item is finally removed physically or surgically the patient may need to be resuscitated.

- Emergency Tracheotomy – If a throat obstruction can't be removed, coughing has ceased and the Heimlich Maneuver isn't working, you'll need to perform a quick tracheotomy:

1. Locate the crevice between the Adam's apple (thyroid cartilage) and the lower Adam's apple (cichloid cartilage) and make an incision horizontally about 1/2in length and 1/2in deep.

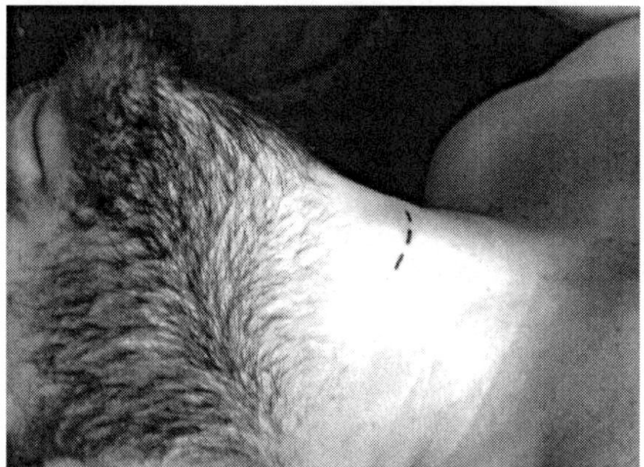

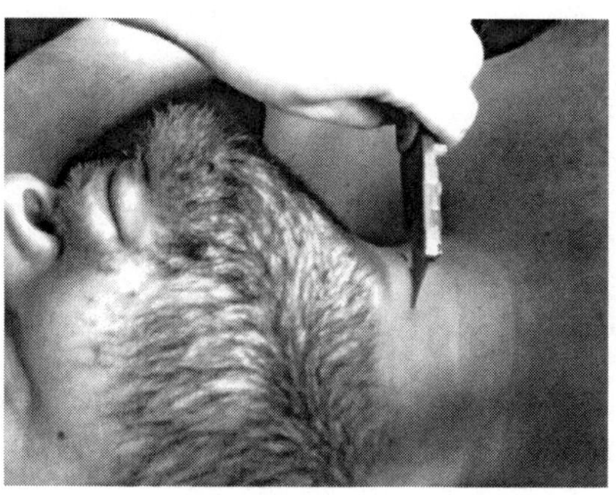

2. Pinch the incision open or place your finger inside to open it.
3. Separate the neck muscles vertically between the fourth and fifth tracheal rings and insert a sterilized tube about 1/2in to 1in like a hollowed-out pen.

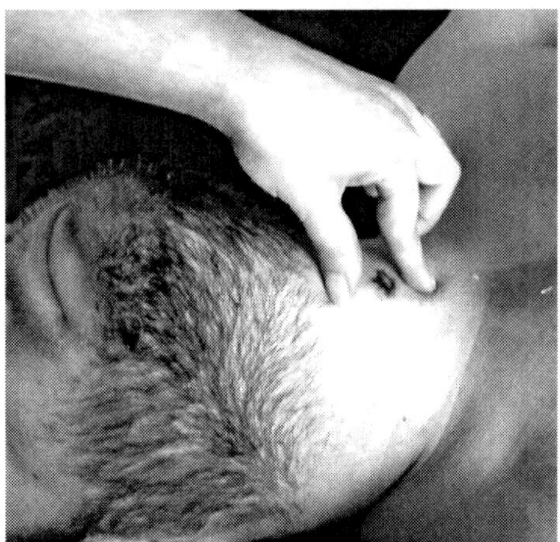
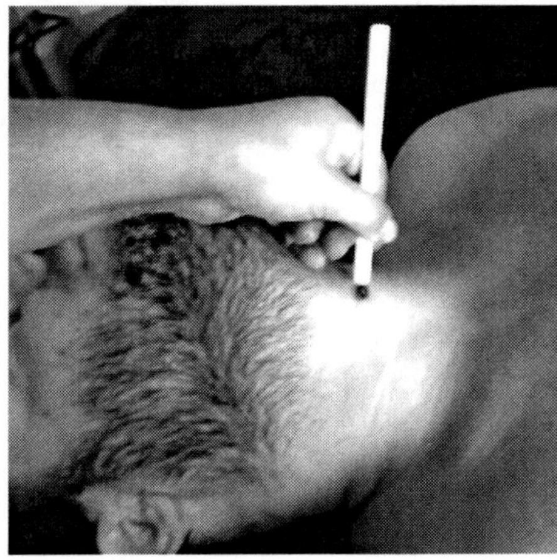
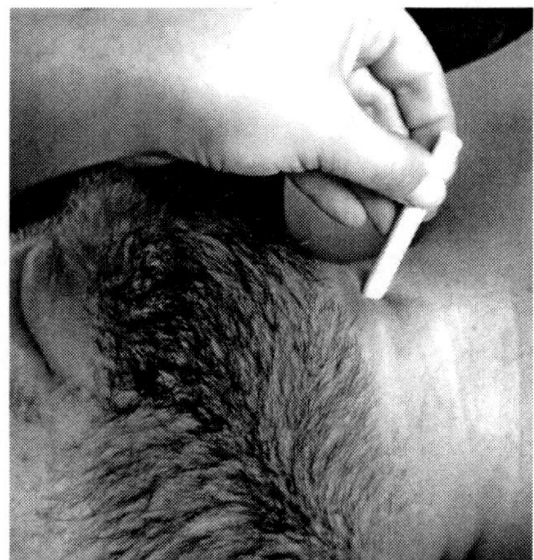

4. Blow into the tube with a few quick breaths of air, followed by a breath of air every 5 seconds. You'll see the chest rise and collapse. Eventually, the victim should regain consciousness and begin breathing on his own with some difficulty.
5. Perform CPR if after 30 seconds to a minute there is no response. If they regain consciousness and breathing you can refrain from blowing into the tube and/or performing CPR. It's important to prevent the victim from panicking and attempting to remove the tube. Although the life is saved, the patient isn't out of the woods yet; the lodged obstacle still needs to be removed.

- Casting – Casting is the process of binding two broken bones back together in order to minimize movement of the area to help facilitate melding or re-growth of the bones. First, make sure the bone is actually broken before casting. There are a few signs to figure this out without the use of an x-ray machine: Was there an actual snap? Is the area sore, swelling or tender with bruising? Of course, if the bone is actually protruding from the skin (compound fracture) it's broken.

1. You'll first need to reset the bones so that they're once again properly aligned. Do this by pulling the two pieces away from each other (as tendons tend to constrict the pieces so they overlap) and resetting them in a natural-looking position. On a compound fracture you'll need to sterilize the area, make an incision through the tissue only, just forward of the puncture, with a sterilized scalpel or box cutter and reset the pieces by hand, suturing up the puncture and incision afterward.
2. Prepare a mix of plaster by pouring Elmer's glue or any type of white wood glue into a bowl.

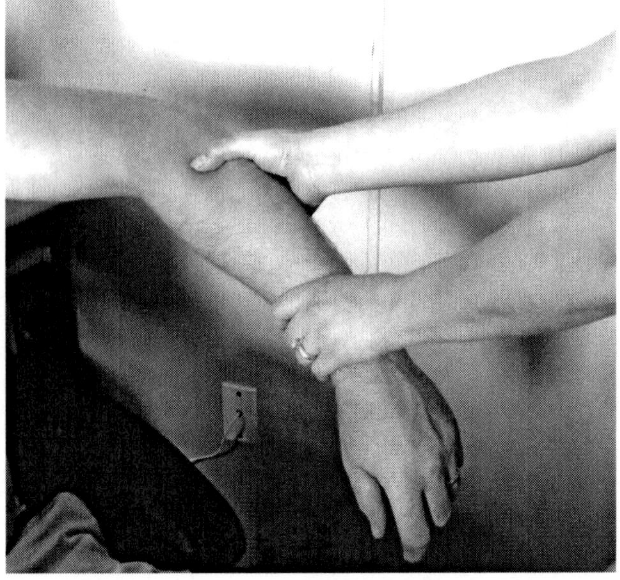

3. Then add (2) cups of flour and (1) cup of water.
4. Stir until the mix is thick and without lumps.
5. If you have a roll of bandage, unravel it and submerge it in the mix. If not, cut (don't tear, it'll roll up and not lay flat) a cotton T-shirt or thermal shirt into long strips and submerge in the paste.
6. Coat the entire area to be cast in Vaseline or petroleum jelly, especially areas with hair.
7. Remove the bandage or strips of cotton from the mix and wrap the entire area with one layer. The mix will take about 15-20 minutes to dry. Just keep the patient calm, relaxed and the cast still.

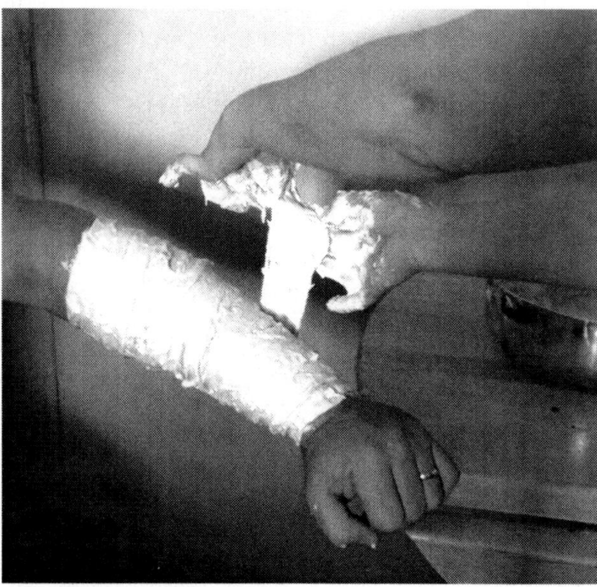

8. Once the first layer dries, repeat for a second and third layer.
9. Remove the cast in about 6-8 weeks by cutting with a pair of strong scissors.

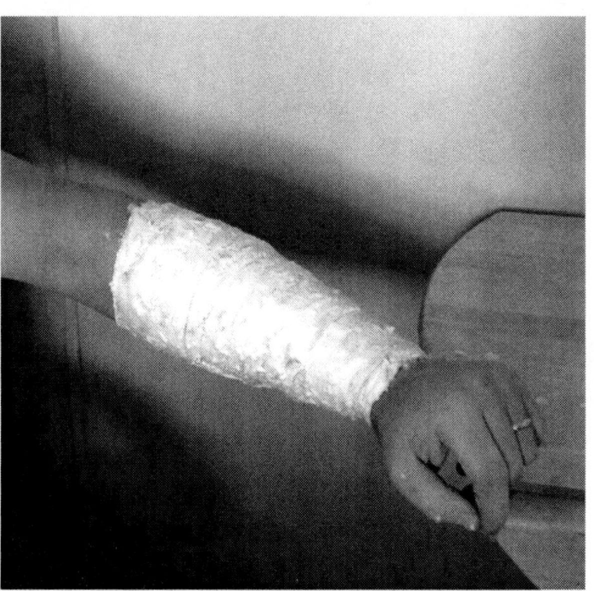

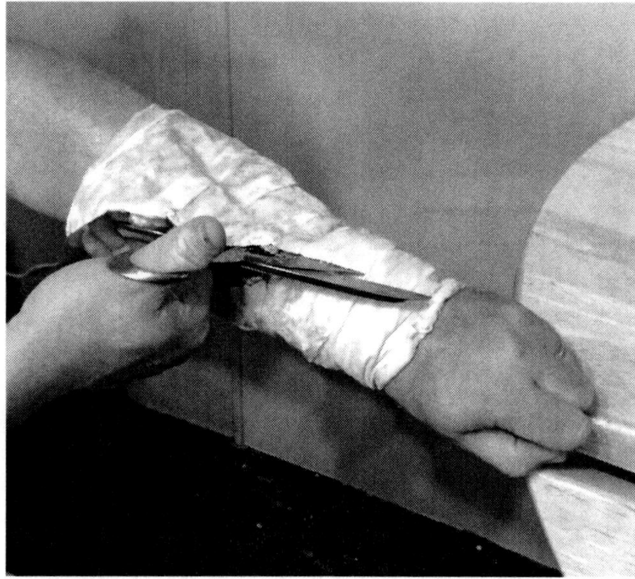

SURGICAL

The only 2 surgeries that I've performed are on a swollen and infected appendix (appendicitis) out in the middle of the Amazon jungle in order to stave off a burst and infection, and an emergency tracheotomy. So that's really all I can comment and thoroughly instruct on here. But I advise you to research other surgical methods.

- Appendectomy – The victim will know if his appendix is infected if there's a sudden and sharp pain around the belly button. This extreme pain will travel down and to the right towards the inner groan area. He may be nauseous, have a temperature, and the area under duress will be swollen. A good test to see if it's appendicitis and not just cramps or food poisoning is to lay flat, stretched out and cough or laugh hard. If there's pain that's relieved when contracting into the fetal position, it's probably appendicitis. The condition is more predominant in males in their late teens to early twenties and does require a surgical procedure known as an appendectomy to remove the appendix:

1. Locate the affected area which should be 2/3 over from the belly button to just above and in front of the right hip bone and just outside of the stomach. In other words, if you draw a line from the belly button to just above and in front of the right hip bone, and mark 2/3 from the belly button, that's the point. Another way to pinpoint the spot is the *333* rule. A 3rd down, a 3rd to the right making a 3in incision. The incision should be diagonal to the torso and slightly arched, angled out and up towards the hip following the curve of the belly. Usually there's a bump or rise in the exact area caused by inflammation which can greatly help you to locate the incision point, but at least with the *333* method you're in the right area.
2. Sterilize the entire area with a topical antiseptic.
3. You'll be cutting through 4 layers of the abdominal cavity (skin, fascia, muscle and the peritoneum or the inner wall or membrane).

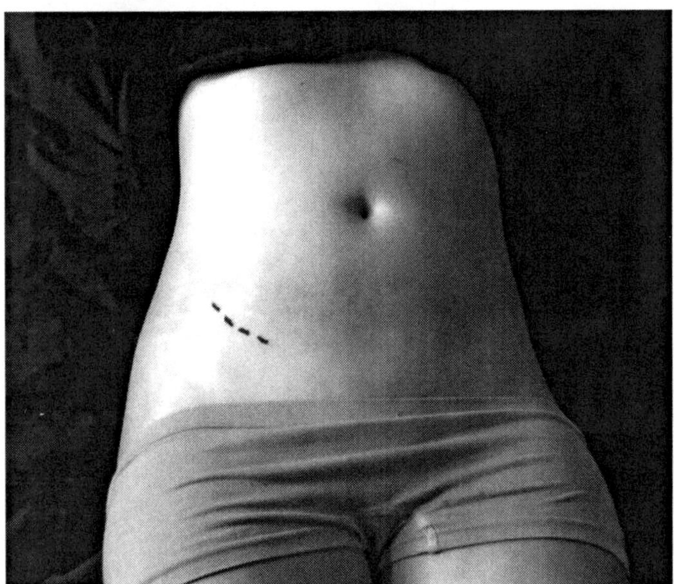

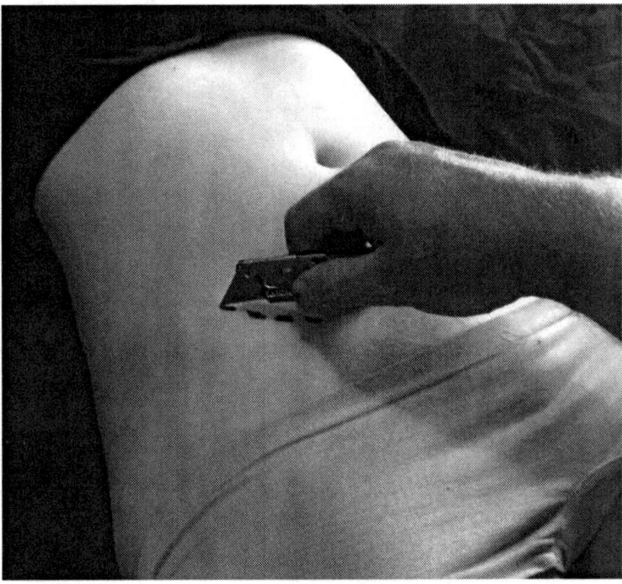

4. Once inside, separate the incision as much as possible with retractors to view the internal organs. You should see the sack connected to the very beginning of the large intestine, curled up like a finger about 1/2in-3/4in thick by 4in or so long when stretched out.
5. Pull the appendix out through the incision point.

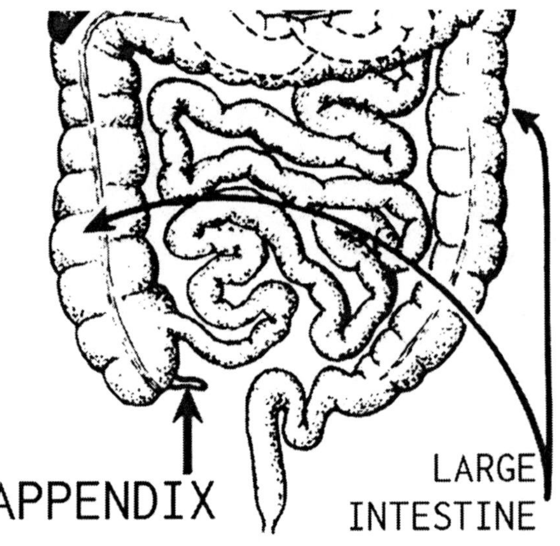

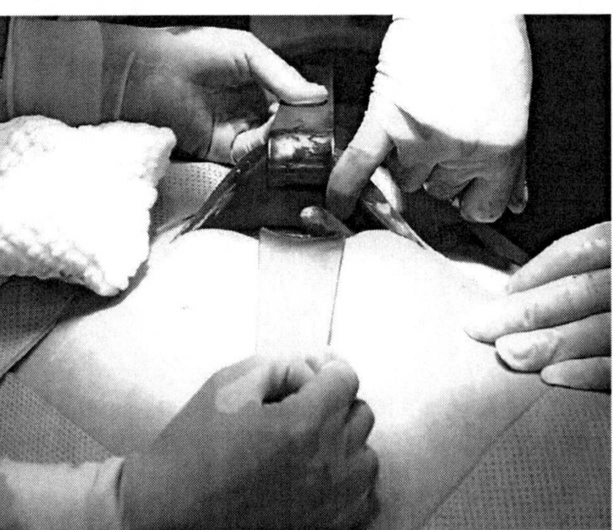

6. Tie a sterilized piece of floss around the bottom or base where it connects to the intestine or clamp off with hemostats.
7. Cut off the appendix just above the string or clamp.
8. Sterilize the cut area with an antiseptic, cauterize the cut and remove the clamp or string.
9. Close up and cauterize each layer, finally stitching up the skin as described above.

- Amputation – Amputating a limb or appendage is actually a relatively simple ordeal; that's why throughout history and wars military surgeons would prefer to amputate rather than surgically save the limb, which is a much more time-consuming ordeal. When to amputate should be determined based on the severity of the damaged area in comparison to the rate of blood loss. If the wound(s) are so major that the patient would bleed out and die before surgical corrections and/or sutures can be made, amputation may be the best option. Either way, if you're going to amputate, it needs to be done quickly before gangrene (decomposition and infection) sets in, which is usually between 2-3 days.

1. Prepare the patient by giving him/her some type of pain reliever in large doses to ease the situation they're about to undergo. At the very least, place a stick or piece of wood between the teeth to bite down on, avoiding additional injury to the tongue, mouth or teeth.
2. Sterilize the area properly along with any cutting or suturing tools and material as needed.
3. A joint is the best location to make the amputation, if the damaged area isn't too far away. This is simply due to the fact that the amputation can be conducted without the need to cut through bone.
4. Place a tourniquet around the limb a few inches up (towards the heart) from where the cut will take place. This will minimize further blood loss to the area.
5. Now the correct 'surgical' way to perform the following feat is to make an incision with a scalpel or, in our case, a sterilized box cutter, cutting through the skin, veins, artery(s), muscle(s), tendons, nerves and finally sawing through the bone(s) (radius and ulna, if it's a forearm) if needed. That said, the entire process can and, in the case of battle-fatigued army surgeons, has been performed by simply hacking through the entire limb with a hack or bone saw.
6. Lastly, cauterize the entire cut surface as described above. Sealing up the artery(s) and veins in the process. If you have a tight enough tourniquet in place, nothing should move or retract much.

MEDICATIONS

- Ibuprofen is a must, it relieves pain, tenderness, swelling and stiffness, reduces fever, headaches, muscle aches, arthritis, toothaches and backaches by halting the production of the substance that causes pain, fever and inflammation. When digging through cabinets, Ibuprofen may be labeled under any of the following names:

Addaprin	Dolgesic	IBU-200	Ibu-Tab	Nuprin	Saleto	Ultraprin
Advil	Genpril	Ibifon	Ibuprohm	Provil	Samson 8	Uni-Pro
Arthritis IB	Haltran	Ibren	Menadol	QProfen	Sup Pain	WalProfen
Cap-Profen	IB Pro	Ibu	Motrin	Rufen	Tab-Profen	

- Acetaminophen does all of the above and is known by its brand names:

Acephen	Arthritis MS	Dolono	Halenol	Masophen	Pediacare	T-Painol	Uni-Ace
Aceta	BF-Paradac	Ed-APAP	Infantaire	Meda Cap	Pediapap	Tactinal	Uniserts
Actamin	Bactimicina	Elixsure	Liquiprin	Neopap	Q-Nol	Tempra	Vitapap
Adprin B	Bromo Seltzer	Feverall	Little Fevers	Pain-Eze	Redutemp	Triaminic	XS
Anacin	Panadol	Genapap	Lopap	Panadol	Ridenol	Tycolene	
Apacet, Apara	Comtrex	Genebs	Mapap	Panex	S-T Febrol	Tylenol	
Apra	Conacetol	Gericet	Mardol	Paramol	Silapap	Tylophen	

- Aspirin is another pain reliever and fever reducer that also reduces swelling and prevents heart attacks. Some common names include:

Acuprin	Aspidrox	Easprin	Fasprin	Magnaprin	Norwich	Uni-Tren
Anacin	Aspir	Ecotrin	Genacote	m. Aspirin	Ridiprin	Valomag
Aspirin	Bayer	Ecpirin	Gennin	Migralex	Sloprin	0-Order
Ascriptin	Bufferin	Empirin	Genprin	Miniprin	St. Joseph	Zorprin
Aspergum	Buffex	Entercote	Halfprin	Minitabs	Uni-Buff	

- Morphine is what's known as a narcotic pain reliever that completely dulls the pain receivers and perception center in the brain. It was used extensively in WWII and Vietnam and is the alkaloid found in opium which is the dried sap of the poppy plant (Papaver somniferum). Poppy plants are a weed that normally grows wild in most fields around the world. It's a rather beautiful bluish-green to green podded plant with a long slender stock. The flower is multi-pedaled and can range in color from white to red to pink to purple to an almost bluish-purple tint. To extract the opium, simple slice into the pod before it's flowered and collect the sap that drains out.

Otherwise, watch for labels that may read:

Avinza	Kapanol	MSIR	Roxanol
Kadian	MS Contin	Oramorph	

- Antibacterial – For the laymen we call these antibiotics. Basically, bacteria is classified into two groups, gram-negative bacteria which include things like Escherichia coli (E. coli), Salmonella and Gonorrhea, and gram-positive bacteria which accounts for stuff like Streptococcus (strep throat), as well as most pathogens (viral, bacterial, prional or fungal); and with the possibility of an outbreak ending the world, it's these that we're more interested in fighting. The antibiotics are also split up to work on each set of bacteria, usually independently, although some antibiotics do work on both equally:

Gram-Negative			Gram-Positive		Gram-Negative & Positive			
Aminoglycosides	Mandol	Claforan	Cephalosporins	Sumamed	Carbapenems	Amoxil	Pentids	Truxcillin
Amikin	Mefoxin	Vantin	Duricef	Zitrocin	Invanz	Principen	Pen-Vee	V-Cillin K
Garamycin	Cefzil	Fortaz	Ancef	Biaxin	Doribax	Geocillin	Pipracil	Veetids
Kantrex	Ceftin	Cedax	Keflin	Dynabac	Primaxin	Tegopen	Negaban	Bicillin
Mycifradin	Zinnat	Cefizox	Keflex	Erythocin	Merrem	Dynapen	Ticar	Pfizerpen
Netromycin	Suprax	Rocephin	Cubicin	Erythroped	Lincosamides	Floxapen	A-Cillin	
Nebcin	Omnicef		Lipopeptide	TAO	Cleocin	Mezlin	Beepen-VK	
Humatin	Cefdiel		Cubicin	Ketek	Lincocin	Staphcillin	Ledercillin	
Cephalosporins	Spectracef		Macrolides	Trobicin	Penicillins	Unipen	PC Pen	
Ceclor	Cefobid		Zithromax		Novamox	Prostaphlin	Suspen	

NOTE: Penicillin for those that don't know is the best drug ever <u>discovered</u>! I say discovered because it's natural. It was found in the early 19th century as a fungus growing on bread, not invented by some geeks in a lab. It kills everything under the Sun, yet in America you aren't allowed to have it without a prescription; and doctors won't prescribe it unless you're in real trouble. In Mexico, however, we can purchase it at any drugstore over the counter without a prescription, no problem. Here (in Mexico) it's labeled as: Acimox, Alvi-tec, Amobay, Amoxiclav, Amoxiclide, Amoxivet, Amoxivet, Ampiclox-d, Ampi-tecno, Ampliron, Amsapen, Amsaxilina, Augmentin, Binotal, Brenoxil, Bromixen, Clamoxin, Gramaxin, Marovilina, Moxlin, Penbritin, Polymox, Pylopac, Servamox and Trifamox ibl (Pentrexyl and Amoxil being the most popular). Because it is a fungus, it grows naturally, so we don't need a lab (or a prescription) to manufacture it ourselves:

1. Rub a slice of bread or citrus on a dusty surface and store in a Ziploc bag with a tablespoon of water at a constant 70°F for 3-5 days or until a blue-green mold appears. This is not actually Penicillin, it's just a mold known as Penicillium chrysogenum; however, this certain type of mold secretes (poops) Penicillin.

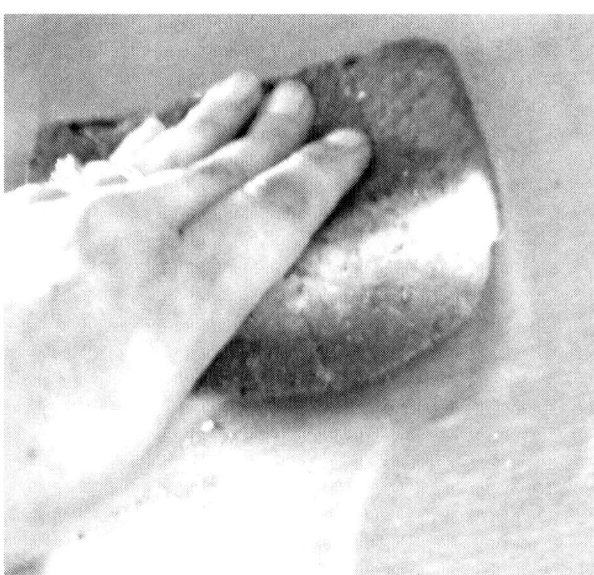

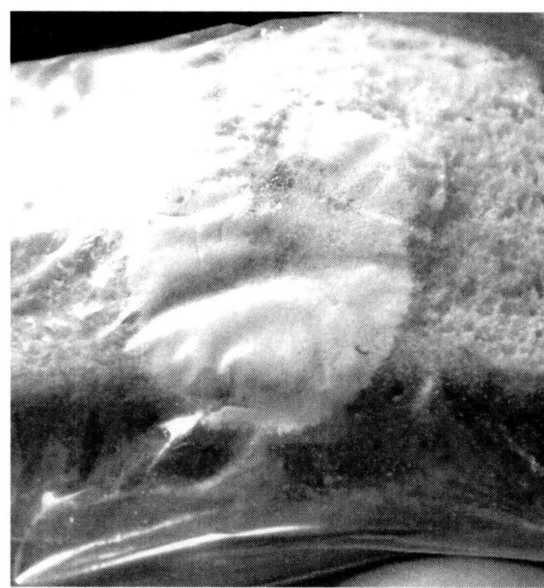

2. To maximize the amount of Penicillin harvestable, we want the little buggers to eat and poop as much as possible. So we'll need to cut the bread or citrus into small cubes, placing them inside a sterilized glass container and store in a dark location for another 5 days, again at 70°F temperatures in order for incubation to occur. (Don't we all prefer pooping in the dark after all?)
3. After 5 days you'll notice the entire surface covered with a very thin layer of white penicillin spores.

4. In a sterilized jar, mix 1 cup of milk, 2 tablespoons of sugar, 5 tablespoons cornstarch (made by grinding the white innards of corn kernels), 1 teaspoon of salt and a cup of pee or pine needles (to lower the pH levels). Boil the mix for 10 minutes, or until a paste-like thickness is achieved, or cook at 315°F for one hour to kill any other fungus or bacteria in the mix which is otherwise harmful to the penicillin.
5. Once cooled, scrape off and add 1 tablespoon of incubated penicillin spores and let the jar rest undisturbed on its side (for maximum air access) for 7 days again in 70°F temperatures to further incubate. The result will be semi-pure penicillin in a liquid state and should be ingested as soon as possible, 1/2 teaspoon per day for 7 days or kept cool and stored for no longer than 2 weeks.

- 'Medical' marijuana – At this point, why the hell not, right?
- Dramamine stops nausea, dizziness and vomiting for whatever reason, which can be deadly if you have no access to clean drinkable water. Look for labels reading Dramamine, Driminate, Travel-EZE, Travel-Wise, TripTone, Uni-Calm or Wal-Dram.
- Merbromin, which was called Micurecrom or Mercurochrome when I was growing up, is a topical antiseptic and is much more efficient at its job than alcohol or hydrogen peroxide during surgical applications. Watch for the larger spray bottles with names like Merbromine, Sodium mercurescein, Asceptichrome, Supercrome, Brocasept and Cinfacromin.

Real medical care and emergency or surgical self-help is the most difficult subject to learn, short of going to med-school. For some reason, there aren't any books available on how to perform surgeries, treat major injuries, or cure dangerous sicknesses. Now, I'm not talking about common first aid here; I'm talking about the knowledge base which doctors and surgeons acquire in order to work on patients. The major in-depth publications out there don't have a chapter on such topics; or if they do, it simply says "call 911," or "go to a hospital as soon as possible," both of which will be non-existent in your case. Because of this, I foresee an enormous jump backwards in medical knowledge, technology and advancements once the collapse occurs, which is very sad. It's sad that this knowledge, or any knowledge, be it medical, surgical, automotive, mechanics, electronics, agriculture, wood working or basket weaving isn't freely distributed among the people.

PREGNANCY & BIRTH: THE NEW SILENT GENERATION

I don't think I need to teach you step-by-step about sex and how to reproduce, or include detailed drawings and pictures on the subject in this book; but I will remind you that humans have been making and having babies very efficiently for hundreds of thousands of years before such things as doctors, hospitals or epidurals were ever even conceived of. Having a baby isn't an illness or even a medical condition; it's simply a natural process, which is why it's not located in the medical category. Yet, it's the only 'natural process' for which humans "need" or are "required" to go to the hospital for, even though there's nothing wrong with them.

There are, however, more and more women today, realizing and not falling prey to this fraudulent act perpetrated by our medical system, who are having babies at home with the assistance of a mid-wife. Midwifery is a practice that goes back centuries, with even healthier results than hospital births today (hospitals are full of bacteria, viruses, staphylococcus infections, etc.). Basically, a midwife is simply a woman who has experience, herself, and/or has overseen the birth process before. But any woman who has had a baby, herself, can coach you and/or your mate with great results in the new world.

Let's start with positions. In the wild, most animals pop out kids standing up with little loss to daily activities. Giving birth lying on your back isn't natural; no animal lies on its back to pop out an infant. Can you imagine a dog or, even better, a gorilla (which is closer to us genetically) lying on its back, legs up, pushing? The most natural position for pushing of the abdominal region is in the squatting position, as with defecation (pooping). Can you imagine pooping laying on your back, legs up, pushing? Of course not, it's absurd. So why would we do it in labor? However, if squatting isn't comfortable enough for you, or you find yourself becoming weak or dizzy, lie on your side, or on all fours. I find water births to be one of the most natural methods for humans. It's an easy transition for the baby and for the mother, since humans are programmed to relax in warm water. The contractions will be more tolerable; and, therefore, labor will occur much more quickly. The transition from a liquid environment to a liquid environment is not only much safer (the baby won't breathe until it feels the air), but an almost surreal way to give birth (the baby literally floats into its mother's arms).

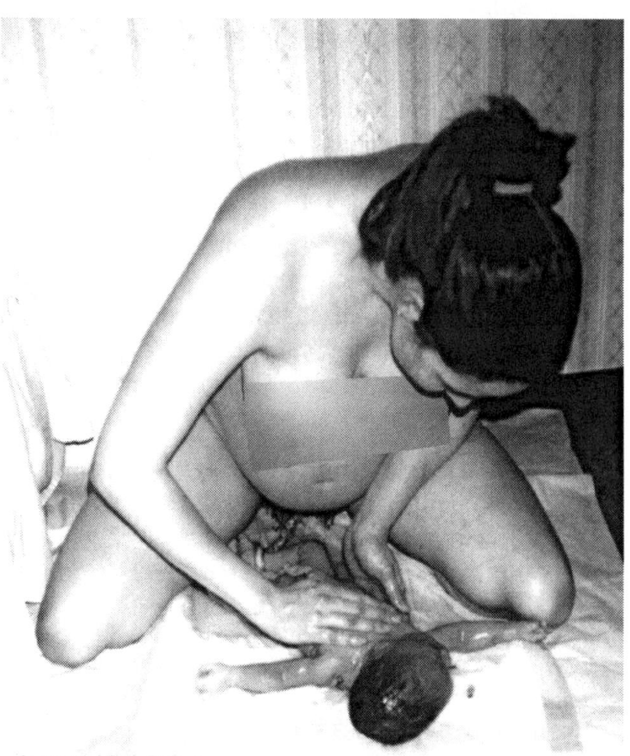

Sourse: Lisa J. Patton

When do you know if it's time? 95% of the time you're water won't break until you're at least 9 centimeters dilated, in which case you will be giving birth within 24 hours. The amniotic membrane warms, protects and cushions the growing fetus in a bubble of liquid, shielded by a second sac that surrounds the baby. Once you start going into labor, the force or pressure of the contractions on the outside layer (chorion) of the amniotic sac (which is comprised mostly of fetal urine), causes it to rupture. In fact, sometimes the water doesn't break at all throughout the birth. This is ok; you can remove both bags after birth. The only problem would be an extra half inch or so added to the diameter of the infant. If necessary, the bag can be manually broken with a sterilized crocheting hook once it starts protruding from the vagina.

Once your 'water breaks' your body will proceed in a certain fashion. You will have more contractions, your cervix will efface and dilate and your baby will move down the cervical canal to be born. The average labor for a first- time mom is about 12-18 hours. When you begin feeling significant contractions, you can begin timing to see which stage of labor you are currently undergoing. Timing contractions is extremely simple. Get a watch with a second hand on it, a pen and paper and note the time when a contraction starts and stops. This is the length of your contractions or how long they last. Then, note the time the next contraction starts; this is how far apart your contractions are. There's no need to time every set of contractions; just retime another set every few hours to see the difference and if you've entered into a new stage or not.

Stage 1. With contractions just starting, it's difficult to tell if you've entered stage one or are just experiencing cramps. If the "cramp" (contraction) occurs in equally-spaced durations (20 minutes or more) you're in stage 1. This phase will last several hours, with the contractions finally happening only 5 minutes apart.

Stage 2. You'll feel contractions 4-5 minutes apart and lasting up to a minute long. It's important during the first two stages to remain mobile so that the body continues with the labor process, rather than relaxing. It's also important at this point to get to a clean, comfortable, protected and secure area to give birth. Place several clean towels or blankets around the area, clean and sanitize the vaginal area and wait. The 411 method says if contractions are 4 minutes apart, lasting 1 minute long, for at least 1 hour you're going into labor.

Stage 3. Stage 3 is the most intense but quickest stage, lasting no more than an hour or two with contractions occurring every 2-3 minutes. Shaking and vomiting usually transpires in the new mother-to-be; this is normal. This stage is brutal on the woman. She needs to work hard absorbing the pain while attempting to relax her abdominal muscles, often sweating profusely as she rapidly burns through calories. A cool wet towel on the forehead and cool water or ice chips can be a lifesaver. In the end of stage 3 she'll be fully dilated.

Stage 4. This stage is all about resting without contractions before the main event.

Stage 5. The last, but not final, stage lasts about an hour or two at the most (depending on the woman's position), and results with the birth of your baby; contractions will dial back to around 4 minutes. You can begin pushing when the urge arises; otherwise, do nothing. Very little pushing goes a long way. Or try panting. Panting is a controlled series of slight pushes of the abdomen; try it right now and you'll feel what I'm talking about. Either way, don't just push for the sake of pushing or because you saw a doctor on some sitcom yelling "Push! Push! Dammit, Push!" In fact, you shouldn't even push unless you can't help it.

Stage 6. Stage 6 witnesses the baby coming out. It's important to do several things during this stage:

1. When the top of the head becomes visible, have the midwife or father place a hand over it to prevent it from popping out (don't push on the head) and push slightly on the perineum (the surface area between the anus and vagina), which will also lower the risk of the baby shooting across the room. You really have no idea how easy these things just come out once they get going. If you're alone, place your own hand over the head as best you can.

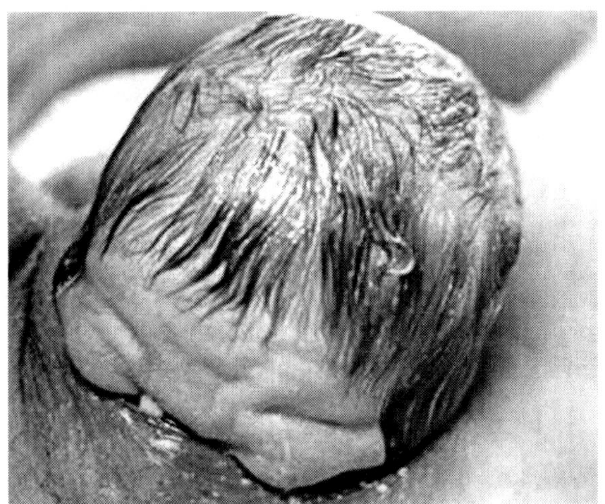

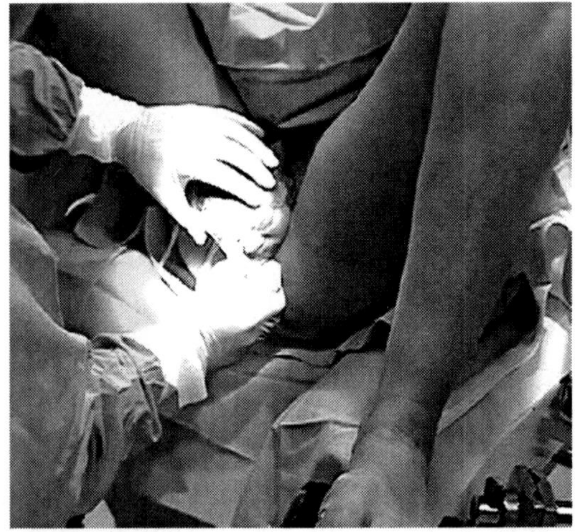

2. Once the head is completely out, have the midwife or husband cup under the baby's head (don't pull), to

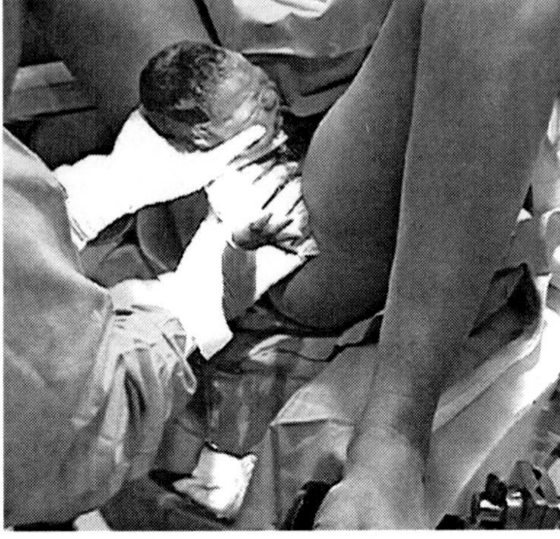

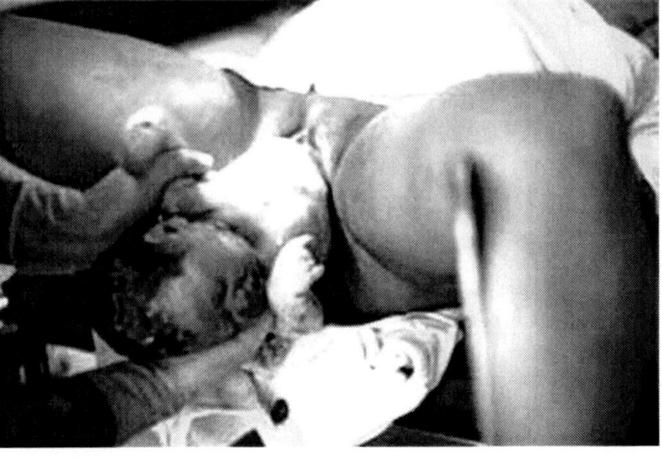

support and gently guide the body while it comes out all on its own.

3. When the little tike is completely out, gently stroke downward on the baby's nose to help expel the excess mucus and amniotic fluid. If the baby is having trouble breathing, place its nose in your mouth and suck out any blocking fluid gently.

Stage 7. The afterbirth.

1. Place the baby skin to skin with the mother, the head slightly lower with nose pointing down to help facilitate the draining of the mucus and cover both with blankets or towels.
2. When the placenta has birthed, place it in a plastic bag next to the baby and do not cut the umbilical cord, yet. Don't pull on the umbilical cord either; wait for it to exit on its own.

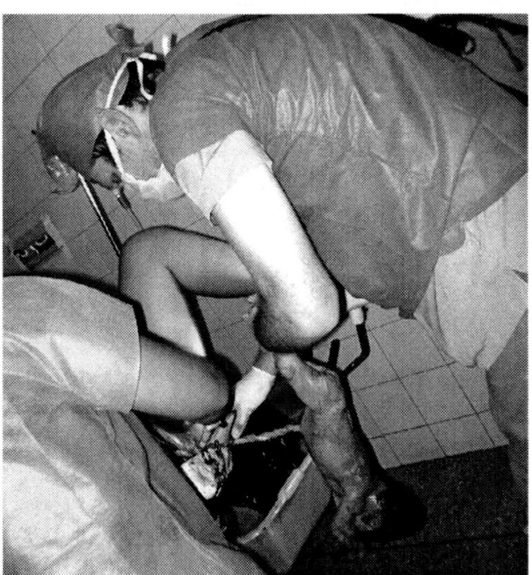

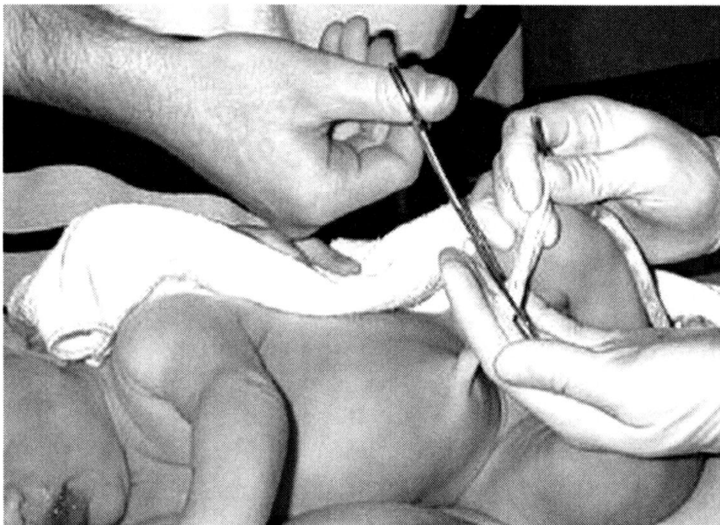

That's it, you're done. Now it's important to just rest, relax and bond with your new little one in a few minutes of relief without pain. After 10-20 minutes, though, if the placenta still hasn't birthed, it will be time to push again, just a little, to expel it. You have a couple of options with the placenta and umbilical cord, cut or don't cut. If you don't cut, they will both dry up and fall off on their own within a week or so. This also provides the baby with needed extra nutrients during the first hours. If you decide to cut, you also have a couple of options:

1. Tie 2 sanitized strings, yarn or tiny plastic zip ties, several inches up from the baby a couple inches apart; and cut with a sterilized instrument.
2. Wait a couple hours until the cord stops pumping or pulsating; the cord will turn white and start clotting. At this point, you can either cut with a sterilized instrument, this way you don't have to tie it off at all, or burn through it with a candle rather than cutting, as it will not only sterilize the area but cauterize the wound as well. Hell, you can even chew through it like every other living mammal on Earth if you'd like. Again, either way, within a few days the remaining inches of umbilical cord will dry up and fall off on its own.

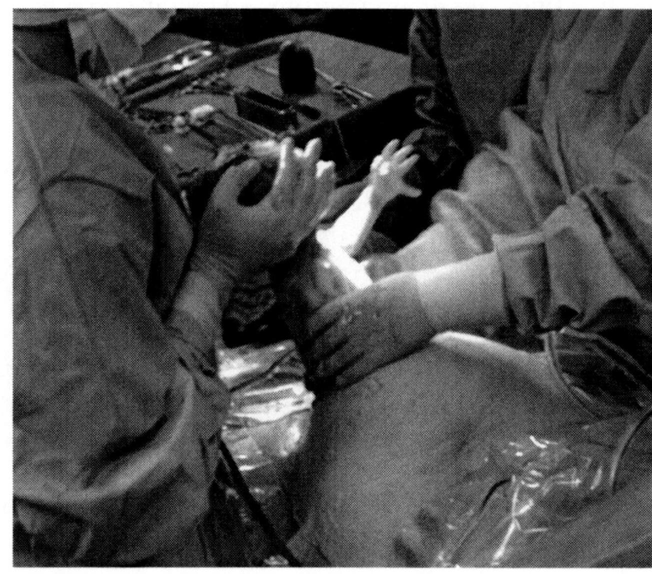

A C-section should never be attempted by anyone other than someone who has performed the surgery before successfully. A C-section involves cutting a several-inch-long incision horizontally into the abdomen area much like we did removing the appendix, though, over towards the center several inches. Sterilize all of the instruments (even the yarn or string) in boiling water. There are multiple layers that need to be cut through before reaching the uterus, all of which have passing blood vessels that will also need to be cut and cauterized to prevent bleeding. The amniotic fluid sac will need to be drained in a sanitary fashion to prevent infection of the host, so that the deliverer's hands can get around the child. If the head is in the pelvis, remove it first; if the butt is in the pelvis, remove the head first, guiding the butt up and out of the pelvis. Once the head clears the incision, extract the fluids from the nostril cavity (this is more important than in natural birth). Guide the rest of the body out, check for umbilical cord placement and place skin-to-skin with the mother and cover. Remove the placenta from the cavity, cut and tie the umbilical cord as instructed above, sterilize the cuts and suture each layer up individually with dissolvable stitches, cauterize or sew with stainless steel .096 wire or smaller as a last option. Know that the SS wire won't dissolve and will remain in the body forever, or at least until an experienced surgeon can remove it at a later date.

Another fear is of the umbilical cord getting wrapped around the baby's neck during natural birth. Although the chances of this occurring are extremely minute, it's easy to resolve if it does transpire. You'll be able to see if the cord is wrapped around the neck or not, once the head has penetrated the vagina and the shoulders are starting to stick out. Either way, it won't be tight and can easily be lifted up and over the head with little effort. Never pull on or try to work the baby out.

Finally, if in doubt, do nothing. Labor will occur safely without your help. If you don't know what to do, and do something anyway, you're more likely to cause damage to the baby or mother and accomplish only death.

LIGHT: LET THERE BE...

Eventually, there will be no more batteries, no more solar panels, no more generators, and no more artificial light. Batteries, even rechargeable ones, eventually die, panels eventually stop charging, and motors eventually lock up. So, once again we fall back to Mother Nature and fruit power to build portable flashlights:

1. Stick a penny halfway into a potato and a galvanized nail about 1/2in away.
2. Remove an LED from any electronic apparatus and simply connect one prong to the penny and the other to the nail.

The dissimilar metals (the anode and cathode) in the electrolyte insides of the potato create an electro-chemical reaction which creates usable current (around 2 volts), enough to power a 1v LED. This, for all intents and purposes is a basic battery. We can then connect it in series with other batteries (potatoes) to harness a larger voltage (thereby powering larger devices) by connecting the copper element of one potato to the zinc element of another. The same setup works with tomatoes, limes, grapefruits, oranges, lemons or any other high pH (high acidic) fruit.

By blending up the fruit, adding it into a salt water solution (dissolved salt water), and pouring it into several cells, say a large ice tray, you'll completely maximize and amplify the batteries' voltage and amperage by

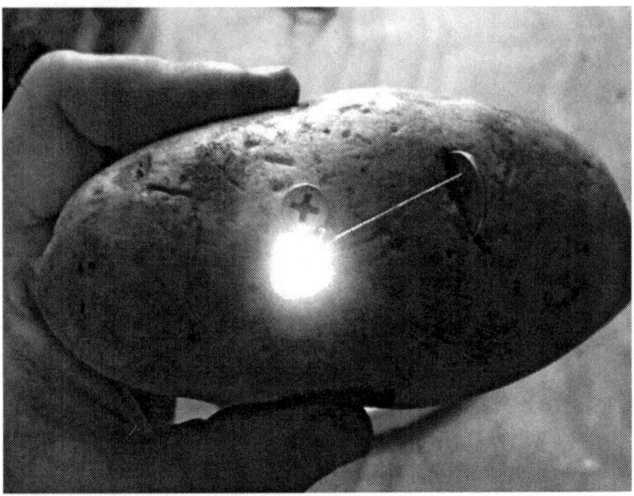

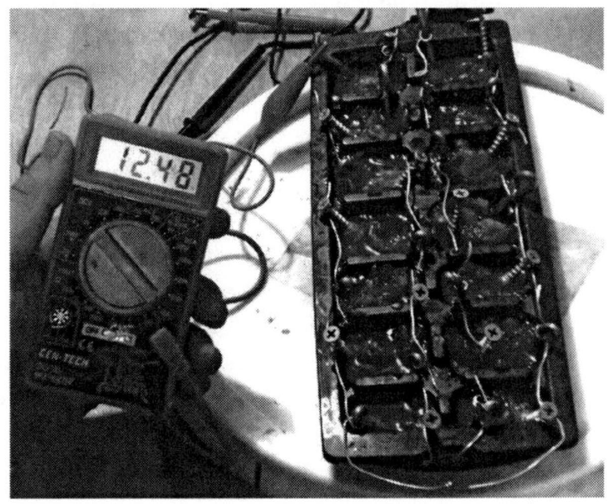

several times, building a fruit battery comparable to that of any 12v car battery. My great, great, grand daddy was making this type of battery in clay pots around Biblical times--it was called the Baghdad Battery.

TRAVEL: PIMP MY PONY

Man has always felt the need to explore 'new worlds' and it seems only fitting that we end this book with the discovery of our new world. In fact, Earth very well may be a completely different and new world both physically, socially, and possibly even spiritually. And, rest assured, there will come a time when venturing outside of your area will be once again 'safe,' possibly safer than it has ever been. There's no need to hurry, no place really to be, so it makes no difference what form of transportation you use to achieve this goal.

- Car – As time passes you <u>will</u> really want to get away from combustion motors all together. Combustion technology isn't even close to being efficient or practical; and it's only due to auto manufacturer and oil company control that the method of outdated transportation has lasted this long. Take a look at the widespread development, adaptation and usage by the masses of any other technology, for example message delivery techniques, in comparison:

Pre-1900 – Telegraph	Pre-1900 – Covered Wagon
1905 – Telephone	1905 – Combustion Engine
1950 – USPS Mail	1950 – Combustion Engine
1980 – Cell Phone	1980 – Combustion Engine
1990 – Computer Email	1990 – Combustion Engine
1995 – Chat Rooms	1995 – Combustion Engine
2000 – Blogging	2000 – Combustion Engine
2005 – Instant Messaging (IM)	2005 – Combustion Engine
2007 – Blue Tooth	2007 – Combustion Engine
2009 – Texting	2009 – Combustion Engine
2011 – Smart Devices	2011 – Combustion Engine

And yet there are other (non-combustible) vehicles and vehicle technologies out there like the electric car and air and magnetic motors, that are available and far more efficient; but the car manufacturers and oil companies keep buying up the patents and killing production on them. I've built/converted numerous cars to run on electricity, air, hydrogen, ethanol, methanol, biogas and biodiesel; and the point is, petroleum based combustion (or any combustion system) is a really horrible technology for several reasons: (a) today it requires a fuel source that we have almost completely depleted to function, (b) there are over 200 moving parts in a combustion engine. This equates to 99% more probability of something breaking, compared to say an EV (Electric Vehicle) which has only one moving part. In other words, an automobile with a combustion engine will break 20,000 times more often than an automobile with an electric engine, and (c) in a post-apocalyptic world there will be no gasoline and no spare replacement parts, what you got is what you'll have to live with.

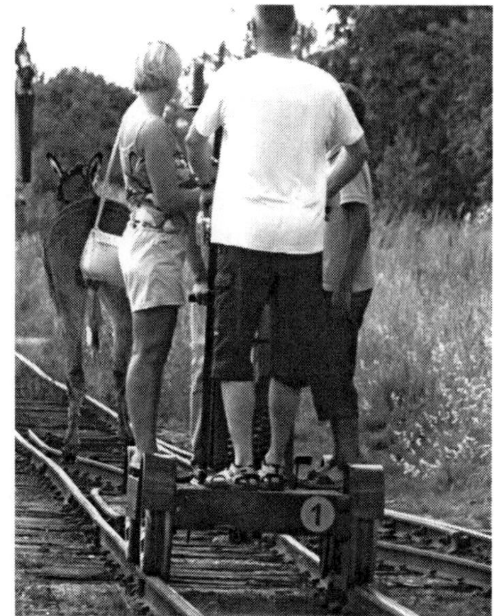

- Horse – So, we're back to square one, then, huh? Actually, yes; in fact, quite literally. The best means of long distance transportation in a new developing world would go back to horses, carriages, donkeys, yaks, etc.
- Bicycle – For shorter distances, bicycles are best; there should be plenty of spare parts around, if not they're easy enough to build.
- Railroad – Within a few years, most roads will completely deteriorate making traveling long distances by car impossible anyway. We can see this yearly in May and June when the respective Departments of Motor Vehicle shut down multiple lanes to repave and asphalt areas that have broken down from washouts and freezing temperatures during the previous winter. Imagine if the DMV were no longer around to fix the roads every year. Potholes would turn into massive pits; and cracks would transform into abrupt drop-offs. On the other hand, railroad tracks don't require such annual maintenance and can be easily utilized with a homemade handcar or mule-powered railcar. Also, if there are any quarantines or barricades still around, legally, due to some form of martial law or criminally in nature, these will be focused and located on major interstates and city limits, not railroads.

- Bicycle-powered railcar – A combo pedal/railcar is a better option, at least for short distances.

- Hot air balloon – Although it's most likely that the materials will no longer exist to make such means of transportation a truly viable option, I felt the need to at least include it as a subject matter here because of the simplicity of hot air travel (fill a large inverted bag with hot air). And who knows, I may be wrong, but we may see a time where our only method of long distance transportation is carried out in hot air balloons. Many historians believe ancient man already had flight in this fashion before we re-invented it.
- Sailboat – Another option would be by boat, sailing the seven seas (maybe soon to be seventeen seas) just like our forefathers did. This is a great method of transportation in itself, making long distance travel extremely accessible and a trip very quick. We're actually lucky that our planet is mostly water. No matter what you decide, you'll need to know about navigation and telling time without the use of a compass or watch, both of which may not be around anymore, or may be useless in the aftermath.

NAVIGATION

What to do without your navigational GPS system telling you where to go? Well, everyone knows that the Sun rises in the east (more or less) and sets in the west (mostly), at least for now, that is. But did you know that in the northern hemisphere most tree branches grow on the south side of the tree? This is because as the Sun spans the sky in the south, the branches naturally grow directionally to receive the most light. If you look at a large tree you'll see that, generally, there are more branches on the south side. Some other well-known directional rules of thumb that may help you out in the end are:

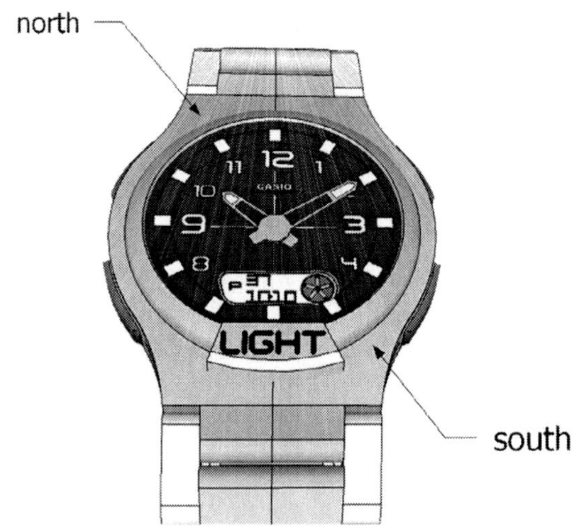

- Wristwatch compass – If you have the type of watch that has hands on it and it actually still works, point the hour hand at the current position of the Sun. Now divide whatever time it is in half (8:00/2 would be 4:00), the answer (4:00) would be north, which means the opposite (10:00) would be south.
- Moss – Moss grows more on the north side of rocks for the opposite reason that a tree's branches grow more on the south. That is moss, just like any other fungi, doesn't like direct sunlight.
- Sun – We can determine precisely without guessing, which way the Sun moves across the sky by watching the direction of which way the shadows of objects traverse on the ground. The shadow of an object will always travel on the ground west to east or opposite of the direction of the Sun. This also works for the Moon's shadow. (Yes, the Moon casts a shadow, actually a very bright one, which you'll be able to see when all the power goes out.) This method is a valuable time-saver, as shadows will move in minutes during which time the Sun moves in hours.

- Moon – The Moon follows the Sun across the sky east to west. If there's no Moon, you can watch the direction of the stars as they also take the same path.
- Satellite dishes – Most satellites orbit the planet over the Clarke belt (the equator), transmitting data to both northern and southern countries. Therefore, most dishes point south towards them (in the northern hemisphere).

- Mile markers – If a highway runs north-south and the mile markers/exit numbers are getting higher, you're heading north (south if they get lower). On east-west highways, the numbers usually get larger as you head east.
- Compass – Can't leave out the old compass method. Don't have a compass? Of course not. Well get to building one! Take a paperclip, needle or other thin metallic instrument and rub one end of a refrigerator magnet along one half of the needle about 30 times. Place the needle on a small piece of plastic and the plastic it in a calm container of water (or hang it from the top of the container with a thread if you don't have water).

Of course, if there's an EMP, the wristwatch method won't work. If there's a meteor strike, all the trees will be vaporized, so that method won't work. If there's a physical poles shift, the North Star, Sun and Moon will no longer be or move in their respective locations/directions (who knows where they'll actually be now), so those methods won't work. If there's a magnetic shift, your compass won't work. In the end, basically, you can forget about knowing which way to go, which is fine; because you shouldn't care which way you're going, anyway, unless, that is, there's an ice age! In which case, just head towards the Sun.

TIME

I promise that you'll have very little need now for time. Time is a device made by man for the benefit of society, and with society gone, well… That said, we do have a natural sense of "time," but it doesn't require the use of clocks. We used to separate and name the parts of day, i.e. *mid-day* or *noon day* (now *noon*), when the Sun reaches the highest point in the sky; *day break* or *Sun rise*; *mid morning*; *mid evening*; *Sun set* and *mid night*. You can then break these up further into new hours. Maybe your hours are 80mins long; and your minutes 28secs long, the sky's the limit, literally.

Another important tool is how to tell when it's going to get dark. A good rule of *thumb*: fingers = 15mins. If you hold up your hand to the horizon and the Sun is 1 finger away, it's 15mins until sunset. 2 fingers, 30mins, 3, 45 and an entire hand minus the thumb equals 1 hour. Tides are also good because they come in (and out) every 12hrs and 25mins.

COMMUNICATION

As you voyage across the newly-remodeled globe, you'll learn that new languages have formed or are emerging in grouped regions far and wide. This is a strange phenomenon that occurs whenever humans became separated or isolated (Tower of Babel, American English-British English, Jamaican English-British English, South Creole-North Yankee, Ghetto Black American-African, etc.), transpiring within as little as a few years. Historically, communicating with native speaking people was carried out with either drawing in the dirt with a stick or on rocks with charcoal. We can however make ink instead (which would also be a good item of trade):

There are many ways to make ink using natural ingredients with 4 basic factors: a pigment, like lamp black, which can be made by placing a bowl upside-down over a candle or by collecting the suit or creosote oil from a chimney; a carrier like water; an adhering/binding agent like honey or tree sap, which not only forces the ink to stick on the paper, but the ingredients to each other as well; and a preservative like salt, lime/lemon juice or some other acid. Finally, by adding egg yolk and vinegar to the mix, you'll make the ink 'permanent' or staining so it doesn't wipe away. Paints, dyes and stains can be made the same way with the same products.

1. Add 1/2 tsp lamp black, 1 tsp salt, 1 egg yolk and 1 tsp tree sap/honey, 1 tsp vinegar and mix thoroughly.
2. Store the paste in a sealed container until ready to use, adding water as needed to form a more sticky applicable consistency, but not to the point that it's watery.
3. Dip the quill (feather) of a turkey, hawk, vulture, eagle or other large winged bird into the ink, letting capillary action draw the liquid into the hollow tube, filling it completely.
4. When you're ready to write, simply slide the quill pen along the surface of the paper slowly (slower than writing with a normal pen), letting the papers sponging ability soak up and draw out the ink.

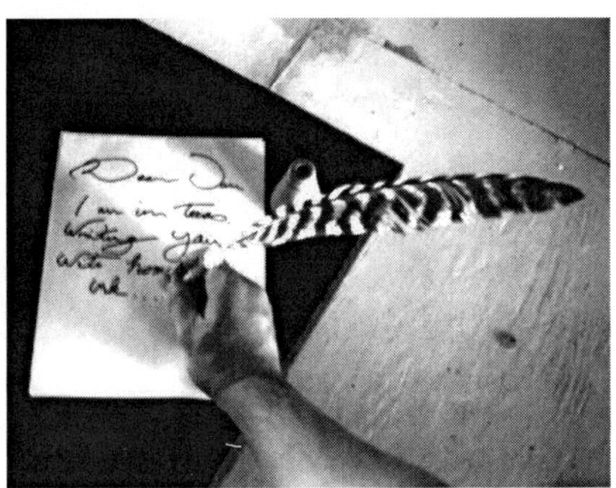

THE ~~END~~ BEGINNING

Congratulations! You've survived an apocalypse (and reading this book). Hopefully, you're in a nice place, free from all the corruption, crime, tyranny, lies, control, sadness, pain, suffering, cruelty and evil. Of course, what kind of prophet would I be if I didn't tell you about this new world? I foresee that I will name this new Earth Concordia, in light of a new, hopeful age. Before we get into that, though, it's important to note only English-speaking people call the planet "Earth." Other cultures, species, religions and societies call it many other names like Aarde, Dunya, Erde, Jorden, Maa, Pamint, Terra, Tierra, Toka, Yird, and Zeme (the list goes on), but none of which translate into the word "Earth." Each have their own reasons, stories, history and etymologies for naming it a different name with a different meaning, respectively.

On Concordia there will be no countries, states, borders, divisions; everyone will have enough and be happy with what they have. They'll get along with each other, the planet and the rest of the inhabitants, animals, insects, vegetation included and share equally. This can only be accomplished if we live in a sustainable way, which could only work if the 'sustainable societies' were based on smaller populations where the people knew each other and community decisions were made by direct democracy. It's easier in small, familiar groups to get people to work for the good of the group versus for personal gratification and self-interest as seen today around the planet. For example, if you pollute the water, use up all of a resource, or act irresponsibly in another fashion, it has a direct and personal effect on you, your family, your friends and neighbors, which isn't the case today.

The question, then, is how to get people to think long-term, act responsibly and do the right thing. The truth is that they won't, especially if they are the people alive today and all the luxuries they're used to were suddenly lost. They will burn coal and oil if they have it or try to take it away from somebody else if they don't. I've described such activities in the last 10 chapters in the same way, rather than saying "we need to switch to solar now!" (which would be impossible anyway), so that the transition is simpler for you when it arrives. The only foreseeable solution would be for a 'good' strong dictator or monarch (a benevolent despot) to force everyone at gunpoint to do the right thing. Actually, if the world as we know it collapses completely, if the power plants quit working, food stops being mass-produced and the oil quits being pumped, there won't be any need to do anything for quite some time because we won't have the ability to do much harm to the planet anyway.

At the time of publishing, it seems that the beginning of the end was already in motion; as if on cue, in preparation for 2012, starting on January 1, every month saw epic and extraordinary, unprecedented change and crisis scour the planet. And I see such occurrences only getting worse and more frequent from now until 2013:

January – A sort of Biblical rash of fish and bird deaths are witnessed around the world. Official reports blame "fireworks" and "cold snaps" for the enormous amounts of dead and dying aerial and aquatic life, both of which weren't present in most of the below locations. Other headlines say it's due to "climate change" and "environmental conditions," which, in itself, should raise a red flag to developing, apocalyptic like changes in the very near future. Also, keep in mind that humans occupy just .3% of the entire planet. That means, the real number of sudden dead animals would be closer to 300 times the 5 million 6 hundred thousand cases reported:

- January 1, 2011, "hordes" of dead fish found in a creek near Cuckoo's Hollow, Peterborough, England.
- January 1, 2011, thousands of dead fish are found floating on the surface of Spruce Creek, Florida.
- January 1, 2011, 50,000 to 100,000 found dead near Paraná, Brazil.
- January 1, 2011, 2 million fish found dead on the shores of the Chesapeake Bay in Maryland.
- January 1, 2011, 50 birds found dead in the streets of Stockholm, Sweden.
- January 1, 2011, hundreds of dead fish wash up on the shores of Coromandel Peninsula, New Zealand.
- January 1, 2011, 100,000 fish mysteriously wash up dead on the shores of Arkansas River near Ozark, Missouri.
- January 1, 2011, 2,000 dead birds fall from the sky near Beebe, Arkansas, about 125 miles east of Ozark.
- January 2, 2011, hundreds of dead fish found in the Brecon Canal near Abergavenny, England.
- January 3, 2011, 500 dead birds fall in Point Coupee Parish, Louisiana, 300 miles south of the Beebe.
- January 4, 2011, Washington AFP announces world-wide bee populations down 90% in the last 20 years.
- January 5, 2011, over 700 birds mysteriously fall from the sky in Italy.
- January 5, 2011, 200 dead birds found on bridge near Tyler, Texas.
- January 5, 2011, 40,000 dead crabs wash up on Kent coastline in the UK.
- January 8, 2011, thousands of fish found on the shores of Lake Michigan near Chicago, Illinois.
- January 8, 2011, over a hundred dead birds clustered together on a highway near Geyserville, California.
  January 9, 2011, 30-50 dead birds are found in Frog Hollow, Missouri.

February – We witnessed the historic governmental disbandment of several countries as people rose up in protest to overthrow their respective leaders all over the world, including Tunisia, Egypt, Yemen, Libya, Syria, Algeria, Armenia, Bahrain, Iraq, Jordan, Morocco, Oman, Azerbaijan, Djibouti, Kuwait, Lebanon, Mauritania, Saudi Arabia, Sudan, Ivory Coast, Italy, India, Thailand, China and Western Sahara.

March – The United States itself nearly shuts down and a 9.0M earthquake and tsunami hit east Japan. Emergencies are declared at four nuclear power plants affected by the quake. The subsequent multiple 7. aftershocks, tsunami and nuclear plant explosions completely devastate the country, ultimately killing almost 27,000 people and prompt the world to brace and prepare for radiation dumped into the ocean to reach us.

April – Over 300 historically *"rural aiming tornadoes uncharacteristically focus on and hit communities across the U.S., which typically don't experience any tornado activity."* During the month of April, tornadoes struck every single day (never before seen), killing over 300 in just one day alone. This strange 'natural' event of almost 6,000 severe weather reports (double the average of any month ever recorded) can only be explained and defined using words like epic, tribulation, reckoning, upheaval, turmoil, chaos, pandemonium and *apocalypse.*

Is the end closer than we think? Major earthquakes in Asia, New Zealand (on the same day); massive flooding in Indonesia, Australia, Brazil (three opposite points of the Earth on the same day). Catastrophes indiscriminately, simultaneously and increasingly sweeping the planet without concern for race, religion, government or color. In reality, it may not be just one of the before-mentioned events at all that will decimate the planet, but rather all combined. At the very least, it will be very interesting times that this generation lives in.

JP5

CHAPTER 1

PREPARING FOR THE END: THE PREQUEL

Preparations can be done in a matter of minutes, hours, days, months, or years, with, of course, the greatest time frame being the most efficient. I'm not one of those authors, however, who will sit here and say you need to sell all of your worldly goods and act NOW! Because you can make enough preparations, with the help of this book, to get you and your family safely through the events, probably with only a moment's notice. Surviving the aftermath is a different story, though; and that's where longer, broader arrangements come in handy. I've put together several inexpensive and even free things that you can start doing now, with your family, to prepare you for what's to come, along with a list of items and supplies that you'll need during and after the catastrophe.

PREPARATIONS LIST

The amount of time you'll be holed up in your shelter will vary from a few days (in the case of super hurricanes, tornadoes or tsunamis) up to possibly years (which would occur in an economic or government collapse). It's important to stock-pile as much food, supplies, gear, tools and materials to last everyone in your group the duration, and possibly even longer. Having extra quantities of every item will also come in handy if you're to take in unexpected refugees, to use as currency for trading, in case some supplies are damaged, lost or stolen or as a 'just in case' resource to fall back on when time comes to rebuild. The list I've put together below will provide one person with a 2-month supply plus an extra 2 month supply (for the above reasons) per person, which means you'll need to multiply the quantities I list by the number in your group.

In order to make a good preparations list, one needs to document what will be used on a daily basis and determine which to use and in which form these items will take up the least amount of space, as well as what can be stored safely for extended periods of time, taking into consideration and calculating for future events, conditions and circumstances. I did exactly this for 2 years, annotating for which situation (or situations) and uses each item was best utilized and applied, testing and trying out every one along the way. The result is a superior preparations list that will provide you with enough supplies suitable to sustain you through any and all previously-described, possible apocalyptic events:

Food:

- [x] Water – (120 gal.)
- [x] Beer/wine – (55 gal.)
- [x] Rice – (30 lbs.)
- [ ] Wheat – (100 lbs.)
- [ ] Beans – (20 lbs.)
- [ ] Nuts – (5 lbs.)
- [ ] Seeds – (5 lbs.)
- [ ] Oats – (16 lbs.)
- [ ] Sugar/honey – (60 lbs.)
- [ ] Salt – (50 lbs.)
- [ ] Salami – (20 sticks)
- [ ] Powdered milk – (20lbs.)
- [ ] Powdered eggs – (30 lbs.)
- [ ] Dried fruit – (10 lbs.)
- [ ] Dried vegetables – (10 lbs.)
- [ ] Dried meat – (20 lbs.)
- [ ] Candy – (5 lbs.)
- [ ] PB&J – (80 lbs. ea.)
- [ ] Coffee – (200 lbs.)
- [ ] Cigarettes – (100 cartons)
- [ ] Canned sardines – (20 lbs.)
- [ ] Cheese – (5 lbs.)
- [ ] Canned tuna – (50 lbs.)
- [ ] Canned ham – (50 lbs.)
- [ ] Canned chicken – (50 lbs.)
- [ ] Spam – (25 lbs.)
- [ ] Canned vegetables – (50 lbs.)
- [ ] Canned fruit – (50 lbs.)
- [ ] Canned pastas – (15 lbs.)
- [ ] Canned stews – (15 lbs.)
- [ ] Boxed noodles – (10 lbs.)
- [ ] Formula/baby food – (40 lbs.)
- [ ] Vinegar – (1 gal.)
- [ ] Cereals – (50 lbs.)
- [ ] Potted fruit plants – (4)
- [ ] Seasonings – (2ea.)
- [ ] Pet food – (150 lbs./pet)
- [ ] Multi-vitamin packs – (8)
- [ ] Multi-mineral packs – (8)
- [ ] Mason jars w/lids – (24)
- [ ] Extra medications – (8)
- [ ] Energy/granola bars – (90)
- [ ] ____________________
- [ ] ____________________

Supplies:

- [ ] Toilet paper – (200)
- [ ] Duct tape – (4)
- [ ] Zip ties – (100)
- [ ] Rope – (100ft.)
- [ ] Candles – (50)
- [ ] Cotton balls – (10 bags)
- [ ] Toothpaste – (10)
- [ ] Toothbrushes – (2)
- [ ] Petroleum jelly – (4)
- [ ] Soap – (2)
- [ ] Shampoo – (1 gal.)
- [ ] Dish soap – (1 gal.)
- [ ] Bleach – (3 gal.)
- [ ] Laundry soap – (10 lbs.)
- [ ] Washboard & bucket – (1)
- [ ] Towels – (4)
- [ ] Bedding – (1 set)
- [ ] Sand bags – (100+)
- [ ] Tampons/pads – (30)
- [ ] Hygiene protectors – (150)
- [ ] Pots & pans – (2ea.)
- [ ] Plastic Tupperware (2ea.)
- [ ] Sewing kit – (2)
- [ ] Pencil – (10)
- [ ] Paper – (100)
- [ ] Books – (10)
- [ ] Card deck – (1)
- [ ] Seeds – (100ea.)
- [ ] Root cloning gel – (2)
- [ ] Musical instrument – (1)
- [ ] Baby wipes – (25 packs)
- [ ] ____________________
- [ ] ____________________
- [ ] ____________________
- [ ] ____________________
- [ ] ____________________

Gear:

- [ ] Compound bow – (1)
- [ ] Arrows – (24+)
- [ ] Shotguns – (2)
- [ ] Rifles w/NV scope – (2)
- [ ] Side arms – (2)
- [ ] Ammunition – (1000ea)
- [ ] Solar batt. charger – (2)
- [ ] Snares & traps – (12ea)
- [ ] Tarps – (12)
- [ ] Clear tarps – (20)
- [ ] Fresnel lens – (2)
- [ ] Dynamo radio – (2)
- [ ] Dynamo flashlight – (4)
- [ ] Lighters – (20)
- [ ] Life jackets – (1)
- [ ] N95 dust mask – (2)
- [ ] Goggles – (2)
- [ ] Sleeping bag – (2)
- [ ] Compass – (2)
- [ ] Topo maps – (2ea.)
- [ ] R&R maps – (2ea.)
- [ ] Jeans – (20)
- [ ] Backpacks – (2ea.)
- [ ] Walkie talkies – (2)
- [ ] Short wave radio – (2)
- [ ] NiMH batteries – (6ea.)
- [ ] Waterproof containers – (12)
- [ ] 55gal. drums – (12)
- [ ] 5gal. buckets – (20)
- [ ] Plastic bottles – (50)
- [ ] Dog food or sand bags – (50)
- [ ] Ziploc bags – (100)
- [ ] Garbage bags – (100)
- [ ] Scuba equip. (1 set)
- [ ] Fishing line – (2 rolls)
- [ ] Fishing hooks – (50)
- [ ] Fire extinguisher – (1)
- [ ] Kevlar vest – (1)
- [ ] Riot gear – (1 set)
- [ ] Signaling mirror – (2)
- [ ] 12v solar panel – (2)
- [ ] Solar shower bag – (2)
- [ ] Repelling figure 8 – (2)
- [ ] Repelling caribiner – (2)
- [ ] RJ11 Lamp – (2)
- [ ] Faraday cage – (1)
- [ ] ____________________
- [ ] ____________________
- [ ] ____________________
- [ ] ____________________
- [ ] ____________________
- [ ] ____________________

Tools:

- [ ] Tri-fuel generator – (2)
- [ ] 1000w inverter – (2)
- [ ] 3' crowbar – (1)
- [ ] 3' sledge hammer – (1)
- [ ] 4' bolt cutters – (2)
- [ ] Rock bar – (1)
- [ ] Shovel – (1)
- [ ] Pick – (1)
- [ ] pH soil tool – (2)
- [ ] Soil moister tool – (2)
- [ ] Manual grain mill – (1)
- [ ] Roof screw bits – (2ea.)
- [ ] Wire – (100ft.)
- [ ] Dynamite – (20)
- [ ] Pipe wrench – (1)
- [ ] Adjustable wrench – (1)
- [ ] Hatchet – (1)
- [ ] Chainsaw – (1)
- [ ] Chainsaw chains – (3)
- [ ] Lock pick set – (2)
- [ ] Survey meter – (1)
- [ ] Dosimeters – (1)
- [ ] Geiger counters – (1)
- [ ] 1/8in. electrodes – (20)
- [ ] Hack saw – (1)
- [ ] Hack saw blades – (20)
- [ ] Leather gloves – (3 sets)
- [ ] 12v cordless drill – (2)
- [ ] Drill bits – (4ea.)
- [ ] Tin snips – (1)
- [ ] Box cutters – (4)
- [ ] Box cutter blades – (100)
- [ ] Glass cutter – (2)
- [ ] Glass pliers (1)
- [ ] Gerber utility knife (2)
- [ ] ____________________
- [ ] ____________________
- [ ] ____________________
- [ ] ____________________
- [ ] ____________________

Automotive:

- [ ] 12v air pump – (2)
- [ ] Tire repair kit – (2)
- [ ] Slime fix-a-flat – (5)
- [ ] Extra oil – (1qt./cyl)
- [ ] Extra wiper blade – (2)
- [ ] Garden hose – (50ft.)
- [ ] Extra U-joints – (2ea.)
- [ ] Extra belts – (2ea.)
- [ ] Extra spare tires – (2)
- [ ] Winch – (1)
- [ ] Road maps – (2ea.)
- [ ] 1/2in Tow chain – (1)
- [ ] Deep socket set – (2)
- [ ] Full gas cans – (50gal+)
- [ ] Full water cans – (10gal+)
- [ ] Tire chains – (5 sets)
- [ ] Extra fuses – (6ea.)
- [ ] Hand crank drum pump – (1)
- [ ] ______________
- [ ] ______________
- [ ] ______________
- [ ] ______________
- [ ] ______________
- [ ] ______________

Medical:

- [ ] Suture needles – (6)
- [ ] Dissolvable thread – (1)
- [ ] Hemostats – (3)
- [ ] Scalpels w/blades – (2)
- [ ] Retractors – (2)
- [ ] Mechanical cutter – (1)
- [ ] Forceps – (2)
- [ ] Prep wipes – (6 packs)
- [ ] Tweezers – (3)
- [ ] Scissors – (2)
- [ ] Super glue – (24)
- [ ] Latex gloves – (10 sets)
- [ ] Stainless steel pot – (1)
- [ ] Tampons – (24)
- [ ] Bandages – (100ft.)
- [ ] White cotton towels – (6)
- [ ] Morphine – (6)
- [ ] Penicillin – (6 packs)
- [ ] Antiseptic/iodine – (1 gal)
- [ ] Motrin/Advil – (4 packs)
- [ ] Tylenol – (4 packs)
- [ ] Aspirin – (4 packs)
- [ ] Ki tablets – (1 pack)
- [ ] Radiation lotion – (1)
- [ ] Sudafed – (4 packs)
- [ ] Medical marijuana – (2 lbs)
- [ ] Dramamine – (2 packs)
- [ ] Edible/medical plant book
- [ ] ______________
- [ ] ______________
- [ ] ______________
- [ ] ______________

Clothing:

- [ ] Rain poncho – (3)
- [ ] Rain pants – (1)
- [ ] Rubber boots – (1)
- [ ] Rubber gloves – (4)
- [ ] Tennis shoes – (2)
- [ ] Hiking boots – (2)
- [ ] Utility pants – (1)
- [ ] Cargo pants – (1)
- [ ] Zip-off pants – (1)
- [ ] Jeans – (1)
- [ ] Wool sweaters – (2)
- [ ] Wool socks – (2 sets)
- [ ] Wool gloves – (1 sets)
- [ ] Wool hats – (2)
- [ ] Wool scarf – (1)
- [ ] Flannel shirts – (1)
- [ ] Fleece shirts – (1)
- [ ] Silk shirts – (2)
- [ ] Silk socks – (2 sets)
- [ ] Cotton T-shirts – (4)
- [ ] Cotton socks – (6 sets)
- [ ] Down coats w/hoods – (1)
- [ ] Wind breakers – (1)
- [ ] Cotton underwear – (6)
- [ ] Thermals – (3)
- [ ] Extra glasses/lenses – (2)
- [ ] Wool blankets – (2)
- [ ] Down blankets – (1)
- [ ] Washable diapers – (6)
- [ ] ______________
- [ ] ______________
- [ ] ______________

A few notes to keep in mind concerning the above lists:

FOOD

- One gallon per person per day is enough water for washing, bathing, cleaning and drinking (sterilized as previously described). Add another gallon/day per potted plant and pet. As far as alcohol, which is next on the list; trust me, you'll need plenty if the world ends!
- I should also mention that many grains come pre-packaged with the larval eggs of many bugs already growing inside, since these eggs are laid on the plants themselves before harvesting. As stated earlier, there is nothing wrong with eating these bugs and will actually be an additional food source. Just make sure to keep your bags of grain and other foods sealed up tight so they can't get out, or others in.
- I try to stay away from canned soups unless they're condensed; otherwise, they're filled with mostly just water. Stew, on the other hand, is packed with potatoes, meat and who knows what else. On the same note, you can get stew cubes that turn whatever you can put in a pot into stew.
- Edible potted plants provide a source of food afterwards as well as oxygen during.
- Since jars are too fragile to transport or carry, keep them in deep storage or bury or hide for later use.
- A good assortment or mix of minerals and vitamins is essential; you can also go with a multi-vitamin and multi-mineral assortment, available at any pharmacy. On a side note, most minerals and vitamins (with the exception of vitamin C and B-complex) are fat soluble not water soluble, which means they break down and are stored in fat. With this in mind, it would be a good idea to consume these on a daily basis before leading up to the event so that your body already has them on hand during the event when needed most, rather than after.
- As I stated earlier, to someone that's addicted and used to drinking 8 cups of coffee a day, they would gladly pay out the rear for a container of coffee; the same goes with cigarettes. So even if you personally

don't drink coffee or smoke, I would suggest keeping an abundant amount supplied to sell or trade afterwards. This goes for toilet paper also. For some reason, we're addicted to it as well.

- Officially, the shelf life of canned food is two years from the date of processing. This is, however, only the 'shelf life,' which simply means the quality and taste (not the safety or protective qualities) of the food stored, will begin to decline after two years. The safety qualities and nutritional value is rated to last ultimately indefinitely at room temperature (75°F or below). Canning is a high-heat process that renders the food commercially sterile. Some cans of food have even been found and tested microbiologically safe in 100-year-old sunken shipwrecks! So if the can is intact, not dented or bulging, it will be edible for as long as you can store it.
- All stored food will need to be in containers and/or on shelves where it won't vibrate off, break, or topple over in the actual event, during an earthquake, for example. Cabinets and pantries that are attached to the walls itself, with doors that can be locked or a lock can be installed, work the best. What you don't want is stacked supplies sitting on shelves that are just set against the wall. If you have this type of shelving, screw a strip of molding around the front edge of the shelf and the unit to the wall. On that note, you never want to keep glass items or supplies kept in glass containers for the same reason. All supplies should be in plastic containers or paper wrapping, stored in plastic or metal containers.
- For long term food storage, consider growing fruits and vegetables in a garden and raising chickens, turkeys, ducks, geese, rabbits, pigs, goats, donkeys, etc. In this manner you'll always have a massive food supply on hand without having to stockpile anything. But I'll discuss this more in my next book. When choosing plants and animals, consider the region and conditions they'll be living/working in, for example, white-colored animals vs. dark, long-haired vs. short.

SUPPLIES

- Tupperware can be used to store and/or waterproof items or to preserve and protect food; but it can also be used as dishware to eat in/on, preventing storing of breakable dishware. Glasses/cups, on the other hand, are a different story. I find that the non-spillable coffee cup with the wider triangular base and small tubular top make better drinking containers for the simple fact that they're not breakable and don't fall over, possibly wasting already limited amounts of water. Plastic yogurt containers with the same properties also work well as cups. Actually, I'm not sure why we still design and use anything other than containers with wider bases to store liquids; they always get knocked over, spill and break.
- Zip ties are a multifunctional device, much like duct tape or super glue; the applications are endless. For example, keep the larger 1ft ties to use as handcuffs or the common 8in ties as a quick tourniquet.
- Make sure to stock up on plenty of books, paper and pencils, interactive children material (that doesn't take up much space), even a musical instrument. In a time of darkness and doom, you'd be amazed how a little music or entertainment can raise the spirits, which is a must in any survival situation.
- An assortment of fruit and vegetable seeds will come in handy upon reoccupying the outside world.
- When tying the ankles and waste areas of jeans with wire, they make excellent sand bags, floatation devices, packs (knapsack) or as pillows. Similarly, aside from bags of dog food, you'll want to stock up on empty dog food bags, which again make great sand bags for flood protection, fortification or food storage. The term 'sand bag' can be misleading; in actuality, the bag can be filled with dirt, gravel, sawdust or any other aggregate to soak up and stop the infiltration of water.

GEAR

- The goggles listed need to cover the entire eye area without letting any air in, protecting the user from viral airborne bacteria and/or nuclear dust. This can be achieved with welding goggles, swimming goggles, dust goggles, motorcycle glasses or chemical or medical eyewear.
- Snares are great for the aftermath; but mice and rat traps are good for providing an ongoing source of food during and inside your shelter occupancy. Rat traps don't just catch rats; they'll trap squirrels, rabbits, chipmunks, birds, mice, lizards, snakes, etc., which are all exceptionally tasty. On a side note, peanut butter makes a great rat trap bait for any animal. Similarly, 'bear traps,' also known as foothold traps come in many sizes with the "bear trap" being the most common and largest. In actuality, the fox size will be more adaptable to our needs because of a broader range in medium sized animals available.

- As far as backpacks, you'll need a couple small school-sized backpacks for transporting gear and supplies short distances or while working, and a couple large travel backpacks for long distance.
- 55-gallon drums, 5-gallon buckets and waterproof containers w/lids can be metal military grade or plastic industrial or commercial grade and can be used for many things afterwards. For now, pack all cans, bottle water inside in rice, wheat or corn to keep everything safe from rats and water. Metal garbage cans also work well for this and are fairly cheap. Also, stock up on any store bought containers; 1 gallon milk jugs, 1 liter soda containers, plastic energy drink bottles, and any other plastic bottle-like container with a lid, any size, anything that will hold water, even shampoo, ketchup or dish soap bottles.

- All batteries (lead and nickel) are rechargeable, despite what the manufacturers say; even the disposable ones labeled "non-rechargeable" will take a charge if you have the right charger. You can also charge batteries with a solar panel. For 12v cordless drills, connect the 12v panel right to the battery terminals or run right off the panel, without a battery.
- Roof screw bits look like small sockets that fit into a cordless drill. You'll want to keep the 3 different-sized bits since the roof screws come in 3 sizes. Sheets of metal roofing will come in handy for fortification, shielding and shelters, not to mention trade.
- Tarps make good blankets, shelters, stretchers, beds/hammocks, signs, etc. If possible, get good quality tarps and don't leave them in the Sun (most plastic is solar degradable, not biodegradable, which means it will break down if left in sunlight, not when buried underground).
- As far as the 'clear tarps,' these can be in the form of paint drop cloths, cargo tarps, weed barriers, greenhouse covers, etc., and range in a whole spectrum of survival uses including water catchment, heat blankets, solar stills, rain protection, tarps, etc.
- A Fresnel lens is a must in any survival situation for starting fires, distilling water, even for cutting wood or metal. IF you can't find a Fresnel lens, at least keep a magnifying glass handy.
- A standard-sized flashlight will last up to 14 hours on one set of batteries. On average, you'll use a flashlight four hours every night when the power goes out. This means that you'd go through a pack of four batteries (per flashlight) every three nights (not to mention radios or any other battery-operated device you may have). At that count, you'll be in the dark in less than three months with 100 sets of batteries. And if the store doesn't have 100 packs of batteries (which is absurd to think it would), or you weren't intelligent enough to stockpile batteries beforehand, you'd be stuck with what they had left, which, during an apocalyptic event, is probably 5-10 packs, IF you're lucky. That's less than a week of light, not to mention how heavy it would be to carry 100 packs of batteries around on your back, or how much space they'd take up in your shelter. On the other hand, Dynamo flashlights and radios don't need multiple sets of batteries or extra battery chargers. They charge their own internal battery or diode by cranking the handle several times. With a good Dynamo device, 100 revolutions will give you 10-20 minutes of operation.

- An RJ11 lamp is a low-powered, usually LED lamp that plugs into and runs off the low electricity from a common phone outlet. So when you lose power, in any of the possible scenarios, you may still have light through the phone line. Making one yourself is just as easy, simply cut the cord of a phone, strip back the wires and connect any of the two to the pos and neg terminals of an LED flashlight. If you don't have an LED flashlight, pull out an LED from any appliance. On this note, you can wrap the prongs around a 9v battery from any smoke detector to make your own LED flashlight.

MEDICAL

- Retractors are used to help spread open the skin for easy access.
- Mechanical cutters are able to cut inside the body without danger of injury to the surrounding areas.
- Forceps hold objects or organs too small for human fingers or for holding multiple objects at a time.
- Tweezers come in handy during surgery as well as daily occurrences.
- Tampons absorb significant amounts of blood and fluids during surgery for their size.
- Cotton towels and cotton T-shirts also make good absorbers as well as bandages when cut into strips.
- Sterilizing all of the above instruments, linens, bandages and swabs in boiling water is critical.
- KI or Potassium Iodate (KI03) pills are anti-radiation tablets that protect the thyroid from damage caused by radioactive iodine during fallout. If you don't have tablets, topically (skin) apply tincture or iodine or betadine.
- Lastly, I've left several lines in each category to add anything else you may need. Maybe special personal things like prescriptions and medications, as well as supplements, such as Lactaid or anti-acid pills. If you suffer from hay fever or asthma (which are both societally-stimulated conditions), you'll want your medications initially. But by the time they run out you shouldn't be afflicted with such problems any longer. I mean, I've never heard of anyone dying from hay fever or asthma, in the old times.

One problem with a catastrophe is that it's unexpected; so we have to prepare for it even though we're not sure when or if it will ever come. The above list, if purchased all at once, could cost a couple thousand dollars, which begs the question, what justifies such an investment? Well, just that, it's an investment, or rather, an insurance policy. As mentioned before, you have insurance on a range of things from car insurance to snowmobile insurance to pet insurance; this is just another life insurance plan. On the other hand, the investment isn't lost like all your other insurance premiums. You still own the goods and supplies and can still actually use them in your daily lives IF nothing were to ever occur; whereas, money you pay out to providers goes into their pockets and ~~may~~ will never come back. For example, by purchasing four months' worth of food, you have four months' worth of food. And by eating the food on a normal basis today, with the oldest dates from your stockpile first and then replenishing that month's worth the following month when you go grocery shopping, you'll always just be four months ahead on your groceries is all. The same goes for batteries or any other perishable goods. If this isn't an option for you, at the very least, keep a backpack full of the essentials in the list near the door at all times.

You may notice a lot of items left out that would usually be in other typical survival preparation lists. This is because many of these items 'should' be plentiful and free after the collapse (as you see in *Chapter 9 and 10*); and, therefore, I see no good reason to spend your hard-earned money buying them up now. It is better to spend your cash on more of the things that will be used quickly, won't be replaceable, will be very valuable to trade and/or will be hard to acquire in the future, rather than, say, fencing, Tupperware or a vehicle, which practically everyone has, making those items easily acquired when everyone's dead. Land is a catch-22 in this line of thought. On one hand, you may need a well-stocked place to fall back on when TSHTF; on the other hand, it may be better to use the money you would have spent purchasing land and outfitting it on much-needed supplies. When the end finally does come, you can just acquire any of the land previously owned, that would now be free for the taking. Really, the main point I'm trying to make is, in the end, when the event finally does rain down upon us and you're hidden away in your shelter, if you have any money left in your bank account or wallet, you're an idiot! There's no need to store up on greenbacks, since they'll rapidly lose their value in the aftermath of any collapse. Gold is great, but it's too heavy to store and move. Diamonds, on the other hand, are lightweight, small, strong, and, therefore, can be easily carried and stored. Also, their authenticity can be easily proven by the age-old method of cutting glass, whereas, proving a gold piece is real and not costume jewelry to the common person during a trade in the new world, can be difficult, to say the least.

SELF-PREPARATION

Another, and possibly the main, problem with an apocalyptic event (other than everyone dying) is that it displaces people from their homes and daily routines, forcing them into a lifestyle of extreme, or at least uncomfortable, existence. Activities you may have never even conceived of doing, like walking through the woods barefoot because your shoes wore out, or suturing up a wife or child, may now become a daily occurrence. There are a few basics that you can begin doing, learning, and getting used to today, to prepare yourself and your family for what's to come though:

- Learn to shoot skeet and bird with a shotgun; learn to site in and shoot moving targets with a rifle; learn to use and practice using a compound bow; and get comfortable carrying and shooting a handgun. I carried a concealed 9mm every day for 5 years; so trust me when I say that a firearm which uses a 9-round clip and two extras gets extremely heavy after a few hours.
- Get out and hike; you'll be doing a lot of walking, especially if you need to go south for more climactic temps. And I don't just mean walking around the neighborhood, shopping mall or track; real terrain is uneven and wears on the feet quicker and differently than flat surfaces. Because of this you'll need to build up different leg and feet muscles than you currently have or would regularly need.
- Learn to swim. An astonishing 36%, or more than 1 out of 3 Americans (60% of whom are African Americans) and 54% worldwide don't know how to swim, which can literally mean life or death in an apocalyptic event or major crisis.
- Learn to repel. It can't hurt to learn as many things as possible. Repelling is just another one of those talents that you'll never know when you'll need.
- At least learn basic first aid, or better, basic surgery, as mentioned earlier.
- When the Sun goes down, don't turn on any lights. If you need to go to the bathroom, cook something, or perform any other after dark activities, do it without light. You'll need to get some practice and feel comfortable and confident moving and working in the dark. You'll actually notice after awhile that there is, in fact, light to see by. It is hardly ever really, completely dark, or even too dark to see by. Regardless, we always feel the need to turn on a light, even if we're good about turning it off afterwards. After a few days, you'll separate and begin performing daytime activities and nighttime activities, which later will come in handy as your eyes grow custom to and stronger in the dark.
- Turn off the heating and AC day and night. Get accustomed to and used to acting, thinking, preparing and compensating for activities based on the temperature and time of day. Similarly, if it's cold outside, take off your shirt, especially women (ok, women can just dress in lighter layers with cooler clothes.) Let your body get acclimated to nature and natural temperatures and away from manmade ones.
- Learn how to use a chain saw and axe to saw/chop down and split firewood.
- Walk around inside and outside without socks and shoes. Over the years we've grown exceedingly dependent on shoes. The best rule to live by, and this goes for everything, is to always ask yourself, what if I didn't have this item? What would I do? How would I survive? If the immediate answer is always accompanied with a negative feeling or even a slight sense of panic, regardless of what you answer, it's most likely that you're dependent or addicted to it and should immediately remove it from your life. I mean, just try to go a week, two weeks, two months without alcohol, cigarettes, coffee, toilet paper!
- Use your left hand! It's true that people are right or left handed, but that only means that that hand has a slightly quicker connection to the brain than the other. You can easily learn to use both hands to do all

jobs equally which will give you a greater range of control and ability over your life and things around you. By starting to use them both now, you'll build up the necessary hand and arm muscles needed later.

- Similarly, deprive yourself of the electronics you rely on so much today, such as microwaves, computers, hair dryer, curling iron, iron, printer, fan, cell phone, music, iPod, washer/dryer, dishwasher, garage door opener, doorbell, vacuum (I'm sure you didn't even realize how many things you actually relied on). I went up to Wyoming a couple years back to do an onsite evaluation for an off-grid doomsday cabin for some folks. It got late so we decided not to trek back to the vehicles but spend the night there, when the client actually said *"I'm not sure that I can fall asleep without my cell phone."* When I asked why not, he said *"I don't know. I guess because it gives me comfort."*
- Eat directly from cans and prepare and eat entire meals by mixing canned foods. You'll soon start becoming very creative, gastronomically speaking. Like I said, the wife and I lived 100% off canned food for 2 years in preparation for this chapter; and I can honestly say she can now make dozens of great 5 Star meals from a can of SPAM, corn and some weenies.
- Take some hunting and fishing trips with experienced hunters and insist on cleaning the carcass of your kill yourself so that you know what to expect. So that when the time comes you won't hesitate, delay or argue about moral obligations, wasting a good shot or even letting valuable days pass before finally succumbing to the act out of shear hunger. Hunting teaches two lessons in one:

    1. How to kill another living thing. Killing is a horrible experience that I wouldn't wish on anyone, the worst part of which comes directly before and directly after actually pulling the trigger or slitting the throat. This feeling, however, diminishes with each kill; so it's important to at least experience it once so you know that you can do it again.
    2. Hunting is made up of so many variables (tracking, senses, tactics, skill, experience), which are impossible to teach through a book.

- Visit a farm, learn how to milk a cow, a goat, butcher a chicken, hog, etc. In most cases, the farmer will welcome you with open arms. I know if I had someone who wanted to butcher my meat for me or milk one of my fatties for free I'd have gone for it in a second.
- Run. Build up some endurance. You may be running for your life soon. I've always found it funny that people buy a car which includes, and is based on, what I like to call all the 'maybe' factors... *"Maybe I'll need to tow something, so I'll need that towing kit;" "maybe my truck will roll so I need that roll-bar;"* or *"maybe I'll run out of gas on the highway so I need AAA."* Well, I say maybe you'll be running for your life so you need to build up your endurance.
- Don't shave or cut your hair. Learn and get used to long hair on your neck, legs, nose, face, ears, and head. Or conversely, shave your head and hair, get used to how that feels as well.
- Do yard or automotive work without gloves. Most people's hands are too sensitive to conduct the manual labor that will soon be needed to survive. Wearing gloves only further adds to this debilitating factor.
- If you don't know how to work on cars, it's essential you learn quickly. Take an automotive community college class and learn basic car repair. Similarly, take first-aid, welding, cooking, preserving, or any other adult education course available at your local community college.
- Don't eat food or water for a couple of days. See how fast your thought processes slow and dilute and how your body feels and reacts to such a situation; then you'll know how well, or rather poorly, you'll perform and the importance of gathering/fighting for food while you still have energy.
- Spend a couple of nights outside in rainy or cold weather; learn the importance of sleep deprivation, shelter, and warmth, so you can obtain such things before it gets cold, dark and rainy.
- One of the main issues I see when bringing interns out into the wild is that everyone thinks they're tired, and doesn't want to work to get food, shelter, water, warmth, etc. while they still have the energy/health. Then when they start getting cold, hungry or wet, they want to get up and acquire these things; but by that time, in most cases, it's too late. So it's critical that you experience and understand first-hand what these things mean before such a situation occurs so that you force yourself to act before you're too tired.
- Sleep on your bed without blankets, pillows or sheets; then sleep on the floor without blankets, pillows or sheets, then do the same on the concrete and/or dirt. You'd be surprised how many people have never slept without a mattress, blankets, sheets or pillows in their entire life.

- Garden. Growing a food source with your own hands isn't as simple as it sounds. And notice that I don't just say "learn" how to garden, because learning just isn't enough. It takes trial and error to really know and be able to grow your own food consistently.
- Ride a bike again, the same as with hiking; this will build muscles in your hands, legs, butt, back and feet that you haven't used since you were a kid, muscles that will prove vital in the up-and-coming days.
- Take a cold shower once in awhile, because warm water will most likely be a thing of the past. You may find it's actually enlightening, waking you up for a moment from your robotic, sheep-like trance.
- Turn the fridge off at night. This will give you a better idea of how and which foods perish and what conditions/precautions you'll need to take/make in the future when there's no, or rationed, electricity.
- If you do decide to buy land, look for places people or realtors tell you "no one can or would ever want to live here," because those are EXACTLY the places I want to live, places that no one would ever want to be or go. This way you 'may' avoid the mass migration of panicked, unprepared people looking for hand-outs and shelter. Use the 'likely cities to be attacked' map in *Chapter 4* as a reference.
- Learn a trade, or even better, learn as many trades as possible before time runs out. Then, not only will you require nobody's specialties and, therefore, not need to pay anyone for their services, but you can then charge for your services. This is a way of life that has been all but forgotten in our developing disposable world with commercial franchises offering replacement warranties and Indian operators.
- Place locks on your wheels and gas cap. Also, it may be worthwhile to have your tires filled with foam. Solid tires are leak-proof and can run over road spikes without difficulty.
- Lastly, as I've already mentioned, it's a good idea beforehand to formulate a group with close friends and family right now, even just in jest. If they survive, they'll remember their bond. Pair up and make an 'apocalypse pact' with a good friend, co-worker or brother (*apocalypto* buddies!) to help and stand-by each other (as long as possible) when the world ends, or if either swims out into the deep end of the lake.

CHILD PREPARATION

Preparing kids can be a little more difficult because they don't really understand why you're taking away their Xbox 360 or cell phone. In fact, some of the following preparations that would need to be accomplished may even seem borderline abusive to folks in 'today's' society. Still, soon such agencies/beliefs will be a thing of the past and the child will still need to know how to survive, regardless. So to get right to it:

- Make the child's life rough/uncomfortable without all the luxuries, comforts and even some of the 'necessities.' That way, the aftermath won't be as shocking or as disruptive to the kid. Hell, if you parent like me, the aftermath may even seem brighter.
- Don't let them taste chocolate, chocolate milk, candy, soda and the like. Then they won't develop a taste/addiction for such things.
- Keep them away from the Internet, I-devices and such, or at least not depend on them.
- Take them hunting, fishing, hiking and swimming. Teach them how to gut, skin and eat raw meat, fruits and vegetables. It took me 3 years to re-teach my ~~body~~ mind not to get nauseated eating raw meat off the carcass (just like every other animal on Earth does). In fact, I have cousins who, from a very young age, were taught to be vegetarians, and I feel really bad for them. They were never given the chance to eat meat, cooked or not. I'm not saying being a vegetarian is wrong; but I do think that not allowing your children to have a choice in life is unfair, whatever that choice is. I mean, what if I force my kids to be meatatarians like me and never eat fruits or vegetables? You may think this is a silly concept, but the brain can be programmed to become nauseous at the sight of anything. My cousins get sick just smelling meat, because it's been programmed into them for so long. Even if they wanted to change now, they couldn't. IF something does happen, they're going to have a really hard time, because surviving in the wild (which it will be) is all about diversifying. The animals with the largest variety of dietary requirements/options have the easiest time of fulfilling them.
- Only give infants 'toys' made from common items like toilet and paper towel tubes, blocks of wood, Tupperware, pillows, rocks, sticks, etc. This may all seem ridiculous to you but 'common items' are exactly what children have been playing with for hundreds of thousands of years, and when all is gone, that's what they'll be playing with again.

- And lastly, but most importantly, and this goes for all family members or friends, make sure to pre-arrange a spot outside of a major city, where everyone can meet up just in case everyone or anyone gets separated in all the confusion.

PET PREPARATION

I've always made it a general rule to never feed any of my animals--that goes for the dogs as well. Everyone is responsible for acquiring their own food; and that includes us. I mean, I don't see them going out and killing a rabbit and bringing it back for me to eat; so there's no reason for me to do the same. Not to mention, there probably won't be much dog food lying around afterwards, anyway. The important thing is to prepare them now for how it will be later. How inhumane, right? The inhumane thing to do would be to not consider them in this transition, abandon them, and let them starve to death or fend for themselves when there's no food or you can't acquire it in the next world, when they don't even understand what's going on in this one.

The fact is that dogs have been hunting and killing their own meals for hundreds of thousands of years before humans ever came along. They're actually much better designed for it than we could ever be. The problem is that the 'humane' people of the world have been feeding dogs for so long they've grown to rely on us for food and have abandoned their hunting instincts and skills in the process. Animal activist groups are just starting to realize this now and is why they're always saying *"don't feed the bears"* or *"no feeding the wildlife."* It's because if you do, these animals will also grow dependent on humans for food, just like dogs have, and when you leave or run out of food (or the world ends), what then? In all fairness though, dogs have no choice but to depend on us now; we've concreted over most of their hunting grounds and killed off most of their prey in the move for bigger and better cities and urban areas. So you'll now need to rebuild and re-teach these traits back to the dog, breaking that dependency, if you want to prepare him to find his own food in the future:

1. The first step in this process is to stop feeding them. Now food is worse than cigarettes, coffee and toilet paper combined, in that it seems you can't just quit eating, *cold turkey*. But you do need to stop feeding them manufactured food. Instead, place a dead mouse, rabbit, bird, squirrel, or any other source of natural prey that's abundant in the area, uncut, unprepared and warm in the feed bowl instead. At first, they'll sniff it, push it around and just play with it, but probably not actually eat it.
2. Now, cut the head off, leaving the body, head and blood in the bowl. Again, they'll smell it first, but this time will probably, eventually eat it. No matter what, carnivores are carnivores; and they'll always remember the smell and lure of blood.
3. Do this for at least a week; and then remove the bowl and place a caged animal of the same origin in its place instead. Let the dog look at it, smell it, jump around it and bark at it, before you break its neck and place it back in the bowl uncut. Hell, if you're really motivated, you can break its neck in your teeth in front of your dog. (Yes, what *doggies see, doggies do.*) Now you may say, well, now I AM having to go out and catch my dog's food for him, just like what you said not to do! Yes, unfortunately, this is what you'll have to undergo for not thinking for yourself and following what all the other mindless robotic-sheep have done for so many years, it's what I had to do too for the same reason. But I woke up and so can you.
4. Eventually, the dog will begin to understand what he needs to do to eat; and you can just let the animal out of the cage at feeding time. If the dog doesn't catch and kill his prey, he'll go hungry that day. Hunger is a strong educational motivator.
5. After a couple more weeks of that, you can take the animal away from the 'normal' feeding area, out into nature and let loose its prey in front of him. The rat, for example, will run under a downed log; a squirrel will run up a tree, a bird will fly into the air; a snake will slither into the grass, and the dog will learn to look in these locations for its source of food. The best age to train them to do this is around 5 months.

You'll only have to do the above to one set of dogs because they'll teach their offspring how to hunt just like they've always done in nature throughout history. Our dogs routinely come home from hunting on the ranch with their entire head and upper shoulders covered, caked, soaked and matted in blood. As a pack (20+ strong), they're able to take down some of the biggest prey in the area, usually eating out the insides first by chewing through and crawling completely into the stomach cavity. Then they spend hours at home cleaning off the last of the kill's nutrients from each other's fur. As far as health, they may be the most overfed (fattest) dogs in the U.S.

SHELTER PREPAREDNESS

Basically, there are three types of shelters that can be built (or one shelter with all three elements) that will withstand and protect its occupants from most of the major, global catastrophes:

- Underground – Which for the most part would protect against viral pandemics, meteor showers, nuclear radiation, flood (if situated above 220ft elevation), super hurricanes, tsunamis or volcanoes, earthquakes, terrorist attack, invasion, global warming/cooling (ice age), magnetic polar shift and, of course, the chaos caused by an economic or governmental collapse.

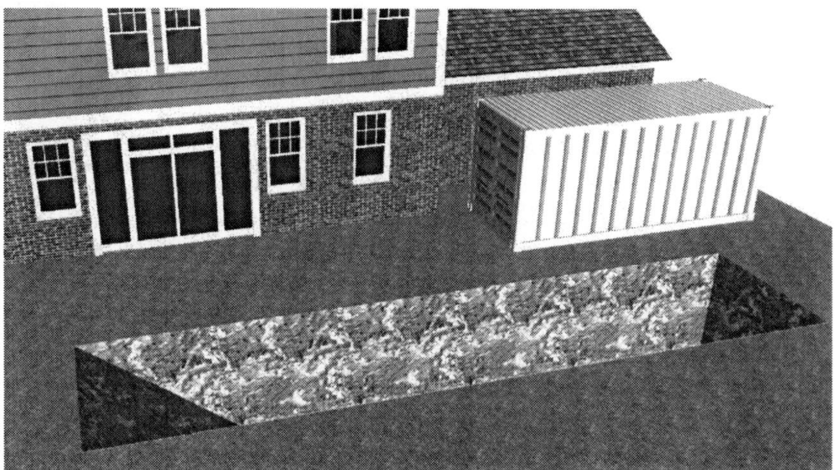

1. Dig a hole in the backyard 12ft-16ft deep by 10ft wide and 22ft long, tapering out one side for stairs. Usually a rented backhoe, bobcat or bulldozer will handle the job very efficiently; but you may have to call in a pool installation contractor and get a pool permit from the city.
2. Purchase and place a 20ft steel shipping container inside the hole, back-filling around three of the four sides.
3. You can build wood or concrete stairs or a ramp down to the entrance to help facilitate bringing down supplies or leave dirt if desired. Shipping containers are the large boxes you see on trains or ships that bring all of the 'much needed' goods to our capitalist country, mostly from China. They're too expensive to send back empty, so they're often sold to us for between $1000-$4000 each with delivery.
4. Don't just backfill the backyard flat, pile up the extra dirt on top making a small mound which will provide several feet more mass to your shelter.
5. Position all of your goods, water and supplies along the front of the container allowing for one of the two doors to open, and cots or sleeping and living facilities towards the back where there's the most mass (protection).
6. Lastly, when it's time, occupy the underground bunker, shut the door behind you, and push the supplies in front of both doors. You can also weld or bolt a

couple of bar padlocks between the two doors in order to lock it from the inside. On this note, I would remove the locking feature from the outside as well, just in case some smart ass (like me) feels the impulse/need to lock you in.

- Remote – A well-hidden, well-stocked cabin (like the now available Agua-Luna Ranch cabin shown in the photo on right) in the desert or woods isn't as protective, but is an inexpensive option to weather out nuclear war, economic/government collapse, viral outbreaks, terrorist attack and invasion. Taking up residence in a large sailboat or other ship actually isn't a bad idea either, since being out in the middle of the ocean is about as remote as you can get. You'll have a means of transportation after the cataclysm itself, not to mention a boat that would ride out the melting of the polar ice caps, viral outbreaks, terrorist attack, invasion, economic/governmental collapse and global warming/cooling. A boat floating on the open sea, however, would be a literal sitting duck and, therefore, would have no chance during an asteroid impact or tsunami.

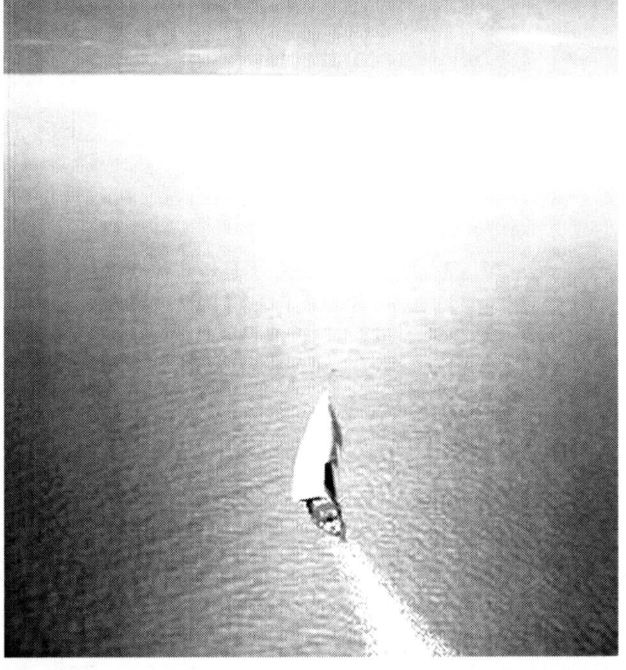

- Fortification – As a last resort, at least by stockpiling food and bricking (not boarding) up the windows and doors in your office or home, you stand a chance from viral epidemics and economic/government collapse. As an added bonus, you can build a makeshift nuclear bunker to protect against fallout in your own home or office (or someone else's) as well:

1. Try to pick a space against the wall with an electrical plug and an Internet terminal, preferably in a basement, cellar or any other location that has at least one wall underground.
2. Push a strong office or conference desk against the wall directly over the plug and terminal.
3. Remove the hinge pins or hinge screws from several doors (as described in *Chapter 9*) and place them on top of and around the desk. If a desk isn't available, place the doors on top of a couple file cabinets, dressers or other furniture making your own table.
4. Push any extra cabinets, furniture, boxes, bricks, books, sandbags, water supplies, food supplies or any other object with significant thickness and mass (the heavier the better) around the tables forming a barricade.

5. Make sure to leave a small void (vent) a few inches thick by a foot wide on top of one side and bottom on the opposite side so that convection air current can begin, providing the shelter with circulation and fresh air.

6. Make it long and large enough to accommodate all occupants lying down, especially in hotter conditions (one can stay in a lying position, comfortably 30 times longer than standing and 20 times longer than sitting), which works with our table/door method as both are typically longer than wide. A small piece of cardboard can help bring fresh air in by fanning the exhaust air up and out the top vent.

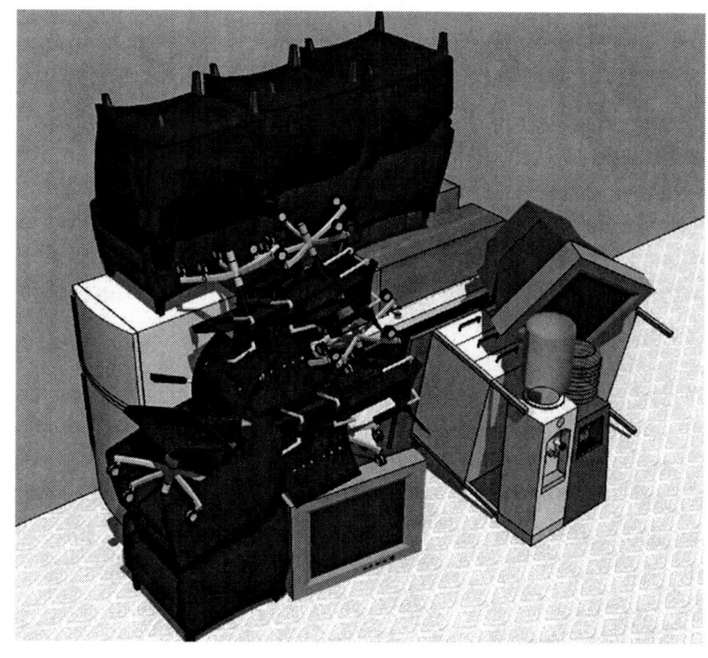

Air isn't contaminated with radiation, only the dust particles traveling in the air. And these dust particles can't travel through walls or dust filters. This is why the blockade isn't built to seal out air from entering, only any dust from settling on or near you, which releases penetrating x-ray-like radiation in all directions. This radiation can penetrate through walls, filters, buildings and your body, killing you from the inside out. Putting mass between you and the dust is the only thing that can absorb the radiation before it gets to you. If there are additional floors above you, and your table or door shelter is at its weight limits, adding additional furniture and supplies (mass) to these floors will add further shielding. The same goes for the other side of the wall, if it's not underground that is. With every inch of mass your barricade grows, the more radiation it blocks out. For example: If the shelter were made out of 5in of steel, 16in of brick or blocks filled with concrete or sand, 2ft packed earth or 3ft loose earth, it would reduce the amount of radiation penetrating your shelter by 99%. The point is that you cannot breathe radiation, only the radiation-soaked dust in the air; so it's important not to contaminate the only clean area in the house/building. If the building is sealed fairly well (doors and windows closed), the air vents in your barricade should be safe, if not just stuff cotton shirts in the vents. Which brings me to your next problem...

You'll probably get a few morons who didn't read this book (probably no more than 2 or 3 though) and, therefore, made no preparations of their own themselves, seeking shelter during the actual fallout or immediately afterwards (when the danger of contamination is at its highest), trying to break into your home/building/shelter, or wanting to loot your supplies (wall mass), essentially allowing radiation and fallout dust in, ruining all your hard work and possibly killing you and your family in the process, just because they weren't smart enough to pre-prepare or know when it was safe to come out of their own shelters. Because of these idiots, it will be mandatory to lock up the building, barricade the building's (or at least the floor/room you're in) doors and windows with metal, bricks or sandbags and seal with plastic painter's drop cloths or tarps. If the air in the room becomes stale, turn on a heater or air conditioner (if power is still on), as they have dust filters already installed. If there isn't any electricity, open two windows on opposite walls, make an incision in the plastic, insert the air conditioner and heater filters, widen the incision and re-tape the area.

MENTAL PREPAREDNESS: WOMEN VS. MEN

Many people, especially men, will have a really difficult time adapting to this new environment. I mean, you have to imagine, you've just worked more than half your life getting into a good university and getting a good degree on time to marry you're the love of your life, land that great job and are now working overtime everyday saving up for that dream home, dreaming and planning for a future with your wife and newborn infant, when all of a sudden those dreams are destroyed, literally. All that education is wasted (a degree in anything other than agriculture won't help you in this world); the company that employed you is completely obliterated; the love of your life is most likely dead along with your kid(s); and you're presently realizing that you're kind of out of your element, surrounded by thugs and have no idea how to survive in this environment. Add to this, a sudden stop and loss of societal infrastructures that once provided for and protected you and such 'comfort' foods and products like coffee, coke and cigarettes; it's no wonder that there will be a massive spike in suicides following the event. Anyone who has experienced a catastrophe (fire, flood, tornado, earthquake) which has completely destroyed their home and all of their personal property, recorded memories and possessions and/or lost loved ones in war or another unforeseen manner, knows exactly what I'm talking about.

Women, you will have it rough in the same and different ways, possibly even worse than men; because society has lied to you all these years, making you believe that you're equal to men when, in fact, you're not. It's a complete falsehood perpetrated, I believe, by a government willing to at least verbally accept the results of the feminist movement, women's rights and the belief in equality, while structurally, infra-structurally, governmentally and corporately ignoring it all (as we well know). What I don't understand is, why? Why the deceit, lies and misleading efforts? Why does society feel a need to brainwash you to believe that you're 'strong and independent' while the men continue to take complete and total care of you? It's a ruse. For example, speaking in percentages (there's always the exception), the people who feed you are men, they (farmers) raise, herd (cowboys), kill (slaughterers and meat packers), transport (truck drivers), stock (grocers) and prepare (butchers) the food you buy in the grocery store every day. When there's something wrong with you, your doctor or surgeon is the *man* you go to. Fire? (men,) police? (men,) military? (men.) When a pipe breaks in your house, I know that you don't fix it yourself; you call a plumber, who's a male. When something's wrong with your car, do you fix that yourself? Hell, no! You take it to a mechanic who, of course, is a male. Who mows your lawn? Who built, painted, bricked, carpeted and sheet-rocked your home? Who repairs your electrical problems? Who fixes your leaky roof? All men. You claim to be equal while maintaining reliance on men. Why don't you fix your roof yourself? Your broken pipes? Your car? Why don't you butcher, gut, skin and quarter your own meat? Because you cannot, and that's ok. But don't lie about it.

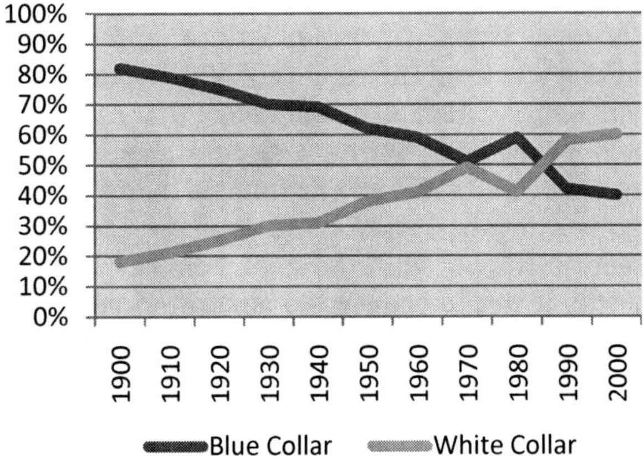

Now before I'm proven wrong by the extremely small percentages of women who can and will do these things themselves, for the most part 98.7% of women not only don't, but can't and won't. This is why females interested in becoming firefighters, police officers and soldiers aren't required to run the same distances as men to pass the respective physical tests, aren't required to do as many pushups, sit-ups, or carry a 200-pound dummy up 7 burnt-out floors; it's because physically, they cannot. So if anything were to ever happen to this structure that allows men to take care of women without women sacrificing their notions of equality, women would find out the hard way that, indeed, they're not actually equal, that they've been lied to all these years and will be forced to depend on a male once again for survival and safety. In fact, men, you may even consider having more than one wife in the aftermath. Polygamy has always been a strong, healthy societal factor throughout history and the world, presenting a binding relationship where the man can care for multiple women. Actually, just recently in the United States did we outlaw such martial practices (although they're still practiced in Utah, as well as most other countries). Now, ladies, you may think we've just jumped back a hundred years; and you'd be right. That's exactly what will happen; and that's exactly what I've been trying to tell you. You're finally catching on!

And men will have to rise up to the challenge and take charge, take care of and protect their vulnerable females and children as well as themselves. Again, it is something that society has done for these men all this time as well. You see, we've been slacking as men and have also been slightly misled ourselves. Although the above tasks and jobs are filled by males, most men don't know how to fix their own car, their own roof, their own pipes, or butcher their own food either. I blame this fact again on society and capitalism. For the last hundred years with the "advancement" of society (the boom of commercialism, capitalism, automation and technology) the percentage of blue collar workers decreased from 82% in 1900 to 40% in 2000. If I were to take an educated guess, I would speculate that as the extremely small percentage of self-sufficient females increased, the percentage of self-sufficient males decreased at the same rate, including their ability to protect their women, children and their possessions as well. In this way, you see, there seems to be very little difference between the sexes today, other than the physical act of sex itself (and even those lines are being blurred). Conversely, society has directed women away from marrying and reproducing with the "ruffians" (blue collar workers) who actually have all of these survival qualities and can protect them during the end times. Hence, most of these types of men aren't married with children or are divorced or separated from their mates and, therefore, no longer responsible or influential in and for their lives, and therefore will be the ones cornering the husband, his wife and two kids in their own home, after the collapse. Instead, women chose or are led to marry men who are "book-smart," handsome, well-educated, have/had a good (office) job and can 'better provide' for them in this environment. Unfortunately, these same qualities also mean he will <u>not</u> be able to 'better provide' for her in the next.

If you disagree, you're either very naïve or greatly mistaken. Today's 'men,' if you can call us that, don't raise our children. Society, in the form of a babysitter, daycare, state-appointed teacher, in-laws, social workers, other parents and sometimes, in rare cases, the wives themselves, raise our children. You wake up and are out of the house by 7:30A.M., maybe giving the kids a quick kiss and a few deep words of wisdom like "have a nice day at school," or "did you do your homework?" as you run out the door, IF you see them at all, that is. That's 10 minutes of good quality time checked off, congrats! Then mom drops them off at daycare on her way to work 45 minutes later. Kids get out of school around 3:00P.M.; but mom can't pick them up until 6:00, so they go to daycare or a babysitter. Dad's home by 7:00 from working overtime, if you're lucky, and is able to really instill some ethics, morals and values between commercials of Survivor and CSI before the kids hit the sack at 8:00. In total, you spend no more than 2 hours out of a 24-hour day on average with your child, or 1/10th of the 18 years, which is typically only 1/4th of your life with them before they move out at 18; all in the name of 'better providing' for them. In the end, it doesn't really matter anyway, since you hire out all the plumbing, auto maintenance, roofing, electrical work, etc. and don't really have anything of importance to teach them anyway.

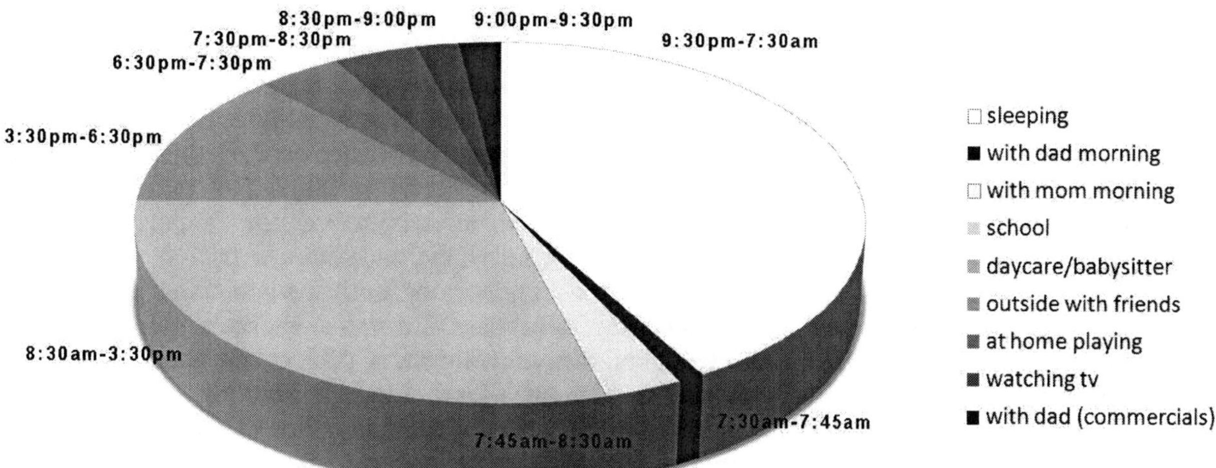

I'm sure I may get many bad reviews from women saying I'm sexist. Truth is, I haven't worked in almost 10 years. For the most part (except when we were self-sufficient), my wife has been taking care of me. I mean, I run a 'non–profit' organization out of Mexico (no income). She not only supports, feeds, cooks for me, cleans after me, but also pays for my projects abroad. To be honest, I deplore and want nothing to do with the monetary structure we've, so I have a great thing going here. I love that women are at least equal to men and can now generate an income to support their families. I don't have to do anything but be a stay-at-home husband. But that doesn't mean I'm blind and ignorant to the truth. If some major catastrophe did occur and society fell, I would have to step up and provide/support/protect us. And it will, unfortunately, all good things must come to an end.

In the end, I foresee adults, unable, unwilling and unmotivated to do anything to prepare themselves and their loved ones for what's to come. These people are exactly the ones I describe in this book as robotic-sheep. They'll be the first to be fed upon (figuratively and literally), abused, misled, taken advantage of, raped and killed for their 'stuff.' To have survived such an event and not even have a chance, what a sad thing. The question is, are you one of these people? If so, are you willing to change, prepare, act? In the end, it can only be up to you.

With all this evidence, all these predictions, all these possible scenarios from so many sources for so long, how can we ignore the slightest, smallest, teeny-weeny, itsy-bitsy chance that something just maybe, might occur in 2012, or in the immediate future? Are you not willing to at least conceive the possibility? Is your family not worth at least that? But I encourage you to do your own research, find your own facts, don't take my, or anyone's word on the matter, for or against. I promise you, you'll be surprised with what you uncover. The ~~following~~ previous chapters provided you with first-hand information, gathered from, and provided by, people who have lived through actual catastrophes; what occurred, what to expect, what to do to survive; how to prepare before and during an event of global proportions; and how to live in a new world. I truly hope you take it all to heart.

ABOUT THE AUTHOR

Dan Martin currently lives with his wife Lucia and their many dogs on a Hacienda in Mexico. He enjoys bouldering, scuba diving, surfing, and spending time in nature. Dan was born in Detroit, Michigan in 1974, the eldest son of the eldest son, five generations long. The offspring of divorced parents, at thirteen Dan went on to live with his father high in the Rocky Mountains where he learned to hunt, trap and be self-sufficient. At age seventeen, Dan joined the military, was stationed in Japan, Diego Garcia, Hawaii and eventually deployed to Desert Shield and Iraq. He received a degree in Environmental Sciences from the University of Hawaii; and upon arriving back in the States, attended UT studying physics/engineering. He then volunteered with Habitat for Humanity, Greenpeace and as a missionary translator in Mexico. Dan then went worked for Boeing Aerospace on Air Force C-17's attending San Antonio Community College, taking undergraduate courses in Pre-Med, Sociology, World History, Mechanics and Psychology, earning enough credits for a Ph.D. and another Masters degree.

In Mexico he met and married Lucia and re-entered the U.S. Eventually he quit his high-paying career at 25; cashed in all investments and 401Ks; sold his homes and personal belongings, to move out into the desert and leave the world, family, friends and "the robotic-sheep" behind. For the next eight-years, the two lived 100% off-the-grid, completely cut-off from society. No electric lines, no telephone lines, no garbage or sewer service, no mail, no city water, no cell service, not even a road to the property. Dan built their octagon home alone without walls, completely open to the surrounding landscape so that they could live "with/in nature". They lived off rain water catchment, hunted, raised, bred and slaughtered goats, chickens, catfish, wild pig, deer and fowl for food, made their own fuel and grew underground hydroponic fruits and vegetables.

In 2008, Dan finally left the ranch after not seeing another person for six-years to give university seminars around the world, conduct workshops and sustainable and renewable energy projects in Asia and South and Central America, and host interns and volunteers in Texas and Mexico on the subject. I personally had the chance to visit the Agua-Luna Ranch and actually met Dan Martin in 2009. The ranch is amazing. He accomplished everything from building enormous arches to worm composting, bee keeping, mining, natural heating and cooling, methane and hydrogen generation, and wind, water, and solar electricity.

Dan Martin then became a consultant performing hundreds of similar sustainable projects, teaching others about making their own renewable fuels and ways to harness alternative energies, building with natural materials and living independently. He has designed and overseen dozens of projects for governmental agencies as well as private corporations and overseas clients. The Agua-Luna Ranch is now for sale and available to someone looking to become self-sustainable or survive the *"crisis."* Eventually, Dan would again build a second completely self-sufficient homestead and create the non-profit organization Agua-Luna in Mexico, composed of interns and volunteers who travel with Dan to third world countries. They live with and learn from the people and cultures that haven't stopped living life self-sufficiently (which is why we call them "third world").

For the last three years, Martin has written and published dozens of do-it-yourself style guides on the subject--from how to make your own ethanol, to how to build your own solar panels and wind turbines. These books are all available on Amazon or on his website: *www.Agua-Luna.com*. Dan Martin has also drawn the attention of established newspapers, websites, and magazines from several countries, and has been the source of half a dozen radio and television interviews.

In 2010, he began writing *Apocalypse, How to Survive a Global Crisis* in preparation for 2012, which is an accumulation of his life's work, education and experiences, in addition to his sustainability guides in preparation for the possible end of the world.

Dan Martin grew up in Detroit during the '80s when it was at its worst, fought in Desert Shield/Storm during the '90s and has since lived in Mexico through the Sinaloa-La Familia Michoacana Cartel wars, making him a virtual expert on survival and humanity at its lowest and most dangerous.

Apocalypse is the first of a three-part series, showing the reader first-hand knowledge and hands-on experience through the eyes of the author, step-by-step how to be self-sufficient. He illustrates how being entirely independent from society is not only possible in today's world, but may even become imminent in the next. His views of humanity and insight into possible future events are eye-opening to say the least; yet, he always manages to follow up with creative and resilient means to handle and resolve the dilemmas that arise. Never has an author managed to capture and awaken so many souls with so few breaths!

- Arnold Williams

Correspondence with the author should be sent to Martin@Agua-Luna.com
Or visit Dan Martin at www.Agua-Luna.com or www.Facebook.com/Dan.Martin.Author

A NOTE FROM THE AUTHOR

I've come to the conclusions outlined in this book over 20 years of experience and intense pondering. Many of my critics reviews of this book say my narrative of society and how its existence before, during, and after the end times are "violent," "vile," and even "vulgar." And I know this, I don't deny it. In fact, I'm the one that said that. Many of the topics and content I discuss in this book, no one should ever have to think about, let alone visualize. It's disgusting, disturbing and possibly even demented, but that doesn't mean you won't or don't have to think about it in a post-apocalyptic world. My response to their statements? I must point out that the current world is all those things and more. It is only described and depicted by myself as such in an attempt to portray the world as closely as possible to the truth. I'm not inventing anything here; I'm simply documenting the existing facts as accurately and descriptively as possible. Something most writers and news agencies shy away from in fear of public outcry, uproar, and bad ratings. I truly hope that the next world won't have the same attributes as this one; and maybe it won't, but I'm not naïve enough to believe that the transition won't be filled with horrific deaths, sufferings and violence beyond anything I, or anyone, can imagine or even write about. But you have to keep in mind that the end of this world isn't necessarily a bad thing; in fact, in this day and age, it could only be better for humanity. It's like a hurricane. It comes in, cleans everything; and we start anew again--better, stronger, healthier.

And then there are those who will surmise from this book that I'm anti-government, which is partly true, but not entirely. I don't believe we need anyone to rule over us, or that that this specific government should be overthrown and replaced with a new one (which would be just as bad), as DuPont, U.S. Steel, Heinz, Standard Oil, the American Legion, Singer Sewing Machine, GM, Chase Bank, J.P. Morgan, The United States Rubber Company (now B.F. Goodrich) and Goodyear believed in 1934. Mine is a fairy tale concept; it will never happen. There will always be an entity that takes control of the masses; it has always occurred throughout human existence. In that case, I would prefer it to be socialist or even communist in nature. I lived in a military ruled world for over 8 years and enjoyed every minute. Free housing, medical, food, entertainment, gym. If you need a tool or a lawnmower, you check it out for free or the work is done for you at no charge. No worries, very little crime. It's the civilian sector that has its issues: laying off the masses at will, scamming first-time homeowners, overcharging for basic goods and services, committing bankruptcy at the drop of a hat, regardless of the effect such actions have on employees, the public, the community or stockholders. If we could all work for the military, many things described in this book wouldn't transpire. The U.S. Military is top of the line; and I have nothing but the highest respect for them and the structure itself, if it just weren't for their connection to the gosh darn government is all. And you may hear how I speak about the human infestation, the human-caused extinction of animals, pollution, man-made climate change, deforestation, acid rain, etc., but wonder why I don't feel the same about things like war, famine, pandemics, drug abuse, murder. It's because the latter helps the former. If anything, I'd prefer more war, famine, drug overdoses; anything that decreases the number of men, helps the planet and increases the number of animals.

LIFE AS 'WE' KNOW IT: EPIC SADNESS

As you may have noticed by now, I'm a big fan of and for the complete and utter annihilation of the human race from the face of this planet; but what you may not know is why. Since humans began forming major cities and intricate societies, we've managed to be directly responsible for the extinction of the North African Elephant, Chinese River Dolphin, the Bali, Javan and Caspian Tigers, Long-Horned Bison, Mexican Grizzly Bear, the Japanese and Falkland Island Wolfs, Sea Mink, Japanese Sea Lion, Caribbean Monk Seal, Broad-Faced Potoroo, the Eastern and Lake Mackay Hares, the Toolache and Crescent Nailtail Wallabies, Dodo Bird, Desert

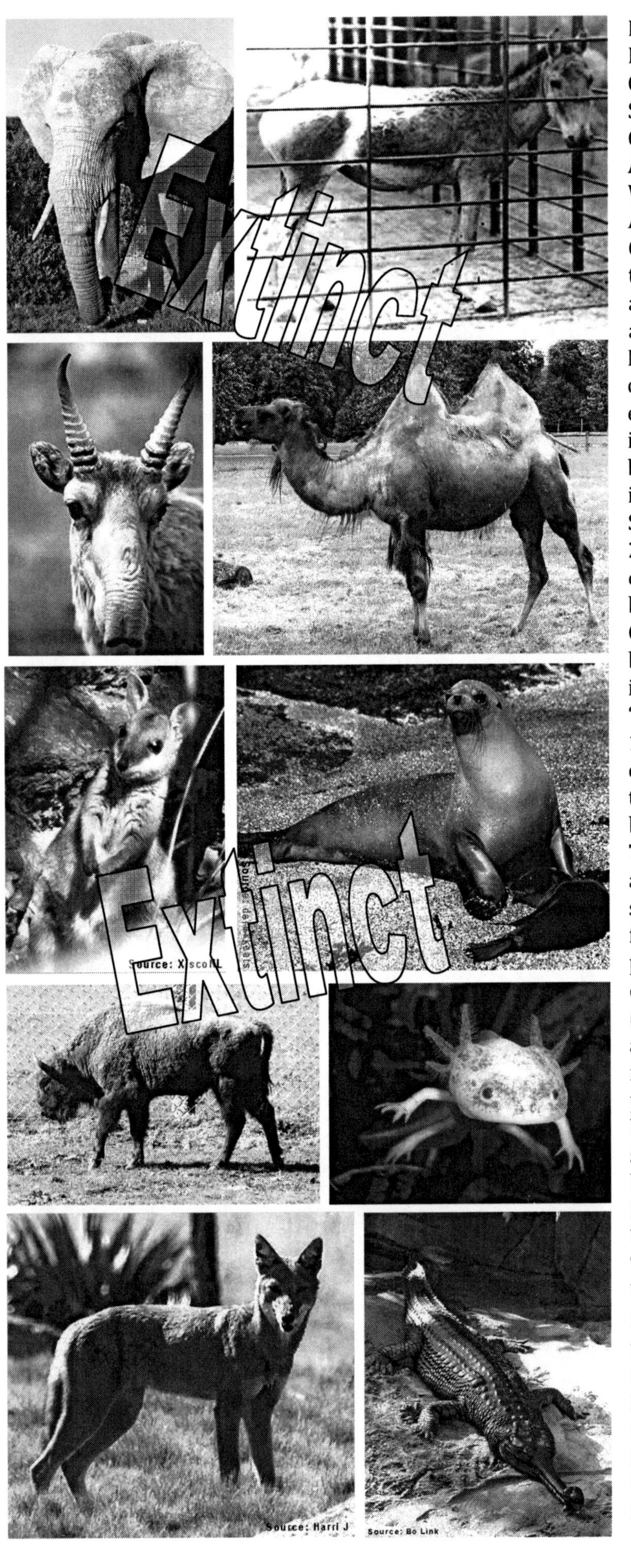

Rat-Kangaroo, Thylacine, the Desert and Pig-Footed Bandicoot, Lesser Bilby, Red-Bellied Gracile Opossum, Steller's Sea Cow, Sardinian Pika, Marcano's Solenodon, the Christmas Island, Balearic and Tule Shrews, Aurochs, the Caucasian and Carpathian Wisents, Bluebuck, Bubal Hartebeest, the Arabian, Red, Queen of Shebas and Saudi Gazelles, Schomburgk's Deer, Pyrenean Ibex, the Quagga, Tarpan and Syrian Wild Asses and almost 50 different species of mice, rats and bats, including Darwin's Galapagos Mouse. Now mind you, these aren't "'errors of past generations." The Saudi Gazelle went extinct in 2008 due to "hunting by humans of its native lands." The Chinese River Dolphin became extinct in 2006 because of "human industrialization," and the Pyrenean Ibex and Sturdee's Pipistrelle disappeared, both in 2000, due to poaching, disease and competitive food sources, all of which were brought on by man and man alone. Conversely, we've driven the buffalos to the brink of extinction (less than 200 in the wild) in the 19th century through 'market' or 'commercial' hunting in only 10 years from 1873 to 1883, something thousands of years of time failed to do. Bison were killed in the thousands for their hides and bones, the bodies and meat left to rot on the ground. The U.S. Government not only sanctioned and actively endorsed the wholesale slaughter of bison herds, but promoted and funded it as well, for several reasons: (a) "to provide the then-developing ranchers non-competitive grazing lands for their cattle," (b) to eliminate 'obstacles' on railroad tracks, and (c) "to weaken the Indian resistance by removing their main food source in order to pressure them onto reservations." But the buffalo are merely one species of a wide spectrum of life forms we've terrorized, brutalized and genocized. We've driven the Mountain Gorilla, Bactrian Camel, Ethiopian Wolf, Saiga, Takhi, Kakapo, Arakan Forest Turtle, the Sumatran, Indian, Black, Northern White, Southern White and Javan Rhinoceroses, Brazilian Merganser, Axolotl, the Leatherback and Green Sea Turtles, Gharial, Vaquita, the Philippine and Solitary Eagles, Brown Spider Monkey, California Condor, Island Fox, Chinese Alligator, Dhole, Blue Whale, the Asian and African Elephants, Giant Panda, Snow Leopard, African Wild Dog, Malayan Tapir, Tiger, Steller's Sea Lion,

Marcher, Bornean Orangutan, Gravy's Zebra, Tasmanian Devil, Cheetah, Blue-billed Duck, American Bison, Jaguar, Manned Wolf, the Tiger and Great White Sharks, Okapi, African Grey Parrot, Striped Hyena, Narwhal, Gaur, Lion, the Polar and Sloth Bears, Dugong, Komodo Dragon, Hippopotamus, Mandrill and the Fossa so close to the brink of extinction, that in the immediate and imminent future, even if we wanted to, we wouldn't be able to stop it and save them now if we desperately tried. In fact, the Hawaiian Crow, Wyoming Toad, Socorro Dove, Red-tailed Black Shark, Scimitar Oryx, Catarina Pupfish now only exist in zoos. And I wouldn't feel so harshly if we had only just killed them without making them suffer; but it seems we enjoy orphaning, abusing and maiming gorillas, sharks, minks, snakes, alligators, chinchilla, whales, lynx and elephants to name only a few, for their hands and feet and tusks and teeth and skin and oil and fur. We transport and relocate dangerous predatory or competitive species, intentionally or unintentionally, to abnormal, non-natural locations that feed upon or devastate food supplies. We run over and over and over millions of squirrels, deer, rabbits, possums, birds, skunks, coyotes and who knows what else per year on our some hundreds of thousands of miles of roadways (an estimated 220 million animals die each year by motor vehicle alone). We destroy their homes and breeding grounds in the name of deforestation, suburban neighborhood development and oil. (Over 12 billion trees are cut down each year and another 6 million tons of coral reef damaged or harvested for souvenirs.) We murder them just for the 'fun' of it or to mount their heads and bodies and antlers on our walls. We force them off our land or slay them for fear that they'll attack livestock. We mass produce them for meat; we pump them full of drugs and force them to live in caged filth. We domesticate, manipulate and create new species of dogs, felines, birds and even rodents, and then perform hideous tests on them all in the name of science and make-up. We lock them up, place them in zoos and circuses and TV shows and force them to perform

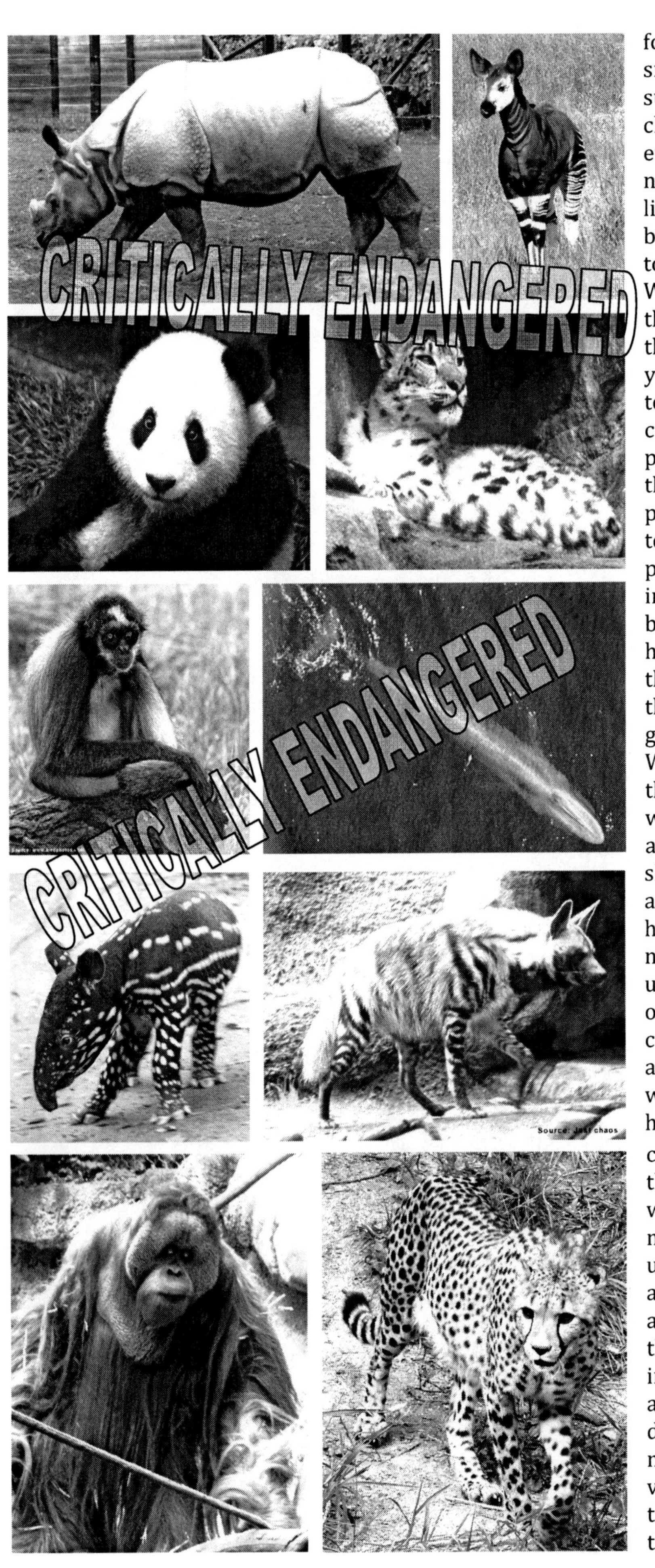

for our amusement while wearing tutus and smoking cigars. We spay and neuter them, surgically stopping them from having children. We literally sell them into slavery, even physically placing chains around their necks and buy and sell them at auctions just like we did the Africans. We hit them, we beat them, we molest them; we force them to fight or race for our enjoyment and profit. We give them man-made diseases, we use them as weapons; and the funny thing is they've all been on this planet for millions of years before us and outnumber us 10^100 to 1 (that's 1 with 100 zeros). We make coffee tables, couches, jackets, gloves, purses, necklaces, belts and shoes out of them. We shoot them with slingshots, paintball guns and bb guns; we make toothpaste, dog food and other food products with them. And then there's insects (not to mention funguses and bacteria), another life form for which we have no regard. We despise them so we trap them, we poison them; we exterminate them. We burn them with magnifying glasses and dissect them for school projects. We roll them up into little balls and flick them across the floor (rolly pollies). So when you ask how I can be so willy-nilly about taking the life of humans, maybe you should ask yourself why you're so willy-nilly about smashing an ant, fly or cockroach. A human's value for animal life is nil, so I have no value for humans. We've completely and utterly disrupted the natural flow of all other life on this planet without regard or concern for anyone other than ourselves; and that's not even the worst part. The worst thing is WE DON'T EVEN CARE! We have no regret, no remorse, no consideration; no loss of sleep. We don't think about the animals on this rock one way or another in our everyday life, for the most part, unless it's because they're unwanted guests in our cabinets, or flying around our head when camping, which is another perfect example. We not only kill them in and around our own homes, we go into nature, into the wild, and kill them in and around their own homes as well. It's despicable. Who do we think we are? I mean, really, what makes animals any less valuable then you? Why do we do these things to them? Why do we experiment on them instead of on ourselves? Why not kill humans to make belts and purses from rather than animals? Why not hunt us for fun instead? Because we can. We can no longer make slaves of, conduct scientific tests on, eat or mistreat humans, but we can animals. It's as simple as that. And until we evolve past this as well, there's really no hope for us. Maybe this next cycle will bring on change, maybe not.

I see humans with our 'almighty' cerebral cortex and our ability to shop as spoiled children, who take whatever they want, do what every they want, eat whatever they want, destroy the planet if we want. We don't share, listen, learn with or from any of the other inhabitants. And if I feel this way about you, how do you think animal activists feel? Environmentalists? Terrorists? Aliens? God? One day, someone or something will come and drastically change our lifestyle, if not in 2012, soon! Ecclesiastes 3:19 says: *"Man has no pre-eminence above a beast: for all is vanity."* In fact, God created plants and animals <u>first</u> (Genesis 1-24), and us, second (verse 26), making us their "ruler" like a king rules a kingdom; and yet, if that king killed his people in the numbers we do, didn't protect them or provide for their well-being and showed no concern for their existence, whatsoever, what kind of ruler would he be? Regardless if all this was done intentionally or unintentionally, you can't deny that if there were no humans on the planet, such inhumanities would cease overnight. If we can't make some radical change literally "overnight," I'd rather just hand this planet back to them in its entirety and let God know we failed as rulers. If you're like me and want to help the planet, the best thing we can do for it as humans, is kill ourselves. It is really the best thing for them. We see literal proof of this throughout history. For example, when the North American Indian population was devastated by wave after wave of epidemics (from European diseases) during the 17th and 18th centuries, the numbers of American bison skyrocketed rapidly. But no, the animal extinction rate has risen to one thousand times its natural level in just this century alone. So I say, bring on the apocalypse, It can only get better from here!

THE TRUTH: IT WILL SET YOU FREE!

It's been my experience that people *can't handle the truth*. I've seen this firsthand in the reactions of my interns, workshop participants and volunteers over the many years of teaching the many, many diverse areas of self-sufficiency. For example, dogs sniff butts; that's what dogs do--dogs love it. They do it to each other to say hello; they do it to us to let us know they care; and they do it because, well, they just like smelling things; and yet, people freak-out every time they do it to them. I also get a lot of interns and volunteers that gross-out over the thought of drinking pee or making fertilizer out of human poo. Or when we're on site and a bee ('the most dangerous, deadly, vicious, blood-thirsty creature on the planet') buzzes around the group. I've actually had people (that weren't allergic) run off seemingly for their lives while swatting violently in the air screaming "aaaa, a bee, a bee!" No kidding. But I'm sure that you've probably seen the exact same reaction in a similar situation yourself. This is how society has brainwashed us to be, to feel 'weird', uncomfortable, or freak-out with things that happen in nature. In the end, I worry that those reading this book, those that really do want to prepare themselves for the end, be it on December 21, 2012, or beyond, won't have the dedication, intelligence, knowledge base, experience, guts or will to wake up and realize how the world truly is.

ROBOTIC-SHEEP: *MOO?!*

Similarly, many of my interns that I tell to do something don't even have the capacity to accomplish the simplest choirs on their own. When I ask why they weren't able to complete the task, they explain some or other short-term reason for their incompetence, which tells me why they didn't do it at that moment, but not why they still haven't done it. This just shows me that they don't have the capability of thinking for themselves; they can't troubleshoot a situation or plan the next step if things don't go as planned; they always need someone standing over them telling them what to do all the time like robots or sheep. They need government, leadership, all aspects we shouldn't need in the next world. But this, in fact, isn't their fault. Today you don't have to do anything for yourself; for example there are arrows telling you where to go and park in the grocery store parking lot; the door opens automatically, no thought process there. Hanging signs direct you to exactly which aisle has what you're looking for, or a clerk is readily standing by waiting to show you right where it's at, no need to look yourself, no need to figure anything out for yourself. The amounts are all barcoded and automatically calculated for you. Hell, the cashier doesn't even need to add up anything anymore. The products are even bagged 'for your convenience' and taken out to your vehicle if you'd like. A recording instructs you that you forgot your seatbelt, and a GPS-controlled computer program verbally instructs the return route step-by-step to you. In the end you have to ask yourself, did you even go shopping? This is just one of millions of examples how humans don't think for themselves, just like 'sheep' and 'robots'.

I even get e-mails telling us that my guides are lies or "a scam," that you can't make hydrogen from water or you can't live off the grid. Again, their minds are so closed to any information outside of what they already have deemed to be true, regardless if it actually is or not, that it is preposterous to even contemplate anything else. But you can't blame them. Society has had, say, 20-70 years (depending on their age) to brainwash them into believing one thing; and I only have the time it takes you to read this book to teach them something completely different, sometimes even opposite or contradictory. It simply can't be done on my end.

I believe this book is a message from God, the problem is that I don't believe in god/God one bit. But I suppose that makes little difference if there is, indeed one; I suppose he doesn't much care if I believe in him or not. I'm not saying that this book is meant to be a warning for us to "change our ways before it's too late," because it's not. You always hear that *"God sent a sign so that we would change our ways."* But believe me, it's WAAAY too late to even consider changing as an option. It's gone far past that point. The events and 'signs' of the '60s were the "warning"; this is simply Him saying game over. Thanks, for playing. See ya next time.

IN CLOSING

People ask me all the time if I personally, honestly think the world will end on December 21, 2012; and, you know, at the end of the day, probably not. I really hope so. I think humans are an infestation on this planet, like flees on a dog's back, like a pandemic; and one day the planet <u>will</u> shake us off, but logically, mathematically, probably not in 2012. That's not to say something won't happen on or around those days. The Mayan calendar is a very sophisticated astrological device that has predicted through math, solar, and lunar eclipses many, many years into the future. Not only that, but they built, base, and end their calendar on such events. Who am I to argue with a culture that's been carrying out mathematics thousands of times longer than I have? So, yes, I do believe something will happen around December 21, 2012, (when Obama's term comes to an end), maybe even the collapse of many societies and governments like we're seeing today already, possibly even our own. It happens all the time, bringing an end to the world, but only "as we know it." Either way, if it doesn't happen in 2012, it's bound to occur soon after; and the readers of this book should find and have peace of mind knowing that they're more equipped, more aware and better fit than most to survive an apocalypse or global crisis, whenever it comes.

As you may have noticed, this book doesn't focus much on how to prepare you beforehand to survive an apocalypse, but rather what to do during and after the event. This is because (a) There are enough 'how-to prepare' books out there already; there is no need for me or anyone else to continuously repeat over and over the same information; (b) I don't believe that by providing you with the information, you will do anything with it, anyway. It's only until after something catastrophic has occurred, or the event itself is imminent, that we begin thinking or doing something about it. But for those who do want to go out right now and spend up this year's grocery bill on supplies, I do include a pre-preparations list in *Chapter 1*; and (c) It doesn't really matter how prepared a nation is to handle a major catastrophe beforehand. Japan *"had the most advanced early warning system in the world"* prior to the 2011 Earthquake, according to Hiroshi Inoue of the National Research Institute for Earth Science and Disaster Prevention; and you see how far that got them. *"If there was any place in the world ready for a disaster of the scale and scope of this historic calamity, it is Japan,"* said Stacey White, senior research consultant at the Centre for Strategic and International Studies.

Regardless of what happens, I'll continue teaching others how to be self-sufficient and independent from society, before, during and after, regardless. It's what I teach, lecture, and discuss at seminars and workshops all around the world to thousands of people all the time; it's now what I do. If any of you want to shed your worldly possessions and exit stage left from society like we have, feel free to contact me. At the very least, IF many of the scientists and prophets are wrong, it can't hurt to know how be self-reliant and how to provide for yourself, your children and your wife. My next book only focuses on this. It is jam-packed with DIY sustainable and permaculture projects, teaching you how to homestead and live off the grid, make your own fuel, food, energy and home, and live with nature. It's due out at the end of this year, early 2012, so make sure to check it out.

Lastly, this book is all about getting as much information to the masses so that EVERYONE, not just government officials, the elite and wealthy, may have a chance to survive before, during, or well after 2012. And although most people don't have the option to pack up all their belongings, quit their job and perform a major lifestyle change in order to prepare for the end times, the information in this book is beneficial to all people, whether anything actually happens on December 21, 2012, (or at any other point in time), or not. This writer's advice: With the help of this book, prepare if you can/want and if you can't or don't believe the hype, that's ok, too. At least, read and be knowledgeable of what YOUR options will be on *day one* of the event. It can't hurt to be prepared mentally, at least, if being prepared physically isn't an option. You also may notice that I have not included any chapters on how to save our world. That's because there is no saving of this world. In my opinion, like the destruction caused by hurricane Katrina in New Orleans, it's better to wipe everything out and start over. Before Katrina, New Orleans had the highest murder rate per capita in the world. Now, it's one of the nicest developing cities in the United States.

Unfortunately, this is just a small taste of the information available to you; but because of the wide limits of distributing the data, I'm limited to what I can publish at one time. I can only hope to expand this knowledge base with future editions and parts; so if any of you have any other catastrophe survival information, DIY self-sufficiency projects or know, first-hand or otherwise, or would just like to offer your story or support, I would love to hear from you and possibly incorporate it in future volumes.

Thank You,

Dan Martin
Agua-Luna Founder
www.Agua-Luna.com

"There comes a time when a house has been so damaged by termites that you must not only kill the termites... but demolish the house... and build again."

- Doctor Hippocrates Noah

Get ready, get a good seat, and witness the most violent display of *nature* that *mother* has to offer. When it's all over, I'll be sure to leave a light on for ya!

MORE BOOKS BY DAN MARTIN

Dan Martin has written and compiled dozens of Do-It-Yourself books on complete Self-Sufficiency available on Amazon.com or www.Agua-Luna.com, including:

- DIY Solar Panel
- How to Build a Hydrogen Generator
- How to Natural/Passive Heating & Cooling
- How to Live Off-the-Grid
- How to Build a Wind Turbine
- How to Build a Solar Water Heater
- How to Make a Cheap Solar System
- How to Make Ethanol Fuel
- How to Build a Compost Toilet
- How to Build a Free Home
- How to Build a Bio-Digester
- How to Make Methane Fuel
- How to Build a Solar Stove
- How to Make BioDiesel
- Convert Your Car to Electric
- How to Build a Solar Cooker
- How to Build an Arc Welder
- How to Build a Super Cooler
- How to Build an Automatic Feeder
- How to Retire Early

Books that are Coming Soon:

- How to Make a Woodgas Stove
- How to Build a Jet Stove
- How to Build an Alcohol Stove
- How to Build a Home Composter
- Fish Farming
- Hydroponics
- Livestock Management
- How to Convert Sea Water to Potable
- How to Build an Underground Home
- How to Gun Powder
- Homemade Ink
- How to Recycle at Home

All books are available in electronic form to conserve paper and minimize deforestation. For easy and speedy delivery, visit: **www.AGUA-LUNA.com.**

CPSIA information can be obtained at www.ICGtesting.com
Printed in the USA
LVOW020049101211

258719LV00002B/31/P

9 781427 651853